Judge the Best

Part Five of Above all Others:
The Lady Anne

By G. Lawrence

This book is dedicated to Anne Boleyn.

From the ranks of nobility she rose to become a Lady, a Marquess and Queen of England. From her came arguably the greatest sovereign of England, Elizabeth I. Anne Boleyn changed the course of history, and although she paid the ultimate price, her name has never been forgotten.

For many long years, Anne has been my obsession, my torment and my joy. I fell in love with her as a child, and like so many others whose lives she touched, both during her lifetime and after, I have never ceased to find her fascinating, alluring and remarkable.

In this book, I must say goodbye to her.

Queen Anne Boleyn said, upon the scaffold where she lost her life, that if any should interfere on her behalf, she wished them to "judge the best".

It is my hope that I have done this, given this extraordinary woman a voice, and done her the justice she was not accorded in life.

"So freely wooed, so dearly bought,
So soon a Queen, so soon low brought,
Hath not been seen, could not be thought.
O! What is Fortune?

As slipper as ice, as fading as snow,
Like unto dice that a man doth throw,
Until it arises he shall not know
What shall be his Fortune!

They did her conduct to a Tower of stone,
Wherein she would wail and lament her alone,
And condemned to be, for help there was none.
Lo! Such was her fortune."
Thomas Wyatt

"Riches I hold in light esteem,
And love I laugh to scorn
And lust of fame was but a dream,
Which vanished on the morn

And if I pray, the only prayer
That moves my lips for me
Is leave this heart that now I bear
And give me liberty!

Yea as my swift days near their goal
Tis all that I implore
In life and death, a chainless soul
With courage to endure."
Emily Bronte, The Old Stoic

"Men are so simple and yield so readily to the desires of the moment that he who will trick will always find another who will suffer to be tricked."
Niccolo Machiavelli

"If any person will meddle with my cause, I require them to judge the best."
Anne Boleyn
Upon the scaffold, The Tower of London 19th May 1536

Prologue

The Tower of London
The Evening of the 18th of May 1536

Twilight bathes the Tower in eerie light.

There is a bright glow from the heavens. It radiates, a serene, twinkling blaze, illuminating the faces of those who hurry home to dwellings within the Tower walls. Doves and wood pigeons coo in the trees, and blackbirds warble, their calls sounding over the hushed, still world.

They, like the people hastening home, know something is coming.

The strange light washes over those people, flowing across their careworn faces and the baggage they carry over their shoulders. It lingers on piled wood held upon forked sticks, borne on the sturdy backs of men, and brushes across bundles mothers hold close to their hearts; sweet, sacred babes they whisper to, trying to calm, as they bear them to the safe warmth of their hearths.

They will sup this night on broth and bread, huddled about their fires, telling tales of the fallen Queen who rests so near. All of London is afire with my tale; how I came to my throne, how I won and how I lost. How I fought and how I failed. How I held the King's love for so long, and how, in the end, love came to be destroyed. Some will tell their children I was a witch who seduced *Bluff Harry* from the path of righteousness, and how, with my death, all will be made well. Others will say I was a force for good, remembering that I helped many in my brief time as Queen.

But some will fall silent, for those wise, quiet souls understand something others do not… after tomorrow, more things will alter than simply the changing of queens upon England's throne.

This light is strange and unsettling, yet somehow it offers peace. It calls to me… a silent, yet keening voice upon the balmy breeze whispering of hope, rebirth and release. My women tell me that on the day my brother and friends died, Katherine's tomb at Peterborough became suddenly illuminated. The candles set about her resting place burst into glaring, unnatural radiance. That same light has travelled far… taking up the path from Katherine to me.

Is it Katherine herself, come to tell me that even now, she has not left my side? I know not, yet I take comfort from the light. Its ghostly blush flows through the diamond windowpanes of my most comfortable prison, lighting on tapestry and sumptuous furnishings placed here by Henry for my coronation. The light strikes against bright blue thread and glittering gold, upon the brown throne standing in the midst of my great chamber, waiting for its Queen.

I do not heed the chair's silent call. The throne is mine no more.

Memories assail me of times when I was happy and careless. If I look to the centre of my rooms, I can almost see Henry, with his hand outstretched, waiting for me to take it, so we might dance to the beating thump of our hearts and the surging rush of our souls. Once, I danced here, believing I had been granted all I would ever need. Long ago I twirled in this chamber wrapped in the arms of the man I loved, knowing all would be well.

Now I sit at the window, watching the platform on which my life will end.

Dust whirls upon the scaffold, caught in the breeze. It glitters like gold in the burnished lustre of Katherine's light. Five steps lead to its platform. Five steps to take towards Death. It is a stage, born of the unearthly twilight of my life. Perhaps such a thought is fitting. I lived my life on a stage set before kings. I played many parts. I learned much… but not enough. That much is clear. Tomorrow, I walk the boards for the last time.

But if this glow from the heavens tells me anything, it is that souls who have been stolen from life do not leave. Have I not known this for a long time? I heard the steps of the dead at my back… felt Katherine beside me. The faces of the dead stare out from behind these whitewashed walls, and ghosts wait behind the fluttering tapestry, watching me. The living and the dead cannot see each other, yet I, who rest between those two states, can.

I am truly the only ghost here, for I am within and without each state of being. I am become dusk; that unearthly state where all becomes unclear, unformed… wavering between states of being. I am twilight. I am the wolf light.

I feel a presence at my side. There is a brief sigh and I almost feel a hand upon my shoulder. Enemies no more, are Katherine and I. She is satisfied. Now, she comes not as a foe, not as the restless voice of my conscience, but as a friend… a companion who understands all I have endured, for she suffered the same.

I wish I could take her hand, but I alone know she is here. I would not wish to disturb my friends into thinking I have lost the last of my wits. When first I came here, my mind collapsed. I could not understand what I had done to bring such a fate upon me. But God heard my cries. He allowed me to regain my composure, so I might face Death with courage.

But still, Katherine lingers, and I am glad of her company. Many times when I was Queen, I stole from her example. I should have learned to emulate her better, but my character would not allow me to. Yet she is with me, her failed, flawed pupil. Katherine grants me courage.

Soon I join you, my mind murmurs. *Soon my story ends.*

Beginnings and ends… I always thought they were two separate entities; one which took a story into birth, and the other that ended it with death. Now I know better. They are not separate. They are part of the same being; a circle drawn in the sands of time by the hand of God. An ouroboros; a snake devouring its own tail… the circle made by compass grass, where a strand of life grows on brittle sand and under glaring sun, blown by the breeze to sketch a circle in the dust over and over and over…

A perfect circle etched in sand. Round and around the fragile stem weaves and scratches, casting dust from one story into another.

The end of one is the beginning of something new.

Katherine's tale was joined to mine long before I knew it. I thought Henry was the one I was bound to, but I was wrong. It was Katherine. All this time… it was she.

For now as I stand, facing the end of my life, I know it is the beginning of something new. I am a particle of sand in the drifting, careless winds. From this circle I will roam, held fast by the hands of the wind, to take up a part in a new tale… to come to another beginning.

I do not die tomorrow. I will linger, as Katherine does, in the minds of the people, in the halls of court, in the hearts of those who loved and hated me. Memories endure even when lies bid them to retreat. I will not be forgotten. Life will be mine no more, but existence will remain. I will be remembered.

I watch the guards as they patrol. The gates have been locked. All strangers have been removed. I cannot get out. Even at the close, my enemies fear I will find some means of escape, or manage to reach the King.

They fear without reason. Henry will have me dead.

But he does not understand what I now know.

That this is not the end.

Chapter One

Greenwich Palace
July 1534

A ghost watches me.

A figure, fallen from the last rays of sunlight streaking through the palace windows, stands in the shadows. Her face seems familiar, yet I do not know who she is, or how she came to be here. And yet still she stands. Still she watches. The gloom conceals her face. The sunlight from the window blinds me. She is a creature of shadow. Who is this woman who dares to come before me, unbidden and unwelcome?

"Who are you?" I demand. My voice rings in the empty room… a shrill noise, interrupting the still, muffled calm.

She smiles gently, yet I fear her smile. It is too calm, too collected. She is confident, assured… everything I pretend to be, yet am not.

"I am you," she says, "the same soul, the same fate… twisted, bent and broken into another form."

"I shall call the guards."

My threat has no impact. She laughs; a low chuckle which sends a shiver down my spine. "Call all you want," she says. "Here, there is no one to hear you, but me."

"What do you want?"

"To see you." She steps forward. I think sunlight will reveal her, but it does not. Somehow, she remains hidden. Her gown flutters in a draught. Silk whispering in the darkness. The same sound comes from the tapestry, rich with golden thread, depicting images of Solomon and Sheba. It moves as though there are people waiting behind it.

"Then you have seen me," I say. "And now you can go."

"I can go nowhere without you." She steps forward another pace. "You and I… we are bound together, do you not see that? Do you still not understand?"

"I do not know who you are," I reply. "And you are nothing to me."

"Perhaps," she says. "Perhaps I am everything."

"You speak in riddles." I make for the door, my heart hammering in my breast. "I will call the King's guards, and you will be thrown in jail."

"You seek to remove or silence all who would speak against you," she says. "But it will not make you safe. I am the only one who can protect you."

"The King, my husband, will protect me."

"The King, our husband, will not."

My lip curls. "*Katherine*," I breathe. "How did you escape your swamp? When the King hears you are here…"

"I am not here. Neither are you." She pauses to glance about the chamber, her eyes lighting on furniture and ornaments that once were hers. "You think this is real? It is not. There is a fabrication built around you, Anne Boleyn, so thick, so deep, so compelling that you cannot see it. A world has been made, brought into life by your wishes. But fantasy is fading. The old world grows strong again." She stares into my eyes. "Time is running out."

I have to swallow in order to speak. "What do you want?"

"To give you a message."

"Speak, then, and have done with this!" Angry heat rises in my gullet, rich and burning, warming my chilled blood.

"*She is my death, and I am hers,*" quotes Katherine, her deep blue eyes resting on me as words I spoke once to my brother trip from her lips.

"You want me to be kind to your daughter?" I ask. If Katherine knows I said this about Mary, this must be why she is here.

She shakes her head. "That is not my message."

"Then what is?"

She smiles again, and her old, tired face shines with beauty. It has not abandoned her. Even in trials of sorrow and separation, Katherine has not diminished. The fire of her soul is bright. It burns in the faded light.

"You are my death," she says. "And I am yours."

I frown at the shade. "I was not speaking of you when I said that."

"I know…" She smoothes her dark dress, never breaking contact with my eyes. "Not for the first time, *Madame de Pembroke*, you had a good notion but allowed it to lead you to the wrong path."

"What do you mean?"

"You are my death," she says. "As I am yours."

*

I sat up in bed, startled. My eyes flashed about the chamber. Mary Howard was beside me, fast asleep, with Margaret Wyatt and Bess Holland wrapped deep in soft slumber on pallet beds upon the floor. My eyes darted about, searching for the mystifying ghost of a still-living woman who had come to haunt my dreams.

There was nothing there. Nothing in the shadow, nothing in the light. Katherine was not in my chamber. She was still at her house in the fens, wasting away in lonesome darkness. Relief flooded through me and I sat back, caressing the bump on my front. My child, almost seven months grown, was warm beneath the clammy, shaking touch of my hand.

It was a dream, Anne, I told myself, flooding my lungs with shallow gasps of blessed air as the fear and confusion of my nightmare departed.

Then I felt it.

It was not the dream that woke me. It was pain. Sharp and grinding. There were cramps, anguished and tearing, in my back and belly. A rush of moisture broke from between my legs.

I grasped Mary Howard by the shoulder, my hand a desperate claw, shaking her awake. "Mary." My voice shattered from my throat, fraught and harsh. I could hear a wail of panic riding my breath. "Mary, wake! Something is wrong."

Another flash of agony thrust into me, and I doubled over, groaning.

"My lady?" Bess was fast on her feet. Her pallet bed shuddered against the rush-matted floor as she skittered from its warm blankets. "What is wrong?"

"The child," I panted. "My son… Get doctors… midwives. He is coming."

I rose, trying to stand, to walk… trying to do anything to relieve my agony, not just of body, but of mind. Terror coursed in my veins as blood. As my ladies helped me onto my feet, I saw the linen bed sheets were wet. My waters had broken, but it was too soon. When I dared to glance at my women, I saw fear in their eyes. The stink of dread rose, drifting amongst the scent of night-breath, sweet-perfumed sheets, and sweat.

My child was coming. If born now, he would not survive.

I stumbled about the chamber, tears blinding me, my hands clasped about my stomach. "It is too soon," I whispered to Mary Howard.

"It will be fine, Majesty," she said. "You are strong and so will your son be." Her face sought to bring me comfort, but I could see she did not believe her own lies.

"Get my mother," I gasped as another wave of pain crashed upon me. Mary ran to find my mother and I clutched the bedpost.

My fingernails bored into the wood. Hopeless talons scraped dark oak. As Mary raced in with my mother and Mistress Aucher in tow, I stared into their eyes. "The baby is coming," I said. I did not need to say more. They read my fright as easily as an English Bible.

"Anne…" My mother took me in her arms. "It will be well. Perhaps you were mistaken about the date of conception."

I allowed them to comfort me. I swallowed their pretty lies. They prepared a pallet bed on the floor and made ready for the birth. Dawn was not yet risen, and as my women scampered about the chamber and Mistress Aucher took charge, all I saw were wide, white eyes flashing in amber candlelight.

They knew. They knew just as I did that it was too soon. They knew what I would face. I would go through the motions of childbirth only to bear Death from my womb.

"Does Henry know?" I asked as they walked me about the chamber.

"He knows," said my mother. "And is most concerned, waiting for news." She smoothed my hair from my face. "He only wants you to be well. That is his sole concern."

Is it? When Elizabeth was born, that was indeed all he had wanted, but I had reason to suspect this time he may have contented himself with a son born and a mother lost, if that was the price God demanded.

I stumbled on, trying to persuade myself that all would be well.

I knew it would not.

*

My women carried out bloodstained bed sheets, their faces sorrow-bowed, their eyes wet with tears. They did their work silently as I lay on the bed, trying to recover my breath. Trying to pretend I was not there. That this was not happening. That all was well.

My hands clutched my stomach, but there was nothing left inside me. I was empty. Not just of a child, but of hope and joy. Yet still the bump remained, as though I were pregnant now not with new life, but with dead dreams.

There was silence.

Palpable… solid… Silence bore down upon me, weighting my shoulders and crushing my heart. For hours I had toiled, enduring the pain, pushing and panting, waiting desperately to hear the shrill call of my son as he entered the world. But when he slipped from my body there was no sound.

No thin, high scream. No merry chuckling from Mistress Aucher, my mother or my women.

Nothing but silence.

They washed me and put me into my state bed. "My son," I croaked. "Let me see my son. He is mine. Give him to me."

Faces glanced at each other, drawn with stark sorrow. They did not want to answer me.

I felt my soul had sailed from my body, as though I watched all this from afar. There was something trying to whisper the truth, but I would not, could not hear it.

My mother waved the others away and sat beside me, taking my hand. Her flesh was cold. "Anne…" Her voice inhabited the same gentle realm as when we were children and she told us stories of happiness, chivalry and honour. "Anne, there is no easy way to…"

"*No!*" The scream erupted, shattering the stagnant silence. Mary Howard and Bess jumped. "No!" I shouted again. "Where is my son? Where is my boy?"

"Anne, he is dead… born dead."

I glowered, my heart unwilling to believe her. "You are trying to trick me," I hissed.

Pushing her aside, I staggered to my feet and lurched towards the bundle they had placed on a table beside the baptismal bowl. "You are trying to keep me from him," I shouted at my shocked friends and companions. "You would deceive me. You work with my enemies! You would steal my son from me!"

Mad with grief, lost to reason, I reached the table and Mistress Aucher tried to hold me back. "Stand aside!" I screamed. "Go to! I am your Queen!"

"Let her see him." My mother's voice cracked. My head whipped about. She was weeping.

They stood aside and I hastened to him, snatching the still bundle into my arms. I gazed down on the tiny face. He looked as though he were sleeping. Small eyes closed. A perfect rosebud mouth, so like Henry's, set in a face which echoed the sharp angles of mine. A fuzz of red hair was plastered to his head.

He was perfect, beautiful, wondrous… Why would they keep my son from me?

It was as though another part of my consciousness ruled me then… grief and sorrow, too hard, too strong to be mastered, reigned in my mind. I was stupid without the rest of my senses, but I could not call them back. Everything but anger and sorrow was numb inside me; frozen in my heart.

I put a finger to his face. I could almost see him nuzzling it. Almost see his mouth opening to yawn. They were mistaken. My boy was not dead!

And then my reluctant eyes saw the sheen of blue about his lips; the pallor under his rosy skin and red hair. He was not moving, not breathing… Dead before he had lived.

He was my lost son.

My eyes dragged unwillingly from his face to stare blankly at my mother. I could not accept what I saw. She covered her face with her hands and a tight, raw sob emerged.

I gazed at Mistress Aucher and she stared back, wary lights in her eyes. She wondered if I had lost my wits... If the wicked spirits and mischievous fairies that waited in birthing chambers, ready to claim lost children and dead mothers had claimed me.

"I am so sorry, Anne," she whispered. "Until the last we thought there was hope. We did not even baptise the boy until we realised… but we may have been too late."

"Someone has done this," I murmured, ignoring her confession that she might have condemned my child to eternal limbo. "Someone has murdered my son." I rounded on my women, the motionless body cradled in my arms. "Who has done this?" I demanded. "Who has killed my child?"

Horrified faces stared aghast at me. "Majesty… no one did this. It was not his time to be born."

I knew not who said it and I did not care. I knew the truth. Someone had murdered my baby.

I turned on Mistress Aucher. "Was it you? Who *paid* you to kill my child?"

Suddenly my mother was at my side, trying to take the bundle from me, trying to calm me. I pulled away from her, staggering to the end of the chamber with my back to the wall, refusing to surrender my son.

"No!" I sobbed. "You shall not take him from me! He is my son! My little boy..."

My legs gave way and I fell to the floor, keeping the head of my dead child safe from harm as I dropped. I wept over his body with no sense of time.

Ages passed. The world was destroyed and made new again. Civilisations rose and fell, men were born and died. About us, stars swam in infinite blackness, armies marched and histories were made as I curled tight about my son. If tears could have made life, my son would have been granted a thousand lives.

Then I felt a hand on my shoulder. A presence knelt beside me.

Dumbly, I gazed up into Henry's eyes. Never had I seen him look so sad and old. So lost and so worried. "They have killed our son," I whispered. "They wanted to take him from me, Henry, but I would not let them."

"Anne… give him to me."

I did not want to relinquish my child. If I let go of my son, somehow, he would truly be dead.

But the grief in Henry's eyes burned too with love. Tears slipped from his light lashes, washing the sea-blue of his eyes into an ocean of sorrow and compassion. "Give our son to me," he said again. "I will care for him. You must rest."

"They told me he was dead," I murmured. "But they are wrong. I feel his heart, Henry. I feel his *life*. They want to take him away. They would use him to destroy me."

"No one will harm you, Anne," Henry murmured. "I watch over you both." His hands prised our son gently from my wretched grip. "You must sleep, my love. When you are rested, we will see our son again." He tried to smile, but it slipped upon his face, distorting into a jagged wound. "You must be hale to feed our boy," he said, his voice breaking.

"Yes," I said, feeling suddenly more tired than I ever had been. "You will watch over him. You will keep him safe from my enemies."

Henry pulled the bundle into his arms and glanced down. For a moment, something flowed through his eyes that I could not read; the darkness of a shadow thrust back to the borders of his mind long ago. He turned his eyes from our son, but hugged him close to his heart. Henry put his hand to my cheek. It shook as he caressed my face. "Get into bed, Anne," he murmured.

Suddenly docile, I obeyed. My women shrank from me as I stood and I stared at them, baffled. Were they afraid of me? I could not understand why. My mother gave me a bitter drink, swimming with herbs, and I fell asleep. When I woke, I understood the truth I had not wanted to face.

My son was dead. A stillbirth. Born before his time; my enemies had not killed him, I had.

They told me it was not so, that many women face such trials, and there was nothing I could have done. They said I was not to blame.

It mattered not what they said. The guilt was crushing. *I must have done something.* I must have not taken the care I should have. I must have offended God, for why else would He steal away the life of my perfect little boy?

Guilt and sorrow consumed me. Where reason had abandoned me in the moments after the birth of my boy, these hollow emotions took its place. I wrestled in dreams of darkness, running after a tiny child as he raced through a long, dark labyrinth, always just out of reach, but always just within sight. Through black corridors and endless, aching turns I stumbled, trying to find him. I could not. When I woke, there was nothing but blankness. My heart was in the shadows, lost with my lost son.

Henry sat with me, day after day, night after night, trying to console me. My son was taken away. They never told me where he was buried. He had not been baptised in time, so they could not have laid him to rest in consecrated ground. When I asked Henry, he would not tell me. He thought it would upset me to know where my son lay; buried deep in the cold, dead ground with no hope of Heaven.

For if Rome's dictates were true, my son would never reach God. His soul, unwelcomed by the Almighty, would float in the state of limbo where all un-baptised souls go. With Noah and with Abraham, my son would drift through all the eons of existence, never seeing the light of God, never knowing the comfort of Heaven.

Never would I know my son, for I was baptised and he was not. I would attain Heaven, as he would linger in a realm beneath Paradise.

Never would I see him again, in this life or the next.

Chapter Two

Greenwich Palace
July 1534

Silence.

That same restless, throbbing stillness that fell upon the world when my child was born dead reached out with skeletal hands and took hold of my women. The crushing quietness of muffled words and unspoken, hollow grief bore down upon me. It was a palpable stillness, a grinding weight which tunnelled into my soul.

They brought me broth and bread. I left it untouched, congealing in its bowl, until they took it away. No one would let me speak of my son, fearing that if I did, it would bring the madness of grief upon me once more. Henry commanded them to say nothing of our child and they obeyed.

They tried to distract me with news of court, of Elizabeth, but nothing reached me. I wanted to speak of my boy, but when I tried, their faces turned away, snapping to one side as though a phantom hand had slapped them. The glimmer of wary concern ignited in their eyes and they tried to lead me to other subjects. They stole words from my mouth and pushed me into a realm of silence. I was alone; raw and naked, abandoned on a stark, lonely hillside where rain and wind lashed my flesh… lost in the kingdom of sorrow.

No one talks of dead babies. No one speaks of souls lost to God.

Mothers are supposed to suffer in honourable silence, never showing the depths of their loss. They are supposed to recover, to forget, to carry on. I could not.

Henry came each morning and night. He read to me, trying to take my mind to another place, one of hope and rebirth. "You need not fear," he said one evening when his efforts failed to draw me from staring at the wall.

"Fear what?" I asked, turning my long neck.

"For your reputation as Queen." His eyes were puzzled, wondering what else I could be upset about. "The birth will not be announced. It is not practice to proclaim stillbirths, so no one will know."

No one will know? I thought. When I had proudly displayed a fine, round belly for months? What did he think? That people would see me return to court and believe I had been mistaken? That I would forget our son, our child, our hope?

"Tell me where you have buried him," I said.

"It will do you no good to dwell on it." Henry set his book on the bed. "This accident will be forgotten, and we will conceive a new son."

"*Accident*?" Hard with accusation, the word hissed from my lips.

"We will have a new son," he insisted, ignoring me. "God will be generous."

He would not hear me. My son was buried in an unmarked grave, resting beside the bones of other babes lost to God. Churches and monasteries had special plots for such children, usually beside hospitals where unmarried mothers went for aid. Was my son resting beside thieves and murderers? Beside witches and heretics? Where was my son?

"We will tell the court you were mistaken," Henry said again, holding my hand. "That way, no one will question our capacity to make a son."

I stared at him with barren eyes. Was this all he was concerned with? What others would *think*? I cared not. Grief plunged inside me; an endless cavern topped with a crumbling cairn of ice-cold stone. I cared not what others might think of me. All I could think of was my child. My perfect, beautiful, dead boy.

"Norris and the others miss you." He smiled, trying to coax me from my empty shell. "They protest there is no merriment at court without their Queen."

Merriment… had I ever laughed? I could not remember. It seemed impossible.

Henry left me that night and his visits became spare. He did not want to witness my sorrow. He would set aside this *accident* and go on with life. He would believe in his own tale and think we had never had a son.

I became feverish. Sorrow and loss, the trials of birth, lack of sleep and food weakened me. Dreams came. The old witch from Hever whispered that I would bear sons, but they would bring me no comfort. I saw blood running down the walls of the white tower set upon its dusty planes. My son's face haunted me. He called out in my nightmares. My sister laughed at me, her giggles becoming shrieks of ancient pain as she stood surrounded by fair-haired children with flashes of Tudor red in their locks.

Many nights I awoke screaming for Henry, but he was not there. My husband was busy elsewhere, entertaining whores in his opulent bed.

As the days wore on, and Henry came less frequently, I sat in my chambers as my women tried to distract me with embroidery and books, whiling away the days until I could be churched and return to court. But my son's face was before my eyes, whether I was asleep or awake. I saw flashes of his eyes, his hair, his skin. They leapt before me when I looked into the glass of windows, or the glossy sheen upon wine. Sometimes I heard him crying, and darted from my bed with hungry eyes, desperate to find him. But as I stood panting in the room, my feet upon the cold boards of the floor, the little herbs laced within the rush mats tickling my feet, I knew there was no one there.

Mistress Aucher said it was common, when one had gone through a time of trauma. She told my mother it would pass. I could not believe her. Each flash was too raw not to be real.

Nothing was said to Henry. My women covered it up, making excuses for my strange behaviour. They did not want Henry to think I was possessed by an evil spirit.

In the light of day, too bright, too glaring… I took to staring at the walls, imagining what my son would have been like, what he might have become. I saw him playing with Elizabeth in the long gallery at Eltham Palace. I dreamed of my children and when I awoke, grief came new and bleeding and bitter.

Grief is not of one moment.

"This must end, Anne," said my mother one day. I glanced up with dull eyes to see she was alone. My other women had been sent to the antechamber. "What you have endured is horrific, and believe me when I say I understand, for I have lost children too. But you must return to us. You have a daughter to care for, and a realm to oversee." Her face puckered. She knew something she did not want to tell me.

"And Henry has gone back to his whore." My voice was flat. I cared not for him, for anyone. My heart was as empty as my womb. All I wanted was to curl up about my grief and hold it to me. It was all I had left.

She nodded. "We all experience sadness in different ways," she said. "The King masks his behind a wall of gaiety, as you embrace yours. But you must leave your son behind, Anne, and reclaim your place at court before…"

"Before Henry forgets me."

Again that nod. Again that worried face. My mother believed I was driving my husband away.

I turned my face to the wall. Should I care for Henry's feelings? Should I care about his whore? Should I care that, at a time such as this, when my hopes and dreams had been shattered and my son stolen by Death, my husband sought comfort in the arms of another woman rather than offering it to me?

But something in me did care. A part of me was scared. Perhaps there was something left inside me besides hollow emptiness.

"Help me to dress," I croaked. I stood in the centre of my chamber as my women dressed me. Like a child I allowed them to softly guide my arms and legs. Purkoy, delighted to find me standing, danced about my feet.

I tried to remember who I had been before this. I tried to set my face as she had… that woman who had mastered the world and moulded it to her liking. I tried to steal the darkness of mourning from my heart, from my eyes.

You must wear your court mask again, the shadow of my old self murmured. *You must give Henry hope.*

I listened to her. Ductile in her hands, I allowed her to take over. She would speak for me as I retreated into the recesses of my soul. The old Anne would take control.

I called for Henry and he came. "I am so sorry," I said. "I thought I was careful."

"We are young," Henry said. "Sons will follow."

"We are young." My hollow voice echoed. "And sons will follow."

"You must return to court," he said. "And when you do, nothing will be said of this event."

"Thank you," I whispered.

I must go back to court. I must cease to speak of our son. I must snatch my husband from the arms of his mistress. I must survive.

But even as I thought those words I knew I was leaving part of me behind. The part that sorrowed. The part that grieved… The broken one.

The broken one would remain tucked inside my soul, curled in a ball, lost in a labyrinth of perdition, with her son.

Chapter Three

Greenwich Palace
July 1534

"The Act will allow the King to tax his people in times of peace and war," said my mother, sitting on my bed with a bowl of chicken broth and rice in her hands. Food for invalids. My mother was concerned for my health.

"And how has it been received?" I asked, stroking Purkoy who was deep in slumber, curled up in a soft ball at my side.

My mother was trying to distract me with news of Cromwell's plans. She had brought up such matters with hesitation, but I welcomed them… I would accept anything that would stop me thinking of my dead child; anything to keep the old Anne Boleyn in charge and prevent the broken one from emerging. I had to keep her locked away, contained. If I fell apart, there was no knowing how long it would take to stick the shattered remains of me back together again.

I was but one moment from oblivion. If I allowed myself to fall, I might never stop.

"There are those for and against," she said, wiping the spoon on a chunk of bread. "As ever."

Cromwell wanted to make Henry rich. Although Henry's father had left him more money than it was believed any man could spend, Henry needed more. He was a spender as much as his sire had been a hoarder, and with rumours of invasion, from hostile Spain and irritated Rome, Henry needed money for arms, ships and men.

The Subsidy Act would allow Henry to demand taxes from his subjects at any time. Previously, kings had only been permitted to raise taxes for the purpose of war, but Cromwell argued they should also be collected to maintain peace, for were the two aims not the same? Before the loss of my child, Cromwell had assured me that this money would be put to good use, much like fines extracted from the clergy before their submission. I trusted Cromwell, for he, like me, was generous to charitable causes. He provided food, vestments and coin from his London houses to the poor, and those who benefited praised him. His ideals were humanist in origin; that those blessed with riches should be generous to others who were not. He promoted the notion of relief for the poor, and support of scholars, and there our interests met. I thought him a social reformer, much as I was.

I had therefore supported this Act, and my mother, knowing this, brought me this news in an effort to cheer my battered spirits.

With this money and all that had been gathered before, Henry could support his people and defend his realm. Poor scholars with aptitude could be put through school and university, widows and orphans would be cared for, and our shores would be kept safe. This was a worthy goal.

But if this news was welcome, shortly there was more that was not. Trapped inside my lying-in chambers until I was churched, I was reliant on others for news of the outside world. My women did not want to say anything that might upset me, but when they failed me I could turn to Jane, my sister-in-law. Jane would not hold anything back. It was not in her nature. She fed from gossip and her blood ran thick with rumour. I was grateful for her honesty. It was a fragile time, and I needed to know all that was going on.

"They say Lady Mary was hysterical," she whispered as we sewed.

I stared at the pattern of acorns and honeysuckle I was embroidering into a cushion. I had started this before I lost my son. The acorn was the symbol of new life, and honeysuckle of love. Long had honeysuckle been one of my personal emblems. None knew it, but I wove it upon my gowns to remind myself of that horrific night in France when I had been attacked. Honeysuckle had grown in the arbour where I had struggled to defend myself. As much as it was a symbol of love, it was also a personal reminder that love might be perverted… made a thing of evil. Sewn into my gowns, into cushions and bed hangings, it reminded me never to be made a victim again.

"Hysterical… about moving houses?" I asked, running my needle through the cloth. Jane had been regaling me with the latest exploits of Henry's bastard. "The Lady Mary always knows how to make the worst of everything."

"She feared riding behind the Princess as a servant, Majesty."

"She needs to understand her place." I sighed. "And this is why Chapuys decided to make his parade through London?"

The hapless hare, in response to Mary's wailing, had taken it upon himself to make a gesture of support. Proclaiming he was taking a pilgrimage to Walsingham, Chapuys had gathered sixty horsemen. They were supposed to be nobles, but anyone with eyes could see they were Chapuys' servants dressed up to pass as lords. This did not matter to the hare. He desired a spectacle, so all would see they were off to see imprisoned Katherine, drawing attention to her plight. They rode through London, apparently making for Walsingham, but it soon became clear they were heading for Kimbolton Castle, and for Katherine.

Everyone in London would know the ambassador was off to see forlorn, abandoned Katherine, and Chapuys ensured this, for they set off loudly, their numbers bulging with trumpeters and minstrels, and processed through London by a most bizarre route… which only made sense if you understood the hare wanted everyone to see them. It was confrontation Chapuys was looking for. By the second day, reports of his little pageant had reached Henry, and, understanding what Chapuys was up to, he sent Cromwell's men after the ambassador. Stephen Vaughan, freshly returned from Antwerp, was now constantly in Cromwell's employ and had been sent to intercept the hapless hare.

"Vaughan rode ahead to Kimbolton," Jane continued, her emerald eyes flickering to my face, "and brought back a message from Katherine's steward that the party were not allowed to visit."

Steward… said Katherine's voice in my mind. *Jailer, more like.*

"But the hapless hare did not listen?" I asked.

"He did not, Majesty." Jane smiled, her needle poised in the air. "Does he ever? Chapuys rested his men and went on the next day. Another messenger was sent saying His Majesty had *expressly* denied permission for him to see Katherine, and it would invoke the King's ire to attempt to do so."

"I wonder if this was part of his scheme. The hare must have known England's people would not like to hear that Katherine is being denied visitors."

"Indeed," said Jane. "Katherine sent loyal servants out to welcome Chapuys, Majesty, and they presented gifts of game and venison, along with many bottles of fine wine, begging them to make good cheer, for *she* would be happy to see him."

"Naturally," I said. "Katherine would do that. She knew if Henry continued to deny Chapuys access, she would prove that she is a prisoner."

"They brought a fool with them," Jane continued. "He had a padlock hanging from his hood, to make it clear that Katherine was being held captive. Chapuys reached the moat and declared he was not permitted to enter, so all of Katherine's ladies, and the Dowager herself, hung from the windows speaking Spanish and Latin to their guests. That way, they declared, they were not flouting the King's orders, for no one had left the house, and none entered it."

"What more did you find out?"

"The fool led a mock assault on the castle, Majesty, pretending he intended to swim the moat and rescue them." Jane tucked her silver needle into the cloth. "He waded in as far as his waist whilst everyone watched and laughed. He was dragged back by Katherine's guards, but as they did so, he threw the padlock across the moat, shouting, 'next time I bring the key!' Chapuys' men fell about laughing and a crowd of local people who had gathered looked on in amazement."

"And now everyone has heard of this."

"They have, Majesty. The whole court is speaking of it. The King is enraged."

"Then I pity Vaughan," I said. "For Henry's wrath will fall on him and Cromwell."

"Chapuys took an alternate route back to London," said Jane. "They stopped at Walsingham, to prove that had been their true purpose all along, and ensured as many people saw on them on the way back as on their way out. Vaughan tried to explain that it was Katherine's steward who did not allow them access."

"But no one believed him," I finished for Jane. "Everyone who saw that spectacle understands what Chapuys was trying to proclaim; that Katherine is a prisoner and the King her keeper."

I frowned. It was time for me to rejoin court. Had I been at Henry's side when this occurred I would have advised him on a better course of action. It was almost time for me to be churched, and so much the better. When I was away from this room, I might be able to pass a day without hearing the call of my son. I might be able to allow the old Anne, the one I pretended to be, to take over, for good.

I had to forget. *I had to.* What other choice was there? To become lost in a kingdom of shadows and wraiths? To leave the world behind?

I had not that option. I must rejoin life. I had to set sorrow and misfortune behind me and look to the future.

I would tell them I was well, and my son was of the past. It would be a lie. Each time I closed my eyes I saw him. But I would not tell. I would keep my secrets. I would bury my son deep in my heart.

Chapter Four

Greenwich Palace
July - August 1534

Two days later, on a blustery morning where clouds scampered in the skies, I presented myself at the boundaries of the palace chapel and Cranmer blessed me. He did not include the words spoken after Elizabeth's birth that tied me to the soul of my child in life and death. Gentle Cranmer knew that according to Church doctrine, my son and I would never see each other again.

My return to court was not as it had been after Elizabeth was born. There was a quiet Mass, but no giving of alms, no feasting, no dancing. Since it was to be a secret that I had delivered a stillborn son, such events were impractical. Besides, I was in no mood to celebrate. But as soon as I was ready to receive guests, I sent for Cromwell.

"I hope you did not suffer from Chapuys' little fiesta last month?" I asked as he took a seat. Thin bands of light from the windows spilled into the inner gloom. Particles of dust danced in them, silver against the golden light.

"Poor Vaughan endured more scolding than I, Majesty," he said, lowering his large, stocky frame into a plush crimson seat. He gazed at me with sympathetic eyes and I waved a hand.

"Please," I said in a strangled voice. "Do not speak of my child."

"If you so wish, Majesty."

"It is still too close… Too raw. When first it happened, I was lost. I cannot allow myself to go astray again." I stared into his eyes and he blinked to see the grief hidden there. "I have to make the best of what I have," I murmured. Those were Henry's words, Henry's thoughts.

"And the King needs you, madam. He has been quite lost without you."

I was not so sure that was true, given all Jane and my mother had told me of Mary Perrot and Joanna Dingley, Henry's whores, but I said nothing. "Has Vaughan recovered from the fire of His Majesty's choler?"

"He is a sturdy man, Majesty. It would take more than a grand ticking off to fell such a tree."

"Then I am glad. It was not his fault."

"No," said Cromwell. "Majesty, I fear I am to blame."

"But the commands came from the King, did they not?"

"They did, but I should have advised him to allow the visit. Once the ambassador was prepared, there was no stopping him. All this has done is confirm to England's people, and perhaps the Emperor, that Katherine is indeed a captive, as they have long supposed."

"I thought you might have caught scent of it before it happened. Lady Rochford tells me you are often with the ambassador."

"Someone has to preserve ties with Spain, Majesty. I play the friend to keep a line of communication open. And with the Emperor ever a threat, we must play nicely."

"Please… do not think I doubt your motives, my friend. I just thought it unusual that with your fine nose for subterfuge you were caught unawares."

"My nose failed me this time, my lady," Cromwell admitted. "Chapuys said nothing. He knew that if he did I would have tried to stop him."

"And now England sings the ballad of Katherine's woes."

"Many join Chapuys in protesting she is ill-treated, Majesty," he agreed, running a fat finger over his shaven chin. His skin had that raw look many men gain after shaving; angry pink spilling into mottled red. "Katherine claims she is a prisoner."

"Is it not true, in some ways? She has little money of her own, no access to the property the King has confiscated. She is surrounded by people who have sworn the oath of succession, binding them to us. Truly, Katherine has few friends left."

"But she makes her bed more uncomfortable than it has to be, Your Majesty," said Cromwell. "Has she not always? She could have retired to a convent in honour when all this began, but she refused. Now, she will not eat or drink unless she sees what goes into her food, and only leaves her room to hear Mass in the gallery. She surrounds herself with the few loyal servants she has left and refuses to see her steward or anyone else." Cromwell snorted. "Her papist addiction to bodily suffering holds her prisoner, madam, not the King. She wears her odorous hair shirt and fasts hard and heavy, proclaiming all she does is for God, when in fact her suffering is made for spite. She would make it seem as though *the King* is doing this to her, rather than the truth… that she inflicts suffering upon herself."

Cromwell smoothed his black doublet. "Chapuys is the only one left at liberty who still speaks for Katherine. Everyone else is sworn to uphold you, madam, or they are in the Tower, like Fisher and More."

"Chapuys believes his position protects him," I said. "Perhaps he is right. If the King became angry enough to arrest him, the Emperor would finally have the incentive he requires to invade. It is clear his aunt and her misery are not enough to stir him into action. I think Chapuys wants to goad the King into doing something… something Charles of Spain could not ignore."

"I had the same thought."

Cromwell sat back, accepting a goblet of wine from Nan Gainsford and offering a charming smile in return. She blushed, even though she was no stranger to the wiles of men. Cromwell had a way about him. He was not an attractive man, but he possessed that indefinable quality we name charisma. He drew people to him. So often he was still and quiet as a mouse lingering at the edges of its hole, waiting for a chance to scamper over the floors. But the still waters of his surface ran deep. There was mystery in Cromwell, and all who engaged with him wanted to know his secrets. He was an alluring man.

"I intercepted one of the ambassador's letters some time ago, and he was not complimentary about me." Cromwell reached inside his doublet and took out a length of parchment. I unrolled it and read. He was right. It was not flattering.

"*He is a man of wit, who understands affairs of state,*" I read aloud. "*Cromwell's words are good, but his deeds are bad, and his will and intent incomparably worse.*" I lifted my eyebrows and Cromwell smiled.

"So, you see, Majesty, we are not as good friends as many would believe."

"But you will continue to court him?"

Cromwell inclined his head. "For the sake of England, Majesty."

"Let me know if you hear of anything that could be used to remove him. A different ambassador might be a better friend to us, or at least less devoted to Katherine."

"I will see what can be done." He tucked the letter into his doublet. "I do have one other matter to raise with you, Majesty," he said. "If you pity Vaughan, he has lately put a request to me on behalf of his wife."

"Which is?"

"She is a talented silk-woman, in need of employment. Vaughan hoped, in view of the services he has done in the past, you might take her into your household. She has made many costumes for my entertainments over the years, and is a skilled woman."

Cromwell's lavish entertainments were becoming legendary. He spared no expense and anyone who had attended one spoke in hushed tones of reverence about it… much to Henry's annoyance.

"And her character?"

"As virtuous as the Virgin," he attested. "She is a good woman, Majesty, dedicated to the new learning and reform, much like her husband."

"Good," I said. "I cannot have any in my household who would be questioned about their morals. Bring some of her work to me and I will see what might be done." I paused. "Poor Vaughan deserves some reward."

As Cromwell went to leave, he turned back. "May I say, Majesty, if I may be so bold, you have a courageous spirit, one I much admire."

I swallowed as the hidden woman within me screamed. She wanted to be set loose, to run the corridors of court, wailing for her child. I thrust her back, chained her to the floor of my soul, and smiled.

"Thank you, Cromwell," I said.

*

Two days later, I was back at Henry's side. But I was not the only one. Joanna Dingley seemed to be falling from favour, although Henry still paid court to her, but there was a new toy for my fickle husband. Mary Perrot, the woman who had been his mistress some years ago, and had a son by him, was at court and Henry was pursuing her.

"The parrot was once one of Katherine's ladies," Jane whispered as we watched Henry flounce about his whore. He looked faintly ridiculous; an aging man playing the fresh gallant, simpering at her jests and all but dribbling at her feet.

My loyal ladies had taken to calling Mary Perrot, *the parrot*, as a jest, but there was something of the exotic birds of the New World about her. She was always overdressed, for one thing, and far too talkative for another.

"They call her the *Imperial Lady*, sister, for she sympathises with Katherine and her daughter."

I watched the overdone parrot as she laughed at one of Henry's jests. Her giggle went through me like a knife. It was a tinkling sound, which ended in a breathy sigh, like the noise impish sprites might make when up to mischief. She sounded like a child. To me, the noise was irritating, but Henry and other men clearly found it attractive. What fools men can be to the wiles of women! Whenever the parrot saw me watching, she would put her hand on his arm, or his coat, seeking to demonstrate that my husband was her property. She might as well have gone all the way and pissed on Henry like a bitch marking her territory. At least that would have been honest.

The parrot was witty, young and pretty, all qualities Henry was attracted to. She was also related to me by marriage, as one of her cousins had married into the Ormonde line, and she claimed kinship with the Dukes of Norfolk, through her great-grandfather. It was said that her husband cared more for deer than for his wife, which gave Henry ample opportunity to pursue the pasty parrot whilst her husband was chasing other game.

I had learned, too, about her son, John. Widely rumoured to be the King's bastard, although Henry had never acknowledged him, he was being educated at St David's in Pembrokeshire, Wales. He was said to much resemble Henry, both in physical appearance and character. Mary Perrot was proud of her son, and talked of him endlessly at court.

As for my husband… Henry must have thought misery had made me blind, deaf and dumb, for he made no effort to hide his flirtation. In the dark days inside my chamber, he had attempted to console me, but now Henry seemed to forget our shared sorrow as easily as he might forget what robe he had worn to bed. Perhaps this show of favour to another woman was also about demonstrating his displeasure. There was a cold streak of spite in my husband. I had disappointed him. I would be punished.

Sorrow can be like that. I had been told to bury mine, as Henry had his. But sorrow is a worm. Through layers of sticky repression it will creep, rising to the wet surface, and from there working ill. In not acknowledging sorrow we force it underground, but that which has been buried undead may not die. It finds a way out, and transforms. In Henry it had become malice. In me, emptiness.

I despised him, but I was also afraid. If other women stole his attention, they might lace his mind with the plots of my foes. The parrot had once been one of Katherine's ladies. If I allowed this wench to steal my husband away, what harm would she do? In the darkness of her bedchamber, what might she whisper in his ear? How would she paint me in his eyes? What might she convince him to do? Set Lady Mary into the succession ahead of my daughter? I needed no more enemies, and certainly not one so close to Henry. I had to draw him back to me.

This would be no easy task. I was not the merry mistress anymore. I buried my heart. I swallowed my soul. About court I presented myself as fresh, wild and happy to entice my husband to me. But a part of me had died with my son.

At night, when only close friends attended on me, I went to the elaborate silver cradle Henry had had made for our son, and I wept. My hands shook as I stroked the silver Tudor roses and precious stones encrusted onto its shimmering surface. My fingers curled about the gold-embroidered bedding, pulling it to me, as if I could absorb my son into my soul.

Bitter tears streaked down my face by night, but as dawn emerged, I had to pretend all was well. I donned my mask and became another woman. Henry did not want me languishing in grief. I had to resume my position as Queen, and more than that, I had to push myself into the costume of the mistress once more to win him from the arms of his lovers.

Once, long ago, I had said to Henry that I would be merry to at last be able to discard the cowl of the mistress and wear only the garb of a wife and queen. But that cloak I had thought discarded had never left. Like an enchanted garment, embedded with a spell of magic, it came back. Only Henry could banish it.

But he would not. I could not be just Henry's wife. Anne, the mistress, still lived. She had to. It was not Henry's Queen who would strike aside her opponents.

How I wished George or Mary were there to console me! But Mary was still in the country and George was in France, bargaining to postpone the meeting with François and Marguerite. I felt alone. Were it not for Purkoy and my ladies, I might have relinquished all hope.

"How goes the questioning of Fisher and More?" I asked Cranmer, turning my eyes from Henry and his whore. I sipped from my goblet and then swiftly took another. Wine allowed me to forget my troubles… for a while.

"Slowly, and with great pains, Majesty." The good man sighed. "More tells Cromwell he had never understood that God had established the primacy of the Pope until he read the King's book on the subject, the *Assertio Septem Sacramentorium*. And then, More says, as he is led by the wisdom of His Majesty *himself*, he cannot allow the King to be upheld as Supreme Head of the Church."

"More uses the King against himself," I noted. "A foolish play, and one not likely to win his liberty."

"Indeed not, Majesty. More says he told the King at the time of publishing that he should not engage in arguments about papal authority, as if there ever came a time when he was involved in a dispute with the Pope, his words might come back to haunt him. More says he investigated further, spurred on by the King's theories, and found that His Majesty was indeed correct and the authority of Rome had been created in ancient times to prevent schisms in the faith. He said the King had set him on this path *personally*, and he had upheld His Majesty's philosophy, using it to govern his decisions. He protests he made his position on the *Great Matter* clear to His Majesty, and was accepted as Lord Chancellor in the full knowledge that he was opposed to the annulment. He said the King had sworn many times that he would never seek to force him to act against his conscience, and therefore he could not swear the oath. " Cranmer paused. "But he did say he supported the King's right to choose his wife and to appeal to the General Council about his excommunication."

"How gracious of him," I said dryly, making Cranmer smile.

"He said to Cromwell that the King had no authority to create laws which acted against the See of Rome," Cranmer went on. "And could not diminish the authority of the Pope."

"He treads close to treason," I noted. "The King will not hear his authority questioned. Not now."

"His Majesty has all but lost patience with More," said Cranmer. "And Fisher too, for he protests much the same." Cranmer sipped from his cup. "Fisher is, however, ill, and his quarters in the Tower make him sicker still. He continues to protest a layman may not govern the Church, and that His Majesty is splitting the faith asunder, but his protests grow as weak as his body."

"But still they both maintain they did not support Elizabeth Barton?"

"They do. They say they met her and advised her not to speak against the King."

"Cromwell thinks they encouraged her."

"And he may well be correct, my lady, but to a lawyer, such as More, encouragement could mean, or *not mean*, many things." Cranmer drew a long finger about the rim of his silver goblet. "Fisher says that the late Archbishop Warham supported Barton, and he saw no reason to contradict him, since Warham was a man of learning and wisdom. He also protests that he had no need to inform the King about Barton's visions, as the lady herself told the King of them before her execution. More, too, says the same. He claims the King introduced him to Barton, and he counselled His Majesty to be cautious about her prophesies, as More was sceptical about their honesty, but at the time the King was too enthused to hear him. They say that Barton was in communication with the Dowager, and offered support to Lady Mary too."

"My husband talks of going to France," I said. "Perhaps leaving me as regent."

"He worries you are not hale enough yet for the visit, Majesty."

Again, that look I had seen in so many eyes; that wary sympathy. No one spoke of my baby, but everyone knew of him. The silence about my child was conspicuous, tangible. It hung about me... another cloak I would never discard, woven from strands of sadness and wrenching, wretched grief.

"If I am made regent, I shall take care of his rebellious bastard," I said, almost to myself.

Mary had been on my mind. I would not allow her to threaten Elizabeth. Her refusal to swear the oath of succession angered Henry, but it imperilled Elizabeth and me. It was an outright denial of my position as Queen, and my daughter's rights and future. If Katherine was the Queen, as Mary so vehemently claimed, I was nothing more than a whore and Elizabeth was a bastard. It struck at the foundations of my security to have Mary at liberty, and I was determined she would not remain so if I was left as regent.

"What would you do, Majesty? Any harm that came to the Lady Mary would be dangerous for relations with Spain."

"King Charles cares nothing for his aunt or cousin," I said. "He is true to politics, not piety. If I am left in control of England, I will ensure Mary swears the oath, and if not, she may face the same fate as More and Fisher." Cranmer looked shocked and I smiled. "I do not mean I would see her *dead*, Eminence, but sometimes, when dealing with troublemakers, we must demonstrate might."

"Of course, Majesty," he said, relieved. "The same is true of Fisher and More. The King would never *truly* have them executed."

"Would he not?" I asked, glancing at my husband. A ring of pretty ladies fluttered about him, as though he were a fine cock and they his adoring hens.

"I think you misjudge your King, Cranmer," I said, taking a large swallow of wine. "For there are times I think him capable of anything."

*

"I did as you asked, Majesty," said my father. I had been mesmerized by the scene outside my window, and jumped sharply as he spoke.

Summer was spread over England, thick as butter. Golden, glowing light stretched radiant fingers, illuminating fresh green leaves and sweet flowers. At dusk, the skies became pearl and shell, reflecting all colours; pinks, blues… ochre, emerald and lapis. In daylight, the sun was a haze of amber above a wide, warm sky of shimmering magic. The wings of birds were made into a cascade of colour; bright blue glimmering through black feathers, purple lights glinting on sharp, dark bills.

"And failed in your mission?" I patted a cushion, indicating for him to sit. Embroidered with my initials entwined with Henry's, it was a work of art. Along with our sewing for the poor, my ladies and I were making enough cushion covers, bed hangings, embroidered cloth and wall hangings to smother all the palaces of England. My mark was everywhere. Perhaps the pernicious parrot was not alone in attempting to establish her territory.

"Not without trying," he said, sitting down.

"Of that I have no doubt," I replied. "But I know your quarry. She is a tricky hind."

I had sent my father to Lady Mary to try to convince her to relinquish her title and swear the oath of succession. I sent him with promises, from both Henry and me, saying she would be well treated if she agreed. I held small hope. By now, Mary would have heard whispers that I was not to have a child. Whatever she made of the odd silence about my son, she would have understood this could only bode well for her. But the shadows of the Tower were long. Mary also knew More and Fisher had refused the oath, like her, and even if once she had been a princess, the possibility of arrest and execution remained.

"How did she seem?"

"Ill," said my father, taking his hat from his head and placing it on the seat. Twin feathers, one black and one white, clasped against the rim with a golden pin, shook gently as he set it down. "She looked aged, and her skin was grey."

"Perhaps she has her mother's constitution."

"Or her father's."

I frowned. Henry had suffered lately with his legs. His veins were swollen and at times they became inflamed, leading to pain. His men had been commanded to keep this quiet, but if my father, who despite being Lord Privy Seal was no longer a part of Henry's intimate circle, knew, clearly knowledge of Henry's infirmities was leaking into court.

"I am sure you did your best," I said. "Is there any news from our friend in Antwerp?" Some time ago I had asked my father to get word to William Tyndale that Henry was after him. Henry wanted this reformer in custody, but I would not allow that to happen.

"Our friend received the warning, and gave thanks for it," my father said. "And I have further news. He was asked to write a treatise condemning your marriage, and refused. Officially he said he would meddle no more in this affair, but I believe he has too much respect for you to speak against you or, by association, the King."

I glanced at the New Testament open on the table in my rooms. The inscription was dedicated to me. A gift from Tyndale who, even if he would not openly support my marriage as he believed Henry's first was valid, did support me as Queen. It might have seemed a contradiction, but I was willing to accept any support offered.

"Is there news of the revised translation?"

"There is. It might be ready soon, and he has been working on Genesis also."

The second edition of *Tyndale's New Testament* was being widely discussed, albeit carefully, about court. Reformers were keen to get their hands on a copy, for it was rumoured to be a masterpiece.

But even as Tyndale toiled, Antwerp was becoming dangerous for free-thinking men. The Emperor, shamed by his inability to control the rise of Lutheranism in his northern territories, was pushing a crushing foot down upon the Low Countries. Increasingly violent penalties were being introduced, designed to destroy reformers of every clan and creed. The possession of vernacular Bibles, or any tome upholding the works of Luther or the theologians of Louvain, an unorthodox and increasingly popular tribe of philosophers, were now punishable by imprisonment, torture or death. Meetings of 'heretics' to discuss the Scriptures and any incident of iconoclasm were likewise punishable by death. *"The men beheaded by the sword, the women buried alive in a ditch, the relapsed burned,"* so read the ordinance of the Emperor.

Those willing to inform on friends and neighbours were richly rewarded with shares in spoils confiscated from these men of faith. Officials had been warned that clemency or laxity would be harshly punished, and the Inquisition was granted the right to torture, confiscate property, and execute heretics without right of appeal. Printers who published inflammatory works could face branding with a cross, burned deep into their skin, and rubbed in with ashes, so its fire would never die. Judges, if so moved, could order that accused men were also to lose hands, feet, or eyes, as a horrific addition to branding. But printers continued to print, and writers to write. Their pens and presses would not be silenced by unrighteous souls.

Dark days these were, but there were still people of faith willing to risk their lives for the benefit of their eternal souls.

Tyndale had taken refuge in the English House, and there he had some protection. He also had another fortification; his belief that Henry's first marriage was valid. Little as this pleased me, I thought it would keep him safe. The Emperor was not likely to turn on one who had so publicly, to Henry's intense mortification, supported Katherine.

But in sending the gift of his New Testament into my hands, Tyndale had made his motives clear to me. I was the Queen he wanted on this throne.

"I want a copy when it comes out," I said.

"If one is not *immediately* forwarded to you here by our friend, Majesty." My father smiled. "George sent word too, he should be home tomorrow."

I felt a breath escape my lips. "I long to see him."

"He is eager to see you, too," he said. "I informed him about…" My father nodded towards my belly and I felt my heart stagger. "So you would not have to explain."

I cast my eyes away, blinking back tears. Such unusual tact and understanding from my father was almost more than I could bear. Kindness, when one is accustomed to cruelty, is shocking and unnerving.

"It will be good to have him home," I said, pushing back the darkness which strove to claim me.

The human mind is a place of many shadowed corners, where much may be stowed away. It is necessary, is it not? For those who suffer abuse, hardship, sorrow and grief, to hide memories is to be able to continue on, and face each new day. It is not a cure, just a remedy. In truth, I did not know how much harm I was doing to myself.

"Did George say how his mission went?"

"He convinced François to delay the meeting," said my father. "But more than that I do not know."

When my father departed, I sat at the window, staring at nothing. The golden light of the morning had departed and the world had become grey, swathed in mist. When George had left, I had been on the cusp of a new life. With a babe in my belly and a daughter in the nursery, I was secure. Now he was to return to England and would find a different world. My son was lost, my daughter's rights were being questioned, and Henry was busy forgetting his sorrow between the legs of other women.

As I stared at the window, a flash of my son's face washed before me. His tiny eyelids, closed so he would never see the horror nor the beauty of the world; his skin tinged with blue; small hands curled about tiny palms.

I looked away.

It made no matter. He followed me. He was in every window and every mirror; in the reflection of a pond and in my dreams. Did my son haunt me? Unable to find rest, bereft of the solace of God, did he come to me to find comfort?

I had longed for my brother to return, but suddenly I did not. If I could prevent George from witnessing my grief, then perhaps it was not real, and all that had happened had been but a terrible dream.

Chapter Five

Greenwich Palace
August – September 1534

"I cannot express my sorrow," my brother said, putting his warm hand into mine. "All I can do is be here, if you need me."

"You are the only one who will speak of my boy," I choked. "Mother and Father ignore the subject, as do my ladies. I endure their stark sympathy. They look at me with eyes that entice me to speak, and faces that turn from me if I do. They think speaking of it will make my sorrow worse, or will cause me to slide into that realm of suspicion and sorrow I inhabited when my babe died, but this silence is almost more than I can bear."

"It was the same for Jane and me when we lost children," George said. "People know not what to say, so they say nothing. It is better than everyone telling you all will be well, I assure you."

"I *need* to speak of him, George," I murmured, uncomfortably wondering if I, like all the others, had gone silent on my brother when he had suffered. Guilt assailed me, but George, if he noticed or had been wounded in the past by this, did not allow that to affect him now. My brother was a man of many virtues. He suffered from pride and had a reckless way with money and women, but he had a true heart, devoid of spite.

"I know," he said. "So speak of him to me."

I unleashed my heart. I told my brother of my strange fantasies when my son was born dead, of the accusations I had thrown at my women. I spoke of my dreams. At one stage he smiled, and stopped me.

"You omit something," he said as I spoke of a dream I had had of Elizabeth and my son playing together at Eltham. "You make childhood into a happy realm of sunshine and laughter, but that is not the way it would have been. You must include some sibling squabbles between Elizabeth and her brother."

"Henry," I interjected. "I would have named him for his father."

"Your son, Henry," he continued. "They must fight, sometimes, in these dreams, Anne, or they are simply not real children."

I laughed despite myself, and George beamed. "You always know how to cheer me," I said.

"You have a talent for that yourself, sister *spirit*."

"Thank you for listening."

The release was greater than I could have imagined, and I was more grateful than I could say. Something in the dark chamber of my mind had snapped open. Hidden horrors could no more rise unbidden, or sneak out to thrash me. The ancients said that knowing the true name of a being granted power; in speaking of sorrow, perhaps

I had named it, and taken back its influence over my heart. It would always be there, but George had granted me the strength to face it.

"I *am* an ambassador." He grinned. "I am good at listening. Do you not know we are all spies?"

"How was France?"

He shrugged. "François agreed to postpone until April, but he remains no happier with Henry. He blames him for ruining all his good work with the Pope. He harbours resentment." George breathed in deeply. "He thinks Henry made him look a fool."

"The slight was never intended."

"To kings, all slights, real or imagined are intended. They are fragile creatures."

*

"I regret, Majesty, my time has all but been taken up with other commissions."

"Since that is good for your career, Master Holbein, do not grieve." I smiled. "All I wish for is a sketch."

My smile was sad. I had called the painter to me not for a royal portrait, but so I might have something to remember my son. If I could hold him no more, and could not visit his grave, I would take an impression of myself at this time, and remember him through it.

"Just an hour of your time," I said.

"For you, madam, I would give *all* my time," said the good man as he took a seat.

The sketch did not take long, and when Holbein gave it to me, he apologised for it, even though I thought it accurate. It showed me in sad repose, dressed in my nightgown with a cap upon my head, staring thoughtfully ahead. A slight double chin was present, as I had asked for honest depiction and no flattery. The fat that had accumulated in bearing my child had not yet diminished. My breasts sagged slightly, and twisting silver lines, where my skin had stretched, roamed over my belly and thighs. About my middle there was a roll of spare flesh. Henry did not like this, and I had started fasting, terrified that his revulsion at my form, a form which was, as I told myself, only natural after carrying a child, might send him only more frequently to his mistresses.

I was fighting a battle against myself. To keep my husband I had to maintain the figure and allurements of the young damsel he had fallen for, but in order to hold my position I had to become a mother, which does not come without toll on the body. I was being silently commanded to become a perfect being; a wife and mother who was also a slim, nubile maid. It was an ideal that could not be achieved.

It was also unfair. I had never expected Henry to remain the young lad he had once been. I did not love him less for the rolls of fat that formed at his belly, for the grossly swollen veins on his legs, or for the second chin, rapidly giving way to a third, under his first. He, too, was not the Adonis he had been on the day of his coronation when first I saw him.

The only times I thought ill of him for his form were when I was hurt and angry at his betrayals. It is common, when one is wounded, to find a way to strike at the person who harms us, if only in thought. When I loved him, I saw not the body he dwelled in, but the soul within. That is love, when it is true. We love not the vessel, but the heart and soul bound inside.

As I gazed on the sketch, however, I noted something that was not honest. Holbein had begun colouring it, and I asked why he had left the suggestion of fair hair.

"It *is* a delicate portrait, Majesty," he said. "You are in a state of undress… I did not want anyone supposing it was you, if it were found."

I smiled. My raven hair was famous. It was true that if any saw this portrait they would not think it was me because of the hair. "I thank you for your thoughtfulness," I said. "But I do not intend to show it to anyone. It is for me."

Holbein also designed goblets and jewellery for me. A silver cup I owned was his work, emblazoned with my arms and the emblem of the white falcon. But Holbein was not the only artist I patronised. Although I had always been interested in them, I felt drawn to art, music and poetry more in the aftermath of sorrow. Perhaps it is like that for many of us; we seek beauty elsewhere when we find none in the barren days of our lives.

A few years ago, I had recommended Lucas Hornebolte to Henry when the position of court painter had fallen vacant. Hornebolte, a native of Ghent, held reformist sympathies, and was a refugee from his native land. He had been long in England and had commissions from numerous noble houses, many of them my enemies. In truth, I thought Holbein the more talented of the two, but since Hornebolte had been linked to my foes, I thought it might be valuable to have him on my side.

Hornebolte was particularly skilled at manuscript illumination. I loved decorated books, and owned many. Some were poor, cheap copies I had bought with my, then meagre, allowance in France and Mechelen, and others I had purchased at great costs as Marquess and Queen. They were as precious to me as any jewel, and many were in fact more costly.

I turned to my books. I looked on the words I had inscribed in them as a youth, and found myself smiling at my zealous naivety. *"The time will come,"* I had written in Latin in one under a picture of the Second Coming and the Resurrection of the Dead, never knowing that one day I would stand at the forefront of almighty change in England, bringing the light of God to its people. That was how I wished people could see me, but my reputation was at odds with such hallowed thought.

I hid in books, in art and music, seeking the peace my soul required. My musicians played, and I did too, taking to my decorated clavichord or virginals to lose myself in dipping notes and lingering melodies. I showed court musicians the book containing sheets of music I had collected in my time abroad and in England. Some of these works, with a strong emphasis on the wonder of motherhood, were played in my rooms. I listened to prayers envisioned as coming from the mouth of Biblical Hannah, or Anna, when her son was born, and thought on my son and my daughter.

By day and by night I was at court with Henry, but when I could, I went to my rooms. I could never be alone, my women were always with me, but in my books, in contemplation of art, I could feel as though I were alone for a while. At night, when the palace was still, I called for musicians to play sweet songs of hope and joy. I tried to remind myself that all was not lost, that there was still hope.

In such ways did I mourn my child.

Chapter Six

Greenwich Palace
August – September 1534

"Sometimes, when I regard your train of ladies, niece, I think I am mistakenly called Queen," I mentioned to Margaret Douglas as her ladies trooped out of the room. For a moment the girl looked abashed, but as she saw my grin, her shoulders sagged.

"Do you think them too many, Your Majesty?" she asked. "I told my uncle that I do not need so many women to attend me, but he insists."

"He will see you honoured, for he loves you dearly," I said, touching her fur-lined sleeve. "I was jesting, Lady Douglas. I am pleased the King honours you, for you are also in my heart."

It was true enough. Margaret Douglas was a winning creature and I enjoyed her company. Friend to Lady Mary she may be, but she was kind, gracious and warm to me. Margaret did not place herself on either side. She liked us both, she had said, and only hoped one day we might be friends.

A sweet wish… if an unlikely one. Lady Mary had been unwell of late, and in her illness, courtiers visited her and people who lived near Hatfield turned out to cheer her. I did not want my precocious daughter, who was just starting to understand the world, to hear people who should have shouted acclaim for her, screaming instead for her bastard sister.

But Margaret I liked. Her mother and I were in communication, exchanging letters so I could reassure her Margaret was being treated well. And that she was. Henry was besotted with his niece. He saw her as the perfect embodiment of all that was pure and good, and held her up as a paragon of chastity and good behaviour. Henry hoped some of this sparkling virtue would rub off his *Magrett's* shoulders and fall upon his headstrong bastard.

Wanting to honour his niece, Henry had granted her a grand train of ladies. It was fitting for her station, although technically Margaret was not a princess. She might be considered one in England, being the daughter of Margaret Tudor, but in Scotland she was but the King's half-sister, born of noble, not royal, blood. But Henry was never going to allow any man to think Margaret was anything less than royalty. I did not mind Henry's love for the girl, for I loved her too. Although she was traditional in her faith, Margaret at times approached me for guidance, and listened to my ideas.

"I will always remain Catholic rather than Lutheran, Majesty," she said, glancing at me nervously after we had discussed the worship of idols. I preferred to *discuss* rather than *lecture* on issues of faith. Henry believed in shouting until everyone agreed with him, but I believed in gentle persuasion, even though many people would have snorted contemptuously at such a notion from me.

"Of course, what do you think I am?" I smiled. "People like to say that I am a heretic, or Lutheran, but it is not so. I believe in reform, but reform of the Catholic Church to make it better, not to do away with it." I eyed her carefully. "You will find, my lady, many who disagree with reform will paint those who do with a sullied brush. You are a clever young woman, but you must open your eyes. Reformers are not the demons you have been told they are."

"I do see, Your Grace," she said. "And I thank you for talking of such matters with me. Many people are scared to discuss anything to do with faith."

"People are scared of that which they do not understand," I said. "The remedy is to come to understand it, and in doing so, appreciate both sides of an argument." I brushed down my gown of green velvet. "I do not say that you should believe all you hear, on either side," I went on. "Nor will I tell you that all arguments carry the same weight, or truth. But you are wise enough to decide much of this for yourself, and to establish a personal link to the Almighty, allowing yourself to be guided by His love."

It was not only with Margaret that I discussed religion. The subject was debated in my chambers almost daily. Differences in interpretation and new theories on idols, the Mass, transubstantiation and the authority of Rome were often brought up by enquiring minds. We had to be careful, of course… it was easy to stray into regions that Henry would consider heresy, but we talked, we discussed, and ideas flowed through my household like water along a bustling stream.

Some of my ladies immersed themselves in discussion of the Scriptures as others shied away. Elizabeth Browne, the Countess of Worcester, along with Margaret and Mary Shelton, and Mary Howard, my young cousin, relished debate. Elizabeth Browne was a lively soul, blessed with a fine, strong mind and I welcomed her participation, for she often had much of worth to say.

Sometimes, in the evening, Cranmer would visit. At times, he wanted my authorization to accelerate Church appointments, so godly men might be put in place quickly. Sometimes it was just out of friendship that he came calling.

With him, I was perfectly safe. We kept our voices low when we talked of something controversial, but we dared to speak of much… sometimes of subjects of which Henry would not approve.

"I have had much cause of late to think on purgatory and limbo," I mentioned one warm evening as we sat before my hearth. There was no fire, since it was summer, but the fireplace was flush with garlands of greenery and scented flowers from the palace grounds. "I am sure you understand why."

"Of course," said my old friend.

"Do you think it selfish to only think on weighty subjects when they affect me personally?"

"No, indeed, Majesty," said Cranmer. "It is natural for us to find paths to the answers we seek for our own solace. God guides us in this way." He paused and pursed his lips. "Some might say the challenges the Lord of Heaven sends are in fact offered *in order* to steer our thinking. We were granted free will, but our heavenly Father sends lessons that we might learn and grow as spiritual beings."

"Perhaps that is the truth. For I find my mind is filled with questions." I turned to him. "Some reformers deny purgatory. They say God would not allow the faithful, no matter their sins, to burn in fire to atone before entering Heaven. They say that faith alone takes a soul to God, and that repentance before death is all that is required. Do you think this is so?"

"I have long thought purgatory a myth, Majesty…" said Cranmer, his voice low. It was dangerous talk, for Henry upheld purgatory as a canon truth. "… Made up by Rome in order to sell pardons and indulgences to unwitting dolts."

"Do you think the same of limbo?"

"You ask because of your son?"

I inclined my head. "He was carried by a faithful soul," I said. "Should he be denied the glory of Heaven for coming too soon into this world? Should he dwell in limbo, without comfort, never to see me or his father again, for want of a sprinkle of water upon his head?" I shook my head. "I do not think God would be so cruel as to deny eternal peace to babes who have never sinned."

"And it would seem odd, madam, that the founding fathers of the faith of our Lord Jesus Christ, should be starved of the solace of God."

"Indeed, for if unbaptised babes linger in limbo, so do all souls who were not baptised before the coming of our Lord and John the Baptist."

"Privately, my lady, I agree."

"Then you think I will see my son again?"

Cranmer's hand fell over mine. "I do, Majesty," he murmured, clutching my fingers. "And then, you will have all the time in existence to be together."

"I will tell him stories of our reform for England, when we meet again in Heaven."

"He will be proud of you," said my old friend, somehow reading my private, plaintive wish.

Even with Henry, I dared to speak my mind. I talked of limbo and our son, and although he did not agree with me entirely, he listened. It was one of the cornerstones of our relationship. There were many people he would not deign to hear when they spoke on subjects he did not agree with, but with me it was different. Henry respected my mind, even if not always my feelings.

"But," he said after I outlined my theory. "The Limbo of Infants is not a bad place, Anne. The Church assures us that those who dwell there rest in perfect happiness, for whilst they were not freed from original sin, they committed no personal sin."

"Why would God deny His comfort to souls of innocence?" I asked. "Even Rome is undecided on the matter, Henry. Not all adhere to the teachings of Augustine of Hippo, who said unbaptized souls would not attain Heaven, but would rest instead in the mildest of condemnations. Some say the Resurrection of Christ, which removed the stain of original sin, did so to the founding fathers of the faith, to Adam, to Eve, Moses and Abraham. Should not the same be true of our son?"

"The midwives should have been more diligent in their duty," was all he would say.

"They thought, until the last, that there was hope," I murmured. "They would have baptised him before death, had they not thought there was a chance he would live."

Henry fell silent, then started to talk about alterations he was making to Whitehall Palace. When I slipped into speaking directly of our son, idle conversation was the shield he used to batter me backwards.

*

Towards the midst of August, as we went to Whitehall, others were on the move too. Lady Mary came to Greenwich, and on her way, she floated through London on an open barge, ensuring everyone could see her.

Mary incited pity and sympathy. She was a pretty girl, if frail in health, and Londoners adored her. As she sailed down the Thames, her boat rocking on the dim, muddy waters, she stood upon its deck, waving to those who crowded on the slippery banks and the beaches beside the Thames. Henry was not best pleased. He had granted no permission for his obstinate daughter to travel so openly.

Her performance was nothing more than false courage; a way to show the people of England that she was neither intimidated nor cowed by her royal father. I was sure she was not so brave in her heart. It was said openly at court that Henry despised her, and Mary was sure to have heard this. It must have been painful to know that her father thought ill of her, and more painful still to hear her mother's protests and encouragement to maintain her war against the father Mary loved so dear.

There were others keeping up their rebellion too. More had been granted privileges in the Tower, and he used them well. Although Cromwell was checking his correspondence, More sent letters of hope to Fisher, his fellow inmate, and to family and friends. Stokesley, the Bishop of London and More's good friend, had taken the oath along with all other bishops of England. Only Fisher stood firm amongst the clergy. But just because these bishops had surrendered to Henry, it did not mean they would cease to encourage More in his protest.

Inside his cell, More was busy. He was composing a new work, he told Cromwell, called *A Dialogue of Comfort Against Tribulation*, and hoped one day that the King would read it, and understand his pains.

"I want you to assure me that this will not be published," I said upon hearing of this. "Neither I nor the King want to see that man gaining more sympathy." I frowned as Cromwell inclined his head. "I think security is too lax, in any case," I went on. "It would appear his letters have been stolen out and reached wider circulation."

"They were *allowed* to, Majesty," said Cromwell.

I paused, narrowing my eyes. "You would offer him rope to hang himself?"

"I would offer him rope to hang himself."

Chapter Seven

Whitehall Palace and Eltham Palace
August – September 1534

Late that summer, a keening cry sounded over England; the sound of abject despair.

En masse, Observant Friars were expelled from their monasteries. Many were arrested, joining their friends in the Tower for refusing to swear the oath. Others were shipped off by the cartload, separated, and sent to orders that showed more obedience to Henry than the zealous Greyfriars. Henry was done with waiting for the clergy to bend to his will. He would have obedience, or they would die.

Public outcry was heard alongside the wailing friars. The Observants, along with the Bridgettines of Syon Abbey and the Carthusians, were the three religious orders who still served some use to England. To see their brothers arrested or detained for treason was unnatural and abhorrent to the people of England. I, too, was left uncomfortable. These orders actually kept to their vows. It seemed to me we should be persuading, rather than persecuting them, but Henry did not agree.

"They have stood against me, flouted me in public," he growled. "And they shall be taught who their master is."

There was no petitioning for clemency. Henry was done with patience. One hundred and forty-three monks were locked away in the Tower; singled out as ringleaders. Others were all but imprisoned by their fellow clergymen, who were scared of Henry and Cromwell. John Forrest, once Katherine's chaplain, was arrested for a second time and sent to the Tower to await judgement. Along with his refusal to swear the oath, he had visited Katherine and offered her encouragement.

Forrest, along with Fisher and More were the first of Katherine's friends to linger under the shadow of death. They would not be the last.

Katherine was reportedly bitter, but she blamed Clement, declaring the Pope's dithering had forced Henry into direct and abominable action. By now, Katherine must have understood that her nephew was not coming to her rescue. This was what we all thought too, but as foreign affairs erupted that summer, we were forced to re-evaluate our convictions.

That summer Suleiman the Magnificent, Sultan of the Ottoman Empire, Caliph of Islam, sent his Admiral, Khair-ad-Din Barbarossa, to besiege southern Italy. His forces came close to the walls of Rome. In August, Tunis was captured, posing an immediate threat to Spain, Italy and the entire Mediterranean. The Emperor began to assemble an army, sending messengers to Rome to request support for his crusade. Henry swiftly became nervous that rather than gathering troops to battle the infidels, Charles might decide to turn his forces on England.

As though in response to her father's paranoia, or perhaps because of his treatment of the clergy, Lady Mary suffered a fit of hysteria and became seriously ill. Mary had become increasingly isolated, with few servants and only two true supporters outside of the Tower; Katherine and Chapuys. But her mother was a prisoner and the Imperial Ambassador, although he adored Mary, could do little to aid her. She had always suffered painful monthly courses, much like her mother, but this time it was more serious. Her health collapsed in the wake of the expulsion of the Observants, and she languished, some claimed close to death.

"I must send one of my physicians," said Henry upon reading the note from Lady Shelton. He handed it to me and I read. My aunt's concern was justified, I believed, and I understood her fear. Should Mary die, Lady Shelton would be held accountable, but I would be blamed too. My position was fragile. I could little afford more venom poured my way.

"Send Doctor Butts," I advised, thinking that my old helpmate would not only deal with Mary's medical problems but could keep an eye on anything passing from her to the Emperor. "Once he saved me, beloved, when I was struck down by the dreaded sweat. I can think of no other man more suited to care for your daughter."

Henry's brow lifted in surprise, for I was no supporter of Mary, but he agreed. "Butts shall go," he said and turned to Norris. "Henry, see to it this hour, will you?"

Doctor Butts shortly had a report for us. Lady Mary had fallen ill with headaches and cramps in conjunction with her courses, but as the symptoms had failed to alleviate, Lady Shelton had sent for a local apothecary. The pills this man had prescribed had caused a reaction, worsening Mary's condition. Doctor Butts requested permission to consult Katherine's doctor, and it was granted by a worried Henry. In the days that followed, I found my husband often in conversation with his men about the *many* virtues of his bastard. Whenever Mary fell ill, Henry's love for her returned, stronger than ever. It was troubling.

I wrote to Lady Shelton, upbraiding her for bringing the leech to Hatfield. In truth, I wrote in fear that somehow his name would be linked to mine. *"If you cannot exercise good judgement in the finding and ordering of such men,"* I wrote, *"then we will have all such matters conducted through court. I am wont to tell you that the King, too, suffers displeasure for your lack of care for his bastard daughter. If you cannot do the task assigned to you, you will be removed."*

Suffice to say, no matter how contrite and polite her apology, that letter won me no favour with my aunt. I heard unsubstantiated gossip that she had called me proud, disdainful and judgemental.

Katherine asked to join Mary so she could nurse her, but this was a step too far for Henry. Katherine's doctor's involvement was helpful however, as, having dealt with Mary's malady for a number of years, he understood it better than Butts. But he was not permitted to speak with Mary unless witnesses were present, and for the sake of appearances neither was Butts. They were also only to converse in English. Henry believed his daughter was unwell, but his trust only stretched so far. He did not want Mary sneaking out messages to her Imperial cousin.

Doctor Butts wrote that he believed her illness was caused by stress and sorrow, *"and she would be well at once if she were free to do as she liked."*

After Henry read this, he heaved a plaintive sigh. "It is a great misfortune that my daughter remains so obstinate," he said. "She steals all occasion for me to treat her well, as I wish I could."

Butts advised sending Mary to her mother, but Henry would not. "If I surrender, she will not," he said. "I know my daughter's resentful heart. She will read generosity as weakness."

I could have laughed. For how long had I been telling Henry this was the way of things only for him to ignore me? But however long it had taken, I was glad the idea had finally taken root. That was the way with Henry. He liked to believe all ideas were his.

Some took a more pragmatic view. Cromwell told his good friend Tom Wyatt that the deaths of Lady Mary and her mother would be beneficial, putting an end to tribulation with the Emperor. Since everyone believed that Cromwell and I spoke with one voice, this was taken by many as a threat, easily traced back to me.

The hapless hare was suspicious of Cromwell. He was sure, not without cause, that Cromwell had spies in Katherine's household.

"Well, he is not wrong there," said my brother as he, I, and Norris walked in the gardens. "Cromwell has spies everywhere. There is no corner of England that is not infested with his little spiderlings."

"He does good work for the King," I protested. "Do not speak so wild of our allies, George."

"I have come to think that Cromwell is an ally to many… for as long as it serves him," said Norris.

"You doubt his character?" It was unusual for Norris to speak against another man. He was cautious and careful, never stepping far from the path of politeness.

"I harbour *no* doubts about his character, Majesty." Norris smiled, his lips lifted in wry humour.

I was struck by his handsome face. When Norris smiled, he could light up the dullest gloom. He had a hawkish cast to his features; a slim nose and high brow and cheekbones. He was sharp of wit too, but never unkind.

"I am sure you are wrong," I said. "Cromwell does much for the cause of reform, and to protect the King, England, my daughter and me. He believes in our cause."

From the observable doubt on my brother and Norris' faces, I could see they did not agree. *It is his growing power that makes them wary,* I thought. *But if power is used for good, there is no danger in it.*

Later that day, Henry found me with a book in my lap, staring from the window. "You would see that good tome rest upon your pretty lap, never to be taken up and honoured by your hands?" he asked.

I smiled sadly. I had been thinking of our boy. "I find my mind is distracted today," I said, shutting the book.

"You have been distracted for a long time." He sat beside me and smoothed the black silk veil over my hair. "I have sent orders for Elizabeth to be brought to Eltham."

"In the summer?" This was most unusual. Although Eltham was apart from London, and therefore not so close to the risks of plague and sickness that rampaged in the city's streets during the summer months, there was still a danger. Hatfield was more remote.

"I think it would do you good to spend time with our daughter."

I stared into his blue eyes and saw the gentle sorrow there. *He does understand,* I thought. *Even if he says it not in words, he hears my heart.*

"I would be happy to see her," I said, brushing a light finger over his jaw. A rush of love fell upon me. At times like this, when he was once more the caring, considerate man I had fallen in love with, I could barely believe he had ever done me wrong.

*

Towards the end of that month, Elizabeth was taken from Hatfield to Eltham Palace. She travelled in style through London and was cheered as she passed.

It did not matter who her mother was, England's little Princess was adored by many. Even those who despised me admitted that she was an innocent, and when she was shown to the people, they cried out for her.

This brought me solace. Even if I was loathed, Elizabeth was loved.

Mary had gained permission from Henry to travel separately to her half-sister. Doctor Butts thought the hysteria that Mary had suffered was dangerous to her health. Forcing her to travel as a servant to her royal sister could bring on a relapse, he wrote, so Henry caved.

I went to see my daughter settled into her new home, but whilst there, I tried to reach Mary. I sent a message, telling her I would intervene with her father if she would recognise me as Queen. Mary sent my messenger back in no doubt of her mind.

I tried to set this aside as I took my daughter to the long gallery in Eltham. Elizabeth was a bonny one-year-old and growing fast. Most babes her age were shy with strangers, Elizabeth was not. She knew what stories she wanted to be told at night, and had favourite ribbons, dolls and games. Sometimes it pained me to see how easy she was with Lady Bryan and Shelton. She was close to them, but seemed to know I was her mother.

She was sturdy on her legs, the fastest crawler I had ever seen, and pulled herself up to stand using the furniture. She was not yet talking, although she could say "mama", "papa" and "*urse*", which we took to mean, 'nurse', and tried to copy what was said to her. My daughter could nod and wave, and was a master at expressing silent displeasure or happiness. And clearly, she understood what was said to her. Simple commands were obeyed, although sometimes with a scowl.

Elizabeth also giggled often, at the most unremarkable of things. What delight there is in the mind of a child, experiencing everything for the first time! Elizabeth made me feel young, as though part of her sparkling youth had come free of her skin and settled inside mine.

Together we played as sunlight stole through the diamond-paned windows which bore my arms. Her exquisite red hair, lit up like dragon fire, was just starting to tickle her neck. When I passed a hand through it, I was reminded of the touch of silk. Her creamy skin and large, black eyes, so like mine, were captivating. But when she grew restless or annoyed, she was every bit her father's daughter. Henry's petulance lived in her little mouth, and when she furrowed her brow and howled, she looked like Henry in a rage.

I had often thought there was something of the child in my husband. In Elizabeth, I saw that child.

I praised her for her efforts at standing and she gazed back with such a stoical, serious face that I laughed. Seeing me chuckling, she grinned and redoubled her efforts. When she fell, her bottom smacking on the hard floor, she looked at me in distress and started to howl. Then I took her in my arms and sang to her. There was nothing in the world that could calm her like my voice.

"Fowls in the frith," I sang. *"The fishes in the flood, And I mon waxe wood; Much sorrow I walk with, For beast of bone and blood. Fowls in the frith…."*

Elizabeth would fall asleep, not knowing what I sang, but obeying the gentle rise and fall of my rich voice, lulling her into slumber.

Whilst at Eltham, I took inventory of my daughter's clothes, and ordered more, along with a contraption to straighten her fingers and cloth for her bed. My daughter had a wardrobe as magnificent as mine, and I was determined that, in all ways, she would outshine her half-sister.

With Elizabeth, I sought to abandon my trials. Gossip was rife at court about my pregnancy. None of my ladies had revealed the terrible truth, but this did not stop malicious tongues wagging.

The Moors say that we were granted two ears and one mouth, so we may only pass on half of what we hear. But this does not hold that what we pass on must be truth. It may be lies.

Some said I had never been with child at all, and it had all been a falsehood, invented to trick Henry and keep his favour. How anyone could believe this when I had paraded a great belly about court for months was beyond me, and strangely, or perhaps not, gossip that I had tried to dupe Henry hurt me. These people compounded my sorrow. They would make my child a fiction. They would deny his existence, making my sorrow into a lie as well.

But they were not to blame. Henry was. If he had had enough courage to announce that I had lost my baby, we would not be in this situation. But Henry was too frightened of what people would say. They might believe I was incapable of having sons, or worse, that *he* was.

Many times had Henry's pride cost me dear, but never more so than then.

For his pride, I was lost, abandoned in silence.

Chapter Eight

Greenwich Palace
September 1534

A delicate foot slipped to one side as the lady lifted her hands to clap. The strike of her palms was crisp, perfectly in time with the music. As she whirled to one side, her silk gown of crimson billowing with her, her partner leapt into the air like an elegant stag bounding through the forest. His hands on his hips and his cheeks rosy with enjoyment, he pranced after her as spectators cheered.

Mary Howard and Henry Fitzroy. What a couple they made! She as pretty and complex as a fresh spring day, and he as bold as his father. Although still not permitted to share a room, or consummate their marriage, their approval of each other was as obvious as that of my husband for my pretty cousin, Mary Shelton.

Are your present whores not enough for you, husband? I thought as I watched Henry's eyes settle on Mary.

Henry wanted to possess what other men desired. Perhaps that was why he had first turned that avaricious eye on me. Once, I had been like Mary; the centre of all attention and lust. She, like me, was careful of her honour, and navigated the perilous path of courtly love with a light step. A careful foot was vital. Step too far one way and all men would think you were their whore, ripe for the plucking and also for abandonment. Step too far the other and all chance at advancement and patronage were lost as men thought you cold.

It is a strange life to lead, is it not? Katherine's voice entered my mind. It happened so often now that I barely thought it odd anymore. *Where women must play both the whore and the virgin at the same moment?*

We must be what men want us to be, I replied. *Men own this world. We cannot be loose like them, for then we would be set aside. We cannot be too reserved, for then we are ignored. We become the Virgin Mary and the Magdalene in one form. We must be their mistresses and their mothers. Their icons of worship and the demons they fear. That is why we play this game; because they fear us and only in pretence can we become all they expect, removing the peril their fear may bring upon us.*

Katherine fell silent and I welcomed the stillness. Although at times my personal phantom and I agreed, there were many more occasions when she said everything I wished I did *not* think. Perhaps in some ways, Katherine had become the voice of my conscience.

I moved through the ranks of courtiers, accepting bows and well wishes, enduring swift, stolen glances at my belly. No doubt they were taking note of the flatness there. My figure was returning under a regimen of fasting. Henry swore I had become a sparrow, so little did I consume. But I did not want to eat. I wanted to control my body. I wanted something, some power to cling to.

Henry stood with his mistress to one side of the throng, roaring with laughter at something she had said. God's Blood, did he think he was subtle?

I had to watch as he courted you. Katherine returned to plague me.

With me it was different, I thought. *He loves me.*

Loves, or loved? He claimed he loved me once too, before he locked me away in the fens.

It was true enough. Did he love so many that he could not decide which he loved the most? Did he love this straw-haired lass at his side? Joanna Dingley was not present, but the parrot was. Just *how many* women did my husband have? And why? Why did he need them when once he had sworn I was all he could ever want? I believed his problems with his manhood had led to these suddenly more-public-than-ever dalliances. In the past he had been discreet, but I wondered if Henry was attempting to conceal his insecurities by showing off his many mistresses. Surely a man who had two mistresses *and* a wife could not be at fault in the bedchamber? But I wondered just how often he actually bedded his whores, for he was fragile and often reluctant with me.

I also had reason to think again that part of this show was to spite me. And I was not the only one to note this.

Henry kissed the parrot's hand and went to his men. I thought to join him. As I walked past, Mary Perrot and others about her bowed. I noted, however, that all she did was incline her head and slightly stoop her foot, as though we were equals. I stopped and stared. Many of my women, who had seen her flagrant lack of respect, did the same.

"Have you injured your back, Mistress Perrot?" I asked coldly. "Or have you forgotten who is Queen?"

"I have not forgotten," the impudent wench replied. "Nor have many others, *Madame de Pembroke*."

Many courtiers gasped. "Do you have a poor memory, my lady?" I asked, bristling with rage. "Or have you forgotten that to fail to address royalty with the proper terms is treason? Do you seek a cell in the Tower?"

Her face paled under flushed cheeks. She was intoxicated, both with wine and Henry's open admiration. "I have not, Your Majesty." She dipped her leg to curtsey.

"Be of good cheer, Mistress Perrot," I said as she rose. "A strong memory is only of use if one has a head. If you carry on the way you are tending, you will have neither."

I swept away, my head high, as voices broke out behind me, but my heart was thundering. What impudence that sprite had! And it was born from Henry's devotion. As soon as I was clear of the hall, I sent Nan back with a message for Henry.

"I want that whore gone from court!" I screamed as soon as he entered the room. "She failed to bow to me, insulted me and addressed me as *Madame de Pembroke*!"

"She was flustered to be spoken to by you," Henry said, his face red with anger. "She claims you threatened her."

"Are not all who fail to recognise me as Queen traitors by your own laws, my lord?" I asked. "I could, therefore, demand her head. But I will make do with her exile."

"I will not send her from court simply for a silly slip of the tongue."

"You will not send her from court because you want to bed her, often and well," I said scathingly. "Do you have no care for me, for the pain I suffer to see you with other women?"

"Men serve you, do they not?" he demanded. "They flock to you. Why should I, the King, not take part in the games of chivalry?"

"With me, the games of courtly love are but *games*," I retorted. "With you they are not. You encourage this chit to spite me by showing her favour. And if she dares to say I am not the Queen, and you will not punish her, you insult the position that you, yourself, have granted me."

"You should think more on that position, madam," he said.

"For you would not grant me it again?" I demanded, mocking the insults he had offered me in other arguments. "You like to say this, do you not? No wonder your whores think ill of me. You feed them insults to throw at me, and Elizabeth. You would have me compete against these women for your pleasure, and you desecrate the sanctity of our marriage in doing so!"

Henry stormed off. He sent me a note later that night, telling me he would not send the parrot from court, nor demand an apology from her. I was instructed to leave her alone and not interfere again. *"Consider where you came from, madam, and how you have been honoured,"* Henry wrote.

I stared at the parchment. When we had argued in the past, Henry had always come to me. I had rarely gone to him.

This note was his way of telling me those days were done.

*

"She has been sending letters to the Lady Mary," Jane whispered in my ear as I simmered with rage in my chambers. I had sent my sister-in-law to find out all she could about Perrot. Much had I learned about Joanna Dingley that I did not want to know, but what I heard about the parrot was far worse.

The parrot had been one of Katherine's ladies, and had served her with open love and affection. She had been brazenly speaking about her support for Katherine, and had opened discussions several times, saying that my marriage to Henry was invalid in light of my pre-contract to Henry Percy. Apparently, Henry had allowed this to be said in his presence, a fact that chilled me to the bone. Courtiers who disliked me, like the Courtenays, the Poles, and Nicholas Carewe, were encouraging her affair with Henry, hoping to reduce my influence. And the squawking parrot had been writing to Lady Mary. I could guess what was in those letters.

The parrot was a genuine danger.

"Can you get hold of one?" I whispered to Jane as we strolled about my chamber, listening to rain hiss against the windows. Outside, a bright sun burned, glaring from behind dark clouds of rain. It cast a strange light over the world. Light was tinged with darkness and darkness with light. The twin sides of life appeared, blended as one. "I must know what this wretch is saying to Lady Mary," I continued.

"I will try," she said. "George has men who keep an eye on Chapuys' correspondence. Perhaps they would be able to do the same to Perrot's."

"Good," I said. "But do not speak of this to others." I sighed. "I wish my sister were here. God alone knows what business is keeping Mary in the country so long. She has been gone for months, and did not even come when…" I trailed off. An invisible cloth wrapped about my lips. I was not to talk of my son.

His face flashed before my eyes.

I felt Jane's hand on my arm and I looked down blankly. When my son came to my thoughts, my heart drifted from my body, and all that was left was a hollow cave. If you lifted my heart to your ear, I believe you might have heard echoing sorrow, cresting backwards, tumbling into nothingness. There was an abyss within me. It was all I could do to stop myself tumbling in, falling for the rest of my days.

Jane was staring at me with a blazing expression on her face. Her green eyes were alight with vengeance. It was not surprising. Had she not suffered the same as me, losing children and watching her husband run off to mistresses? George was, at least, a shade more subtle than Henry, but the pain inflicted was the same. I think Jane saw an echo of herself in me, and where she could not fly at George, she wanted to attack the woman who embodied both her outrage and mine.

"Jane," I said. "Do not do anything rash. Find those letters. If I can prove the parrot is sending messages to Lady Mary and encouraging her dissent, I can have her removed from court."

"Surely, you wish for more justice than that, sister?"

"Her removal will satisfy me."

"Then I will do as you command."

Unfortunately, Jane did not.

*

Henry strode into my chambers, afire with indignation. He was banishing Jane from court.

"For what reason?" I asked coolly.

"That lady has no decorum," he retorted with equal coldness. "She had a public fight with a minor noblewoman in front of the whole court. I am sending her away to teach her to hold her tongue." He glared at me and my face froze.

I knew what woman Jane would have picked a fight with and why.

"If my sister-in-law has offended Your Majesty, it is only proper she be sent away to think on her faults," I said smoothly, cursing myself. I should have seen Jane's inflamed temper and kept her away from Henry's mistress. He was angry to be shamed.

Curse you, too, Jane! I thought. Had she obeyed me I might be a step closer to getting one of those letters and proving the parrot was a menace. If she had written in outright support for Lady Mary and Katherine, Henry might have been persuaded to see her true nature. After this, I had little hope of getting hold of evidence. Gertrude Courtenay, one of the parrot's companions, was a spy mistress, and no stranger to subterfuge. She would instruct the whore to hide her letters.

"Thank you for informing me of your decision," I continued, struggling to remain calm. "I will see to it that Jane's maid and her dogs are also removed, to relieve any financial burden on Your Majesty."

I had to be careful. Exploding at Henry had only led to him abusing me. He did not like to be called out on his flaws. This situation was mortifying for him. He wanted everyone to believe he was a paragon of virtue. Jane's little scene had upset that fantasy.

I could not fight for Jane.

"Let us hope that some time in the country will calm Lady Rochford's spirits and allow her to see the benefits of reserved behaviour," I said, resuming my embroidery. "She is often too keen to speak before she thinks."

Henry grunted. "Yes," he said, relieved that I was not going to start shouting. "And... how are things with you, sweetheart?" he asked carefully, abruptly changing subject. "You and your ladies are keen to decorate all parts of the palaces. Everywhere I go I see your beautiful creations. Is this something new you are working on?"

He was so eager to talk to me that I felt a great piece of ice in my chest melt. Warmth flooded through misery and I clung to it as a woman may to a splinter of wood upon a rough sea. I thought of the ornament of the ship I had sent to him when we were courting. *I thought then that Henry was the ship that would keep me safe,* I thought. *Perhaps this is a wish that may never come true.* If Henry was the ship on which I, the maiden, travelled, he was also the sea, the tumbling, heaving waves, the oncoming storm.

"It is our badges," I said, holding the dark green cloth out. "Surrounded by the honeysuckle and the acorn, symbols of love and fertility."

"We will make more time to see each other, Anne," said Henry suddenly and gruffly. "There has been so much happening these past few months. It sometimes seems you and I are apart, but you must never think that. There is no one in the world for me but you."

They were just words. But I cherished them.

*

We heard that month that Pope Clement had died. His papal throne was passed to a new man, Cardinal Alessandro Farnese, who became Pope Paul III. Usually deliberations on the appointment of a new Pope took months, but this was passed in just one day. Forty years a Cardinal, and at the ripe age of sixty-eight, Pope Paul III swiftly took his seat amongst whispers of bribery, for none could see how else he had gained his throne so quickly.

On the surface, this was in our favour. Clement had been of no use to anyone, and Paul had, at least in passing, seemed more temperate than his predecessor towards Henry. Pope Paul let it be known that he was anxious to resolve Henry's argument with Rome and bring England back to the Catholic fold. He was also no friend to the Emperor, which brought us hope.

George and my father were much in company with Henry, and since I had accepted Jane's hasty removal from court, Henry and I were reconciled. George did not seem to care Jane was gone. If anything, he was relieved.

"Pope Paul appears more useful than his predecessor," I said to them.

"Could any man be *less* useful?" George asked, making Henry laugh.

"Will you make peace with Rome, my lord?" I asked my sniggering husband.

"On my terms alone will I consider it," he said. "If he ratifies my annulment, accepts you as my wife, and Elizabeth as our heir, until our son is born, I will make peace." He breathed in, extending his growing gut and emphasising the rather overlarge codpiece he was wearing.

Although popular at court, and generally nothing out of the ordinary when worn by other men, Henry's codpieces were becoming ridiculous. Unlike those worn by other men, which were discreet if noticeable, Henry's were getting larger by the day. He had started to wear jewels upon them too, whose sparkling lights drew the eye to his groin. I was certain this was another sign of his increasing fears about his abilities.

"It pleases me to hear this," I said, taking Purkoy into my lap. He gazed up with his huge, liquid eyes. There was a hunger within me to take the innocence I saw there into my heart, to shield me against life's oncoming storms. *If only such a miracle was possible,* I thought. Purkoy glanced up, as though he had heard me. My faithful hound always seemed to know my thoughts.

"Did you think I would allow Rome to have peace on any other terms?" Henry smiled; that boyish expression I had once adored on his face. "No, Anne," he said. "They will bow to us, not we to them."

Henry sent word for his ambassador in Rome to seek a meeting with the new Pope to discuss terms. With this soon to occur, Rome would not move forwards with any of Clement's notions about rousing Europe to invade, or reconfirming his bull of excommunication. Henry was sleeping better than he had for many months, as it seemed sure the Emperor would not be enticed to invade, and Henry sent word that he would grant the papacy a second chance.

I have no doubt when Henry's man in Rome opened that letter he found other ways to word it. From Rome's perspective, they were offering Henry a second chance. Henry thought just the opposite.

Chapter Nine

Greenwich Palace
September 1534

Reaching my apartments later that day, I strolled in accompanied by a merry mood. I felt light. *The appointment of the new Pope will bring nothing but good,* I thought as Purkoy danced beneath my feet, infected by my happiness.

As I turned into my rooms, talking brightly to Nan Cobham about entertaining Henry and his men that night, I found my ladies clustered about the hearth, deep in whispered conversation.

"What has you all so captivated?" I asked, only to stare in shock as they turned as one, abruptly ceased their chattering, and every one of them blushed crimson. I gazed into a sea of red. "What is it?" I asked, handing my cloak to Nan Gainsford.

"Majesty," said Margaret Lee, *nee* Wyatt, stepping forwards. "Your sister has returned to court. She is waiting in the next room with your mother and father."

"At last," I said with a trill of happiness. "Finally she is here." I walked to the chamber Margaret had indicated and felt a hand on my sleeve. I turned to find Margaret's worried face staring at me. "What is it?" I asked. "Is my sister unwell?"

"Majesty…" Margaret's voice failed her. It surfaced as a whimper. "She is with child."

I stared blankly at my friend, at a complete loss for words. "That… cannot be," I stammered eventually.

"You will see for yourself, Majesty," said Margaret, trying not to meet my eyes. "There can be no doubt of her condition."

I pushed through the door to find myself in the centre of a conspicuous silence. My father and mother were at the fireplace, their faces made of flint. I looked at them and they dipped to bow, but as I followed the path on which their eyes wended, I stopped in my tracks.

Mary was near the window. She heard me enter and dropped to an awkward curtsey. There was a gable hood of black silk on her head, rimmed with a pretty pearl-grey ribbon. Her gown was blue, trimmed with silver. For a moment, I was struck by her beauty, but as my eyes travelled down, I stared in horror. With the light from the windows beaming upon her, my sister might have been an angel… were it not for the bold, large, bump sticking out from her gown.

The door behind me opened, but I did not turn. I was transfixed… I had become a statue. And as my brother entered, I felt my heart tumble from my chest, slipping past my shoes, past the floor, and dropping to the bowels of Hell.

I lost my baby, I thought. *And my own sister comes to parade this before me?*

I stood staring at her with my mouth open. Mary's face was bright white. She looked like the moon. Perhaps such a thought was fitting, for there was something of that being's ancient loneliness in her at that moment.

"What," I said slowly. "Is that?"

George came to a sudden stop behind me. From the corner of my eyes, I saw his widen as his face lost all colour. Our mother's expression was much the same; drawn and pale. But Father was a blood moon to Mary's full. He was struggling to contain himself.

"*That*," he spat. "Is evidence of your sister's whoring, Your Majesty."

"I am no whore!" Mary almost shouted, twisting on her heel to face him.

George raced to intercept our father as he lunged at Mary in a sudden, violent rage. "You *are* a whore!" our father shouted. "You have always been a whore!"

"Once, you found that useful, Father," she murmured. Mary swallowed and took a step back as she saw his face. Our mother stepped between them, taking hold of Mary as my sister swayed, pale and afraid.

"Touch her not, Elizabeth," Father hissed through gritted teeth, trying to shake his son off. "Let me go, George!"

Reluctantly, George released him. "It is not becoming to beat the sister of the Queen, Father. Nor does it add to your honour to threaten a pregnant woman."

"*Pah*!" said our father, spitting flecks of white spittle from his mouth as he advanced on his eldest. His hands flew in her face. "The Queen asked you a question, girl. What is *that*?"

"It is not a '*that*'," she said quietly. "It is the lawful child of a good man; my husband."

"Your *husband*?" The words burst from my mouth. "Pray tell me, sister, when was the Second Coming announced, that the dead may walk once more amongst us? When did my good brother William Carey return from the grave? I am most sorry to have missed such a momentous occasion."

"Anne!" said my mother, never one to entertain sacrilegious talk at the best of times.

Mary steeled herself. "I was married, some months ago, to a good man, sister, and have known nothing but love and peace since."

"A good man? *A good man*?" our father exclaimed, marching on Mary as though he meant to stamp on her like a bug. George jumped again and pulled him back. Mary stared at me with fear and pleading in her eyes.

She wanted me to help her. But all I could see was her heavy, swollen belly.

I hated her for it.

All my pain, my anguish, all the misery of losing my child crashed inside me, grinding, making a paste of my heart, until all that was left was fury.

"You are married?" I said coldly.

She nodded. "Yes."

"Yes, *Your Majesty*," I said. "You forget, sister, both my position, and yours."

My family stared in amazement. I had never proclaimed my right, as Queen, to be head of the Boleyns. Yet now I used it. Father's face lit up with approval at my unyielding tone. Perhaps he had expected me to defend my sister, as I had when he assaulted her in France. He was delighted to find it was not so. My mother looked at me with surprise, but unlike my father's face, there was no approval of my harsh tone in her expression.

"Yes, Your Majesty," Mary obediently replied, adding a curtsey for good measure.

"Who?"

"His name is William Stafford, Your Majesty."

"Stafford? Of Buckingham?" It was a faint hope that Mary might have chosen kin of the dead Duke for her husband. And as she spoke the name, suspicion rose in me. Was it possible that that hungry-eyed young pup who had dogged her steps in Calais was the father of this child?

"Of… Cottered, Your Majesty," she said unwillingly, confirming my fears.

"Who is his father?" shouted my own father.

"Sir Humphrey Stafford, Father."

"The son of an attainted traitor," he sneered. "What have you done, girl? Married a no one, with no money or connections, without the approval of your father, family or your sister, the Queen of England? Do you have no wit in that stupid little head? Do you know what ruin and disgrace you have brought upon us? You turn up with some lump in your belly and expect us to accept you? It will not be. That thing is not my grandchild and *you are not my daughter!*"

Mary burst into tears. She fell to her knees and put her head to the floor.

"So, this is why you did not come," I said. "This is what you were doing in the country… Not seeing your children or tending to lands, but spreading your legs for some oafish bastard in the hay ticks? This is what you were doing when I asked you to come after I lost my son?"

She wept into the rushes and then looked up. "Sister," she said, holding out her hands. "I have been alone for so many years. I set aside my happiness to further the cause of your ascension to the throne. William and I met in Calais. He is part of the King's guard there. He admired me and courted me nobly, with honour. He wanted to ask for my hand, but I knew you would not allow it. But *I loved him*. I loved him so much that we married in secret. And although he is poor and without title, though he be but a third son of only a *Sir*, he loves me with all his heart, as I love him."

Mary's hands shook as she held them out, beseeching me to show mercy. "You, sister… my Queen… *you, too, married for love*, you too defied all who stood against you. And be they king or pauper, love is love; something given by God, as unchanging as the skies and seas. I could not live without William nor he without me."

She fell to weeping once more. I drew myself up and felt coldness fall, tumbling down my spine, infesting my blood, festering, rank and rotten in my heart. Never in all my life had I felt so jealous and full of hate. I could have ripped her apart.

"Get up," I said.

She wobbled as she stood. Her huge belly, more than seven months pregnant as she must have been, made her unsteady on her feet. I saw that, and in a flash my hand lashed out and slapped her hard across her pretty face.

She cried out as one of my rings caught her skin. Her beautiful eyes swam with tears as she saw the depths of my rage.

My mother was staring at me as though she didn't know who I was. Only my father was smirking. George looked amazed.

"*How dare you compare your marriage to mine*?" I shouted. "I married the greatest King on this earth and gave this land a princess of royal birth, with the support and approval of my family and God, whereas you have lain with some dirty soldier!"

"I thought you might be pleased for me, Majesty," she said, her eyes flashing with anger as well as fear. "To find happiness after so long. Much as you married for love, sister, I have done the same."

"I am head of this household now, by virtue of title!" I announced. "You should have consulted me, and if not me, then certainly our father!"

"I knew you would not approve…"

"You were right," I said. "And now you have come to plead for us to accept this child? It will never be, Mary." My lip curled. "How are we to know you are truly wed, and this child is not a bastard? You have lied often, and well, apparently in these past few months."

"I am married," she insisted.

"Where are the banns?" I demanded. "Where is the priest?"

"I *am* married," she bleated.

Her eyes went to George, hoping to find some hint of sympathy. She was not likely to find it. George might stop our father beating her, but his pride was deep and delicate. He knew this illicit marriage would affect us. People already said I was too low-born to be a queen, and my family were naught but merchants. This would confirm that in every hateful mind. George turned his face from her.

"We have only your word to confirm it," I said. "And what is that worth?" I shook my head. "Lifted your skirts for him behind the barracks did you, Mary? I hope he paid you well up front, for we could not expect that your flabby, well-used quinny could have granted much pleasure. You are a whore. You have brought *shame* on all of us, and especially on *my* reputation as Queen. *You would have done better to die than to ever bring this disgusting belly before us!*"

"Anne!" my mother gasped.

I rounded on her. "She has brought shame and disgrace on us, all of us!" I shouted.

I glowered at my trembling sister. Her eyes were alight with pain, and I cared not. What would this scandal do to my reputation? What would Henry do when he found out? The King of England, if Mary was to be believed, was now brother-in-law to one of his lesser and most distant, poor cousins. The disgrace would be unimaginable.

But it was not that which set my heart aflame with lust for vengeance. It was Mary's belly. It was her child. It was her standing there in possession of all I wanted and could not have. I was mad with jealousy and rotten, foetid terror.

"You and your husband, *if* that is indeed what he is, are banished forever from this court," I said. "You will never return here, nor to the house of *my* father. *You disgust me*. Get out of my sight."

She gaped, her hand on her flaming cheek, bleeding and scratched where my ring had torn her skin. She looked so young, like an innocent child beaten on a whim. Just a little girl, lost and alone.

"I would rather beg my bread with him," she said in a trembling, yet dignified voice, drawing herself up with all the pride she had left, "than be the greatest queen. And I believe it is the same for him, for he would never forsake me." She curtseyed. "Goodbye, Your Majesty."

Mary left.

I turned to George. "See to it that she leaves with as few people as possible seeing her," I hissed in a sibilant murmur.

He nodded and ran after Mary.

My mother went to reach out to me and I shook her off. "Do not touch me, Mother," I said. "In my present temper, I might strike you as well."

"But with your sister being in that condition that you so recently lost…"

"I am fine," I said, twisting my face away. "And I have no sister."

Chapter Ten

Greenwich Palace
September 1534

The eager young pup that had pursued Mary in Calais was indeed the man she had married; William Stafford, third son of Sir Humphrey Stafford, the Sheriff of Northamptonshire. Distantly related to Henry though he was, Stafford's alliance was a disgrace. He was not a knight, and had no real income or hopes for a title. He was a soldier, nothing more.

His family owned a manor at Cottered, and to there Mary and her husband fled. Stafford was a spearman in the service of Henry's cousin, Arthur Plantagenet, Viscount Lisle, the Deputy Governor of Calais. It was said my sister and her husband would go to Calais and make a life there.

The court was ablaze with gossip. Everywhere I went, someone stumbled to a halt swiftly in their conversation, and from their smug, smirking faces, I knew they were speaking about Mary. Tales of her adventures in France broke out anew, with everyone happily telling each other they had *always* known the Boleyns were whores and whoremasters. My enemies pounced on every scrap of scandal, and much more was invented about my sister. It was said she carried disease, and had passed it to the King. They said she was the greatest whore who had ever lived, and that her incontinent living infected everyone around her.

The only way to bear the disgrace was to alienate Mary. Our father refused to either see or acknowledge his daughter and declined to pay her allowances. Henry was deeply embarrassed and cut off her pension. William and his family had little wealth of their own. My sister quickly became desperate for money.

When she sent a messenger with the papers of her marriage, it was found that she must have conceived out of wedlock, and only married when she had discovered her condition. The dates on the documents could not lie as Mary had. Norfolk almost lost his mind when he heard. Were I not so furious, I might have enjoyed seeing him storming about, tearing his hair from its roots, close to a fit of apoplexy.

"A *whore*!" he shouted. "A whore who has brazenly shown her true colours in the public sphere! She is insane, surely! Who marries for love? What woman would dare thwart her family and kin, just to wed a common soldier?"

I dared to marry for love, I thought. *Yet since I married a king, this was acceptable.* I pushed such thoughts away. I told myself I was furious for the shame she had brought upon our family, but even then I knew this was not the reason.

He gawped at me. "What is to be done with her?"

"She is cut off, Uncle," I said. "And has no income. She is no more a Boleyn."

"Still less a Howard," he muttered.

"Think yourself fortunate, Uncle," I said, "that we are not closer kin. Although that unfortunately takes you a step further from claiming kinship with the throne, does it not?"

I walked away. If I had not wanted to cry, remembering Mary's belly, I would have laughed.

Mary wrote to Cromwell after our argument. He brought the missive to me, thinking I had a right to read it.

"Master Secretary,

After my poor recommendations, which is smally to be regarded of me, that I am a poor, banished creature, this shall be to desire you to be good to my poor husband and to me. I am sure that it is not unknown to you the high displeasure that both he and I have, both of the King's Highness and the Queen's Grace, by reason of our marriage without their knowledge that we did not well to be so hasty nor so bold, without their knowledge. But one thing, Master Secretary, consider; that he was young and love overcame reason. And for my part, I saw so much honesty in him that I loved him as well as he did me, and was in bondage, and glad I was to be at liberty."

Bondage? I thought. Did she mean her widowhood and reliance on our father's meagre generosity? If so, she was conveniently forgetting all the ways I had helped her.

"So that for my part, I saw that all the world did set so little store by me, and he so much, that I thought I could take no better way but to take him and forsake all other ways, and live a poor, honest life with him. And so I do put not doubt but we should, if we might be so happy to recover the King's gracious favour and the Queen's. For well I might have had a greater man of birth, and a higher, but I ensure you I could never have had one that should love me so well, nor a more honest man. And besides that, he is both come of ancient stock, and again as meet, if it be his Grace's pleasure, to do the King service as any young gentleman at court."

A place at court? That was never going to happen.

"Therefore, good Master Secretary, this shall be my suit to you, that, for love, that well I know you bear to all my blood, though for my part, I have not deserved it but smally, by reason of my vile conditions, as to put my husband to the King's Grace that he might do his duty as all other gentlemen do.

And, good Master Secretary, sue for us the King's Highness, and beseech His Highness, which ever was wont to take pity, to have pity on us, and that it would please His Grace, of his goodness, to speak to the Queen's Grace for us, for, so far as I can perceive, her Grace is so highly displeased with us both that, without the King being so good a lord to us as to withdraw his rigour and sue for us, we are never likely to recover her Grace's favour, which is too heavy for us to bear. And seeing there is no remedy, for God's sake, help us, for we have been now a quarter of a year married, I thank God, and too late now to call it again; wherefore it is the more alms to help us. But if I were at my liberty again and might choose, I assure you, Master Secretary, for my little time, I have spied so much honesty to be in him that I had rather beg my bread with him than be the greatest Queen christened. And I believe verily he is in the same case for me, for I believe verily he would not forsake me to be a king."

As I read that, I thought of my sister standing before me, her red eyes alive with defiance. I thought of all I had gone through to win Henry, of all we had endured to be together. But I refused to stack Mary's actions against mine and judge them in the same manner. Spite made it easy to be unjust to my sister.

"Therefore, good Master Secretary, seeing we are so well together and does intend to live so honest a life, though it be but poor, show part of your goodness to us as well you do all the world besides, for I promise you, you have the name to help all them that hath need, and amongst all your suitors I dare be bold to say that you have no matter more to be pitied than ours, and therefore, for God's sake, be good to us, for in you is all our trust.

And I beseech you, good Master Secretary, pray my Lord my father, and my Lady, my mother, to be good to us and to let us have their blessings, and my husband their good will, and I will never desire more of them. Also, I pray you, desire my Lord of Norfolk and my Lord my good brother, to be good to us. I dare not write to them, they are so cruel against us. But if with any pain I could take my life that I might win their good wills, I promise there is no child living would endure more than I. And so I pray you to report by me, and you shall find my writing true, and in all points, which I may please them in I shall be ready to obey them nearest to my husband, whom I am bound to, to whom I most heartily beseech you to be good unto, which, for my sake, is a poor, banished man for an honest and goodly cause. And seeing that I have read in old books that some, for as just causes, have by kings and queens been pardoned by the suit of good folk, I trust it shall be our chance, through your good help, to come to the same; as knoweth the Lord God, Who send you health and heart's ease.

Scribbled with her ill hand, who is your poor, humble suitor, always to command,

Mary Stafford."

"She is in a desperate way, Majesty," Cromwell said carefully. "Would you have me respond?"

I thrust the letter back. Mary's words had cut me, as she had intended. Desperate she might be, but she was striking back at the same time as pleading for mercy; showing me that she was happier in her marriage than I might ever be in mine.

"Take it," I snapped. "And bring me no more from her!"

I ignored the fact that Mary had leapt in her letter from pleading for mercy to outright insolence. I set aside the realisation that she was in chaos, without money or connections and in utter disgrace with her King and Queen. I could not bear to receive anything from her. The memory of her belly was bitter poison to my heart.

Looking back, I regret that jealousy made me hate my sweet sister. Envy blackened my heart. I could not speak of her, think of her or remember her without wanting to rage and cry.

Mary wrote to Cromwell when, I believe, she realized her banishment was no temporary state. She went through Cromwell as she understood his influence at court. Rightly, she did not believe I would open any letter in her hand.

At night, I remembered her belly and wept quietly into the cushions of my glorious bed. Purkoy nestled beside me. He guarded me, but he could not reach the darkness of my dreams.

Sometimes, I dreamt Mary had stolen my child, and he was living in her belly.

I could not deny her enough. I wished I could do her more harm. I was not a Christian woman in those days. George, offended as I to be related to such low connections, refused to see her. I did not petition Henry for her return. I did not help her to recover her husband's position, nor asked my father or husband to show mercy. But for everything I could deny her, she still possessed the one thing I wanted more than anything.

Mary was undone, by me.

And all for the love of my son, who had never drawn breath.

Chapter Eleven

Whitehall Palace
September – October 1534

As I burned with rage about my sister, Cromwell had a much more fortunate encounter.

Passing through the slippery streets of London, Cromwell caught sight of a familiar face. Drawing his horse up, and calling his men to stand, he sent a messenger over, and was rewarded by gazing into the eyes of his old master.

Francesco Frescobaldi was a merchant who had taken Cromwell, then a young man, under his wing. In London to chase unpaid debts, the merchant was astonished to be reunited with his friend, and was even more content with the outcome. Cromwell took Frescobaldi to the Augustine Friars and bought him dinner, as well as immediately ordering his men to look into his debtors. Such was Cromwell's influence that the debts were paid rapidly, and his old master was able to return to Italy a few weeks later with a full purse. Cromwell also insisted on granting Frescobaldi one thousand, six hundred ducats, in payment for horses, cloth, clothing and food that his master had granted him over the years of his service.

"You show loyalty and generosity," I said to Cromwell when I heard. "Soon all masters will be treating their men with undue, bountiful consideration, hoping, Master Cromwell, that one day their servants will rise as high as you, and remember them."

"I do not forget my former masters, Majesty, for each taught me something."

For a moment, I wondered if he was speaking of Wolsey.

"How go your affairs, Majesty?" he asked.

"*My* affairs are not those I worry about," I quipped, for he was clearly speaking of my sister. "The King is enraged and I no less disappointed. My sister will come no more to court. Mary has chosen her bed, and she will lie in it."

Henry tried to distract me with plans for our palaces. My new suite of rooms at Hampton Court was underway. The foundations had been laid before we left for Calais, and now a skeleton of the glory that would come could be seen. My rooms were on the same level as Henry's, a change from the past when queens had lived on another floor to their husbands. There was to be direct, private access to Henry's chambers from mine, and they would be grander than anything anyone had ever set eyes upon.

Whitehall, too, was also being enlarged. It was already a much grander palace than Wolsey, its first owner, had ever envisioned, but Henry would go further. That was his way. With Henry, everything must be bigger, grander, and more impressive. Everyone must marvel at his achievements and be awestruck by his accomplishments.

It was not only castles and palaces that were undergoing improvements and repairs. Foreign policy was too. Despite François' anger at Henry, the French King was making noises of friendship. He proposed sending a delegation that winter, and the suggestion was warmly received.

"You see, sweetheart?" Henry said. "France wants to be friends again. There is talk of arranging a match between our daughter and the Dauphin."

Much as it pleased me to hear Elizabeth might one day be Queen of France, the thought of her leaving me, even in the distant future, sent my heart scurrying for cover. I was anxious, in those days, unnerved and skittish, although I barely knew why. Was it just the loss of my son? It was in some ways, not in others. With my son I had lost my security as well. A part of me wanted to take Elizabeth and Henry in my arms and never let go.

Perhaps even then something was whispering that I did not have as long as I thought with my family.

"No doubt François is fearful of the fleet the Emperor is putting together to vanquish the infidels," I noted, trying to maintain the bright smile on my face. It felt frozen, faked.

"No doubt." Henry grinned, noting nothing of my unease. "But that can only be to our advantage."

*

"Send Doctor Butts to your son, my lord," I said.

Henry had come to me, out of his mind with terror. Fitzroy was sick. The lad was not only his son, but the sole acknowledged proof he could father boys, although if Jane were to be believed, Henry had more than one bastard son flitting about England.

My sister-in-law was most upset, languishing in the country at one of the houses where George stood as steward. She had written to me many times, bemoaning her lot and protesting that any action she had taken was in my interests. I did not reply, to my shame. No matter what Jane had done for me in the past, she had gone too far. With Mary's disgrace the talk of court, I could afford no more embarrassing family members.

Fitzroy appeared to be suffering from that old curse of the Tudor line: consumption. He had coughed and wheezed his way through the past two weeks, taking eventually to his bed, although he had resisted, much to the horror of his friend, Surrey.

"He will not accept that he is unwell," my Howard cousin had said. "Someone must convince him to take care, Majesty."

"And you think I might have more success than you, cousin?" I asked. "I will try, but this may be a task for his father. I can only *ask* Fitzroy to take care. The King can command him."

"Any help, any aid, would be welcome," said the distraught young man.

I did not allow Surrey to put the case to my husband, fearing that his abject terror might infect Henry. My husband was a mass of neurosis at the best of times when it came to illness. Setting him loose on his son might do more harm than good. I worded my explanation carefully, and Henry commanded his son to take care. But the worst had not yet occurred and as autumn started to succumb to winter and freezing white mists flowed over England, Fitzroy had fallen dangerously ill.

"Send Butts," I said again. "No greater faith have I in any physician's skill than in Doctor Butts."

"Aye," Henry said, glancing again at the parchment in his hands as though doing so might alter its information. "You are right."

"And caution the young man," I said, setting my hand on his golden sleeve. "I am sure this malady will turn out to be nothing, but your son is so desperate to impress you, my lord, that he takes undue risks."

"He does, and has no need to," said Henry. "I could not be prouder of him. Does he not know that?"

I smiled. "Sometimes it is hard for us to know what lies in the heart of another, especially if they do not express their feelings aloud. Write to your son, my lord, and when he is well, visit him. Tell him how proud you are, and tell him you love him. It must be hard for the boy, being in a state between beings, as illegitimacy often is, to know where he fits in, in the world."

"He is a duke," said Henry.

"Titles are nothing to the love of a father," I said. "Forget not this moment, Henry. You fear now and wish to say all that you have not said to your son. Remember this time. Tell him of your love. The time we have with those we love is so short, so fleeting. Leave your son in no doubt of your feelings."

His hand closed about mine and his eyes glowed with love. "Sometimes I forget to say what I feel to those I love," he said quietly. "But those I love should never think my love has weakened or abated."

"Do you speak of me, husband?" I asked with a smile. "I tell you to be frank, and you escape into hyperbole."

Henry chuckled, taking me in his arms. "I love you," he said. "Is that clear enough?"

"As I love you."

I wondered later if the strain set upon Henry as Fitzroy fell ill was not in part to blame for his actions towards the Observants. The people of England had not reacted well to their arrests or disbandment, and Henry had faltered in the face of their disapproval.

Insecurity is more dangerous a state than we give credit for.

As his son became ill, Henry's hard resolve returned. Fear brought anger, and Henry offered himself up to it. He knew what was best for England, and England *would* fall in line. Not content with arresting ringleaders and separating the Order, Henry decided to suppress it entirely. The last remaining servants, friars and monks were carted off or turned out onto the streets to find alternative employment, or become beggars. Their church was converted into a mill for the royal armoury.

Later that month a new Act of Supremacy enshrined Henry's title of Supreme Head of the Church in law, finally cutting England's last ties with Rome. Ecclesiastical matters were now in the hands of Henry alone. About court it was said that Englishmen were now to understand the Word of God was synonymous with that of their King.

It was simple to get the Act through Parliament. Cromwell had stuffed the Upper Chamber with lords loyal to Henry, and the Commons was full of MPs dedicated to the new order. Detractors were warned to stay away, or risk losing more than just their livelihoods. Allied in thought and deed, Parliament, the Lords and the King marched on, and all who objected tumbled to the wayside.

Cranmer, Cromwell and I rejoiced. This was the final cut required to set England loose of the shackles of Rome. Reginald Pole called Cromwell *the Emissary of Satan*, and Cranmer and I came under fire too, but it was done. Henry was indeed Emperor and Pope in England.

With this change, more came. Cranmer and his bishops were busy discussing which rituals of the Church would remain and which would be banned. The granting of indulgences to buy time out of purgatory was immediately brought up, since many thought it a scandal, but talks went ahead about idols, the wealth of the monasteries and charitable reform. Some went so far as to question the Order of the Garter, since their devotion was offered to St George rather than God, but Henry adored the Order, and would not allow it to be disbanded.

There were other things Henry would not allow. He believed in the Sacraments, and would not permit the transubstantiation to be brought into doubt. He believed in purgatory and limbo, despite our discussions, and upheld clerical celibacy. He was enamoured of statues, images and the grandeur of the Catholic Mass. He was, in fact, just as Catholic as Pope Paul. He just did not agree that the Pope should be the Head of the Church. Cranmer, who was a great deal starker in his religious outlook, understood he would have a hard task convincing Henry to ban many aspects of traditional religion which the Archbishop and many others considered ungodly popery.

But for all this, Henry had an inquisitive mind. He often invited my chaplains, whom he knew to be ardent reformists, to debate theological matters with him. He and I discussed much at the dinner table, or with our friends. Henry had a quite endearing habit of selecting two people he respected and getting them to take opposing points of view, so he could decide which he agreed with. Although some took this for idleness, I did not. Henry could be lazy, but when he asked others to debate, with him as the judge, it was to delve into their minds and discover new thoughts. Outside our windows at Whitehall, Henry built an open-air pulpit. Four times as many courtiers could attend events held there than could squeeze into the Chapel Royal, and Henry made good use of it. We watched from his Council Chamber as men, usually my chaplains, preached. Hugh Latimer was Henry's particular favourite.

But it was not only at court that Cromwell and Henry made their views known. It had become apparent that the people of England did not understand all that had happened over the past years. Henry made it his mission to instruct them. Pamphlets on the corruptions of Rome and the salacious behaviour of various popes were distributed, preachers preached, and there was talk spread thick on the wonder and honour of patriotism. Believing in Henry was now the same as believing in *England*. Indeed, to many, they were one and the same. What is a king without his country?

What is a country without a king? God requires a sovereign so His will might be done through His instrument. Henry was God's chosen.

Henry was hailed as the noblest king that ever had reigned: the father of England; a paragon of princely goodness; the one who had made England whole again, by his wisdom, courage and virtue; the King who had set us free.

New coinage was commissioned, bearing Henry's face in the likeness of a Roman Emperor, and a third Great Seal was created, displaying Henry's image mounted on a great throne, with his title of Supreme Head of the Church inscribed underneath. An Imperial crown was added to the royal arms, indicating that Henry was only answerable to God, and many started to call him *The New Arthur*. Since Henry claimed descent from this noble King, he welcomed the title, even though it must have brought unwelcome memories of his brother, and father, to his mind.

Henry could never quite forget that his father had thought Arthur Tudor would be the saviour of England. And although it was never said aloud, Henry was desperate to prove him wrong.

Tracts, books and pamphlets flowed from Henry's printers like water, proclaiming his glory and magnificence. Poets, playwrights and historians were called to court to blaze Henry's new titles into art and justify them with historical fact. It became fashionable for loyal subjects to display Henry's portrait in their houses to demonstrate their faith in him. Indeed, portraits were copied cheaply and dispersed in the streets, so Henry would look down upon his people whether they dwelled in manor house, castle or hovel.

I believed in Henry. I thought he would take us into a new time, a new era, a new world. And I was not alone. Gardiner, who had wisely abandoned his previous support for the clergy, hailed Henry as semi-divine, calling him *"the image of God on earth"* and as all this went on, Henry became enthralled by his own magnificence.

Conservatives were not happy. Norfolk, who paid no more attention to the Scriptures than one might to a buzzing fly, kept company with the Poles, Carewes and Courtenays. Allied to our family he might be in theory, but he had more in common with our foes. But even those mired in tradition, lost in the wish to obey Rome, did not speak too loud. They did not dare. The sound of monks wailing in the Tower, combined with the ghosts of still-living Fisher and More, silenced many.

Henry took to wearing a chain with the inscription *"Plus tost morir que changer ma pensee"* or *I prefer to die rather than change my mind*. No one could doubt his conviction. To reformers, Henry had become King David, or Solomon. I think he had transformed into a mythical figure in his own mind, too.

Amidst all this noise and colour, poetry and pageantry, more was occurring. Cromwell was appointed Master of the Rolls, becoming one of the first secular holders of the office. He made good use of the post. The Master of the Rolls was one of the highest judicial positions in England, and brought along with it the grand Rolls House on Chancery Lane. Once, this had been a Carthusian house for converted Jews, but for several hundred years it had been the seat of the Master of the Rolls. The Master was required to keep and maintain the rolls, or records, of the Court of Chancery, which held authority over all matters of equity. The Masters were usually priests, often the King's chaplains, so it was a mark of great favour that Cromwell was offered the post.

And it kept him busy. Cromwell made good use of his new house, for he had too many servants now to keep at court or at his other London residence. Rolls House became his own private court, filled with supplicants seeking justice or favour. Cromwell bought more houses. He was becoming a miniature king himself, with many palaces, all crammed with people waiting to plead for his favour.

But this was not the sole order of business for canny Cromwell. He wanted to root out those who might oppose us, or him, and my uncle was the first of his targets. Comments such as "it was merrier in England before the new learning came," did not endear Norfolk to Cromwell, and my uncle was the most experienced member of Henry's Council after Cromwell, making his conservative views therefore threatening. Suffolk, too, was a danger, but a lesser one. His reaction to our marriage had left Henry in doubt of his affection, and Suffolk was no more the force at court he had once been.

Suffolk fell in line. Although his new wife, Katherine Willoughby, and her mother, Marie de Salinas, were firmly on Katherine's side, Suffolk understood if he was to retain Henry's love, he would have to offer support. Norfolk was less careful. And it was a symptom of the insecurity in Henry that he listened to Norfolk at all. Captivated by his new titles and being the chosen of God, Henry was… at times. At others, he feared what might come, and failed to forge ahead.

Cromwell believed that if Norfolk were removed, more might be done, but with Henry changing his mind as often as his flat-toed shoes, Master Secretary could only wage a partial war against his foe.

Cromwell surrounded himself with intellectuals. His houses became as famous as Henry's for discussion and philosophy. Ballads and books came from this brew, seeping into the streets so the people would know of the tyranny of Rome. Even in times of leisure, Cromwell was working for his King, although he managed to take time to hawk, one of his happiest pastimes, and put on lavish entertainments at his various homes.

At times, Henry would grunt with annoyance to hear people speak of Cromwell's pageants. Although Cromwell often organised ones for the court, and Henry was always invited to his house to see events held there, my husband did not welcome the notion that one of his subjects might be seen to equal, if not outdo, his own court.

It was not only Henry who was starting to be displeased with Cromwell. My brother heard that Cromwell had countermanded one of his orders given as Lord Warden of the Cinque Ports, and was not best pleased.

"He makes me look subservient!" George said, his cheeks flaming. "As though he is my better, my master!"

Pride is a strange master. People who wear his livery brashly are often insecure. My brother was one of them. He was haughty about court, and earned many foes for his pride. But in truth, he was unsure of himself, and this was why he seemed so bold. It was a feint; a mask worn to play a part. I understood, for I felt the same.

"I am sure he merely thought he was saving you time and effort," I said, setting aside my book.

It was a French copy of the Old Testament book of Ecclesiastes with a separate commentary. Illuminated in bright colours, and with bold, black writing, it was stunning. The initial letters of each section of text were highly decorated, sitting in a background of sky-blue and dusky pink, sparkling with gold. At the head of the text, there was a shield combining Henry's arms and mine, done out in seven colours. Produced by Flemish craftsmen working in England, it had been a commission from Henry for me, and I was proud of it. The front cover carried my arms, in enamel on a base of silver, topped with a crown. The four corners of the book were decorated with brass, and each engraved with a heraldic beast; a crowned lion rampart, a dragon, a crowned falcon and a greyhound. Two decorated brass clasps closed it, designed by Holbein. It was one of my dearest possessions. Henry had ordered it for me, knowing my tastes were as French as my lingering accent, and such devotion to detail reminded me of his love.

Sometimes I took it into my hands, not to read, but just to draw comfort from.

Putting it on the seat beside me, I went on. "Write to Cromwell, brother. He is our ally. He would not willing step on your toes."

"He takes me for granted, Anne," he said. "And it will not be borne. I shall write to him, and good Master Secretary will come to understand that he may not soil my authority!"

I sighed as I watched George storm off, but at the time I thought little of this.

What I did not see was that Cromwell was indeed becoming a king. A man who used another as his puppet... A king of shadow and secrets.

Chapter Twelve

Whitehall Palace
Late October - November 1534

Emboldened by her first success in pageantry by showing herself to London on her barge, the Lady Mary gave a repeat performance that October. I was informed later that Mary arranged everything personally. She ordered the barge, planned the route, and made sure to stand on deck where everyone could see her.

I complained to Henry when I heard of the roaring crowds shouting acclaim for Mary, but he did nothing. He was too relieved that his daughter was well and his son apparently on the mend to act against her. "She has every right to *travel*," he noted in a distracted fashion when I accosted him.

"But not to stir dissent." I set my hands on my hips. "She steals love from the people that should be offered to Elizabeth."

Henry would not hear me, so I took matters into my own hands. I demanded that Mary be punished by Lady Shelton, and the girl rapidly found her privileges, such as they were, revoked. Her meal times became stricter and her seat at the servants' table was never left empty. I would not allow them to permit her to escape by claiming ill-health.

"She was well enough to take a trip down the Thames, in an uncovered barge, with her maiden's hair loose and streaming down her back," I wrote to my aunt. *"Therefore she is well enough to eat her meals at her proper place and you will ensure she does so, or face dire consequences."*

Lady Shelton was growing ever more displeased with my orders, but I could never leave well alone. Mary scared me, and Henry's newfound affection for her made me shiver on my throne of glass.

Mary was reportedly distraught, and spoke of preparing herself for martyrdom, like her mother. Katherine had not been idle these past weeks either. Horrified by the royal supremacy and actions taken against holy men, Katherine stirred herself. She assured those she wrote to that she wanted action, but not war. Her soldiers would be holy martyrs, called on by God to protect the faith from those, like *wicked little me,* who would undermine it.

One letter my father intercepted said, *"when the storms of this life shall be over, and I shall be taken to the calm life of the blessed."* Katherine was ready to die, and if she had to, she would take Mary with her.

"A prophecy exists that says a queen of England shall burn upon the stake," I said to Margaret Lee one night as we sat at my fire. The flames' light flickered on the walls, across the tapestry, caressing the darkness. "Therefore I cannot rest until Katherine is gone. For if a queen must die, it will not be me."

"Prophesies only have power when one believes in them," said my wise Margaret.

"And how many *do* believe?" I asked, staring at the flames as they curled their crimson fingers about black sea coal. "There are some who think I cannot go on as

Queen, are there not?" I looked at her. "In truth, Margaret, I am already amongst the flames."

"But nothing can reach you whilst the King loves you."

I nodded, but I wondered. Our problems in the bedchamber were frequent. I had even asked some of my more trusted ladies, such as Margaret, Mistress Aucher and Elizabeth Browne, about remedies for Henry. Elizabeth Browne brought me a tonic of mistletoe, and Mistress Aucher had provided blessed thistle, a plant known for its protective qualities against harmful spells, which could bring spiritual blessings as well as those of fertility, in both finances and a woman bearing fruit. "Carry it to bring joy to your heart and ward off harmful spells," she said when she handed the imported flower to me.

Taking it in my hands, I knew what it would have cost her. The flower was not native to England. It grew in the stony, barren spaces in southern Europe. Cleary my old nurse thought I had need of something to keep me safe. Perhaps she was right. I had many enemies, and they might not shy from wielding the dark arts against me.

"They say it also makes men better lovers," she had whispered, bestowing a cheeky wink upon me.

Better lovers? I thought. *Just a husband who showed up each night would be something…*

Henry came but little to my bed. Dingley and the parrot were often with him, and I feared what they might say. If I did not produce another pregnancy soon, I wondered if I could rely on Henry's love to save me from the flames.

It should have been our surest time, our greatest moment, but all was fragile, teetering on a cliff edge. All was shadow amongst the billowing flame… dust flowing from one circle to the next.

*

"I carry bad news from France," I said to my brother as I entered his chambers. I found him groaning over his desk, working on legal disputes for Dover and the Cinque Ports. George seemed almost relieved to find me there with different tasks at hand. That was shortly to change.

"There has been an incident in France," I said. "Reformers took to the streets, setting up placards which denounced the Catholic Mass as popery. The notices were an unguarded attack on the Catholic faith, and rumours have spread that reformers want nothing more than to burn all churches and murder all traditionalists in their beds. One was nailed to the King's bedchamber door, and others have been found in Orleans, Tours, Blois and Rouen." I sighed. "There have been arrests, and François has come to think this is part of a plot against him. It would seem the once-tolerant King who upheld the reforming beliefs of his sister is backsliding." I paused as my brother's forehead creased with consternation. "There is talk that François will forbid French printers from producing books supporting reform."

"He may, then, grant the Sorbonne licence to take what measures they wish," said George, speaking of the University of Paris, the stronghold of conservatives in France. The Sorbonne was responsible for weeding out heresy and banning works thought to be heretical. It had run blindly into disfavour in years past, when it banned a work penned by François' sister, Marguerite, called *The Glass of the Sinful Soul,* of which I owned a copy. It had been an embarrassing blunder, and the Sorbonne had paid dearly for censuring her work, but now, with François convinced that French reformists were plotting against him, the Sorbonne might be offered more power.

Much as in England, there had been a rise in iconoclasm in France. Reformers stole into churches and destroyed statues and relics. Lutherans and Anabaptists, a sect of reformers who believed baptism was only valid when performed on adults, and only after confession of their faith, who were widely seen and persecuted as simple heretics, were on the march. In response, Catholic traditionalists were baying for blood. François was likely to grant the Sorbonne and his Parliament a free hand to deal with troublemakers, and he was rapidly speaking ill of anyone who supported reform.

"England grows more isolated from Europe every day," I said. "Many kings do not want to accept me as Queen, and Henry fears the forming rifts. If we lose France, I fear what may come."

"No foreign kings truly care for the religious policy of England," said my brother. "They care for politics. At one time it is advantageous to be friends with one country and at another time, with another."

"All the same, Spain will never be our friend as long as I occupy the throne." I tapped my fingers on the table in a haphazard manner. "The new ambassador from France is due to arrive soon," I said. "I want you to meet him, and Henry has agreed. We must woo them, George. I fear this affair has set François against reform, and no matter how hard his sister works to restore his good opinion of it, this will be a problem for us. François is well aware of my sympathies and yours, and if he is against reform, that may lead him to be cool with us."

Little did I know how right I was.

*

The new French Ambassador, Philippe de Chabot de Brion, Admiral of France, took a long look about him and sniffed as though there were something offensive in the air. What that scent might be, I knew not, for there was nothing but perfume wafting from the skin of courtiers, and the smell of delicious food being prepared in the kitchens in honour of his visit.

George had been sent to meet the ambassador, and every courtesy had been extended. Their journey from Dover to Greenwich had taken a few days, and the ambassador had been entertained in the houses of those who supported Henry and me. A huge train of gentlemen had accompanied the Admiral, along with three hundred and fifty horses, and my brother had had the responsibility of finding lodgings and stables for all guests each night. George had struggled with the logistics, even accepting help from Norfolk to complete his task. Not that you would have known this when watching them ride towards London. The arrival of the ambassador seemed like a well-oiled clock, ticking along in perfect working order. They were later than expected, as George had planned the route in stages to allow Brion to rest. But however meticulous my brother's efforts had been, Brion did not seem overly impressed… with England, court, or anything else.

Henry greeted him, and afterwards, Brion was taken to Bridewell Palace to be entertained by Norfolk and Suffolk, invited to dine later with Henry at court. Brion had come to speak of the postponed meeting with François, and we were keen to press forth Elizabeth as a bride for the Dauphin. But as the Ambassador settled into his apartments, he appeared to be in no rush to open negotiations.

The affair of the placards had led not only to arrests, but burnings. François had banned all new books, and the most sacred relics of France had been taken from their churches and paraded about, some being borne by François' sons under a canopy of golden cloth. François had led prayers for his country and encouraged his people to denounce all heretics. More burnings had marked the end of this outpouring of fanatical, one might say hysterical, devotion to the traditional faith.

In truth, although many took François' new stance as a reaction to the slight of the notice pinned to his own door, it was more political than personal. The placards had attacked his Church, his men and, by association, his rule. He could not allow his will and word to be so questioned.

Despite this, I still kept faith that Brion would negotiate fairly. What I and Henry failed to see was just *how* reliant we were now on France. With Spain and Rome our enemies, France was our only friend. And they knew it.

After two days, I was surprised to find Brion had sent no message of greeting to me. It was standard practice for new ambassadors to send a polite note to the Queen. Brion ignored this.

"I am planning a banquet in his honour," I said to Henry, affronted and not a little frightened by this obvious slight. Everyone was speaking of it. It was humiliating.

"Brion is a man of action, not politics," Henry said. "I will remind him of his duty." He rose and kissed my brow. "Fear not, my love, I am sure this is but an oversight. Do not take offence and cause a rift."

"*I* am not the one causing a rift," I pointed out. Why was I being blamed for Brion's impolite actions? "Surely past ambassadors must have advised Brion about protocol? And even had they failed to, I met the Admiral in Calais. He was a model of politeness then, why should he not wish to resume our friendship now?"

Henry had no answer for me.

Chapter Thirteen

Greenwich Palace
November – December 1534

As the days wore on it became increasingly apparent that the French ambassador had no desire to see me. I held tennis matches and entertainments in his honour, but he often failed to attend, and when he did, did not stay long. This angered Henry, since he had taken the time to compete in matches against Weston and Norris. Brion did not request an audience with me, and at the first banquet I prepared in his honour, he spent his time talking to Norfolk and Suffolk, ignoring George and my father.

It was clear to me that the Admiral was courting my enemies, but Henry accused me of being paranoid. "He prefers the company of men to women," my husband said. "It is not unusual in soldiers."

"Are my father and brother *women*, then?" I asked, making Henry chuckle. I shook my head, but I was glad for his smile. There had not been enough merriment between us of late. "I do not think that is the reason, Henry."

"François is our good friend," he said. "Perhaps he just advised his ambassador to be aloof, due to the troubles of the past. It is but a bargaining tool, sweetheart, so when he turns the smile of friendship upon us, we will welcome it all the more."

"I see." I did not think he was correct.

Another reason for my growing suspicion was that Brion made swift and unlikely friends with Chapuys. Even the hapless hare was astonished. Brion, in seeking out Chapuys, was demonstrating that François considered friendship with Spain more valuable than England.

My worst suspicions were confirmed when Henry came to me after a meeting with Brion. As soon as Henry entered I knew something was wrong. Anger made him look old as joy made him young. That night, he was aged.

"Brion proposes marrying Lady Mary to the Dauphin," he said, throwing himself into a chair upholstered with blue buckram.

My heart reeled. "What do you mean?"

Henry snorted. "I said the exact same words to Brion," he said. "I had to remind him that my eldest daughter is a bastard."

"He had forgotten?"

Henry shook his head. "Brion says he was sent with a clear brief by François. The marriage proposed between my daughter and the Dauphin when they were children is the one the French want resumed. Brion says it would be made on the understanding that Mary is legitimate."

"But she is *not*." My voice rose with rage.

"I know that, Anne," said Henry, his tone equally fierce. "And said as much, but that is what they want in return for alliance."

"But… that would mean the undoing of the Act of Succession, and the ruin of Elizabeth and me!" I cried, my tone brittle and disjointed. "You did not agree?"

Henry frowned. "What do you take me for?" Not waiting for an answer, he went on. "I proposed marriage between Elizabeth and the Duc de Angouleme instead, but Brion did not agree."

"Why François' *third* son?" I demanded, aghast that Henry would sell our daughter for a lesser prize. "Why not the Dauphin?"

"Because clearly the French do not wish to recognise Elizabeth at this time." Henry ran his hands through his short-cropped hair. "I think this slight is made to make a point. François has not forgiven us for marrying swiftly and causing him embarrassment with Rome."

"So he would try to force Mary ahead of our daughter in the succession?" I shook my head. "Who do the French think they are to attempt to influence English politics? If the Bishop of Rome is not allowed such authority, the French certainly are not!" I gazed at him with troubled eyes. I could see a glimmer of hesitation and I feared it. "They seek to *dictate* the laws of England, my lord," I said, hoping to rile Henry's temper.

"They do," he said, although he sounded calmer than I, which frightened me. "And they will not be allowed such liberties. Our daughter is the *only* Princess of England. They will recognise that or there will be no alliance."

No matter Henry's assurances, I was shaken. News of the talks leaked into court, and soon all were aware that France wanted Mary, not Elizabeth. Chapuys was reported to be parading about court with a great, smug grin on his face, and Norfolk said openly he thought Mary was indeed the better match, "given her age," he hastened to add, but he fooled no one.

François had claimed to be my friend, but he knew that any child of mine would promote reform in England, and he did not want that. Returning Mary to the succession would restore traditional Catholicism along with her, and wedding her to a prince of France would allow him to control her, rather than the Emperor. As talks went on, Brion threatened that if Henry did not agree to their terms, François would wed his heir to the Emperor's daughter instead, leaving England alone in Europe.

I could not have been more mortified or afraid. The French were openly demonstrating that they had no love for me, and did not recognise me as Queen, or my daughter as Princess.

France had betrayed me.

It is hard to explain the myriad of emotions that came to me with that realisation… the homesickness, the yearning, the sorrow… France had been the seat of my youth, the place where I had blossomed from a child into a woman. I had learned much at Mechelen, but the years I had spent there were fewer than those in France. My voice still sang with a foreign lilt when I spoke, and I preferred to read and converse in French when able to. France had burrowed deep into my heart, and never had it left me. To find that the country I loved so dear was now opposed to me was a brutal, horrible shock. It was as though someone had informed me that memories of my childhood were false, and in telling me the true tale, had stripped away an intrinsic part of my identity.

The place I kept safe for France in my heart was shaken. It became brittle. I could feel parts of it sloughing away; a dune of sand slowly eaten by the desert winds, blowing its particles through the arid wasteland, fading gradually into nothing.

I could not turn to Spain, the other great power of Europe, and with me as Queen, Katherine's usurper, neither could England. I had never thought that François, no matter the enticement, would turn so blatantly on me. This was a public, ineffable, damning strike against me and my daughter. Had François sailed to England and slapped me about the face, I could not have been more traumatized or insulted.

England and I were in the same position; becoming gradually isolated. George was often busy, and Mary and Jane were banished. I had my friends, and my ladies, but Margaret, now a married woman, was frequently pregnant and away from court, and my other ladies, no matter how I loved them, were separated from me by virtue of my title. There were few I could confide in. I had to put on a brave face, and pretend I was untouched by these negotiations. Nothing could have been further from the truth and everyone knew it. The parrot was heard saying to Elizabeth Grey, the Dowager Countess of Kildare, that of course the French wanted Mary, for she was the King's *true* daughter, and a virtuous, beautiful woman. The Dowager agreed. She was Henry's first cousin and in league with my foes. The Poles, Courtenays and Carewes joined in, saying that Mary should be restored to the succession.

And Henry did nothing to contradict them. I began to wonder if he thought as they did.

We went ahead with all the plans for the visit. The feast to celebrate the end of the talks was due to go ahead in a few days' time. I would have to sit beside Brion, this odious monster who denied my daughter's rights and existence in the succession, and pretend we were friends.

I would have to keep a careful hand on my temper, for if I met him in the mood I was presently in, I believed I might murder the man.

*

Henry believed Brion could be swayed by smothering him with hospitality. I was not so sure. The detestable ambassador had finally deigned to call on me twice, and although he was all cool politeness, it was obvious he did not relish my company. He said afterwards, to Chapuys, that he had only visited me because Henry had asked him to. Henry flatly refused to talk of marriage for Mary, but the message was clear. Friendship with France was no longer reliant on me or my efforts. I was superfluous at best, and at worst, standing in the way.

Like Henry, Cromwell attempted to charm the ambassador. When Cromwell presented a gift to Brion, the ambassador thanked him, but mourned later to Chapuys that whilst Henry had shown him many pretty sights on his trip, he had not seen the prettiest of all: the Lady Mary. "I would I had seen the most singular and valuable gem in all his kingdom," Brion loudly declaimed, going on to flatter Mary to Chapuys, saying that France was her *servant*.

Henry and I had many arguments. I shouted that Mary should be married off to a minor nobleman, to show her bastard birth. He screamed back that even if she was a bastard, she was still of royal blood, and could not be disposed of so lightly.

Each time he left me, I heard the tinkling steps and breathy giggles of the parrot as she was whisked along the dark corridors to his chambers. Her laugh rang out like my death knell in the corridors of court.

I had never felt so alone.

As plans went on to entertain the loathsome French Ambassador, Cromwell and Henry arrived in my chambers. "More is being placed in harder confinement," Henry said, kissing me. "Thomas thought you should know before my command become public."

I smiled at Cromwell. He understood where Henry always failed to, that when anything ill was done to Fisher and More I would be held accountable.

"More has upset you more?" I asked. "His name is so apt, do you not think?"

Henry grunted, taking wine from Frances de Vere and drinking almost the whole goblet in one huge mouthful. A dribble of red wine escaped and trickled into his short beard. I had to try hard not to curl my lip in revulsion.

"More has been abusing his privileges," he said, drawing the back of his hand over his wine-stained lips. "I was generous enough to permit his daughter and wife to visit him, as well as allowing him to exercise in the grounds, but it would seem More has been made too comfortable. He has been using his time to write inflammatory tracts."

I looked to Cromwell, who nodded. I wondered if this was the rope of which he had spoken. Should I have said something? Told Henry that the security about More had been left lax on purpose, to allow him to incriminate himself further? Perhaps I should have, but at the time I thought More was getting a just reward for his bloody work. And no one had *made* him write these tracts, whatever they were. Cromwell had simply granted him the liberty to think he could do so without harm. A slim distinction between right and wrong it was, perhaps, but when our enemies plunge themselves into danger, often we do not discriminate between good and evil.

"We allowed him writing materials," Cromwell said. "But, Majesty, rather than use them to write to the King and admit his guilt, More has been exchanging letters with Fisher, and writing new works. Some of these have been smuggled into London, where they have been printed and distributed."

"More never could stand another having the last word," I said. "What are these works?"

"The one that has been sent out is called *A Dialogue of Comfort Against Tribulation*," said Cromwell. "We have men searching for it, amongst More's friends and kin, but copies are already circulating."

"More will be kept under close guard, not allowed visitors or be permitted to attend Mass outside his quarters," said Henry. "I want that done today, Cromwell." Henry glowered at his servant.

Thomas when he likes you, Cromwell when he is angry, I thought. Was it not the same for me? I was Anne when he loved me, *madam* when he was enraged. It was Henry's way of dividing us up, compartmentalising us, fitting us into slots where he could make sense of us. We were only ever one, and not the other. One day I would learn this to my peril.

"Of course, Majesty."

Henry departed with Weston to play tennis, and I was left with Cromwell. As Weston departed, Cromwell's eyes were on him. He did not like Weston. He thought him frivolous and annoying. The fact he was friends with Gardiner and Norfolk did not help either.

I glanced at him. "What is in this work?"

He frowned. "Much," he said. "The book, Majesty, centres on the kingdom of Hungary, in a time between the invasions of Suleiman the Magnificent. It is a fictional dialogue, like many of More's works. He never did have much imagination."

"He does adore that format."

"Indeed, Majesty. The subject is that comfort may only be found through God, and the dialogue itself is a narrative on worldly power, the transience of pleasure, and the redemptive power of Christ. It is as much a treatise on politics as it is on religion, and its conclusions on power are not entirely flattering."

"I can understand, then, why the King is so enraged."

"He is also angered because in passing an eye over it, he saw it was one of More's best works."

Given the body of More's accomplishments, this was quite a statement.

"There is something else, madam. Something the King would not want me to tell you."

"Something against me, then?"

"Something against you."

"Which was?"

"More's daughter went to him on one of the permitted visits," said Cromwell. "Apparently, his family believe you are the sole reason he is in prison. My guards told me that she spoke bitterly of the entertainments in your chambers, telling him all you were concerned with was dancing and sporting with men."

"Is that all?" I asked. "There are many who look down on a woman for having a little diversion. Women are allowed no enjoyment, apparently, but the same is not true of men. They are never censured, for only women fall."

"More said he pitied the misery that would shortly be yours," said Cromwell. "And that whilst your 'dance' might now spurn heads from necks like footballs, it would not be long before your head would dance a like dance."

"Thomas More is a fool," I said. "To say this within hearing of his guards? He threatens his Queen."

"This is another reason the King is determined to reduce his privileges."

"The King is most protective of me."

"Because he loves you, madam."

Thomas More rapidly found himself in less comfortable arrangements. Straw mats, provided weekly for the floors and walls of his chamber, were not ordered anew, he was prevented from hearing Mass in the Tower Chapel, and no visitors were allowed. Henry's men stormed out to capture the works that had slipped out into London, and More's houses were searched. One of the items found was a note More had written to himself, saying that it would be wrong to betray a secret entrusted to him. None knew what this secret was, but it made Henry infinitely more suspicious, and with France boring into my husband's personal sense of security, this was not a good time to rile the King.

As well as his *Dialogue of Comfort*, another work appeared. *De Tristitia Christi, On the Sadness of Christ*, was, as it transpired, More's last work. His books were filled with venom against heretics. More compared them to Judas. Heretics claimed love for Christ whilst betraying him, More wrote. They could repent and come back to God, but whilst they remained lost in sin, *"the air longs to blow noxious vapours against the wicked man. The sea longs to overwhelm them in its waves, the mountains to fall upon them, the valleys to rise up to him, the earth to split open beneath him, Hell to swallow him up after his headlong fall, the demons to plunge him into gulfs of everlasting flame…"* The lists of heavenly punishments went on and on. At times, Thomas More could be an insufferable, long-winded author.

I could only shake my head that this man who professed such faith and devotion to God failed to see that reform was not wickedness. Wickedness was allowing the Church to continue in such an ungodly way, robbing from the poor and coveting the wealth of kings. And those who questioned the Church were not like Judas. If anything, they emulated Christ, for he had dared to question the religion of his forefathers, and had transformed it. If anyone was betraying Christ, it was people like Thomas More, bound in servitude to blind, mistaken faith, and never acting for God.

But we did not know that more had been snuck from the Tower than just More's work. If More was to die, as seemed increasingly likely, he would not allow his greatest enemy to survive.

There was a plot against Tyndale, of which we knew nothing until it was too late.

Chapter Fourteen

Greenwich Palace
December 1534

At the start of December, as bright-breasted robins hopped on the first falls of snow and jaunty blackbirds rummaged in drifts for worms, we held a feast and a dance for Brion… who I was starting to hate more than any man alive.

I processed to the head of the hall with Henry, my black eyes snapping as we passed row upon row of bowing courtiers. I was in cloth of gold and purple, the royal colours blazing from my skirts, catching the light of the candles. Henry was dressed in the same colours, so we might show unity.

I was uncomfortable in my gown. Although I had lost much of the weight that had accompanied my lost pregnancy, I was still wider about the middle than I would have liked. My ladies said I was as thin as I had always been, but I did not feel so. Cloth of gold and purple were also not colours that suited me. I had selected them for their royal symbolism, as clearly the ambassador needed reminding *who was Queen*, but I looked better in fresh colours; greens, reds, silver and white. Purple and gold clashed against my olive skin and raven hair, making me look gaudy and overdone. But at times people needed to remember I was no more a mere lady of court. Sometimes it felt as though I was constantly reminding people of this.

Whilst I live, chuckled Katherine. *They will never see you as Queen.*

I ignored my personal phantom and went on with the night. The air was cold, bitter as chastisement, but black sea coal burnt bright in the glowing hearths. Diamonds shone on my cloak, glinting in the flicking light. My sleeves were long and hanging, lined with soft ermine and silver fox fur. Furs nuzzled my neck too, and their softness brought comfort as I watched the night's entertainment unfold.

Mummers performed as we feasted on carp and whiting. Trout cooked with herbs and presented as though alive, were set beside pink salmon and bream. Broiled herring with pepper and vinegar steamed on the tables, alongside succulent haddock in green sauce. Sallats of fresh green herbs, glistening with oil, sugar and vinegar were laced with strips of white and purple carrots, young oak leaves, Alexander buds, whelks and capers. Seethed shrimps, cooked in ale, salt and savoury, were piled in little mountains upon green-glazed platters. Boiled cockles in ale, pepper and vinegar were served bobbing in broth. Piles of clinking muscles, dripping with butter and garlic, and dressed with parsley, were prised open by eager diners. Crabmeat dressed in red wine, ginger and cinnamon, was served re-stuffed in their shells. Whole lobsters, oyster chewets, sturgeon in vinegar and white fish fricassee were brought out to great cheers. Pike in mustard, marjoram, thyme, parsley, rosemary, ginger and cinnamon was presented roasted whole to the King. There was carp and bream, trout pate pies, baked seal and roasted whale meat. There were herring, mullet, plaice and lamprey, trout, pike and eels. Fried beans with butter and garlic stood beside purple-black laver bread and sallats of lemon, egg and herbs. Tarts of cheese, fish, spinach and eggs shone golden-brown on the tables, and peas royal, baked artichokes, buttered worts on diced bread, and spinach ball fritters with dates and currants, filled the bellies of the gathered masses.

We finished with soft cheese on crisp wafers, oranges in rosewater syrup, peach pies and tarts of lemon and candied orange peel, laced with pretty, purple borage flowers. Possets of sugar, cinnamon, ale and sack shimmered before us like gemstones.

As the feast ended, I felt dizzy. I had drunk deep of Henry's fine wines, attempting to honour the ambassador and conceal my revulsion for him. Brion had condescended to raise a glass to me during the meal, but he did so with a sour cast upon his face. Henry appeared oblivious to Brion's downturned lips and furrowed brow, but I was not. What could I have ever done to so offend him, or his master? Had I not always been a friend to France? Had François not counselled me himself on the importance of queenship and love?

But then, I thought as I lifted my almost empty goblet, *François also counselled me there would come times when politics would force him to act against me*. Was this one of those times? Should I see the rudeness of his ambassador and his horrific negotiations as but temporary measures?

I knew not, but the more I drank the darker my thoughts became. Wine has a habit of stripping away the surface of sorrow, for a while, only to plunge the drinker into a deeper realm later. It is strange we forget this so easily.

"My love," Henry murmured. "I will fetch Brion's secretary, Gontier, for you. The Admiral may have no love for England, but I think his servant will prove more malleable."

I inclined my head. Although France was no England, it was just as possible for seemingly insignificant men to rise from the lower ranks and become useful later on, much like Cromwell.

Henry got up, leaving the ambassador and me to talk stiltedly. I watched my husband as he moved through the crowds, stopping now and then to talk to a favourite, or a friend. He drew people to him. Henry was a magnetic force, luring people with unseen charm.

As I watched, I saw him drift towards a most beautiful girl; a young wife of one of the French lords. It was as though he could not help it, as though he was caught in a spell. Her skin was white as milk and her hair golden as ripe corn. She looked at him with appealing, wide-eyed surprise as he held her arm to stop her from curtseying. I saw the familiar look of desire glinting in those blue eyes. That look that had once been mine alone.

I felt as though my heart would break and tears sprang into my glorious eyes. And then, without warning, I laughed out loud.

At times, sorrow springs from the body in ways that make no sense. Once my brother had told me when I was of two minds, I should always follow the trail of laughter rather than tears. It seemed my body, unable to express its heartbreak, had heeded George.

Brion, who had been talking, stopped short and stared at me in indignation. It was not as though he liked my company in any case, and now I was laughing in his face. "My lady," he said coldly. "Do you mock me?"

Suddenly the affronted expression on his ignorant, proud face was all the joy I was to have in the world. I laughed hard and heartily.

My father, standing not far away, stared as though I had lost my senses. People were turning. There was a febrile, unnerving edge to my laughter. I sounded like some unearthly being.

I touched the ambassador's arm. "No, no, dear Admiral," I said gaily in French. "I laugh because the King had gone to bring your secretary to introduce to me, but instead has met a most beautiful lady who has made him forget all other pursuits. Such is the way with the King!"

Tears jumped out of my eyes and I giggled again. I sounded hysterical. Perhaps that was just what I was. Henry should have honoured me, or at least had the courtesy to save his lust for private moments rather than flaunting it before court. But he could not help himself. I was laughing as much at myself, at my foolish notions of love and devotion, that once I had believed in without question, as I was at the ambassador's shocked face.

Brion was puzzled. Obviously, he could see nothing amusing in the situation. I took another pull on my wine. My laughter died.

Brion went back to his dull tale. I listened not, but nodded where I was supposed to until the time when I could call my ladies to me, thank the ambassador for regaling me with his *so interesting* tales, and leave with my head held high. However bold my appearance, my feet were unsure, trying to walk as my head swam with wine. Desperately, I held back the tears until I was alone.

Henry was still deep in conversation with the pretty little maid. He did not notice I had gone.

What is harder than to have known love once, and to have that taken away? I thought. *What is worse than continuing to love someone who once loved you?*

That night I wrapped my arms around little Purkoy and cried deep and hard into his soft fur. The lovely creature whimpered at my distress, nuzzling me with affection until I slept. In the morning, Purkoy was still there, watching over me. Sometimes it felt as though he was the only one who was on my side.

The French left the talks promising they would relay our proposal of marriage between my daughter and the house of France to their master. But before leaving, Brion took the time to dine with Chapuys.

Although Henry insisted that negotiations would continue, and we would win, I was not so sure. The French had shown where their preference lay. It was not with me.

Sometimes, in those dark and wearisome days, if felt as though everyone I had ever loved was destined to betray me.

As Brion left, our parting was as cool as the winter mists.

*

Later that month, as we began to prepare for Christmas and the first snows started to arrive, George had a blistering argument with our cousin, Francis Bryan. The fight began, I suspect, from jealousy.

George was highly favoured by Henry, and Bryan, like any courtier looking for elevation, was likely to resent this, but I had the feeling the argument was an indication of something more. Since the French delegation left, Henry had been cool with George. Perhaps he blamed him. George was our ambassador, and so we should have known, from the start, that they were intending on asking for Mary's hand. But my brother had had no idea this odious match would be proposed. It seemed to me, therefore, that Bryan had picked a fight with my brother on purpose in an attempt to distance himself from Henry's ire.

George and Bryan fought in public, at court, and were both scolded by Henry afterwards for disturbing the peace. They were told to shake hands and put their squabble behind them. They did so, but they would never truly be friends again.

And my sweet brother soon found his way back into Henry's heart, so Bryan's stance against him was foolish. Henry adored George. My brother was charming, learned and gallant. He was witty and clever, cutting at times, and far too proud, but he was charismatic and engaging. It was hard to stay angry with him. As Henry's anger departed, he informed my brother that he would lead the negotiations about Elizabeth's marriage. Bryan went about with a face like a dog left out in the rain.

But I wanted answers. I wanted to know why I had been betrayed. I wrote to du Bellay. My old friend was more forthcoming than I had expected, and informed me his master was worried that English merchants who supported Chapuys and Katherine would surrender to Charles if an invasion occurred. François reasoned that should the Emperor actually decide to invade England, it would be better to have been seen on Mary's side, rather than ours. This explained much, but I was still unhappy. France had insulted me and threatened Elizabeth. I could no more be a friend to them… yet without France's support, where could I or England turn? Not to Spain… not to Rome… Katherine had brought political value in her marriage. What had I brought to England? I had no foreign connections… and those I thought I did have, were no more. The only possibility left, I reasoned, was the Schmalkalden League of Hesse and Saxony. But they were not as powerful as France and Spain.

Henry set out to make friends with the Lubeckian and Hamburg merchants, part of the Hanseaic League. They sailed up the Thames, responding to his invitation to dine at the palace, their banners streaming in the breeze. With the looming threat that Imperial ports might close against us, England needed these merchants to continue trading. Many were Lutherans, and whilst Henry despised Luther, he enjoyed the heaping of praise they lavished on him when they met that day at the palace.

If France, Spain and trade were not enough to worry about, I had more concerns. Henry barely visited my bed, preferring to spend time with the parrot. The talk about court was that he was in love with her, and this unnerved me. An enemy in Henry's bed was dangerous, but what if he should decide he was really in love with her? She was married, that was true, but I had failed to give him a son, twice, and with his infrequent trips to my bed, was not likely to succeed.

A terrible thought was dawning in my mind. Like a cursed fog it crept. I tried hard to banish it, but it crawled over me, consuming my thoughts.

Henry was going to keep mistresses. No matter how much that hurt or how little I could understand it, that was the truth. If this was inevitable, it would be better to have one of my supporters in his bed rather than an enemy. A terrible, painful thought, rising like a blood red sun over the desert, dawned; I had to place someone in Henry's bed… someone who would speak for me.

I had to become a whoremaster, in order to keep my husband's love.

Chapter Fifteen

Greenwich Palace
December 1534

"It falls to the King to decide these matters," I said to Cromwell as he showed me his plans. Henry was to make Cromwell the Vicar-General of England, invested with the power to investigate religious houses. This was a new post, created by Henry, and its purpose was to bring his Church in line. I supported the notion. Poor practices would be abolished, dissenters would be rooted out, and reform would begin in earnest. It was the revolution we had been seeking, and finally Henry had agreed to move forward with it.

"But for my part," I went on, "I am in favour of this examination. I would have our Church stand against corruption and it would seem many religious orders have fallen into sins, that by their very existence, they should oppose."

I looked from the window. Snow was falling… a wide, white blanket of glittering light. Evergreens had been gathered from the parks and the halls of court had transformed into a forest of twisted ivy and shining, verdant holly. Robins hopped over the frosted earth, their red breasts brilliant against the white sheets of winter. Old gossips claimed that a robin had pulled a thorn from Christ's crown in pity, and thus had stained his breast, marking his ancestors as the blessed of God. Their presence that day made me think that the Almighty was watching us, and approved of our plans.

The sun was barely visible over the last line of shadowy trees. Sullen mist crept across the parks. The trees were bare, and through the empty avenues of the forests, the song of birds and call of wild beasts could be heard clear and sharp. Life was waiting, under the cover of snow, waiting for a chance to break free, to unfurl frozen leaves and stand strong once more. I wondered if I was doing the same… hiding under a blanket of brash confidence, masking my true nature with shadows and lies. If ever there was a time to break free, it was now. If ever there was a time to stand strong, I would stand for my faith.

Cromwell nodded. "I believe the same, Majesty," he said smoothly. "And you are right that His Majesty has the final say. But I brought this to you so your good opinion may stand with mine when these matters are presented to the King. His Majesty wishes to believe his clergy are the best of all men, but you and I are aware of their corruption."

"It saddens me," I said, turning from the window. "But I have long suspected that the Bishop of Rome and his cardinals have encouraged the pursuit of earthly pleasures amongst the clergy. It is no more a place where men and women go because they have a true, spiritual vocation, but a place they are bundled off to if there are too many children in one household, or if they desire a life of ease. You have my support, Cromwell. I would have this country become a great leader in all matters spiritual and temporal, and with His Majesty now assured as the spiritual head of the Church, I see greatness coming from his hand to heal this nation and all others."

Cromwell smiled. "We think alike, Majesty," he said. "And when a prince is born and the royal nursery is filled with legitimate heirs, the whole world will see God's beneficence shining on England."

Cromwell was in some ways so unassuming. He seemed to blend into the background with the skill of a creature born to camouflage. But in other ways he was so forceful, so skilled in getting people to understand his cause and his will. I wanted so badly to trust in others. My circle of supporters was smaller since I had assumed the crown.

I wanted a friend.

I licked my dry lips. "I believe we have a good understanding of each other," I said slowly. "You and I dedicate ourselves to the same offices in support of reform and rejuvenation."

He bowed. "Of course, Your Majesty."

"I wonder if I may talk to you about a matter most delicate," I said. "I wonder sometimes who a queen may trust?"

"Your Majesty," he said. "I am your servant, and that of the King."

"The King finds the need to have… company," I said, blushing. "There are rumours that one of his present companions was brought to court through your offices."

I had heard this not long ago, from Bess Holland. Like many men in Henry's service, Cromwell was rumoured to have helped his master procuring jades, Joanna Dingley amongst them.

Cromwell was not one to betray emotions, but his eyes grew wary. "Your Majesty," he said, but I held up my hand. It shook. Glistening rings of emerald and diamond shimmered in the sunlight.

"Please…" I said. "It was brought to my attention that the company you provided for the King during my pregnancy was, if not a friend to me, not important enough to become an enemy. If you did have a hand in that matter, I would say to you that I understand the choice was careful and made in order to help me. And however much it might hurt to know that my husband is unfaithful, I would thank you for your care and caution." I stared into his eyes. "You were trying to help me, I think… You provided a woman who was no threat to me."

His face was a mask, but a little glint in his eyes betrayed that this was indeed the case. He nodded.

I felt a rush of anger flow into my blood and I crushed it. The world was not as I wanted it to be, but that was not Cromwell's fault. If he had supplied Dingley for Henry, he had done so smoothly and carefully. He had protected my honour, tried to keep the unpleasant truth from me, supplied Henry's needs and ensured that the selected girl was no serious contender for Henry's affections. In a deeply unpleasant affair, he had done well. Dingley had been meek and mild, and although I worried about her connections to Norfolk, it was clear she was no menace. The same was not true of the parrot. *The Imperial Lady*, as she was known about court was a true threat to my position.

"Your Majesty," he said. "There was an office that needed to be done, and I tried to ensure the best outcome." He paused. "You are, and will always be the King's greatest and only love," he said, his voice scarred with something akin to admiration

I nodded, tears leapt to my eyes and I dashed them away. "You did well, even if I could not see it at the time," I said. "But Mistress Perrot is a different matter."

"I had nothing to do with her coming to court, Majesty," Cromwell rushed to say. "She was brought by Carewe, for he knew of His Majesty's past affection for her."

So that was who had brought the parrot to a new cage. Carewe. I was not surprised. The man despised me. I wondered if he had coached her… told her not only how to draw Henry to her again, but groomed her to oppose me. If so, the parrot was even more dangerous than I had thought. She had to go. I had to play Carewe at his own filthy little game.

I braced myself. What I was about to do went against all my natural instincts. I had done many things I was not proud of, and this was one of them.

"My cousin, Mary Shelton, is a vibrant young lady," I said, my voice shaking. "Her family are devoted to reform, and loyal to me. I was wondering if the King might have exhausted the pleasures of company and conversation with his last friend, and might be persuaded to keep company with another?"

Cromwell regarded me with steady eyes. There was sympathy in those dark tunnels, mingled with relief. Clearly he had feared I would eventually discover he had brought Dingley to court. I thought back to the day I had exploded at Henry and blushed. That must have been just the kind of scene Cromwell had tried to avoid, and I had been too foolish, too much a girl still lost in fantasies of love, to understand.

He nodded slowly. "I will see to your request with all delicacy," he said. "I would add, Your Majesty, some are brought to the crown by virtue of blood. Some, such as you, were born to wear it, by virtue of courage and strength." His eyes gleamed against the amber candlelight. "I am your most humble servant… and admirer."

"You admire me for setting aside the fantasy of love and devotion?" I asked, shaking my head. "Do not flatter me for this, Cromwell. It is no virtue. I ask this of you only because I am forced to. This is not the way I would have my life, or my marriage."

"In recognising necessity, my lady, and setting it above our most ardent wishes, a soul shows itself wise."

"I wonder if wisdom ever keeps company with joy."

As he bowed, I rested my hand on his shoulder and squeezed it. "You have my admiration too… Thomas," I said. "You are a good friend."

"So shall I always be, to you, madam, or may God strike me down."

*

As we marched towards Christmas, I found myself often wrapped in my furs, walking in the gardens. The world was silver. Paths crackled beneath my feet and birds warbled in the desolate trees. A still hush had fallen, transforming the glory of autumn into the graceful death of winter.

In the parks, Henry's servants hunted wood pigeon with nets and arrows. Maids in the kitchens plucked the pearl-grey birds, loosing plumes of soft feathers into the air, like snowflakes, and gathering them to stuff mattresses and cushions. The birds were made into pies, or roasted on the spit, coated in ginger and honey, and brought to our tables each night.

Curlews sang, pausing only to dip their bills into the muddy tracks along the Thames. Geese flew into England, honking and jostling on the waterways, and scaring young children who sought to poke them with long sticks. Wild falcons, their feathers lapis and slate, glittering against the faded skies, swooped upon prey like arrows. Shrews bustled in the hedgerows, their long noses rooting through the dead leaf litter for insects.

I relished the cold, the breathtaking chilled air and the beauty that surrounded me. My women did not. It was their duty to follow wherever I went, but they did not welcome my morning walks. I tried to interest Purkoy in accompanying me, but although he was, at first, quite excited about the snow, and raced about in it like a madcap creature, he soon felt the cold bite into his delicate skin, stopped dead still, and emitted a howl like a wolf about to be slaughtered.

My little Purkoy was not made for the hardy outdoors. When he did accompany me, out of steadfast loyalty, he would shiver and gaze up with his huge, liquid eyes, begging me to take him under my warm cloak. Although I scolded him for cowardice, I always lifted him. Purkoy was my friend. We all like to try to make life easier for a friend.

One morning I had risen, and another day of embroidering bed hangings surrounded by the stuffy, stale air of the palace loomed despondently before me. I had wanted escape, peace and some time to walk by myself. That morning, Purkoy declined to accompany me. His soft bed by the richly tiled fireplace was far more tempting than hurting his paws upon the frozen ground. He looked so content, curled in his blankets, that I did not press him to accompany me.

I left him and my ladies in my chambers, and with just one guard, went out to feel the bite of the chilled air. The snow and its majesty were but little disturbed as I crunched along, feeling the snow resist, then yield to the pressure of my boots of Spanish leather. The freshness in the air almost took my breath. It was as intoxicating as fine wine. I thought of my good fortune. I would never have to march out by necessity, as so many in the town and country would, to break ice to water their beasts and family. For me there was only enjoyment in this frozen world.

I will ask that the kitchens give out more than just scraps from court feasts, I thought as I walked. In this weather there would be many in need. I did not want poor widows or beggars leaving empty-handed and bellied.

I spent an hour walking. One of Henry's men, Edward Seymour, followed me, shivering in his boots as he tottered along, trying not to disturb me as he bashed his hands against his sides to warm his blood. Seymour was a growing favourite of Henry's and Cromwell's. Indeed, Cromwell had paid some debts for him, since he was sure the lad had a promising future. Cromwell liked to support 'new' men. I think he saw himself in them. Since Seymour was also my cousin, I often agreed to him attending upon me.

Eventually I smiled at Edward, feeling pity. His grin was tinged with relief as he realized I was going back to the palace.

"Come then," I said. "Let us return whilst you still have fingers and toes left."

He bowed. "My lady, you are as beneficent as you are beautiful." His pale eyes were watering and his nose was a mighty shade of burgundy. I laughed as we turned for my apartments.

Returning to the palace was like wandering into a great hug from a giant with smouldering arms. I started to strip the furs from my shoulders before I even reached my chambers. Henry's huge fireplaces were a feature in almost every room. They were a display of wealth and luxury, but also practical and clever. Ambassadors in particular were grateful for them. Hailing from warmer climes, they often struggled to keep patience with England's weather.

I smiled as I remembered Henry's boyish face as he unveiled those plans to me… so long ago, it seemed. His eyes had lit up with the idea, and his hands, so strong and capable, had been unable to restrain themselves from flying about as he moulded the air with his designs.

My heart flooded open to this memory, when I was full of certainty that all we needed was to be together. Was I so wrong? Could we not be happy? Perhaps, if the world was not always getting in our way.

As I wandered into my chambers, I was lost in thought. But then I stopped and stared at the ghostly scene before me.

The room was empty. Not of furnishings, or hangings, but of people.

My rooms were never empty. My women were always in attendance and gentlemen servers too. Petitioners arrived each day, maids of honour flitted about, chamberers cleaned and noble guests came to call. But the beautiful chamber was utterly deserted. Candles flickered uncertainly, wary to be so alone. The fire burned with no one to warm. Had I wandered into a dream?

Edward stopped behind me and also stared in amazement. "Where is everyone?" I asked in the hushed tone one adopts when alone.

Seymour had no answer, but his hand darted to his sword and he moved in front of me.

"Is anyone here?" My voice was eerie. It bounced from the walls, disappearing into the silent chasm.

A shape appeared in the far doorway. For a moment, the great shadow loomed like a demon of my dreams. I could see blue eyes, like fire, glinting in the gloom.

Then the figure stepped into the light. It was Henry.

I let out a laugh, a sudden, high expulsion of relief. My breathing resumed and I walked forward, so relieved it was not some creature of my nightmares, that I failed to see the pain on his face until I was right before him.

A greeting of love and affection stalled on my lips. "My love," I said gently. "What is wrong? Where is everyone?"

He took my hands, looked at them, and then at me. His face softened as he saw my concern. Henry was a sentimental man; proof of genuine affection touched him deeply, most likely as he was so used to hearing sycophantic falsehoods. He yearned to be loved for the man he was, not the crown he wore.

"Beloved," he said gently. "I have sent your ladies away to spare them having to give pain to the mistress they admire and love. That task falls to me. And much as I wish to spare you any hurt, I must tell you of a horrible accident."

My eyes widened. "Who?" I said, fears leaping into my head. "Elizabeth?" I was weak at the thought. His arms reached out as the blood drew back from my flesh.

"No, no," he said holding me. "Our daughter is well and hearty, and your family too. But you must come with me. This will not be easy."

He walked me into my bedchamber. On the bed, on a velvet cushion of crimson, as though sleeping, was my little Purkoy.

But he was not sleeping. Even in slumber, Purkoy would move his ears, twitch his nose and scamper after imaginary rabbits.

Purkoy was dead.

With a strangled cry, I rushed to the still body of my dog. As I touched him, I felt the stiff muscles and the hideous rigor of a body touched by the hand of Death. My hands roamed, quivering over him. His underside was battered and smashed, thick with blood. They had laid him out so I would see his good side, but as I took hold of him I saw the bloody horror underneath.

One of his beautiful eyes was sealed shut with caked blood. The side of his head was crushed like a rotten apple. I could see shards of skull, winking white in the guttering yellow candlelight. One of his legs was twisted at an impossible angle, broken and bent. I fell back. My legs gave way, and I slumped to the floor, my hand against my mouth as I started to cry.

Purkoy had been my friend. My simple, loyal friend, who had never asked for anything but to be with me. I stared at his body in horror. It could not be. He was so alive, so vital. How could it be that my friend was so far from me?

Henry came to me. I think even he was surprised at the depth of my sorrow. Perhaps he had been expecting the rage to which I was so prone to escape, but I was weakened by grief. I leaned back into the arms of my husband and wept. There was blood on my hands. I curled my fingers about my palms so I could not see it.

Purkoy… *dead*? How could this be?

Henry held me until I had cried myself quiet. He sat on the floor with me, his fine clothes on the rushes as he comforted me.

"Henry?"

"Yes, beloved?"

"How did this happen?"

Henry brought me close. "There was an accident. Purkoy fell from an open window. We are some floors up. He was too small to survive such a fall."

I pulled myself up. "But… my windows are never opened in winter."

Henry reached out to stroke an idle piece of hair come loose from my hood. "Today they were," he said. "I do not know what to tell you, my love. Two of your women came to me. Mary Shelton and Jane Seymour said Purkoy had been sniffing out of the window. The next minute they turned, and he had disappeared. They were afraid to tell you, so came to me. They are good girls, your women. They were mortified to think they would bring you pain."

"But, Henry," I said, an idea forming that was so monstrous I could hardly entertain it. "Purkoy hated the cold. He would have stayed on his cushion by the fire, especially if the window was open. He would not have gone near it."

Henry shook his head. "Mistress Seymour said she thought he was looking for you." He stopped as my eyes flooded with tears. "Come, Anne," he said, stroking my face. "The dog was your loyal friend until his last breath. Even though he was no great hound, he died trying to ensure his mistress was well. You have this gift to inspire all men and beasts with the same wish, it seems."

There was such a gentle note to his voice that I sank into his arms. But as I lay in Henry's embrace that afternoon, there were suspicions and fears in my heart.

Purkoy's death had been no accident. I had ordered those windows kept closed and Purkoy would have never abandoned his bed for the chill air of the window.

Was there someone, within my own household, who wanted to cause me grief? Someone who would have pushed my little friend from the window when I left, knowing what his loss would cost me? Had someone hated me so much that they were willing to take the life of an innocent, to bring me anguish?

Was there someone close to me, who, far from being my friend… was my bitter enemy?

In the days following Purkoy's death, I was shaken. I was sure my dog had been murdered. I thought of all the times he had helped me; granted me love and affection when there was none to be had from Henry. I thought of all the times I had told my ladies that he was my only true friend, and as I thought of this, I became certain.

Someone had killed him in order to hurt me.

My temper became as fragile as my trust and my heart. Norfolk came to speak with me, wanting me to aid him in a plot to oust Cromwell from court. Norfolk had uncovered that Cromwell was slandering him, although much of what he had said was, in fact, true.

"As my blood-kin, Majesty, you are honour bound to aid me," Norfolk said, leaning on his odious cane. Encrusted spittle sat hunkered at the edges of his mouth. I despised him.

"It is interesting, Your Grace, the times you choose to remember our bond and the times you do not."

"I know not of what you speak, Majesty."

"*Hah!*" I cried out, my temper snapping. "What of all the times you have supported the King's bastard over my legitimate daughter? What of all your whispered conversations with Chapuys, Uncle? All your fine dinners with the Poles, the Courtenays and Nicholas Carewe? Do you think me ignorant or blind? You would use me as you use all women. But I will not be your tool, old man. And for my part, I would rather have one Cromwell than a thousand Howards! I would rather have one useful man than an army of incompetent dukes!"

As Norfolk quitted my chamber, I heard him speaking to Henry Percy, my old suitor, who was on a rare visit to court. "That woman is no Queen!" Norfolk shouted. "Queen Katherine was a true queen! Anne Boleyn is nothing but a *grande putain!*"

What Percy made of this, I knew not. My old suitor had been ill, and when I met him at court upon his arrival, I had been shocked by the spell of deathly winter that had fallen upon him. His marriage was unhappy, and he was in constant debt. Unlike George, Weston, or any other who incurred debt at court, Percy was not favoured enough to relieve his concerns. After hearing Norfolk, Percy took sides with the conservatives. His physician, his most intimate companion, told courtiers that his master was indignant at the treatment he had received from Henry's government. Quite what this treatment was I never did discover, but I took Henry's part. My husband rewarded useful men, and Percy was nothing of the sort. And my foes knew it. They did not welcome Percy into their ranks, so he drifted on their borders, like a wraith.

Norfolk's bluster earned him a stern scolding from Cromwell, sent by Henry. But however satisfying it was to know Henry was protecting me from slander, it did not stop my uncle's insult being repeated about court.

That night I stared into my mirror, counting the lines of worry fast-forming about my eyes. A great whore… that was what my uncle had said. That was what Henry's people called me. Yet I had only taken one man to my bed; my husband.

"How easy it is to defame a woman by calling her a whore," I said sadly to Cromwell the next morning. "The mere mention of the word calls her character, temperament, and virtue into question, expelling all good that might have been hers. There are few words for the same state when applied to men, for promiscuity is only a sin if women undertake it."

"Majesty, your uncle is opposed to all women, that much is clear, especially if they have the spirit to stand against him. Do not take it to heart. All men know of your virtue."

"If you want my help in reducing the influence of my uncle, it is yours."

"I would appreciate your aid, my lady. The Duke is too concerned with his own plots, and not enough with the King's wishes." He gazed at me with compassion, but I could see he was excited. Norfolk's influence with Henry was degrading by the day, and should he be plucked from court, there was much Cromwell might achieve without Norfolk hindering him.

I allowed Cromwell to comfort me, but a time would come when I would remember this conversation, and curse myself for having put such a useful notion into his head.

Perhaps because he understood my sorrow over Purkoy, Henry brought Elizabeth to court that Christmas. I welcomed my daughter as the earth greets the first sunrise of spring.

What joy is there to compare to the presence of one's child in one's arms? What more happiness than hearing laughter, so sweet and innocent, spill from the tiny mouth of one's child? Elizabeth was the embodiment of innocence; that state that once I rested in, and had lost. But in her, it lived. I hoped she would never be forced to part with it.

I sang to her. I told her tales that my mother had told me. We sat together in the wild afternoons of winter, bundled up under a blanket on a seat in the long gallery with candles lit against the falling light. As the wind screamed and the rain lashed the palace walls, I sang to my daughter of chivalry and love. We played with her rattles and dolls. Together, we whiled away hours, as my rich voice sang softly in the candlelit gloom, until her pretty black eyes, so like mine, closed as she fell into slumber.

With her in my arms, I could forget much.

But if I could forget some things, there was much I could not. I needed to speak to Mary Shelton, and convince her to become Henry's mistress. Yet how could I ask a girl to whore herself for me? How could I go against my soul and provide a woman for the empty space I longed to fill beside Henry?

I wrestled with my conscience, but as I held Elizabeth, I knew I had no choice. No matter how terrible, no matter how much it hurt, I had to do it. The parrot had to be removed. There was no other way, and if I could not hold my husband to me on the merit of my own charms, or on the strength of our love, I had to find other means.

Tension ran high during Christmas, not only in my heart but in court. The court was no more simply a place of song and dance. The talk was of reform, religion and rebellion. There was dissent everywhere, and everyone could feel it. It seeped through the walls, through every crack, blighting merriment with a stain of evil. Fears about France and Spain, the rise of Lady Mary in the world and the rejection of Elizabeth assailed me. But one thing troubled me more.

Henry shied from my bed. Without him, how could I produce this son who would make me safe? How could I protect my daughter?

Chapter Sixteen

Greenwich Palace
January 1535

"I want it taken to my sister," I said quietly to the messenger. "But I do not want it known that I have sent her anything. I will require you to swear it, upon your honour."

The man nodded and swore, taking up the case containing a golden cup and a purse of money. Publicly, I could not be reconciled to Mary, but my sense of isolation had deepened in the wake of Purkoy's loss, and I wanted to make amends. Mary and Stafford had gone to Calais as Stafford had a post there.

Long, hard and often I had thought on my bitter, unjust words, especially in the aftermath of my uncle using the same slanders against me. I could only think ill of how I had treated my sister. How distance brings clarity to a disturbed mind! She had married for love. How could I disgrace that when I had done the same?

I had become my own father; abusing my sister just as he had in France. That thought, perhaps more than any other, shook me.

Some time later, I learned that Mary had received my presents with joy. She sent a message back, telling me she had recently borne a daughter, and named her Anne, for me.

Oh, the guilt that was mine then! My sweet sister had named her child after me, when I had brought her untold unhappiness. I could not bring her back to court, for Henry paled even to hear her name, but I sent a message saying we would keep in touch, with discretion, and Mary responded warmly.

She wrote to me of her life in Calais. She was happy, and even though they were poor, she and Stafford were a good match. He was kind, cared nothing about her past, and adored his tiny daughter. It brought some peace to my heart to know this. I hoped one day to see her in person, perhaps when we finally went to France, if the postponed meeting ever took place. There I would explain my reasons... the darkness of my jealousy and the malice born of my terrors.

I was not the only one giving presents that New Year's. Although it was the traditional time for nobles to exchange gifts, one in particular raised eyebrows. Lord Darcy, one of Katherine's silent supporters, presented a sword and a golden brooch, bearing a forget-me-not flower upon it, to Chapuys. Since this coincided with Henry and the hare speaking about the fleet the Emperor had assembled to battle the infidels in Tunis, and what the Emperor's intentions towards England were, I had no doubt Lord Darcy's gifts were a signal to the Emperor that he was his supporter.

The hapless hare was also dining with Norfolk and William FitzWilliam on a regular basis. The old rift between Chapuys and Norfolk seemed to have healed, and the three were together often, sometimes with Gardiner and his little shadow Wriotheseley in tow. Perhaps it was good the hare had friends at court, for Henry was rapidly turning against the ambassador, although he could not show it openly.

"I am certain the Emperor is considering invasion," Henry said one night as we dined.

"You do not believe he is only against the infidels?" I asked, spooning chicken broth onto Henry's plate.

"That is what he would like us to think."

Sometimes Henry seemed as paranoid as his late father, but I did not dare bring up the comparison. "And Chapuys denies this, of course?"

"Of course, but he cannot fool me. I will have our coastal fortifications bolstered. No foreigner will land on English soil carrying designs on my land."

Henry was doubly suspicious of the Emperor as Charles had recently sent arms and soldiers to aid the Earl of Kildare, an Irish lord and Henry's sworn enemy. Henry thought that the Emperor might try to sneak men in through England's back gate. Chapuys protested that the Earl and his men were protecting Spanish fishing rights in the Irish Sea, and that was why men had been offered. This led to a mistrustful Henry lecturing Chapuys on his new coastal defences, and ships, boasting that the Emperor had nothing, *nothing*, to the fleet England possessed.

Chapuys could only answer that his master was not thinking of invading, but added he would never recognise me as Queen. Cromwell told him there was hope that the new Pope would honour our union, and declare my daughter legitimate. To such a notion, Chapuys simply smiled.

As Henry's focus was fixated on Spain and the Emperor, mine turned to Lady Mary. In truth we were looking at the same problem from alternate angles. If the Emperor invaded, Mary would be set upon the throne, mayhap with a Spanish husband to keep her Imperial cousin sweet. And the French were supporting her too, endangering Elizabeth. With Henry's zealous belief that England would soon come under attack colouring my thoughts, I sent a deluge of missives to Eltham, warning my aunts and Lady Bryan that Mary was to be kept under stricter watch than ever before, as there were rumours she might be stolen out of the country, or her cousin might attack on her behalf.

My aunts did not welcome my commands. Mary was already under strict watch, they informed me, and to tighten her restraints still further would engender ill-feeling from the common people, who adored her.

But I would not relent. Paranoia is a dangerous creature. It is not one being, but many. It is a host of rats stowed upon a ship. In the darkness of the murky holds they breed, and sight of one means many more lurk nearby. Such a beast is paranoia. It multiplies and grows, becoming stronger as it sups on terror. The stringent measures I had my aunts take caused Mary's health to collapse. She became mistrustful, jumping at every word, and in her fragile state, her old troubles returned.

Once more Doctor Butts was sent, and Katherine pleaded to nurse her daughter. Chapuys was dispatched to Henry to read him a letter Katherine had sent, begging to be granted access to Mary. Henry refused. He feared Katherine might be seeking means to escape England, and would take Mary with her. When Chapuys made a counter-offer, that Mary should be reunited with the Countess of Salisbury, her old governess, Henry declared the Countess was an incompetent fool.

Henry received all messages on Mary's health with a mixture of worry and suspicion, not knowing if this illness was a trick to dupe him into doing something foolish that would allow Katherine and their daughter to fly from his clutches. In the end, it was said Mary would be permitted to move closer to Katherine, but not to see her. If anyone understood what sense this made, I did not, but it seemed to calm mother and daughter.

Finally convinced that his daughter was telling the truth, Henry also learned of the measures I had taken. Forgetting that he, too, had feared she might flee, he came to me in a grand temper, berating me for my interference.

"It is none of your business!" he roared.

I stared at him. He had not bothered sending my ladies away, or his gentlemen. I could almost hear those hateful words he had spoken last summer, saying that I should be grateful for the position he had granted me and *would not do so again*, about to emerge from his lips. I would not allow him to do that to me in front of the court. Not again.

I drew myself up. "You are as much indebted to me as ever man was to woman," I said loudly, causing many courtiers to stop pretending they could hear nothing. They gaped with mouths open so wide they could have been used to collect butterflies.

"I am the cause of your being cleansed from the sin in which you were once living," I said boldly. "By marrying me, you have become the richest monarch that ever was in England, both in wealth and spirit. Without me you would never have had this. It is because of *me* that you have moved to reform your Church, my lord, to your great personal profit and that of your Kingdom. You owe me much."

Henry stared at me, his cheeks burning. Everyone was gaping.

"I took measures against Lady Mary to protect both you and our daughter," I announced. "It was feared your bastard might try to escape England and bring wicked war upon our people, so I ensured she was unable to. I have done my *duty*, my lord, as your wife, as your Queen, and as the mother of our daughter, the heir to England's throne. Scold me not for taking care of my family. You are right when you say I owe you much, but you owe much to me also. That should never be forgotten."

I stood, bold and beautiful, strong and fierce. From the corner of my eye, I could see Norris gazing at me with unbounded admiration. The faces of Weston, Heneage and Brereton were much the same. My ladies looked as though they might laugh. Only Henry seemed astonished.

"We will speak of this in private," he said. "Later."

"As you wish, my lord." I sat down calmly and clicked my fingers for the music to resume. I could have laughed! Henry was trying to save his pride. He had accosted me, but where once I had fallen apart, this time I had triumphed.

As he left, I heard him talking angrily to Norris… saying that I was getting more like Katherine every day, and he knew not what he had done to deserve two such troublesome wives.

I could almost feel Katherine at my back. If I turned, I was sure I would see her there, smiling.

I do not need his good opinion, I thought. *As long as I think well of myself, that is enough.*

I felt like the girl I had once been. False confidence had been my friend for so long, that when true courage came, I was almost undone by its power. I felt mighty, and strong, once more. I would not be crushed into this weak, feeble creature who cried and wailed. I would stand. I would fight. I would hold respect for myself.

Henry did not seek to bring up the matter again. Not in private and not in public. If he admitted he might have been mistaken, his self-image would shatter like a glass thrown to the cobbled floor. But where he had vanquished me before, I swore he never would again.

*

I was not the only one to endure a royal scolding that season. Henry turned on Norfolk and my father some days later, for not taking harder measures against a Carthusian monk who had preached a sermon criticizing the royal supremacy.

Perhaps it was this which stirred Henry into action, as soon Cromwell was granted full authority by Henry, as the Head of the Church, to wield the authority conferred upon the Crown by God. There were many facets to this power, but Henry wanted one used with immediate effect.

Cromwell was to begin a massive undertaking; a survey of all the religious houses in England, to uncover abuses, ill practices, slovenly behaviour, allegiance to Rome and mortal sin. Commands would be issued, requiring all clergymen to personally take the oath of succession, as well as their religious orders as a whole, and to ensure that none of them followed the doctrine of Rome, or demonstrated obedience to the Pope. Religious orders were further informed that the emphasis would no more be on the manner of their apparel, shaven heads, fasting or getting up at all hours of the night for Mass, but would instead rely upon *"cleanliness of mind, pureness of living, Christ's faith not feigned and brotherly charity"*.

Relics were to be investigated, and taken from display if found to be false. This would cause uproar, I was sure, as monasteries grew fat on the coin of pilgrims. But I welcomed the notion that sober charity and prayer would supplant the worship of what were widely believed to be false relics.

Restrictions on monasteries would also be more strictly imposed. Enclosure was one of them. Certain orders were enclosed; their members were not supposed to tarry beyond the boundaries of their houses. This was widely ignored, but Henry meant to enforce it, saying, quite rightly, if solitude was the term of service offered to God, that should be honoured.

Houses beyond help would be dissolved, and their wealth would go to the Crown, to be used for charitable purposes. But those that required guidance would be offered it, and those doing well would be upheld. Those that I hailed as good provided medical care, education, alms and employed many people on their farms and estates. The Church was one of the largest landowners in England, exceeding even Henry in wealth and estates.

Closing, or suppressing, monasteries was not a new event. My husband's idol, Henry V, had begun the practice and under Wolsey some had been investigated and closed, although the Cardinal had used this as a means to fill his own coffers rather than to redistribute wealth to the poor. But this examination would be larger than any conducted before, and more thorough. I welcomed the proposal. My brother, however, was more critical.

"Cromwell's men have also been told to gather information on the possessions of each house," said my brother one night as we sat with a chessboard between us.

"Only so they can uncover false relics being used to extort money from the unwise," I said, playing with one of my bishops.

"Think that, if it brings you comfort, sister," said my brother, toying with his eating knife as he watched what my move would be. "But this vision the King has of a fortified England, safe from invasion, will not come without a great influx of coin. The King is obsessed. He thinks the Emperor is poised to invade. Where do you think the money for all the ships he wants, all the walls, all the arms and all the soldiers will come from?"

I frowned and sat back, abandoning the game. Cromwell had visited me only that morning to assure me that anything confiscated from churches, unless they were false relics or useless icons, would be used by Henry for charitable purposes. I had also been told religious houses that were shut down would be converted into schools. Henry's fortifications had not even been mentioned.

"His Majesty wants new castles built up and down the coast," George continued, his hazel eyes fixed on mine. "The money for that is not in the royal coffers, but soon it will be."

"But that is what the bill for raising taxes in times of peace was for," I protested. "I assure you, brother, everything taken from monasteries or churches *will* go back to the Church or the people. I have Cromwell's personal assurance on this."

"Anne," said my brother, setting his goblet on the table and leaning forwards. "You must uncover your eyes. Cromwell is misleading you. Wealth taken from monasteries *will go* to the King. What the King chooses to do with it is up to him. He is under no compulsion to support the needy. He will use it for defence."

"Even if some is used for military purposes," I said sternly. "More will be given to the poor, or to re-found religious houses."

"Not if Cromwell is in charge. He wants to make the King rich, and himself, too, in the process."

"You are allowing resentment to colour your thoughts," I said, although I had to admit my heart was not at ease. "His interference in your affairs last year has led you to distrust him, but I assure you, brother, Cromwell is as dedicated to true and godly reform as we are. He will make sure those funds are spent well."

"Oh, I am *sure* he will." George's tone was scathing and his eyes were heavy with scorn.

George left me uneasy. I sat staring at the half-played chessboard after he departed. Was he right? *Was* I being duped? I had believed Cromwell without question, but as I thought back to the fines demanded of the clergy after their submission, I had to confess I did not know if they had been spent on charity, as I had been assured. Was it possible I was being lied to? Was my brother correct in his assumption that the riches of the monasteries would go straight into Henry's purse?

I called my brother to me again the next day and asked him to provide men for me to use. I wanted to quietly investigate where the money from the fines of the clergy had gone. I wanted answers. I wanted to know if, and for how long, I had been being blindly led astray.

When answers came back, I did not like them. There was no proof that money from the clergy's fines had gone to aid any notable cause. And there was more. People were talking about the enforcement of enclosure.

"How are abbots to collect rents due to their houses?" Norris asked quietly. "How are they to sell their produce? Monasteries *rely* on a certain amount of contact with the world. Without that, how are they to live?"

"But if solitude and prayer is what was promised to God, Norris, this is what should be offered."

"Pardon my impudence, my lady," he said, his earnest eyes on mine. "But I do not think God intended for his servants to starve to death, or run themselves into bankruptcy."

"I am sure the King has a plan," I said. "He is utterly dedicated to his Church. There is time to perfect a plan, as any such commands will only go forward after Cromwell's investigations. When anything new is done, there is always a period of confusion, Norris. His Majesty will set it straight, and we will enter a new time, with him leading us."

"I am sure you are right, Majesty," said Norris, sounding anything but certain.

In truth, I felt the same.

I had to support Henry in public. All he was doing was done, at least in part, to protect me, Elizabeth and England. I could not allow anyone to think I was unsure. But in private, I made up my mind to keep a close eye on Cromwell, Henry, and what was being done with the wealth of the monasteries. Even to the detriment of my position or that of my daughter, I could not allow evil to be done in God's name. And if certain people had lost the path in the forest of faith, and were veering off down dark gullies, I would lead them back. For what good was any of this, if we were not doing God's work?

The Lord is a clement master, but He does not like men doing ill in His holy name. I would not allow my soul, Henry's, or that of our daughter to become tainted. I would not allow the faith to be abused so wicked souls might profit.

*

As Cromwell began to gather his men, and I sent George's out to investigate, Henry took measures too. At the end of January he started to style himself *"Henry VIII, by the Grace of God, King of England and of France, Defender of the Faith, and Lord of Ireland. Supreme Head of the Church of England."*

At the same time, Henry's men unleashed a tempest of words against the papacy. Doctor George Brown preached on the subject of bishops, saying all who would not burn their papal bulls of appointment were traitors. Cromwell took advice from loyal bishops as to whether the King could unmake bishops at will. Cranmer formally rejected the authority of Rome over England and some bishops followed his lead.

Anti-papal sentiment rang from the preaching pit at Whitehall, spreading through England like a blanket of fog.

Cromwell was enthused about his survey, and deep in work much of the time. But I interrupted this and called him to me. "I am disturbed by the tenor of this survey," I said. "It would seem some have taken this to mean *all* religious houses will be shut down."

"Only those who show poor practices, madam," was Cromwell's reply. But I was not fooled. George's men had not come up with a great deal, as Cromwell was not a man to be caught out when it came to numbers and finances, but what they had uncovered thus far led me to believe I had indeed been led awry.

"Those that suffer from greedy abbots, or slack practices should be re-made into either new religious houses or colleges," I argued. "Those houses could again be vital to the welfare of England's people as once they were, Cromwell. They cannot be simply disbanded."

"I assure you, madam, reform is my wish as well." He smoothed his doublet upon which a heavy chain of gold hung. It was not only Henry who was swift becoming a man of vast wealth.

"Reform is better than closure," I continued. "The monasteries have for too long played no part in the life of England's people. That is the reform I wish to see. For them to take on the ancient and hallowed office, granted by God. To aid poor people and educate the worthy."

"And it will be done, Majesty. But where and when any confiscated funds will be spent is not up to me. His Majesty will decide that, and he, as Head of the Church, will surely act in accordance with the wishes of God."

I nodded, knowing he had a point. Henry's conscience was sharp and he paid close attention to it. But at the same time, I wondered... Cromwell was shrewd. He had a way of sneaking into people's minds. Many words that sprang from Henry's mouth of late were, in truth, born in the mind of his chief advisor.

"I will speak to the King," I said.

"I think that a fine notion, Majesty, for it is good that the King hears all points of view. His focus is on England's defence, but perhaps you can get him to see the value of supporting the poor."

"*None* of that money should be used for warfare," I insisted. "The taxes raised for defence should pay for our fortifications."

"But with Spain looming close..."

"It matters not if a thousand infidels are at our gates!" I said loudly. "This is a matter of morals, Cromwell, not money! Money that was once in the hands of the Church should be returned to the people, where it belongs." I gazed at him with growing displeasure. "That money was raised *from* the people, granted so the Church might support those in need. Would that not be what God would want, Cromwell? Jesus Christ was no man of war. That money should be redistributed to aid Henry's people, not stolen away to line the pocket of the King!"

I stopped abruptly. I had gone too far. *Curse your tongue, Anne Boleyn!* I thought. It always got the better of me. "Forgive me," I said. "I feel passionately about this issue and became lost in my zeal."

"Of course, Majesty," said Cromwell. "And your piety does you credit. Speak to the King. I am sure that, guided by you, this will indeed be the path he takes. I have tried to tell him this myself, but he is so obsessed with security of late that perhaps this godly use of such funds has become lost to him. You will have more success, I am sure."

I agreed I would speak to Henry, but as Cromwell left, I wondered if he had *actually* attempted to talk to his master, or if he, as my brother suspected, would be happier to make his King rich, than see others profit.

Chapter Seventeen

Whitehall Palace
January – February 1535

At the end of January, I decided to take up my most unwelcome role as whoremaster.

Mary Perrot was too dangerous to be left keeping my husband warm. There were rumours that she was writing to Lady Mary and Katherine. I doubted Henry knew of this, but if I attempted to say anything he would only explode. He was lost in affection and would hear nothing said against her. I needed the parrot gone. I was not enough for Henry, but perhaps someone else could be.

Henry flirted with my cousin often when he came to my chambers, usually finding her in company with her friends, Mary Howard, Margaret Douglas and Bess Holland. Mary Shelton was a bright, clever woman of wit, who was also blessed with beauty. She was young, being but sixteen, but confident, and therefore seemed older than her spare years. When she smiled, her cheeks dimpled like a charming infant, but when she talked, all men listened. She shone like a searing torch in a darkened chamber.

The book of poetical warfare was still going strong, and although Henry did not contribute, he called on poets to write verse that he might add to. No one dared breathe a word to Henry, but his poetry was poor. It was not his greatest skill. He had many, to be sure, but his poetry was often stilted, pretentious, and did not possess that pleasing flow which captures the mind and carries the soul. But since Henry was unaware of this, he persisted. Oftentimes, I found my ladies tittering over his work, and I knew their giggles were not for embarrassment at the sentiments of love, but at his slack, ungainly expression and overblown, antiquated ideals.

He brought Mary to him when he called on my chambers, ostensibly to peruse this book, but that was not the only reason. Henry wanted Mary Shelton. I had seen his eyes rest on her too often to be in doubt. At the moment, he seemed satisfied with Mary Perrot. Joanna Dingley was absent from court, some said because she was to bear Henry's child. Henry had no doubt ordered her removal as he did not want to cause a scene which might embarrass him. Knowing he had wasted his seed on another woman did distress me of course, but I was about to upset myself further. I had to wound my own heart, and betray my morals, which I had held sacred so long, in order to survive.

My cousin Mary entered my chambers and I took a deep breath. *Now is the time*, I thought. *I must ask my merry, pretty cousin to whore herself for my benefit.*

I hated this necessity. I loathed myself for it. How many times had I counselled my women against loose morals? And here I was, about to ask a virtuous girl to help me by spreading her legs.

It saddened my heart to see her pretty face and chestnut hair covered by the becoming French hood that I had made all the more popular as Queen. Mary aped my style. She admired me. Her figure resembled mine; tall and willowy. She had little breasts and large dark eyes. We were cousins, but she looked more like my younger sister. Yet I was about to take on a role no sister ever should.

I felt like a hypocrite, because I was.

But this was not just for me. I had to protect my child and my position. There were whispers of rebellion, and great support for Lady Mary and Katherine. I could not afford an enemy to rest so close to Henry, poisoning his mind. But this would have to be handled carefully. Henry was a prudish man. He liked everything ill he did to be quiet and discreet.

"Cousin," I said. "Come and sit with me a while, I would talk to you."

Obediently, she came to my side.

"I must speak to you of something of great delicacy," I said, "something I wish to share only with you."

"Your Majesty," she said softly before I could continue. "I know what it is you wish to ask. For loyalty and love, I will do this. But I want you to know that I should never have thought of doing it unless I was asked to by you. I hold you in the greatest reverence, both for your title and because of the wealth of my admiration for you."

I gaped, stunned. "How do you know?" I breathed.

She took my hands. "Cromwell," she said and I blushed deeper. "Please, Your Majesty, do not make yourself uncomfortable. I would that this were not necessary, but I understand, as you do, that there is more to marriage than four legs in a bed, as they say."

I saw nothing in her eyes but sympathy. It humbled me. "And Your Majesty has granted such beneficence to my family and to myself, shown the people of England the truth of the Word of God, and led the King to embark on a revolution of change, and all for the betterment of the faith. You have been an example to us all. If you were to ask me to lay down my life for you, I would, but since you ask this of me, I will do it."

I grasped her hand. As tears gushed from my eyes, I fell from the chair to kneel at her side, and, in a manner most unbecoming a queen, wrapped my arms around my cousin and wept. Mary held me as gentle as a mother should hold her child.

She wiped my eyes with her sleeve. "My family owes all that it has to you," she said. "I am no man to wage battles for my lord, but a woman may fight for a cause where a man would be unable." She paused. "If I can attract the King to my bed and keep him on the side of all that is right and good. If I can keep the wolves that would support foreign powers and sinners away, I will."

"Mary," I murmured. "I am so afraid."

I was unsure where that admission came from. Was, even then, my heart frightened that Henry might seek to replace me? France had abandoned me, England detested me and Spain was hostile. I had little political worth, and I brought much ill. My only strengths were Henry's love and the possibility of a son. But he gave his love to others, and his seed too.

Yes… I was afraid even then. I was trapped in marriage, and never would I own my liberty again. The only course was to keep striving; fighting for Henry's love with whatever weapons came to hand. I could not go back. I could not retreat. For as long as it took, however much blood was spilt, however badly I was injured, I had to keep fighting. Henry could and should have been my ally in this battle. But at times, he was my enemy.

"Be not afraid, my lady," Mary said, holding me to her breast. "You have many friends, and when a son is born, you will be revered as you deserve."

"You speak such comfort when I ask such a filthy thing of you."

"We are on the side of the angels, madam," she said warmly. "God will forgive us. He knows sometimes hard choices must be made to counter evil. He will not forget your sacrifice. God will know you do this not for yourself, but to prise the King from the clutches of evil."

Would He? I knew not.

"You are my great friend," I whispered. "And all that you do will not be forgotten."

She wiped my face with her silken sleeve. "I serve you, Majesty," she said stoutly. "And I will never betray the trust you have placed in me."

I wiped my eyes and looked with appreciation on the beautiful, intense face of my cousin. Never had I felt such gratitude.

To my shame, due to the jealousy that would later infest me, I would not always show Mary Shelton my appreciation, as I should have.

*

I told Mary Shelton I did not want to know anything that went on between her and Henry. I commanded her to never tell anyone I had asked her to undertake this task, and to be discreet with Henry, whilst working to oust the parrot. She agreed, and I attempted to turn a blind eye.

But I could not help myself. A horrible, hungry, grating, insistent *need* to know consumed me. Seeking truth is like that sometimes. Ignorance would be easier, lighter, more freeing… there is good reason it is said to be bliss… yet we cannot remain ignorant when we know something is going on.

When my other women were engrossed in court gossip, I went to Mary. I could not keep hurt and envy from my voice as I quizzed her. I had set Mary on this path, but I resented her. I was grateful to her even as I hated her. I was not one woman in those days. The whoremaster told me her swift progress was good, for was it not what I had wanted? The woman, whose heart was shattering into dust, told me to punish my cousin.

Did you ever do the same? I asked Katherine. *Mary Perrot was one of your women, once. Did you select her for Henry, thinking she might draw him away from me?*

Never would I have stooped so low.

Never had you the need, I replied. *You had the might of Spain behind you. I have nothing. I have been forced into this by Henry. If I do not provide a woman who is loyal to me, he will take from the offerings of my enemies.*

Tell yourself that, if it brings comfort.

In vain did I attempt to cast out Katherine's voice and reconcile myself to the idea of Mary in Henry's bed. I was a lost soul, brought low by all I had suffered and all I feared. My temper was fragile, glass in my hands. My heart a blackened, motley mess of distrust and anxiety.

And just as I could not restrain my ill feelings for Mary, I could no more contain them about Henry. He was the reason I had had to tear my heart from my chest. The reason I was forced to go against my morals. Some days I could not even meet his eyes, fearing he would see the loathing in them.

Mary knew of my mixed emotions. She was careful, tactful and discreet. I stopped pressing her for details, but when I saw my husband blush as she entered a chamber, I knew. I could see infatuation in Henry as the skylark sees the first light of dawn. Towards the end of January I was certain she was entertaining him at night.

I wept bitter tears, knowing I was the author of my unhappiness. But results came swiftly. The parrot was distressed to find she was not called for as often as before, and Dingley remained in the country. Henry became warm towards me, often coming to my chambers on surprise visits. It was then I knew that Mary had done her work. I had a friend in Henry's bed, speaking well of me.

This helped my fortunes, but not my heart. To distract myself, I threw my efforts into welcome work when Cranmer came to me with a mission.

"Jean de Denteville has written, madam," he said, speaking of one of François' men. "He believes the noted scholar, Nicholas Bourbon, is in some danger in France. There is talk he will be detained for his beliefs."

I had heard of Bourbon. Marguerite de Navarre was an advocate of his, and he was a friend of Erasmus. Bourbon preached humanist principles and supported reform. Given François' growing predilection for persecuting reformists, I could understand how this gentleman had encountered trouble.

"How can I help, Eminence?" I asked. "Would you have me write and attempt to protect him? I am willing to try, my friend, but King François has made it clear he has little friendship to spare for me."

"But perhaps if you intervened with the King, my lady, something could be done?"

"I will speak to His Majesty."

"Thank you, my lady." Cranmer was wearing a strange expression.

"What is it?"

"You seem troubled, Majesty."

"It is nothing. There have been some issues between the King and me, that is all." I gazed into my friend's eyes and tears leapt from mine. "Of late he has been sweet and kind, but I worry sometimes that he no longer loves me. Once I thought our love was the strongest element on earth; stronger than steel or iron, mightier than the crashing waves of the ocean, or the sun in the skies. I thought nothing could come between us. But now… he puts things in the way of my love, and I do the same."

Cranmer reached for my hand. "It is easy, in times of strife, to believe that this is the way everything will remain," he said. "It is easy to suppose, when one is lost in darkness, that light will never return. But you know this is not true, my lady. All that is good or ill are but temporary states. The wheel turns and everything changes. You and the King are the strongest couple I have ever met, Majesty. You fight and bicker, but in the end, you always return to each other. There have been sorrows, and this has put strain on you both, but you must turn to one another rather than thrusting love away." My friend patted my hand. "When you are united there is nothing you cannot achieve. If you wish to heal this rift, do so."

"You are right," I said. "I should talk to him."

"You should. But if you cannot find the words to put this right, talk of other things. Become friends again. In that way each of you will be reminded of how and why you came to love the other."

"You are a wise man, Cranmer," I said. "Perhaps it is a pity for women that you became a priest. I think you would have made a fine husband for a fortunate lady."

A fleeting look of something I could not place fluttered across his eyes. If I did not know better, I might have thought my good friend had a secret he was loath to share.

Chapter Eighteen

Whitehall Palace
February 1535

Religion was on everyone's mind that winter. How could it have been otherwise? With Cromwell readying his men for inspections and the monasteries quivering in their comfortable shoes, with the new Pope proclaiming the old Pope's sentence of excommunication on Henry still held, and the Spanish making a ruckus in their harbours with their formidable fleet, faith and religion were all of which anyone could speak.

Some men added to the growing controversy without intending to. Doctor Carsely, a canon of Wells Cathedral in Somerset, was reported to Cromwell for leading prayers for Katherine. When this was investigated, Cromwell excused the man. "He is close to eighty," he said to Henry and me. "And fast losing his wits. He said afterwards that he had meant to lead prayers for *you*, madam, and forgot himself."

"Tell the canon I forgive him his slip of memory," I said.

But even if this one man had made a mistake, others spoke ill and meant it. Although it was illegal to speak against me, or the supremacy, many dared to. In some minds they were one and the same evil. A vicar in East Sussex was found with a little book in his possession which argued against the supremacy, and a friar at Blackfriars in London earnestly declared he wished to see all supporters of the new learning upon a stake, with Henry joining them to die a "violent and shameful death". Not surprisingly, these people were swiftly arrested.

At court, discussion on religion was more temperate. Henry loved to sit as judge when matters of faith were debated. Few dared to argue against him, but I was one. Sometimes it was necessary to argue with Henry, so he might understand opposing viewpoints. One was the transubstantiation of the host. Traditional religion held that this was the moment when the wine and bread of Mass become transformed into the body and blood of Christ, and whilst I upheld that miracle, I wished Henry to understand why others did not.

Henry was a passionate man, and men with such temperaments can, at times, find themselves caught up in a maelstrom of ideas. People sometimes said Henry was easily led, but this was not exactly true. He was firm in his beliefs and ideals, but he could also become so fanatical about a new idea he rushed ahead with it, refusing to listen to anyone who opposed. Of late he had been angered about those who would doubt the transubstantiation, and I wanted to demonstrate to him that even though some radicals thought it should cease to be used in the Mass, most reformers, even those who did not believe the miracle, thought the ritual should remain.

At times, Henry only saw in shades of black and white. But there were many hues of softer, less glaring, colour. If my husband was a painter, I would be his palette.

"It is shown, in the glory of the Mass…" I said to Weston who was attempting to take the other side of the argument, with little success since he did not understand the points I had given him before we began the debate. "… That wine and bread *are* transformed by the will of God into the body and blood of Christ. But even those who do not believe in this wonder do not wish to see it banished from the Mass. Am I correct in thinking so, Master Weston?"

"You are, my lady," said poor Weston, hastily glancing at his notes. I had never seen eyes move so fast. Weston looked as though he had a host of crawling spiders in his sockets.

Realising the man I had selected to put forth these issues was not capable, or perhaps was too afraid Henry would lock him away in the Tower for speaking on the heretical beliefs of others, I went on.

"For whilst all good souls believe in the transubstantiation, even those who question it would not take it from the Mass, knowing that such rites and rituals serve to refresh the minds of the godly, and bring us back into contact with God the Father. Those who argue for its removal believe too much emphasis is put on this ritual, detracting from the Mass. And for those who do not understand Latin, as the Mass is spoken in, this may well be the truth."

I looked up at Henry on the dais. "I put it to you, my lord, as our judge, that if all men could understand the Mass in their own tongue, there would be no confusion. The superstitious influence of the Mass, which radical reformers dislike, is born from hearing God's Word in a foreign language. Read the Mass to a man in his mother tongue and he will understand not only the ritual and rites, but the wonder of God. In that way alone can man find his way to God the Father; in perfect love and understanding."

"The Queen argues well," Henry announced, "and manages to be as kind to heretics as she is to poor Master Weston... who clearly did not read his notes before standing to debate."

Everyone, including Weston, laughed. The young man did not mind being called out. He had a gentle soul. That was one of the reasons I was so fond of the lad.

"The Queen makes an interesting point," said Henry. "That even those who deny the power of the host do not deny its use to lead us to God. For my part, never shall I be convinced that the host is anything other than the transformed body and blood of Our Lord, presented to God anew in each and every Mass. But the Queen has given me much to think on."

Henry leaned forward, his eyes twinkling with enjoyment. "Do you think, my lady, that the common man, if granted the Word of God in his own language, would take the wrong path as many learned scholars have done, and believe in that which we take to be heresy?"

"It is the office of the Church, led by you, Majesty, to translate to the common man that which he fails to understand. I do not say we should give all men the Bible and no guidance, for even the most learned pupil requires aid from time to time. What I do say is that allowing the common man to hear the Mass in his native language would bring him closer to God and strip away superstition that has prevailed for so long. When all men may hear their God, and understand Him, they will be brought to greater understanding of their faith. This breeds only comfort and consolation. They will require the clergy, led by you, to guide them so they might understand the more difficult aspects of their faith, but I believe having the light of God shining upon them would lead only to greater goodness."

"So you would have all men who are able to, reading the Bible?"

"I would, my lord."

This was a contentious point. Many thought only nobles or heads of households should be allowed to read the Bible, should it ever appear in English. I did not. Some distrusted commoners, thinking them ignorant. But if they were this was not their fault. How is a man to educate himself if he is not granted the means to do so? I wanted there to be more trust, more faith in the people of England.

"For what harm is there to man in the Word of God?" I went on. "For the majority of people, intense study of the Bible is not required. They can read the Word of God, and understand the stories and parables. Academics and scholars will study the harder passages and in those where the Scriptures conflict, scrutinize God's meaning, and reveal it. But for the common man, a *general* understanding will suffice, and for clarity, this should be conducted in their own language."

"My Queen would make every man a wise one," said Henry with affection.

"I would have everyone know the true comfort of their faith," I said, "to possess a close understanding of God, bringing solace in times of hardship."

Henry enjoyed these discussions. I was careful when selecting subjects, and engineered them so that even topics he was revolted by could be worded so as not to cause offence. And as these meetings became more frequent, he became more affectionate. There had always been many elements in our relationship. The physical attraction we had held for each other might have faded somewhat, becoming habit rather than need, but the fire of our minds burned strong.

That night he came to my bed, and it was as easy as it had been when Elizabeth was conceived. When he was confident, there were no problems. In the darkness, as he stroked my body and groaned against my shoulder, I felt pleasure for the first time in months. Our marriage was not perfect. There were more people in this relationship than there should have been, but at times like this, when I held my husband close and felt his need for me, and *only* for me, I thought nothing could tear us apart. Even Death would not separate our souls. We were joined, bonded, we were as one. When we were united, we were stronger than any tempest, and when apart, weaker than a new-born lamb.

*

I turned a restless hand to charity that winter. Somehow, with Henry and me on better terms, I was made sadder by the notion that he had not given up my cousin.

I had thought that his betrayal and coldness were the worst things I could endure, but it was not so. Having him with me was wonderful, yet that sweetness was soured by his need for other women.

When Henry was entertaining my cousin, I spent time with my chaplains. Latimer, Shaxton and Skip were the three I admired the most. With them I discussed welfare for scholars and the poor.

"I want standing orders of money offered to those who come pleading for their families," I instructed, "as well as prompt handling of petitioners. Too often cases are left hanging. We must do better, gentlemen. I know you all have much work, but *this* is where our dedication should be. The poor deserve our aid, and as they are granted it, you will instruct them in the faith."

My ladies spent a considerable part of every day sewing for the poor. Pregnant women received blankets and sheets, and clothes were distributed in London and on progress. Money was also granted to poor widows, those who cared for orphans, and women with many children. Warm vestments, blankets and baby clothes were our most common tasks, but we made richer items for the palace, and hangings for the Royal Chapel. Whilst I understood more and more the reformers' cry to strip churches bare of all frippery, leaving the honest soul alone to converse with the Almighty, I also liked to see the house of God decorated. God appreciates beauty. He had made much that was wondrous to behold.

I was also a generous patron of education. It was important to me that promising young men were supported through university, for if they had the right religious outlook, they would lead my daughter's generation into the light of true faith. Doctor Butts found and recommended men for me to support, and my chaplains did likewise. Even those who might have been enemies came to me, knowing of my support for scholars. One was Thomas Winter, Wolsey's bastard son. He returned from Padua when his money ran out, which threatened his education, and went to Cromwell, who sent him to me.

"I am well aware, my dear Winter," I said. "That you are beloved of the King, and have many friends who wish you well. Reckon me amongst their number."

In truth, Henry had been too busy shooting with his new crossbows to grant an audience to the son of his once most-beloved friend. Winter made Henry uncomfortable. He looked so like his father. Henry did not care to keep company with Wolsey's ghost.

People were surprised that I granted Winter funds to continue his education. They presumed I would hate him, as I had his father. But I did not judge a person for their kin. Were that true, I would have despised Mary Howard for her father, or her mother. Winter was not accountable for Wolsey's sins, and he was dedicated to the new learning and humanist ideals. In aiding men like him, I supported the future, and perhaps there was a part of me which understood he deserved help since I had been responsible for the fall of his father.

I also supported universities, setting up funds, and promoting them at court, and took a keen interest in appointing men to teach from the Bible, offering lessons to common people so they might understand their faith better. This service extended to the sons of leading courtiers, like Norris, whose heir studied at Syon Abbey with my ward and nephew, Henry Carey. Grammar schools were set up to teach the rudiments of language, maths, writing and reading to poor lads, the basics of reading to noble or merchants' daughters, and free pupils, paid for from my purse, were maintained.

Although Cranmer, some years ago, had advised me to make my charity publicly known, I had not. I could not bring myself to publicise it. Charity is not charity if one seeks acclaim. It is just another purchase. Charity, when treated like that, is no godlier than a whoremaster procuring jades for his customers.

Some of my charity was, naturally, noted, such as public giving of alms and events such as the Maundy ceremonies. But all else I did, I would not shout about. Perhaps it was one area in which I outdid Katherine, for she had never made a secret of her work.

That is what a queen does, said her voice. *Promotes herself to her people.*

That is not what this Queen will do. If I have played the whoremaster once, I will not again.

From Kimbolton, Katherine insisted she would wash the feet of the poor on Maundy Thursday, and I sent a command that she would not. The ritual of cleansing and alms giving on Maundy Thursday was reserved for royalty, and I would not allow Katherine to undertake it. When her servants shared this news, there were grumblings against me. Some brought up an old prophecy about Henry, that he would begin his reign as a lamb and end as a lion, saying that restricting Katherine in this way was but one of the signs this would come true. Others made up ditties, singing them in the streets, mocking my attempts to *play* Queen, whilst England's *true* Queen languished in the fens, unable to aid her people.

But if the majority of Henry's people noted nothing good in me, some did. William Marshall, a writer and social reformer, dedicated a book to me entitled *The Form and Manner of Subvention or Helping for poor people, Devised and Practised in the City of Ypres*. It was a treatise on recent policies introduced in Ypres that were said to be of good note.

"My very mind, intent and meaning is (by putting of this honourable and charitable provision in mind) to occasion your grace to be a mediatrix and mean unto our most dread sovereign lord… for the stablishing and practising of the same or of some other, as good or better, such as by His Majesty or his most honourable council shall be devised," said the dedication. Marshall wanted me to take it to Henry and his Council.

Upon reading this, I sent it to Cromwell with a note, asking that the practices in the book be examined to see if they might be used also in England. I took a copy to Henry. He was delighted with it, and called for me when he had read it so we could discuss the ideas.

"I find many worthy ideas in this tome," said Henry, tapping a finger, fat as a sausage, on the leather cover.

"And if any monasteries must be closed, there will be funds to enable much to go ahead for the good of your people," I said.

"I have been meaning to speak to you about that," said Henry. "Thomas said you were adamant about those funds going back to the people, but it will be necessary to use some for defence of the realm."

"I am sure both aims can be achieved," I said smoothly. "What of the taxes set in place only last year? Could they not be called on to use for fortifications?"

I caught a distant flicker of insecurity in his eyes and touched his hand. "I feel uncomfortable, Henry, in the notion of taking from the Church to give to war. Our Lord was a man of peace. No doubt God understands the necessity of protecting your people from harm… but there is something that feels wrong about this. Do you not feel the same? For if you, with your conscience and spirit so close to God do not waver, I will be led by you."

Henry stared at my hand. I could smell indecision wafting from him like perfume. "I think you are right," he said. "And truly, I never thought about it in that way until now."

I sat back, pleased. If Cromwell was trying to persuade Henry to rob the churches and give nothing back, I had at least planted a seed of doubt in my husband's mind.

Chapter Nineteen

Whitehall Palace and Greenwich Palace
February – March 1535

"You should not fill your book with idle posies!" I snapped at Mary Shelton.

Her prayer book was in my hands. I had seen her scribbling in it at prayers at church that morning and handing it to Tom. When he had laughed quietly, I knew it was no prayer she had shown him. When we reached my chambers, I demanded the book, and she surrendered it most unwillingly. I found a witty poem in it, deriding the possibility of love at court.

"You should spend your time in church with God, not with Master Wyatt!" I shouted.

In truth, I was not angry about the poem. I saw it not, but I was seeking an excuse to shame Mary. I was jealous, resentful, and wanted to spite her. It made no sense, but emotions often do not.

Mary endured her scolding with grace, but was relieved to take back her book and fly to her friends. Later in the day, I took her aside. "Mary," I said. "I do not know what possessed me this morning. I should not have upbraided you, for oftentimes have I written in my book of hours. If you are a sinner, I am too."

"I understand, my lady," she said. "Sometimes, when we are fractious and ill at ease, we find trifles become as mountains."

How did this young girl understand so much? *It is not her fault,* I told myself. *If you want someone to blame, Anne Boleyn, blame yourself.*

But a few days later, I was scolding again. Not Mary this time, but one of her suitors. Weston was courting her, even though he had a wife he claimed to adore. When I saw his attentions increase, I was angered… infuriated on behalf of the wife I believed he was betraying.

"My cousin may shortly become engaged to Norris," I said. "And you have a wife, Weston. It is not fitting that you pay so much attention to Mary. Think on your wife and be grateful for her love!"

"You seem to be often in a temper, Majesty," said Tom that afternoon as we strolled through the long gallery. Outside, rain was falling steadily from the skies. It was no deluge or tempest, just a seemingly unending stream of soaking mist that drenched the unwary… a common occurrence in England.

"I do not like to see honest women made fools of," I retorted. "Men should honour their wives." Seeing his face fall, since his wife and he had separated some time ago, I touched his arm. "I do not mean in cases where there is no love, Tom," I said gently. "That is why I rarely scold you or George. But Weston claims to love his wife, and she him. Should he not save his affection for her?"

"Some men cannot resist flirtation when it is offered," said my friend.

My eyes dragged to Henry. Standing at the end of the hall with Mary, he pulled a silk cloth from his sleeve and offered it to her. When she tried to hand it back, having wiped her eyes after laughing, he refused, pushing it into her hands with a sloppy smile.

"As I have daily proof," I murmured.

Inside me, the broken one wailed.

*

In late February, Gontier, Brion's secretary was back at court to continue negotiations.

"You have taken a long time to return," I said scathingly when he came to pay his respects.

My quarters were crowded with enemies and friends. Henry was trying to convince Mary Shelton to dance as Weston played on his lute. Everyone was watching me, as they always were... eager to see if I would explode.

"Your delay has caused the King great suspicion," I went on. "He does not like to be insulted by a king he once considered a great friend."

"I assure you, madam," said Gontier. "We took the time that was needed."

"If your master does not ally the concerns of the King, and mine too, we are left in a precarious position," I said, and leaned forward. "And I am left in a position more fragile than before my marriage. I thought France my friend, but it would seem your master, François, has forgotten the promises he made to me."

I looked around. Everyone wanted to know what we were saying; my friends because they wanted France to support me, and my enemies for the opposite reason. I could feel eyes burning into me. "I can say no more," I said in a low voice. "Not with everyone watching."

I withdrew, my heart pounding. Henry took hands with his mistress and started to dance.

*

Cromwell was away from court that March. Illness, brought on, I suspected, from too much work granted him rheum in the eyes. I dispatched Doctor Butts with a solution of eyebright, and Cromwell sent a message back, expressing gratitude.

Cromwell was not the only one absent. He had long been working against those who would oppose him on the Council, granting leaves of absence to his detractors, and not hurrying them back to court. He had also been annoying Norfolk, embarking on a constant campaign to oust him. Cromwell succeeded. Norfolk left for his country estates that spring, declaring he was sick of court and sicker still of Cromwell. This weakened Gardiner's position further, since he relied on the Duke for support. Gardiner was not a favourite of Henry's, especially given his support for the clergy in the past.

And Gardiner *loathed* Cromwell. After all, he had been forced to surrender his position as Henry's secretary to him. But Gardiner was canny enough not to show it openly, and professed friendship, knowing the favour Cromwell enjoyed in Henry's eyes. Cromwell reciprocated, but their show of affection was false as Norfolk's teeth, and everyone knew it. With Norfolk gone, however, Cromwell grew bolder. He started to taunt Gardiner openly in Council, mocking him for having supported the clergy over the King. When Gardiner accused Cromwell of trying to undermine him, Cromwell acted as though he was surprised and hurt.

Little battles, little wars… all fought in the close confines of court every day. Little did we know what would come of them.

That Maundy Thursday I went out amongst the people to give alms. To my chagrin, Henry countermanded my orders that Katherine should not distribute Maundy money. "She *is* the Dowager of Wales," he reminded me. "It is traditional that royal ladies grant money to the poor. My grandmother did in my father's reign, even though she was only the King's mother. To stop Katherine doing this will only cause trouble with Spain."

I had agreed, with poor grace, consoling myself that Katherine had not much to give. But I was further upset when I learned Henry had sent her money, through Cromwell, to grant to the poor.

"How am I ever to be recognised as Queen when Katherine is promoted in my place?" I asked Nan Gainsford.

"Your offerings are *far* more generous than the Dowager's ever were, my lady," she replied. "The people will see that."

When the time came to distribute the purses, I felt some satisfaction when I saw the look of surprise on the rude faces before me. When they felt the weight of the purses, they were stunned, and happy. As we walked away from one group, I heard one lady. "That's more than the last Queen gave, whatever you say," she said, talking to a filthy man, pitted with pox scars. The sickness had robbed him of his lashes and brows, and pinned one of his eyelids to his cheek. He was nodding in agreement, testing the weight of the bag against his palm.

"This is for you," I said to a little boy, slipping a silver ring from my finger and onto his. "Soon I hope God will send me a son like you."

His mother was overcome. She flung herself to the floor and grabbed my skirts. Guards moved to pull her back, but I held up my hand. She looked up. She was not much younger than I, with deep blue eyes and fair hair. She had a pretty face, but her skin was grey and her hands were coarse and reddened from years of hard work. Her gown was ill-fitting, tight and drab. She gazed up with tired eyes that shone with gratitude. That ring could feed her family for a year.

I kissed her head. Although the girl smelt unwashed, I did not care. I wanted Henry's people to see that I was not this evil Jezebel they had been told I was.

"You have my blessing," I said. "May God's light shine upon you. Your lad is a fine boy, Mistress. I hope to have the same blessing as you one day. My daughter is a beautiful girl, and I adore her, but every mother loves her sons. We become used to caring for men, do we not, Mistress? And so we long for boys, so we might continue our good service."

The woman laughed and put an arm around her son, executing a clumsy curtsey. "God bless you, good Queen Anne," she said. "God bless and keep you."

How it touched me to be named *good*! A simple kindness means a great deal to a heart that has known slander and hate. Before we moved on I touched her shoulder. "Take care of your little boy. Use the ring wisely. Buy bread, for all men must eat, but feed his mind, too. Send him to school, for this new world holds many opportunities and men can rise higher than the station they were born to, if they have love for God and our King."

We moved on, putting heavy purses into grasping, grateful, often desperate hands. There were shouts of "God bless you, Queen Anne!" and "God bless the King and Queen!"

Many nights I lay awake, wondering feverishly where Henry was and what, or *whom*, he was doing. But that night I simply fell into the heavy, dark arms of sleep and felt the coolness of simple and happy dreams wash over me like water in a crystal stream.

I do not fully recall my dreams, but I remember smiling faces, happy laughter, the grateful mother and her handsome son, looking up with eyes that sparkled with new hope.

And perhaps God was watching me, and approved, for later that week, when I looked for my monthly bleeding, it did not appear. I wrapped my arms about my body and smiled as I lay in bed. Each morning there was no sign of blood. No cramps, no sense that the world despised me.

I was with child.

Chapter Twenty

Whitehall Palace and Greenwich Palace
March- April 1535

That Easter George took pity on Master Smeaton and gave him one of his books. "It was a poor thing," said my brother. "But he admired it, and has no means to purchase such items."

Books were expensive, and even many crude, cheaply produced ones were out of Mark's reach.

"Which tome did you grant him?"

"The one Wyatt gave me when I married," he said. "*Liber lamentationum Matheoluli*, a translation by Lefevre."

"The book about the ills of marriage?" I asked, arching an eyebrow. "Does Mark think to wed? And do you mean to frighten him off?"

"No," said George, with a smile. "He simply admired the book, so I gave it to him." My brother toyed with a small pie of beef and barley on a golden platter. "In truth," he went on. "I think he reads little. To him, the worth of a book is in its ownership, not its contents."

"Books have no worth if left upon a shelf. They must be *read*."

"I agree, sister," he said. "But we are in a minority. Do you think Norfolk has ever opened even *one* of the books in his great library? Surely not, for then he would have absorbed some of their wisdom, and I doubt his mind is prepared for the onslaught of original thought."

I giggled. "Does our uncle still sulk in the country?"

George inclined his head. "And wails about his woes. I'll wager his reedy voice is only the more penetrating from afar to the King. Norfolk thinks Cromwell was trying to oust him."

"He is not mistaken." I frowned.

"Have you altered your good opinion of our Master Secretary?"

"I find much that worries me," I admitted. "But nothing certain. Cromwell says it is up to Henry to decide what happens to the monasteries and their wealth, and he is correct."

"But the King must come to the right decision," George said. "Which is where you enter, sister."

"I will attempt to guide him."

"Do," urged my brother. "Men think it is easy, Anne, to pull something down and start anew. At times, it is the only way, but sometimes it is better to take a foundation and build upon it. I think Cromwell is urging the King to tear everything down, telling him they will start afresh. This is not the way it should be done. The way I think reform should progress is slower, but will, in the end, be better for England."

"You know I concur," I said. "But this has to be handled with tact. Henry is obsessed with Charles' fleet. He is drawn to the lure of the monasteries' wealth because he thinks it will save England."

"What will there be left to save if the poor starve and the streets become clogged with beggars set loose from the monasteries?" George shook his head. "I do not say I have always been a good man, or that my heart has always tended towards charity. I am a sinner, and have far to go before I can call myself a saint. But this is wrong, Anne."

"Of course, but I know not if Henry is pushing the notion or if it is Cromwell."

"Either way, influencing the King to do good will produce the desired outcome."

"And that outcome we will have, once the investigations are done," I said. "It would be premature to act now, and if Cromwell is influencing Henry, it might be foolish."

"Bide your time, then," he said. "But do not forget."

"What have I ever forgotten that you have remembered instead?" I asked, laughing. "Men think they are the masters of all, but women are the keepers of memory."

"And the fell mistresses of love," he said affectionately, kissing my lips.

It was not only my brother who found joy in giving presents. That Easter, I gave Henry one of the greatest gifts I could imagine when I told him I suspected I was with child.

"You are sure?" he asked, delighted beyond measure.

"It may be too early to tell," I said. "But my courses have ceased and I am constantly nauseous."

"God be praised!" he said, taking hold of my waist and starting to dance across our bedroom floor.

"Henry!" I giggled. "Set me down!"

"Never will I let go of you," he said, dropping to his knees and staring up at me. "Never."

For a moment I wondered if he *had* been thinking of letting me go.

Emboldened by my condition, which to Henry was synonymous with the favour of the Almighty, Henry declared to Chapuys that he would not allow Katherine and Mary to meet. He then sent a message to Mary, saying he had *"no worse enemy in the world but her"* and accused her of being the source of all his misery. Publicly, he declared his daughter's conduct was a calculated move to bring about rebellion or invasion, and said he would have no more to do with her. In his exuberance, Henry also brought Elizabeth to court, so we could spend the spring with our daughter.

If it had never before been clear to me how to win my husband's love, it was now. I decided to go one step further, and mentioned to Henry that I thought there were too many women at court without true purpose. It was a lie. Men outnumbered women ten to one, but I hoped to be rid of a little bird who had long been twittering in my ear.

"Mistress Perrot, for example," I said lightly one day. "She has no purpose and she and her husband are a strain on court finances."

Henry glanced at me, but he did not look angry. Content with Mary Shelton, he had no further need for the parrot. "I will see to it," he said.

And with that, the parrot was gone.

Joyous, I took Elizabeth into the gardens every day, and together we played. I showed her birds in the skies and the bright catkins on the trees. Watching my daughter with a spray of yellow buds in her hands, her black eyes mesmerized by the blossoms, brought a joy like no other.

Each morning, I rose into the blurred and fuzzy grey dawn, where the world wears that loose, baggy, look, as though God's mind, still slumberous, has not yet formed its thoughts clearly enough for the world to possess shape and clarity. The day still had dew upon it as I went to Elizabeth and dressed her myself. We took to the gardens when it was sunny, and played in the long galleries when it was not. Above us, the dawn became a haze of gold, cresting into a wide, warm skyline of pink and shimmering pearl. Wet afternoons allowed us to huddle together, playing at the fireside. Grim nights brought me to her bedside, where I told her stories until her eyes fluttered and closed.

If only I could have just been a mother, and a wife.

If only I had been allowed to know joy and keep it.

Chapter Twenty-One

Greenwich Palace and Hampton Court
April 1535

On the first day of April, the Lady Mary was moved closer to Katherine. Chapuys had not relented in his mission to reunite mother and daughter, and despite my urging to keep them apart, Henry made a partial surrender, thinking it might appease his people and the Emperor. As had been promised some time ago, Mary moved from Eltham, where Elizabeth was, to Hunsdon, thirty miles from Kimbolton Castle, but was still not permitted to see her mother. This did not content Chapuys, however, who pressed for Mary to move closer still, but this was denied.

"They are close enough," Henry said.

In truth, they were so close in spirit that no miles would make a difference.

It was not only the ex-princess who was moving. That month, Cromwell's investigations began. It was a cautious start, but Cromwell wrote to bishops, the nobility and Justices of the Peace, commanding them to imprison those who *"had been seduced with filthy and corrupt abominations of the bishop of Rome or his disciples"*. In these letters Cromwell described himself as Henry's *eyes*, whose task it was to remedy the abuses of the clergy. All his letters carried Cromwell's stamp, and Henry's.

Some said Cromwell was becoming as powerful as his master. Others whispered he desired nothing less. I wanted to believe in him, but even I had cause to deliberate on his motives. Power is a slippery beast. It crawls into the heart and whispers it is not enough. There must be more. More and more, for power is never satisfied. I wondered if Cromwell was reaching too high, influencing Henry into sin. But I could prove nothing. I had to watch, I had to wait, and see what would unfold.

Many quaked to discover Cromwell's letters on their desks, for the twin stamps of Cromwell and Henry seemed to signal that a new power was dawning. But if some shook to see these letters, others did not. There was unrest, and it was growing.

"We need a sign to show what will happen to those who disobey," Cromwell said as we wandered in the fresh spring air in my gardens at Whitehall. "All who support Rome are traitors," he continued, tearing a straggly thyme twig from its nest of branches and rubbing it into his palms. "And, Majesty, the King is determined to make a public demonstration."

"So the rebellious Carthusians will be executed?" I asked. There had been whispers of this for some time.

"They will, Majesty, but only those who refuse to swear the oath."

"Of course…" I stared at him with puzzled eyes. "For what reason would you execute others?"

Cromwell shrugged. "Some may only have sworn to save their bellies from the hook."

"We cannot delve into the souls of men, Cromwell," I said. "If men swear and refrain from treason, this should be enough."

I wondered if he thought the same. The new regime was fixated on dominating and controlling the thoughts of Henry's subjects as well as their actions.

Cromwell's men started to visit monasteries, and the inventory of goods also got underway. This, in particular, was taken as an ominous sign. It was widely rumoured this inventory was the true purpose of their visits, and Cromwell and his men were less concerned with corruption than they were with coin.

Cromwell's survey eventually became known as the *Valor Ecclesiasticus*. It revealed in ferociously accurate detail the wealth, property and rents of England's religious houses. Cromwell said it would grant Henry means to tax his clergy more effectively, but detractors claimed it was a means to convince the King to dissolve *all* houses and keep the riches for himself. The clergy owned perhaps two-thirds of England in land and estates. It would have been a tempting prospect for anyone, but for Henry, who was fixated on security, and maintaining the ostentatious show of his position, it was perhaps far too alluring.

*

We moved to Greenwich in the second week of April, but within a week were forced to hurry to Hampton Court when one of my women was struck down with a pox.

Frances de Vere, the wife of my cousin, Surrey, seemed to only have a cold at first, but rapidly developed a cough and a fever. Her eyes waxed red and little spots erupted inside her mouth. Within a few days, a red-brown rash appeared on her creamy skin. It was then we knew it was something more serious.

Henry, fearing it was plague, carted the court off to Hampton Court as soon as possible. I was separated from Frances and he refused to allow me to see her.

"You are carrying our child!" he exclaimed in horror when I spoke of nursing her.

"I do not think it is plague, Henry," I said.

"Even if not, it could still be dangerous."

Perhaps Death was listening, as plague did break out in London. Frances, however, recovered and her rash was gone in little more than a week. But one morning as my ladies pulled off my nightshirt, I saw the same rash upon my belly.

In fright, I called for my doctors. Fever settled upon me, and the same hacking cough Frances had experienced infested my lungs. Henry was wild with terror, but he was not allowed near me. Hampton Court was shut off and the court hunkered down to see if the dreaded sickness would come upon us.

It did not. A few more of my ladies contracted a fever and the rash, but they recovered, as did I.

When my rash receded, Henry came to my chambers at night. He needed reassurance, for in the depths of his heart he was troubled by many things… France's offer to Mary, the unrest in England and Cromwell's investigations… they all weighed upon him. He needed me to confirm that he was right, and I tried to offer support.

But we were merry too, each night talking of our boy, this new life growing inside my body. To Henry, my pregnancy was proof that he was righteous.

It was but a few days after I was recovered that it happened. I was sitting with my women, making clothes for the poor, when I felt a lurching pain in my lower abdomen. At first, I thought I needed to go to the privy, as I had suffered from loose stools in the days after my recovery. But then there was a sudden rushing sensation between my legs and I stood abruptly, dropping the tunic I had been sewing to the floor.

"My lady…?" Nan's voice was scared. She could see the pallor on my face.

"It hurts," I groaned, doubling over.

They took me to my bed and brought the doctors. Within an hour, bright red blood was flowing from between my legs. The doctors gave me potions to stem the bleeding. They poked and pulled about down there, but their worried faces told me the terrible truth.

My child was dying.

"Do something!" I sobbed. "What use are you? Save my child!"

But there was nothing that could be done. Over the next few days the bleeding came and went. Each time it vanished, they clapped themselves on their backs and told each other all was well. Each time it returned they hastened into work again.

Over and over, they raised my hopes and dashed them to the ground. In the end, all I could do was lie on my bed, feeling my child leave me, slowly… agonisingly slowly… over the course of a few days.

I stared at the cloths they removed. The blood called to me, asking why I was not doing more to save my child. I curled up, my hands about my belly, begging my baby to stay. "I have so much to show you," I whispered, stroking my belly. "So much love to offer you. Please… please do not leave me."

But my child could not, or would not hear me. Within a week, the bleeding stopped. I experienced no more nausea. My breasts were tender no more. When I told the doctors this, they looked at each other and left the room.

They left it to Henry to tell me I had lost my baby. But rather than be kind, he was furious. "You took too many risks!" he shouted, standing at my bedside like a tower of rage. "You should not have kept company with Frances when she showed signs of sickness!"

"Am I to send away every woman or man who coughs?" I demanded, tears racing down my cheeks. "Do you think this horror was my aim, husband? Do you think I wanted to know this pain?"

I doubled up, pulling the covers about me as though they could protect me from his wrath, and I cried. Hot, bitter tears of loss and abandonment flowed. My child was gone, and in the hour I needed him most, my husband was not Henry. He was the King.

"Anne…" I felt a hand on my shoulder and I shrank from it. "Anne, I should not have said that. I forget you feel as deeply as I."

I threw off the covers. "*How*?" I demanded with hatred in my eyes. "How can you forget? Have you listened at last to my enemies, Henry, and decided I am without feeling? I am none such. I have a heart, and it is broken."

He pulled me to him and held me. "We will bear the loss together," he said. "It will not be spoken of. The pregnancy was not announced in any case… so none will know of this, my love."

As he moved away, I saw tears in his eyes.

I watched him leave with a blank expression, and a barren heart. Another child not acknowledged. Another grief I was not permitted to express.

Another secret kept to save Henry's pride.

Chapter Twenty-Two

Hampton Court
April 1535

In dreams, my children found me.

Abandoned by the memory of the living, lost to the light of the world, they came to me in darkness. Sometimes those visions were sweet; images of three children playing together… Elizabeth and her brothers. I saw them in the gardens at Hever, Greenwich and Hampton Court, racing along gravelled paths, trying to catch each other, as laughter rang out, caressing the skies. Sometimes I sat upon a stand, watching my two, fine, young sons as they donned glittering armour and competed in the joust. Sometimes I watched them with their father, their faces the image of his.

But more often, nightmares came. I chased my lost sons along dark paths in a maze of blackness. Hands tore at my clothing and pulled me backwards. I could not find them. I could not defend them. Their wailing screams, pleading for my help, ruptured my soul.

At times, my dreams made no sense. They came as brief, passing images; visions of childbirth… my son's perfect, dead face… flashes of bright red blood glistening on glaring white cloth.

These flashes started to assault me when I was awake. I would be sewing and crimson thread became tissue and blood. As I stared into books, hoping to find peace, words blurred into grey fuzz, and the parchment became the cloths placed between my legs in those awful days of loss and pain. I saw my dead sons in windowpanes. I became unwilling to sleep, unwilling to do anything. I was haunted. My appetite slipped away like a thief in the night.

I needed time to grieve. I needed understanding and companionship. I needed Henry to take my hand and lead me back to the world. But he did not. He had convinced himself that my pregnancy had never been. Perhaps it was easier for him that way. It was not for me.

I had no outlet for grief. I was expected to immediately become the merry maid again, entertaining in my chambers, calling young men to adore me from far and wide. I was expected back at Henry's side, to meet dignitaries and ambassadors. I was to smile and wave and sing and dance and laugh and play.

Sometimes, when I sat with a fixed smile upon my face before court, I thought I might shatter into a thousand pieces. Once, I had said I ruled an empire of glass. Now that empire was within me. I was glass; brittle, fragile, sheer… I felt transparent. All eyes would see through me and in my chest witness not a heart that beat with life, but a wizened core, blackened and dead.

And along with all this, there was guilt.

Guilt is a raw, rubbed wound that never heals. It festers, leeching into your heart and soul, dragging aside sense and reason and infecting them with venom. This time it was worse than when I lost my first son. Perhaps it was because this child had had so little time to live. Perhaps it was because this time there was a reason. When I had lost my first son, there had been no discernible cause. No trail I could follow back and say, *this*, this is the moment I lost my babe… Without firm reason for my loss, there had been fewer ways to blame myself. But this time, as Henry had so kindly mentioned, there *was* a reason.

I found myself running over and over the sequence of events, from Frances' first show of illness to the day I felt the pain, trying to find a moment where I could have saved my child. Over and over and over and over went my mind, tumbling on a wheel of horror and dismay.

I do not know if Henry ever understood that his words had such an impact. If he had not suggested I was to blame, perhaps I would not have fallen so hard on myself. But that which is spoken may not be unsaid.

A second lost baby. A second silence. How can silence be so powerful as to break a woman's heart?

A new lowness fell upon me. I hid my sorrow under bright gaiety, but anyone, had they gazed into my eyes, would have witnessed not happiness there, but stark, barren emptiness. My heart had become a desert, where nothing lived. Only sand, the broken, fractured, miniscule remains of dreams, dwelled there, billowing in the light wind… spiralling in the sultry air.

Everything was stale and broken. The dreams I had nurtured were unwinding like a ball of wool. Everything was dust, slipping through my fingers.

*

"Take it away," I said, turning my head from a spray of red rowan buds my ladies had collected from the gardens to decorate the bare hearth. I could not look on the colour. I could not bear it. Every time I saw it, a flashing image of white cloth and bright red blood swam before my eyes, making me sick and dizzy. I had told them not to give me gowns of crimson anymore. I would wear green and white and silver and gold. I could not wear red. Not for a while. Not until these visions left me.

I did not tell them why. No one could think me unhinged.

My ladies were fearful to upset me, and removed the offending branch. They brought my brother in to cheer me, knowing that he, unlike my husband, could restore my spirits.

"You need time," my brother said, sitting beside me. "Time to grieve."

"I am not permitted such luxuries," I said, my voice desolate and cold. "Henry says nothing will be announced, and so he makes it as though it never happened. Just like the last time."

I put my face into my hands and wept. For a time, there was no noise in my chamber. My ladies, anxious to obey Henry's instructions, made no move towards me. Only my brother's hand on my back gave me any indication that I was not utterly, and completely, alone.

"I want you to do something for me," I said when I was able to draw breath.

"Anything."

"You translated works for me before, from Jacques Lefevre," I said. "I want more. I want solace, George."

George agreed. He set to work to translate the *Epitres et Evengiles pour les Cinquante et Deux Semaines de L'an*, the *Epistles and Gospels for the fifty-two weeks of the year*. Eventually his work would be turned into illuminated manuscripts for me.

"Pourge therefore the olde leven bread," said Lefevre's work, taken from Saint Paul, *"so that you maye be new dough. As ye are sweete bread. For Christ, our Easter lamb, is offered up for us. Therefore let us keep holy days not witholde leve, neither with the leven of maliciousness and wickedness, but with the sweete bread of pureness and truth."*

I wanted only part translations… passages, snippets of truth, which I could scan quickly to bring me comfort but not read for too long lest the pages transform into something else, something darker. George did not question me, for I think he understood. He, too, took comfort in the work of scholars and in the Word of God.

When I was well enough, I called my chaplains to my chambers and set them to work. I wanted good books from learned men, so I might draw wisdom and succour from them. Thomas Tebold and William Lok were my agents on the Continent, procuring volumes for my library, and seeking out banned books for me to consume. And consume them I did. This was no mere habit or hobby. These books were my salvation; the only release I had from the horrors I had faced. But if I found comfort in words and thoughts and facts, Henry hid in fiction.

He would not speak of our children. He would not acknowledge their existence. He liked to pretend we had conceived no child but Elizabeth and spoke brightly of the day our son would join his sister.

But for me, the idea of becoming with child filled me with ghastly terror. I was afraid; afraid to become pregnant again if I was to face the same nightmare as before.

Henry chattered away about our little girl and the sons who would shortly come, bemusing his own mind into blocking out the trauma of losing two children. But for me, there was no escape.

I understood my duty. I had to have a son. But part of me wanted to rise from my chair when Henry spoke. Part of me wanted to flee, taking to the stables and a swift horse, galloping away on its back, never to return.

Chapter Twenty-Three

Hampton Court
Late April – May 1535

At the end of that month, a gaggle of Carthusians appeared before the King's Bench at Westminster; three priors and two priests. Charged with denying the royal supremacy and upholding the Pope and Rome over their King, they faced a sentence of death.

I had reason to dislike the Carthusians, and their brothers, the Observants, who, I had been told, when asked if my daughter had been baptized in cold water or hot, had replied, "hot water, but not hot enough." The Carthusians also dabbled in scandal rousing and obscure prophesies. They said Henry was the cursed *Mouldwarp*, prophesised by Merlin, who would bring about the destruction of England, and added for good measure that I would burn to death for my sins.

If they will not swear the oath, I told myself, *they are traitors.*

I knew their arrests were justified, but I worried about the outcome. Cromwell wanted to make examples, so all men would fear to defy their King. I wondered if we should attempt to convert them, to show the people of England that the new leader of their Church was a merciful, Christian prince. But Henry said they had had enough chances.

Cromwell had led their interrogations personally at his Rolls House in London. One of the accused, Richard Reynolds, was part of the Bridgettine house of Syon, where my young ward, Henry Carey, was studying. Syon had become a hotbed of treasonous talk. Some men of Syon claimed Henry was a whoremaster who bedded every maid at court, whether they wanted him to or not. Others said that he had meddled with my mother as well as my sister, and Mary and I were in fact his offspring.

More men claimed the Emperor or the Pope would invade England soon, and God would have His revenge. John Hale, one of the accused, was said to have declared Henry was *"more foul and more stinking than a sow, wallowing and defiling herself in any filthy place. For however great he is, he is fully given to his foul pleasure of the flesh… And look how many matrons be in the court or given to marriage, these almost all he has violated, so often neglecting his duty to his wife and offending the sacrament of matrimony… And now he has taken to his wife of fornication this matron, Anne, not only to the highest shame and undoing of himself, but also of all his realm."*

The wife Hales was concerned about was not me, it was Katherine. Whilst I had unbounded sympathy with the notion Henry was offending God by keeping mistresses, I had none with the idea that I was another of his jades. But people like Hales would never support me. To them, I was the Devil, and Katherine an angel.

The monks were found guilty, and sentenced to be hung, drawn and quartered. One exemption was made, ostensibly because the pardoned man, Robert Feron, was but a youth, but everyone knew he had really been spared for turning King's evidence to escape death. The condemned were to die on the 4th of May, and Henry refused to hear any petitioner who came begging for their lives.

I watched Henry as a bishop was screamed out of the room for daring to ask for mercy for the accused. It was not only resolution that I saw on his face, but sorrow. Grief twisted and curled inside him, oozing from his skin, transforming into another being. Henry might have liked to think he had forgotten his sadness, but he had not. It was there, under his skin, as mine was. It was a trapped beast.

But trapped beasts are canny creatures. Those who seek to ignore the monsters within often find that the beast has found a means of escape; by wearing their skin… by overcoming the soul of their host.

There was a monster inside Henry. My mistake was not to understand how dangerous it was until it was far, far too late.

*

As the condemned monks were taken back to their cells to wait for death, Cromwell visited Thomas More. Henry still harboured love for his friend, and this was one reason why Cromwell went to More, but there was another. All over Europe there were cries for More's release, and with him, Fisher. Both were upheld as paragons of virtue. Whoever thought this must have missed More's bloodthirsty career as Chancellor, but all the same, More and Fisher were respected men. Henry little wanted to offer the Emperor another excuse to come for England.

Cromwell and Henry both believed that the sentence of execution on the Carthusians might sway Fisher and More into terror, allowing Cromwell's men to extract the oath, but if they believed this, they were fools.

Cromwell asked for More's opinion on the succession and supremacy, and More replied that he had already given it. "I have discharged my mind of all such matters," he said. "I will not dispute the King's titles, nor the Pope's, but I am, and always will be, the King's true, and faithful, subject."

When Cromwell pointed out this would not satisfy Henry, More smiled. "I may be condemned to perpetual imprisonment," he said. "But not of my duty and obedience to the King."

"I have done no one any harm," he went on. "I have said no harm and thought no harm, but thought everyone good. If this is not enough to keep a man alive, then I long not to live. I have been ill many times since coming to this prison, and more times than once thought I might die of natural means in this cell. I am not sorry for it, but rather was sorry when my pangs and pains passed. My poor body is at the King's pleasure, and I wish that my death may do him good."

After this visit, Cromwell became so ill that he had to excuse himself from court. He insisted that his papers were brought to his room, so he might work in bed. He wrote to the new Pope, explaining the reasons for Henry's separation from Katherine and the annulment of their union. He pressed not only for the Pope's understanding and acceptance, but for his espousal. Cromwell asked for a public testimony of the Pope's support, knowing that if it was offered privately, it would not satisfy the Emperor, Katherine, or any other opponent we faced.

Henry sent constant messages to Cromwell, not enquiring about his health, but commanding him to come back. "There is too much going on for Cromwell to be ill!" he said one day.

Cromwell now, is it? my mind asked. *Thomas when you love him. Cromwell when you do not…*

"He cannot help falling ill, Henry," I pointed out. "No matter his many talents, he is mortal, like the rest of us. I think he has too much work. The strain is making him sick."

I sent Cromwell some artichokes, a treat of which I knew he was fond, as well as another tonic for his eyes. Cromwell was approaching fifty, and his eyes pained him. He had a pair of spectacles which he used when working, and hid at all other times, as though if any witnessed their existence it might make him suddenly cursed with old age.

By the time May arrived in full bloom, Cromwell was back, but he was visibly ill. "You should take more care of yourself," I said when he visited. "You do too much."

"Yet there is always more to be done, Majesty." He passed a hand over his brow and smiled wanly. "Work is like that. It is a hydra. Chop off one head and six more appear. The more one takes on, the more there is to do. But fear not, my lady. I will be well."

When Cromwell felt haler, we went out to hawk. We rode out, spaniels and greyhounds panting as they raced alongside our horses, their pink tongues steaming in the early morning air. Greyhounds took the larger birds when they fell; herons, crane and bustard. Spaniels would capture struggling pigeons, ducks and geese. Beaters came to flush game from the reed beds, their hands clasping cudgels and long wooden staffs. Local children turned out, eager to earn a penny, and their laughter was as effective as the sticks they held at startling birds into flight.

At the river marshes we would stop, listening to the thump of a skin drum ringing in the distance, calling time for the beaters. Courtiers took it in turns to fly falcons from their wrists, with those of highest rank leading the hunt. Over the water, shimmering silver and black, our birds flew, their wings sharp against the skyline, eyes fixated on their prey. Titbits of flesh were offered to each successful bird, so they might be rewarded but continue to hunger for more. Dogs raced into the rippling water, upsetting its silent passage as tiny waves broke and crashed on the surface and against the banks of the river.

Wagering was part of the sport. One courtier would bet against another that he would win this match, or a lady would swear to outdo another. In the afternoon we would sit beside fires lain under trees, and sup on fresh meat cooked over the flames, dripping with fat and blood. Fine bread, cheese and pies baked that morn in the kitchens would accompany our feast of flesh, and Henry's musicians would play as we rested on cushions and blankets of wool and velvet, under gaily coloured tents which provided welcome shade.

As the meat was sliced up, I had to look away. Cooked flesh, I could see without problems. Raw meat invoked flashes of blood on cloth.

As blue dusk fell, with it came silence. It was as though the world were holding herself still, to give us a moment in time to stand, to draw in courage. As we rode home, weary and happy, I would listen to the merry chatter in quiet contemplation, sensing a peace, stolen from the eternal world, as it settled in my soul.

It was not so in the palaces. There I was not free, not whole. There I felt haunted, anxious and watched. But in England, in the wild and open spaces, with the wind against my skin and the promise of rain ever close, I could find solace. Even for a short while, it was welcome.

When not hunting together, Cromwell often joined Henry and me for card games. On many an occasion, thinking it a clever jest, Henry would hold up a knave and exclaim, "I have been dealt a Cromwell!"

The jest, although amusing the first time, rapidly became tired the more Henry used it. But that was his way. Whenever he had a thought he believed clever, he would wear it thin. Norris cheekily told me that at times he had to grit his teeth, and force a laugh, to please his master.

Sometimes, if the day was fine, I would take my women and Henry's men into the gardens. At Hampton Court, Henry's heraldic beasts, sitting atop poles painted in stripes of green and white, had been joined by a new friend. My secondary badge, that of the leopard, stood alongside Henry's, his fierce eyes watching over the gardens. In the great hall, if one looked up to the magnificent ceiling, one would see my arms, and the entwined initials *H&A*. The gatehouse, too, held these symbols, and my badge of the white falcon, surrounded by roses, was everywhere. Long had Katherine's emblems haunted me, but now there was a conscious effort to remove them. If only it were so easy to remove Katherine from the minds of the people, as it was to strip her from wood, plaster and stone.

Sometimes I would put my fingertips to a necklace or brooch that once had been hers, and wonder if anyone saw those stones on me and remembered her. Her shadow was with me. Everywhere I went, there she was. Pearl chokers, made before I became Queen, hung about my neck, along with strings of sapphires, rubies, and diamonds. I wore golden emblems depicting our entwined initials, but even as I hung them about my long, white swan's neck, I wondered if any could still see the vision *H&K* rather than *H&A*.

In the gardens, we would sit in alcoves and bowers. We ladies would spread out our thick skirts and sit upon flowery meads, listening to Tom, George or Surrey recite poetry. Oftentimes, we women had to defend ourselves from charges of cruelty in love. If we were distant, or failed to surrender our virtue to gallants who came hunting, we were named cold and cruel. Of course there was no true way to win this game. If a maid submitted she would be used and discarded. The object was to walk the fine line between the two states; never giving in and never allowing the men to give up. To survive at court, a woman had to be simultaneously both virgin and whore.

As I quipped and rebuffed the men who swore to love me, I felt an echo of my old self return. I remembered the bright young girl I had once been, before sorrow had come to live in my heart. For a time, lost in these games, I could forget. But when I entered my chambers again, saw the bed on which I had bled, that girl departed, leaving behind a sadder woman, a frailer soul... one who was not as sure of herself as that damsel had always been.

We tarried at Hampton Court as preparations for the public executions of the Carthusians went ahead. On the 4th of May, the Carthusians and their allies were taken from the Tower. More and his daughter were brought out to watch their ungainly march towards death. Cromwell thought this might move More to swear the oath, but it had the opposite effect. He became more resolved. But if this horror did not frighten More, it did others, just as was intended. The execution of Elizabeth Barton and her followers had not produced the desired effect, but the spectacle of men of God being dragged to their deaths silenced many.

Still in their habits, they were hauled on hurdles through London to Tyburn. Those awaiting death were forced to watch as each of the accused was half-hung, cut down before they lost consciousness, then castrated and disembowelled whilst still alive. Sometimes, mercy was offered by allowing a condemned man to drift into unconsciousness before starting to rip his innards out. Not so for the monks.

After their entrails had been burnt in their faces, as they writhed and screamed upon the block, they were beheaded. Their bodies were cleaved into quarters, so they might be displayed in London, York, and other prominent cities. Feet and hands were strung up on gates; heads were stuck atop spikes on London Bridge; one chunk of a man was taken to the Charterhouse Monastery and hung upon the gate, to scare the monks into submission.

My brother, father and uncle went to see the grisly task done. Henry wished to attend personally, but he was kept away by his Council who said that if he did it would incite trouble. My family were sent as his representatives. They had no choice. To refuse would be tantamount to treason.

George told me that as clergymen watched their brothers die, they continued to preach, asking God to spare England from its fell and evil King. They told the crowds to defy Henry, and follow instead the truth and light of Rome. Their defiance only served to make Cromwell and Henry more resolved to act against monks still awaiting trial.

Unlike my husband, I did not want to witness the bloody entrails, glistening purple and red in the sunlight. But it was not only for revulsion that I did not attend, but for worry that this path was not the right one.

My kin were joined by Fitzroy and others. My brother said that if you glanced about, it was as though the whole court had come to Tyburn. "Although many people wore disguises," he said as he sat on my bed later. "Most of them not very convincing."

"Why were some in disguises?" I asked, pressing a hand to my head. In the aftermath of my miscarriage, I was often weak and ill, but I also knew it was not this alone which assaulted me. Some part of me was full of guilt, shame and fear.

George's handsome face was flushed with wry disbelief. I laughed a little and cuffed him. My ladies sat sewing nearby. There was a gentle hush upon the rooms. If the conversation was less grisly, it would have been a lovely, calm evening.

"They came in disguise because there are many in Europe who will speak out," he said. "They will say England is a tyrant; that we execute not traitors, but men with powerful minds, to placate our ignorance. They will call us heretics and murderers. It is already being said, sister, and it will continue. Courtiers will turn up at executions to demonstrate loyalty, but they will wear disguises so that if any foreigners ask, they can pretend they were not there."

I raised myself upon my elbows. "But the monks are traitors. They speak against the King and the oath… against my daughter and me."

"Of course they are," he said. "But you know as well as I that men in other countries with purposes and designs of their own will see it differently. They will say, 'look at the King. He is become a tyrant. We have excuses to march into England'. That is what the King fears. He knows treasonous mouths must be stopped, and treasonous minds must be cut from their bodies. Truly Anne..." he paused and kissed my fingertips. "... This has to be done. They have had ample opportunity to swear the oath and they have refused. No matter if this causes problems abroad, it will protect England. This will lay the foundations of the new world we want to build. It must be done ... besides..."

He cut off and offered me a roguish smile "... if any man were to threaten my dearest sister, I should give them short quarter!" He jumped up and drew the short sword at his belt. My ladies giggled, glancing at my handsome brother with admiring eyes. He noted their interest and, elated by the opportunity to show off, continued. "Let them come!" he said, parrying an imaginary foe. "None shall take my sweet sister *spirit* from me!"

"George," I said, laughing. "Stop, you will scare my good ladies."

"They shall not take you!" he cried, thrusting his sword out, the blade shimmering in the last light of day which fell through the windows. I watched him with great affection, knowing he was trying to draw me from dark thoughts.

"Come," I said and patted the bed. "Tell me, have you heard from Mary?"

"She and William are well in Calais," he said. "Do you want me to send word to her?"

"Tell no one. But I have sent her a letter, and some money."

George whistled, his lips a pert little rosebud. "Does the King know?"

"No one knows but you." I put a hand to the linen coif on my head, adjusting it. "I cannot call her back to court, but I will name her my sister if any ask it of me. I owe her that much."

"You have forgiven her?"

"Her... but not myself." I smoothed the coif, tying its ribbon tighter about my chin. "I was too hard on her," I said. "Too harsh."

"She disgraced our family."

"She did, I do not deny it. But she only wished to find happiness, and that is a quest I understand more and more. Perhaps it was selfish of her to not think of our family. But perhaps it was selfish of us to never have realised the hardships she bore as a widow."

"Her duty was to her family, not to her own desires."

"If that is true," I said. "Is not *our* duty to her? She is a part of our family, is she not? We lapsed in our obligations, George. We left her on the fringes and expected her to simply wait. We are as much to blame for this as she was."

My brother's face was sceptical. He did not agree. It was strange to speak of honour and duty, and include woman in such talk, for many would say that all duty and honour are due *from* the lower members of a household *to* the higher, and women are usually kept at the bottom of any hierarchy. As such, Mary was to blame for not giving consideration to my father or me. But what are duty and honour in a family if they extend not to the whole?

We were bound to each other, we Boleyns, in chains of love, affection and duty. And if Mary had failed us, we had failed her.

Chapter Twenty-Four

Hampton Court
May 1535

May is the most beautiful of all spring months; the time of birth, renewal and new life. Blossom erupts upon trees in a dizzying display of white and pink, and hawthorn leaves mist hedgerows with glorious green. Sudden storms burst from sultry, sticky skies, causing flashes of dazzling blue and streaking silver to rupture the midnight heavens, swathed in gowns of cobalt and black. Rain comes in deluges, making scents of the parched earth and hot cobblestones rise, as perfume, into the nostrils. And sometimes the rains stay away for days, weeks at a time, causing farmers to watch the skies with a prayer upon their lips.

On good days, maids take their spinning and sewing outside, sitting by their doorsteps, chattering to neighbours. Bluebells flood the forests, a miasma of blue and purple bobbing gently in the soft wind. Butterflies flutter, alighting on jack-by-the-hedge and heartsease. Lovers gather forget-me-nots to give in the hope they will always be remembered. Children are sent to collect garlands of branches and blooms, singing at the doors of neighbours on the way, and carrying the garlands into their church. Primroses crowd hillsides like spectators at a royal joust, and horse chestnuts become a mass of fresh leaves as their blossoms grow in steeples, granting them their common name of the candle tree. Horses are decorated with flowers, and young maids divine their future husbands by making sweet-scented balls of cowslips and wool, chanting the names of the boys they think to marry as the ball is tossed between them.

Honey-bees flirt with flowers, as white spiders hide inside fresh, sweet blooms, waiting to trap them. Swallows swoop in the skies and cuckoos sing from amongst the confusion of heather upon moor lands. Crops and hayfields spring into life, and orchids, delicate in their frail beauty, emerge, nestled in the shady places, bringing light and colour to the gloom. Buzzards wing, shimmering gold against clear blue skies, and hawkers go out in search of herons.

A beautiful month… when the most bloody deeds in living memory had occurred…

As the enormity of what Henry had done erupted about Europe, I was blamed. How could it be otherwise? To many, I was a creature of black and white, but never grey. Those who did not love me, hated me, and believed I was a witch who had stolen Henry from Katherine, and England from Rome. If there was bad weather, I was accountable. If there was plague, it was my fault. And now these monks had died, in such bloody and graceless ways, I was the one to blame.

I was their Salome, their Judas… their Devil. It was assumed I had asked for their executions, and thirsted for the blood of Fisher and More. It was not so. They died for Henry's pride, and for his fears.

Hoping that the deaths of the Carthusians might have tempted Fisher and More away from their obstinacy, Henry sent his Council to them, with Cromwell leading, urging surrender. He did not get the result he desired.

Cromwell did not want either man to die. It would be much more valuable, he said, to get them to conform, for then they could lead the way for other doubters of the supremacy. Fisher and More were not about to grant his wish. They would die for the faith just as they had lived for it.

Fisher declared Henry was not the Head of the Church, all but signing his own death warrant, and More refused to be moved. Both were willing to swear allegiance to Henry and to me as his wife, but they would not accept the royal supremacy. They believed the Pope was the only leader of the Church. They would not say it, but to them, Henry was nothing more than a pretender.

Their spoken affirmations, however, somehow sneaked from the Tower and were being talked of in London. In response, Henry sent his men out to preach. Both men were denounced as traitors. Their sins, of pride, malice, traitorous thought and even suggestions they were thinking of rebelling, were proclaimed far and wide. It was Henry's mission to defame Fisher and More in the eyes of his people. He convinced some, but not all… never all.

Henry played the merry, confident monarch about court, but he was unnerved. In doubt, he clung to me. Each evening he would go over and over the reasons for More and Fisher being detained, and I consoled him. The distance that had grown between us upon my miscarriage evaporated like May's morning dew as the hot sun rose, bloody and glaring, in the skies. Henry could not do without me. Every day I was at his side, holding at bay the wraiths of men not yet dead, and the ghosts of those he had sent into Death's arms. I was his shield, but I wondered how often he thought on the fact that his people always blamed me? Sometimes, I believed he understood and was grateful. At other times, when the monster within him was in control, he thought that was my rightful place.

Henry sent fresh deputies to France. It was a sign of favour towards me. France had hardly been friendly of late, but Henry understood I wanted alliance with them. As another token of esteem, my brother and Norfolk led the mission. George was to persuade François to make a public commitment to me as Queen, and accept Elizabeth as a bride for one of his sons. Henry wanted François to send whichever son he chose to court, so he might be raised according to English custom. The implication, never spoken, was that Elizabeth and her husband might one day rule England as King and Queen; a safeguard in case I never bore a son. Cromwell told Norfolk and George before they left there was to be no compromise. Elizabeth and I would be recognised.

With More and Fisher remaining unmoved, Henry made plans for their trials. But others had heard of this. On the 22nd of May, Fisher was made a Cardinal by the papacy.

"I will cut off Fisher's head and send it to Rome!" Henry shouted. "There can it go to be anointed with his Cardinal's hat!"

Henry repeated this threat, hoping his fright would be seen as resolve. He forbade Fisher's hat to be sent to England and stormed about court, telling anyone who would listen of all the woes Rome had inflicted upon him. The Pope asked men to intercede for Fisher and More, sending du Bellay and pleading with the King of France to speak for them, but nothing would sway Henry, not even the thought that he was sending François into the arms of the Emperor, by distancing himself from the morals of other kings.

A deadline was set. More and Fisher must swear the oath by St John's Day, the 24th of June, or they would die.

In the meantime, more monks were sent to trial. Cromwell put on pressure to convict, just as he had before. Henry's supremacy meant that he possessed the power to be rid of his enemies.

He meant to do just that.

*

George arrived home from France on the 25th, and rather than going to Henry first, he came straight to me. "François will not be moved," he said, taking his cape from his shoulders and cracking his tired back with his hands. "They want Mary, or nothing. They will not send one of François' sons to England to be educated by the King, and they will not speak about a meeting until their terms are accepted."

"François said this?"

"François would not deign to meet me in person," said my brother, throwing himself into a chair of green silk, trimmed with Venice gold. "He allowed me to converse with Brion and the Cardinal of Lorraine."

"He insults us," I hissed, fury gathering as a storm in my soul. "Over and over, he slights us, and we are supposed to just sit here and take it?" I got up. Anger brought me energy where grief had sapped it from me. "The King of France is a false friend," I declared. "And I despise him!"

"I have grown none too fond of him either," said my brother. "But where do we turn for support in Europe if not to France? The Schmalkalden League is not strong enough, and Spain will never accept us."

"Will not accept *me*, you mean," I said. "Even if France is our most likely ally, I will turn to them no more. They have rejected my daughter and imperilled my position. We will have to find a way to reach Spain or encourage the King to make friends with the Emperor's rebellious subjects in Germany."

By the time George had left to report to Henry, I had let loose many unguarded words about François. I was furious, insulted and frightened. Once he had told me there would be times when policy and politics would get in the way of our friendship, but to demean my daughter was a step too far, and François should have known that. The only possibility left to make England secure was to make peace with Charles of Spain, but how could that ever happen? With me on the throne, I did not see how we could come to terms with Spain.

Unless I die, murmured Katherine.

"Unless you die," I whispered, putting my hand to a diamond at my throat that once had been hers.

*

George told us more about the meetings in France. Upon his return, Brion had apparently failed to inform his master that Mary was out of the question, and François, upon hearing this from George instead, refused to give up the notion. This had meant the talks went badly from the very beginning. But we could not allow others to know this. In an effort to fool Spain into thinking all had gone well, Cromwell met with Chapuys and showed him a document which said that France supported me as Queen. It had been sent with George for François to sign, but the French King had refused. No one was about to tell Chapuys that, of course. Cromwell, therefore, decided to try to dupe him.

"I suggested that England was keen to make friends with Spain," he told me. "Even though we had the support of the French."

"And did the ambassador believe you?" I asked. "He must have seen the document was unsigned."

"He was wary," said Cromwell. "But we need Spain, Majesty. With them, we know where we stand and on what terms. The French switch sides faster than a coursing greyhound."

"I do not see how Charles would ever accept my daughter and me."

"It will require some careful handling," said Cromwell. "But there is word that Katherine is ill. If she were to die…"

"The sand would be wiped clean," I said, thinking of my dreams. *I am your death as you are mine…* the whisper came from nowhere and I shivered.

"The sand would be wiped clean," Cromwell said, seeing nothing of my unease.

"How go your investigations?" I asked, wishing to turn the conversation from this ghoulish notion.

"They go well," said Cromwell. "Or badly, depending on your point of view. The abbots and monks are not pleased, but the King is. My men have uncovered many ill practices, Majesty, and I suspect there are many more to come."

"When one mouse is seen, many more hide inside the walls."

"The inventories, too, are making headway," Cromwell went on, his eyes lost in thought. "The dissolution of the monasteries will fill the King's coffers," he said with an unpleasant smile. It was a curiously unguarded remark for Cromwell, and I saw him start as he noted my icy stare.

"It should be used for worthy purposes. The King agrees with me on this, Cromwell." I eyed him with disapproval. "I thought that was what you wanted too."

"Of course, Majesty, but when the King is invested with this wealth, he can decide what it will be used for."

We always seemed to reach this point, where I all but accused him of thievery and he set the responsibility on Henry's shoulders. But I had enough to worry about without pitying monasteries about to be caught out for peddling false relics and hoarding money. For now, I set my concerns aside. But they would return.

*

Two weeks later, I made it my mission to show the French they were well and truly out of favour. If François would exclude my brother from his presence, I repay the compliment with his ambassadors.

"Anne," my brother laughed when he heard my plans for a gathering at my estate at Hanworth. "You are bolder than a cock on Christmas morn!"

"If they exclude you, we will reject them," I said. "The King and Cromwell agree. France will play no further part in our affairs until they are willing to play nicely."

The party at Hanworth was joyous, and the French ambassadors were omitted from the guest list. It was a clear, public snub, and did not go unnoticed. Ambassador Dinteville also found he was not invited to court and tried instead to visit Cromwell. He waited at Cromwell's house in Stepney until ten of the clock one evening, but when Cromwell arrived home, tired and still ill, Dinteville was told to leave.

Henry, too, railed at France and his *good brother*. "Spain, at least has always maintained the same stance," he said. "But François once supported our marriage. I see now he is a fickle friend."

In the presence of my ladies and several of Henry's men, I tore the French hood from my head, tossed it to Norris, and asked to be brought an English gable one. There was a lot of laughing, and a few shocked faces. Married women were not permitted to display their hair as maidens were. When a gable hood was brought to me, I set it upon my head.

"There," I said. "This hood will not give me a headache as the past one has."

"You find England comfortable, my lady?" Norris asked, his bright eyes dancing.

"England is a better choice than France," I said. "All the French do is copy the Italians. They have no true style, manners or thoughts of their own. In England we think our own thoughts and make our own way. Better to be English than French, my lord. Better to be original and honest, rather than dull and disreputable."

Although I did not wear it all the time, given that it was intensely unbecoming, I made sure people saw me wearing my gable hood. When the French Ambassador sent me messages, I returned them unopened. Wherever I could, I made scathing remarks about the French, and told my women I wished I could have been brought up in another court, "for the court of France has slid into decline since I left," I said. "King Louis understood what *true* majesty was. His cousin was never meant to become a king. François is a country lord with country manners and a contrary heart."

There was a great deal of laughter about this. Suddenly it became fashionable for everyone to wear English styles. Gable hoods became a common sight, and ladies aped me, telling their gossips they would rather be crowned with loyal England than fickle France.

*

"My man was most thorough, I assure you, madam," said Cromwell a few days later.

I had no doubt about it. Richard Rich had been sent to interrogate More in preparation for his trial. Rich was a strange man; the sweetest face that ever you did see, which served the blackest heart beneath. He looked like a fresh young maid, yet his soul was dark. Of this I had no proof, but there was something about Rich which sent a shiver down my spine. There was something which emanated from him, like a shallow, creeping mist, which fell upon those near him, making them soiled. Sometimes, when people are perfect in appearance, their intense beauty becomes somehow ugly. Perhaps it is a jest, one of God's finest, to play such a trick on those blessed with beauty; that when people are struck by their perfection, they are also repulsed by it. To be truly beautiful is to own flaws. This makes a person real. God likes imperfect things… broken things… Fractured pieces brought together to make something new and wondrous.

But Rich was the perfect man to be sent to trip More into either confession of his sins against Henry, or to dupe him into swearing the oath. Rich was Cromwell's Solicitor-General, and an intrepid commander in his investigations.

After that interrogation, Rich arrived at court with a merry twinkle in his eyes. "He has secured an outright denial of the supremacy from More, which states he does not accept Parliament's authority to bestow supremacy on the King," said Cromwell with a contented smile.

"So, he succeeded where you failed, Master Cromwell?" asked George, his tone none too pleasant and his eyes kindled with deep suspicion.

"He did, my Lord Rochford," said Cromwell smoothly. "And now the King cannot deny any longer that More is a traitor."

"If indeed he *did* succeed," said my brother after Cromwell had departed.

"You think Rich's evidence false?"

"I do." George shook his head. "If More is too clever to be drawn out by Cromwell, I see no reason why he should fall for the charms of *Mistress* Rich."

I snorted at his jest, but rapidly turned serious. "If that is so," I said. "More confessed nothing that would make him a traitor."

"Aside from his failure to swear the oath," my brother pointed out.

"We knew from the start he would never do so. He said as much to Henry when he resigned as Chancellor and he was promised it would not be held against him."

I walked to the window and looked out on the day. Summer was almost upon us, but even the coming of the balmy breeze and the light glow of the sunset, bright, pale pink, and white, could not stir me from my unease.

"You think More should be acquitted?" asked my brother.

"No," I said, staring at the sunset. It was mother-of-pearl spread across the heavens. "He is guilty of not supporting the supremacy, and we cannot allow that, but more and more, brother, it feels as though we are racing ahead without truly considering the consequences." I turned to him. "Men have died for failing to recognise me as Queen, George. If that is the case put against More, I will say nothing, for he knew the consequences. But if he is attained on false evidence, we set a dangerous precedent."

"Only the guilty will die."

"I wish that were true. Guilt and innocence seem to be one and the same at this time. It all depends on the King… not on evidence, confession, or actual sin… just on what Henry believes."

*

At the end of May there was news from France. Not from flighty François, but a request for aid from Marguerite de Navarre.

The Queen wrote to me in secret, using friends we had in common to reach me. Knowing of her brother's annoyance with all things reformist, she begged me to intervene to aid Nicholas Bourbon. Cranmer had already spoken to me of this when Bourbon first got into trouble. Many reformists François had previously protected were in peril. With François no longer sheltering them, they were vulnerable, for they had spoken about their beliefs openly in the days when it was safe to do so.

Bourbon, hearing of Marguerite's plan, wrote to me from his cell. *"A poor man,"* he wrote. *"I lie shut up in prison. There is no one who would be able or who would dare to bring help. You, alone, Oh Queen; you, oh noble nymph, both can and dare, as one whom the King and whom God Himself loves."*

Dare I did, indeed. Through Jean Dinteville, who was eager to regain favour, and had been a school friend of the philosopher and poet, I sent word that I would help. I went to Henry, and he agreed to ask François to consent to Bourbon being sent to us. Since François had no wish to keep Bourbon, he was released and shipped to England.

Bourbon was housed with Doctor Butts at my expense. I took him on as a tutor for my ward, Henry Carey, and also for Norris' heir and the son of my dead friend Bridget. I wrote to Mary, telling her about engaging Bourbon, and she was pleased. Her husband, she wrote, was a staunch supporter of the new learning, and she believed in reform too. She said that Calais was full of those who upheld evangelical ideals, and she had been persuaded of the evils of worshipping idols.

Bourbon, too, was grateful. "You saved me, most gracious lady," he said in French when he was brought to me. "Never can I repay all that you have done for me."

"You can," I said, smiling. "Teach my nephew and the other boys at Syon well. Fill the minds of the next generation with wisdom, Master Bourbon. In doing so, you will repay me a hundredfold. I want my daughter's England to be blessed with the light of Christ. By educating young minds, by setting them on the right path, you can help to craft this future for the good of our people, and for the peace and happiness of my beloved child."

In the months that followed, Bourbon wrote many verses about me. He became a part of the reformist circle at court, and made swift friends with Cranmer.

"Just as the golden sun dispels the gloomy shadows of night and at day-break makes all things bright, so you, O Queen, restored as a new light to your French and enlightening everything, bring back the Golden Age."

Bourbon extolled me as a Frenchwoman, the highest compliment a native might offer, but he also saw me as a significant figure, with international power. He hailed me as a beacon, a light that would illuminate both England and France.

I only hoped I could indeed be this light, this torch shining in the darkness, bringing peace and hope.

At times it seemed impossible that one day the people of England, of the world, might see me, the *true* me, past the shadow and smoke of my enemies' slanders. At times I thought I might become the nightmare they imagined me to be; this evil Queen who called for blood to bathe in, and bone that she might suck its marrow. Yet some, like Bourbon, saw me in another light. A light I hoped to take into my soul, to replenish my heart and feed my spirit.

Chapter Twenty-Five

Windsor Castle
June 1535

On the 1st of June, the Emperor sailed. Four hundred ships carrying over thirty thousand soldiers left the shores of Spain to reconquer Tunis from the Ottomans. As the first reports of battles arrived, suspicions that the French had been secretly working with the Ottomans against the Spanish were confirmed when cannon balls bearing the brand of the *fleur-de-lys* were discovered.

"*That* was careless," Cromwell gloated, almost crowing with pleasure. "The Emperor may well wage war on France, rather than looking to England."

"You think the Emperor will look to England for alliance now?"

"I think the Emperor will look to England." Cromwell smiled. His face had taken on an appearance of youth, despite his long years.

Henry did not want the Emperor victorious in case triumph made him consider sailing for England next, but as Chapuys detailed the fleets' accomplishments, I could see Henry's eyes igniting with the fire of warfare that had always lain within his heart. Henry had always wanted to be seen as a second Henry V. He not only feared his royal cousin of Spain, he was jealous of him.

Another kind of war was being fought in England as Cromwell's men spread far and wide. So much ill was reported back to us at court that I wondered how abbots and bishops could bear to stand in the light of day with such dark sins weighing them down. Slovenly practices, as well as sinister reports of sodomy, orgies with nuns, worship of money over God, and hoarding of wealth, swiftly arrived, and although some declared that Cromwell may have ordered his men to invent crimes, to paint an even blacker picture, it was hard even for those who supported the Church to remain on their side as such sins as these were uncovered.

Publicly, I was firmly behind the investigations. I could not be seen to be anything else. Henry and I needed a united front, especially whilst the Emperor's future plans were as yet undecided. These reports were a vindication of everything we had said about the Church, and it was important for Henry's people to understand our motives. But even as I spoke in support, I wondered if the gossipmongers were right, and Cromwell had commanded his men to invent sin if they could not find it. The more lax a religious house, the more likely it was to be shut down; the more houses that were closed, the more money for the Crown.

With France suddenly on less firm footing than before, George was dispatched to François. A compromise was offered, saying that if the Duc de Angouleme was sent to live in England for six months before marriage, we would be satisfied. My brother returned a week later. He had failed.

"I did all I could," he said. "François seems to think he is not in such a precarious position, and does not require our friendship."

"The Emperor will give life to his disillusionment in that matter," I said. "And when he does, we will witness how well French worms crawl when they come begging for our affection."

Bold words, but they meant nothing. I was aware that I was standing in the way of political alliance with Spain. As long as Katherine lived, there would be no peace. As long as her daughter lived, there would be no alliance. Did I plot to kill them? No. Did I wish for them to be removed? Yes. It is hard to find oneself alone. Loneliness breeds much that is ill. Terrors that would not touch us normally draw close, and fear infects the blood, turning all minor slights into mighty ones. All I had was Henry and Elizabeth, and only one of those people had any power to protect me.

*

With Cromwell's investigations turning up all sorts of scandal, faith and worship were all anyone could talk of. Two days after the Emperor sailed for Tunis, Cromwell had written to Henry's bishops, demanding they support the supremacy and weed out those who would follow Rome. Many came out in public support, knowing that if they did not they would be subjected to inspections. Court was on fire with debate, and reformers were bold. At one of the gatherings in my rooms, perhaps inspired by my sister's secret letters, I spoke to Henry about iconoclasm.

"Whilst I do not hold with men taking matters into their own hands, I can understand the sense in worshipping God over idols," I said. "Do these sculptures not distract the common people from God? For in our churches there are no images of God the Father, only of the saints, Jesus and Mary. Some ignorant souls look to these idols, my lord, and believe them to *be* God."

"I understand what you say, Anne, and I promise to think on it." He ran his finger along my hand. "You always know how to word things, so I might understand my people better." He gazed at me with affection. "But I will continue to keep statues in *my* church," he said. "I do not find they detract from my study of the Word of God."

"Of course, my lord," I said. "You are blessed with learning and understanding. When I say this of others, I mean those who are not educated… those who rely solely on the signs they see in churches to steer them. For, without a Bible in their own language, what have men to guide them? Those who cannot read use signs to find their path. This is as true of a man trying to find an inn in London, as it is for a soul trying to find God in church. That is why we must ensure that the signs they see are the *right* ones. Putting statues of saints before such people makes them believe that this is where God is to be found; inside marble, captured within stone."

"There is something to what you say," he admitted. "I will speak with Cranmer further on this, as he has said something similar."

"If, in normal churches, statues were removed," I went on. "It would allow your people to concentrate on the worship of God the Father, rather than on saints. And at the same time, an English Bible would teach them all they do not presently understand."

"I have long thought we should have a Bible in our mother-tongue," said Henry.

I smiled. What a lie! Henry had been against this for a long time, but now that it seemed almost *patriotic* to have one, he believed the thought had come from him. I did not correct him. It was better to have Henry think he was the author of this notion, and strive ahead with all the passion of the first convert to a faith.

Later that month, after the Emperor had won a stunning victory against the Ottomans, Henry told Chapuys that he yearned for reconciliation with Charles. I doubt he wanted anything of the kind. Charles was nine years Henry's junior, and was now in possession of an Empire that stretched from southern Italy to Austria and across the tumbling, heaving oceans to the New World. He had raised a fleet like the conquerors of old, beaten back the infidel, and now might turn his attention on either troublesome France, or obstinate England. Henry did not like those who accomplished more than him.

It was important to win the Emperor's friendship. Relying on France was impractical, and both Henry and I were unnerved by the Emperor's war skills. We were truly alone; a stone shelf lingering in the wide open seas, surrounded by foes.

When Cromwell heard of the Emperor's victory, I thought he might pass out, for a few moments, he seemed to cease breathing.

The Emperor's triumph stirred people into action. Katherine wrote to her nephew and to the Pope, urging intervention in England, but neither was listening. Chapuys hoped for better treatment for his two beloved women, but it never happened. Henry took to playing mind games with Dinteville. He insinuated that he and Charles were close friends, in regular correspondence, in an effort to get the French worried enough to capitulate, but Chapuys informed his fellow ambassador that no such relationship existed, sullying our chances.

Chapuys might not have welcomed Henry's friendship, but the Emperor did. He had no wish for England to make alliance with France, especially not after he had secured a peace treaty with them, on most favourable terms, upon the discovery of their friendship with the infidels. If France joined with England they would be made stronger, and even if he disliked Henry's treatment of his aunt and cousin, Charles of Spain was not about to let that interfere when it came to politics. In response, we become colder to the French than ever before. The new ambassador, Antoine de Castelnau, the Bishop of Tarbes, was affronted when Henry refused permission for him to use Bridewell Place as an embassy as his predecessors had. Cromwell made a point of avoiding the ambassador, and Chapuys was invited to court each day, so Henry might flatter him.

Henry came to me often. His affection for Mary Shelton was on the wane, and everyone was wondering who would be his next mistress. But as More and Fisher edged ever closer to the executioner's block, as Charles of Spain roared about the Mediterranean, and as France tried to hide behind diplomacy, Henry turned to me. In times of trouble, I was the courage he lacked and the strength he supped from.

At night, as he twitched in nightmares born of dread, I would pull him close. I heard the whimper of a small boy emerge from the mouth of this almighty King, but as I held him, his demons departed. In my arms, Henry of England slept like a baby.

*

As June unfolded, and a flaming heat wave broke over England, almost suffocating the land, More stood firm. Perhaps it was fitting that his resistance should be rigid in this month, for it seemed time had become still, seared into position by the glaring sun.

The hedgerows were ablaze with flowers, the fields a haze of yellow. Hoverflies held still, their invisible wings whirring in the shimmering air. Dog roses scrambled up haw and blackthorn, and swifts screamed through the heavens. Owl chicks blinked in the faded light of barns, and field mice emerged, dashing through the dry dust on the floor of storehouses. The air was rich with scent and pollen, but the heat was oppressive, clinging, and exhausting. England held her breath, waiting for a cool breeze, for a raindrop, for a sign that we were not abandoned to this tyrannical heat for the rest of time.

And it was then we had terrible news.

Tyndale had been arrested in Antwerp.

"Why did he not go to ground?" I whispered to Doctor Butts. "I sent men to warn him."

"That was some time ago, madam," said the poor man, who was just as concerned as I. "It may be that he grew careless as time went on and nothing happened." Butts paused. "But I have intelligence, my lady, that Thomas More may have been working with Bishop Stokesley to have him captured."

"From within the Tower?" I asked, although it was not as unlikely as it sounded. After his harsh incarceration some time ago, Henry had allowed his once-friend privileges again. The hope was that this would make More malleable, but clearly the ex-Chancellor had used his liberty for other purposes.

I called Cranmer to my chambers as Butts left. "We must aid Tyndale," I said. "Much as we did with Bourbon. What can be done? The King is seeking reconciliation with the Emperor. Can we work through those channels?"

"The King wants Tyndale in England, so he might execute him, Majesty," said Cranmer, twisting the rings upon his fingers. "I do not think he would agree to save him."

"Let me work on him," I said, thinking of how reliant Henry had been on me in the past few weeks. I was sure I could convince him. "If we can first ensure Tyndale's escape from the Emperor, we can work on the King's mercy."

Cranmer agreed to aid me, although he insisted it would have to be in secret. I understood. Henry was becoming a changeable beast, and Cranmer, even though he knew Henry loved him, was wary of his temper.

We learned that Tyndale had been betrayed by a friend… his own Judas. Henry Phillips was the son of a Dorset landowner who was also a Member of Parliament. Phillips was an Oxford graduate, with a bright future, who arrived in Antwerp apparently ready to embrace all that was new and evangelical. Tyndale and he had become friends, and had dined together often. Some of Tyndale's companions were mistrustful, but Tyndale believed in his friend.

Tyndale, for all his wisdom, did not understand of the minds of men.

Tyndale did not know the lad was not what he appeared to be. Phillips had robbed his father upon leaving home, and had lost much of that money through gambling. A year later, he had somehow come into money, enabling him to enter the University of the Louvain, a conservative, Catholic institution. None of this did he tell Tyndale, for his friend would not have trusted that an avowed Catholic would be his friend.

Tyndale opened his arms, not seeing the viper nestled at his breast.

Phillips was working for More and Stokesley. He went to the Imperial Court at Brussels and told them he could deliver their quarry. Since arresting someone of the protected English House was a delicate business, they had to wait until Tyndale was outside of its perimeter before making their move.

Phillips returned to Antwerp, borrowed money from Tyndale that he had no intention of repaying, and betrayed him. They ate dinner together one night and set out from Phillips' home, making for the English House. Phillips insisted that Tyndale lead the way through a squat, dark alley. At the end, soldiers were waiting. They took Tyndale to the Procurer General. Later, he was taken to the Castle of Vilvoorde. His possessions were seized and searched, and his books, his most precious belongings, were taken from him.

Phillips rapidly became a poor man again, without means to earn another bag of silver.

Cranmer and Cromwell tried to discover the reason for Tyndale's arrest, and therefore reach a possible defence. They found much. The mysterious benefactor who had supported Friar Peto, he who had preached against Henry, calling him Ahab, seemed to have been the one who gave money to Phillips. The name on all lips was that of Thomas More, working with his friend Bishop Stokesley. There was no proof, but I believed this accusation was correct. More had wanted to do one last service for the God he believed would reward him in Heaven. He had brought Tyndale down.

Whilst Cranmer, Cromwell and I attempted to have Tyndale freed, Tyndale's adversary, More, remained immoveable. He once more failed to swear the oath, and maintained his stance on the supremacy. He declared the oath was a double-edged sword. To use one edge, and refuse the oath would endanger his life, but to take the other, and swear, would imperil his soul.

In thinking on More, I also came to meditate on Katherine. "I think she has cursed me," I said to Cranmer. "I will not bear a son whilst she and her daughter live."

Seeing his face crinkle with doubt, I went on. "Why else would I suffer two failed pregnancies, Eminence? Why would God withhold His blessing?"

"Many women lose children, Majesty," he said. "It does not hold there is a curse upon you."

I looked out from the window into the gardens where a bright moon shone. The paths, the flowers, and the grassy knolls were bathed in bright, silver light. White roses glowed, illuminated into wider, deeper being by the moon's radiance. Red roses were black spaces; deep, unending holes in the fabric of space and time. There was no grey, no half-light. There was only black, only white.

"Believe what you will," I said. "I know the truth."

I voiced these concerns to Henry, who agreed with me. There followed immediate rumours that Katherine and Mary would be executed, as Henry spoke openly of his distaste for them about court. Cromwell joined in, telling Chapuys that everything would be better if both women simply died. But no matter the threat, Katherine was undaunted.

"I am determined without doubt to die in this kingdom," she said to her servants.

If only Katherine would die, I thought. If only this ghost in my mind would become one in truth. People would stop seeing her at my elbow. Peace might be reached with Spain. My daughter would be secure. I might be less afraid.

If only you would die, I thought one evening as the wolf light fell.

Do you never think, Mistress Boleyn, how many say the same of you?

I shook my head and marched out to my privy garden to clear my head in the chilled twilight. Even in my own mind, Katherine always got the last word.

*

Late that May, another three monks stood trial for denying the supremacy. Cromwell was on the board of judges, and would be so again, some days later, when Bishop Fisher was tried. Just like before, with the Carthusians, Cromwell put pressure on the other judges to convict. A special commission of oyer and terminer for Middlesex was convened, commanded to make diligent enquiry into all treasons, and felonies in that county. Commissioners heard cases and determined the outcome. Everyone knew what the outcome would be.

The monks were found guilty and sentenced to death. They spent thirteen hollow days in Newgate Jail awaiting their grizzly executions. Shackled to the walls, and forced to remain standing throughout this time, their punishment for disobeying Henry began long before the time of their deaths.

As the monks waited for the sweet release of death, Fisher was brought to trial. The court was informed that Fisher had denied the supremacy. It did not take the judges long to decide his fate.

On the 19th of June, the monks went to their deaths and three days later, Fisher followed. Henry did not honour his oath that Fisher and More were to swear by St John's Day. He had run out of patience.

Fisher walked from the belly of the Tower, broken in body but not in spirit. He was painfully emaciated. Some said you could count his ribs through his thin shirt.

He had been sentenced to die the traitor's death of hanging, drawing and quartering, but Henry commuted the sentence to beheading. Think not this was through mercy. No… Henry was afraid. No matter his bold words about Fisher's Cardinal's hat, he worried that killing a high-ranking clergyman would bring war upon England. But he would not allow Fisher to live. The cup of Henry's mercy had run dry.

Mary Howard witnessed the spectacle with her father, who had been ordered to attend by Henry. Norfolk had no love for his task. He despised Fisher on principle, for being of common blood, but he respected the office he held.

"He was clearly weak and fragile, Majesty," said Mary when she returned. "He had trouble walking, but as four sheriff's officers made ready to carry him up the stairs, he waved them away. 'Nay, masters,' he said. 'Now let me alone. You shall see me go to my death well enough myself without any help'."

She sighed, for she understood I was none too happy about this fate for Fisher either. Long had the man been my enemy, but this public execution was causing unrest. I feared what it would bring upon us.

"They stripped his gown away," Mary continued. "And there were many gasps, for he was so thin. He looked like a corpse, Majesty… wasted and ghastly. Some said that Fisher was truly Death hiding in a man's form, using his voice to speak."

I shivered and crossed myself.

"He said a few words, telling the crowd that the King was a merciful prince, but was led astray. He declared he wore his finest clothes, for the day of his death was also that of his marriage… wedding his soul to God. They granted him one last chance to swear the oath, and he refused. He lay down, his body upon a straw mat and his head on the block. The executioner was quick and his blade was true. As he sliced Fisher's head from its body a great fountain of blood gushed forth. People at the front had to scuttle back, amazed to see so much blood come from such a thin man."

This was not the only tale told after Fisher's death. His body was guarded through the night, and in the morning it was flung into a grave in All Hallows, in Barking. It was said that the soldiers who laid him to rest did so with little dignity, making jests about him. Fisher was thrown into his pit without a winding sheet, and lay flat upon his belly in the dank soil. His head was parboiled and set on London Bridge, beside the heads of the Carthusian monks. But soon, people were remarking how *good* the head looked. Even after two weeks, it was fresh and clean as it stared down upon London's jostling people. People took this as a miracle; a sign that Fisher was blessed by God. It signified his innocence and holiness, it was whispered, and London Bridge became jammed by masses that came to see it.

In the wake of Fisher's death, Cromwell sought to link him to Katherine. Fisher had been interrogated about letters he had sent to her, which said she despaired of God's mercy. This admission was used to demonstrate that Katherine had a troubled conscience, for only the guilty would despair of the light of God. Cromwell's minions declared that Katherine was beset by a troubled conscience for lying about her relationship with Arthur. Rumours abounded that she and Mary would be arrested, but I knew Henry would not dare. Thinking, however, that the notion of her arrest might frighten people into ceasing to support her, I welcomed the gossip. Katherine lost much with Fisher's death. She lost her knight and defender. She turned on Pope Paul, saying that had he not taunted Henry by making Fisher a Cardinal, he might still be alive.

The day after Fisher died, Henry attended a pageant to celebrate the royal supremacy, seeking to show detractors that he cared not a fig for their protests or miracles. Henry rose early that day, and walked ten miles from Windsor to the village where the entertainment was being held, carrying a two-handed sword. The pageant had been organised by Cromwell for the eve of St John the Baptist's Nativity and it was based on the Book of Revelation. Henry was taken to a small house to view the entertainment, which showed him as a righteous king, punishing wicked clergy members who wanted only to wallow in sin.

So greatly did Henry enjoy himself that he removed his crown and went bareheaded. He sent Richard Page to tell me that I must see it when it was due to be performed again, on the eve of St Peter.

I rewarded Page with a purse of money and sent him back to tell my husband I would of course see the performance. I spoke at court about the righteousness of Fisher's death. But privately I was unsure.

The laws of England were no more being written in ink, but in blood.

Chapter Twenty-Six

Windsor Castle
June 1535

That month I heard that Joanna Dingley had borne a child… a girl, named Ethelreda, in honour of the Saint upon whose feast day she was born.

Relations between Henry and me had been good, but as I heard this all the pain of the past returned. A dark cloud fell upon me, thoughts of vengeance and recrimination poured through my mind. This jade he had courted as I had carried our daughter had been granted a child in my stead.

I could not comprehend why God would reward her and punish me. For this *was* punishment. Even though her child was a girl, and therefore of no consequence to Henry, it was still a babe of his seed borne by another woman.

Why would God reward sinners and punish the faithful? My chaplains had no answer for me. All I could think was that in some way I must have displeased the Almighty. Had He looked into my soul and found it wanting? Had He seen my dark thoughts about Mary and Katherine and chastised me? Was the Almighty displeased with the executions? Or had I been correct when I had said Katherine had laid a curse upon me? Hours did I spend upon my knees, praying to God and asking His forgiveness.

"I will do all that You ask of me," I whispered. "If only You grant me a son. Please, Almighty Father, hear my prayers. Turn my husband from sin. Return him to me."

I had no doubt this child was Henry's; another sister for Elizabeth and Mary, another bastard born… another sign that he cared nothing for our love.

Bitterly, I spoke of Henry to my friend Elizabeth Browne. "The King is fickle and inconstant," I said.

"But, Majesty," she whispered. "Surely you find satisfaction in his love? Men stray. They are weak to the wiles of women. But that does not hold there is no satisfaction in marriage."

I snorted. "The King has neither skill nor strength enough to satisfy a woman."

Elizabeth laughed, but told me I should have a care. I did not. In anger and hurt, I repeated my accusation, and it spread quietly about court. People sniggered at Henry behind his back. He knew nothing of it then, but all his men were laughing at him because of me. That helped my wounded pride, but in the end it would do me no good.

I was a fool. Henry was my only protection, and the Court of England was a gabbling mouth. It passed on all it heard, and embellished whatever was said.

*

As June drew to a close, two things happened. The first was that Henry released Katherine's longest-standing servant, Francisco Felipez, from her service. The second was that my brother returned home again.

Felipez had been found carrying secret messages from Katherine to the Emperor, and his removal was violently protested by Katherine, who swore she could not do without him. But Katherine's howls became muffled under the tempest of trouble George brought home with his baggage.

"I suspect much," he said.

"Of what and whom? The French?"

"Not of foes far away," said George, "but those closer to home." He leaned close. "Cromwell told Norfolk and me not to allow any compromise in our negotiations," he whispered. "That intractability meant that negotiations could go nowhere. The talks broke down."

"And you blame Cromwell? He must have been acting on Henry's orders. You must understand, brother, we cannot sway like the wind. The French must accept Elizabeth. To do otherwise would imperil my position and hers."

"That I understand," he said. "But there was no room for movement, none at all." He sat back. "I think we were set up to fail."

"For what purpose?"

"I do not know, but I think Cromwell has asked the King not to send me to France again," he said. "Cromwell desires alliance with Spain. The Emperor has proved himself the stronger man, and the more dangerous enemy. Cromwell whispers into the King's ear, Anne. Norris and Weston have told me as much. He set us up to fail. He influenced the King to allow no room for negotiation, for he knew that when our talks failed with France the King would have to listen to him about Spain."

A chilly hand drew a finger down my spine. Never had I felt more insecure. I had tried to push Henry towards the Schmalkalden League, but they were nowhere near as powerful as either of these other countries, and however many reformers there were in the world, they did not wield the power that François and Charles did.

"But," I said. "Cromwell must understand that the Emperor will never accept me, and Charles of Spain wailed as loud as any about Fisher's death. He will be no friend to England."

"Not whilst Katherine lives," said my brother with a pointed glance.

"You think Cromwell would kill her?"

My brother said nothing, but I was sure that was what he thought. "I cannot act as ambassador whilst secret impulses are kept from me," he said. "François would not allow me to see him, and he has made it clear that our friendship, such as it was, no longer exists."

"*Curse* François!" I shouted. "And curse Cromwell too if he set you up to fail, brother!"

"Anne, have a care," warned my brother.

"My ladies are loyal, they will say nothing."

"At court, everything has ears," he said, reminding me of Agnes, who had said something similar some time ago.

"I will call him here," I went on, ignoring my brother's concerns. "I will have the truth."

George could not reason with me, and left on other business. When he had gone, I had Cromwell brought to me. "Was my brother sent on a fool's errand?" I asked as Cromwell entered. "Did you send him to France *knowing* the negotiations would fail?"

"Majesty…" Cromwell sounded shocked. "… Why would I do such a thing? It would endanger the very cause we work for."

"That it would," I said, a dangerous note in my voice. "Test me not, Cromwell. For many years I have considered you a friend, but if I find you have turned from me, you will regret it."

A sheen of sweat glimmered on his top lip. "Majesty," he said. "I know not what cause you have to be furious with me."

"What cause indeed?" I asked. "You are one of those, I come to think, who manages to keep a still water upon a raging flow of thought and deed, Master Cromwell. You come to me with eyes as wide as a maiden's, speaking of innocence. And yet I wonder… I wonder if you are my friend."

"If we allowed any slack in our dealings with France, François would pull the rope from our grasp," he said. "Majesty, these demands were made to uphold the status of the Princess and you, as Queen. Your brother is a skilled negotiator. If any had chance of success, it was he."

"Have you told the King not to send George to France again?"

Cromwell bowed his head. "I have, but not for dark designs, Majesty. François is, at present, alienated from reformers. He knows your sympathies and those of your brother, so I do not believe it is in our interests to send Lord Rochford to France for a while."

"And what else is in *our* interests?" I asked, my tone scathing. Was there another reason Cromwell did not want my brother to shine? For a long time Cromwell had been manoeuvring himself into the position of Henry's greatest confidant and companion. George was beloved by Henry. Was it possible Cromwell did not want him so close? Cromwell had become rich in the service of the King, and he liked money. Did he want all favours to go to him, rather than others?

I stared at him. "Test me not, old friend," I said again. "This is not the time to go against me. The King is fast removing those who would deny his power. Think not that I will hesitate to do the same."

Cromwell's watchful eyes seemed hollow in his great head. "I would never think of doing such a thing, Majesty."

"Keep that in mind, then, as you go about your day," I said. "Heads are rolling, Cromwell. Do not seek to join those who would defy their masters."

Chapter Twenty-Seven

Windsor Castle and Reading
July 1535

On the first day of July, Thomas More stood before a jury of his peers in Westminster Hall, accused of treason.

The charges were related to More's violation of the statutes of the King's supremacy. It was called malicious silence, which I am sure brought grim mirth to this man of wit. He was further accused of conspiring with Fisher.

Henry, not wanting to be in London as his old friend was tried, was preparing for a summer progress. This preparation also meant he was already certain More would die. I should have noted the cold, calculated distance he put between his old friend and himself, but I did not.

My brother, father, Thomas Audley, the Chancellor, and Norfolk all sat as More's judges. When a case came to court, it was up to the jury to confirm accusations. Innocence was to be proved by the accused, it was not assumed. If anything, the opposite was true.

Thomas More stuck fast to the old legal defence of *qui tacet consentire videtur, one who keeps silent is said to agree*; he refused to directly answer any questions about the supremacy. As long as he did not deny the supremacy, he thought there was hope.

But there was not.

Richard Rich was the Crown's main witness. Rich described a conversation he had had with More when he and two of Cromwell's men had confiscated More's books. Rich stated that he had put to More that the King was the Head of the Church in England, and More had denied this. "A king can be made by Parliament, and deprived by Parliament," Rich attested More had said. "But as to the primacy, a subject cannot be bound because he cannot give his consent to that of Parliament."

More declared that Rich was lying. "In good faith, Master Rich," he said loudly. "I am more sorry for your perjury than for my peril." He shook his head. "Richard Rich was always reputed light of his tongue," he said. "He is a great dicer and gamester, and not of any commendable fame."

More acquitted himself well, claiming Rich had wilfully misunderstood him, and, wondering aloud why he would impart his opinion to Rich, and Rich alone, when he had not spoken of the supremacy to any other man, not even a friend. "I refer it to your judgements, my lords, whether this can seem credible to any of your lordships," he said.

But for all this, it took less than fifteen minutes for the judges to decide their sentence.

More was condemned to die, sentenced to hanging, drawing and quartering. As he heard the sentence read, he spoke. "Since I am condemned, and God knows how, I will speak freely for the discharge of my conscience what I think of this law."

No one wanted him to, but he had the right to answer. "For the seven long years I have studied the matter, I have not read any approved order of the Church that a temporal lord could, or ought, to be head of the spirituality."

Audley cut in. "*What*?" he shouted, afraid that More's words would get back to Henry. "You wish to be considered wiser, or of better conscience than *all* the bishops and nobles of this realm, who agreed with the King's rights?"

"My lord," More replied in a calm voice. "For one bishop of your opinion, I have one hundred saints for mine. For one Parliament of yours, I have all the General Councils for a thousand years, and for one kingdom I have France and all the kingdoms of Christendom."

"Your malice against His Majesty is now perfectly clear," Norfolk bleated.

"Noble sir," replied More. "Not any malice or obstinacy causes me to say this, but the just necessity of the cause constrains me for the discharge of my conscience and the satisfaction of my soul. I say further that your statute is ill-made, because you have sworn never to do anything against the Church, which through all Christendom is one and undivided. You have no authority, without the common consent of all Christians, to make a law or Act of Parliament, or Council against the honour of Christendom."

More drew himself up. "I know well the reason why you have condemned me is because I have never been willing to consent to the King's second marriage, but I hope in the divine goodness and mercy, that as St Paul and St Stephen are now friends in Paradise, where once they were enemies, so we, though differing in this world, shall be united in perfect harmony in the other."

More glanced about the packed chamber, sticky in the July heat. "I pray to God to protect the King," he said. "And give him good counsel."

Clearly, good counsel was not what More believed Henry had.

As he was led from the room, the axes of Henry's guards turned towards him, showing his fate. His daughter, Margaret, pushed through the crowds to embrace him, falling into her father's arms with a sob.

George's father-in-law, Lord Morely, came begging for More's life. He petitioned Henry to pardon his friend and fellow scholar. He was sent away.

That same day, I had another visit from George. "Cromwell has been throwing his weight around again," he said. "He rebuked Lord Lisle for the forfeiture of some wool by merchants in the Cinque Ports. Lisle was most surprised, for I have jurisdiction there as Lord Warden, and in such matters, Lisle reports to me, not Cromwell."

"So why did Cromwell interfere?"

"Because he wants all suits to the King to go through him," said George. "That can be the only reason. Lisle protested that I would have done the same as him, and he was right. Cromwell was angry that Lisle had not sought his approval, but Lisle did not require Cromwell's authority, only mine."

"This sounds like a squabble amongst boys at a river bank trying to prove whose stick came from under the bridge first."

"Perhaps it does," said my brother. "But it is just another way Cromwell seeks to undermine me and all others. I will not stand for it. Norris says Cromwell frequently tries to send him away, so that only he is with the King. He seeks to isolate the King, move him away from his friends, and ensure that all suits for favours go through him. Soon, the greedy spider will have a leg on every silken strand, with the King in the centre of his web, as his big, fat prize."

After More's trial, with George's warnings about Cromwell in mind, I petitioned Henry to give More's property to my brother. George needed the money, for he was always in debt. It mattered not how many titles and positions my brother held, money slipped through his fingers like sand.

Henry agreed that the bulk of More's wealth would go to George, and Cromwell was unhappy about it.

"It will teach him not to overreach his position," I said to my brother after he had been informed.

"Perhaps," said my brother. "Or perhaps it will push him to further action."

"He has been of use to us for many years," I said. "I do not wish to think that Cromwell has joined the ranks of our foes."

"I do not think he has, yet," said my brother. "But he has grown plump and rich on all the King has granted him, and once a man knows the comfort of a full belly and purse, he does not surrender them lightly."

My brother gazed about at the cases and chests being packed for progress. Henry wanted to leave London the day before More was due to be executed. "You are taking everything in the palace," my brother jested.

"Almost," I agreed.

"You leave on the morrow?"

I nodded. "First to Reading and from there we travel west."

"Cromwell goes with you?"

"He will join us later, if he can tear himself from London."

"Keep an eye on him, Anne," said George. "I thank you for speaking to him last month, but as I understand it, he told Chapuys afterwards that you had threatened him and he was not afraid."

My heart skipped a beat. "Cromwell thinks I may be overlooked?"

"He said the King would protect him against any foe," said my brother. "Even if that enemy be his own wife."

"Did he?" I asked. "Cromwell grows too confident. If this man needs reminding that all he has comes from me, I will nudge his memory."

That night, we sat with Cromwell as he went over some of the reports from the abbeys. Henry was disturbed by them.

"All this will be set right, my lord," I said. "And let us use our time of pleasure for other purposes."

"What do you mean?"

"Let us visit those who support you and the necessity of reform," I said. "We will go to towns that have already shown loyalty, and in showing grace to them, we will encourage more to do likewise." I looked at Cromwell. "And, at the same time," I went on. "We will visit some of the houses listed in these reports. Long have they had no master to oversee them, but this will change."

"I think this a fine notion, my lord," said Cromwell. "If abbots and monks see their King in the flesh it will remind them of their duty to God."

My reasons for sending Henry to monasteries were not quite as I had said. I hoped that if Cromwell's reports were true, Henry visiting their houses might encourage better behaviour, and if the reports were embellished, it might persuade Cromwell's men to have a care, and report only the truth.

"We should also release any who took holy vows before the age of twenty-five," said Cromwell. "Only those with true dedication should serve God. Too often, poor people send unwanted children to the cloisters. This should end."

"I agree, Master Cromwell," I said. In truth I thought sixteen was old enough for people to decide their futures, but I was willing to make concessions to keep the peace.

With the new route of progress agreed, the court was informed and those who had been chosen to play host were sent messages. This did not sail by unnoticed, and it earned me some powerful enemies. They thought that I instigated Henry's reforms in all ways. If only such were true! But everyone could see I influenced Henry. They saw my power.

They feared it, as they feared me.

*

We left Windsor for Reading in early July. The morning was broken by the happy, jumbled song of the birds. The morning light was far off, but I rose and wrapped myself in warm blankets, sitting at the window.

We had been on progress many times before, but this time there was a sense of expectation tangible on the air. Perhaps it was our combined longing to leave behind the stench of death, or to put the sorrows of our lost children behind us. Perhaps in each of our hearts there was a yearning to return to the days when our love had been simpler, cleaner… not weighed down by all the opinions of the world.

Henry came to my chambers at first light. He was eager to leave and wanted to ensure that I had everything I needed for the journey.

"I am well provided for, as always, Your Majesty," I said. On a whim, because he looked so like a boy in his excitement, I kissed his cheek, my hands resting on the glorious purple fabric of his tunic. As my lips touched his skin, warmth surged in my soul. Since I had heard of Ethelreda's birth, I had been cold with Henry, but something broke inside me that morning. Something hard gave way. Sometimes the hardened heart yearns to be broken, longing for the comfort of love to make it ductile once more.

As I rocked back onto my heels, his eyes were soft. Impromptu gestures touched Henry. He stroked my face, then leaned in and kissed me gently. With his touch a jolt of desire hit my blood and my stomach tightened. My hands encircled his neck and pulled him into a deeper kiss.

"Anne," he said as we pulled apart. "There is no one like you."

"That is because there is no one who loves you so well in all the world." I ran my hand down his tunic, to his manhood, pushing my hands into the folds of his clothes. I felt him shudder. "We can still be away from this place early, my lord," I said, my eyes sparkling through my long lashes "But perhaps there is a little time for a man and wife to… break our fast before we ride?"

His eyes clouded with desire and with a grunt and a nod, his servants and mine left the room, grinning widely. As the door closed, he turned, his blue eyes hungry. He walked towards me, items of rich clothing dropping from his body like leaves from an autumn tree. I unlaced the front of my gown as I backed towards the bed. A huge grin lit his face.

"Now, my lady…" he said as I fell backwards onto the bed and he pushed my dress up. "Let us see what you have to offer, for I am a hungry man this morn."

*

Thomas More died on the 6th of July.

Fearful that to execute More at Tyburn would attract more censure, Henry commuted his sentence to beheading, and had him executed on Tower Hill.

It was nine o'clock in the morning when he emerged from his cell to make his way up the ill-built, rickety scaffold. "I pray you, Master Lieutenant," More jested to Edward Walsingham, Lieutenant of the Tower. "See me safe up. As for my coming down, let me shift for myself."

Before the crowds, More spoke of his love for Henry, but also for God. "I go to death as the King's servant," he said. "But God's first." He turned to the executioner. "I am sorry my neck is very short. Strike not awry, for the saving of your honesty," and added, "I pray you, let me lay my beard over the block, lest you should cut it."

The executioner smiled under his black mask, as did many in the crowds. More met Death with a jest on his lips.

With one cut, Sir Thomas More, once Chancellor, philosopher, author, theologian, lawyer, and great friend of the King of England, died. Cromwell was in the front row.

More's head was set on a spike on London Bridge, replacing Fisher's, which was tossed into the Thames. Fisher's body was dug up and he was buried with More in the Chapel of St Peter ad Vincula, in the Tower grounds.

When messengers brought the news to Henry, he paled. For a moment he stood, his hands shaking, as he stared at the report of More's death. As he turned to me, his face became lost in anger.

"*You* have done this!" he shouted, thrusting a shaking finger in my face.

I blinked in amazement. Never once had I asked for his death.

"*You have killed this man, my friend!*" Henry screamed, his eyes brimming with tears. He left, leaving every noble present staring at me.

In their eyes, I saw the same accusation; More and Fisher had died at Henry's order, but everyone believed they had died for failing to accept me as Queen.

It was not so. They had said Henry had the right to choose his wife. They did not die because I wanted it, but because Henry did. They died for the Church, for Rome, and for their faith. They died for the belief that Henry was not, and could never be, the Head of the Church.

It mattered not. I was blamed, and not only by England's people, but by Henry too.

Chapter Twenty-Eight

Reading
July 1535

When Henry's anger abated, he became morose. He did not come to me and I went not to him. I could hardly believe that he blamed me for More's death. When had I demanded it? When had I asked for it?

I had not. But Henry could not accept the blame. He, like everyone else in England, used me. Once again, I was his whipping boy.

In truth, I was disturbed about More's death. Long had I thought he deserved death for murdering innocent men, and yet, the manner in which he had been brought to death, potentially on false witness, troubled me. If More had been executed for burning those men, I might have rested content, but Rich's testimony was suspect, and it disturbed me to think this was the sole reason More had gone to his death.

A story had been told, and on the basis of that had Thomas More died. Stories have power. We tell them all the time. We live in stories. Our world is made by them, crafted from word and brought to meaning by our impressions. It is just as easy to make a world of evil as it is to create one of truth. It just depends on the tale…

I sat in my chambers, thinking of the first time I had seen More, at the jousts to celebrate Henry's coronation. I had been a girl, more interested in worshipping valiant knights than keeping watch on members of the court, but I remembered his bright, merry face. He had told my father that Henry would bring a new era of hope and peace. I doubt he had thought that at his end.

How lightly his story, his life, had touched mine then, and how intricately we had become woven together later. Stories… circles in the sand, never ending… never beginning.

I came to doubt myself. Should I have spoken for my enemy? Protested to Henry that Rich was suspect? Perhaps… but he would not have listened. Henry had wanted More dead, and he had died.

Unlike me, Pope Paul was not of two minds. He wrote to Henry, saying he had *"exceeded his ancestors in wickedness,"* and went on to announce he was compelled to uphold Clement's sentence of excommunication, and declare Henry deprived by papal decree of his kingdom and royal dignity. The Pope reached out to François, who was equally shocked by More's death, to execute justice upon Henry, *"remembering the great armies with which your forefathers revenged her injuries,"* he wrote, trying to stir François into action.

But still the papacy dithered. The Pope clung to the hope that he could convince Henry to return to his arms, and if he deprived him of his realm that would never happen. Rome fiddled as fires kindled, knowing that Henry was still a valuable ally to Charles and François no matter what ills were done in his name.

Cromwell, to everyone's surprise, announced he was *astonished* by the Pope's position. More and Fisher had been tried and found guilty of treason according to the laws of England, he protested.

"Their punishment was much milder than the laws prescribe," he declared. "And many others have, from their example, returned to loyalty. Anyone of sound judgement may see how precipitately the Pope and the Roman court have taken offence at this, but these men opposed England's laws, pretending they were given up to the contemplation of divine things, and endeavoured to refute and evade these laws by fallacious arguments. Let not the Pope be offended if the King acts in accordance with his own right and that of his kingdom."

Strong words, but they convinced few. Only fear swayed Rome's supporters to uphold Henry. Terror of death, dread of dishonour.

More was immediately proclaimed a martyr by Rome. In all honesty, he had died for his faith, so this was true, no matter how ungodly his actions towards his fellow man had been. François and Charles condemned Henry. The Emperor said he "would rather have lost the best city of our domains than have lost such a worthy counsellor." But the two kings did not abandon talks or speak of invasion.

Responding to allegations of injustice, Cromwell had English ambassadors posted in foreign courts extol the reasons for these executions, and told them to inform François and Charles that Fisher and More had spread sedition. He instructed his men to present these ideas whilst upholding Charles, François and Henry as brothers, united against the deceit of the papacy and all traitors. It did not work. Charles and François were horrified by Henry, and had no wish to claim close kinship with him. But abandon their brother-king, they would not. The papacy gnashed its teeth, but knew, without support from Spain and France, nothing would happen.

George was granted More's property, but sold his new house in haste. When he arrived to join us at Reading, he admitted he could not imagine himself walking there with ease, and told me he, too, was disturbed.

"At first," he said. "I thought Fisher and More deserved death. But I wonder now... I wonder if they were not sacrifices made on the altar of the King's pride."

I thought much the same. One day, I came before a portrait Holbein had done of More, and I ran from it. The likeness was so uncanny I felt as though he were watching me, accusing me... his eyes hunted mine and I could not meet them. A part of me felt deep shame and guilt. No matter how much I had disliked him, Thomas More had been wronged. He had worked evil, there was no doubt of that, but responding to evil with evil will never bring about good.

Ill had been done, and I had not stopped it. Was this why God did not bless me with a child?

My brother was anxious to hear Henry was holding me accountable. "You did not command it," he said.

"And yet, to hear Henry, or anyone at court, you would think I ruled England."

"He speaks from fear of repercussions."

"He speaks from *guilt*," I said. "He wants to blame someone else. With Henry there must always be someone else to accuse. He cannot accept he is anything less than perfect." I shrugged, although my light-hearted gesture was far from representative of the foreboding in my heart. "It was the same with Wolsey," I said. "First he accused the Cardinal's enemies of plotting against him. Ultimately, he came to blame Wolsey. The same will be true of More, given time."

Eventually, Henry came to me. I had refused to go to him. Where before, such a public demonstration of hatred might have sent me running to him, like the little pup he wanted me to be, I could not allow it. Condemning me might be easier than accepting accountability, but I could not allow his indictment to stand. I had too many enemies already. I did not need all who had set More on a pedestal to think me the author of his demise.

"I should not have said what I said to you," he said. "I was full of sorrow."

Henry could not meet my eyes. He sat on his chair, a little lost boy, and I felt my heart soften. He was adrift. I saw in him the same maze of dark horrors that lived in me.

"I know that," I said, coming to him. "More was your friend, once, just as Wolsey was."

Henry's arms stretched about my waist, pulling me onto his lap. "Sometimes I think you are my only friend," he murmured. "All others become infected with greed. They pursue their own aims and care not for mine." He gazed into my eyes. "You alone, can I trust."

"And I will never give you reason to doubt me."

I kissed his forehead and stole his cap away to kiss the crown of his head. To my surprise, I found his hair was thin. It was usual for men and women to wear a hat, hood, or cowl, even in bed, so I had not noted this before. Henry was becoming bald. It was a slow but steady march his hair made as it gradually receded, but the fact he had allowed me to witness his vulnerability was deeply touching. Usually he did not like me to see illness, deformity, or signs of aging. But that day he permitted me to steal into a hidden part of his soul.

I made it my mission to distract Henry. Each night I called him to my chambers, and there he found food, drink, women and musicians. I made sure Mary Shelton was always on hand, but, to my unbounded joy, he did not want her. He wanted me.

Perhaps he was right. I was his only friend, the only one who would love him, no matter what he did. The only one he knew he could trust.

That night we reached Reading Abbey and supped with its Abbot, Hugh Farringdon. Housed in a magnificent suite of rooms at the Abbot's house, we passed a merry evening.

As the feast came to a close, I stepped outside. My ladies huddled in the doorway, unhappy to feel the chill of the night.

I looked up. The moon was full, and so bright that the skies were almost as they were in daylight. Clouds in the distance were mountains of shadow, ice and smoke, suspended in the grey-blue skies. Delicate puffs of cloud hung near them, as though a hand had pulled tufts of lambs' wool out and tossed them into the still air.

Only the few, brightest stars could be seen; dots gleaming in the distance, eclipsed in beauty and magnificence by the clouds and the moon.

I stood, captivated, lost to the world even as I marvelled at it.

That night, Henry came to my bed with all the enthusiasm of our younger days. Our reconciliation made him strong and confident. I felt him spill his seed deep inside me and dared to hope that we might once again have a chance to make life, and live happy, as we surely deserved to be.

Chapter Twenty-Nine

Reading
July 1535

My chambers were filled with heat and conversation. Wagging tongues, forgetful of all that had passed of late, spoke of nothing but gaiety. Silk whispered on wood and ladies giggled in dark corners as gallants professed love. Musicians played bright tunes of happiness and merriment, and the sultry air, redolent with fresh scents of the countryside, spilled over us.

Had you come to dance with us that night, knowing nothing of the blood spilt at Tyburn and the Tower, you might have thought it the merriest place in the world. And to see Henry, ringed by a multitude of pretty maidens, his face flushed with wine, you would have thought he had not a care in the world.

Perhaps he did not, for Henry's sins rested on me. The blame I had refused to accept had accepted me. It was there in everyone's eyes. Hidden under the film of wine and good company it remained, lurking. Henry had apologised in private, but his public allegation remained. And it was not this alone that troubled me. Katherine was alone no more. More and Fisher had joined her. Finding Henry unwilling to see them, so deep was he buried in this fantasy of happiness I had created, they turned to me.

These shades did not speak. Like the eyes that accused me, they were silent. But they were there. Always there, watching me.

I sipped from my goblet, trying to ignore the phantoms at my back. How many ghosts would I gather? How many shades would walk in procession about me? And why follow me?

But I knew the answer. They followed me because I felt remorse. They ignored Henry for there was no reaching him.

I stood with Margaret Douglas, and saw her eyes linger on my uncle, Thomas Howard. The much younger brother of Norfolk, Thomas was Agnes' son, and a fine young gallant. He was a talented poet, with a passion for puns, and was a strikingly handsome man. Many women had an eye for him, and it seemed my niece was one of them.

"You like him, do you not?" I asked quietly, staring at Thomas as I spoke.

Margaret started. Her cheeks flushed and her eyes went wide. "Before you attempt to deny it, and make those cheeks a brighter shade," I said. "You should learn to conceal your emotions better." There was a jesting note in my voice and the girl sagged with relief.

"I think him a fine man, Majesty," she said cautiously. "A credit to your noble house."

"Oh… I think it more than that," I said, sipping more wine. "I have read those poems in the book that Mary Shelton keeps. If only a part of what you and Thomas express is true, you are both very much in love."

Her eyes stole nervously to Henry. I understood why. The *actual* Duke of Norfolk would be one thing, his younger brother, however, was quite another. But there were ways and means to all things with Henry. He might not think well of a match between Margaret and Thomas at first, but if I cut through to his sentimental streak, there was hope.

Love was in short supply in this world, and even when it did come, it did not arrive without unwelcome guests sent to try it. If I could help one love prevail, perhaps I would win some victory.

"Answer me true and without fear, for I will keep your secret," I said. "Do you want to marry him?"

She nodded. "But my uncle is sure to disapprove."

I smiled. "Leave it to me and I will ensure you have your choice of groom."

Margaret's smile was like the dusk's sun; brilliant yet waning. She feared to lose love. As I bathed in its light, my eyes were drawn to my sister-in-law. Jane was back at court, but seemed none too happy about it. She had been cool and detached when I greeted her at Reading, and when, later, I had tried to explain why I had not petitioned Henry for her, she was dismissive.

"I was to blame, Majesty," she had said. "I should not have taken matters into my own hands."

From her tone, I surmised she did *not* consider herself to blame at all. I had not sent her to pick a fight with Mary Perrot, but Jane seemed to think I had. She blamed me for her months away from George, and perhaps thought I had riled her into attacking Henry's mistress.

But that, like so many other fantasies, was in Jane's febrile imagination.

*

I could distract Henry from his woes in the country, but everyone in London wanted him to remember them. There was discord. Henry was being named a tyrant, albeit quietly, since to speak such words aloud was tantamount to a death sentence.

A week after More's death, Bishop Stokesley preached in London on Henry's behalf, surprising everyone, since Stokesley had been More's greatest ally. The Bishop was not talented at public speaking and was given to stammering and stumbling over his words. At St Paul's he went before the crowds and spoke about Henry's union with Katherine, calling it ungodly and perverse. Cromwell was at his elbow.

But as one man spoke for us, others decried. A woman named Margaret Chancellor had been arrested in May. Drunk when she was hauled into prison, she had declared I was a "naughty, goggle-eyed whore" and Katherine was the true Queen. When interrogated, she swore she had only said such because she was intoxicated, and remembered not her words. She was whipped, and released. But there were others.

Reports flooded in to Cromwell and Richard Rich of people who had spoken against Henry, me, and the supremacy. Many thought England was seeping into a deathly pit of sin. And as is common, in all times when suspicion reigns, false reports arrived. It did not take much for a man to be arrested in those days, and when he was, it was his word against that of another. Some people disliked and feared the changes in religion, but there were those who accused men on flimsy evidence, for revenge.

The malicious, the drunk, the mistaken, the outspoken, the forgetful... none were spared. It was treason to speak against royalty, and no one would be forgiven for having a feeble memory, or outwardly defying Henry.

Henry Percy was heard speaking against me. He echoed the accusation of my uncle and called me an infamous whore, earning him a spell away from court, accompanied by threats against his life. In France, François started to inform people I was a harridan. He told people "how little virtuously she has always lived," and started to speak of gossip that I had joined a plot, dreamed up by Norfolk, to place Mary Howard on the throne at Fitzroy's side.

Not that I would have put such a ridiculous scheme past my uncle, but I knew of no such conspiracy. Why would I seek to set my cousin on the throne when my daughter was England's heir? And what did François have to accuse me of in terms of my reputation? I had taken no lovers in France, and had refused *him* often enough. It was also intensely hypocritical, for he was one of the most promiscuous men alive. Was it possible he was jealous, even through the distance of years, miles, and sea? I suspected not. François had enough willing women to satisfy any carnal desire that came sweeping across his over-active loins. He was simply trying to discredit me, and he knew the best way was to call me a whore.

Or... had he thought back to the night he had been my saviour, and decided I, like all women in the world, *must* be to blame for a monster attacking me?

Henry reacted boldly. Orders went out to remove the Pope's name from prayer books and priests were to cease to lead prayers for him. Preachers marched forth to ensure that Henry's subjects knew the truth. The King's titles were reaffirmed at every Mass. Prayers were said for me, for Elizabeth and for Henry. Katherine and Mary were to be forgotten. Cromwell's spies were everywhere.

Everyone who would not bow would be punished. Anyone who spoke out would be silenced. Everyone had to prove their loyalty. Everyone had to choose their side.

Chapter Thirty

Ewelme, Abingdon and Sudeley Castle
July 1535

We left Reading for Ewelme, one of the houses of the Duke of Suffolk, and the skies were rich with the scent of cut hay. Warm and sweet, it flew on the wind like a flock of birds. Scythes swept in hayfields and the earth came alive with ancient songs as churls chanted to keep time. In the hands of experienced men, the scythe became an extension of their arm; sweeping effortlessly out at ankle height, slicing through the hay with a hiss as golden stalks fell. Hedgers' sickles, too, flashed in the afternoon sun, their bright, well-crafted blades glinting as men laid hedges to keep cattle and sheep safe.

Young grey partridges had grown strong on their infant wings, and bees bustled in fields of purple clover, flying home to their hives, ready for men to plunder their sticky, amber riches. Some errant bees took on human habitations long-since abandoned, making homes in empty rooms where generations of ghosts dwelled. Farmers collected honey to use for food, although some was always put aside for mead and megethlin.

In the woods, sow badgers were weaning cubs, teaching them to gather grubs from the thick leaf mould. The call of the blackbird sounded in the hush of dawn, and robins sang to the trees. Jackdaws hopped about the waysides, their bright, beady eyes searching for grubs and beetles. May bugs winged into the air, making an unsettlingly loud buzzing noise, as they flew on delicate wings, with their downy antlers testing the skies for trouble. In oak forests, purple butterflies floated in the dim light like petals. Maids hung fresh washing on hawthorn hedges, infusing the already sweet air with the scent of soapwort. Honeysuckle brightened the gloomy shade and fleet-footed deer stepped delicately through bracken and bramble, ready to fly at any moment.

At Ewelme Suffolk greeted us. His new wife, Katherine Willoughby, was seven months with child and took that excuse to fail to attend many of the feasts given in our honour. I knew her pregnancy was not the reason. Katherine Willoughby was the daughter of Marie de Salinas, one of the Dowager's greatest friends. Like her mother, she supported the former queen, not me. When I did see her, the sight of her belly made me sad and anxious. I needed her state, yet I feared it. The twin sides of my soul were in conflict as I gazed upon her belly. I was glad she did not come into our presence more than she did. It was agony to look upon her.

One morning, I stood beside my horse, doing nothing more than breathing in the air and feeling the sun radiating upon my riding hat. A plume of white feathers crowned my cap, and I could see them, dipping and bending in the wind. My horse nuzzled my hand, his nose as velvet in my palm. I felt at peace, as though nothing more could come to harm me. I knew it was only temporary, a state of calm brought on by the peace of the countryside, by separation from the city, but I relished it. For as long as it would stay with me, I wanted to retain it.

"Are you ready, sweetheart?" Henry asked, breaking the spell upon me by speaking close to my ear.

"I am," I said. In that moment, truth be told, I felt I could face anything.

*

As we pushed on with progress, Cromwell was moving too. More's death spurred Cromwell on, as did the wealth of mounting dissent. He understood he had to prove himself.

I was wary, not only for his late, rather suspect, actions against my brother, but for other reasons too. I did not want reform to descend into anarchy where the innocent would be persecuted along with the guilty.

What need had anyone to create falsehoods when there were sins, many and varied, already present in the Church? Pardons, indulgences, payments and debts collected by the Church for services, over-indulgence of food, wine and *any* indulgence with women… Greed, corruption and wanton living, the worship of idols over God and the tyranny of Rome… all of this was what we should be fighting, not phantoms born from the mischief of story-tellers who embellish tales to make everything delightfully scandalous. I believed this was a danger of the path we had taken. In order to persuade his master that the Church was rotten to the core, Cromwell might create stories to shock Henry.

Perhaps the sins of the clergy had become so *normalized*, so commonplace, in English minds that Cromwell sought other means to alarm his King. Perhaps he was simply trying to keep his head upon its broad shoulders. Or perhaps, as my mind whispered, telling me not to be so generous, perhaps my brother was right and Cromwell wanted money, prestige and power. If he could get Henry to move against the monasteries, he could have all he wanted.

But I had kept faith with Cromwell for many years and I hoped something of goodness was left in him. I had been cool with him since our argument, but I was optimistic this state was temporary. He was a wise man, unlike Wolsey, and would not dare to take me on as an enemy. My position was fragile, it was true, but Henry and I were closer that summer than we had been for many months, and everyone could see it. When I was in favour, there was no man who could rival me in Henry's affections. Even when we fought, he still listened to my counsel. No… Cromwell was no fool. He would not dare oppose me.

And my faith in Henry blossomed anew as did my love. Henry was serious about his role as Head of the Church. It was no mere title to him, and no matter what anyone said, was not just a convenient excuse to be rid of Katherine. Henry *believed*. He *was* the chosen of God, and it was his place to set everything right. That was why I believed I could reach him about the monasteries. If the right part of him could be convinced at the right time, dissolved monasteries would be put to educational use, and many might be saved to be reformed.

But although Henry wanted everyone to understand and support him, he would not allow the oath to be demanded from Katherine and Mary. The blood spilled at Tyburn and the Tower had caused enough problems. To demand they swear would be to place a kindled stick to a line of gunpowder. For now, they were left alone.

At the end of July, as we reached Sudeley Castle, Cromwell arrived to catch up on affairs of state. It was rare to see Cromwell out of London. As much as the waters of the Thames, he was part of the city. On rare occasions he had come to Windsor or Hampton Court, but more often than not he was in London. He did not even summer at his country estates. London had been his home as a boy, so perhaps he felt an attachment to it when he returned as a man. But it was also the crucible of thought, commerce and activity, and if any man was born for work and toil, for noise and trade, it was Cromwell.

He greeted me with great affection, which pleased me. I thought perhaps we had left our troubles behind. I wanted him as an ally, so if my warnings had been understood, I would be satisfied.

Henry, too, was happy to see him, but instructed him to keep this, our first meeting for some time, short, as he wanted to get into the park before the morning was spent. Luckily enough, and with his usual gift for reading his prince, Cromwell had brought with him very little of what I am sure was a mountain of work accumulating on Henry's behalf, and suggested that we talk first on the pleasures of our progress, and second on the monasteries.

"It must be agreeable that you keep more private company here than on other stops on this progress," Cromwell said to us. "The peace afforded by the lack of suitable quarters must be welcome, Your Majesty."

I smiled. Sudeley Castle had been neglected for a while, much to our benefit. Once the state rooms had been improved upon by the usurper, Richard III, before the castle had passed to Jasper Tudor after Bosworth, but the castle had not been well cared for in subsequent years. The royal chambers were opulent and comfortable, but some of the castle was uninhabitable, which had led to the rest of the court seeking rooms a mile away at Winchecombe Abbey. Henry had been somewhat distressed to see the state of the neglected parts of the castle, seeing as fortifications pressed heavily on his mind, but the reduction of our households, riding parties, and hangers-on, had afforded greater privacy.

After we had passed time talking of Reading, I turned to Cromwell. "Let us speak of your investigations," I said. "I have told His Majesty that I earnestly hope some of the smaller houses might be saved or reformed as educational establishments, for without the corrupting influence of Rome, there is hope that corrupt men may find the Lord of Heaven through His Majesty."

Henry smiled warmly and squeezed my hand.

In Henry there was great potential for goodness. He possessed a simplicity which called to the better natures of men, something that if allowed to mature, would, I was sure, make him as wise as any of the Old Testament fathers. There were other sides to Henry; malice, spite, pride and suspicion… but there was, too, much good in him. No man is perfect, but most possess something of good. *In time,* I thought, *he will become a father to his people and a true leader in the army of Christ.*

I believed in him. Is love blind? I have often wondered. But I think not. I saw Henry's faults as well as his virtues. Had the best of his character prevailed, much would have been different.

"The investigations go on apace," Cromwell said. "My men have uncovered a great deal."

Henry was scandalised to read Cromwell's reports. His face turned grey as he learned of sordid entertainments and boundless gluttony.

"Let us send men," I said. "I will send mine with Cromwell's, as we discussed. When they see our servants, my lord, they will seek better ways."

It was agreed, but as we went to leave Cromwell that night, I saw him watching me. He knew what I was up to. He did not want my men going with his. He feared what they might uncover.

Chapter Thirty-One

Sudeley Castle
July 1535

Those first few weeks of progress, as we moved from the outer rim of the capital, out and into the glorious country of the west of England, were as happy as I could ever remember. Freed from constant strain, Henry and I were close, and tender.

Release from the shackles of the capital granted our marriage new life. We ignored our problems and our sorrows and laughed, talking of trifles. Our time was taken up by hunting, hawking and feasting under soft-shaded trees. We spoke of Elizabeth, and considered several new country seats for her and her household. It may all sound trivial, but those few months of peace, where I was loved again, meant everything to me.

Each night we feasted on the finest foods, wines, meats and breads that each house had to offer, and every morning we rose fresh and eager to ride out into the clean summer air. There is nothing like a break from all that has weighted heavily on a person to refresh and relax the mind and body.

Some mornings, when we did not rush away with the dawn to hunt, Henry and I would lie in bed, snoozing, jumbled together so you could not tell where he ended and I began. We took pleasure in each other as we had not done in a long time.

"Although it is much a part of you," I said one morning in bed. "I like you more without your crown."

"Treason!" he shouted and kissed me heartily. "There is no one like you, my Anne. Even if I were lost to all but you, I would still have everything I needed. As long as you are mine, all others can leave."

"I love you, Henry," I said and my eyes filled with tears. I did not speak of all we had tried so hard to ignore, but that did not mean I did not remember.

"Cry not," he said, catching my tears with a gentle finger. "God has seen fit to test us, and we will endure. We have come through Hell. In time, I will hold the proof of God's approval in my arms, and we will make this country the greatest any have ever known."

I nuzzled against his hairy chest and kissed it. "You are right," I said. "God rewards the faithful. We must be patient."

Henry slid a hand between my legs. His clever fingers gently rubbed back and forth. "Of course I am right," he said. I moved my legs apart and felt him enter me, slowly but deftly, as his hands cupped my naked breasts. "I am the King," he panted in my ear. "I am always right."

*

"Where is it?" I demanded of my ladies. "I thought you had taken care to ensure all my gowns were packed?"

My ladies were distraught they had missed this gown. It was a work of glory; purple silk and golden cloth. I did not look well in it, but that mattered not. Henry had asked me to match his costume at a feast that was to be held to mark the end of our stay at Sudeley.

It had pleased me he had asked this, for I had seen his wandering eye light on a new lady in my train. Jane Seymour, my pallid cousin, appeared to be the present delight of my husband's lusts. Quite *why*, no one could understand, for she was not only pale of appearance, but colourless of character. Since joining my household, Jane had been meek, and so mild compared to my ladies of spice and excitement that she all but went unnoticed.

Aside, that was, to Henry.

Perhaps it was her humble nature and quiet ways that attracted him. Henry was a man of diverse passions. He usually sought out women of fire and spirit, but now he seemed to want more tepid company. He was tiring of Mary Shelton, and looked for something else, something new. Jane was about as far removed as you could get from women like Mary and me.

But we had been close on this progress, so I refrained from accosting him about his wandering eye. It pained me that he would always seek other women, but what threat was little Jane Seymour? I knew that she admired Katherine, but she had done well from me. Her brother, Edward, was rising in Henry's estimations, and their family would do well at court, although I doubted they would ever reach the upper echelons … Not with the disgrace of their father's scandalous affair with Edward's wife never forgotten. In some ways, I thought I was coming to accept that Henry would always keep a mistress. He had been discreet with Mary, and since the parrot had flown there had been no trouble. What choice did I have but to accept? There was nowhere I could go. Nothing I could do.

No, I thought, looking on Jane as she smiled shyly in conversation with Cromwell. *There is nothing to fear from such a simple flower.*

And Henry had been attentive. As we rode into town and village, dined with our allies and drank as deep of their support as their wine, he saw me in a new light. Finally he understood I did have supporters. He saw that all I had told him was true and vindicated; there *were* many people in England who wanted reform. And as we rode west, and more and more people came out to cheer for us, he understood he was not alone, as once he had thought.

One day soon, I thought. *Henry's people will accept me.*

It was important to show a united front, and this gown was but one of those ways. "We cannot do anything about it having been forgotten," I said. "Lady Rochford, you will make for Greenwich, find the gown and return. You should be able to get there and back in a few days, which will leave us time to make any adjustments to the dress, if required."

"As you wish, Majesty." My sister-in-law looked unhappy about her mission, but what was I to do about that? Should I fetch the dress myself?

"I will let you choose one of my old gowns from my collection when you return," I said kindly. "As a mark of gratitude."

Jane's mouth smiled, but neither her eyes nor, I suspected, her heart, joined in. She left that morning, bound for Greenwich.

Within days, we heard a strange report; my brother's wife had been sent to the Tower.

And there, I thought as I heard what had happened, *she can stay and rot.*

Finally, and who could understand why, Jane had shown her colours. In a staggering turn of her fine coat, Jane was found amongst a group of ladies demonstrating in favour of the Lady Mary at Greenwich.

Father was black with anger when he stormed to my apartments with Mother scurrying behind. "What in all the *seven Hells* was she thinking?" he raged as he strode about. I had sent away my servants. This was not a time for more gossip to breed against us.

"Does Jane often think?" I asked. "If she is no friend to us, we are no friend to her. My brother's wife has been arrested with the other ringleaders. Perhaps she relies on her connection with us to be released, but she will be disappointed. If she supports my enemies, I will be hers."

"If she does get released I will get George to batter her skull like an apple," my father hissed through gritted teeth. "Better yet, I may do it myself."

"Peace, Father," I said wearily. "And speak no more of beating her. There are other punishments. I will not ask the King to pardon her. She must face the Tower alone."

My father chuckled. "I will ask the warden to remove her money and give her a poor cell. I will not protect a daughter who seeks to support that bastard."

I nodded. "Do as you will. I do not care. She is no sister of mine."

My mother looked at me sharply. "What?" I said. "Should I spend all my time worrying on traitors and deserters? Mary, Jane…who next? Tell me not to be soft-hearted to those who would disgrace me and support our enemies."

"I would never do so, Your Majesty," she said softly.

"Then cease to throw looks at me that suggest otherwise," I said, rising. "Tell those guards they can do with Lady Rochester as they feel fit," I said to my father. "I am weary of trying to reach people with reason, but perhaps they will hear us when they are left all alone."

My father nodded. His face was grim, but a long, dark smile bearing no mirth moved along his mouth and cheeks.

I left the room, and did not, could not, look my mother in the face.

*

Despite what I had said, I petitioned for Jane's release after a few days. Henry was not happy. "Why should she not stay where she is?" he asked.

"Her imprisonment brings scandal upon us," I explained. "We need no more of that."

Henry agreed to release her, and her imprisonment was wiped from the documents of the Tower upon my request. I sent a letter, telling Jane to remain in London and I would deal with her upon my return.

George was mortified. He refused to see her and swore he would find a way to finally part with her. Our aunt, Katherine Boughton, Lady William Howard, was also incarcerated in the Tower for taking part in the demonstration.

But it was not only my sister-in-law who found herself in trouble that summer. In a poorly thought-out jest, Will Somers, Henry's fool, was plunged into disgrace after declaring I was a ribald and Elizabeth a bastard. It had been meant as a reflective jest on times and events, but Henry was in no humour to hear it. Threatened with death, Somers was screamed from court and took refuge with Carewe.

Henry became increasingly angry at his daughter Mary, thinking she had had something to do with the protest. He said if she did not take care she too would see the inside of a cell. But this demonstration was a symptom of a rising sickness. Dissent was rife. Whispers of rebellion came thick and fast, growing on the edge of our vision like a crawling winter mist.

Henry sought distraction. In an effort to appease the court's conservative faction, he kept company with Carewe, Neville, Browne and Russell, all arch-traditionalists.

Henry also paid court to his ladies. In anger at me over Jane, he turned to them. About my forty-four-year-old husband flocked a veritable spring garden of pretty flowers, but whilst he was entertained by Mary Shelton, I saw his eyes turn more and more to Jane Seymour.

What does he see in her? I wondered. Perhaps he was seeking a blank slate; someone so unlike me. But I was affronted. Turning to such a colourless cloud of a woman in my place was surely an insult.

As we reached a point where we were hardly speaking, Tom came to me. He had a new poem, he said, one he thought I would like. When I read it, I could not help but laugh. Tom had a canny quill. I read it aloud to my women.

> *"In this also see you be not idle:*
> *Thy niece, thy cousin, thy sister, or thy daughter,*
> *If she be fair, if handsome be her middle,*
> *If thy better hath her love besought her,*
> *Advance this cause and he shall help thy need.*
> *It is but love. Turn it to a laughter.*
> *But ware, I say, so gold thee help and speed,*
> *That in this case thou be not so unwise*
> *As Pandar was in such a like deed;*
> *For he, the fool, of conscience was so nice,*
> *That he no gain would have for his pain."*

The poem was a rebuke to women who had thrown themselves at Henry, or been tripped into his bed by their families.

Mary Shelton was bright red as I finished reading, but I put my hand on her shoulder to show everyone I did not consider her one of these women. We laughed about the poem, but in truth, was I not one of those Tom censured? I would not deny my sins. I had sent Mary into my husband's bed. *But*, I reasoned, *others, who undertake such sins freely from greed have more reason to hang their heads than my sweet cousin or me.*

Chapter Thirty-Two

Tewkesbury and Painswick Manor
Late July 1535

"Here my grandsire won his crown back," Henry said, gazing upon the fields of Tewkesbury.

I smiled to see the fierce pride in my husband's eyes. We had spent four days at Tewkesbury Abbey, in the company and care of the gracious Abbot, John Wakeman. Despite, or perhaps because, the Abbey was due to come under investigation soon, we had been well cared for. The Abbot had spared no expense, and Henry had praised Wakeman's Master of Spices for the delicate touch he showed with the dishes presented each night at dinner. Riding out to look upon the alleged field of battle where his grandfather had triumphed, Henry wore a wistful expression. He longed to be remembered for martial prowess, just as his Yorkist grandfather was.

"Men will remember you, my love, not only as a king of warfare in battle, but as a soldier of God," I said. "Your fame in military matters is already well-known and admired, but your battle to restore and purify the Church will be remembered with as much acclaim."

Henry smiled. His hand stole to mine and would not let go. Like a puff of winter mist, Jane was forgotten. We were close once more.

To further please Henry, and as a mark of friendship, I appointed Cromwell my High Steward with an income of twenty pounds a year. Although this sum was nothing to him, given his mighty array of titles and positions, I hoped this appointment would bring us back into harmony for good. Cromwell was richer than he had ever been, and not only in grants and appointments. Petitioners who waited for days at his Rolls House all carried gifts, and whether or not they got to see Cromwell, those presents went to him. Money, meat, fish, drink, potted pears and exotic fruits, along with cloth, coin, land and estates all flowed into his hands.

I had brought the mighty Cardinal down, only to replace him with a layman.

Cromwell seemed pleased at the appointment and Henry with him. Henry liked it when we loved the same people.

Cromwell came to me a few days after this was announced, finding me inspecting my bows before the hunt. "I wonder, Majesty, if you would consider lending your house at Havering to Chancellor Audley?"

"What need has he of it?"

"Plague has broken out in London, and he fears contamination. I am afraid the same sickness has been sighted in Bristol, and may impair the King's plans to visit the city."

I waved a hand. "Tell Audley he may use my house," I said, then frowned. "Why did the Chancellor not ask me directly?"

"He did not want to trouble you, madam, with more petitions than you have already. He knows you are seeking rest, although with all we are achieving, that seems a distant goal."

I smiled. This progress was indeed as much about politics as pleasure. We had visited many supporters, and were soon to see some of the religious houses under investigation.

Later that week, Cromwell sent a book of physic to my rooms, with a note to say he thought I might find it interesting. It was about fertility and conception. The message was discreet, and the gift thoughtful, therefore I was pleased. As I thought about his petition for Audley, however, I came to realise how deep and ingrained Cromwell's influence had become. All petitions were now going through him. Anything men wanted from Henry, or from me, headed first for Cromwell's ears, and only then to ours. In a short space of time, Cromwell had made himself indispensable. The thought made me wary.

That year Henry acquired new houses. His passion for property was rooted deep in his soul. There could never be enough houses, palaces and castles to satisfy my husband. Chobham Park in Surrey was purchased from Chertsey Abbey, and immediately extended. Manor houses at Hackney and Humberside were bought, some with coin and one by exchange with Percy. But Henry did not forget his old holdings. At Hampton Court, Wolsey's dining hall was converted into the great watching chamber, and at Greenwich Henry's privy chamber was transformed into a wealth of tapestry, sculptured decorations and every floor soft with carpet.

Henry was spending more than ever, and when I looked at the lists of work, tools, goods and ornamentation purchased, I wondered how he was able to afford this. I had been told all money was urgently required to fortify England.

It seemed Henry was confident that soon enough more money would be his than he had ever dreamed.

*

We rode on to Gloucester, and made a ceremonial entrance to the city. Welcomed by the Mayor and local dignitaries, we passed three days at the Abbey, surrounded by cool walkways, gracious gardens and heavenly ponds. We took time to visit the shrine of Edward II. I spent time in the Lady Chapel, a place known to pilgrims as a place where women might go to ask for intercession for fertility. I went to the altar each day we were there, to bow my head and ask for aid. Henry spent his time hunting at Coberley and Miserdon, but each night returned to ask of my prayers.

In the third week of July, we arrived at Winchcombe in Gloucestershire. Here was the seat of Hailes Abbey, a famous pilgrim centre. Whilst Cromwell was with us one night, we talked of the Abbey, upon which a cloud of superstition and suspicion had fallen. The Abbey had a relic, a vial of blood, which the monks claimed was the Holy Blood of Christ. It had brought them great wealth and influence.

"And think you this relic is false?" Henry asked Cromwell.

Cromwell smiled. "Your Majesty, should this prove to indeed be the Holy Blood of Our Lord Jesus, it should be a miraculous wonder, but..."

"But what, Cromwell?" I asked, running my finger about the rim of my silver goblet. The crowned falcon on the cup seemed to wink in the guttering light.

The shadows and flames of candles danced around the room and lit briefly on Cromwell's face. For a moment, he was revealed as a creature of both shadow and light. We are all such beings. The darkness within is matched, twinned with the light. It is rare to see both at the same time, however, for within us, one element reigns usually stronger than the other.

"During my time on the Continent," he said carefully, "and especially during my service as a soldier in the wars in Italy, I saw no fewer than *fifteen* such relics, each claiming to be the blood of our Lord." He sighed with unfeigned weariness, his eyes steady on Henry's. "At the same time, Majesty, I counted twelve fingers the clergy claimed to be from the hands of St Peter, and two heads, both apparently belonging to Saint Catherine. I am sorry to say this, Majesty, but for every real and holy relic there are a dozen fakes set up by men to make money from the faith of others. And even if all these relics were real, would God not be more pleased to find us worshipping His Word and truth, rather than idols?"

I nodded. "This surely bears investigation, my lord," I said. "It makes a mockery of faith if men worship the bones and blood of common people, more likely than not pilfered from consecrated ground."

Henry looked away, staring into the golden flames. "Investigate this claim," he said. "I will not have my people duped. If it be a holy relic, it may stay and do glory to our kingdom. If false, we will suffer no more of our people to be fooled."

"I will send my men with yours," I said to Cromwell.

Cromwell agreed, and Henry was excited that I would take so vested an interest, but I sent my men for another reason. I wanted my chaplains to keep an eye on Cromwell and his men.

Soon, it was found that the blood was indeed false; a strange, gummy substance crafted from the blood of a duck and melted wax, made fresh by the monks each week to run red and slick. I went to Henry and the false relic was taken from display. It was not a permanent removal. The monks were granted time to protest their case and produce the true relic, which they claimed they had hidden somewhere safe. They said they had displayed the false idol because of fear of what might happen to the real one.

"They say that they grew afeared about the rise of iconoclasm, madam," said John Skip, one of my men. "And hid the relic to save it from harm."

"But they could not produce it?"

"They said only two men knew where it was hidden," he said and frowned. "The monks were unwilling to bring it out whilst Cromwell's men were there. They feared that surrendering the vial would lead to its destruction."

"You will take a personal interest in this, Skip," I commanded. "Keep in contact with the Abbey. I want to hear when they have found the true relic, if it exists, but you will also tell them that if it is proved true, I will protect their Abbey." I paused. "And say nothing to Cromwell or his agents."

"I will do all you command, Majesty."

I liked Skip. He had a plain face but a worthy heart. He was passionate and devoted to his God, but was wise to the ways of man, too. I knew I could trust him. He had found nothing untoward about Cromwell's men, but also said he thought they had restrained themselves in his presence.

Henry was pleased to discover that the false idol was proved so. "This will be the start of a great wave of change," he declared.

"As I have yearned for," I replied.

But when account books and inventories of the religious house were delivered, his eyes lit up, not with the zeal of faith, but with the contemplation of coin. I murmured to him, as I looked at the figures over his shoulder, that I would be pleased to see such wealth redistributed to make good religious houses greater, create university places, and help the poor.

Henry liked my plans, but added ones of his own. "I will see to the betterment of my country," he said, "in many ways. More defences, greater castles, more ships... in this way will we maintain peace."

I heard his plans with a weighted heart. Would he ever understand? Of course one of the duties of a king is to keep his people safe, but what of the safety of the present, by aiding poor people, or ensuring the future, by educating scholars?

Henry did not look to the future, unless to look for a son, and even that aim, I was coming to think, was less about securing England and more about building his legacy. Henry felt the eye of history upon him, and wanted to prove that he, and no other, was the greatest King England had ever known.

*

By late July we were at Painswick Manor, a place perfectly situated for excellent hunting. A vast forest stretched from the Manor, out and over the countryside; a blanket of green leaves and murmuring branches coruscating under the light of the moon. It shimmered, beckoning, pleading for us to come. We took to our beds early, so we might hunt from first light to last the next day.

Cromwell was on another kind of hunt. As we made ready to pursue beasts of the forest at Painswick, he and his men were at Bath Abbey, investigating their possible sins and definite assets.

Grey dawn welcomed my eyes as I awoke. Slipping into my clothes, with some of my ladies helping me and others seeing to my bow and arrows, I felt at peace. There was something about the stillness of the morn that brought this to my soul; something about the quiet, the hush, the growing light and lingering dark. Cobalt blue stretched in the dark skies, flanking and swirling about patches of black and shimmering pearl-grey. Birds were starting to sing, hesitantly, but true. Everything was muted, still and tranquil.

Dripping trees, bowed with morning dew, whispered as we rode into their domain. Hooves crunched on bracken and briar. There was a slight noise of leaves and twigs unfurling from their night's rest; a crackling noise, light and delicate on the fragile breeze, the sound of the world awakening.

We met the rest of the hunters in a glade. Shining emerald leaves swayed in the wind, and delicate blooms fluttered at the fringes of the clearing. Breaking our fast on hunks of crusty bread, fresh, soft cheese and salted meat, we inspected deer *fumays* and talked over plans for the hunt. Local foresters were brought in to show us the trails harts took through the trees, and local children, who were not supposed to be there, huddled at the edge of the woods, their eyes wide and sparkling to see so many nobles suddenly appear like fairies upon their lands.

"Here, Thomas," Henry said, turning to his new page who was, as ever, hovering at his elbow. "You will carry the royal horn this day."

Thomas Culpepper took the ceremonial horn in his hands, an expression of awe upon his handsome young face. Whilst not of great use in the hunt, being too clumsy for practical use, Henry's horn was magnificent. Reportedly made of unicorn horn, it was carved, depicting *fleurs-de-lys*, lions and rings of gold. The horns Henry's huntsmen used were vugles and ruets; French-style horns made of metal and ivory. They sounded calls, combinations of long and short notes, which all hunters knew, telling the riding parties and packs of hounds where to go, how far ahead they were, and when to stop, or rush forwards to take the kill.

Granting his ceremonial horn to Culpepper was a great sign of favour, and the young man did not miss this. He had recently been rewarded with a new tunic of satin as well, and Henry was fond of this young man. Culpepper had come from the household of Viscount Lisle, and his elder brother, also named Thomas, was in Cromwell's service. It may seem confusing that two brothers would bear the same Christian name, but with infant death so common, some parents who wanted to keep a name alive in a family, chose to hedge their bets, and name two sons with the same name. The Culpepers had advanced at first through their connection to my family, as they were related to me through the Howards. Joyce Culpepper had married my uncle Edmund Howard, and had been the mother of the bedraggled children I had visited so long ago at their house.

Culpepper was a beautiful young man, there was no other way to put it. His skin was fresh as new grass, and his body as graceful as the wind. He took the horn reverently in his hands and tied the cord about his neck and shoulder. "Thank you, sire," he said to Henry. As he looked to the other pages, I saw his eyes light up with glee that he had been honoured, and they had not.

Henry turned to his men and began eagerly discussing the hunt, the harts, and the route we would take. As I listened to Henry talk to his huntsmen in animated joy, I gazed over the dark earth. The air became still, breathless as fear. Puddles shone; long, dark mirrors laced along the black earth. On the pools' surfaces, I saw the clouds, racing each other in the heavens. Birds were shots of rapid blackness, darting into and out of view on the water. Like my eyes, the pools were black and deep, wide and long. They stared up, as though something had taken them by surprise, and had become frozen, with nothing to do but look to God, and ask how such a fate had befallen them.

Henry's men had gone into the woods two days before our arrival, seeking the best quarry. A hart of ten years was most desired, and the finest specimen amongst those available was even more sought after. Younger stags were known as *rascals*, and were not pursued, for the honour was not as great to take a young, inexperienced hart, rather than a grand master in his prime.

The time of *tempus pinguedinis* was upon us, the *time of grease*, where rich summer had made deer fat and tender, and the time of their rutting was coming. By now, harts would have lost their antler velvet and would be in peak condition; swift enough to give a good chase, but not as vicious as they were in winter, when their mating instinct took over. The huntsmen had found several harts for Henry to choose from, and we had inspected their droppings, or *femays*, to note the size of each animal. Tracks in the damp woodlands were found and followed. These *fues*, along with *froyeis*, the frayings of bark on trees, and twigs disturbed by their silken bodies, were our clues to find our game.

We set off into the woods, lymers and huntsmen leading the way. The air smelt of earthy, decaying leaves and mud, fresh fallen rain and refreshing dew. Hawthorn, recently cut, sent the pungent smell of death tumbling into the air to contrast with the fine perfume of sweet flowers and leaf mould. The forest was deep and dark. Spindles of light broke through the clustered, green leaves. Dust sparkled in the gloom, as did moisture, lighting from leaf and bark, shimmering like silver. The hounds snuffled close to the ground, picking up the scent of piss, sweat and shit. We had chosen our quarry, a fine beast of more than ten years; a stag, who had fathered many, and would this day surrender his wild throne. Small groups of hounds and men were sent ahead, to line the trail this hart would take as he fled, and drive him into our path.

Ducking under moss-covered branches, deep in the dripping darkness, we came to the nest of the hart. Henry's Master of Game knelt beside the patch of earth, setting a hand to it. As he looked up and nodded, the lymer at his side barked. The nest was warm. The stag had been there only a short while ago. The chase was on.

"*Ho moy, ho moy*!" called the Master of Game to his lymers, keeping their attention fixed on the scent. The huntsmen ran ahead, their feet pounding on the wet earth as they kept their eyes focussed on the ground to watch for droppings. The tracks were light upon the earth. If they were deep, that meant our quarry was running, but the hart was not aware we were after it, as yet.

As we rode on, the tracks became deeper, and huntsmen blew horns to call running hounds from the rear. Tipping their heads back to howl, the hounds cried out, shattering the silence of the morning.

We flashed through the trees, the sharp-barbed wind racing past our ears, blood pounding in our veins. The hounds had the hart cornered in a glade. He was huge; a mighty beast with a coat that was almost white, like the pagan agent of another realm whose presence signifies change.

He was trapped. Snapping, growling dogs surrounded him. Smokey, terrified breath plumed from his nose and mouth as he lowered his antlers, stomping the damp earth to threaten the hounds. His black eyes were feral with fright. Sweat poured from him like water. The stink of terror and rage rose, outmatching the sweet scents of the forest. He bellowed, a mighty, crashing sound, and turned to face his foe.

Alighting from his horse, Henry approached the beast with his short hunting bow in hand. He pulled back, muscles straining against the weight of the bow. Henry's eyes narrowed on the stag. The stag stared back, undaunted even in the face of death. Henry's bow was quick and his aim true. His arrow flashed into the hart and as it staggered, kicking at the slathering hounds gnashing at its hooves, Henry's men fell upon it with swords.

Bleeding, wounded, but still not dead, the hart fell. His voice cried out; a single, aching call, resounding in the woods, floating through the air. The last cry of a noble creature done to death.

I watched him fall; watched his knees shake and his powerful form crumple. As he slipped to the earth, and men about me started to cheer, I walked to the stag. It was dangerous to approach even a felled hart. They were formidable creatures who could stab the unwary with their antlers, or crush a hound's skull beneath their hooves, but strangely I had no fear.

He lay upon the dark earth, puddles surrounding him. As I knelt at his side, I saw glimmering light in his black, liquid eyes. I put a hand to his face, smelling the overpowering stench of fear-laced sweat, piss, shit and blood. In the darkness of his eyes, I had the sense he was watching me. I stroked his hairy jaw and a bubble of pink, blood-filled liquid emerged from his nose.

With a sigh, he died. It was not a cry, nor a scream. He accepted death, and rushed to meet it. I felt a sorrow unlike any other come upon me and knew not why. More times than I could count I had been a part of such hunts. I had often loosed the killing arrow. I had taken life. But this time there was something different. I felt sorrow.

As the light left his eyes, he watched me. As the steady glow of life's fire became replaced with the dullness of death, it was as though he was trying to tell me something.

I moved away as the unmaking began. The hart was cut open, so his entrails might be removed and his body cleaved up for Henry to share between his favourites. I watched from the edge of the glen as huntsmen took out their assortment of knives for cutting bone, hide, and removing the more delicate, desired organs, hoisted the hart up, and set to work.

Blood fell, dripping from the hart. I watched as a drop fell into a puddle of water. In the gloomy light, the water was black as ink, black as blood. As the drop of blood fell, the water rippled, tiny waves cresting out from the centre, heading swiftly to the sides and back again.

Black falling to black. Blood on blood… A ripple in a pool.

I turned away. I had no stomach for the hunt that day.

Chapter Thirty-Three

Berkley Castle and Thornbury
Late July – August 1535

"I have sent Rich to inform the Duke of your dissatisfaction, my lord," said Cromwell.

"Suffolk should have more care about his claims," I noted.

Henry grunted in agreement. The Duke had recently boasted he had set some religious houses right, and restored them to better practices, but upon investigation Cromwell's men had found just the opposite. I was pleased Suffolk would suffer a reprimand, but there were other actions Cromwell was taking which left me less pleased.

George informed me that Cromwell had been seen with Carewe and Gertrude Courtenay. I hoped Cromwell was merely making overtures to my foes in the name of bringing peace to court, but my brother was distrustful.

"He has tried to undermine us in the past," he said. "Perhaps he continues to do so. Carewe and Courtenay promote traditional religion, and would have us return to the Pope's chains."

"They do not truly fear us, George," I said. "They fear losing *tradition*. They want a Church ruled by Rome, and a country overseen by nobles of ancient houses. Cromwell, being of low birth, stands for everything they hate. He would not truly ally himself to them."

"In the shadows of court, strange friends are made, if only for a time," said my brother in an ominous tone. "They may dislike Cromwell, but they see how close he is to the King, and note his influence at court. That cannot be ignored. Many a time have people made alliances with enemies in order to gain what they want."

"And what do they want?"

"Speak not like a fool. Cromwell wants what Wolsey wanted; all others removed so he might control everything."

"He cannot unseat us," I protested, but my voice was not as sure as my declaration.

"Wolsey had me and others sent away, and the King agreed to it." My brother tossed his cap into a chair of crimson silk, anger clouding his handsome face. "When the King is in company with a friend, no one could doubt they are in his favour, but when he is separated from them, he is easily manipulated." George sighed. "Since Wolsey died, and increasingly, since More went to the block, the King has become only more suspicious of his friends."

"He cannot doubt your loyalty."

"Can he not? They say his father was as miserly with his friendship as he was with money. Perhaps the King draws on the influence of his blood." My brother had a strange light in his hazel eyes. "Wolsey was his friend. More too. He claimed to love Katherine and Mary. The Carthusians and the Observants were orders he declared he supported without question." My brother paused, staring not at me, but from the window. "It seems to me that the King protests often about friendship," he said. "But he will discard it without a moment's hesitation if something of greater use comes along."

"More once said much the same."

"He was a wise man."

I ran my hands down my gown of fresh green velvet. "Cromwell has been careful and polite of late," I said. "I would give him the benefit of the doubt."

George nodded. "Do that," he said.

"But you will not?"

"One of us should keep watch. There is something I cannot see here, and it nags at me."

"Cromwell does not have as much influence over the King as he would like to think," I said. "Wolsey… even More, had more than he. Henry will keep his hand upon all that happens in his kingdom now. That is the way of things."

"Think that, if you wish," said my brother. "I will think otherwise. Between us, we may find the truth."

*

On progress, I received a note from Cranmer, informing me he had made a new friend. A Scottish reformer, Alexander Aless, who was also a theologian and doctor of medicine, had taken up residence in London.

"Cromwell thinks well of him too," wrote my old friend. *"And he has many ideas for England. It would seem the tide of reform has reached Scotland, too, my lady, and there are many men there willing to make changes for the betterment of their country. Aless is keen to meet you, and to know what you think of the Schmalkalden League. I have told him that you love to meet with those whose minds are open to the sweet cause of reform, and would ask permission to bring him to you when you return to London."*

Just after reading this note, I received another. As Cromwell had warned, plague had broken out in Bristol, and Henry's fear of sickness, never far from the surface of his skin, meant we could not visit the city. Instead of a royal entrance to Bristol, a party of delegates came out to meet us at Thornbury. Henry was presented with gifts of livestock to feed his household on progress and I was given a gilt cup and cover with one hundred marks to accompany it.

"I thank you," I said, taking the fine cup into my hands. "But I desire to demand or have no other gift than to be able to return to Bristol one day and see your fair city for myself."

The meeting was a success for many in Bristol had listened to Latimer when he had preached, and were converted to reform. We went on that night to Acton Court, where Sir Nicholas Poyntz entertained us. Knowing since last summer we were to come to his house, Poyntz had built a whole new range for our visit, an eastern wing, done out in classical style, holding lavish furniture and sumptuous hangings. Poyntz's father had once been Katherine's Vice-Chamberlain, and his uncle, John, a great friend of Tom's, was a member of my household. Poyntz was close with Cromwell and a dedicated reformist. Henry wanted to honour him and did so with more than just our visit. At the end of our stay, he knighted Poyntz.

That night we feasted, eating from blue and white tin-glazed earthenware and drinking from Venetian glass goblets. Later that night, as I went to my rooms, I could hear people talking and laughing in the grounds, wandering about the moat whilst they drank, their shadows long on the inky waters. I sat in my chambers. They were familiar, being done in a French style to honour me. I was satisfied. Henry was close to understanding that whilst we had many enemies, there were converts to our cause.

From Acton we moved on a bare six miles to Little Sodbury, home of Sir John Walsh and then on another twenty-two miles to Bromham where Sir Edward Baynton, my Vice-Chamberlain, played host. Again, they were passionate reformists, and we engaged in many interesting discussions in their houses.

Bromham was the more impressive of the two houses. Baynton had made great improvements to his former manor, and there were rooms enough to house seven hundred guests. Whilst the privacy afforded to us at smaller houses departed as we reached Bromham, it did not seem to matter. Henry and I had grown close once more.

Whilst at Bromham, Henry came to my chambers. "I have something for you," he said, holding out a package of velvet with a crimson ribbon about it.

I swallowed. Although the flashes of memory that accompanied that colour had abated, there was still something in the shade to make me uncomfortable. But I could not show that. I had to pretend. If Henry was to know that I suffered from these blinking lights of memory, he might think I was possessed by malevolent spirits. "For me?" I asked, standing. "What more could you give me?"

Henry smiled and passed the package to me. Unwrapping it, I discovered a pendant with a central diamond, and the initials *H&A* intertwined in gold over it. There were rings, too. One of gold with a bright diamond bearing the *H&A* cipher. The other two were simple gold bands; one with *The Mooste Happi* about its rim, and the other with a Latin inscription, *"O Lord, make haste to help me."*

I gazed into the bundle of presents, knowing this beauty was Holbein's work. The ring with the Latin inscription was clearly a message from Henry to his Maker, but that he had granted it to me meant we were united in our prayers. The items with our initials on them touched me deeply. I looked up into Henry's eyes and felt my breast beat with the warmth of love.

"They are spectacular," I said, touching the rings with the tip of my finger. "You honour me."

"You are my wife," he said gruffly, looking almost shy. "And I love you."

*

"He is a good, honest man, who has lost his livelihood," said Hugh Latimer, his earnest face pleading. "His wife has come to beg mercy and aid."

"I will see her," I said. "Bring her in."

The woman who came before me was poorly dressed, although clearly not of one of the most desperate, lower orders of people in England. Her hair had been washed and presented under a becoming cap. She was young, but her eyes, although pretty and blue, held a helpless glaze.

"Your husband has lost his cattle to sickness, I am told?" I asked as she executed a surprisingly graceful curtsey.

"He has, Your Majesty," she said in a tremulous tone. "He asked me to come to you, as he thought…"

"That I might respond more to the pleas of a woman, than those of a man?" I asked with a smile and she nodded. "It is true, good Mistress, I have sympathy with the trials of women in this hard world." I nodded to Latimer. "My chaplain has informed me that you are of his Parish, and are good people of abiding faith. He says you attend church every Sunday, and many days during the week. I am encouraged to meet people like you, who embrace reform, and understand that grace and godliness does not come without work and effort."

I smiled wider. "But that, I suspect, you understand from experience, do you not? It can be harsh toil being a farmer's wife. You work the soil, you tend your cattle, and are rewarded by God for your effort. I hope to do the same in England. I will tend the earth and grow the crops. I will wash the water of purity upon corrupt soil, and from it, fresh shoots will come, to nurture the people of God. But sometimes, God sends us trials, as He has sent to you. And in such times, it is the duty of the nobility, graced with more resources and wealth, to aid those who follow the King with loyalty, and who willingly undertake sacrifices of change and alteration, in order to make our new world."

I turned to Latimer, who was looking mightily pleased that his petitioner had not only been heard, but praised publicly by his Queen. "My chaplain has a gift for you," I said. "It is an initial payment, to aid you and your husband in this time of trouble. I have many affairs to deal with, so may not be able to meet you again, but Latimer will watch over you."

The woman was handed the purse. She opened it and her eyes flashed wide.

"Twenty pounds," I said. There was a collective gasp from courtiers standing nearby. It was a vast sum, far larger than this woman or her husband would earn in a year. "This will enable you to get back on your feet, Mistress, and keep attending church to show your gratitude to God."

"My Queen…" Words stumbled on her lips and her face was ruddy. "I know not how to express my thanks."

"Attend church, worship God and love your King," I said. "That is all the thanks that will be required." I nodded to Latimer. "You will come to me if anything else is required for this woman and her family?" I asked and he nodded. "Then all is well. Go home, Mistress, and share this good fortune with your husband."

"I shall, Majesty," she said, her eyes becoming bolder. "And everywhere I go, I will tell all who ask that Queen Anne is a *good* woman, who aided us in our time of need."

From the tone of her voice, I could tell she thought many people would think otherwise. But there was a ferocity in her that inspired my soul. I did not shout about my charitable works, but if this woman, and others I had helped were willing to speak for me, much good could be done to my reputation.

My annual charitable givings amounted to one thousand five hundred pounds per year, the average income of a nobleman. A labourer would earn five pounds a year, and a merchant one hundred. The amount of money I granted to noble causes was therefore a fortune. As Queen, my income was vast, and if I could support the poor, especially those who were loyal to our cause, why should I not? They were a part of the future. They were the blood that ran to our heart.

The next day, emboldened by the audience with the farmer's wife and the new closeness between Henry and me, I made a decision. My efforts with Cranmer and Cromwell to have Tyndale released had not borne fruit. The Emperor, who previously had been reticent about persecuting Englishmen on his doorstep, now seemed interested in keeping this one... because he knew how desperately Henry wanted to get hold of him. Cranmer was concerned that Tyndale would be executed, and had written to Cromwell and me to persuade us to approach Henry directly. Subterfuge, he wrote, was not working, and straight-talking would have to take over.

Cromwell and I were on fragile terms, but in this we were united. We went to Henry together, to ask him to intervene, and save Tyndale from the flames.

"Were he to be brought to England," I said. "You would be able to talk with him. Perhaps when he has seen your generosity, he would change his mind about our marriage."

"He does not recognise you as Queen, Anne," Henry grumbled.

Thinking about the English Bible in my chambers, I did not think this was the case. "And yet I would forgive him," I said. "He could work for us, Henry, and when set right by you, he would be valuable."

"And you concur, Thomas?"

Thomas, I thought. *Thomas today, as I am Anne. Not Cromwell and madam. Henry is in a good mood.*

"I do, sire," said Cromwell. "Besides which, the man is an English subject. It is not for the Emperor to punish him."

I liked Cromwell's train of thought not at all, but I understood his purpose. Any suggestion that another man might steal Henry's authority from him was insupportable.

"Letters will be sent," Henry said. "The Emperor is keen for our friendship. I will ask him to release Tyndale into the custody of your man, Vaughan."

As Cromwell left, I kissed Henry. "Thank you," I said.

"You have long admired this man," he replied. "I would do anything to make you happy."

"There is another I admire more," I said. "You. You set aside the grief and sorrow Tyndale caused you, and intervene to free him. You forge ahead with the reform of your Church, and make even my foes honour me." A wash of love, so strong and deep I thought I might cease to breathe, flooded over me. "Never have I loved as I love you," I said.

His eyes were warm and tender as he took me in his arms. "You are my soul, Anne," he murmured into my hair. "And the only thing that keeps me sane. You set my feet upon the track that will lead from the darkened woods. You keep my hand steady upon my sword." He pressed his lips to my throat. "God forgive me if I ever forget all you mean to me."

Later that day, Henry spoke warmly of the notion of an English Bible. The idea had been put forward some time ago, but Tyndale's translation had not proved popular, due to his slandering of traditional faith. Cranmer was attempting to produce a new version, working with his bishops, but many sections of this were still being perfected. Henry had been tepid about Cranmer's project, but, enthused by the notion that Tyndale might soon be in England, and he could convince him to support his supremacy, he became inspired.

"I greet this with a grateful heart," I said as he told me he would order Cranmer to spur his men on. "Long have you known my opinion."

"And you were right," he said. "I will order it done, so our people will hear the voice of God in their hearts, and understand the grace of our reign."

I could not have been happier.

Shortly… Oh, how shortly, that would alter.

Chapter Thirty-Four

Wulfhall
September 1535

By early September, we were riding into Somerset, bound for Wulfhall, the seat of the Seymours. Edward Seymour was rising high in Henry's estimations, and although my husband thought I saw it not, so was Edward's sister.

Henry was careful. He paid court to Jane only when I was not around. This was his pattern. When aggrieved with me, he would court women openly, seeking to shame, punish, and hurt me. When reminded of our love, he was cautious.

Can you grow used to this, Anne Boleyn? I asked myself as we rode towards Wulfhall. *Can you accept he will always stray, that he will be disloyal?* I knew not. I was addicted to Henry's love. It was my torment and my pleasure, my sorrow and my happiness. But there was another part of me that had started to accept, knowing he would always come back to me.

I was three women. One was the broken woman I kept hidden away; another was Anne Boleyn, a raw and broken heart kept hidden under a wall of bright gaiety and flirtatious fortifications. The last was the Queen; a more pragmatic creature. I think I was starting to understand that Henry, too, was many souls bound in one form.

As we rode up the lane, cattle braying in the fields, and sheep thick against the fences, sheltering from the wind, Wulfhall came into view. Made of red bricks, smouldering in the afternoon sun, and timber frames which had been painted white, it was a handsome house. There was a central courtyard and a large private chapel, gardens with Tudor roses marked out by raised beds and coloured sand, and winding pathways leading into sheltered arbours, and further, away into the dark trails of the forest. Stained glass shone from the chapel windows, marking the ground outside with a myriad of dancing, bright colours. Wulfhall's walls glowed like warm blood.

Wulfhall was grand, but clearly had been improved upon. I suspected it had once been a mere farmstead. In the large courtyard set before the house there was a huge barn, its roof crested with vast timbers, stretching like the ribcage of a mighty whale, burned white by the sun, where, Edward told me, they held dances and feasts.

"I was married there, for the first time," he said, and flushed, clearly thinking it unwise to bring up his first wife, Catherine Filliol, who had rutted with his father and been cast aside when Edward had discovered her incestuous infidelity. She had been sent to a convent, but had died earlier that year, enabling him to marry again. They said that his father had lost his wits, perhaps understanding what the scandal had brought upon his son, and entire family.

I pitied the young man. His sister might be Henry's next whore, which hardly endeared me to her family, but Edward did not deserve to carry such shame. He had two sons, but after Catherine's betrayal, he doubted their paternity. There was talk he meant to petition Henry so he might disinherit them. What a cruel choice for a father to have to make!

I touched his shoulder. "You have a new wife now," I murmured. "Anne Stanhope is a good woman." I paused and sniffed. "People like to talk, Master Seymour. They engage in scandal when there is little else to divert them. Take no notice. This sin was not yours. Others carry the weight of this corruption, not you."

He stared at me, perhaps startled that I would speak so kindly to him. "I will endeavour to do as you suggest, Majesty," he said.

"Whatever people say of us cannot touch us if we remain true to ourselves," I added. "Keep peace within yourself, Master Seymour. The world will follow suit, no matter how long it may take."

Henry was pleased to see me talking with Edward. He had been impressed by the young man and thought he had a bright future. You might think this was all to do with his fancy for Edward's sister, but it was not. Henry rewarded men for talent. If they happened to have a kinswoman he liked, so much the better, but it was not the wiles of a mistress he rewarded but the wit of minds. The same accusation had been levied at my father. Some said Thomas Boleyn would never have risen so far if not for the open legs of his daughters. But if so, my father would still be in favour, and he was not. He had been eclipsed by George, Norris and Cromwell.

"Come, Ned," Henry cried, clapping Edward hard on the back. "Take us to your family."

We entered the manor and feasted that night with the Seymour family. Their table was rich with wild game; venison Henry had sent ahead from his numerous hunts that summer, along with roasted bittern, quail, pigeon and hare. Savernake Forest bordered their lands, and offered plenty of bounty. They might not be the greatest of nobles, but the Seymours kept a fine table. Despite the tasty foods and rich ale offered, there was a conspicuous, cool air at dinner. Edward's father was kept from saying a great deal by his wife. Each time he tried, she placed a warning hand on his arm. Clearly, they wanted no one to see that his mind had come unhinged.

Edward also did not talk to his father more than he had to, and his mother sometimes blushed without cause. Clearly, despite John Seymour's infirmity, the trouble between Edward and his father was not forgotten. How could it ever be? For a father to keep his daughter-in-law as a mistress, possibly fathering the boys supposed to belong to his son? How could that be forgiven?

I watched Jane Seymour that night, starting to understand the nature of Henry's attraction. Jane was seven years younger than me, but seemed like a child. There was an air of innocence about her. But such wiles as any maiden might possess was not what drew Henry to her. She had a compelling way of looking at a man without looking directly at him… a glance, the upward tilt of her downcast eyes… as though she were saying *here I am, yours to command*. She gazed at him in short spurts, allowing her pale eyes to seek him out as if she could not help herself. When he looked into her eyes, he was the only man in the world.

"What man would not feel comforted by such trust in a woman's eyes?" I asked Mary Howard as we whispered about Jane.

"And what woman would not see that trust was as false as teeth made from the leavings of the unfortunate dead?" she murmured back.

I laughed loudly, causing people to stare at me. The air was thick with the scent of sweet herbs, but the smell of wet earth and fresh rain wafted in too. The night smelt new and unsullied, but as I watched Henry glance more and more at Jane, all purity left me. I sipped my wine and entertained bitter thoughts, wondering if I could ever reconcile the women struggling within me.

*

A day later, I found myself in the gardens. Mistress Seymour, Margery Wentworth as she had been known before her marriage, had been talking at me all morning. I say *at*, rather than to, as that was the way it was. Some people do not, apparently, need to breathe between sentences.

Margery was the daughter of Anne Say, making her my mother's first cousin. Although it was hard to find anyone who was not related at court, Margery took our blood connection as an excuse to speak to me at any, and every, moment we were at Wulfhall. She reminisced about the days when she and my mother had been in the household of the Countess of Surrey, and the poems John Skelton had written for her. Margery had once been a great beauty, and the angles of that elegance were still upon her face, but bearing many children for her lord, ten in all, including six sons, had taken a toll. I suspected the scandal of her once beloved daughter-in-law had not helped. It is often not the years a woman has encountered or the suffering of childbirth she has faced which affects her beauty. Bitterness ages more than any other trial. I thought myself ill used by Henry, but what a fate to find that your own husband has bedded his daughter-in-law, and that your grandsons may in fact be no relation to you? You would not have known anything was amiss to see the affection she showed to her frail husband, however. Perhaps she, like so many others, held Catherine accountable, and convinced herself that the wiles of this young temptress had enticed her husband into sin.

Many times it was protested in my lifetime that women were weak, and helpless before sin. But if men were completely unable to resist temptation, were they so strong?

After half a day in her company, I was desperate for escape. I was not alone. As Margery went on and on and on, barely bothering to draw breath, I saw a malevolent flicker in her daughter's eyes. Jane Seymour was no fonder of her mother than I. I believed she may have been treated poorly by her, for Jane did not live up to the paragon of courtly beauty and grace that her mother had once been. When parents fail to see themselves in their progeny, sometimes they become cruel.

Not for the first time, I considered how fortunate I was in my family. My father was never to be trusted, but he worked to further our goals. My mother was the wisest and sweetest of all women, and my brother was my best friend. Thinking about this, I thought on Mary. By letters that I had burned, not wanting scandal to touch me, we had become reconciled. I doubted if she would ever be welcomed at court, and certainly not at Hever, but there was hope for the future. I could never truly abandon Mary. I loved her too well. I hoped that at some stage, if this much-postponed meeting with François ever took place, I might have a chance to see Mary and her husband, and meet the daughter who had been named for me.

I thought about Elizabeth, but thinking on my daughter made my heart ache so greatly I could hardly bear it.

As I walked into the gardens, I took a deep breath of heavenly air, thanking God that Margery had not wanted to walk that day. My ladies were far behind me, enjoying George's japes as I strolled ahead. Wulfhall might not be the grandest of houses, but its gardens were stunning. There was a certain wildness, even in the cultivated areas, which calmed me. The skies were blue as the Virgin's robes, and there was a lightly-scented breeze, carrying floral perfume and the distant, earthy smell of horse dung. I obambulated, lost to the notion of thinking or doing anything useful. I drank in the day, and so was quite unprepared for what I discovered in those gardens.

Turning a corner, I glimpsed two shapes in an arbour. One, a lady, was sitting upon a stone seat where shimmering ivy crept up the legs. Even at this distance I could see her sallow, pellucid cheeks lit up with fire. Kneeling beside her was a man, his face, too, shining with earnest crimson.

It was Henry and Jane Seymour.

I drew back. A willow, its branches thick with long silver-green leaves, dancing and dipping in the wind, concealed me. My heart pounded so loud I thought they might hear it. I glanced back, but the others were far behind. George was reading his poetry to my ladies beside the crumbling ruins of an old building, and my women were sitting, their eyes lost in bliss, for the pleasure of a handsome court gallant extolling words of beauty to them.

I crept close to the tree. From here, I could just make out the soft words coming from the arbour.

"Long have I loved you," said my husband to my waiting woman. "Yet you will not let me near. Do you love me not, Jane?"

Love... My heart shattered at the word. Henry *loved* this pale imitation of a person? My lip curled. Just *how many* women had he professed to love? Sometimes I wondered if Henry fell in love a thousand times a day, with whomsoever he happened to be standing near. I also knew, however, that my brother had protested love to many a woman in the hope of getting her to lift her skirts. *That is it,* I thought. *For he cannot truly love this pallid worm. He wants to bed her, and she will not allow it, so he will dupe her into sin.*

"Your Majesty is so kind to me," Jane almost whispered. I had to strain to hear her. By God's Holy Death! Even her voice was dull!

"You have been so kind, but I am an honest maid. I cannot be a man's mistress."

With those few words, my estimations of the girl doubled. But as she went on, they tumbled once more. "With all the trials you have suffered, Majesty... being ever disappointed of a son by your unpopular wife, and with so many beautiful women about you at court, I am surprised you even noticed me."

"I saw you at *once,*" he said, clearly a lie. Henry had tarried with other women whilst Jane was at court. "But I felt so true and pure a maiden would not welcome my love."

"I welcome it," she said, her cheeks igniting to further flame.

"Then let me come to you," he said. "I will show you how things are between us."

My heart lurched. He had said the same words to me once, at Hever, when I had refused him. Was anything Henry said original, or had he been spouting the same, tired, shallow, meaningless, vapid words to women for years, and each and every one of us had fallen for his lies? Fools we were, for him.

Fools indeed, Katherine murmured.

"I cannot…" Jane said, glancing about. "My brother is here, my mother and father… my lord… I could not. And even if not for them, I could not for my honour."

"Then let me be your admirer," he said. "Let me court you. I shall be your knight, Jane, for I know you have suffered much under the Queen's hands."

"It is true," she said, bowing her head in sorrow.

I blinked. *What* suffering? I barely spoke to Jane, and certainly did not scold or harm her. Was this the suffering of which she spoke? Going unnoticed? If so, then most people at court had harmed her!

"I think sometimes, my mistress sees your affection for me, and hates me for it," she said, those pale blue eyes widening. "I think she wants to hurt me, and I have no protection."

Oh… I certainly was considering harming her now! Jane was playing a part, I could see that. Suddenly, I doubted in her defence of her virginity, *if* it even existed. What was the girl playing at? Did she think to secure richer rewards by holding him at bay for a time before she surrendered? I did not believe for a moment she would reject him. Jane had been long ignored by everyone; her family, her parents… only Katherine had been kind to her…

Katherine… I thought. So that was it. This little strumpet meant to turn Henry against me in revenge for the suffering of her beloved mistress. That was the purpose of those lies. I had never touched Jane, never showed anger, except in passing comment. But she would paint me black as my raven hair, and rejoice to see me ignored or shamed by Henry. And if she supported Katherine, she supported Mary too.

I was forced to retreat further into the bushes as the pair exchanged some sort of love token, and escaped the arbour by different paths. Jane took one that went directly to the house, but Henry took a trail which led him breathtakingly near to where I was hidden. I pressed myself into the tree, seeking to hide in its voluminous branches. As his golden doublet disappeared about a shade-dappled corner, I breathed out. Glancing back, I saw George and the others were on their way.

I ducked to the floor, pretending to be engrossed in studying some pretty, pale-violet flowers spread-eagled along the ground. As I dipped, something near me moved. A shape I had not noted shifted in the trees to one side of the garden. I narrowed my eyes, trying to see it clearly, but like Katherine's ghost in my dreams, he remained in shadow.

I lifted a hand in greeting, and from the gloom stepped Cromwell. I knew not why, but a shard of ice entered my heart as I realised he, like me, had witnessed Henry adoring Jane Seymour.

"Majesty," George cried as he came upon me. "Whatever are you doing down in the dirt? Do you grant your royal blessing to the flowers?"

"I was just looking at these blooms," I said, holding one up. "I don't believe I know them."

"Speedwell, Majesty," said Nan Gainsford, a look of surprise on her face. The flowers were common. There was no reason I should be mystified about their identity.

"Ah," I said. "I quite forgot."

I glanced back to where Cromwell had stood, but he was gone. Leading the others, we went on through the gardens. I tried to put Jane and Henry from my mind, but they would not leave.

That night, I handed out rewards of money to Weston and Brereton, for poems they had written for me. I laughed with my brother. I jested with Tom and Norris and played the fine and happy Queen. But that night, as I waited for Henry to arrive to bless me with his seed, my heart was broken.

So, I said to myself, *you thought you were fine with his betrayals, did you?*

How could any woman be? Katherine's keening voice cried out. *How could any woman in love happily subject herself to such misery? Duty-bound to one man, tied to him by the Church and by God… Fated to watch as he shames us. Forced to stand by him as he betrays us.*

Fate was cruel to women indeed. I sat in bed, trying to hold back tears as I waited. Waited for the man who had broken my heart more times than I could count. Waited for the man who had just that afternoon sworn he adored another. Waited for the man who could bring me security, if he could only hold his nerve long enough to grant me a son.

Waiting, waiting, waiting. Had I ever done anything else when it came to Henry? I had waited for him to notice me, to leave his wife, to take a stand for us, for England, for the faith…

Katherine once said that Clement had thrust us all into limbo, but it was Henry, not the Pope, who had done this to me. Since the first moment he had entered my life, I had been floating in this state between beings. I twisted and curled in darkness, never finding a place to rest. In shadow I billowed and wafted, in blackness I danced and I dreamed. I had nothing to cling to, nothing but feeble hope and shattered love. Elizabeth was my only tether, but Henry cut me loose, time and time again.

Where was my perch? My safe harbour? Where was the security of love? Never had I had these things, and never would I. Henry's love was not a means of liberty, or freedom, it was a haze that held me fast, struggling against invisible bonds, lost in the knowledge that I adored a man who did not, and perhaps would never love me as I loved him.

He took me that night, but as I lay there, under him, feeling him grind his feeble member inside me, I knew I was not the one he was thinking of.

He used my body to make love to Jane Seymour.

When he left me, I went to my chests and brought out a locket with Elizabeth's hair in it. Holding it to my breast, I sat on the floor and wept, crying for the time she had been conceived, when I had believed in love.

I would have done anything to go back to that time. Anything.

Chapter Thirty-Five

Wulfhall
September 1535

"Cromwell says my actions are in conflict with the wishes of His Majesty," Brereton said as we sat together in my apartments.

"And are they?"

The old rogue had a merry shine in his eyes. "I swear to you, madam, they are not."

I laughed a little, sure somewhere along the line these two purposes did conflict. Cromwell was attempting to impose his order on Wales, but Brereton, who held a great deal of power there, was holding him back.

"Perhaps Cromwell harbours a grudge," I said. "He did not like it when you bested him over the Eyton case last year."

"With your aid, madam," said Brereton.

In the year just passed, one of Brereton's retainers had been murdered and Brereton had accused a man of Flintshire, John ap Gryffith Eyton, of the crime. Being influential in Flintshire, Brereton had called on rough men who owed him favours, and had carted Eyton to London. Cromwell had leaned on the justice system to acquit, as Eyton was in his debt, but Brereton had had him rearrested, with my help. Eyton had been returned to Wales, where he stood trial and hanged for his crimes. I had intervened as, no matter how questionable Brereton's methods had been, I had been assured of Eyton's guilt. Cromwell had not been pleased, and Eyton's death had cost him dear, as the money owed to Cromwell had gone to the Crown rather than into his pocket. And now Brereton and he were bashing heads again. Brereton had almost a monopoly over Cheshire and North Wales. Henry and Fitzroy had entrusted him with a great many appointments, and Cromwell was finding it hard to sneak his plots for the Welsh Marches and the borders past Brereton. In truth, Brereton understood the lands in question much better than Cromwell. He had a wealth of experience, and was familiar not only with honest merchants, but with the rogues and pirates who operated there. Cromwell should have left those areas to Brereton, as Henry and his bastard son were happy to, but he could not. Master Secretary was becoming greedy. He wanted a hand in all matters.

"Cromwell despises the influence I have in Wales and the Marches," said Brereton. "Cromwell wants to be master of all, madam. That others hold power is a condition he wishes to cure England of."

I frowned. First George and now Brereton singing the same song. For a moment I wondered if my brother had put Brereton up to this, but dismissed the thought. Cromwell was greedy for power. *That* was the condition that required curing.

"Allow Cromwell's agent in Wales and Cheshire to have better access to that which he requires," I said. "And be friendly to Cromwell."

"I fear he may seek to remove me from my posts for the Duke of Richmond, Majesty."

"I will never allow that to happen. Neither will the Duke. Where else would he hear such marvellous tales of piracy and brigands, if not from you?"

Brereton grinned. "You know all my secrets, my lady."

"Probably *too* many." I teasingly struck his arm with my hand. My ladies, some of them no doubt thinking old Brereton had become too familiar and I had scolded him, looked our way in disapproval. "This is not the first time I have heard such things about Cromwell," I murmured, my tone more serious. "And doubt not, it will be investigated."

"I place all my trust in you, my lady," he said, rising and offering a gallant bow.

As he departed, I stared at the altar cloth I was embroidering, but saw nothing of the glory of its threads of gold. I was thinking about Cromwell. The man was becoming too avaricious, too keen to see off his rivals. Like a gluttonous wolf, Cromwell stalked England. Wolsey had been the same way. His ordinances, which had stripped my brother and others of their positions at court, had been done to separate Henry from his friends and the Cardinal had taken all important or well paid posts for himself. The few remaining he had offered to his friends, or those he knew he could control. Would Cromwell follow the same path?

There is greed in power. What one has is never enough. It is a sickness that infests the heart and soul, bending the bearer to its will. Slowly it grows in the darkness, taking root, until the day comes when there stands a man with power no more, but power with a man to use.

It is a monster, which devours its prey from the inside out.

I had to wonder, if Cromwell wanted Henry separated from his friends, did he also want to remove me? To pluck me from my shell would leave a gaping hole, one which, even then, I was sure Cromwell lusted after. Did he think to drive us apart? I shook my head, lost in angry thoughts. Never, as long as there was blood in my veins, or air in my lungs, would I allow another man to shove me aside.

*

"Katherine has been writing to friends again," said my brother, drawing close and pulling a letter from his pocket.

"The Emperor and the Pope?" I asked, reaching for it.

"Not this time," he said. "Marie de Salinas was the recipient."

"And does she have a copy as *fine* as this?" I mocked with a smile, unravelling the scroll to see my brother's poor hand. "You should have paid more attention to our tutor, George, your hand is never careful. I would recognise it anywhere."

"My hand is no poorer than many at court," he protested. "Just because *yours* is so fine, that is no reason to criticise the rest of us."

I gazed down at the letter.

"My special friend," it read. *"You have greatly bound me with the pains that you have taken in speaking with the King, my Lord, concerning the coming of my daughter to*

visit me. You must await your reward from God, for I have no power to reward what you have done with anything other than my goodwill.

As touching the answer that has been given to you, that his Highness is content to send her to some place near me, so long as I do not see her, I pray you to give my great thanks to his Highness for the goodness which he shows to his daughter and myself, and for the comfort that I have received from this.
As to my seeing her, you must inform his Highness that even if she came within one mile of me, I would not travel to visit her, for I am not able to move around and even if it were possible for me to do so, I do not have the means with which to travel.

But you must impress on his Highness that what I asked for was that she be sent to where I am and assure him that the comfort and laughter which she would bring to me would undoubtedly be very healthy for her. I have experienced this because I have suffered the same illness of solitude and know how much good can come of being reunited with kin. It was entirely just and reasonable of me to make this request, and it so greatly touched on the honour and conscience of the King, my lord, that I am very surprised that it has been denied to me.

Do not, for love of me, fail to do this. I have heard here that the King has anxieties about trusting her to me, believing that I would flee from the country with her. I cannot believe that such a fear, which is so far from reason, should come from the royal heart of His Majesty and I cannot believe that he has so little trust in me. I beg you to insist to his Highness that I am, without any hesitation, determined to die in this kingdom and that I here pledge my life as security that, if any such escape should be attempted, the King would do justice to me as the most evil woman who had ever been born.

Other matters I remit to your wisdom and judgement as a trusted friend, to whom I pray God will give health,

Katherine, the Queen.”

“Marie de Salinas went to Henry?” I asked. I had not heard of this.

“On another mission to move Lady Mary closer to her mother,” said George. “But that was not what I thought you would find interesting.”

“No,” I said. “I understand.”

So, you are dying, Katherine? my mind asked the presence within it.

What care have you for me? she responded. *Have you not long thought that when I am gone, you will finally be Queen? That when I am dead, your children will no more be questioned?*

I had indeed thought all those things. Many was the time I had wished Katherine dead. But, as I read about her frail condition, regret entered my heart.

Perhaps it was because her voice had been so long inside my mind. Perhaps because with her dead she would become a martyr to the people. Perhaps it was her proud, unending calmness, even in the face of death… but something in me was uneasy.

I thought back to the dream I had had on the night before I lost my son. *You are my death,* she had said. *And I am yours.*

A shudder passed through me.

That night I dreamt of a storm which came with no warning and gave no quarter. I stood in the centre of whirling wind and lashing rain. An invisible barrier stood between me and the elements. Rain fell, but it did not touch me. The winds stole my hair to fly in the skies, but did not strike my face.

There I stood, alone, as about me the world was torn asunder.

Chapter Thirty-Six

Winchester, Hampshire
September 1535

I was glad to escape Wulfhall. Glad to get away from the kin of the woman attempting to defile my name in Henry's ears. Glad to escape her too-talkative mother. We rode out one bright, cloudless day with the sun beating on our caps. The air was stiff, breezeless, still… a storm was coming.

My suspicions were proved correct. We reached Winchester through a raging tempest. Weighty cloaks were made heavier still by rain, and sheets of leather had been flung over the wagons bearing our chests, attempting to prevent ruin coming for our clothes, furniture and baggage. But for all our precautions, I felt like a drowned cat when I reached my chambers. Puddles of water were everywhere, and my ladies scampered and slipped, dripping upon the rushes, simultaneously attempting to attend to me and get the chests opened to ensure everything was safe.

"Go to!" I said irritably. "See to my possessions. Check the books first. I do not want them ruined." I turned to Nan Cobham and Margery Horsman. "You two come with me, and send for water for a bath. All other hands to the baggage!"

My ladies chuckled as I squelched off to change.

The summer storm was fierce and wild. The countryside, dried to a husk under the sun, swiftly became a swamp. Roads were flooded, homes became unusable, and farmers risked their lives trying to save herds.

"What a storm!" said Norris that night. "I have never seen its equal."

"Indeed," I said. "Smeaton has a task to try to drown it out."

The lad was playing true and bold, but the feral wind defied him, shrieking over Winchester like a banshee. I shuddered to hear it.

"My lady, are you cold?" Norris asked.

"I am fine, Norris," I said, smiling. "How is it that you always know when my body moves? No one else notices."

I was surprised to see his high cheekbones flush. He looked away, seemingly embarrassed, and I was baffled as to why.

*

In the days of our ancestors, Winchester had been England's capital. It was an ancient seat, with fine houses and a magnificent cathedral. Perhaps it was therefore fitting what occurred later in that cathedral; the dawn of a new age from amongst the old.

As we engaged in indoor pursuits, being banished from the country by rain, Jean de Dinteville arrived. Sent as a special envoy from François and his sister, Dinteville presented Marguerite's compliments.

"My greatest wish," I said, "next to having a son, is to see Queen Marguerite again."

Dinteville brought news. The Pope, he said, was outraged by Henry's conduct, most especially the execution of *Cardinal* Fisher. That summer, Pope Paul, with the backing of the College of Cardinals, had sent out the papal command which deprived Henry of his kingdom, and had written to François asking him ratify the sentence.

"My master, naturally, has no intention of doing any such thing," Dinteville said swiftly, seeing Henry's colour rising. "He thinks that this Pope, much like the last, is embedded in the Emperor's pocket and seeks your aid to free him. My King assures me that if his good brother would join him to assault Italy, together you might free the Pope and satisfy your mutual troubles at the same time."

Good brother, is it now? I wondered. *Now you want something, François …*

Henry did not appear to be listening to Dinteville as he rattled on. I knew Henry. He was worried. A papal command that he be deprived of his kingdom was no light matter. Although, even if issued formally this day, Pope Paul's threat would not come into action for a year… but what if his people heard of it and chose to rebel?

"We will think on these matters," I said after Dinteville finished and a thick, awkward silence fell. "Leave your letters with us, my lord. We will have an answer for you soon." I looked about the chamber, seeing rain slip down the windowpanes like tears. "Leave us," I said to the other petitioners. "The King must consult with his Council to see if a holy crusade to free the Bishop of Rome from the clutches of corruption may be undertaken by England."

Henry glanced at me with grateful eyes. For once he did not mind that I had interfered, and squeezed my fingers hard.

"Let us set aside François' requests," I said as soon as we were left with just Cranmer and Cromwell. "We have no need to insult any of our intelligences by lingering on *that* false friendship."

"That is certain," growled Henry. "But how to counteract this papal brief? Some answer must be given. To allow it to be heard by my people…"

I wrapped my tiny fingers about his. "Your people love you, my lord," I said gently. "Do not allow the blackness of this to dupe your mind into seeing enemies where there are none. The Pope, Rome, France, Spain… they are foes, but your people are not. And, as we have seen…" I waved my free hand at Dinteville's papers, "… all once-enemies may become friends again, when they want something."

"You are right," he said. "God's Blood! In my misery at the corruption of France and Rome I am brought to doubt the love of England!" He stared at me with fierce eyes. "I will not let the Bishop of Rome drive a wedge between me and my people!"

"He will never have the power to do that, my lord," I said. "Your people believe in you, as I do. They know all you do is for their betterment. They would follow you even into death with perfect trust and perfect love."

"Aye," he said, clutching my hand.

"I will put it to the Council," said Henry. He turned to Cromwell. "Gather them. There is no time to waste."

As Cromwell scurried off, I turned to Henry and Cranmer. "I think, my lord, that whilst this affair is dealt with by your Council, we should do something ourselves. Something to demonstrate to your people that they have no need to fear Rome. Something to show that we are just."

"What do you mean, Anne?"

"We are to consecrate three bishops this month, are we not?" I asked. "Foxe, Latimer and Hilsey." I gazed at Henry and saw he was starting to understand my meaning.

Because of fears about how the public would react, the consecration of new bishops had been subtle affairs. But now, we needed to demonstrate our might. We required an open show of defiance and courage, not only to inspire Henry's people, but to inform the Pope we feared him not. Fisher's bishopric of Rochester was presently vacant, and Henry had passed an Act taking back English Sees held by Italian men, and foreign cardinals. Salisbury had been stripped from the odious Campeggio, and Worcester had been taken from Ghinucci. My men were to replace them.

Nicholas Shaxton had already taken Salisbury, but Edward Foxe was to have Hereford, Hugh Latimer, Worcester, and John Hilsey, Rochester. It was a sign of Henry's favour that men I had cultivated would become the leading lights of the new English Church.

"Let us make a grand event of this occasion," I said. "Let His Eminence perform the ceremony, and let us attend, my lord. Together, as a united front, we will show the people the might of their King."

Henry stared as though he were seeing me for the first time. He reached out, a wondering look in his eyes, and gently touched my face. "You always know," he murmured. "You always know how to comfort me."

"I say this not only to bring you comfort, my lord," I said. "But because this is the time for us to act. We have been quiet too long. We should not hide in the shadows. We are in the right, and Rome in the wrong. Let God see our courage, my lord, and perhaps then He will bless our reign."

"You are right," he said. "Perhaps God saw our gentle ways and disapproved! Perhaps this is the reason we were denied our sons."

Cranmer was gazing at me as though I were the best gift anyone had granted him on New Year's morn. I could see he was inspired.

"You would be happy to preside, Eminence?" I asked.

"Joyous to be used for the will of God, Majesty."

Henry laughed. He lifted my hand to his lips and kissed it. Going to Cranmer, he threw his arm about the shoulders of his Archbishop and pulled him close. I did not hear what he whispered, but Cranmer smiled.

Henry bounded up the dais like a young stag and kissed me. "I go to the Council," he said. "But I will come to you tonight."

Watching him almost run off, with a new energy in his gait, I turned to my friend. "What did His Majesty say?"

Cranmer smiled and opened his eyes wide, teasing me. "As a man of the cloth," he said. "I cannot break sacred trust."

"Was it a confession, then?"

"It was, madam." Cranmer smiled wider. "But rest assured, it was one of perfect love and perfect trust from a husband to his wife." I smiled to hear him ape my words about Henry's people.

That night, Henry came to me. Although his Council had found nothing secure they could work on to counter the papal bill, he was suffused with enthusiasm. The thought of defying Paul had inspired him.

Henry arrived with his men, dressed in his nightshirt. There was much ribald jesting, as though we were being put to bed on our wedding night... something that had, in fact, never happened for us.

As Henry all but leapt into my bed and waved his men away, I could not help but grant Jane Seymour a great, fat grin, as she turned to close the door. Her face did not change, but I hoped I had shown her that whilst Henry might protest he adored her, he loved only me.

*

On the 19th of September, Latimer, Foxe and Hilsey were consecrated in Winchester Cathedral. It was a magnificent ceremony. With Henry and me in the royal box, Cranmer officiating, and every prelate and noble within three counties commanded to attend, the Cathedral was packed. Droves of common men and women swarmed to us too, drawn by the lure of alms, celebration and worship of God.

I watched them, *my* men, on the dais as they were welcomed as God's warriors. I had supported them, promoted their careers and brought them to this place. With my hand guiding them, we would bring England to new hope, and new life, for the glory of God and the honour of the people.

Pungent incense poured through the air, and the choir sang. As Cranmer spoke ancient words, conferring the rights of these men upon them, I felt utterly content. My marriage was imperfect, and perhaps would always be so, but there was much to grant satisfaction, if one was willing to see it.

The only thing that delighted me more than witnessing this public, brave, bold ceremony, was to see the Catholic faction looking ill at ease. The appointment of these bishops, as radical in thought as they were able of mind, did not please the old guard of court. They wanted us to backtrack, to slide into the old ways. This was a clear sign that was not about to happen.

I held my head high. This new age was ours and all who did not support us would fall into obscurity, just as the Bishop of Rome had.

Chapter Thirty-Seven

Winchester
September 1535

We had a surprising advocate who took up the task of answering the Pope's threat; Stephen Gardiner.

Gardiner had not had a good few years. After failing to support Henry during the submission of the clergy he had left court, hoping to distance himself from Henry's wrath. He had lost his post as King's Secretary, and had been the subject of investigation by Cromwell, on Henry's orders, on suspicion of doubting the supremacy.

But worms have ways of surviving in their dank little holes.

The crisis of the papal bull brought Gardiner into the Council again, and it was he who came up with the best answers. Chosen to respond to Pope Paul, he had a ready quill and a clever mind, and was keen to show himself Henry's true subject.

Gardiner's first draft was fiery. It declared the Pope had no cause to mourn a traitor like Fisher, and the Bishop's death had been merciful. The final draft, approved by Cromwell, was entitled *De Vera Obedientia, Of True Obedience*. It defended the supremacy and censured Rome, using Scripture as its authority. Gardiner wrote that he, like many other bishops, had sworn an oath to the Pope, but had been deceived. The loyalty of England's clergy was due to its King, he argued, therefore oaths sworn to Rome were unlawful.

Gardiner, inflated by new respect and favour, worked day and night. As Henry admitted himself impressed by his work, Gardiner began boasting, and Cromwell grew annoyed.

"How swift do men forget how far they fell in times of trouble when new opportunities are granted," he said.

"You are finding the good Bishop irritating?"

"I am finding the good Bishop irritating." Cromwell smiled. "We, neither of us, madam, have any cause to trust Gardiner. He has never supported the supremacy, nor your marriage."

"Once he did. Once he asked me to be his patron."

"Those days are long gone, Majesty. It falls to us now to find another post for Gardiner. Once his use is spent in this matter, he should be sent away."

"Are there not enough chairs in the Privy Council Chamber?" I asked, teasingly, "... that you and Gardiner cannot fit about the same table?"

"When he is present, Majesty, space diminishes rapidly."

"The King has been speaking of sending another ambassador to France," I said. "Perhaps Gardiner, having proved his worth here, might become useful there?"

"That would be a fortunate appointment," Cromwell said, his eyes dancing.

I was willing to aid Cromwell. In truth, I was none too sure about Gardiner myself. He had shown how quickly he could switch sides more than once, and I wondered how long he would remain loyal this time. My brother was unhappy not to be chosen as ambassador, but I explained the reasons.

"Besides," I added. "Whilst François reaches out to us now, he still does not hold with our sympathies. Perhaps it would be better to send one of the old guard, to show him that whilst much has altered in England, much also has not."

"And Gardiner is so eager to prove himself that he will not allow any to speak against the supremacy openly," mused my brother.

Within a week of finishing his brief, Gardiner was sent to France.

I never saw him again.

*

Upon his return to London, as he left us hawking and hunting in the West Country, Cromwell suspended the powers of all English bishops to allow his men to complete their surveys. He invoked his authority as Vicar-General to establish a court which would return these powers gradually, making it clear bishops were now officers of the state, bound to serve the King. Like the Whitestaffs, when the King died, so would the bishops' powers. It would be up to the next King to reinstate this authority, meaning that the bishops were not only sworn to offer loyalty, but their future authority and careers depended on it. No more would men of the Church live free and feckless. No… They were lashed to the supremacy, chained to the royal line.

If this was not enough, Cromwell tightened his grip. Privileges were restricted as Cromwell withheld rights to visitation and probate, from which the clergy gathered lucrative fees.

Power and money… Cromwell understood the hold they had on the souls of men.

His investigations, too, were gathering pace, and as men poured into abbeys, monasteries and nunneries, complaints washed into court, detailing how unscrupulous agents were gathering evidence. As we heard more and more reports that Cromwell's men were lying, exaggerating or fantasising in order to condemn religious houses, I became increasingly disturbed. Henry, however, accepted all the reports as truth, and was mortified.

"I read here of *orgies*!" he said, his cheeks pink.

Why do you find it so surprising that monks might breaks vows and keep mistresses, husband? I wondered. *You have done the same.*

"And drunken cavorting," he went on. "Of intoxicated monks wagering at dice, fornicating with fellow brothers and granting children to nuns!" He shook his head, looking queasy. "It is well I am here to set this right."

"It is," I replied. "But let us remember, beloved, not all houses are of equal sin. Disband the fallen, by all means, but we must preserve those that can be redeemed. England cannot be left without abbeys and priests! We must *reform*, my love, not destroy. Did Christ not welcome the corrupt into his hallowed presence and bring them to goodness? It is up to you to show the same mercy."

Henry agreed. The evidence allowed us to issue a full-scale order of reformation. It was needed, but I was afraid that we might descend into a fever of righteous indignation, attacking those who had committed only minor crimes with the same wrath as those who clearly had fallen into an impenetrable pit of sin.

It is all too easy, when a wave breaks, to be swept along.

Many houses *were* guilty. Abbots and abbesses were usually elected by fellow monks and nuns. If the order was subject to laxity and pleasure, its members would choose one whom they knew would look the other way. In many monasteries, a luxurious standard of living was offered, and in nunneries it appeared the doors were not kept well locked, as pregnancies seemed rife.

But when I looked over Cromwell's reports, something nagged at me. It took me some days to discover what this sensation, that of a thought lingering at the edges of the mind, unable to find a path in, wanted. But in time it became clear.

Cromwell's reports were *all too similar*. It might be reasonable to suggest the sins of man are often the same, but the fact that the *same sins* were found in *each and every* house of worship troubled me. It suggested Cromwell's men were indeed fabricating their reports.

It also suggested Cromwell might have asked them to do so.

This was not reform, I realised. This was the first trumpet blast of war… a war on the Church, led by Cromwell. I wondered if his eyes, like Henry's, had lit upon the treasures of the monasteries and noted rich pickings for a soldier of fortune.

Once a mercenary, always a mercenary, I thought. *And he would make my husband a pirate too…*

Chapter Thirty-Eight

Winchester
September 1535

Is it possible? I thought as I sat upon my horse, sick to my stomach.

I had vomited each morning for a week. My breasts were tender and I shied from Henry's exuberant touch at night. I did not want to say anything as yet, for fear of exciting Henry's hopes and shattering them if I was mistaken, but I was coming to think I was with child.

The thought filled me with as much excitement as dread. The loss of two children hung upon me, and although the flashes of memory had abated, they had not gone. I could wear red without fearing I might lose my mind, but my nights remained troubled by visions of my children. Fear was within my soul. A clammy-palmed wraith whose hands shook and heart hammered to think that I might have to face loving a child within me, and losing it again.

I tried to set aside such fears, but the clammy presence in my soul persisted. *What if you lose another child?* he whispered. *What if you have to face another dead baby… another streak of scarlet blood upon a cloth?*

I needed a son, but the thought of bearing not life but death from my womb again made me cold. No… I would not tell Henry until I was sure, and I would take care. If there was a child growing under my heart, I would keep it safe. Never again would I face the ghastly anguish of seeing my child born dead, nor endure the slow, lingering blood of death leeching from the midst of life.

For that reason, I was not as active on the hunt that day as I might have been. My snail's speed allowed me to keep pace with my ladies and some of Henry's men… who were less interested in chasing game than they were with pursuing each other.

Two were Mary Shelton and Norris. Their horses close together, they chatted brightly as they rode. Norris was a widower, and my cousin had been suggested as a bride for him some time ago, but he had seemed reluctant until now.

As my husband's Groom of the Stool, Norris knew Mary had been his master's mistress. This, perhaps, had put him off, since if she was still sharing Henry's bed, any children she bore would be suspect. It certainly did not appear as though he was concerned about not having a virgin wife, for now that Mary had been gently abandoned by Henry in favour of Jane Seymour, Norris paid court to his fiancée happily.

A strange feeling entered my heart to see them. It was an ugly, creeping, uneasy sensation.

What has Mary to recommend her above all others? I thought with a bitter tone.

Jealous? asked Katherine.

It was no use arguing with Katherine.

As we rode on, ducking under branches just starting to display the golden blaze of autumn, I understood Katherine was right. I was jealous. Norris was not only a fine man, but he had been my good friend. I resented someone taking my place. He had always adored *me*, looked up to *me*, told me I was beautiful… It sounds shallow, but I envied my cousin her suitor. When one is alone, as I so often felt, the solace of an admirer is hard to set aside.

Part of me had grown reliant on Norris. The thought of him being taken away by another woman was painful.

*

"Will I never be permitted to decide anything for my daughter?" I demanded. "Will everything always have to go through your Council? Through men who know nothing of children?"

Henry glared. Lady Bryan had written from Hatfield to say that Elizabeth was able to drink from a cup by herself, and therefore had no further need for her wet nurse. I had started a letter to Lady Bryan on how Elizabeth should be weaned, as I had been reading medical texts for some months in preparation for this momentous event in my daughter's life. But Henry had stopped me.

"This must be agreed by me and my Council," he said as he stood over me, casting a shadow across the letter containing my maternal advice and wisdom.

"And as but her *lowly* mother, I have no say?"

"It is unlikely to be countermanded, Anne," he said, a strained note of immense weariness throbbing in his voice. "The Council will agree, but our daughter is a princess, and therefore everything she does must be sanctioned by them."

"Do I have no authority over her care, as her mother?"

"You do," he said, glowering. "And as I have just explained, your commands will not be rejected." He sighed irritably. "You complain when our daughter is not accorded full respect as a princess," he pointed out. "Yet each time you think you are being passed over, you lash out as though Elizabeth were your daughter alone. She is not. She is mine and she is England's. Understand that, madam."

He turned and left. I looked down at my letter. I could concede that Henry had a point. I did indeed strike like a snake when I thought anyone was not offering Elizabeth full rights and honours, but this was no matter of marriage, or the succession, this was her *weaning*. Should not such a simple, intimate moment in my daughter's life be mine? If I had breastfed her, as I had yearned to, I would have decided when to wean her. But because she had been torn from my breast, I could not.

As Henry promised, the Council agreed. Upon hearing this, I went back to my letter, and included all the recommendations I had found over the past few months, as well as personal messages to Lady Bryan, and my aunts. I lectured them on choosing the right milk, recommending goat above cow, as I had heard from many sources it was purer. I told them I expected the introduction of poultry and other white meats to be gradual. The best times to wean a child were either in the spring or autumn, when the moon was increasing, so I told them to start immediately, since autumn was upon us. I instructed them to only allow Elizabeth a little wine, as whilst it was common to start a child on ale and wine at the same time as meat, I had read that only small amounts should be permitted. I sent recipes for barley broth, and told them Elizabeth should be fully washed twice a week. It was said that too much play could over-heat the blood, and not enough could make a child dull, so I instructed them to play with my daughter as they saw fit, and to be strict with her tempers, so she might grow into a woman with more control over her rages than I or her father were able to exert over ours.

When I sealed my letter that night with dripping red wax and the imprint of my royal stamp, I was satisfied, but there was an ache in my heart.

I missed my daughter. It was a raw, constant pain. How would my Elizabeth have changed since the beginning of summer? It was my duty to be at Henry's side, but continual separation from my child was a hard price to pay.

I called my ladies to play cards, and as we took to the table, I noted there was someone absent. "Where is Jane Seymour?" I asked Margaret Douglas.

"She was taken unwell, Majesty," said Margaret. My niece was no skilled liar. Her cheeks ignited and I realised Jane was not ill.

She was with Henry.

*

With relations with France improving, at least whilst François was keen to draw Henry into war against the Emperor, I took it upon myself to write to my old friend and mentor, Marguerite de Navarre. I was sure Marguerite would embrace all that we had done in England. If we could not trust her brother, I knew we could trust her.

I had heard much of her since I had left France. Marguerite took her humanist principles seriously, even taking to the streets, so she might hear petitions of unfortunate souls in person. She called herself *"The Prime Minister of the Poor"* and none could doubt her devotion. She was a tender, loving soul, who brought solace to many and protected reformers. If Margaret of Austria had been my mentor in the ways women may control power, Marguerite was the paragon of what power should be used *for*.

Marguerite had a daughter now, Jeanne of Navarre, but, like me, Marguerite had lost her son to bitter death. I felt this connection of sorrow brought us closer together.

My letter was full of hope, extolling her virtues and letting her know that I hoped to give a son to my lord, as well as see our countries come together as friends. As I sent the letter, I took heart from it.

I could not run scared from the possibility of losing my child. That, in itself, might bring this pregnancy into danger. I had to be strong, like Marguerite, and hand myself to God. In God would I trust.

I did not know that man, not God, would let me down.

Chapter Thirty-Nine

The Vyne, Hampshire,
and Windsor Castle
October 1535

"You are sure?"

"How many times will you ask, Henry?" A merry smile eclipsed my face. He had asked four times already. "I am sure. I am with child."

A joyful bark came from his mouth as he leapt, pulling me into his arms. "God has heard our prayers," he said, burying his head in my hair and knocking my becoming cap of purple velvet awry. "You said it, did you not? When you asked for the ceremony for our bishops? You said God would approve!"

I laughed, wrapping my arms about my husband. It was a hard task. That summer, hunting and hawking had not stripped weight from Henry as they had in other years. He had never been a small man, but now I felt like a slight fairy embraced by a great troll when he took hold of me.

"I will go to church and give thanks," he said, kissing me over and over.

"I will come with you."

We processed to Mass in the chapel at The Vyne with joy in our hearts. Everyone remarked upon it, saying that Henry had never looked so young. Young he might appear, in his joy, but not so was he in body. His legs had caused him constant irritation that summer. Veins had grown large and swollen in them, no doubt because of the extra weight his form was forced to carry. They stood out; hideous, lumpy blue lines coursing over white flesh. At times, when I looked on them in bed, I shuddered.

Although he made it clear that he adored me, as before when I fell pregnant Henry decided we must separate. "There can be nothing to disturb our child," he said, gazing at me with faint disapproval, as though I had been the only one who had ever wished to share a bed. "In the past, we have been too eager, too careless. It will not happen again. Our son will be born in perfect health."

"We were together in the first months when Elizabeth was within me," I said. I was not particularly sad to think that Henry and I would not share a bed. His problems with his manhood had abated during the summer, but it was a struggle at times to be together. But at the same time, I did not want little Jane Seymour curled up beside him.

Jane might pretend to be humble and meek around me, but from what I had heard at Wulfhall, she was clearly duplicitous and sly. I little needed to lose my husband to an enemy. But Henry would not be moved.

"We will separate," he said. "Until you are churched. God has shown His approval. I will not risk His ire."

And my fears about Jane, were, as I swiftly realised, justified. In addition to her royal knight, Jane had supporters. It was only to be expected. People had flocked to me when I was the most important person in Henry's life. Now, they went to Jane. They hoped to secure influence and favour, and I had no doubt, many of them hoped to use her to reduce my power too.

Gertrude Courtenay and Nicholas Carewe supported the Seymours, or at least, would support them until they got what they wanted. Bryan, who was Carewe's brother-in-law, had joined this motley band and the Poles, along with the Dowager of Kildare were in league with them too. Their aims were clear; they wanted the Lady Mary restored to the succession and less, if any, reform. They wanted the Pope to again be England's spiritual leader, with Henry as his malleable lapdog, and no more common men like Cromwell taking posts that surely, in a sane world, *only* nobility should possess.

Their dislike for the gentry, as Jane was, and for the lower classes, as Cromwell had hailed from, was so obvious that I wondered about this alliance. Cromwell, I believed, was making nice with them as he saw the benefits of keeping communication, even with enemies, open… But what of Jane and her brothers, Thomas and Edward? Had they convinced themselves that all this attention and affection was genuine? Or were they simply looking for a ladder to climb, caring not for the rungs they must use on the way up?

I did not care for Jane's new friends, or the way I had heard her speak to Henry. In her own way, this submissive little worm was even more dangerous than the parrot had been.

And I was not well. Pregnancy, if it suits any poor woman, did not favour me. I became weak, fractious, weary, and depressed. I did not want to hear music, or read books, sure signs of despair, but took instead to staring from the window, thinking of times I had felt my heart sing with joy, knowing I loved and was loved in return.

Disillusionment is a cold, stark place to dwell.

"A penny?" asked a voice at my side.

I turned to see Norris, and my heart leapt in my chest, descending to flutter like a little bird.

What is wrong with you? I asked myself, blushing as his handsome face turned quizzical. *Are you so starved of affection, Anne Boleyn, that the slightest hint may steal your heart from Henry?*

"A penny?" I asked.

"For your thoughts, Majesty."

I smiled sadly. "You would use the words of Thomas More to bring comfort to me?" I asked. Although the phrase had been around as long as any could remember, More had popularized it in his book *Four Last Things*.

Seeing his face grow disturbed, I went on. "I do not think you would want to hear them, Norris," I said. "No one wants to hear of sorrow. Courtiers come to my chambers for lively discussion and dance. That is what my people expect from their *most happy* Queen."

"It is the Seymour girl, is it not?" he asked gently, sitting at my side. "You are sad the King has gone to her."

"I am sad the King would go to anyone else. Once, he told me I was everything he needed, and I believed him." My eyes flashed to the window, and behind me, my son's face looked on in sympathy. "I was a fool."

His hand touched mine, and I felt a spark dart through my blood. I looked up, my cheeks warm, to find him gazing on me with the gentlest of expressions. His hawk-ridged nose and high cheekbones caught the shadows and the light. His eyes, which I had always thought blue, I realised now were grey. Golden lights shimmered at their centres, and reflected the colours he saw, transforming into ocean blue, emerald green, or, as he looked at me, dark grey, like a storm upon the tumbling sea.

"You were not a fool," he murmured. "Or if you were, no more fool than the rest of us who fall in love."

"You will tell me she is nothing," I said, my voice turning harsh. "You will tell me she is a tool for the King. That he uses her and I should not be sorrowful or afraid to see him with another woman."

"I would not," he said. "I would tell you to take heart, for although the one you love is not faithful in body, he is in his soul. I would say that many other men both admire and love you. You are not only Queen of England, but to all who know you, you are Queen of their hearts."

"I am not Queen of my enemies' hearts," I countered.

"I said all who *know* you," he insisted, a winning smile on his lips. "Your foes do not, otherwise they too would fall for you."

"Norris…" I whispered, hardly trusting myself to say anything. My heart and soul were lost, yet he had the power to draw me back to the world. "You have always been such a good friend."

For a moment, we just stared at each other, an unspoken admittance of something more hanging between us, but as one of my maids laughed nearby, our eyes snapped from each other's, and the spell was broken.

"Come," he said. "If you sit here, looking broken, then Carewe and his trolls have won, have they not?" He smiled. "Play for us, Majesty. Lose yourself in music. Then sorrow will not be able to reach you."

I did as he asked, to make him happy. But as I played, I did not leave the world behind. One face, one voice, came to me.

Norris had helped me. When others would have told me lies to cheer me, he did not. There is nobility in honesty. He offered me a moment of truth in a world of lies. And amongst the lies and deceit, the pain and grief, there was, in this cold world, a sincere, good heart that beat for me, as mine did for him. I knew that now.

It would never become anything more. Unlike Henry I honoured my marriage vows, and the oaths of love. But love does not have to be expressed physically to find form.

The world would not understand. People thought the only way to express love was to take a person to bed, but there are many ways to love. What I felt for Norris was not the same emotion I had for Henry, but love comes in many guises, and just because it comes in different forms that does not mean it cannot run as strong as another, older, and more familiar kind of love.

I needed to be loved. I hungered for it… and in Norris' eyes there it burned, for me.

*

After four days at The Vyne, mostly spent hawking in the marshlands, we made for London. We reached Windsor by nightfall, and to hear the excitement of my ladies about drawing baths, you might have thought we had been living in caves for the past few years.

Talks immediately resumed about a meeting in France, and a match between Elizabeth and the Dauphin. I had to swallow a great, hard lump of pride in agreeing to play nicely with François. Not that I had any real choice.

But this is not about you, Anne, I told myself. *This is for Elizabeth.*

A royal betrothal, even if it came to nothing, as so many did, would ensure my daughter had international recognition. Even if I had to swallow my own soul, I would protect Elizabeth.

"Shall we bring our daughter to court, this Christmas?" I asked Henry. "When the French ambassadors see our fine girl, they will fall in love with her, as all others do."

Henry smiled, but he was distracted, scribbling away on a bit of parchment. Quick as a slip, I pulled it from him. "What has you so removed from me?" I asked in a teasing voice, scanning the parchment rapidly. My heart fell. It was a love letter, and it was not to me.

Henry tried to snatch it back, but by the time his hand made contact with the parchment, it had fallen from my hand onto the floor.

"You love her *above all others*," I said in a dull tone. "Was that not once what you said to me?"

I laughed. It was an eerie sound, floating from my mouth as though I were not the source, but something buried deep inside my soul was. It was the broken one, curled in a labyrinth of perdition inside me.

"I am writing on behalf of Norris," Henry blustered, his cheeks red. I arched an eyebrow. Did he expect me to believe these lies?

"Norris adores Jane Seymour, does he?" I asked lightly. "Some competition for you then, my love."

Henry's face turned purple as he struggled to control himself. "You should not excite yourself," he said. "It is bad for the baby."

"Do you suppose that all actions that are bad are mine alone, then?" I asked, my voice calm and numb. "For you never seem to think that you might affect my emotions. You run to your little whores, and when I find out, you blame me. It is very convenient for you, is it not? To blame me for your sins."

"Enough!" he shouted. "I will leave you. When you are calm we will talk again."

"Am I the one blustering, shouting and growing red in the face?" I asked mildly. "I think that is *you*, husband. And the reason you grow so wild is because you know I am right." I pointed a finger at him. "God rewarded us, Henry, when we followed His wishes. If anyone is putting our child in danger it is you, for you are the one who betrays sacred vows, sworn before man and God."

He left and as he went my anger drained away. It gave me strength, and courage, when it lived inside me, but when it left, I was emptier still.

"Ask Norris to come and speak with me," I said to Mary Howard. As she departed, my voice dropped as I spoke to myself. "I am in need of a friend."

Chapter Forty

Windsor Castle
October 1535

"I know not what you thought you were doing, Lady Rochford," I said to my brother's wife. "But you will not do so again. Think yourself fortunate I petitioned the King on your behalf at all. My father wanted to leave you to rot."

"I am grateful for Your Majesty's intervention," she said humbly, her eyes on the floor.

"I only did so to prevent scandal staining our name," I said. "Not for you."

"I understand." Jane glanced up, her emerald eyes shining with tears. "Majesty," she said. "I would beg a favour."

I stared coldly at her. "You think you deserve more from me?" I asked. "I allowed you to retain your position and freed you from the Tower. You think to ask for more?"

"I would ask you to intercede with your brother, Majesty," she murmured. "If you can find it in your heart."

"Because he has mentioned casting you off?" I asked. "Are you so surprised? You disgraced our family and humiliated him." I stared at her. "I will not intercede with my brother. Your relationship with him is your own business, and you have had more than you deserve from me already."

As Jane left, tears blinding her, Cranmer brought in Alexander Aless. The Scot was a reformer, keen to make links with England.

"I understand you support the German Lutherans, Master Aless," I said, looking at this high-browed man. He had a large forehead, and eyebrows which hung so low he looked as though he had a permanent frown, but not one of censure. It was as though he were constantly scrutinising the world, as any good scholar might. He had come to England with copies of books for Henry by the Lutheran philosopher Phillip Melanchthon, and was a keen follower of the idea of having vernacular Bibles produced for his people.

"I am sure you see their worth too, Your Majesty," he said in a heavy, charming brogue. "My good friend the Archbishop has informed me you are a guiding light in England."

"My charitable friend Archbishop Cranmer is often too kind," I said, smiling at him. "But it is true that I see the value of new friends, especially those who think the same as us in some ways, even if not in all."

Aless nodded. "I understand His Majesty is not fond of the followers of Luther," he said. "But I also understand he is considering a Bible in English."

"He is," I said.

"And has come to consider this, because of *your* intervention, madam."

"I would never claim to influence the King," I said, although everyone knew it was a lie. "But we have talked, and I have told him my opinion. My husband is a wise and learned man, as well as a mighty King. He likes to hear all that is said, and unlike some other monarchs, does not close his mind to new thought."

Also not entirely true, but I held hope.

"It is the wish of all subjects, my lady, that they might have the blessing of such a sovereign."

Aless told me much of changes occurring in Scotland, and the rise of reform there. It brought me hope that one day we would see reformation in all the lands of Christ. Hope that the power of the papacy was waning, and soon all of Christ's subjects would find a personal link to God.

*

As the winter winds tried to reach us early, there were rumblings of discontent.

Although reformers had been delighted to see Henry and me consecrate our new bishops in such a public, bold way, conservatives were not. There was word that Katherine was writing furiously to her nephew and the Pope, asking for aid. All the Holy Father could do was to lead prayers for Katherine. He offered seven Lents of pardon to all who would say three paternosters at three of the afternoon on St John's Day, and it was said those prayers were for Katherine, Mary, and all who kept the faith in England.

Henry reacted by swearing he would rid himself of Katherine in the next session of Parliament. Gertrude Courtenay was seen heading for Chapuys' London house that night in a rather poor disguise, off to tell her ally that Henry was threatening their mutual friend.

But suddenly, and to everyone's overwhelming surprise, the Emperor became friendlier. As he travelled to Rome, to give thanks for his victory that summer, there was word that he was speaking calmly, even well, of his royal brother.

"What is that Spanish fox up to?" I wondered aloud as George and I walked in the gardens at Windsor. It was a bright, blustery day. Wind whipped about the trees, spilling leaves to tumble and spiral through the air, but it did not feel ominous. There was something playful about the wind, as though autumn had grown weary of the strain in England, and had decided to gambol a while.

"Most likely he fears the new closeness between France and England," said my brother, pulling up the collar of his cloak to keep the wind from his neck.

I snorted. "Closeness… Perhaps we are in some ways, but far removed in others." I sighed. "I feel so… displaced, since François slandered me."

"It is to be expected," said George. "France was your home and François your King. It is an unsettling thing for a man to lose faith in his monarch. The King is the seat of all stability and grace. When a man loses faith in him, the world trembles."

"And what of when women lose faith in their kings?" I asked. "Two have I been failed by now: Henry and François."

George glanced about. "Fear not," I said. "I know how to go unheard."

His expression of wry disbelief amused me and I chortled. "I know how to keep my voice unheard, *sometimes*."

George smiled. "Your honesty is part of your charm, sister. Norris notes it often."

Something in my heart sang. I busied myself with a ribbon on my skirts, much to my brother's bafflement.

"Have you truly lost faith in the King?" he asked quietly as we moved on.

"As a husband," I said. "Yes. As a monarch… I know not. Sometimes he is so strong and virtuous that he fills me with golden hope. At other times, when he is led by others, I am not so sure." I sighed. "His tempers and personality are as changeable as his virility in bed."

George guffawed so loudly that Cromwell and Cranmer, deep in conversation on the other side of the garden green, glanced up. I took my brother's hand, pretending we were playing, and laughed with him. It did my heart good, even if it was at Henry's expense.

"Perhaps things will improve," said my brother.

"There is not much sign of that," I said. "The people are agitated, George. They mutter in the shadows. The investigations make many uneasy, even those who pushed for them, like me."

"Because you think Cromwell will convince the King to keep the wealth for himself?"

I nodded. "But I will reach him, somehow, if I can prise him from the claws of that Seymour wench long enough to talk. If the wealth of the monasteries was granted to the poor, there would be less dissent. I can do nothing for what they think about Katherine and Mary, but I can do what is right."

Something, some whisper of the zealous young girl I once was, who held such high, lofty ideals, came surging into my soul. It was good to feel her. For too long had she been absent, buried under layers of pain and misery.

"I will make him see," I said.

"If you can control your temper long enough to speak with him."

"Perhaps in loss of faith, there may come loss of love," I said. "And then I shall be free of him. Even if I have to remain at his side for the rest of my life, if I loved him no more, there would be no pain."

"Would you want that? A loveless marriage?"

"Not at all," I said. "But if I must be forced into one, where my husband runs after pretty girls and plain alike as he descends into crumbling dotage, then at least if I cease to love him, I will be free not to care. I will become as Katherine was, and take up causes in which I know I may do good for England."

I looked up into the skies. "If I cannot have love and happiness," I said. "I will grant them to others."

"Where is my Queen amongst this rabble?" Henry shouted over the din in my chambers. Abruptly the music ceased and the giggling gaggle of courtiers who had been playing *Blind Man's Bluff* fell still. Weston, who was blindfolded, almost fell over. Henry sounded angry, but as the chaos quietened, a great roar of laughter burst from his mouth. "You play like children," he chuckled indulgently as he passed, Culpepper and Richard Page at his back. He came towards me on my throne, spying Norris and Tom at my feet.

"Sweetheart," he said warmly, making me arch an eyebrow in surprise. We had not made up from our last fight, but it appeared Henry had forgotten this.

"My lord husband," I said. "I am thrilled to find you here. We thought you were… otherwise engaged."

Henry skirted my suggestion that he had been with Jane Seymour and sat down. "I have word from Kimbolton," he said, his face an unpleasant mask of gloating glee. "The Dowager is ill. Her servants think she will not last the week."

I attempted to hide my disgust at his joy. I could understand it, of course. Katherine put our marriage, daughter and relationship with Spain in peril. Her death would remove all those problems. But even if he felt happiness, did he not think it distasteful to display it? This was a woman he had lived with for twenty years, and once had claimed to love.

Having been set in Katherine's place, as her true *inheritrix*, I wondered if, one day, should I die in childbirth, or of natural causes, Henry would be as merry to see me go. I had given him as much trouble as Katherine.

"That is good news," I said. "But nothing should be said at court."

"Of course," Henry said, a shadow of his former anger resurfacing. "That is obvious."

Obvious was Henry's new word. He repeated it often, like a spoilt little boy. He had used it against Cromwell of late, making Norfolk snort with amusement. Henry thought he was pointing out *how very clever* he was, by protesting after any wise person had said something that it was *obvious*. He was using it to cover his inadequacies, of which there were many.

"But when she is gone, Anne, finally will we be free." Henry sat back and sighed with contentment. His eyes were drawn to Norris. "Here again, old friend?" he asked. "Whenever you are not duty-bound to be with me, I find you with my wife."

"My Queen is the wisest of women," said Norris, the faintest hint of a blush on his sharp cheekbones. "She has been counselling me about the match with Mistress Shelton."

"Ah," said Henry. "She is a good girl, that one." His eyes grew soft, no doubt remembering intimate tussles. "You would have a fine wife, there, Norris."

"So the Queen tells me," he said.

"You should come to me if you want advice about women, Norris," said Henry, rising from his chair. "There is much I could teach you." He winked and I had to grip the armrests of my chair to keep from leaping to my feet and slapping him about his fat, arrogant face.

Henry moved off through the crowds and I turned to Norris and Tom. "Do not listen to the King," I whispered. "If you want to know how to satisfy a woman, ask a woman."

Not a man who thinks that the source of a woman's pleasure lies in being lied to, I thought. *Nor one who has to cover up his inadequacy by shaming his wife.*

Chapter Forty-One

Greenwich Palace
Late October – November 1535

"At last, I have it for you, Majesty," crowed Cranmer as he entered my chamber bearing a book. "The Coverdale Bible."

Miles Coverdale was a scholar who had produced an English translation of the Bible, based largely on Tyndale's work. There was hope amongst our faction that this rendering might prove more acceptable to Henry, since it was not penned by Tyndale, leading the way for an accepted English Bible.

George Constantine, he who had been suspected of working for Thomas More, had found this book for me. He had written to Brereton, his old school-friend, admitting that he had accepted freedom in return for promising to spy for More, but had not done so. Safe, now that More was dead, Constantine had recently returned to London, and Brereton had found him a position as Norris' servant. Norris had spoken well of Constantine, and Brereton too, so whilst he had made suspect deals with papists in the past, I was certain he would not do so again.

All people deserve a second chance.

I held out eager hands, and smiled as I read the dedication. It was to Henry and his *"dearest wife and most virtuous princess, Queen Anne."* The binding had my initials embossed on its dark leather cover. The frontispiece was designed by Holbein, and showed Henry as an Old Testament King, in the model of King David. He was enthroned above all lords, temporal and spiritual, holding a sword and a Bible to demonstrate his dual powers. Henry was handing the Bible down to three bishops. In the past, all such images had shown the Church as above the King, but here, Henry conferred spiritual authority on his clergy, not the other way around. It was a unique, revolutionary image.

"I shall place it in my chambers," I said, "so all who visit may partake of its wisdom."

"The King remains unconvinced about allowing it to be widely published," Cranmer said. "But he has agreed, Majesty, to our notion about printing it in Southwark. He says it may be read by the nobility alone, as they will understand it better than the common man, but I think we are one step closer to having a vernacular Bible that all men may draw comfort from."

I smiled. I was as enthused as he, even though I had had to ask Cranmer to take this petition to Henry on his own. Henry had remembered his anger at me for confronting him about Jane Seymour. Our relationship was strained, but I reasoned this was not my fault. Henry had made his bed, and I was not in it.

"This brings me hope, Eminence," I said, running a finger over the vellum. "Hope for the future."

*

In November, the childless Duke of Milan, who had been ailing for some time, died. This brought up fresh strife, as the duchy of Milan had been claimed by both François and Charles. And it was not only they who were troubled.

"The Pope is trying to convince them to join forces against England," said George. "He thinks that this could be the best way to unite them, by promising they will each have a stake in Milan."

"Surely they are more likely to fight each other than link arms as brothers and sail for England?"

"Which is perhaps why the Bishop of Rome is so keen to draw them swiftly into negotiations," said my brother, taking a goblet of wine from his wife with little more than a second glance. He had grudgingly accepted Jane's return to my chambers for the sake of appearances, but they met little and spoke less. "Paul thinks to call his dogs and set them on England."

I watched Jane move away, and start talking to Jane Seymour. She hid it well, but her heart broke each time George treated her as though she were invisible. How could I not understand? Henry did the same to me.

If only I could be free of my love for Henry, I thought.

"Perhaps if Henry could be persuaded to support French interests in Milan, they might finally accept Elizabeth," I said thoughtfully.

"If we can get him to think on anything but his *poetry*." My brother pulled a weary face of distaste and I chuckled. Of late, Henry had become quite overcome with his own brilliance, as he alone saw it, in the hallowed realms of poetry.

"The King's verse grows no better?" I asked. "I remain unsurprised. He has never learnt that words will not obey even a king and rhyme where they have no cause."

"Neither has he learnt that that *middle* of poems are just as important as the first two, and last two, lines," said my brother. "There are all sorts of rubbish thrown in between."

I cackled like a merry witch. "Oftentimes, brother," I said. "I think it may be my fault. When he wooed me, I was so lost in love that I praised his efforts more than they deserved. I should have told him straight when his poems were unpleasing, for now he lingers over a verse for the Seymour whore all day, and emerges with something that sounds like a tavern ditty sung by drunkards."

"Not that she would say a thing," said my brother, glancing at her. "She cannot read, can she? So she knows not what a good or bad poem is."

"Perhaps that is why he likes her so. She is easily impressed."

"As we see by her admiration of his clothes," said my brother.

"They grow more tasteless by the day," I agreed. "Sometimes I have to cover my eyes when he enters a room, for they are assaulted by the glare of garish hues." I tittered. "He will never learn that tawdry show becomes not a king."

We had kept our voices low, but as the two Janes turned to take a turn about the chamber, I saw the eyes of my sister-in-law light up. I swallowed, hoping that she would not dare repeat what she had just overheard. To laugh at Henry's clothes or his poetry was to mock the King. If Henry heard, we might swiftly be on worse terms than ever before.

*

"Take also this," I said, stepping from the dais and removing a golden chain from my waist. Lord Grey stepped forward, amazed at his good fortune. "It is worth one hundred marks," I said, "and I would have you take this purse as well."

Grey was going to Ireland on a mission for Henry. Ireland was proving troublesome. Rebels had risen there, and Henry feared they might be in league with Rome, or the Emperor. Grey had considerable forces, and gifts from Henry for undertaking this mission to bring unruly Ireland into line, but I wanted to show my support too. A personal gift from the Queen was a mark of favour. I wanted our representative in Ireland, the very country I might have been banished to had I married James Butler, to know I supported him.

"You are generous, my Queen," Henry said, reluctance in his tone as he praised me.

"The Queen is uncommonly generous to all," Latimer chimed in, his voice trilling with admiration. "She intercedes in matters high and low, and although she is too humble to promote her good works, I cannot help but sing of them."

"My chaplain is too kind," I said.

"No man could be kind enough about you, Your Majesty," Latimer protested, turning to Henry. "The Queen has helped poor scholars, men whose families have deserted them, poor widows and orphaned children. She is a light in the darkness."

"Your chaplain thinks you are a woman without fault," said Henry once Grey and Latimer had been dismissed. His tone suggested he did not agree.

"There is no such creature," I replied. "What good I do, I do not do for praise. I do it because it is right, husband." I looked at him. "I know that you are angry with me, and I with you," I said. "But will you hear me on a subject?"

"If it pleases you."

"Cromwell's investigations," I said. "I worry his men have become too zealous. We spoke before, Henry, about the lesser monasteries. We agreed, did we not, that not all religious houses should be shut down, and those that would, would be made into educational establishments? It seems to me the cause of reform has been lost to that of revenge. This will do no good. These houses and their abbots have erred, but they are not beyond redemption."

Henry grunted, a faraway look in his eyes. "I have had words with Cromwell of late," he said. "The man exceeds his authority, and sets members of my court against each other. I like it not."

"Then you will look into what I have said?" I asked. "I know you are angry at me, but do not let that colour this request. I make it not for myself, but for our people."

Henry nodded, although he would not look at me. "I will look into it," he said.

Chapter Forty-Two

Greenwich Palace
Late November – December 1535

My chambers were a riot of colour and celebration. My pregnancy was known. Although it was usual to wait until the fourth month when the child quickened to make an announcement, news had slipped out. I called for musicians and dancing each night. Even if Henry and I were on bad terms, I would celebrate our child.

The news that Katherine was unwell had brought hope. Even those who had no cause to fear the Dowager believed her death might see England safe from the threat of invasion. Reformers celebrated, and even some conservatives quietly did the same. Her death would liberate us of the ire of the Emperor, and once she was gone, this reluctant nephew who had shown little interest in defending her, might well become an ally.

I gazed out over the sea of men and women. Bess Holland, Margaret Douglas and Mary Howard were together, as usual, as were the two Shelton sisters. Each had a gaggle of adoring men dancing attendance. Jane Seymour stood with her good friend Francis Bryan, and her brothers, Edward and Thomas, sipping wine and as usual, saying nothing. My sister-in-law hovered near George, eager to beg a scrap of his time. Also as usual, George ignored her.

Smeaton was singing as Weston, a most accomplished musician, played the lute. I listened with great appreciation, but another was less impressed. Nicholas Bourbon was standing on the edge of the company, his brow furrowed.

"I hope you are pleased with England, Master Bourbon," I said. "Does my ward, Carey, do well at Syon?"

Bourbon bowed, deep and graceful. "He does indeed, Majesty," he said, using the tone of reverence he kept for me alone. "He has a fine mind and a ready enthusiasm. I find him a most pleasing pupil."

"It would seem you are less pleased by our songbird," I said, nodding to Smeaton who had finished his song and was accepting praise, with a rather smug expression, from those near him.

Bourbon adopted a wry face. "He writes good songs," he said. "But, Majesty, he overdoes them. Even the most beautiful song may be rendered tedious by exaggeration. Even honey, if taken too much, becomes bitter. Beauty, when it is at its best, is simple, pure…"

I smiled. "Like your poetry."

"If you have read my poor verse, I am honoured."

"Read, and greatly enjoyed," I said. "But try to be kind to the lad. He wishes himself other than he is. He wants to be a nobleman, and never will he be so."

"The greatest misery comes from an inability to accept what one is," said Bourbon. "The young man should take pride in what he has accomplished, rather than dwelling on what he thinks he lacks."

"True," I said. "But all men strive, Master Bourbon, to become more than they are."

"If you would pardon my impertinence," he said. "I would say, Majesty, that to strive for one's ambitions is a fine thing, but to wish to become something other than what we are is not. Why not accept who we are, and work to be the best version of that person?" He lifted his goblet to his lips. "If the young man cannot accept who he is, it will bring only misery and pain."

Seeing my father watching me, I excused myself.

"I have been thinking," said my father, drawing close, "that we should look again at George's marriage. Jane has caused us mortification and shame, and there is no fruit to come from that woman's barren womb. It puts our family line in peril."

I frowned. "Many have said this of me, too, Father," I told him. "Would you advise the King to set me aside?"

"*You* are with child," he said. "*You* have borne a living child. You have proved your worth as a woman. Jane has brought nothing to our family but her money, and George has spent that."

"If my brother shared her bed rather than dallying with his mistresses, perhaps she would have a chance to bear a son."

"Then she should be more enticing," said my father. "It is no one's fault but the wife's if a man strays."

"Are men not responsible for their actions, then?" I asked lightly. "This is a strange thought to me, Father. If men truly have so little control over themselves, perhaps the laws of England are awry? If women control the actions of men, perhaps we should be in charge?"

He scowled and I smiled sweetly. Gone were the days when my father could shame me, or treat me like a child. Woman I might be, and therefore weak in his eyes as well as those of many other men, but I outranked him.

"God did not want the world in chaos, Majesty," he said, "so He handed the reins to men."

"Ah," I said. "And note the vision of perfect peace, harmony and sweetness that our world is in after eons of the rule of men. You are right, Father, I quite forgot that poverty, hunger, greed, adultery and corruption had been vanquished long ago by the power of men."

"Sarcasm is the refuge of the slow-witted," he muttered.

"Sarcasm is the weapon of those who must fight against what is perceived as normal," I retorted. "By showing people the laughable state of much they hold as normal, we alter perspective, do we not? And if the Lord Jesus Christ used sardonic wit to make a point, as my friend Archbishop Cranmer has told me on more than one occasion, why should I not emulate him?"

"Majesty." My father bowed and moved away. He did not have a retort that was safe to use, and so he retreated. I cared not.

"You father wears a scowl as deep as a ploughman's rivet," said Tom's voice near my ear.

"He finds his children no longer fear him."

"The fear of every father."

"No," I said. "The fear of every man or woman who wants to dominate the world and everything in it. Fear lends control, does it not? But when those they seek to dominate rise up and defy them, they find their fantasies crumbling into dust."

There are many kinds of power in this world. One, particularly common and always false, lies in comparison; women are weak, so men are strong.

But here's the rub. For them to stay strong, we must be kept weak. Educations restricted, means and freedoms limited, minds and bodies degraded from worth or ownership by common opinion. For they fear what we may become, if we were granted the same freedoms. They fear we would become greater than they, making them the weaker sex, and we the stronger.

If a woman demonstrates strength, the illusion crumbles. That is why some men fear women, why they seek domination; our fragility is their strength. When we are weak no more, they have nothing.

The same is true of races that hate each other, of rapists who must master their own fear by inflicting it on others. It is true of men who beat their wives and women who abuse each other. It is true of those who would bully, those who would violate. They suppress others to mask their greatest and truest fear; that they are nothing, that they are worthless… empty…

But there is another kind of power; one which comes not from subjugating others but from upholding yourself. From knowing yourself, recognising and accepting the darkness and the light within you, and attempting to do the best you can with both elements, that you might leave the world with more than you took from it.

I grinned inwardly as I thought of Henry. His was the false power. He had tried to diminish me and I had stood against him. No more would men beat me to the ground, abusing me with my own emotions.

"Your father certainly does not seem to have the King's trust, as once he did." Tom sipped thoughtfully from his goblet.

"His Majesty has new men to advise him, like my brother." I set back my shoulders. "The old is on the way out, Tom, and the new dawns in an unhurried, clear sky."

*

Cromwell came to Henry and me with bad tidings. There was rebellious talk, he said, amongst the common people. "I have sent men to gather information," he said. "But there is talk of your people misunderstanding the greatness of Your Majesty's ascension to your rightful role as Head of the Church."

Henry looked simultaneously full of anger and tiredness. "Understanding of the Act of Succession will see all these mutterings put to their rightful place," I said.

Cromwell nodded. "I have ordered arrests," he said. "But we must be on our guard. If any would turn to revolt, we must be prepared."

Henry paled. "Think you it would come to that?" he asked with wonder. "That my subjects would rise against me?"

Cromwell nodded slightly. "There are always those who would listen to the devil on their shoulder," he said carefully. "But rest assured, Majesty, I shall root out any canker in your realm. Traitorous actions, words or deeds will be silenced."

"It is Katherine and her daughter," I spat angrily. "They spread division and unrest."

Henry nodded. "The lady Katherine is a proud, stubborn woman of very high courage. If she took it into her head to take up her daughter's part, she could easily muster a great array, and engage in war against me as fierce as any her mother ever waged in Spain."

"She would not dare to raise English men against an English king," I said.

"The majority stands true to Your Majesty," said Cromwell smoothly. "English men and women are loyal. They will not follow the Dowager in pursuit of a crown for Lady Mary." He paused, his eyes flickering from me to Henry. "Give me time to root out the evil in this land, but allow your hearts to feel no mercy, and we will bring an end to this dissent."

"The people must accept the new order," Henry said. "And when our son is born they will truly understand we do God's work." He touched my belly as though it were a talisman against evil.

"Yes," I said covering Henry's huge hand with my own. "Once our son is here, the people will see the true path. Our son will blaze a trail for the men and women of England." I looked at Henry. "Why not send a delegation to the Schmalkalden League again, my lord?" I asked. "Perhaps England's people fear that we have no friends."

"We could send a delegation to Wittenberg," said Cromwell.

"Speak to Alexander Aless," I said to Henry. "He has a good understanding of the German Princes."

Henry frowned, but agreed to send envoys. As Cromwell left, he bowed to Henry and me, and to my belly.

Inside me was the hope of England. That December, I was careful. I ate what I was told. I drank what was instructed. I spent time reading devotions, thanking God for His blessings, and asking my ladies to do the same. I became quiet, introspective.

I was not the young, spirited girl who first came to this court, who thought of little but her dresses and opinions. As we grow older we find that life is made of more compromises than we ever would have thought possible when fired by the passion of youth.

Youth is uncompromising, adventurous, and brash. Age is concessionary, careful and cautious.

We do not care about the enemies we make when young. Now… I could count them like grains of sand on a beach.

I slipped often into thinking of the past. Perhaps it is only natural. When we are young we look to the future. When we grow older, we think back, for we have more past than future.

Elizabeth came to court, and I spent almost every day with her. Henry had been distant and angry of late, but with the arrival of our daughter, he seemed to soften.

"You are the best of mothers," he said, his tone defensive and grudging as we sat in the gardens, watching Elizabeth play with little stones on the path.

"I would never claim such a thing," I said. "But if the best of motherhood lies in love, I will accept your compliment." I touched my belly; a soft, small lump was starting to form under my clothes. "For there is no one in the world I love as I do my children."

"Do you love me, still?" he asked.

"You think I do not?"

Henry looked away. "You busy yourself with other men," he said gruffly. "You act as though you care not."

My soul cried out at this unjust accusation. Had Henry not sought other women? Acted as though he cared nothing for me? It is so easy to take our sins and place them on others. Was this another of Henry's tricks? Trying to blame me for all that was sick in our relationship?

"I busy myself with others because you desert me," I said. "You left *me*, Henry."

He looked away, his hands becoming fists at his sides.

"Should you come back, and respect me as a husband should his wife, I would have no cause to seek companionship elsewhere." I stared at him. "You were all I ever needed, Henry. If only I could have been that to you."

He seemed angry and comforted at the same time. "Men require different companionship, from time to time," he said. "Katherine understood."

"Katherine did not love you," I said, unsure if that were actually true or not. "And so she could look the other way with ease. Her heart was safe because she never offered it to you. Mine is not."

More anger in his hunched shoulders. Henry liked to imagine the whole world adored him, no matter the evidence to the contrary. "Yet still," he said. "You have flocks of admirers."

"Courtly love is not love," I retorted. "You know that well enough. Men praise me, but they seek patronage, not pleasure." I turned to him. "With you, it was not so. The love you offered me was true, for once you held your heart out, and begged me to keep it safe. I would have held your heart forever in my hands, Henry, and never seen it come to harm. It was not me that removed that heart from my hands. It was you."

"My heart is in your keeping," he said gruffly. "And always shall it be."

He rose abruptly and went to our daughter. Gathering her up, he put his face close to hers, and she giggled as his short beard brushed her peach-soft skin. Elizabeth set her small, chubby hands to his face and nuzzled against him. As he turned, our daughter in his arms, I saw the sheen of tears in his eyes. But whether my husband was moved by the sweetness of his daughter, or by our conversation, I knew not. Once I could have read Henry as easily as the English Bible. Now, I never knew what might come from his heart, or his mouth, to either comfort or crush me.

Somehow, Henry always seemed to know when I had grown strong. In our arguments, threatening me with abandonment, or telling me I was not a proper queen, he could reduce me to nothingness. But I rose. Like the falcon who wings through stormy skies, I rose time and time again to stand strong. And that was when he would bring out his second weapon; love. Henry used love against me, reducing me, diminishing me, until I was rendered weak.

It was a powerful combination, and souls stronger than mine had been crushed by it. It was abuse of emotion, abuse of love. Henry wanted to control me. As his wife, he thought it was his right to be my master, and he had learned how to exert authority over me. Just as a man may seek to defeat a woman by beating her, Henry thrashed me with emotion. Shame… Misery… Fear… and the hope and comfort of love. Those were Henry's weapons.

But I was quick to his tricks now. I could not deny that he still had the power to bring me low, but reduce me again, he would not. If this was the game I had to play, if I was trapped on this board, I would be the Queen. Never again would I allow myself to be someone's pawn.

That was what I told myself. I had found the second kind of power. I had sipped from it, nibbled it, finding strength within myself. But I was not yet filled by it. I was not yet complete.

I rose and went to my family. Hesitantly, Henry offered me his arm. I took it and we walked through the snowy gardens, chattering away to Elizabeth. Her words were few, but she was far advanced compared to many children her age. Everyone remarked on it.

As we turned a corner and Henry burst out laughing at one of my jests, I saw Jane Seymour talking to Cromwell. They looked up, and Cromwell made a hasty excuse, scurrying away.

Although that day made me happy, for Henry and I had made a peace, of sorts, I was haunted by Cromwell's frightened eyes. Why had he not wanted to be seen talking to Jane? I could only think of one reason.

Cromwell wanted to use her against me. Jane, such a blank canvas, might well be used to whisper in her royal lover's ear, promoting Cromwell's cause above mine.

But Cromwell did not know everything. He did not know Henry was annoyed about his talent for surpassing his authority. He thought his royal master was firmly in the palm of his hands. He was about to find this was untrue.

Chapter Forty-Three

Eltham Palace and Richmond Palace
December 1535

When not at court that winter, my daughter was housed at Eltham Palace. On a visit, I went the chapel to pray for Elizabeth with my ladies. As we went to leave, Margaret Lee noted that Lady Mary, who had been behind us, had dipped her skirts and acknowledged me before retiring.

"She curtseyed and had her ladies do so likewise, I would swear it, my lady," said Margaret, breathless with excitement. "I think she seeks to make amends."

I was astounded. Nothing had allowed me to think Mary might be softening. I had made many gestures, and every one had been rebuffed. But her mother was ill. Perhaps, knowing this and knowing too that I carried a child, had made her more aware of her precarious situation. In some ways I had sympathy. I, too, understood that life does not always work out as expected.

"Take a message to her," I said to Margaret. "Tell her I am distressed that I failed to see her bowing to me. Say also that I am heartened by her homage and hope to act as an agent for friendly correspondence between her and her father. Tell her this is an office I would embrace willingly and warmly."

Margaret went to do my bidding and when she returned, she came to Elizabeth's chambers. I did not note her arrival for a moment, as I was playing with the fastening of a new purple cap for my daughter. Lady Bryan and I had gone over the garment in particular detail, as we did with all of Elizabeth's sumptuous clothing. The cap had made many trips back and forth between court and my daughter's household, but no matter what, it never seemed right.

Finally, I had the style just right. The pretty cap was plumed with delicate white feathers, which fell across Elizabeth's face and tickled her nose. She played with it as Lady Bryan and I smiled to see how interested my little girl was with pretty fabrics.

"Her mother's daughter," said Lady Bryan, her eyes glowing with affection.

No royal child had ever been as beautifully dressed as my Elizabeth. If I could not be with her every moment of the day, I could surround her body and encase her skin in all the care my hands and purse could afford. I hoped she could feel my love warming her through these clothes.

Margaret stood near the door, hesitancy flowing from her. She was struggling to work out how to not give offence.

"What did she say?" I asked and sighed. "I can see it is not something you wish to relay. Fear not. You are not accountable for the words and deeds of others."

Margaret spread her hands, as though seeking absolution from the Almighty. "I gave her your message, Majesty, and she said the *Queen* could not possibly have sent that message as she was so far from this place. She said I should have referred to you as *Madame la Marquis,* and the curtsey she had made had been to God her Maker, not to her father's mistress." Margaret paused as my face darkened. "I am sorry, Your Majesty," she hurried on. "This is my fault. I mistook her intention. I have caused this schism."

I almost laughed. Poor Margaret! How could she have caused this rift, so deep and wide that none could ford it?

"None of this is your fault," I said, struggling to keep a hold on both my temper and my laughter. I was assaulted by a mangled mess of the two much of the time. "Lady Mary is at fault, not you." I expelled a fraught breath. "She is a stupid girl filled with wanton fancies, and she will unmake herself, perhaps unto death if she does not take care."

Lady Bryan's face tumbled to hear Mary abused. Mary had been her first charge and she was fond of the girl. Lady Shelton also looked on with disapproval. We were not as intimate as we had been. And all for this girl… this child who sulked and stomped through her idle days, refusing to accept that the pristine world in which she had once lived had altered. I was running out of patience. It was time for Mary to grow up.

"Your Majesty…" Lady Bryan said "… please offer mercy. She does not mean to insult Your Majesty."

I rolled my eyes. "If all this is an accident, Lady Bryan, then the King's bastard should take more care. It is dangerous to be so clumsy."

"Of course, my lady, but…"

"I want her books taken from her," I said, cutting in. "All but the Bible and she is to have no additional privileges."

Lady Bryan looked at me sadly. "She has none now, Your Majesty. We have not allowed her to hear private Mass, she eats with the servants in the hall and I have expelled those who would call her by her old title, or speak of the Dowager. She is only allowed to write to her mother if her letters are inspected, and every day she serves the Princess… But we will continue to carry out your commands until the girl starts to pay the respects expected of her."

"See that you do," I said imperiously. "I want regular reports on her insolent behaviour, so I can show her father what a nuisance this *cursed bastard* has become. When my son is born she will have to accept her place. Then, she will be begging for the help that I offer her freely now."

"Yes, Your Majesty," Lady Bryan said, sweeping sad eyes to the floor as she curtseyed.

I left Eltham with rage bellowing in my heart. Mary was a constant, irritating symbol of dissention. She was showing the common people and nobles that they could flout us and survive. Mary and her stubborn mother were little sparks that could kindle a mighty fire. She had power, and she knew it. If it were up to me, I would have had her arrested already. Perhaps a few weeks in the Tower would show her who was truly in charge. But whilst Henry wavered between love and hate for her, there was no such option.

Mary stood, her spark as bright as the flint's first flame… even as Katherine steadily started to fade.

"I have a task for you," said my husband, marching into my chambers as I dressed. Henry never cared for formality when he wanted something.

We had come to Richmond two days ago. It was not one of my favourite palaces. For so long it had been the seat of Lady Mary that I seemed to hear her voice as well as Katherine's everywhere I went.

Once, Richmond had been known as Sheen Palace; a royal manor of the Yorkist and Lancastrian kings, inherited from their Norman and Angevian forbears. Henry's father had torn down the old palace and replaced it with a new one, rich with towers, turrets, a grand great hall, and gracious dwellings. There was a vast chapel, privy gardens, a close gallery and the palace had running water, with pipes pumping in water from a conduit in the fields nearby. Henry had plans to install flushing privies, as he had in Hampton Court, for he would never miss the opportunity to outdo his dead father, even if the man could no more marvel at his accomplishments.

"What is this task?" I asked, gazing at Henry in the mirror as he stood behind me. The two Janes were combing my raven hair, and the light from the windows fell, shimmering emerald green and sapphire blue upon the black patina of my hair. They stepped aside as Henry took a tress in his hands and passed it through his huge fingers.

"Like silk," he murmured.

I smiled at his unabashed admiration, glad that Jane Seymour was present to witness it. No one had hair like mine. Most women at court were golden or fair of hair, portly in figure and plump of cheek. My black hair, even under my gorgeous hoods and veils, shone out, setting me apart. The same was true of my lithe figure, sharp cheekbones and wide, black eyes. When I stood beside the women of court, I was a stately, graceful raven amongst a horde of golden, twittering starlings.

But the years had taken a toll. I had never been conventionally good looking. I was no wide-eyed doe. The toil of bearing children, the sorrow of their deaths and Henry's lack of care had worn my beauty. But my hair and eyes never faded. If my cheeks sometimes seemed hollow and my figure over-thin, at least I had my greatest assets to fall back on. Besides, no other woman could match my ready wit.

"You have mislaid your purpose," I teased, smiling at his reflection as he stared at my hair.

"I was lost in contemplation of your beauty." Henry smiled and took a seat on a stool beside me. "I want you to go to Syon Abbey."

I lifted my eyebrows. Syon had had many visitors of late. Cromwell had sent his men early that month to investigate the house, and had called personally on the nuns and monks in early December. He had been followed a week later by my chaplain, John Skip, and my ally Doctor Butts. The very next day four academics went to Syon along with Lord Windsor, who had a sister there. The next Thursday, the Bishop of London had gone too.

These visitors were united in purpose; to compel the order to accept the supremacy, swear the oath and submit to Henry.

Syon was home to the Bridgettine Order, and was named for the Biblical City of Zion, the City of David. It was one of England's wealthiest abbeys, with a huge library, boasting enviable collections. The Bridgettine Order had been founded from the Order of St Augustine, and their holy saint was a visionary who had once seen a vision of the Holy Christ displaying his wounds. The Order were devoted to the Passions of the Christ and the honour of the Virgin Mary, and had been brought to England during the reign of Henry V, who had laid Syon's foundation stone. Nuns and monks dwelled separately, with an abbess ruling the sisters and an abbot the brothers, but since the Order was dedicated to a female saint, the Abbess had as much, if not more, influence than her counterpart. Agnes Jordan was the present Abbess, and she, along with her Order, had proved resistant to the supremacy. Some had come out in support of Henry as Head of the Church, others had not. They who had not were the most vocal, causing problems for us.

One Syon monk, Richard Reynolds, an eminent doctor of divinity, had once facilitated a meeting between Thomas More and Elizabeth Barton at Syon, which Henry believed had only set More more firmly on the path to treason. Reynolds had died at Tyburn with his Carthusian brothers.

Meetings between Cromwell and the Bridgettine Order had not gone well, and neither had they been receptive to any of the other men sent to them. Cromwell's men had attempted to convince, to coerce, and when that failed, to blackmail and threaten them, but the Abbess and her loyal followers stood firm. They were proving a nuisance. Their continued defiance made a mockery of Henry's authority, and since the community were well-respected, and popular, their treasonous example set a dangerous precedent.

I knew Syon well. My ward, Henry Carey, was studying there alongside Norris' son. My husband obviously thought that I might have success where his men had failed, possibly because, as a woman, I might have better luck in reaching the rebellious nuns, but also potentially because I had supported Syon with my generous patronage.

"Cromwell had no luck bullying them?" I asked.

"His men are too brash," said Henry, a disgruntled glimmer in his eyes. "They threaten the monks and nuns, making them only more resistant."

"And you think I will have more success?" I smiled. "I am not always known for tact."

Henry chuckled. "But when something is important to you, you argue well. I would have you reason with the Abbess. If we can get the nuns, at least, to accept our supremacy, we are half-way there."

"I will only be permitted into the nuns' house. The Abbot might meet me, but I cannot go amongst the monks."

"If you only convince the Abbess to accept," he said. "I would be most happy."

"You steal my motto." Suddenly I let out a slight groan as a wave of nausea came over me.

"You are unwell?" Henry asked anxiously, putting his hand to my belly.

"No more than is to be expected," I said. "Your son saps my energy, but I have enough left to undertake this task."

"If you are not well, I would not have you exert yourself."

I put my fingers to his lips, stalling his protests. "For our cause, Henry, I will always have strength."

"My Diana," he murmured, leaning in to kiss me.

"When would you have me go?"

"As soon as you can. There are whispers abroad. Syon's continued resistance brings others out to speak. I would have them silenced."

"I will go today, and fear not, husband, where your men have failed, I will succeed."

I arrived at Syon with my ladies that afternoon, only to be told the nuns were at choir. As a married woman, I could not be admitted. "I will wait," I said to the novice who escorted me through the grand, shadowy halls.

"They will be some hours at prayer, Majesty," she said.

"Then I shall do the same," I said. "We will wait until your Abbess is ready to receive her Queen."

The novice scurried off, her footsteps echoing in the halls. "Settle into your seats," I said to my women. "We are likely to be left for a long time. They will try to avoid us, but I will not return to the palace until we are seen."

Eventually, the doors to the chapel opened and I was admitted. I found the nuns, sixty in total, prostrate with their heads upon the floor. This angered me. It was a traditional practice of Rome, one that Henry had already criticised, since it glorified the *act* of worship rather than the object. Seeing me, the Abbess, Agnes Jordan, came over and greeted me. Her welcome was not strikingly friendly, and she gazed at me with wary eyes.

"The King has sent me," I said. "There have been many ill reports about lax standards at Syon which are being repeated at court."

"None are true, Your Majesty," she said stiffly, her back rigid.

I drew her to one side of the chapel. "I believe you," I murmured. "Long have I held the house of Syon in my heart, for I know that whilst we differ on points of theory and practice, your order is one of the faithful, one of the shining lights of England."

"Then why have you come?" she asked, surprise stripping her of not only her ability to dissemble, but apparently of the capacity to remember my title.

I paused and glanced at the nuns. Although many still had their heads to the ground, others I could see attempting to lean backwards to hear what I and the Abbess were saying. "These are troubled times," I whispered. "Cromwell and his men are greedy, my lady Abbess. They seek evidence for the King, and sometimes, in their rush and zeal, they create it. I am sure I have no need to tell you this."

Agnes inclined her head, her eyes wide with amazement. "I had heard, Majesty, you were fully behind the investigations."

"I am behind the *purpose* of the investigations," I said. "I believe there is much that requires change… but I am not behind the methods these men use."

I stared into her pale blue eyes, seeing the colours of the stained glass reflected in them. "I would have *reform*, my lady, not obliteration. No matter what you have heard, I was not to blame for the executions of the Carthusians, or the expulsions of the Observants. I confess, at the time I thought them justified, for those who stand against His Majesty cannot be allowed to rebel. But of late, I have come to question much. I fear, in their quest to stamp out corruption, Cromwell and his men have become lost. They forget the great good that England's religious orders bring when they are properly governed. They forget that reform does not mean destruction." I rocked back on my heel. "I would remind them."

"Then… you are for Rome?"

I shook my head, irritated. Why did people see only in black and white? Opposing Henry or Cromwell on one issue was not the same as supporting Rome.

"The King *is* the Head of the Church," I said. "God made David his King, did he not? And guided David's ruling hand. The same will be true of our King. Unlike Rome, he will not look aside as sin holds sway. He will root it out and make our houses of religion clean. Ungodly orders will fall, but I would preserve those who are doing good yet require guidance. I would have those who work with their communities in peace, offering medical care and aid, kept alive. To me, holy Abbess, reform must be tempered by control. Cromwell wants extremes. I desire moderation."

"Why do you tell me this?"

"Because the King wants Syon to accept his supremacy," I said and went on as I saw her face harden. "If it comes not, Syon *will* come under attack, much as the Greyfriars and the Carthusians, and if the King is convinced by men who have nothing but greed in their hearts to move against Syon, there will be little more I can do for you… Syon will fall." I touched her arm. "But if you submit, I swear I will do all I can to protect your order. We can become united in this goal; to keep the worthy orders of England alive; to preserve all that is good as we weed out that which is rotten."

The Abbess looked away, her eyes lost in thought.

"Will you work with me?" I asked.

"I hardly know what to say," she said. "Since the start of this month, both I and the Abbot have encountered nothing but threats, blackmail and promises of riches if we will submit. But never have any of the King's men said anything as honest as your words, my lady." She gazed into my eyes. "Will you swear to me, on the Bible, and on your faith, that if I agree you will protect us?"

"I swear on my life and on my soul," I said. "On the faith I hold dear and on the lives of my children, I will do all within my power to uphold Syon and other deserving houses, and protect you from dissolution."

"Then I place myself under your protection," she said. "With a grateful heart." She paused. "But I cannot compel any of the sisters to go against their souls."

"I can arrange a meeting between your sisters and Cromwell. Tell the sisters that the question will be put to them, on whether they accept the supremacy. If they accept, they are to remain seated, and if not they are to leave the chamber. Ask them to remain seated, but say nothing. In that way, any who object can say that they never *said* they supported the supremacy, which will satisfy their consciences. This will be enough to persuade the King."

"That is a lie, is it not, my lady?" she asked. "Our order is sworn to honesty."

"For a lie to be a lie, it must be spoken," I said. "Please, allow me to guide you. There must be some sign of hope for the King. He is already talking about disbanding Syon. If you are separated, sent to other orders, or offered pensions to leave, then this great house, and all it might offer England will be lost."

I breathed in. It was dangerous to speak like this. The Abbess might well betray me, but I had to take a risk. "The saints and Christ died for their faith," I said. "I ask you to live for yours. England needs you."

She fell silent, her eyes lost to contemplation. "We are taught that glory lies in death," she said quietly, "for that was the path our Lord took to save the world." She gazed at me with steady eyes. "Death and glory," she went on. "Martyrdom and sacrifice… These are the cornerstones of faith, so we are taught. But today I think otherwise. It is my duty to protect these women, but we also owe a debt of service to the people of England. Without us, what will they do?"

She looked to the altar, and the cross on which an image of Christ hung, suspended in the air, his bleeding wounds glimmering against the light of the sun. "To live for faith, rather than to die for it," she pondered.

"Something must remain," I pressed. "The Lord never intended for all His faithful to die, otherwise who will instruct the children? Who will lead the path of the righteous? We cannot allow everything good to crumble, only to be replaced by that which is ill."

"We cannot," she said. She drew herself up and set her shoulders back, like a knight preparing for battle. "I will do as you say, Majesty."

"Then you have my thanks." I looked across at the hall of nuns. "I must lecture them, with your permission," I said. "There must be a solid reason for your submission. If it is said you and I talked alone, Cromwell will grow suspicious. He will know we made a bargain."

"Say what you will," she said. "I will explain later what we must do in order to survive."

I went before the nuns and lectured them. "The enormity of your wanton *incontinence* cannot be measured. You should cease to use Latin prayer books you do not understand." I nodded to Nan Gainsford who nudged forward a boy dragging a chest of English primers. "Read the Word of God in English, and you will understand your faith and Lord better."

I rebuked them hard and strong, for this was what was expected. My words would be reported to Henry and Cromwell and I could not allow them to think that I wavered in my support for the supremacy, or the investigations. My secret purpose was safe, as long as I played my part in public.

In truth, it was ridiculous to claim that the nuns did not understand Latin. The majority of Syon's clergy hailed from noble houses, and would have been instructed in Latin from childhood. But the theory that lack of understanding led to disobedience was deeply rooted in the reformist cause, and it would lead Henry to think they had defied him from ignorance.

They listened with ill grace, thinking me a shrew, but as my speech came to a close, and with the help of the Abbess, the primers were accepted. I went back to Henry and told him of my success. He was pleased and said we would wait to see if I had made an impression on the nuns.

Some days later, Cromwell and his men went to Syon and the Abbess did as I had asked. The Abbot and his monks refused to attend the meeting, but the nuns came. They remained sitting as the question was asked, and although a few offered resistance, Henry was pleased to learn that the majority had accepted the supremacy. William Latimer praised me about court, telling everyone how I had reached the nuns through reason, bringing them closer to God. Latimer was a touch over-generous in his praise, but it was useful to me at this time, so I did not contradict him.

"You see, Thomas?" Henry asked Cromwell when he returned to Richmond. "My wise Queen can convince anyone of anything!"

Cromwell smiled, but I could see he was displeased. Further resistance from Syon would have meant he could easily convince Henry that they, like the Greyfriars and Carthusians, were rebels. The wealth of Syon would then have been his, to toss into the already swollen coffers of the Crown.

Cromwell had failed. He knew it, and when Henry came to understand what he had lost as Syon slipped through his fingers, the King might not be as pleased as he was now. This put Cromwell in danger.

As Cromwell smiled and complimented me, I was reminded of the day Wolsey came back from France to find me in Henry's arms.

Circles in sand have a way of repeating themselves. This was a new fight, a new battle and a new opponent, but an old war.

Our armies were assembled. The field had been decided. The fight for Henry's favour had begun.

"Let battle commence," I murmured as Henry left with his arm about Cromwell. "You will find me no slack opponent, Thomas Cromwell."

Chapter Forty-Four

Greenwich Palace
December 1535

"Another young man of promise, my lady," said Doctor Butts as I perused his lists of men seeking financial aid to study at Cambridge.

"And *another* who wants to enter Gonville Hall," I noted, glancing up with a teasing grin. "Does every one of these men seek to study in your old college, Doctor?"

"Many, madam," he said with a smirk, completely unabashed to be caught out. "I cannot help but retain loyalty to my old college. I would have it filled with good men, with your help, Majesty."

Ever since the days when he had saved me and my family from the sweat, I had nurtured great affection for Doctor Butts. Together, we had done much for the cause of reform, and he had brought many of my chaplains into my household. Latimer was one, and Shaxton and Skip were both ex-students of Gonville Hall too. Cambridge seemed to breed reformers, probably because Butts supported so many there with my money. It pleased me that a new generation of scholars, priests and doctors would emerge from the educated womb we had created.

Another of my chaplains, Matthew Parker, had proved rather reluctant at first to take up the offered post. He possessed a mild temper and gentle sensibilities, and was therefore perhaps unsuited for court life. I had recently had him appointed dean of the college of secular canons at Stoke-by-Clare in Suffolk, and Hugh Latimer, ever a watchful man, had asked him to take care not to disappoint me. Parker had replaced William Betts, another of my chaplains, who had died some months ago. When his post fell vacant I could only think Betts' soul would be pleased that Parker, a fellow ex-student of Corpus Christi, would take it. Cranmer spoke well of him, but Parker was reluctant to place himself in danger. John Skip wrote to Parker almost every day, and eventually the man was won over. Assured of my protection, he came to court.

I found him immediately endearing. He was a large, powerfully-built man, who looked more suited to warfare than the Church, but hearing his soft voice and seeing his gentle nature, I came to understand he was a man of peace. He was also moderate, and agreed with me about the monasteries. I found great solace with Parker. There was something infinitely caring in his soul.

Henry was also fond of Parker, finding his natural humility and reserve pleasing, and sometimes sent him gifts of game for his table. But for all his humbleness, Parker was a fine preacher and I had him speak before Elizabeth's household, as well as mine, often.

One of the reasons Henry liked Parker was that he did not seek to make trouble. He stuck to subjects Henry found acceptable, not attempting to speak on iconoclasm, transubstantiation, or purgatory. Parker's tact was notable, but I knew his sympathies were more in line with mine than with his King's.

He also did not speak too long. An hour and a half was more than enough for Henry in one sitting.

But if Parker was moderate and cautious, many of my men were not. They were marked leaders of the new order, and as such came into conflict with traditionalists. Conservatives spread rumours about them, some that were true and others which were pure fiction.

In truth, some did have shady pasts. The deceased William Betts had been associated with a scandal in Oxford in relation to banned books, and Latimer and Parker had been involved with the case of Thomas Bliney, a martyr who had died for the reformist cause, but was widely viewed as a heretic. They held a united front, but disagreed amongst each other often enough. Foxe, Hilsey and Cranmer found Latimer too extreme. Indeed, he was accused of being a Lollard in some quarters, and Shaxton was more a traditionalist than a reformer. But I did not mind private debate, as long as in public we stood united.

I was not one to close my mind. There was much in the reformist cause I agreed with, and an equal amount I did not. But I was willing to hear all... a virtue not common at court where everyone guarded their opinions and stuck to them like mussels to the rocks of the shore.

Court, at that time, was a hotbed of ideas and theories. It excited me. The pursuit of knowledge is not the preserve of but one man. It takes many to form a new world. My clergy were innovative, passionate men, and I encouraged them to share thoughts and ideals.

It was not so simple anymore to speak of reformists and conservatives. Even amongst evangelicals there was disagreement. New factions seemed to form each day. There were Lutherans, who were coming to be called *Protestants* because of the manner in which Luther had nailed his protestations against the Catholic faith on the door of his church. There were Anabaptists, who believed that only adults should be baptised, so they might fully understand the pact they made with God. There were evangelicals, like me, who followed the teachings of the old Church, but wanted reform. There were those who believed not in the act of transubstantiation, nor the worship of icons, but upheld other Sacraments.

The old way, of one unified practice of religion, was being torn apart, and in its place was a multitude of people, all coming to God in their own way. Of course we could not allow everyone to make their own faith and follow it. There had to be order or all would fall to chaos, but I, unlike so many others, did not shut my ears. I listened and I learned. If only all men could do the same, the world would be a different place... a kinder place... a more welcome existence.

I smiled at Doctor Butts. "I will grant allowances for all these men," I said. "Speak to my treasurer, he will grant you the funds."

"That is more generous than I dared to hope, Majesty," said Butts, his face alive with happiness.

"We work for change here and now," I said. "But we must not forget the future. These men will lead it. It is important they are chosen well, so they might guide my daughter's generation to a better world."

"We can only hope that time will come," said Butts.

"Hope alone does not suffice. We must act. We must *make* the world as we want it to be. God will aid us, but we must take the first steps."

Leaving Butts and returning to my chambers, I entered to find Henry almost alone with Jane Seymour. His men were to one side of the chamber, along with my sister-in-law, but Henry and Jane were close together. As I entered they snapped apart.

"Should you not be at your duties, Mistress Seymour?" I asked, quivering with anger. "If you have not enough to occupy your time, I can ensure you are granted more offices."

Jane hastily withdrew and Henry was angry. "Can you not restrain yourself and flirt with your whores in private?" I asked waspishly as his men and my women took to an adjoining chamber. "You could at least show respect for me by *attempting* to hide your passion for that witless worm."

"Speak not," Henry growled.

"And so in silence, do I become the wife you wish for?" I asked, sneering. "You would have another Katherine. You would have me hide my love and attend only to duty whilst you make a mockery of our love."

"You could never be a wife or Queen as Katherine was," he said, his voice and temper rising. "She was reserved and modest. You flit about your chambers, flirting with all and sundry, disgracing yourself."

"Then I match my husband well, do I not?" I crossed my arms over my chest.

"I should never have married you," he said. "Repeatedly, you have cursed my seed with your venomous womb. Perhaps the men who whisper that you are my sister are right."

"If there is sin in that matter, my lord," I said, swallowing the sting of his barb. "Then it is yours alone. Unlike you, and your saintly Katherine, *I* did not rut with one of your relatives. Our marriage was absolved of sin by dispensation, and if God censures either of us, it is you, for your infidelity."

Henry stared at me with eyes of evil. I held my head high. No more would I be abused into submission. He left.

By the end of that week, Henry and I were barely speaking.

*

The first of December had seen the first payment of a new tax, set at ten per cent per annum, on all clerical incomes. Smaller religious houses protested they would not have anything left, but they were largely ignored. Other houses, less given to protest, surrendered their money and with it their courage, knowing if Cromwell's men came knocking, corruption was bound to be discovered. Like Syon, they submitted for survival.

Friction between Spain and England had led to some of England's most vital markets in the Low Countries coming under threat. Trade continued, but there was constant concern it would cease, bringing poverty. This, combined with the Hanse merchants threatening to close the Baltic, troubled many. With its rich reserves of grain, the Baltic was crucial, especially since England's harvest that year had not been good. Supplies were short. It was said that half of England's crops had been lost, first to the glaring sun and then to the unending rain, making it the worst season in more than eight years. Parliament found it impossible to levy the taxes that Henry had declared he required to build fortifications, and the plague, which had come calling in the summer, had not abated.

It was said I was a witch, an emissary of Satan, sent to bring England into company with famine, death, plague and war… the heralds of the apocalypse.

Those who spread such rumours evidently ignored everything I did to aid the poor. They were too busy selecting what *'evidence'* to follow, and ignoring everything that did not fit their theories, to see sense.

Strife was our companion and conditions for rebellion were ripe. Hunger may make even the most loyal man a traitor. Common people did not understand the break with Rome, or the new religious changes. They thought Henry was on a path to destruction, and would take England with him. Many wanted him to take Katherine back and return to Rome, a series of events inexorably shackled together in many minds. Without me, there would have been none of this chaos, men said. Were I to be removed, peace and amity would be restored.

Henry's preachers went out, spreading word that if England was being tested by God, we would rise to the challenge. But even as the words *"whom the Lord loves, he chasteneth,"* were cried from the pulpits, people were muttering that this was no test from the Almighty, but a punishment.

Talks were going on to prevent one of the apocalyptic heralds coming for England: war. François wanted Henry to join him in the conquest of Milan, but the Pope was equally keen to see François and Charles unite against England. Ambassadors at every court in Europe barely had time to sit down, so busy were they with plots, negotiation and subterfuge. Disinformation was rife.

Although I despised their King's comments about me, I put my support behind the French. I also asked Henry to pursue alliance with the Schmalkalden League, although he told me that Gardiner had attacked the notion, saying if we allied to the League, they would dictate all that Henry did. My husband was already angry, as the League had asked for more money than he was willing to offer, and also wanted him to defend the Lutheran doctrine they upheld. Henry was never going to support Martin Luther. He despised the man. Henry thought the German Princes were testing him, trying his patience, and, since I had suggested alliance, he blamed me for the failure of the talks.

When Henry was angry with me, I was to blame for everything.

And it was amongst this chaos that the hapless hare came to court one afternoon. He went to Cromwell, who was becoming Henry's gateway to the world, asking for permission to see Henry, and it was granted. The hare found Henry in the jousting grounds and said that he wanted to see Katherine, as she was rumoured to be dying. He also put forth the notion that Lady Mary should be allowed to see her mother too.

"The King embraced Chapuys," said Norris when he and my brother came to update me. "The King had already heard that Katherine was on her deathbed and was overjoyed by it."

"The ambassador did not look as delighted as the King," said the dry voice of my brother. "The King discussed England's relations with France and Spain, and was not cordial about François. The King said that when Katherine died, the Emperor would have no further cause to meddle in England's affairs."

"Chapuys was shocked," said Norris. "He said that Katherine's death could bring no possible good. He was sent away, but later the King called him back, to say he had word that Katherine was in extremis and even if he left immediately Chapuys was unlikely to reach her in time."

"He told Chapuys that Katherine is ailing fast," said Norris.

"Is it so surprising?" I asked. "She is over fifty and refuses to take much food or drink, for fear of poison."

"Chapuys says she has suffered pains in her belly and has become unable to take food," said my brother. "The King professed concern, but seemed more merry than sorrowful. He slung an arm about Chapuys and led him about, parading him before the French ambassadors."

"When Chapuys left, however…" said Norris, leaning forwards. I caught the scent of his skin, a mixture of rose perfume and his own scent. It was beautiful, intoxicating. "… with permission to visit Katherine, His Majesty sent a messenger after him, to tell Chapuys that her death would remove all barriers to friendship with the Emperor, and the King was considering allowing Lady Mary to visit her. The King asked Cromwell to send someone with Chapuys, and Vaughan was dispatched."

"I doubt he was sincere about Mary," I said, sitting back so Norris' scent could not distract me. "Henry would be too worried this sickness is a feint, and that Katherine means to steal Mary from England."

"That was just what Cromwell said," my brother noted. "You think the same."

"We do not," I said. "Cromwell would destroy the faith, as I would heal it."

"Allow me to offer an amendment," said my brother with a droll grin. "You think the same in terms of *politics*, not policy."

"I am not sure even of that," I said. "Cromwell and I are on opposing sides. I do not see how both of us may survive this struggle."

Only a few months later, I had good reason to linger on the importance of those words.

Chapter Forty-Five

Greenwich Palace and Eltham Palace
December 1535 – January 1536

Chapuys wasted no time. Mary's request to see her dying mother was flatly denied, despite Henry's declarations he would consider it, but the hapless hare could not worry for his princess now. He had to make haste to reach his Queen.

Katherine's physician sent word to court that she was close to death. This had come about, he wrote, after Katherine partook of a draught of Welsh beer. Earlier in December, Katherine had rallied, and her doctors were encouraged, but after that cup of beer, she went into a rapid, steady decline. The beer, a favourite tipple of Katherine's, was rumoured to have been poisoned. Naturally, my kin were blamed.

Chapuys made haste, but the hapless hare was outstripped by another of fleeter foot.

We spent Christmas at Eltham, with Elizabeth, and passed a merry time with our daughter. On New Year's Day, I handed out golden medals bearing my image to Norris and my husband's other men, and Henry presented me with yards of gold and green satin. Lady Lisle, who had given me Purkoy, sent a gift of gold beads with matching tassels.

"Lady Lisle was going to send you a new puppy," Norris whispered in my ear. "But I instructed her not to."

My eyes swam with tears. Considerate, caring Norris had known I would find such a gift unbearable. I had not kept a hound since Purkoy. I could not. He was irreplaceable.

Sometimes, when I was low, I could almost feel his wet nose nudging my hand; almost feel the brush of his silken coat against my cheek. Many mornings, when I woke, I looked for him without thinking. I missed my little friend.

"She toyed with sending an ape," said Norris. "But I said that would be unwise."

I laughed, pulled from depression. I hated apes. They reminded me of Katherine and her pitiful, rocking capuchin.

"What does she wish in return?" I asked.

"She would like a livery kirtle," he said. "In Your Majesty's colours. That way all will know she is a part of your household, even in Calais."

"I will find a suitable one," I said, making a note to tell Margery Horsman to send one.

And as we celebrated, a visitor came to Kimbolton Castle.

It was early in the evening. Snow was falling, covering the fens with shimmering light. A knock rang upon the door of Katherine's house. Cromwell's men, who had the report from her servants, told us later that Katherine's stewards were much amazed to see a woman, clearly a noble by her gown and jewels, standing bedraggled at their door. She explained she had fallen from her horse, and required aid and shelter to recover. They let her in, and presented her to Katherine, but no introduction was required. They fell upon each other with tears and laughter, for this traveller was none other than Marie de Salinas, Lady Willoughby, Katherine's oldest friend.

News of Katherine's illness had travelled swiftly and although the Dowager was not allowed visitors, especially ones like Salinas, who were her loyal supporters, Marie had risked all and gone to her friend. Armed with the pretext of her fall, she won her way into Katherine's house, and once there, she would not leave.

Later, Marie would claim to Katherine's steward that the letter permitting her visit was on its way, but everyone must have known Henry would never have granted permission. Perhaps some concern did fall upon the man, for he tried to stop her, but Marie slammed Katherine's door in his face. I could not help but admire her spirit.

By all reports, Katherine could not sit or stand, but had to lie in her bed near the fire. She could not eat or drink, and the pain in her stomach had stolen sleep from her, but she was overjoyed to see her friend. Salinas vanished from the house as quick as she had arrived. She had fulfilled her mission to see her friend one last time. No doubt Katherine told her not to stay, so Henry would not punish her.

Chapuys joined Katherine on the 2nd of January, amused and cheered to hear of Salinas' adventure. They held their meetings before witnesses, so their discussions could be reported to every man and woman in England, and so that Henry would not attack Katherine's friends, assuming they conversed of treason. Vaughan was called in, as were a very surprised Bedingfield and Chamberlain, Katherine's stewards. True to her oath never to deal with her captors, Katherine had not spoken to, or seen either of those men for more than a year.

"It is a relief to me, my friend, that I may now die in your arms and not disappear like a beast," Katherine said to Chapuys.

"Stay with us, my Queen," Chapuys urged. "The peace of Christendom depends on it."

Katherine smiled gently, and led him to other topics of conversation. After an hour, she sent Chapuys away, claiming she needed rest. That afternoon, Chapuys was recalled, and they spent hours talking. Whenever he tried to leave her, fearing to make her sicker, she would not allow it.

Chapuys stayed for four days, reassuring Katherine, for she had entered a time of unrest. She was worried for her daughter, and England, she said, and wondered if the problems in England had not, in fact, been caused by her refusal to stand down as Henry's wife.

Katherine had at last come to understand that her pride had driven Henry to break with Rome. Chapuys denied this, and told her that even if the break with Rome had occurred for her resistance, it was Henry who had made it so. He also said that God sent heresies to confound the wicked and laud the righteous. It was not for either of them to question the Almighty.

Katherine seemed reassured, but the truth was that she was correct. Katherine was as much a catalyst for the royal supremacy as Henry, or me.

Just as Cromwell and Henry were ready to start celebrating her demise, Katherine improved. Chapuys decided to leave, so he might petition Henry to allow a visit between mother and daughter.

But the hare hoped too soon.

On the 6th of January, Katherine knew Death was close. She could feel Him at her back, waiting. At midnight, she started to ask what time it was, knowing that Mass could not be sung, and the Sacrament may not be administered, at night. Her confessor, Jorge de Athequa, offered to break the rules, explaining that God would understand, but Katherine was not one to surrender, even to Death, until she was ready.

She waited until dawn, confessed, heard Mass, and took the Sacrament. Athequa forgot, in this moment of sorrow, to extract from Katherine the last confession that she had never truly been Arthur's wife. It seemed strange to me that Katherine would forget this, at this crucial time.

Perhaps she did not. Perhaps, in this last moment of truth, with her immortal soul in question, she could not bring herself to lie.

Katherine dictated her requests for her possessions. She did not make a will, since, as a married woman, as she considered herself, her property was Henry's. Katherine asked that she be laid to rest in a house of the Observant Friars, with five hundred Masses to be sung for her soul. She wanted Henry to make gold and silver that he owed her available, and asked some of her servants to embark on a pilgrimage to Walsingham to pray for her soul and give alms along the way. A golden collar that she had brought from Spain was marked for her daughter to inherit, and her ladies were granted money, and expenses.

She dictated a letter to Henry. It arrived some time later at court.

"My dearest Lord, King and Husband,

The hour of my death now approaching, I cannot chose but, out of the love I bear you, to advise you of your soul's health, which you ought to prefer before all considerations of the world or flesh whatsoever. For which yet you have cast me into many calamities and you yourself into many troubles. But I forgive you all and pray God to do likewise. For the rest, I commend unto you Mary, our daughter, beseeching you to be a good father to her. I must entreat you also to take care of my maids, and give them in marriage, which is not much, they being but three, and to all my other servants, a year's pay beside their due, lest otherwise they should be unprovided for until they find new employment.

Lastly, I want only one true thing; to make this vow: that, in this life, mine eyes desire you alone.

May God protect you,

Katherine, the Queen."

Katherine fell to prayer, begging God to save Henry. The extreme unction was administered. As the winter skies flowed white over Kimbolton, at two of the clock on the 7th of January, Katherine, Princess of Spain, Princess of England, and once Queen, died.

We heard of her death when her letter arrived at court. Henry read it, and in an excess of joy leapt from his chair, crying, "God be praised! We are freed from threat of war!"

He bounded over and kissed me. It was as though someone had told him his son was born, rather than the woman he had once claimed to love had died.

At first, I celebrated with him. I rewarded the messenger with a handsome purse of gold and laughed with Henry. But, as the enormity of what had occurred washed over me, I fell heavily upon a stool and burst into tears.

"My Queen weeps for joy!" Henry announced to my ladies who were flocking about me, trying to ascertain what was wrong. "For she knows England is safe!"

As Henry raced off to celebrate, I looked up at Nan Gainsford.

"*Do* you weep for joy, my lady?" she asked.

"Nay," I murmured. "For sorrow. What was done to Katherine might one day be done to me."

My ladies all assured me, cutting over each other in their haste, that nothing like that could ever happen. Henry loved me, they said. England adored my daughter, they said. Peace would come from Katherine's death and all would be well. Their words flowed over me like water. How many times had Henry said he regretted marrying me? How many times had he threatened me?

I walked to the table and took up the letter. Katherine had, to the last, been not only an opponent of courage, but of grace. Her last letter to Henry was beautiful. Finally I understood. She had loved him.

"So," I whispered. "You are gone."

There was no answer in my mind, but I felt a presence at my side.

I am your death, as you are mine.

The words that came were not spoken. They were born from my memory, from the dream in which Katherine came to me, standing amongst the desert, the dust, in the shadow of the great tower of blood. I shivered and set the letter down.

My mind was silent but I could feel her. Feel her close. Katherine lingered. Her soul could not yet rest.

Katherine had departed my mind, only to follow me as a ghost.

Chapter Forty-Six

Greenwich Palace
January 1536

There were immediate rumours of murder.

About court, people swapped tales of unnatural death and delighted each other with horror, scaring their audiences with stories of Italian powders that could be slipped into drinks, leaving no trace… and with every tale told, the name of Boleyn was whispered.

Had Katherine been murdered? I could not believe it of Henry, but what of Cromwell? Had he sought a way back to favour by ridding me of the woman who had always outshone me, even from her gloomy houses?

My father and brother helped matters not at all, for I heard they had said Mary should follow her mother's example.

"Why did you say such a thing?" I demanded of my brother.

"We *didn't*," he said, sinking into a chair. "We were passing comment on something the King had said. Chapuys reported we said this, but those words did not pass our lips, I swear it, sister."

I sighed. There was nothing to be done. No matter what, in some minds we Boleyns would always be guilty of whatever evil came.

If I was inclined to do away with Katherine, I would have done so years ago. When I was her lady-in-waiting, I had ample chance, should my obviously so-wicked heart have pushed me to poison her. I had served at her table, brought her wine and beer in bed. If I was the witch they all supposed me to be, and had known what the future held, surely I would have grasped the opportunity long ago and delivered us all from a great deal of trouble.

But people care not for reason when rumour is unleashed. The stories became wilder and wilder. Chapuys became utterly convinced someone had murdered Katherine, and pressed Henry to investigate. But Henry was in no mood for trouble and toil. He was beside himself with joy. Henry had lived in a private hell of horrors for more than a year, imagining every moment we were about to be invaded. Now, there was no cause. Katherine's death had freed him. We were at liberty.

Chapuys, upon his return, was shocked to find a court in celebration rather than mourning and was made only more sceptical when Cromwell informed him the rumours of poison had originated in France.

To the disquiet of the hapless hare, Henry organised jousts and masques, and ordered matching yellow costumes for us, in which we appeared before court. Yellow is the symbol of rebirth and renewal; the colour of spring.

"For this is the spring of our lives, Anne," he said, quite forgetting how angry he had been with me of late. He took me in his arms. "This is truly our beginning."

"And I am finally the undisputed Queen."

"You always were."

We processed to Mass that morning, taking Elizabeth with us. In her father's arms, she gazed about with her large, black eyes, calmly taking in all the acclaim and glory. That afternoon we feasted and after, Henry commanded all my ladies to his room, and held a dance. Elizabeth was brought in and passed around until Henry almost snatched her from Norfolk, saying, "The Princess is mine alone!" as he roared with laughter.

He was so merry, lost in joy. So much court did he pay to my daughter that I felt foolish about what I had said when we heard of Katherine's death. When he was like this, I was sure there was no one else in the world for Henry but me.

After days of dancing and celebration, Henry ordered a joust, swearing he would compete. I did not attempt to reason with him, although given the turn of later events, I should have. I did not tell him he was no longer the young knight he once had been, or that his reactions were getting slower. I told him he *should* compete, for I wanted everyone to see how joyous he was that Katherine was gone, and I was the undisputed Queen of England.

Even in the minds of those who opposed me, there could be no further doubt. Henry's first wife was dead. The path for friendship with Spain was clear, and France, seeing this, would have to fall in line.

Henry continued to court Jane, but everyone could see that some of the passion had gone from his wooing. The Seymours and their allies were not best pleased, which, of course, delighted me.

On orders from Henry, Cromwell reached out to France, informing them of Katherine's death, and making it clear that since the impediment to friendship with Spain had now been removed, François was no longer in any position to dictate terms to England. Gardiner and his man Wallop were sent further instructions, telling them that England would now pursue alliance with the Emperor, and if François did not want to lose all allies in Europe, he would have to be much more polite and conciliatory than he had been in the past. Chapuys suddenly found himself frequently invited into Henry's company, and more often than not was ushered into meetings in full view of the French ambassadors. The anguish on their faces was greatly soothing to my ruffled spirit and battered pride.

Henry was delighted to find himself suddenly in a position of power and influence. "We will play both sides," he said to me one day at the lists as I tied a green ribbon about his lance.

I had been watching him ride, and seeing me in the stands, he had brought his horse over to accept my favours. It was a public gesture of love and respect, and although Jane Seymour was present, and of late she had sometimes tied her ribbon about his lance, that day he chose me.

"You will keep them guessing?" I asked, looping the silk ribbon into a pert bow. "Keep them on a knife edge for many months, my love, to richly pay them back for all they have done to us."

Henry laughed. "It is all France and Spain deserve," he agreed. "They have toyed with us, but now the game is ours."

"Let them squirm," I said, with a broad grin. "Show them who is master, my beloved."

"The King wants to play both sides, Majesty," said the voice of my sister-in-law in my ear as Henry rode off. "Yet Cromwell seeks alliance only with Spain."

"Why?" I asked. "His Majesty has told him that he wants to delay a while, to see which side will grant the most benefit."

"The King has told him this, indeed," whispered Jane. "But Cromwell does not heed his commands. I heard him blatantly voicing disdain for France in the company of Chapuys just this morning. He suggested that Chapuys should come to the Augustinian Friary between their houses in London to meet him, but the ambassador refused, saying he had to attend a Mass for the soul of the Dowager."

"What else did you hear?"

"That Chapuys told Cromwell to write to him instead," said Jane. "But Cromwell was unwilling to put what he had to say on parchment."

For fear it would be read, I thought. What was Cromwell up to? Henry was right. George was right. This man was overstepping his authority. He thought he was the King, and we were his subjects. Knowing that Henry was already angered at Cromwell's growing arrogance, I stowed Jane's information away, preparing it for use later on.

As I watched Henry ride in the joust, his armour gleaming in the early morning sun, I thought back to all the hundreds of times I had watched him. I thought of the day he had been thrown from his horse by Suffolk, and the terror I had experienced then… a terror that had told me, even though I had resisted long and hard, that I loved this prince.

And now we were united again, in love and in duty, I would not fail him.

Cromwell wanted to make himself a king, just as Wolsey had. He thought to stand behind the throne, pulling Henry's strings. It would not be. England was Henry's, and Henry was mine. No matter how long and brutal we argued, no matter how often we hurt each other, our love was deeper than any other. And our commitment to each other, although strained and battered, had not died.

I would not allow another Wolsey to rise.

*

"I do not understand the problem," I said to Cranmer. "Katherine left her property for the King to deal with after her death, did she not?"

"In a way, madam," said Cranmer, frowning. "But the King wishes to use her funeral to accentuate that she died his brother's widow. If she died a widow without a living husband, then it was her right to decide where her property went after her demise."

"And if His Majesty makes a claim to her property, it will seem as though he was her husband," I said. "I see."

"Rich has been set on the task," said Cranmer. "He is a wily fox, that one, although I cannot admit any affection for him."

"I feel the same," I said. "There is something disturbing about his company. I need to bathe when he has been near me."

My gentle friend smiled. "The cloud of the evidence against More hangs over him," he said. "There are many who believe Rich lied to obtain the evidence that sent More to his death."

"So said my brother," I noted. "And I have wondered too. At the time, Cromwell spoke for Rich, and at the time, I believed him."

"But now you do not, Majesty?"

"Sometimes I know not what or whom to believe anymore," I said. "I always thought I was a creature of court, Eminence, born to live here, fated to dwell in these shades of brilliant light and infinite darkness. As time wears on, I wonder if I was as suited to this life as I thought." I smiled. "I find myself enamoured with honesty," I said. "Perhaps because I have grown sick on a diet of lies."

"I was told you wept at the death of Katherine," said Cranmer. "The court was speaking of it with surprise."

"But you were not?"

My old friend shook his head. "Your heart is known to me," he said. "Even for an enemy, you would sorrow."

"I am not sure that is true of all my enemies, Eminence, but for Katherine…" I trailed off, my eyes seeking to express what my lips could not say. "Perhaps it was for fear and relief that I wept," I said. "Since I became Queen, even before that, perhaps, I have felt as though Katherine was with me. As though she stood at my elbow and everyone could see her and compared us. I thought I would experience only relief when she passed, but it was not so. I feared that should the King tire of me, he might treat me as he had her."

"The King loves you, Majesty."

"Sometimes," I said. "Sometimes I think he loves me, at others I think he hates me. At times, I think he might like to be free, to choose again, to pick another wife, one who would be kind and gentle all the time. One who had no opinions of her own, but would echo back his thoughts, pleasing him with flattery."

"You speak of the Seymour girl," said Cranmer, shaking his head. "She is a *diversion*, Majesty, that is all. She is not you. The King often says that there is no one like you and he is right. When troubles come, does he go to his fair shade, or does he come to you? When he feels joy, he does not go to her but to you. His Majesty is bound to you. You are the one he turns to in strife and in happiness. It is only when you argue that he goes to others. He does not love the Seymour chit, for she is a child. You are right when you say that she but echoes his own thoughts back to him. She is an empty cave, that one. The King stands and shouts and all he hears in return is his own voice. He comes to you for just counsel, and receives it. He goes to her when he is bruised, and needs comfort." Cranmer paused. "But he would never do to you what he did to Katherine. You are the light in his darkness, the path in his grim forest. Without you, he is lost. He knows that."

"You bring me great comfort," I said. Cranmer was right. I was the tonic that Henry needed to bolster his strength and courage. I was the stability he sought when his world trembled. Were it not for the necessity of carrying his children, Henry might never have strayed.

*

Despite frantic requests from Chapuys, the Courtenays and the Carewes, it was decided that Katherine would be laid to rest in Peterborough Abbey, rather than Westminster. As Katherine's body was taken for examination and embalmment, I began to think about Lady Mary.

The girl had lost much. Perhaps everything. Her mother had been a huge part of her life, and I knew she had loved her. Henry had softened towards Mary, sending her a purse of money and a kind note. He also had not reiterated his demands that she recognise me as Queen or Elizabeth as his heir.

Pity moved me. I wrote to Lady Shelton, instructing her to relieve pressure on Lady Mary. I told her that I had hoped harsh measures would bring forth obedience, but in the light of her loss, and in hope of a better relationship in the future, I would have her treated gently. I asked my aunt to inform Mary of this, and to tell her that she needed to submit whilst there was still a chance to gain from her submission. I told her also to officially inform Mary that I was with child, as another incentive to surrender.

But I had not been alone in thinking of Mary. People feared that Katherine's demise would lead to harsher tactics being used against her daughter. Chapuys had written to my aunts, passing on a titbit of gossip in the hope that it would make them kinder. The rumour was based on something that Henry had apparently said to the Marques of Exeter, husband to Gertrude Courtenay.

"The ambassador said, Majesty, that the King had expressed doubts about the legality of his second marriage," wrote my aunt. *"And that the King had said he had been seduced into marriage by witchcraft, and for this reason considered it null. Considering the source of this gossip was the Courtenays, and knowing their restless tongues are often full of deceit, I took not much stock in this report. The ambassador himself sounded dubious about it, but it was reported to us at Hatfield in the hope of making us treat the Lady Mary better. I thought, no matter how unworthy or untrustworthy the source, I should repeat it to Your Majesty."*

I stared at the letter. Had Henry really said this, or was it poison dreamt up by my enemies? I felt cold. I bound the parchment up and hid it in a chest, hoping that if I could not see it, it did not exist.

But I was haunted by it. Was Henry thinking of destroying our marriage? With me pregnant I could not believe it, and yet there was a possibility he had expressed such sentiments. He had said things like this to me in the past. After an argument, had he gone to his men, not only complaining about me, but seeking ways to remove me?

He came to me that afternoon, and I could barely speak to him. I told myself to be witty, to be quick, but I could not. My smile froze upon my face.

The Lady Mary was unmoved by my efforts. She repeated anew that she knew of no other Queen but her mother, who, although dead, was still the Queen. I grew annoyed, and wrote to Lady Shelton again. *"If I have a son,"* I wrote. *"She knows what will happen to her."*

I told my aunt to resume harsh treatment, and my orders were not welcome. My aunt began to turn from me, disliking my shrill commands. I heard that Lady Shelton had not done as I commanded, and George informed me that one of his men at Hatfield had said he thought Lady Shelton was taking money from Chapuys in return for allowing his servants to meet Lady Mary in contradiction of Henry's orders.

I asked George to find evidence. Henry was presently disposed to be kind to his errant daughter, but if I could prove Mary was working against us, this might change.

*

Reports came from Savoy, a state in which François had intervened. The Emperor opposed him, and war was rumoured. Italy and Milan became Europe's focus, and England slipped to one side. Henry did not care to see that his realm was not as important as he might have liked. But I believed that if the Emperor's gaze fell elsewhere, all was well.

As Katherine lay in state, awaiting her funeral, I sat upon my gracious throne, trying to pretend I was happy. But I was not. I was distraught, bereft… I knew myself to be alone, and only the child in my womb protected me. *If I am taken from this throne,* I thought, *will they take my daughter from me too? Will I become as Katherine, locked away in little rooms, never to see my Elizabeth again?*

When Katherine's corpse was opened for examination, her heart was found to be black and hideous. It was cut in half, and washed, but the blackness remained. People said she had died of a broken heart, and this was their evidence.

Sometimes, I set my hand against my own heart, and wondered if it, like Katherine's, had died. Was this what Henry did to the women he loved? Claimed their hearts, and turned them to rot and ruin?

Katherine's body lingered at Kimbolton for almost two weeks after her death, whilst Henry attempted to seize what little property she had left. On the 15th of January she was encased in a lead coffin, and her body had begun to decompose. She was returned to the chapel, to lie for another twelve days as Masses were sung for her soul. Suffolk and Elizabeth Browne, the Countess of Worcester, along with the Countesses of Oxford and Surrey, and ladies of lesser rank, were chosen as her mourners. Lady Mary could not attend. It was not normal for royalty, even of bastard birth, to attend funerals of close kin.

As we waited for the once-Queen to be laid to rest, a strange series of accidents occurred. The first was that I woke one morning to billowing black smoke, and had to be rushed from my chambers. It was said one of the coals from the fire had escaped and set light to the carpet. In my fright and slumberous confusion, I called for my women to bring Purkoy, only to remember he was dead.

We stood outside the palace, watching white smoke curl from the windows. The early morning air was cold, and I felt frozen. *Was this an accident?* I asked myself. The memory of Purkoy and what had been done to him was fresh within my mind that morning. I had to wonder if this destruction of my chambers was indeed an accident, or if it had been done either as revenge for Katherine, or as a clumsy attempt on my life, and that of my unborn baby.

Henry found me outside, shivering in my fur-lined gown, and took me to his rooms, bellowing at everyone that they should have more care of their Queen.

The second event was even more serious.

On the day before Katherine's chivalric banners were made ready to fly above her funeral procession, the second accident occurred. It was a mishap that might have altered the course of England's history and the path of my life.

On the 24th of January, whilst competing in jousts to celebrate his freedom, Henry fell from his horse.

Chapter Forty-Seven

Greenwich Palace
January 1536

I was sitting in my rooms when the news came, my hands busy sewing a nightgown for my unborn child. Henry had visited that morn in a bright mood which matched the sunny skies.

"Will you join me today?" he asked, picking up the gown I was working on and smiling to see my preparations for our son.

"I may attend in the afternoon," I said. "But if you will excuse me this morning, beloved, I am not feeling hale."

"It is only proper that you rest," he said, stooping to kiss my forehead. "I will see you later, but only if you feel strong enough."

"I love to watch you ride," I said. "Do you remember the day you fell from your horse and I came running to your side?"

He laughed. "There was no man or deer who could have beaten you. You were with me before I even knew that I had fallen."

"I thought I had lost you, and my heart could not bear the pain."

"And I have not fallen since," he said. "You placed a spell of luck upon me that day, I think."

I shivered as he spoke of spells, remembering Chapuys' letter. But Henry, lost in his desire to get onto a horse, noted nothing.

"Ride well," I said as we parted. "Show foolish boys what a true man can achieve."

I thought later that perhaps I should not have spurred him on, but at the time, I simply returned to my embroidery. Taking up the gown, I gazed upon my work with satisfaction. Golden acorns spilled across a hem of white linen, and a sky of blue was picked out in azure above. My child would have a beautiful array of garments to greet him when he arrived. And with Henry and me on better terms, and Katherine gone, I felt lighter than I had in months. I told myself that Henry's threats to remove me had been spoken when he was angry and he did not mean them. How often had I let slip unguarded words… insults about his ability in bed, poetry and clothing? When I was at peace with him I did not think such wild, horrible thoughts, and it was the same for him.

At least I hoped it was.

But there were reasons to rejoice, and I would not ignore them. God had listened. All the hours I spent on my knees after the deaths of my sons, and the effort put into our reformation had been rewarded. This pregnancy was a sign God loved us. This time I would not fail.

My ladies and I had thrown ourselves into work on bed hangings, clothes for my Elizabeth and for my waiting son. I had sewed so many *H* and *A's* entwined that I had started to dream of our initials. The palaces were decorated by the symbols of our love. I was not going to let anyone forget that Henry and I were joined by bonds of a love everlasting. There was no love like our love. We fought, we scrapped, we wounded each other, but always we came back.

Our love was a drug. We were addicted.

Thinking thus, as I sewed, I whiled away the hours. Just as I was preparing to rest, there was a commotion outside the door. With a distraught servant dogging his steps, begging for him to tarry so he might be properly announced, Norfolk barged into my chambers.

My uncle looked wild. His hair was uncovered, and he had run his fingers through it; it spiked like the coarse hair of a sweaty boar. He glanced about, his eyes feral, his mouth gaping.

I rose from my chair, thinking for a moment that he might be there to kill me.

"My lord?" I asked, my hand on the back of my chair. If he meant to murder me I could throw it between us.

"The King is *dead*!" Norfolk cried.

I stared at him. The room went silent.

Henry… *dead*? How could it be?

"What?" I asked, my voice emerging as a hard, tight curl from my mouth. "What do you mean?" Everything was numb. I could not feel my body. There was no thought in my mind.

"He was thrown in the lists!" Norfolk went on. "His horse collapsed on top of him, crushing him. He is dead!"

"It cannot be." I swayed, feeling all the blood in my body leave my flesh and flood to my heart, so it might thunder in my chest, beating out a refrain for the lost heart that once had beat in time with mine. My ladies, seeing me close to fainting, ran to me, bearing me to a chair where they thrust my head between my knees.

When I looked up, I could feel my face was grey. "He is dead?" I whispered.

"We have to move fast," said Norfolk. "There will have to be a regency council established for the Princess and the child you carry."

I put my hand dumbly on my belly. Henry was dead?

I could not think. I could not imagine a world without him. A dull shadow fell upon me, sapping my energy. The light had left the world. The sun had died. Endless night would fall, blanketing the world in darkness.

Norfolk let out a noise of exasperation and threw his hands into the air. "You are the *Queen*!" he shouted. "Stand, and take command, or our enemies will!"

Even through the pain and the fug of sorrow, I knew he was right. This was a fragile moment. The future of my children now depended on me.

I stood. "Take me to the King," I said.

"He is dead."

"You will address me as *Majesty*!" I shouted. "And you will do as I say!"

Norfolk took me to a tent in the tilting yard. There was a huge crowd about it, full of milling people with pale faces. My hands shook and my blood quivered as they parted, allowing me to enter and see Henry lying on a makeshift bed. Doctors were flapping about him, but at first sight, I could see he was not dead.

"God be praised!" I shouted, making them stare. "I was told the King was dead!"

"We thought he was," said my father, rushing to me. Taking one glance at my drawn face he led me to a chair. "When first he fell, he went down so hard we thought he might not rise, and his armoured horse, seventeen hands high, fell upon him. He was wearing nearly a hundredweight of armour. The horse rolled on him."

"So said my uncle," I said, glaring at Norfolk, who looked utterly flabbergasted. "You told me the King was dead!"

"No one thought he could survive that fall," said my father.

"When we moved him in here, Majesty," said Doctor Butts, "we found he was breathing. He remains unconscious, but he lives."

"He lives," I breathed. "He *lives*."

Relief washed over me. I was dizzy. Henry had been taken from me and restored within an hour. The thought that I had lost him had been unbearable, and now that I knew he was alive, if gravely injured, I knew not what to feel. Should I be relieved, or fear to lose him again? Should I rest easy, or start planning to protect our children from my enemies?

My mind felt strangely blank. Finally I understood limbo… a state of non-being, floating between worlds. If Henry lived, all was well. If he died, much, perhaps all, was lost.

"Can I speak to him?" I asked. "Just for a moment. I would not get in your way, but I cannot be here without…"

"Of course, Majesty," said Butts, waving back the other doctors. "It will help him to hear your voice."

I went to Henry. They had removed his armour. His face was deathly pale and there was blood on the back of his head, matted in his hair. A thin line of crimson had dribbled from his mouth, running down a crease in his skin. A flash of memory rose, and I had to force it down, down into the pit where the broken one lived; into that labyrinth where I stored all dangerous things.

One of his legs was uncovered, and I stared at it in horror. Henry had suffered from his legs, but now, those risen veins were swollen, distended and hideous. Stretching from his calf up to his thigh, they were lumpy, erupting from his flesh like earthen fortifications upon an old hill fort. And one had burst. The doctors were trying to stem the bleeding coursing from his thigh, but blood pumped out, rude and red, brilliant against his white skin.

"Can you stop the bleeding?" My voice was desiccated, reedy. I thought I might be sick.

"We will do everything we can," Butts said. "But should His Majesty recover, this may be the end of his days of competition."

I bowed my head over Henry. Taking his hand in mine, I started to whisper. I knew not what I said, for the words poured out of me like water. I spoke of my love for him, of how I needed him, of how our children needed him. I pleaded with God to bring him back. "For what will England do without her King?" I asked. "What will I do without you, my love… my only love?"

On and on I spoke. On and on I prayed. When I looked up, my eyes glazed by tears, I saw the same in the eyes of many others. Moved to grief by my entreaties to the Almighty, they stared at me with admiration and sorrow.

If it had never been clear to some that I loved my husband, it was now.

"You cannot leave me," I whispered. "Do not go, beloved. You must be here to rule England, and see our son born. I cannot do without you. All the petty arguments, they are nothing, do you not see? All that matters is that you are here, and we are together. I cannot live without you."

I started to sob, and my father led me from Henry's side. "Go and rest," he said.

"I will stay with him."

"You should protect your child," he said. "Norfolk was a fool to tell you the news as he did. He might have put you in danger."

I had not even considered this. My hand flashed to my bump. *Please,* my mind begged. *Please, little one. All will be well. Stay, and I will keep you safe.*

As though hearing me, my child moved under my hand. It was the first time I had felt him quicken, and it did not cause alarm. It was the sleepy movement of a child in perfect happiness.

"My child is well," I said. "And my place is with my husband."

"We need to make provision," said my father. "In case the King does not survive."

"The King will live."

"But if he does not…"

"*The King will live!*" I shouted, causing heads to twist about and eyes to stare. "Make whatever plans you think necessary to protect my children, Father, but speak no more of death. It is treason!" I turned to the doctors. "When you think he is strong enough, he will be moved into the palace," I said. "He cannot remain here, in the night air, it will make him sick."

"We thought the same, Majesty," said Butts. "But the crowds outside must be moved."

"I will address them."

"Majesty," said my father. "Are you strong enough for this?"

I stuck my chin in the air. "I am the Queen," I said. "This duty is my office to perform as my husband lies unwell."

I went outside, and as I stepped before them, the anxious masses fell silent. "The King lives," I said. "And he will recover. We thank you for your care, but the noise is disturbing him. In an hour he will be taken into the palace to recover. I would have all of you disperse so we might take him to his chambers without further problems. News will be given this evening, and any time there is more I will tell you all. But, for the sake of His Majesty, the King we love and revere, please go now."

As they started to drift away, I held up a hand. "Please," I said. "Do not seek to scare the rest of court or England by passing on this news for purpose of shock or scandal. If you must speak of the King's fall, say also that he is well, that he is a strong man… that no one can compare to him. Your King will be recovered in a few days, and when he is, he will not wish to hear that anyone has passed on false gossip and alarmed his people." I eyed them with my great, black orbs. "And neither will I."

I am sure some there thought I was about to be announced as regent. They thought Henry was dead, and we were concealing his demise.

Cromwell was hovering. "In half an hour," I said. "Go about court and tell everyone that the King is awake and jesting about the accident."

I did not need to explain myself to Cromwell. If Henry was thought to be gravely injured, there might be immediate problems. Someone might take this chance to rebel, to place Mary on the throne. He bowed, and left to do my bidding.

I turned to my father. "Ensure Elizabeth is safe," I said. "See to it personally, Father. If anyone decides to seize this moment to set Mary on the throne, we must be ready. Dispatch guards to Hatfield. Tell them to let no one leave and no one enter. If anyone plans to harm my daughter, they will pay dearly for it."

As my father ran off to order his men, I glanced back at the tent. "You must live," I murmured to Henry. "England will be mired in war if you do not… And I will be lost without you."

Chapter Forty-Eight

Greenwich Palace
January 1536

I sat by Henry's bedside. I did not get in the way of his doctors, but I would not leave. My ladies, unable to remonstrate with me, brought my meals to his chamber on the ground floor, which was as far into the palace as we had dared move him. They asked me to rest. I would not.

At first I had only thought of my heart, of the pain and suffering I would endure if he was taken from me, but now I thought on what Henry's death would mean for England.

Visions of fire and blood and rebellion roamed in my head.

War would come. The babe in my belly was unborn, and none knew what sex it might be. My enemies would not wait another five months to make up their minds. Many of them had never thought me fit for the throne. They wanted Mary. If Henry died, we would see another war such as that between Lancaster and York, in the days of my grandparents. But this time, it would be no shadowy queen such as Margaret of Anjou was to me, struggling to protect her child. It would be me, fighting to uphold the Church of England, hold off Rome, Spain, France and English rebels, and save my children from murder.

I was petrified. Was I strong enough for this? Strong enough to hold England together? To act as regent? Could I protect Elizabeth and my unborn child?

Father informed me when his men were ready, and he sent them to Hatfield with strict instructions to guard the house, but not to allow news to leak out. We did not need Mary's passionate supporters to take to arms and march to her aid.

Much ran through my head in the hours Henry lay there, unconscious and bleeding. War, famine, struggle, invasion… tortured thoughts, wild visions, everything that could and might go wrong raced in my blood like droplets in a crushing waterfall. There was a torment of noise in my mind; a grating, whirring, mechanical sound, as though bone and blood had been replaced by cogs and gears.

But all the time, there was a voice; a begging, pleading, terrified voice. All it wanted was for Henry to open his eyes.

I had thought many times that I loved him not. I knew, at that awful time, this was false. *No matter what he does, I will always love him*, I thought. My sorrow was mighty and great. It loomed over me. I stood in shadow, deep and unyielding, and could not find the light of the sun.

"I love you," I whispered, holding his hand.

"I never knew…" A strangled whisper emerged from Henry's mouth. I let out a cry and leapt to my feet, astonished and terrified to hear him.

"The King is awake!" I almost screamed at the doctors. They came running, but Henry was not done amazing us.

"I never knew angels were so dark of hair," he muttered, gazing up with eerie, unfocussed eyes.

A burst of laughter exploded unguarded from my gullet. I leaned on the bed, weak with relief. Henry was not only conscious, he was jesting!

"What does he mean?" asked Butts, looking at my flushed face in confusion.

"It is nothing," I said, grasping Henry's hand and squeezing it tight. "It was something he said to me a long time ago, when a similar accident happened."

The doctors were relieved. I think for a moment they had thought their master was seeing things, or that he was indeed so close to Heaven that he had witnessed the agents of God. But with my words, they sagged.

"I heard you," Henry whispered, blinking and making as though he meant to sit up. I pushed him down.

"You heard me?"

"Your prayers," he said. "What has happened, Anne? Everything is so dark."

He sounded drunk. Words slurred in his throat. I kissed him, tears of happiness running down my cheeks. "There was an accident, my love," I said. "Your horse fell and you were injured. But I am going to make you better."

"With your magic, Anne. *My* Anne..." He smiled and fell into the arms of sleep.

Wiping my eyes, I stood and grinned wanly at the room full of physicians. Never had I seen men look more relieved in all my life. "Tend to him," I said. As I spoke, the room swayed. Black spots broke out in front of my eyes. Had Butts not caught me, I would have fallen.

"You must rest, my lady," he said. "The shock of this could be dangerous."

"I am well," I said, groping blindly for the chair beside Henry's bed. "I will stay a while."

"My lady," said Mary Howard. "We have prepared a bed in the next chamber. Come now and rest. You will be only a room away, and if the King wakes, you will be roused as quickly there as if you sleep on that chair."

I allowed them to take me into the next room, but I would not change out of my gown. I wanted to be quickly on hand if I was needed. I fell into sleep as swift as my husband. My hands wrapped tight about my belly, my last words were to our son. "Rest easy, little one," I murmured. "All will be well."

*

"You are sure our son is fine?" Henry asked as I sat by his bed feeding him chicken broth laced with saffron and expensive, imported wild rice.

"Our son is strong," I said. "Fortunately the shock of Norfolk's message did not do any harm."

Henry had been told of this by my father, and was furious with my uncle. I could understand his rage. The bumbling ass might well have endangered my baby and me by telling me Henry was dead and we had to make ready for war. What a fool he was! Although a cynical part of me had to wonder if Norfolk had intended to bring harm upon me.

"I will have words with your uncle," said Henry, taking my hand. "And even with that shock, and your disquiet to see me so ill, you did not leave."

"I will never leave you," I said. "Not as long as you have need of me."

Henry's eyes clouded with sentiment. "How now," he said, running a hand gingerly over his leg and wincing. The bleeding veins had been covered by thick, soft bandages of linen, but his wounds were itchy. "I am well," Henry said, attempting to insert a finger into his dressing.

"Leave that alone," I scolded, tapping his knuckles with my spoon.

"It itches."

"That means it is healing."

I was not sure if I was telling the truth. Whilst Henry had slept, they had dressed his wound again. His legs were frightful. The physicians assured me that this would heal in time, but I had trouble stopping myself retching to see Henry's legs. The doctors were right, never would he joust again.

Henry sighed and sat back. "What news from court?"

"Only the unbounded relief and joy of all your friends and subjects," I said, smiling as I took another spoonful of broth to his mouth. "You gave us a scare, my lord, but when you return to court, it will do your heart good to see how happy your people are to see you. They love you with all their hearts."

"Perhaps it was a fool's errand to joust," he said with a grunt after he had swallowed the mouthful of pottage.

"It was an accident, Henry," I said. "Accidents may befall any man, young or old."

"I am not old!" he snapped, his eyes irritable. Henry was not talented at bearing physical pain or infirmities. They made him feel weak, something he could not endure.

"I simply meant the accident could have happened to anyone, at any time," I said soothingly. "Think of the joust that claimed Bryan's eye, my lord. Chance takes us ever by surprise. You will be fit and hale soon, and although, for the sake of my nerves, it would please me if you did not compete again until our son is born, I would not like to think I would never see you on a horse again, riding like Saint George himself; a warrior of God."

Henry smiled softly. "For you," he said. "I promise not to compete until our child is born."

I congratulated myself. Making it seem as though his failure to ride again for some time was for the comfort of a lady appealed to Henry's sense of chivalry. It would buy time for Butts and the other unfortunate physicians who might have to tell Henry that to compete again could risk his life.

"That would please me," I said, and then made a face. "I must excuse myself," I said.

"You are unwell, sweetheart?"

"I must to the privy," I said, blushing. "Our son leans on my bladder."

Henry chuckled as I raced off. But it was not urine I needed to pass. Since Henry's fall, I had suffered from loose stools, almost like passing water. I was sure it was due to the stress of the situation, but it was most vexing. Court gowns were not made to be removed swiftly, and even with my women's help, I barely got upon the privy in time.

I clutched my belly as I passed the stool. I had been suffering cramps for a few days too. I believed they were in league with my other problems, but something, a little thought that I would not allow purchase on my mind, nagged, whispering that I had felt pain like this before... During a time I never wished to remember.

Chapter Forty-Nine

Greenwich Palace
January 1536

On the day of Katherine's funeral, I awoke feeling pensive. Henry had been moved to his bedchamber, and there was every reason to feel merry, but I did not.

I was not sure what it was. Perhaps it was Katherine, her ghost coming to haunt me as her voice had once sounded in my mind. Perhaps it was just the release of all the pain and fear I had endured over the past week, or the sapping of my energy from the loose stools and cramps. But I could not seem to point to one event and say, "This is it; the reason I am sad".

Sadness had simply taken up residence in my heart.

Katherine had lain at Kimbolton for three weeks whilst Cromwell arranged her funeral. Her servants had hunted out scraps of black cloth to wear about their arms for mourning, as it had been said nothing would be provided by the Crown. In actual fact, garments were supplied, but were not dispatched until a few days before the funeral, due to everyone's focus being on Henry. Katherine's coffin had been taken by trundling wagon to Sawtry. Placing Katherine under a canopy, the Abbot and his monks prayed for her soul and lit over four hundred candles, illuminating the church with blazing, brilliant light. Mass was celebrated, and forty-eight poor parish members carried candles for her soul.

Then, Katherine had made her last journey. They took her to the Benedictine Abbey of Peterborough, where she was received by the Abbot and the Bishops of Lincoln, Ely and Rochester. The chapel was hung with banners proclaiming her descent from the royal houses of England and Spain. Pennants, bearing Katherine's arms and her father's, were displayed, and about the chapel golden letters were hung, spelling out her motto: *"Humble and Loyal"*.

Loyal, Katherine certainly had been. I am not so sure she honoured the other part of her motto.

Masses were sung, and Katherine's confessor, Athequa, was allowed to serve as deacon. Sir William Paulet represented Henry, and Suffolk's daughter, Eleanor, was chief mourner. One of my men, Hilsey, Fisher's replacement as Bishop of Rochester, preached a sermon against the power of the Pope and the marriage of Katherine and Henry. On her tomb, the arms of Spain and Wales were quartered.

Everything displayed, everything said, all proclaimed that Katherine had never been Queen of England. Her funeral was a pageant, used by Henry to make this clear.

On the same day that these rites were being performed, I rose from my bed and went to Henry. I had been unwell the day before, with more cramps and unpleasant privy experiences, so had stayed away, thinking if this was a sickness, I might pass it to him.

But when I awoke with sorrow, and could not divine the cause, I wanted him. Since his accident, my heart had wound back the hands of time and fallen in love with him all over again. Coming so close to losing him had brought into sharp relief how intrinsic he was to my life.

This was God's way of showing you how wrong you were, I thought as I dressed. *You thought you could leave behind the love you bore for him and become free by doing so. And yet, this is false.*

I wished many things were different, and that morning I made up my mind to make what I wanted come true. Henry's first thoughts had been of me. In the days of his recovery we had nestled close to one another, allowing our hearts to heal in the glow of each other's love.

I had hope… so why did I feel so sad?

Henry will dispel it, I assured myself. He would take me in his arms and make all things well.

But when I got to his rooms, I found he could not take me in his arms. There was another already occupying that space.

The guards on the door had tried to stop me, but in my usual brash manner, I marched past. Flinging open the door, I was about to make a merry jest, but it died upon my lips.

Henry was out of bed, sitting on a chair. But he was not alone. In his arms was Jane Seymour, her little, pale hand playing with the collar of his nightgown. His arms were around her, and through the sheer fabric of his gown I could see he was aroused.

My stomach lurched. My eyes refused to look away. I swayed in the doorway, and suddenly, without warning, fell to my knees, emitting a horrific howl.

What a fool I was! What a fool to think that this accident might have reached his heart as it had mine! A fool to believe that he might have wished for reconciliation and happiness. A fool to think he needed me as I needed him.

I heard Jane break from his lap and run for the far door. My ladies were in a confused crowd behind me, staring as Jane fled. Henry, flustered, red of face and fumbling, tried to gather his robe about him. I felt hands on my back as my women tried to get me up, but all I could do was kneel, sobbing on the ground.

Henry drove them away and tried to pick me up, but my legs would not work. I stumbled to a chair and stared at him.

"I came to see you," I said, my voice hard and numb. "I felt low and thought our love would calm me." A brittle chuckle fell from my lips. "I am the mother of all fools… To think for one moment that a false heart such as yours could possibly feel as mine does."

"I love you," he said gruffly.

"Do not defame the name of love," I snarled. "There is no love in you! How could such virtue and glory live in your festering, rotten heart?"

Henry looked as though he might strike me, and I lifted my face. "Go ahead," I whispered. "Hit me. There is nothing more you could do to hurt me now."

He left and my ladies all but dragged me back to my room.

After an hour, the cramps in my abdomen grew worse. Blood started to flow. Small pieces of liver-like tissue started to come with the blood, and as I was taken to bed, screaming and crying out in fear for my child, the doctors and midwifes were sent for. They fed me cinnamon comfits in a syrup of althea, trying to stop the child from coming. They laid me down in my bed, warmed by bedpans, and poured fresh spring water down my throat, followed by ale with shredded purple silk in it, as well as the treads of eighteen eggs and a conserve of red roses. They put toasted bread soaked in muscadine wine upon my stomach, sprinkled with powder of cloves and nutmeg, and bound it to my belly.

Nothing worked.

I had to go through it all again. All again. Like a nightmare… like one of the flashes I had endured of blood on cloth, of the face of my perfect, dead boy, I had to relive it all. I went through the motions, pushing on contractions and straining against the shoulders and hands of my women, knowing that my child could not live. Knowing that I was about to lose another baby.

Blood came thick and heavy. I was weakened by the flow. The doctors whispered in the corners of my room; they knew a miscarriage at four months was dangerous. Most women, once past the first few months, were past peril. I, in losing my child at four months, might be in danger of my life.

When my child had passed from me, they hastily baptised him, and rushed to stem the bleeding. They fed me infusions of oak bark and leaf, and placed pads soaked in sage and water horehound between my legs. Vervain was hung about the chamber, and sage burned, to remove wandering sickness and dispel evil spirits who might come for me and my child.

When it was done, I lay on the bed with my face turned to the wall. Hangings of crimson cloth of gold surrounded me. The colour made me feel sick. One hundred and eighty badges bearing Henry's arms and mine watched me. Two great arms of the King and Queen were joined in a garland and topped with an Imperial crown. Fringes of Venice gold and silver twinkled in the candlelight. I was surrounded by symbols of our unity, but I knew I was utterly alone.

Silence fell.

I knew silence now. We were old companions. Silence was within me and without. It surrounded me, suffocating my heart. Everything was dead… my children, my hope, my love. I was no more of the living, but of the dead.

Numbly, I went to the table and looked down at the unmoving form. I swayed, weak upon my unsure feet. My baby was tiny, no bigger than the span of my hand. His head was impossibly large. His skin was smooth, but a horrific blue-grey colour; the skin of death. His hands and feet were formed, and there was just enough evidence to tell that my child would have been a son.

My son who had died as he felt my heart expire.

I wanted to take him in my arms, to hold him close and to tell him I was sorry. Sorry for all the pain and fear he must have experienced through me. Sorry for the life I had promised that he would never have. Sorry for his death, and sorry for not saving him. But they took me away. Away to stare at the wall. They bundled my son into blankets and took him away too.

The broken one became strong. She lusted to be set free. The shell of Anne Boleyn encased her, just, but my control over the darkness within was about to be tested.

Henry came to me later, limping on one leg. He stood over me in silence as I lay curled up, like a baby, weeping bitter tears. "I see that God will not give me male children," he said. "When you are up I will speak with you."

"God took our child," I whispered, turning to him.

Henry shrank from my accusing glare. "You were not careful enough," he said.

"It was your fall!" I cried out. "It was my fear that you were dead and the way my uncle told me." I paused, seeing his face darken. "And it was my love for you," I whispered. "My heart died to see you loved others."

Henry looked away.

"Our child died for your sin," I said, half-rising in bed and pointing a shaking finger at him. "*Your* sin, Henry."

"I have committed no sin."

"You have sinned against me and all you swore to me," I said, my voice harsh. "You murdered our child, for how could my heart feed him when it died within me to see you in the arms of another?"

"You are without sense," he said, his cheeks flaming. "I will see you when you are well."

"*Your sin*," I said again, mad with grief. "Your sin killed our boy."

"You will get no more boys from me," he said and without another word, he left.

I listened to the sound of him thumping along the corridor, and the cane he carried pounding along with his steps. It sounded like two hearts beating in unison. Like the two hearts Henry and I had once been.

But no more. No more.

I fell into dreams of blood and dust. Of the tower and arid planes. As I watched blood stream down the tower, and saw the dusty earth break and crack under my feet, I held a bundle in my arms.

Another child. Another sorrow. Another reason for my heart to dry and crisp under the unyielding sun.

*

How strong are the hearts of mankind that when one suffers as much as I had, they continue to beat?

In the days that followed my child's death, I rose from my bed and picked up my embroidery. These garments would not keep my child warm, but they might keep another safe. My ladies, seeing me return to my work, thought I had lost my mind, and tried to take the tiny garments away.

"I will give them to Elizabeth Browne," I said, speaking of my friend who was with child. "I will have to unpick the royal symbols, but they should be used. We cannot let them go to waste."

Numbness was my refuge. My salvation. It was the only thing keeping the broken woman imprisoned.

Mary Howard ducked down beside me, her face crumpled with grief. "Madam," she said, disturbed by my hollow voice. "Are you sure?"

I looked up at her and the others. I marvelled that they should hold some of my sorrow. Perhaps the strand they held was what kept me clinging on to sanity. Were if not for them sharing my grief, as my husband evidently did not, I might have lost my wits.

"Do not grieve," I said gently. "It is better that this child, conceived when Katherine still lived, did not survive. I shall be sooner with child again, and this time none will doubt my son, because Katherine is gone."

They were amazed to hear me comfort them at such a time, and took to their duties in silence. Later on, I heard Margaret Douglas return. Apparently she had been to Henry.

"I told His Majesty that his wife needs him," she whispered to Mary Howard and Bess Holland. "And that her courage extended even as far as to comfort us in her time of need."

"What said the King?" asked Mary.

"He said his Queen was the strongest, most courageous woman he had ever known," she said. "And then he turned from me and wept. He promised to see her tomorrow."

And he did. I heard his shambling steps in the corridor before he entered, his cane clipping against the wooden boards under their herb and rush matting. He sent away my women and sat beside me as I sewed. I greeted him blankly but then fell silent, picking out the royal acorns and ciphers from the linen cloth.

"Others could do that for you," he said gently.

"The task is mine, as is my sorrow," I said, looking up. "And none can take it from me. If this was the last of our children I am to bear, allow me to grieve, husband. Do not steal my sorrow from me, as you did with our other children."

"How did I steal your sorrow?"

"By commanding me not to think or speak of them," I said. "By running into the arms of other women. By betraying all that was good between us."

I reached for a cushion of pins and he shrank from me. "You shrink from my touch?" I asked. "Do you think me cursed, as Katherine was?"

His face crumpled and he put it into his hands. From behind his fingers I heard a noise of hollow, bleak grief. It was the same sound I had made to see him with Jane. I reached out and touched his hand, and this time he did not shy away.

"Join your sorrow to mine," I said. "And let us fear no more to speak of our children. Only together, Henry, may we master this."

He said nothing, but pulled me into his arms. There we sat and there we stayed, a huddled mass of arms and legs, as we wept. When he was called away to have his dressings changed, he took my hand. "Bid me do anything for you," he said.

"Ask my brother to come," I said. "I would have his company until I might have yours again."

"I will send him." He paused as he was about to leave. "This is not the last child we will have, Anne," he said. "I was angry and sad when I said that. I meant it not."

"That brings me comfort," I said, although nothing could really reach my heart but sadness.

"Soon, we will have a son," he said. "One that Katherine cannot curse."

I wondered at his tone, but when my brother arrived he told me that Henry had taken up a new refrain; Katherine had laid a curse upon us whilst she lived, and the death of our child was the last sting in its tail. Henry had taken my idea, and claimed it as his own.

"Many couples suffer setbacks," said my brother, his hand warm on my shoulder. "It does not mean you are under a curse."

"It is strange, is it not, that Henry does not refer to the old curse," I said. "The one they say was placed on the house of York by the Poles when King Edward killed his own brother."

"He blames Katherine."

"Because he does not want to accept blame." I stared at the wall. Where the tapestry ended there was a gap before the next hanging, where crumbling plaster could be seen. It reminded me of the desert in my dreams.

"It was an accident, more than likely brought on by the stress of hearing the King was dead."

I nodded, but my heart was full of resentment at Henry and at God. I had done all that God had asked. I had heard His voice in the wilderness and sought to bring a truer faith to His people. Was the loss of my children a sign that my union to Henry was not lawful in the eyes of God? I knew that Henry, too, must be thinking the same. And that scared me. If Henry came to truly believe that I was not his lawful wife, as Katherine had not been, would I be put aside too?

Henry's demons had returned. I had seen them in his eyes. He had witnessed this pattern too often with Katherine to allow it to pass unnoticed, and Henry was a deeply superstitious man. Was God frowning on our union? I was sure Henry was questioning everything; me, his faith, his standing with God. His accident had driven home the fact that he was young no more. He was forty-four, I thirty-five. Our time for bearing children was waning. I had little time left.

Would Henry grant me that time? Would we indeed have another chance to make a son? He said so, but what did he whisper when my back was turned? Did he tell tales of witchcraft and magic, saying I had seduced him into marriage? The thought was laughable. I had never pursued him. He had hunted me. But the truth was not a constant to Henry. It was flexible, bending to his will. He believed what he wanted to believe.

Witchcraft, in itself, was not seen as a crime. There were many who practised arts akin to those of witches; cunning men and women, alchemists, doctors, scholars… there was only a penalty for witchcraft if a person had done actual harm, of which there was evidence. In cases brought against high-ranking people, like the Duke of Buckingham, witchcraft was a crime because it was linked to treason. Three royal women had been imprisoned in the past for wielding the dark arts. Joan of Navarre had been held for three years on charges of sorcery by her stepson, Henry V, but everyone knew those accusations had been brought about as he wanted her money. Eleanor Cobham, the Duchess of Gloucester, had been accused of practising harmful witchcraft on Henry VI and was sent to the Isle of Wight for the rest of her life. Most people believed Eleanor was guilty as charged. And Jacquetta of Luxembourg, the Duchess of Bedford, and mother of Elizabeth Wydville, Henry's grandmother, had been accused of witchcraft to bring about the union of Elizabeth and Edward … but the case against her had been crushed, and she had been released.

But treason was not what Henry was accusing me of, if he had indeed accused me. He seemed to think I had cast a spell upon him… or perhaps this was what my enemies thought… thought no woman could have power unless she turned to Satan.

But there was another reason. Canon law provided means for a man to escape his marriage if sorcery could be proved.

I leaned on George. He was my rock, my safe harbour, the one person I knew I could rely on. My father had no sympathy, only worry and a look in his eyes that accused me of murdering my own child. But Henry was sweet. He came to me, often finding my brother reading to me.

My male family members visited in secret, permitted by Henry to come to my chambers through private routes, guarded and designed only for royalty. Until churched, I was not allowed male visitors, but seeing my sadness, Henry granted permission for George to come to me.

Court was alive with gossip. I could hear it even through the walls. They said I could not give the King a child, that I had a defective constitution, that I was being punished by God. They ignored all the strain I had been under this time, and the sickness I had endured the last. They blamed me.

Should I have expected anything else? The same had happened to Katherine. The same curse, the same loss… We were as one, she and I. Finally I understood what she had meant when she had told me in my dreams I was her sister of Fate.

It was true. We were joined. Bonded by the same nightmare. Twisted into the same grief.

When I rose, people barely bothered to drop their voices when speaking of my inability to give Henry a son. Every word hurt. Every voice bore deeper into my gaping wounds. People had often thought I was without a heart. It was not so. Never, in all my years, had I been so aware of my heart. My three lost children were within it. Grief consumed the rest of me.

I was an eaten woman, being slowly consumed from within.

I saw a dark tunnel opening before me. I knew that darkness well. It was the space in which my horrors waited for me; those I suffered now and all those I had shoved into the recesses of my mind. It was where the broken one waited.

I turned from the tunnel. I swallowed my heart. I brought out the fiction of Anne Boleyn once more, and plastered her upon my face. Quiet and subdued I was, for the first days after my loss, and then, as I started to find it easier to throw my sorrows and nightmares so deep into my mind that I could not access them, it was easier for the old Anne, this construct of me I had made to protect myself, to come forth.

But darkness does not leave us. If we do not confront it, it simply lingers. It settles down to wait for its chance. A chance to break through the armour we have built about it. A chance to rise again, to swallow us, to eat us… to claim us.

The broken one waited. Waited for her chance.

Chapter Fifty

Greenwich Palace
January 1536

"The Emperor has written to the King from his seat at Naples," said George, taking several plump red grapes from a glazed bowl and popping them into his mouth.

"To say he is desirous of friendship?"

"Indeed." My brother swallowed, washing the grapes down with their fermented counterparts. "He told Chapuys to inform His Majesty that he was sorrowed by Katherine's death, but wished for better relations with England to stand against France."

"It pleases me to think of François sweating upon his throne."

"It seems the Emperor may be willing to accept you as Queen."

"Now that he has no other option." I ran my hands over my gown of green silk. Once more, I did not want to wear red. "And Lady Mary must be accepted as legitimate before he agrees to sanction our union." I rolled my eyes. "Which does my daughter no good, or me. Legitimizing Mary is the same as saying I have lived as a whore with Henry these past few years. As good as saying he was always married to Katherine, and all we have done has been wasted. The King's pride will never endure that and I shall not accept it."

I shifted uncomfortably. The pads awash with herbs between my legs were bulky and awkward. I was still bleeding. Mistress Aucher had fed me little more than beef, beans and herbs known for their restorative qualities for days, trying to build up my strength and restore my blood, but I was still weak. I wished my mother was with me, but she had been taken ill at Hever and could not come. My doctors assured me I was not in danger of my life anymore. They were saturated with relief about this. For a time, they had thought I would die.

I sat back, putting a cloth to my forehead. I was feverish. Out of danger I might be, but my miscarriage had brought scorching heat to my flesh along with grief. "The Emperor called Henry's resolve to keep Mary a bastard his 'theological error'," I said. "Henry was not best pleased."

"There is more. Charles proposed marriage between Lady Mary and his brother-in-law, Dom Luis of Portugal."

"Henry will never agree. He has grown more suspicious than ever and this is simply a move to ally Spain with Portugal. With such friends Mary might take the throne."

"Few would support a woman."

"They would not be supporting a *woman*, would they? Mary would sit upon the throne, ruled by her husband and cousin. She would be simply the blood giving lawful right to the throne, not the master of it."

*

Two weeks later there was further news. The Emperor wrote that he had convinced Pope Paul not to proceed with the declaration of Henry's privation of his throne. This had been done, Charles wrote, to show Henry that he desired friendship.

In light of this, Henry showed kindness to Mary. He sent her money, and ordered her moved to another residence, one that was better kept, but also further inland… demonstrating he remained worried about her potential for escape. He sent more coin for her to distribute as alms as she travelled, along with messages of comfort and love.

I could understand Henry's wish to bring Mary solace, but the death of another child had put me in a fragile position. Seeing this attention, people might think he revered Mary above Elizabeth. As it was there were far too many people in the world who thought Katherine's daughter a princess and mine a bastard without Henry adding fuel to the fire.

In many ways, Mary was a greater threat to me now Katherine was dead. With Katherine alive, those who supported Mary's legitimacy had fallen on rough ground. To assert Mary's claim, Katherine's would have had to be upheld too, by association. But now Katherine was gone, this problem was no more. Mary could be declared legitimate in virtue of the length and honesty of her parents' union. If Henry accepted Mary was born in good faith, she could be restored to the succession, and, since my only living child was, too, a girl, Mary, as the elder, could supplant Elizabeth as heir.

This was my enemies' plan. Mary was their hope for the restoration of alliance with Rome, and a traditional future for England.

Had I carried my son to term, Mary would have been relegated to the back of the stalls. Since I had failed, she was set in the front seats. This joust for the succession could be decided by Henry. Only he could safeguard my child's fate.

And what of me? Had I borne a son, I would have been secure, but without that blessing I was left to rely on Henry's love. I was no princess of Spain or France with powerful friends in foreign countries, or means to extract promises that might bring wealth or trade. All I had to rely on was me, and the love Henry and I shared. At the moment, as the harsh, barren hurt we had inflicted on one another in the aftermath of our loss dissipated, Henry showed love and affection, but what if he should listen to all who hated me, and set aside another wife, to take one who might grant him children?

As I pondered, Henry came to me. "France and Spain turn cold towards each other," he said. "And both look to England for warmth."

"You said you would play them against each other for a while," I said. "Is this still true? The court whispers that alliance with Spain is certain."

I sat back in my chair, relieved that that my fever had passed and I could think clearly again. Under the care of Mistress Aucher, I had recovered in body. My mind, I tried not to think upon.

Henry chuckled. "As I would have them believe," he said. "We have been so long at odds with Spain that it will take a great effort to convince anyone that we mean to join with them. The French are, by nature, suspicious. We will make grand gestures of friendship towards Spain, and see what comes. It is about time the French had a lesson in good manners, in any case." He paused. "We are talking of holding the meeting with François in May."

"I would be willing to go, as long as I am recognized as Queen."

"I shall accept nothing less." He leaned back, pleased with himself. "And Spain will recognise you as Queen," he said. "On that score, I will settle for nothing less than absolute submission."

It was easy to believe him. So easy to assume that he was doing this for me and Elizabeth… So easy, when he was with me, to have faith.

But when he left, I wondered. Was this for me, or did he do this to heal his pride?

*

"I will do all I can to aid you," I told my poor aunt.

Lady Katherine Daubeney, *nee* Howard was trying to secure a separation from her husband. Seeking this on grounds of cruelty, she had turned to me as I seemed to be the only member of her family who looked on her claims with a kindly eye.

"Your husband is in debt, is he not?" I asked.

"*Perpetually*, Majesty."

I smiled and it was returned. Katherine was no wilting wallflower. She despised the way her husband treated her. Something I could sympathise with. She was not the only one who had petitioned me of late. Dame Anne Skeffington, widow of Sir William, the Lord Deputy of Ireland, had sent a letter asking for my aid. She felt her children had been undone in their inheritance by her husband's faithful service in Ireland, and was sending a petition to Cromwell that she wanted me to support. Whilst I had nothing but sympathy for these women, undone by different means by their husbands, it was pleasing to know that I was valued at court, and that they recognised I was still a force of influence upon Henry.

"I will ask my father to make money available to Lord Daubeney," I said to my Howard aunt. "In return for an amicable agreement of separation."

As my aunt left, I spent time with Elizabeth Browne. My friend was with child, but although the fourth month had come, her child had not quickened.

"Perhaps you were mistaken in your dates," I said soothingly.

She nodded, but her pretty face was pale. "I think, at times, that my child will not quicken for the sorrow I felt for you, Majesty," she said.

I blinked back tears. "All I could want, would be your safe delivery and good health for your child."

I walked to the window and saw a sight I wished I had not; Henry, walking in the gardens with his usual band of sycophants prancing about him, but there was a lady on his arm: Jane Seymour.

When Henry and I were apart, I had no way of knowing how often Jane was being thrust in his face by my enemies. What was she telling him? That God looked on his second marriage with no more liking than his first? That she, submissive, placid, dull-as-a-drain Jane would make a more pleasing wife?

Carewe and Edward Seymour were deep in conversation at Henry's heel and behind them Lord Montague, the Dowager of Kildare, and Gertrude Courtenay wandered, contented smiles upon their faces.

Just as I went to turn away, thinking I could stand no more, I stopped. Rounding the corner was Cromwell, chatting away to Thomas Seymour and Francis Bryan. With them was Chapuys.

So, I thought. *You there too, Cromwell? Where once you swore to walk my path, now you stroll one forged by papists. How long do you think they will endure your company? They like not that a peasant should stand beside them.*

The wolves were at my door. Only Henry could keep them at bay. But he was too busy running with the pack to think of me.

Chapter Fifty-One

Greenwich Palace and Whitehall Palace
February 1536

Another child was in my dreams.

Three sons haunted my nights, sometimes with Elizabeth, sometimes alone. Flashes of memory resurfaced in the daylight. I saw the tiny body of my last dead son in dreams and waking moments; his large head and little body… his small hands curled up into tiny fists… I had to turn my face from him, and thought I might choke on my guilt each time. I had to pretend, had to throw grief into the deep well inside, and hope it would not crawl up to consume me.

But to the court, another miscarriage for the Queen was already old news.

Some people had evidently believed that the moment Katherine breathed her last Henry would race back to the bosom of Rome. They were horrified to find anti-papal sentiment at court did not slacken but increased in the wake of Katherine's death. I was amazed to think anyone would nurture such a false belief, these people who thought Henry was a loose leaf, blown by whatever wind keened strongest that day. Had they forgotten our years of struggle and study to prove Henry was the Head of the Church? Had they missed that he had executed friends, monks and bishops? Were they unaware of all the laws passed, the insults brayed on both sides… all the strife, trouble, and heartbreak we had endured to make this dream reality?

Did they know their master not at all?

Perhaps not, for conservatives were shocked to find Cranmer taking to the pulpit at St Paul's Cathedral to deliver a searing sermon in which he named Pope Paul the Antichrist, and Henry the hallowed saviour of the faith.

Cranmer was usually so mild and tactful in his sermons that many were caught off-guard. His address was powerful, evocative, patriotic and magnificent. It showed clearly that if the King's marriage had been the starting point for this religious revolution, it had not been the sole or most important reason.

Henry was determined that everyone would understand he had been right all along; he had brought England to a greater seat of power than it had ever known.

This glittering vision was not a true representation of reality. The Emperor and François were poised to make war. Rome was only being held off by Charles of Spain, and England was a stewpot of contention. But Spain and France *were* both eager for friendship. Henry took this and moulded it into a sculpture of perfect desperation. He wanted his people to witness the vision of England *he* saw; a country in an awesome, ineffable position of power.

All who expected Henry to scurry under the Pope's skirts, begging for mercy, were as mistaken as they were blind. Henry was not about to surrender.

But trouble was looming. Early in February, a woman called Joanna Hammulden was arrested for slandering me. Someone had said that she, an experienced midwife, was worthy of serving the Queen, to which she had replied, "provided it was Queen

Katherine," for she would never serve a harlot. She added, "it was never merry in England with three Queens in it," a clear reference to me, Katherine and Jane Seymour, whose affair with my husband was known in some circles, and said she "trusted there would be fewer Queens soon."

She was arrested and punished, but she was not alone.

Rumours were forming, calling me wicked and loose of morals. Since this had always been said of me, I thought nothing of it.

I should have.

*

"I must to Whitehall go," Henry said one morning. I sighed and he caressed my face. "It is necessary," he said.

"I wish I could join you."

I was weak. My fever had fallen, but I had not yet ceased to bleed, and this was making me nauseous and feeble. I was pale and shaky. I could only sit in my bed or in a chair, trying to ignore the visions of my child. He was always there. There were many ghosts about me now.

"Soon you will," Henry said. "When you are churched, come to Whitehall and I will acquaint you with all that has happened."

Henry was about to oversee the final session of Parliament. The bill to dissolve lesser monastic houses was about to be put to the Lords and our five-year battle to have Henry's rights as Head of the Church enshrined in law was about to be won. If there were any problems, Henry had to be there to solve them. He would hold Shrovetide there, without me, as I could not re-join the court until purified.

I looked up to see his eyes lingering on Jane Seymour. I stared at him, not with accusation or the burning grief that had, I was sure, led to the loss of my child, but with the blank, stark stare I had worn in the days after that loss.

Henry blinked to see my expression. It disturbed him. It was not as before, where I had accused him in heat and fire, for to that he had a response of equal ferocity. This was silent, numb, and striking. He did not like this blankness, this empty stare, my dead eyes. It laid bare my barren, empty heart, showed plain the void within me. It cut through the fiction we had both created. He knew he might lose me to the aching maw of darkness.

No matter what, Henry could not allow that to happen. He could not play the villain.

He did not look at Jane again. He paid her no special attention in my presence.

I think he had finally realised how much he had hurt me and although I was certain he would not cease to lust after her, he would not do so obviously, or in front of me again. Would this suffice? No… but perhaps it was enough to keep the darkness at bay.

We parted with affection. "When you are recovered, we will be together again," he said, kissing my hand.

Recovered… When I ceased to bleed and became ready to bear a child again… that was what he meant. Would I ever cease to bleed? In body, yes. In my soul? I knew not. Grief is a wound that never heals.

Some people think grief comes for a spell and then departs. Perhaps with some deaths, this is true. But I do not hold with that notion of sorrow. Some sorrows never leave. They are etched in our souls, branded upon our hearts; we cannot leave them behind for they will not go. Some people become consumed. They lose themselves to sadness. Others refuse to acknowledge grief, so it festers inside them, birthing a monster.

And some of us recognise sorrow, but lock it away. We contain it, but it is always there. Like Pandora's Box, when this secret chest is opened, chaos is unleashed. There was a room in my heart where my children lived. A chamber bound in darkness. It was where I kept everything that wanted to hurt me, everything that might have broken me. Only I had the key and I only dared to open the door a crack.

That chamber in my darkened heart was filling. One day, I would have to open the door wide and face what lay within.

Henry seemed to forget our dead children so readily. Perhaps because he had suffered similar losses with Katherine, they did not affect him as they did me. But even as I pondered this, I knew it was not so. Henry refused to acknowledge grief. It dwelled inside him, twisting and curling. Making a monster. Birthing a demon.

Recovered… would I ever be? I doubted it. There are some experiences we carry for the rest of our lives. Some events that shape us. Dark times and deeds and events linger in us, rising like oil over water.

My children were within me and about me. They were in my bed, where they were brought to life and where they died. They were in the hope of a golden morning's dawn, and the cool darkness of dusky twilight. They were the velvet black of night, and the soft dreams that come between the realms of waking and sleeping. They were in my hopes, dreams and fantasies. In the tang of sorrow that came with each morn, and the wrenching pull of grief's claws when a flash of memory resurfaced. How does one recover from losing children? No parent should have to bury their child, but still crueller is the fate of one who never knew her children before they were taken from her… The fate of a mother never permitted to weep beside her children's graves.

I never found out where they lay, but sometimes, after I was churched, in the months before my arrest, I would be found in the chapel grounds at Greenwich, wandering as though simply enjoying the day, as I searched for my children. At times, as birds sang to the dusk, I would stand in the chapel grounds and murmur to my babes, telling them the soft stories and happy tales I never got to recount in life. Sometimes I stood in silence, holding back the tears, as I asked God to show mercy and take these children into His Kingdom.

"For one day will I join you there," I murmured. "And we will get to share everything we did not have a chance to in life."

On the day I said those words, I remember turning my head sharply to one side. For a moment, I had thought I heard a sigh, and felt a hand rest on my shoulder. When I looked, there was nothing there.

You know what I say is truth, I said to Katherine. *For are you now not surrounded by your babies in Heaven?*

Katherine answered me no more, but I believed she heard me. I believed she was with me. It is strange to think that one who has been an enemy in life, might, in death, become a friend.

Our souls were bonded. No more would I deny it. Her ghost was with me, and always would it be, from the time I sought to take her place, to the moment of my death, and beyond.

*

I was churched without ceremony. Cranmer spoke words of blessing over me as I carried the taper to the door of the chapel, and offered up my child's chrisom cloth in payment for purity, and it was done.

Much as ever before, my child was not spoken of, yet my failure was all that was on anyone's lips.

In the desperation of sadness and fear, I turned to my friends. One day in the gardens, I stood at the archery butts watching Norris compete against Weston and George.

"Will you not try your hand, Majesty?" Weston asked, smoothing his yew bow.

"I am not yet hale," I said.

"This is good for us, Weston," said Norris. "The Queen is unmatched in the bow." He smiled. It was like witnessing the first golden dawn of summer. "All men should fear to compete against our Queen," he went on. "For she can strike the hardest target, and have it fall to her power."

"Flatterer," I said, brushing his arm with my hand. I had meant to cuff him, to scold him… but it was more like a caress.

I moved away swiftly to talk to George. As I walked I could feel Norris' eyes, watching me. Sometimes it felt as though every eye of the world was upon me, but when Norris watched, I knew it was not with dislike. It was, in fact, just the opposite.

In every glance between us there was the respect of love, and yet in our every action there was understanding of duty. Norris was Henry's best friend, and I his wife. There was no question of betrayal by our bodies, but whether my heart was solely my husband's anymore was another question.

Long had Henry held my heart, and that was a bond unlike any other. Carried with that love was pain… pain of sorrow, the agony of his betrayal, and my fears that he would set me aside. There were our years of steadfast commitment, our shared love for Elizabeth and, when we were at peace, our love for one another.

My love for Henry was no more a simple creature. It was one of many heads and hearts. There were times I hated him, found him laughable, thought him cruel. There were times when I knew I could not live without him.

Henry was deeply burrowed in my soul. My love was not something that may one day be forgotten. There is something about sharing life with someone that digs deep into the heart and soul. No one could replace Henry, but as I looked for comfort and found it not with him but with others, a shadow of another love came to me.

I welcomed it. Norris' love warmed me. It was like waking from a troubled night of broken rest amongst cold sheets, only to find the warm summer sun on one's face.

Did Norris truly love me? I knew not, but in every action, word and conversation there was enough evidence for me to think he did. A wounded heart seeks solace. I found that with him, in him.

*

"The King has taken to checking and double-checking everything Cromwell sends," said my father with cheery, undisguised relish as he came from Parliament. "He trusts him completely no more."

"That is good," I said, hoping Henry had heeded my warnings.

The bill to dissolve small religious houses, those with an income of less than two hundred pounds per annum, was poised to go through Parliament. On the basis of Cromwell's, somewhat questionable, investigations, they would be dissolved on the basis of corruption, but there were many, myself included, who wondered if his motive was money rather than morals. The official line was that confiscated property and coin would be put to better use… but what that use was, was not specified. Indeed, many estates were already earmarked for distribution amongst nobles, and Henry had promised some to me and my family. Anything granted to me would be used to further my charitable aims, but I had to question whether all nobles would do the same. Not all of those at court were as dedicated to humanist principles as they protested.

A second act was to follow the first, granting leave for the Crown to confiscate property, land and goods of the suppressed abbeys and dispose of them in whatever way would be most profitable. A court would be set up, known as the Court of Augmentations, overseen by Cromwell's cronies, which would control this second wave of attack.

These were revolutionary ideas. Never before had a layman ruled the Church, and never had a king taken upon himself the power to dissolve so many religious houses and profit from their destruction. I was unsettled.

It was the duty of nobles to protect the needy. That was why God had made some rich and some poor. It was in keeping with humanist and religious morals to do so too, and Henry understood that, even if he liked the idea of having more money to spend on his ships, on his court, and on his castles.

I had spoken to Henry about allowing exemptions to be made. Henry had welcomed the idea, but Cromwell had not. If the King granted licences for smaller religious houses to continue to exist, albeit with a watchful eye looming over them, the amount of property and money that Cromwell might be able to extract not only from the smaller houses, but larger ones, like Syon, which I knew he had an ravenous eye upon, was reduced.

Cromwell liked money. It had granted him power, freedom and favour. His relationship with Henry was close, there was no doubt of that, and the trust he had been shown by his sovereign was remarkable, but money bought much that favour could not, and Cromwell was well aware of its power.

As Parliament wore on, I made preparations to move from Greenwich to Whitehall. I needed to be there to advise Henry. I set myself into this task; to save what good was left within the Church. If I did this, I reasoned, God would bless me. No more would He take my children. This quest was my salvation.

The night before we left, I had a strange dream. I dreamt of a storm. As a falcon I flew against it, the winds battering my wings and rain lashing my feathers. I saw my brother, caught in the maelstrom, his hands flailing against the dark tempest, his form floundering in the storm.

I caught him in my talons. Against the wind we strove. But I could not hold him. The wind was too strong and I too weak. From my grip he fell, and as I dived to him, we were flung backwards, against a cliff I had not seen.

Smashed against rocks, we fell to pieces, shattering as though we were made of sand, falling to the earth as sparkling particles of silver dust.

Chapter Fifty-Two

Whitehall Palace
February 1536

I arrived at Whitehall for the feast of St Matthias, and was taken to Henry with all speed. He was not in his chambers, but his men greeted me with a hearty cheer, flocking about me to speak words of friendship and greeting.

"You look stunning, Majesty," Norris said quietly in my ear. "I think sometimes you become more beautiful with every dawn."

My cheeks coloured and my heart leapt. "As always, Norris," I said, finding peace in his warm eyes. "You know how to flatter a lady."

"With you it is not flattery, but truth," he said, handing me a goblet of wine.

"Sweetheart," Henry said as he entered some time later, finding me amongst a throng of men. "You are more beautiful than ever."

Unlike Norris, I doubted him, for his eyes strayed to pallid Jane.

"My men have sorely missed you," he announced, leading me into the company. "Norris has been quite lost without you!"

I did not welcome the glint of jealousy in Henry's eyes, and from the slight flush that rose becomingly on Norris' cheeks, I understood he did not either.

"I merely said, my lord, it was sad at court with no ladies," Norris said. "But of course I miss the Queen's fine counsel and company when she is not with the court."

"As do we all, Norris," said Henry, patting the seat beside him. "You are churched?" he asked gently as I took a seat.

"I am, and restored to full company with the world, my lord."

"Then I shall come to you tonight," he said. "Now that Katherine is no more, we will not suffer her curse."

It was strange, at times, to see how a thought, once it had entered Henry's mind, could possess him so completely. Repetition is a powerful tool. I often wondered, when Henry repeated himself, driving his friends to distraction, if he was attempting to convince them, or himself.

As Henry moved away to talk to George and Brereton, Norris came to me. "There have been rumours that you should know of, and should also know are false," he said, handing me more wine.

"That the King will abandon me and seek a new wife?"

He blinked. "I did not think any other would dare repeat them to you."

"I know the minds of my enemies. They think to spread falsehoods and make them true by repetition."

"Like the King?"

I had to smother a giggle. "Perhaps," I said. "But I thank you for telling me this."

"The Courtenays spread rumour that the King will seek a new wife, one of the daughters of François, but you should not be alarmed," said Norris. "The King has said nothing of the sort, and Cromwell has gone out to dampen the rumours at court, although…"

"Although?"

Norris leaned closer. "Although, madam, he has, whilst protesting the King is dedicated and devoted to his marriage to you, also declared that he never supported your union."

"He tries to keep both sides appeased," I said. "He will shout praise for me to keep Henry happy, and protest he never supported me to endear him to my enemies." A trill of panic fluttered through my heart. Once I had said I would not envy one who got on the wrong side of Cromwell. I was now in that position.

"One thing he did of late failed to rouse their affections. Chapuys especially was outraged," said Norris. "Cromwell demanded property from the Lady Mary that had once been her mother's. He said that a necklace in her possession, which reportedly holds a sliver of the true cross, was part of the Queen's jewels that the King demanded from Katherine before we went to Calais."

"I assume the Lady refused to give it up?"

"Indeed. She said she would rather die than part with it."

"Mary would rather die than do many things, so it would seem," I said dryly, making Norris smile. "But I see no cause to separate her from this comfort. Cromwell only does this to try to convince the King that he is on our side, and yet at the same time, he blusters in support of my enemies." I sipped my wine. "He will be uncovered soon, and shown to be the false friend he is, to *all* parties."

I glanced at Henry, noting his inconstant eyes on Jane. "But the King has said nothing to suggest he was thinking of another marriage?"

Norris stoutly shook his head. "He has nothing but praise for you, Majesty. He declares you are the bravest woman who ever lived, and he is honoured to have such a soul as his Queen." Quietly, he added, "As he should be."

"Good," I said, feeling more than a little relieved.

That night, a grand procession of Henry's men escorted him down the halls of Whitehall and to my chamber door. Our coming together was awkward, and it took many hours before our aim was achieved. Henry said he was tired, but I persevered. Tempting him with my allurements, speaking softly of my love and admiration, I brought him to life. As he spilled his seed in me that night, I hoped, hoped for a child I might carry to term. Hoped for a future that could not be cursed by my enemies.

Hope… a strange beast. It can live in the most barren wilderness and survive without anything to sustain it. It lives because we will it to, and endures because we need it to. It is the grass that grows in the desert, the animal that struggles on whilst bleeding to death. It is the agonising joy that love brings and the last lingering light of the sun, glimmering against the storming night.

I held hope in my hands, warming its fragile, cold body with my courage.

*

At the end of February, Cromwell made ready to release his *Compendium Compertorum*, a document which held the full list of all monastic abuses. This sordid tome would lend weight to the ongoing arguments in Parliament. I gained a copy, and whilst I found many of the abuses horrific, I also had to question the frequency with which those abuses occurred.

Once the bill passed, royal consent had to be granted for the houses to be suppressed. With Henry and me on good terms, I had hope of convincing him to grant exemptions and use any dissolved houses for educational purposes. If Henry supported me, there was little Cromwell could do, but I wanted to speak to Cromwell. This man had once been my friend. If we could come to the same way of thinking once again, I would be in a better position at court and he would profit from my support. I wanted him to understand that even if exemptions were made, many unworthy houses would still close, so there would be money for him and the nobles who supported him, but I could not stand aside and allow complete obliteration of England's religious houses. I would not be silent.

If I could not bring Cromwell on side, I would become his adversary in truth.

Chapter Fifty-Three

Whitehall Palace
March 1536

"You requested my presence, my lady?" came Cromwell's soft voice as he was escorted into my chamber by Nan Gainsford.

"I did," I said. "Will you take some ale, Master Cromwell? I have much to speak to you about, and would not want your throat to run dry."

He smiled warily and accepted a cup of cool, frothy ale from Margaret Shelton. "Come," I said, gesturing to the cushions beside the hearth.

The day was cold and bright. A cloudless sky stretched above Whitehall, bringing a chill to the late winter air. Hoary frost lingered on branches and twigs, sparkling in the sunlight. As Cromwell took a seat on the cushions, I went to my throne. I wanted him to labour under no illusions of his place.

"I wanted to speak to you about the suppression of the lesser houses," I said.

"You have read the report?" Cromwell asked. "There are so many abuses, Majesty, that I admit I was astounded. I see no other option but to disband them and take their property for the King. He will make good use of it, much better than that which the abbots and monks put it to."

"Whilst I agree the offences are numerous and shocking," I said. "You have long known that the suppression of *all* religious houses in England is not dear to my heart. Where would the poor be without the charity of the abbeys? Where would sick folk, without coin to pay a doctor, turn when they are in need?"

"The King and I have already spoken of this, Majesty," he said. "And have agreed that part of the confiscated wealth should go into trusts to aid the poor, and building hospitals to help the sick."

"Yet there is no solid promise of these great aims in anything I have read," I said. "It seems to me that it will be left to the conscience of the nobles to act as they see fit. We can *hope* great lords understand the necessity of using their power, influence and riches to aid those less fortunate, but there is no provision to force them to do so. This troubles me."

"Do you have no faith, madam, in the consciences of the nobles?"

I smiled. "Come, Master Cromwell… play not the fool with me. You know as well as I that men may promise to do much for others when they catch sight of riches soon to come their way. But if they hold true to their promises when their coffers are filled is another question. For some, too much is not enough, and when a rich man gazes into his purse, he always thinks it empty." I twisted the rings upon my fingers. "If the wealth of the monasteries is granted to nobles and to the Crown with no hope of charity coming from it, then how are we doing anything different to the past corruptions of the Church? The clergy stole from the people and hoarded their riches, growing fat on them. Is not the same being done again? The same vice, the same evil? How are we doing God's work if we repeat the same sins, albeit with different beneficiaries?" I gazed down upon him. "And it is not this concern alone which troubles me."

"What more is there, Majesty?" Cromwell asked.

"The *uniformity* in the reports," I said, noting a flicker of uncertainty in his eyes. "It seems strange that *all* monks and *all* abbots engaged in *exactly* the same level, amount and types of abuses. That they are all drunkards, gamblers and lechers. Am I to believe that only the most despicable of England's people are drawn to the worship of God? That all men who take the cloth are bound to the same sins? The marked similarity in your men's reports troubles me, Cromwell, for they are all so very alike. *Too* alike, one might say."

"I assure you, madam, my men have acted only as instructed, and were diligent in their duty."

"Perhaps too much so. Do you not think that their zeal to provide the evidence you needed might have caused them to fabricate or exaggerate?"

"I would stake my honour and my life upon their honesty, Your Majesty."

Despite his calm words of reassurance, there was a thin sheen of sweat on Cromwell's upper lip. The voice may hide many things, but the body does not lie.

"Do you ever think of your old master, Wolsey, as you walk these halls?" I asked, as though on a whim. "I do. I think of the days when this was his house. Many people do not know it, but there was a time when he and I were united in purpose, before he decided to attempt to sway the King against me, before his corruption and ungodly behaviour were discovered." I paused, noting a fresh outbreak of pearling moisture on Cromwell's heavy brow. "As Wolsey discovered, Master Cromwell, those who have much to hide never rest easy. And yet for all our differences, I would have stayed a friend to the Cardinal, had he remained so with me."

I stared at him for a moment and then smiled. "I should not take up all your time, Master Secretary," I said. "I am sure you have much else to do."

"I am much occupied," he admitted, gratefully handing his cup to Nan. "And rest assured, my lady, I will look into your concerns. If I find that any of my men have been overzealous, I will discipline them."

"I am glad to hear that," I said. "But know, too, that I will investigate. If there is anything hidden, I will uncover it."

*

Elated, in the aftermath of threatening Cromwell, I was swiftly brought crashing to the earth. From Norris and George I heard that the Emperor was willing to become friends with England again, but only on the condition that Lady Mary was restored to the succession as heir presumptive.

"The King told us not to say a word," said George, "for fear of frightening you."

"But he surely did not agree?"

"Of course not," said my brother. "He said he would not for anything be held as a liar and dissemble in the eyes of God, and therefore could never agree to placing a bastard daughter above his legitimate one."

I tried to smile, but it froze. Was this not the actualization of all my fears? I had thought that many in England would attempt to persuade Henry to restore Mary, but that this demand had now come from Spain was harrowing.

"Norris, give us a moment, will you?" George said. Norris departed to pay court to Mary Shelton, and my brother kissed my cheek.

"What was that for?" I asked, touching my cheek where the warmth of his love lingered.

"To cheer you," he said. "Anne, you must have known that this demand would arise at some stage. But there lives no danger in it as long as Henry refuses. Cromwell would have England allied to Spain, but this is not the only option open to us. France has not been a true friend, I agree, but perhaps we have enough true friends, and may settle for a temporary one."

"As long as I have you, I have all the friends I would ever need," I said, touching his shoulder. "Often have I considered how empty my life might have been without you, George."

"You will never have to do without me," he said. "Even after death, just as the spirit of Samuel came to Saul, so shall I return to you."

I shivered. "Speak not of death."

"It is with us every day as we live," he said, nodding to the mourning rings upon my fingers. One for each child I had lost. One, worn for my first dead son, was of gold and jet, with a Tudor rose as its centre. The other two were plain golden bands, with the dates of my children's deaths inscribed inside. Many mourning rings bore symbols of skulls, but since Henry had asked me not to speak of our children, mine did not. They were not obvious, but they remained; a silent reminder against my flesh to a world that would not acknowledge my children.

"Death is the natural end of life," I said. "And you are right that it never leaves us. Every day, brother, my children wait for me in little things. I pick up a cup, I see a flash of crimson, I hear the thin cries of a child in the street as I pass, and they are with me. They hide in little things, insignificant things, and when they spring from them, as though in play, I lose them anew, and my heart is crushed again."

"You have Elizabeth," he said, taking my hand. "And you will have more children. It is likely that the quick succession of pregnancies you have endured weakened you. It would be well to wait for a few months before attempting again."

"I have not that option…" I said, glancing up to look about the room.

Smeaton was playing for my ladies, and they were gazing on his fine looks with happy relish. I sometimes wondered if the manner in which men treated women at court did not rub off on the women too. Sometimes it seemed we were all objects, rather than people. *Things*, rather than souls.

"… Especially if the Emperor continues to demand Mary's restoration, I have not the option to wait." I looked at my brother. "Even if it kills me, George. I cannot wait. Neither can Henry."

Chapter Fifty-Four

Whitehall Palace
March 1536

My brother was a busy bee that March. His seat in Parliament kept him occupied as the suppression bill was discussed, and there was more besides. That month, my father secured letters patent extending his lease of the Crown property of Rayleigh in Essex, and George was instrumental in securing this honour, as he had an interest in it too. With the patent granted, George was brought in as a joint tenant with a share in the rebate on rents. There was talk, too, of what property would go to whom when the bill passed. A handsome settlement was promised to my father and brother, and Henry wanted me to take a share too.

"Anything I am granted will be put to good use," I said. "And I thank you for thinking of me, but I am troubled, beloved."

"In what way?"

"I wonder if all your nobles will see as I do, that this wealth should be put to charitable use," I said. "I fear, with no provision for this in the Act, there may be abuse of your generosity."

"You suspect your own family?" he asked with a grin.

"Not my brother," I said echoing his smile. "But there are men who will not act with good in mind, my lord, no matter what they promise."

"Cromwell has already said as much."

"*After* I spoke with him on the matter."

Henry smiled and kissed me. "I have thought the same," he said. "And I will ensure that this wealth is used for good. Trust in me."

"I trust you with all my heart, you know that. But other men, I trust less."

"Such as Cromwell?" Henry's gaze was questioning.

"Long have I placed absolute faith in him, but I have to admit, of late I have noted his attitude towards you has altered, and I like it not." I sighed. "Did you not say that you thought he was overstepping his authority? This is what I speak of. Cromwell should be ruled by you, my lord, but of late he prances about court as though he were King. We saw this once before, with someone you raised to a position of ultimate trust, and we were let down. I fear we may bring the same devil back into our lives in another guise."

Henry crossed himself to hear mention of the Prince of Darkness. Yet sometimes we have no cause to look for the Devil. Evil enough is done by the hands of men.

He fell silent, but I knew he had not missed my allusion to Wolsey. He had been bitterly disappointed by his friend, and Henry did not like making the same mistake twice.

"I will keep an eye on his doings," he said.

*

Early that March, Edward Seymour was appointed a Gentleman of the Privy Chamber. Although Henry had spoken well of him ever since the summer, I was certain his promotion had more to do with Henry's increasing ardour for Edward's sister.

Henry had made some effort to hide his liaison, but as we lingered at Whitehall, waiting on the verdict of Parliament, he became rapidly less careful. Perhaps he thought a decent amount of time had passed since I had lost our child, or was simply tired of playing the good husband, but for whatever reason, Jane and her brothers were constantly with him, and everyone was talking about it.

Many, like me, were amazed that Henry should be so lost in lust to such a woman. Others were further astounded that she had managed to hold his interest. But the reason for her allure became clear. Talking to Bess Holland, I found out much.

"Jane tells the King *constantly* of her virtue," said Bess, her plump lip curling. "She portrays herself as a virgin, and says she cannot become a man's mistress."

Was Jane sincere, as I had been? Had she learnt that to be a man's mistress was to submit to the censure of the world as he took all the glory, or was she playing a role, one which many knew had worked in the past, in order to gain greater rewards? I could not believe she would refuse him forever, but perhaps her brothers and my enemies had counselled her into holding out for a while to increase Henry's lust. Certainly, it seemed to be the only explanation of how she had captured his interest. She had little else to recommend her.

And it hurt. My feelings were more exposed than Katherine's had ever been. She had married for politics. I had married for love. I was stripped, naked before the world, whereas she had hidden beneath layers of duty and honour. Katherine had been able to distance herself from her husband when he hurt her. I could not. I had to put myself between Henry and Jane, and force him to choose between us.

This was no short order. Everywhere Henry went, Jane appeared. I heard that she spoke to him about the unrest in England, questioned the legality of our marriage, and conversed on my unpopularity. Gossip was seeping through the walls of court, saying that a nullity suit might be offered to Henry on the basis of my pre-contract with Percy. I was sure Jane, Bryan, and their minions were spreading this about. Some of my women thought Jane an ardent supporter of Lady Mary, and believed that she might have written to her, offering solace and support. I had no reason to doubt them. Jane had loved Katherine. There was good reason to suppose she might transfer that affection to the last of Katherine's blood left in the world. Henry had appointed rooms for Jane to use at Greenwich and Whitehall, and courtiers flocked to her, their noses catching scent of a new power.

The more I heard, the less I liked. And then, there was more.

Bess told me that whilst I had been recovering at Greenwich, Henry had sent Jane a present; a purse full of sovereigns and a letter. "Jane kissed the letter, my lady," said Bess. "And returned it unopened. She took to her knees and told the messenger to repeat her words to the King without qualification."

"And what did she say?"

"She begged the King to consider she was a gentlewoman of good and honourable parents, without reproach, and had no greater riches in this world than her honour. She said she would not injure that for a thousand deaths, and if he wished to make her a present, she would that he would do so when God enabled her to make a good marriage."

A cavernous quiver ran through me as I heard my own words come back to haunt me. My enemies, who had no doubt groomed Jane, were using my own stance against me… Inflating this girl with the notion that she, like me, could refuse a king and perhaps rise to become a queen.

I had spoken out of honesty, an honesty, which at the time I had thought might cost my family their posts at court, and might see me thrown from Henry's presence as an unwanted toy never played with. But this aping chit was using my protestations to play her own game. And what did she want? A position as *Mistress en Titre*, or my throne?

The notion of that pallid wraith taking my place was almost laughable. That insipid Jane Seymour should take up the throne of queens? But as I thought about laughing, I felt like weeping. For how long had I thought Henry was attempting to mould me into the meek, humble wife he wanted? For how long had I known he was tired of my lashing tongue and the passionate nature of our union? Our relationship was as changeable as the restless English skies. There were two sides to Henry; the knight who adored me, and the old monster who longed for peace. The man who was willing to hear and respect me, and the demon who wanted domination and control. Henry's power was in the comparison between us. Every time I grew strong, he was rendered weak. It did not have to be this way. We could stand strong together, sup from the true power I had started to nibble at… but which of Henry's dual sides would win?

The demon wanted a wife as Katherine had pretended to be; subservient, mild, chaste and simple… a little shadow at his back…

Could Jane be this to him? She would always be weak, so he would always feel strong. I had shown the world how a mere lady might rise to become Queen, but I was no man's serf. Jane was anyone's willing slave. I was sure she had been set on this path by my enemies, by Gertrude Courtenay, Carewe, Chapuys and perhaps even Cromwell.

Jane was taking all that had enticed Henry about me, and joining it to her own wiles… her submissive nature, her meekness… she was unmarked parchment. She would become everything and anything he wanted. She would be his lump of clay.

And she came from a fertile family of many sons. Henry would have noted this, indeed, he had remarked on the good fortune of the Seymours many times. Could it be that my enemies were not just preparing to send in a mistress, but were setting up a potential queen?

It might not be hard to remove me, were it not for my friends and allies. I had borne only a daughter. I had lost my sons. Henry's past relationship with my sister might be used to invalidate our marriage, or my agreement with Percy. Infertility could give Henry good reason to part with me, but would he?

Was he so lost in lust, that he had forgotten our love?

At the moment, I thought not. But something had to be done. Secretly, I called for my printer from Southwark to meet me at court, and gave him a commission. I wanted pamphlets, decrying the King's relationship with Jane, to be secretly distributed. Henry liked his liaisons secret, so he did not suffer shame, but if everyone knew of Jane, and understood he was once more betraying his lawful wife, he would have nowhere to hide, and neither would she.

My printer was willing, for he had done well from my patronage. He assured me the pamphlets defaming Jane as a whore, and Henry as an unchaste King, would be ready in a month or so, and even suggested a few slanderous ditties that might be added, so people could sing them about the streets of London.

I laughed when he said this, and agreed, but as he left to undertake his task, I became morose.

Was it possible? That Henry might set me aside, after all we had been through, after all we had been to each other? Part of me could not contemplate this, but another was not so sure. I had to steal him away from her.

Dust off the cloak of the mistress, I told myself. *Once more you must play all parts, Anne Boleyn. You must be the mother and the maiden, the virgin and the whore.*

All things to all men, that was what I had to be. A combined creature of allure and dignity, of sexual wiles and queenly honour.

I resented this. Resented having to play the merry mistress as well as the dignified Queen. But what choice did I have? None… not if I wanted to keep my husband, my daughter, my throne, and my power.

Chapter Fifty-Five

Whitehall Palace
March 1536

It is strange, or perhaps not, how, when in times of trouble, we turn to worldly pursuits to bring comfort. My mind was in a state of unrest, and so I turned to something that had always brought me great pleasure. Looking back, I wonder if some hint of what was to come was in my mind, for I started to make provision for my daughter.

I turned to cloth and clothes. For the bulk of my life, ever since my mother took me on her knee to show me stitch and fabric, I had been drawn to clothing. I had made myself famous for my style and grace, and now, as my world shook, I turned to that comfort again.

Reams of cloth came to my chamber so I might make glorious clothing for my own body, and that of my daughter. I spent lavishly. Purple cloth of gold, black and tawny velvet, damask, miniver and Venice gold braid were ordered, along with kirtles of white satin and nightgowns of damask in shades of green, black and ochre. Velvet slippers of midnight hues, ribbon for my hair and Elizabeth's, lambskin, fur, and feathers… all came… all were purchased by my purse. I slaved to produce stunning garments. Elizabeth had a new satin gown, caps embroidered by my needle, and kirtles in shades of russet and green, which would set off her colouring to perfection.

But it was not only for comfort that I ordered these items. If I was going to compete with another woman for Henry, *again*, I had to make the best of all I had.

It was not only me ordering new gowns. Jane Seymour arrived in my chambers wearing better fabrics and cloth each day. I had no doubt wealthy patrons were sending her riches to enhance what spare beauty she possessed. She looked more attractive, I had to admit, in her new clothes, much better than she had when first she had come to court wearing garments clearly made for her shrewish mother. But I had access to fabrics and furs she could not wear by law. I was determined to outmatch her.

I was fighting not just for my husband, but for my throne… for Elizabeth. Who would protect my daughter if I did not? If I was cast aside, we might be separated, just as Katherine and Mary had been. I would not allow that to happen.

But despite my fears, there was no sign that Henry was seeking to replace me. He was affectionate in public, and made everyone aware he was not about to restore Lady Mary to the succession. When he saw the clothes I was making for Elizabeth, he admired them and brought his men over to do the same. As he praised me, I saw Edward Seymour's brow furrow, as though someone had demanded he solve a complex riddle.

Such things pleased me, but I was less happy when I heard that Cromwell had allowed Jane to stay in his rooms with her brother. Cromwell's chambers adjoined Henry's by a secret entrance. Cromwell had granted my foes every chance to sneak Jane in to see Henry without my knowledge. One of her brothers, or her sister-in-law, Anne Stanhope, were always on hand to act as chaperones, guarding her much-vaunted virginity, but Henry had access to her now, away from the watchful eyes of court, away from me.

It was entirely possible this was done at Henry's command, but I was certain the idea had been Cromwell's. He was scared of me and what I might discover about his dealings with the monasteries. He wanted Jane closer to Henry than me, and had provided an opportunity for that little worm to wiggle her way into Henry's heart.

There was an echo here of our courtship. There had been a time when, putting aside his lust to make me his mistress, Henry had courted me only when members of my family were present. A time he had declared he respected me too much to sully my reputation. He was doing the same now with Jane. He was removing the stain of the mistress from her… was he thinking of making her his wife?

The clothes I ordered that winter were my armour. There was a battle ahead. War trumpets sounded in the distance. Armies were gathering. If I had to fight, I would.

*

"For my part," I announced to a gathering of courtiers in my chambers. "I always *adored* the Hapsburg court of Burgundy."

An entertainment was being held, a re-enactment of a pageant I had seen in Mechelen, although on a more modest scale. My maids were dressed in white linen gowns, with tissue of gold trimming their hems. They danced whilst Smeaton played, tripping through steps I had taught them as they enacted a scene of chivalric love.

Suddenly, the court had become Spanish. Talks were going on, and although Henry was not about to restore Mary, we believed much good would come of them. To show my husband and everyone else that I could rise above the insults of the past, I had returned to my love for the Hapsburgs. I might have had little spare for Charles, but I had loved his aunt.

I spoke warmly of the Archduchess, and all she had taught me. When Henry joined me, flowing to the place where all light and beauty were to be found at court, he was pleased. "My Queen is the most generous of all women," he said, patting my knee. "For she sets aside all slights of the past, and looks to the future."

"I am glad we are to come to rapprochement with the Emperor," I said. "I loved his aunt like a mother, so I hope to think on him as a brother."

"And so shall he be, if our plans come to fruition," said Henry.

I glanced at Cromwell, chatting to my brother and his wife and I smiled. If all things *I* had planned came to fruition, another Wolsey was about to fall.

Later that night, as I prepared to receive Henry in my bedchamber, Jane Seymour was combing my hair. I did not like to have her close, but much as I had sat above Cromwell when he came calling, I liked to remind her of her place.

As she pulled the ivory comb through my dark locks, she caught a snag and tore out a chunk of my hair. I gasped in pain and my hand lashed out, at first simply to deliver a smack to her wrist. It was not uncommon for masters to chastise servants in such situations, still less for a queen to rebuke her women. But as my hand flashed out, my eyes followed. Dangling from her throat was a pendant, held by a long golden chain, tied about her neck by a ribbon. Hidden inside her gown during the day, it had come loose, and hung before my eyes. As I saw the image on the centrepiece, I wondered if she had intended for it to be seen.

It was a miniature of Henry.

I caught the pendant as she tried hastily to retrieve it and pulled it towards me. Jane, her body lumbering across my shoulder, made a slight noise of distress. It angered me and I tore the necklace from her throat, snapping the delicate ribbon.

Holding it in my hands, I rounded on her. She was staring at me with wide eyes, her face even paler than normal. I stared at the portrait. Henry had sent me a bracelet bearing his image when we were courting, and I owned many more he had given me since. Now he had granted one to this girl. I almost laughed. How many such items did Henry have, to use so he might convince foolish women that he loved them? Were there *drawers* of them in his chambers?

"A pretty bauble," I said, wondering when I had come to sound so like Katherine. "What an expensive little whore you are, cousin. What did this trinket buy the King? Your maidenhead?" I sneered at her. "Although by what I have heard about you at court, there is nothing left to purchase."

"It is not so," she whispered. "Please, Majesty, may I have it back?"

"It is not yours," I said. "And neither is the man whose image it holds." I stepped forwards. How I longed to strike her!

"The King is my husband, cousin," I said. "I would advise you, rather than disgracing your family still further by making yet another daughter of the Seymour line into a *husband-snatching jade*, you should find your own husband." I shook my head and laughed. "If any would take such a witless, colourless, oafish whore as his wife!"

Several of my ladies, who had no love for Jane, laughed. The girl was utterly mortified. "Get out," I said. "And come not near me again. I do not want my person contaminated by you."

Less than an hour later, Henry arrived, but he was not, as had been his habit, escorted by his men or in his night clothes. "You will cease to abuse your women!" he roared, not bothering to wait for my ladies to leave.

I was sitting at my mirror. Without turning, I held out my hand and allowed the necklace to unravel from my palm. The chain ran, sliding from my skin, until I caught its end. The little portrait bobbed in the air between us. "When will you cease to abuse our love?" I asked quietly.

I turned. His face was almost purple in the candlelight. His hands were at his sides, clenching into fists. But as he saw the necklace, and his face clouded with unrest, I realised he had not been told the full story. No doubt Jane had run to her lover with a tale of woe, weeping that her mistress was cruel, unreasonable and malicious. She had not told him about the necklace. That was a mistake on her part. She did not know her man as I did.

Henry was suddenly embarrassed and looked away from me.

"If you must give the same gifts that once you gave to me out of love, to others for lust," I said calmly, "have them conceal them better. She wanted me to see this,

Henry. She wanted me to be hurt and you allowed her the means. I would beg you not to do so again, if you have any respect for me."

I got up and put the necklace into his hands. "You may grant your image to any you think worthy," I said. "But know that when you give yourself to others, I am heartbroken."

He left without another word, and did not come again that night.

I went to the wall. Hanging there was a gilt clock. It was a pretty thing, made for Henry and for me. Ornamented in a classical style, it was intricate and delicate. The weights that hung below were inscribed with our initials surrounded by lover's knots, and our mottos, *Dieu et Mon Droit* and *The Most Happy*.

I stared at it for some time, thinking of the past. There had been a time we were knotted together, bound to each other's souls. There was an echo of that still, even now. I could hear it, a whispering voice on the wind… a murmur of something born that will not die.

The next morning, he invited me to the archery butts, and we took turns shooting against each other. There was no further mention of my abuse of Jane. And I never saw that necklace on her again.

I thought I had won a victory. I thought I had shown him what she was. But all I had done was push Henry to conceal his ardour with greater cunning. His lust for her did not die, nor did it retreat. He hid it, and in doing so, concealed his true, and dark, intentions.

Chapter Fifty-Six

Whitehall Palace
March 1536

"Do you think to add weight to your moral reputation by offering a room to a court whore?" I asked Cromwell as he entered. "Do you think to transform your chambers into a brothel?"

Cromwell started. At court, it was usual to at least *start* with polite greetings before heading into more dangerous waters, rarer still that someone would actually say outright what they meant.

"My lady, I know not of what you speak."

"You gave your rooms to the Seymours," I said. "So Thomas and Edward might use their sister as a tool for their ambition, and sneak her into the company of my husband through your secret doorway."

In the aftermath of my assault on Jane, Henry had gone oddly quiet. No more did he attempt to berate me about my behaviour. My success, if that is what one may call it, had led to me deciding the time was ripe to confront Cromwell. I had no power to dismiss Jane. It was up to Henry who would serve in my chambers, and he would not rid me of his jade. But Cromwell was another matter. It was about time the man learned I was no idle adversary.

"Do not attempt to deny this," I said. "And besides, although it adds nothing to your character, Master Cromwell, it is not unusual to find men acting as whoremasters for their King. I just did not expect such behaviour from you, since, as the Vice-Regent of spiritual affairs, I thought you might wish to be seen as a man of morals, rather than of depravity."

I set my hands on my hips. "I cannot tell you to do otherwise. The rooms are yours, after all, but you should know that I do not look on this with a kindly eye, and you have brought me to question you in this matter, and many others."

"If I have offended, madam, I can only protest that I am the King's servant."

"It is good to hear you say this, for I thought you might have forgotten," I said. "You overreach your authority on so many matters one might come to believe that you thought yourself the King."

Cromwell shifted uncomfortably. It was dangerous to accuse a man of thinking he was as high as Henry, and it had the effect I desired. I wanted Cromwell uneasy. This was no time for subtlety, this was war and I was about to fly my pennant into the wind.

"I admit myself mystified, Majesty," said Cromwell. "I know not of what you speak."

"I speak of many things, *Master* Cromwell," I said, accentuating his common title. "The King has not decided which of Spain or France he will offer his gracious friendship to, but you attempt to decide the matter for him. The fate of many lesser monasteries is by no means settled, yet you have already started handing out favours to your slathering minions. You once professed friendship to me, yet you allow the Seymours space and time to trip their little whore out in front of the King."

I eyed him with a dark expression. "I once thought you a true advocate of the faith," I said. "But your actions have shown you are not. You have fallen to sin, Master Cromwell. You are a slave, mastered by greed, avarice, lust and power. I see plain that you care nothing for the faith, for you are willing to destroy it in return for riches. There was one who once betrayed our Lord in return for a bag of silver... do you take from his example? And tell me, what would your late wife, a woman I have heard spoken of with great respect for her upstanding character, think of you providing jades for the King?"

A faint hint of colour in his usually controlled cheeks told me what I needed to know. His wife, dead these many years, would have been ashamed of him. A sliver of that shame touched him now, even through all the layers of self-preservation and guile he had built about his soul.

"I am tempted to extend my investigations," I went on. "My men are looking into your reports, Cromwell, but I wonder if I should ask them to look back further... into the accusations against More and Fisher. Rich was sent on your order, was he not? My brother found it strange at the time that a man as clever as Thomas More could have resisted incriminating himself in conversation with you, and yet fell for the wiles of Richard Rich, a man who is so incapable of concealing his slimy nature that all who have sense avoid him. It seems remarkable, does it not? Almost as if this intricate web were made of lies, rather than truths?"

I could almost see the heat evaporating from his body, rising in waves at his neck, floating into the air. "Majesty, by your reckoning, I am indeed at fault," he said, "but I swear to you that all I do, I do for the King."

"All you do, Cromwell, you do for yourself. I know that, and my husband is no dullard. Soon he will understand too." I shook my head. "You thought to pit yourself against me, did you not? You thought to undermine me, using the Seymour wench as a tool. You worry I will support France over Spain, and fear I will steal the plunder you aim to pillage from the monasteries. You have tried to sneak past me, but it will not work, Master Secretary. I have a keen eye... I can see a snake in sunlight. I would advise you to cease supporting the Seymours, and work for me again, or face the consequences." I waved a hand. "You can go."

Cromwell bowed and made for the door.

"Cromwell?" I called. He turned and I met his eyes. "Take a moment, in the days that follow, to think upon your old master," I said. "Remember the Cardinal."

As Cromwell left, he stumbled and had to catch the wall for support. I went to the card table with my ladies and enjoyed a raucous afternoon of laughter and wagering. I could not laugh enough. It was a dangerous move to call someone out at court, for I had revealed much, but Cromwell had seen how close Henry and I had been of late, and he knew my power over my husband. By calling him out I had, I hoped, given him good reason to fall in line.

"And I win again!" I announced, smacking my hand, flush with four kings, down on the table as my ladies squealed with delight and horror.

"None can best you today, Majesty," said Nan with admiration.

"No," I said, setting my smiling face on the arch of my interlocked fingers. "They cannot."

*

"A dinner party of my enemies," I said to my brother. "Chapuys should have invited me as guest of honour, should he not? And served *spleen* as the first course!"

I laughed. Despite the fact my brother had just informed me that Chapuys had invited practically every person at court with a grudge against me to his house, I felt elated. Cromwell had been meek and subservient since I had accosted him, and Henry was attentive.

The dinner party the hapless hare assembled had included the Courtenays, and Henry Pole, Lord Montague. Montague was the eldest son of Margaret Pole, the Countess of Salisbury, Katherine's friend. His brother was the infamous Reginald Pole, who was still abroad writing his *In Defence of the Unity of the Church* against Henry. Courtenay and Montague were peers of the realm, and they had been joined by Katherine, the widowed Dowager Countess of Kildare, Henry's half-cousin.

"Did you find out what their conversation was about?" I asked.

"No," said George. "But I would wager it was not flattering to you or any of our faction."

"Well, if Montague managed to speak on any other subject besides his lineage I would be much astonished," I chuckled.

George laughed with me. Montague was notorious for speaking long, dreary, and often about his royal connections to Edward IV, but as George finished laughing, he looked at me in surprise. "What?" I asked. "You think that I should be downcast? That I should hear of my enemies uniting and quiver in my velvet slippers?"

"I did expect you might be a little less merry," he admitted.

"That is what they want, is it not? They want to drive me into restless sorrow and have me wallow in it, slowly drowning. But they know not who they deal with. Perhaps I had forgotten, too, George. I may be older, but I am no weaker. If they want a fight, I shall give them one, and they will see which dog they should have wagered on… Not the large one that all thought would win, but the small, canny beast who rises from the earth to snap his opponent's throat." I slipped my arm through my brother's and smiled. "Yes," I said. "They will have a fight."

"Then know that Cromwell will be one of the dogs you face," he said. "You say he has been humble since you confronted him, but I hear much of his plans for the monasteries and Spain."

"Then he has chosen his side. As I have mine. I will not allow him to destroy the religious life of England, George." I sniffed. "They like to call us names, our enemies. It is perhaps therefore ironic that the ones who will save the Church will be the Boleyns."

"Perhaps they will cease to call us more Lutheran than Luther."

"I care not what they call me," I said. "I care what God sees. He will note that we are on the side of good."

"And when He does, He will reward you with a son for England."

"I hope that may be the case, but even if it is not, at least I will know I did all I could… that I did all that was right. I have done much wrong in my life, but perhaps, with this, I can make amends."

I almost turned. Once more I had felt a hand on my shoulder, offering support. Katherine approved of me. I almost laughed that our two souls, disjointed and separate for so long, should be brought together over religion. I felt her approval. It cheered me.

"What do you mean to do?" asked my brother.

I looked up at the grim evening sky. March had been both bright and wet, alternating her days as though she cared not to choose whether to allow England to bask in warm sunlight or drown in a deluge of rain.

"The time for dealing in the shadows is done," I said, looking out the window to see the Lenten Moon rising high in the heavens. "It is time to enter the light." I looked at my brother. "My almoner is to preach in a few days. I have a sermon I would have him perform. Soon, we will have more allies."

"What allies?"

"The Church itself."

Chapter Fifty-Seven

Greenwich Palace
April 2nd 1536

The day before my almoner, John Skip, took to the pulpit, I was informed that Chapuys and Cromwell had met, although no one knew what had been said. But from this, I understood Cromwell was seeking to bolster his position with support from the Imperialists. Since Henry remained undecided about Spain and France, I stored this information away, ready to use against Cromwell.

That afternoon, George and I were closeted with Skip and my chaplains, preparing the speech. I wanted it to be perfect. It had to show my position clearly. This was the first trumpet blast of war; the moment when my armies rode into battle. The first strike had to hit Cromwell hard and true. I wanted him staggering, caught unawares, his forces divided, and plans askew.

On the 2nd of April, I walked to the royal chapel with my ladies. Everyone was there, and as I took my place beside Henry, I smiled at Cromwell. Little did he know he was about to get the greatest surprise of his career. What we were about to do was dangerous. My almoner was about to accuse Henry and his advisors of pursuing personal gain over morals, but Skip was undeterred.

"I would not be a true follower of Christ if I balked from speaking out for his Church," said my good man when I had asked him if he was ready for what might come.

"You are a soldier of God, and you will have my protection."

The passage chosen for the sermon was from the Gospel of John; part of the story of Christ's time on the Mount of Olives, when the Lord of Heaven had taught some of his last lessons to his disciples. The verse ran *"Which of you can rebuke me of sin? If I say the truth, why do you not believe me? He that is of God heareth God's words. Ye therefore hear them not, for you are not of God."*

It was a condemnation of Cromwell, and a strike at Henry, for failing to heed the godly over the greedy. No one missed the allusion as Skip began to speak.

In the sermon, the congregation was identified as the 'you' in the verse, and in particular, those who would counsel Henry to destroy the Church. Skip accused them of sycophancy, and of pushing Henry to do anything that would line their pockets, even to the disgrace of God. The 'me' of John's verse was the Church, and all who supported moderate, rather than radical, reform.

Skip bellowed that the attack on the clergy had gone too far, and the people who would sway the King to believe this was necessary were working for greed, avarice and lust for gold. Skip declared that whilst the Church had strayed into sin, and should be punished, to attack the clergy as a whole was unjustified and hypocritical.

"I would that men would use more temperance, and first amend their own lives before they taxed other men to do the same," Skip blasted, staring at Cromwell, then at Henry with brimstone in his eyes. "Nowadays, many attack the clergy for sin, but they look not to their own, and only seek to do so as they would have from the clergy their possessions."

Skip also took a moment, not at my urging, to criticise Henry's liaison with Jane Seymour. I was surprised, but not at all displeased. Skip used the example of King Solomon, a historical character Henry had already been much compared to. Therefore, everyone knew my chaplain was speaking of the King.

"In the latter end of his reign, he became very un-noble and defamed himself sore by sensual and carnal appetites in the taking of many wives and concubines," Skip said. "And also by avaricious mind in laying too great or sore burdens and yokes upon his subjects, pressing them too sore thereby."

Henry shifted awkwardly, his great, round face red and angry. Cromwell was trying to act as though he was untouched by these accusations, but I saw him pass a hand over his brow and wipe it on his handkerchief. *Is the chapel too warm, Master Cromwell?* I thought. *Or do your many sins keep your blood hot?*

Skip went on to ensure that everyone knew where I stood, saying that the King should "be well wary what he does after the counsel of his councillors for some time for the malice they bear towards many men or towards one man, as of a multitude, they would have the whole multitude destroyed."

Skip used the example of Esther, the Jewish wife of the Persian King Ahasuerus. Ahasuerus was deceived by his advisor, Haman, into agreeing to massacre his Jewish subjects. "But," Skip roared. "There was *one good woman*, which this gentle King, Ahasuerus loved well and put his trust in, for he knew she was ever his friend, and she gave unto the King contrary counsel."

The story of Esther was famous, and popular, especially amongst women. The Bible more often told of wicked, fallen women, so any agent of goodness was welcomed by our sex. No one misunderstood. Henry was Ahasuerus, led astray by Cromwell, his Haman. I was Esther, and the clergy were the Jews about to be slaughtered.

I would give good counsel to the King. I would save his people. I would defend the Church.

Skip finished by urging for good and godly reform. He said that funds seized by the Crown should be put to good use, such as supporting the decaying universities of the realm. "How necessary the maintenance of them is for the continuance of Christ's faith and His religion!" he exclaimed.

Skip's sermon was a call to arms, led by me. It challenged men not to consider worldly rewards they would gain here and now, but to think on their eternal souls. It called on Henry to reject the enticement of personal gain and work for his people, and it, too, named Cromwell and all who supported him, as enemies to the faith.

To drive home his point, Skip altered part of the story of Esther. According to the Bible, Haman offered to pay the King to cover the cost of the archers who would slaughter his people, but Skip reversed this, saying that Haman had promised to raise ten thousand talents for the Crown from the deaths of these people, adding that the King had told Haman he might take that money for himself when the massacre was done.

Haman, of course, failed, due to Esther's intervention, and was hanged on a high gallows… a warning of what might come to Cromwell.

As the sermon ended, the congregation were almost in a state of riot. Everyone was talking, and several of Henry's leading counsellors, Montague and Courtenay included, looked ready to make war. Cromwell excused himself, his face grey.

Straight after, Skip was hauled before the Council, accused of spreading malice, slander, presumption, lack of charity, sedition, treason, disobedience to the Gospel, and inciting anarchy.

"I want my almoner released," I said to Henry when I heard Skip was being attacked.

"The man spoke wild!" he roared. "He all but accused me of ungodly, avaricious behaviour!"

"He accused you of nothing more than having poor counsellors," I said calmly. "The offence, as my almoner readily pointed out, is not yours, my lord. Sin lies on those who would pilfer England for their own gain." I stared at Henry. "The Dissolution Bill is passed, but it awaits your royal consent, my lord. Will you dissolve all religious houses in England, for the glory of your coffers, or will you look to the welfare of your people, and only disband some, leaving others to be reformed for the glory of God?"

"You, who have supported reform so long and viciously, now place yourself as a knight of the Church?" he asked in an incredulous tone.

"You know well enough that I have long said this wave of destruction is not to my liking," I said. "And you, yourself, admitted it was not to yours either."

I gazed at him. "I know you, my husband. Your conscience vexes you. I see it in your eyes. You know that outright dissolution of all the houses of God is not what the Almighty wishes. Your soul is so close to the spirit of God that you feel this, do you not? Skip spoke on my authority, Henry. It is my role, my duty, and my *right* as Queen to advise you where others cannot. Who else would dare to stand against Cromwell and others who, like pirates, would steal all that is good or might be made good from the Church? You say I have long supported reform, nothing has changed. I support reform, I support the dissolution of some houses, but I will not sanction acts that would impoverish the poor still further, and steal from England the next generation of learned souls who would lead her in the light of God."

I could see I was winning. "When I sued for Cambridge University to be exempt from the tax levied upon them, you understood me," I went on, speaking of a petition I had put to him the month before.

The University had been required to pay the First Fruits and Tenths, a tax on clergy taking up an ecclesiastical position in England. It was a portion of income, annates, and a tenth of their revenue thereafter. Universities were required to pay too, but if the charge had been levied, it would have diminished the number of scholars in each and every college. Understanding me, Henry had exempted them.

"There are men telling you that the only good that can come is to make the rich richer," I said. "It is not so. We have a duty of care to England, my lord. A duty many of your Council have forgotten, for their convenience."

"I will have your man released," he said. "And I will think on all you say. Perhaps in their zeal, Cromwell's men have been too fanatical."

"When sheep stray, my lord, it is for you to bring them back to the herd."

Henry suddenly smiled. "I thought some of my men might succumb to apoplexy," he said. "Upon hearing Skip speak."

Henry could be merry now, now that I had absolved him of blame and placed it upon Cromwell.

I chuckled. "I am glad that you have heard me," I said, putting my hands about his thick neck. It was like hanging from a tree.

"I am glad I have a Queen who is so devoted to my people that she will risk my wrath by speaking out for them."

"I cannot ever be anything less than honest."

"How well do I know that," Henry laughed. "And if, at times, I seem not to appreciate that quality in you, know that somewhere, deep down at times, I always do."

"So you will release my man, and hear what my chaplains have to say about houses that deserve your protection?"

He kissed me. "I will."

Skip was released from the Council that hour, much to their horror. They had thought he would spend time in the Tower for his impudence, but Henry ordered him back to my household. And if my foes thought I was about to rest there, they were gravely mistaken. That afternoon I called for my chaplains, and spoke to them about preaching in support of moderate, controlled reform.

"Make earnest petition for the salvation of deserving houses," I said to them.

"Do they deserve such protection, Majesty?" asked Latimer.

"Did Christ abandon the fallen?" I asked. "Did he turn his face from the tax collector, or refuse to speak to lost women? If Christ could offer grace to those who slipped into sin, so can we. Help me to do God's work. Do not be carried away by the lies of those who would profit from destruction. We take not the road that is easy and quick, but the path of what is *right*. And what is right and just takes work, gentlemen. It is all too easy to destroy. I ask you now to aid me in rebuilding the Church. This will be our sacred task."

They promised to speak for moderate reform. Hugh Latimer, Henry's favourite preacher, was apparently so convinced that in his next sermon he spoke of not dissolving *any* monasteries, but of putting them all to educational use. Latimer used Luke's parable of the vineyard, saying that the vineyard confiscated from bad tenants had not been burned down, but handed to better owners. Monasteries should be used as places for good men to study and serve England, he said. Education should be the use their wealth was put to.

Cromwell left that service pale as a ghost.

My chaplains and preachers trooped out, as my army for God. But there was another I needed if I was truly to succeed. Cromwell controlled the Commons, the Lords, and held sway over the Council, but the Church would become my ally.

And if I was to stand with the Church of England, I required its leader to understand my will.

I sent for Cranmer.

Chapter Fifty-Eight

Greenwich Palace
April 1536

The battle lines were drawn. Once, I had destroyed an impediment to my marriage, now I sought to remove one who stood in the way of the true faith.

Skip's sermon, and the advance of my preachers into the streets, had brought hope to the Church. In the days that followed, archbishops, bishops and abbots all came, begging for my protection. But, even if I was working to shelter them, I was not about to let them get away with their past sins.

I lectured one delegation on the numerous abuses which had brought this fate on the Church, and chastised them for continuing to look to Rome.

"When all know that His Majesty the King is your true and just leader," I said fixing a glittering eye upon them. "You have failed in many ways, gentlemen, and failed not only the people of England, who should have been your first and primary worldly responsibility, but also failed God, who put His trust in you."

Some looked abashed and others did not. No doubt they had heard Skip's sermon, which had been shared and published throughout England, leading to unbounded amazement in some quarters about my support for the Church. On the basis of this, they had expected me to welcome them with open arms. It was not so. No more would England's clergy gain respect simply for their titles. I wanted to see them working for God, for the people and for Henry.

"My opinion is that the dissolution of your houses falls upon you for your just demerits as a deserved plague from the Almighty God," I said. "Who, abhorring your lewdness, derideth your blind ignorance."

There was muttering at the back. "But," I said. "Until such a time as you shall cleanse and purify your corrupt life and doctrine, God will not cease to send His plagues upon you to your utter subversion." I looked at each of them in turn. "Hear the whisper of God in your hearts," I said, "and show the King that you will work towards goodness."

That night, I was sent a message. All the abbots present at that meeting had offered substantial sums to add to my trusts for the support of poor scholars and preachers.

"They also offer you the right to the best livings in their gift," Latimer said, "for they understand you will treat them more kindly than Cromwell."

"It is a start," I said, sitting back and stretching my arms. I was tired. It would have been a gross understatement to say that the past few days had been busy. My body screamed out for rest, but my soul was energised. "I leave it to you, Latimer, to appoint men to oversee this wealth they promise. Ensure it is put to good use. Let us put this into the fund for scholars, as they ask, and other funds we will use for the poor."

"As you wish, Majesty," he said.

"And appoint someone with impeccable bookkeeping and morals to oversee these affairs," I said. "My enemies will seek any way to trip me after this. I want every penny accounted for. No one will assault me for lack of morals if I come to be inspected."

"I will appoint a good man and a second to oversee his work," said Latimer. "Nothing will be allowed to go astray."

"What will you do next?" asked my brother as Latimer left.

"Persuade Henry to allow a great deal of exemptions on the merit of education," I said. "The Church is our ally now, brother. They understand what they must do to keep our protection. We will have our reformation, and it will be magnificent. Generations will look back on this time and note how ill it might have gone. They will know all that was done to save England from the assault of corruption and tyranny."

George was smiling. "What is it?" I asked.

"You have never been more a queen than you are now, in this moment," said my brother. "I am awed by you, Your Majesty."

As I stared at him, astonished, my brother swept into a deep, respectful bow.

*

"They cannot *all* be saved," Henry said, his face growing red. "I have already told Cromwell as much when he came to tell me that perhaps more should be preserved than we had thought."

So, you switch colours on the field of battle, do you Cromwell? I thought, vastly pleased that he had been sufficiently scared to run to Henry with a pacification deal in mind. Woman I might be, but I had a unique hold over Henry. Cromwell was afraid I might not only persuade our changeable King to salvage many religious houses, but I might too convince Henry to arrest him, much as I had with Wolsey.

But Henry was on the side of dissolution. He might say he would hear my pleas, but I knew I would not be able to save as many houses as I might like. Henry wanted their money. He lusted for it as he did for Jane Seymour. His father had set him up well, but over decades of reckless spending the royal coffers had dwindled. Henry wanted money to defend his lands, but he also wanted it so he might continue living in glory and riches. It was the right, if not the duty of every king to do so, but this, to me, was not the way.

"I do not speak for *all* the houses," I said. "But there must be further and more impartial investigation of some." I took out a letter and handed it to him. "I offer the sum of two thousand marks from my own purse to reprieve the closure of the convent at Catesby," I said. "And I wish to secure the continuation of the convent of Nun Monkton too. Other houses will I speak for, if I am assured of their dedication to you, as Head of the Church, and to their vows. Any that must be disbanded, I will ask to be put to educational use."

Henry looked displeased. "Is it not my right as your Queen to speak for your people?" I asked.

"It is," he replied shortly. He did not like that I was pilfering his plunder.

"Then I shall continue to do so," I said.

I should have seen his greedy slip of mind, his lust for gold. I thought Cromwell was leading him astray, but that was not wholly true. Henry had a mind, he had a will, and when it was set on something, nothing, not even love, would stand in his way.

*

"I bear ill tidings," said my father, handing his travelling cloak to Elizabeth Browne. "Your mother is most unwell."

I glanced up from the reams of parchment on my desk; more petitions for houses that wished to be protected, as well as a thank-you note from Cambridge University and a request from Lord Stafford, who wanted me to support his quest to attain the manor of Ranton Priory in Staffordshire. I was in demand, and many people recognised my influence, but my petition for Catesby Convent had not gone as planned. The nuns had written to Cromwell as well as to me, and he had told Henry that they could not support themselves. Henry turned down my request to save the convent. Although this was perfectly reasonable, I resented that Cromwell had intervened. But as my father spoke, every other worry in the world left me.

"Is she in danger of her life?" I asked, my heart floundering.

"I know not." My father sank into a chair and gazed at me with hollow eyes. "She is very sick, Your Majesty."

"At such a time as this, I am your daughter first, not your Queen," I said, taking his hand in mine. "You have sent doctors?"

"I have, but I came to ask if Butts could go. He is the most skilled of the King's physicians."

"I will ask him to go to Hever this very day," I said. "Should you not join her?"

"The King makes increasing demands on my time as Lord Privy Seal," he said. "He wants peace with the Emperor, and through Cromwell, entrusts this to me."

"The Emperor dances to our tune now. He has even said he will support my marriage."

"You should understand he does this for he fears the King might be persuaded to set you aside and take a French bride," said my father.

I dropped his hand. "This has been spoken of?"

"Not to me," my father said, shaking his head. "But Chapuys and Cromwell have had many a meeting of late. I think Cromwell is trying to gain Imperial support. When he has it, he will go to the King and tell him it is clear you cannot bear a son." He gazed at me with troubled eyes. "Your strike against Cromwell is well known. You must prepare for his counterattack."

"Cromwell has been trying to persuade Henry to allow more monasteries to be saved. He is in retreat."

"Do you know the tale of the Battle of Hastings?"

"Of course," I said. "Unlike Mary I paid attention to my tutors."

"Then you will know that the Norman knights pretended to retreat from the Saxons," said my father. "They ran, and as the Saxons charged after them, they turned on them. The Saxons thought the day was theirs, but in affecting retreat, the Normans won."

"And in such a way you think Cromwell will turn on me?"

"I do, and you should prepare yourself." My father rubbed his brow. "You are most vulnerable when it comes to the providing of an heir. That is where he will hit you. He will whisper that you are infertile, and cannot give the King what he wants. He will use your sister against you, and tell the King that his second marriage is invalid on the basis that you and he are related, just as Henry and Katherine were."

"And what would you advise I do?"

"Find a way to thrash him again, and quickly," said my father. "You must defame him in the eyes of the King. He has come to lean on Cromwell, but Master Secretary is not as yet invincible. There are chinks in his armour. One of those is the annoyance Henry feels for his talent for overstepping his authority."

"He has often spoken of it."

"Use that against him. You have the support of the Church, but that will not be enough. They are not as strong as once they were, and Henry wants their money. You are interfering with that ambition. If Cromwell can convince him you are wrong, and not only in this matter, but others, he might still triumph."

"Cranmer is coming to see me today," I said. "I will have his support too, but I will think on all you have said."

"I have told George to help you. Not that your brother requires convincing to come to your aid, but you will need help."

He rose and made to leave, but I stopped him. "I will ask Butts to go to Mother today," I said. "We will ensure she recovers."

My father nodded, but his face chilled me. I saw fear, and for my father to betray any emotion was rare.

Before Cranmer arrived, I sat down and wrote to my mother. I told her of my love for her, and that Butts would be with her soon. I told her all was well at court, and I hoped soon to have a son. I told her of Elizabeth and all her little, enchanting ways.

I told her nothing of sorrow and fear. I did not wish to worry her.

Chapter Fifty-Nine

Greenwich Palace
April 1536

"Money taken from the abbeys will be used for the betterment of the poor," said Cranmer.

The Archbishop had come to Greenwich on my urging, but as he opened his mouth I heard Cromwell and Henry's lies.

"That is what we were all *told*, Eminence," I said. "Yet I fear that is not what will happen."

"You doubt the King, Majesty?"

"I doubt the honesty of his advisors." I stared at Cranmer. "And, Eminence, I think you do too."

He narrowed his eyes. "It is true, that of late I have cause to question some things," he admitted. "Especially since Skip preached. Your Majesty's sermon is spoken of throughout England. Many are surprised to find you a sudden advocate for the Church."

"As you well know, old friend, I have always supported the Church, as long as they adhere to the true path of God."

"Many houses do not, Majesty."

"That I know, and I speak not for all, but for some. Those that can be saved I would have reformed, and those that cannot I would have disbanded and transformed into educational establishments."

"And His Majesty agrees?"

"The King commanded that there would be a provision in the Act to save houses he believed in," I said. "And so he does support this... but he has been seduced by the allure of money, Eminence. I would save him from himself."

"You are the true Esther," he murmured.

"I would not claim any such thing," I said. "But the King must see reason. What good does it do the poor to disband all lesser houses? Many do good work, and if some are corrupt that does not hold that all are."

"I do agree," said Cranmer. "I have thought, for some time, that Cromwell's men have gone astray in their task. They see not what may be lost, in what might be gained."

"And when one of us strays, Eminence, is it not up to the others, and to the King, to bring them back?"

By the time Cranmer left, I had convinced him. He swore he would write to Cromwell and tell him that he feared mass dissolution would do no good. As Archbishop of

Canterbury, Cranmer was duty bound to think of the people of England. The Church of England was now truly my ally.

On the 13th of April, I went to Westminster Hall for the Maundy Thursday ceremonies. Taking on the role of Christ, who had washed the feet of his disciples, I cleansed the feet of poor women and presented them with golden cups, old kirtles from my wardrobe, and purses of money. Later, I took to the steps outside the Cathedral and distributed alms. The amounts doled out that day outdid not only all of Katherine's offerings to the poor on past occasions, but mine as well. I was going to show the people of England that I was firmly on the side of the needy. I required their support.

The ceremony was a success, and the people were quite beside themselves with glee. I heard voices cheering for me, and whilst some still muttered that I was no Queen, there were increasing numbers of those who applauded me.

Skip's sermon was famous now, and many in London had heard of it. To people who considered me a heretical whore, this seemed like an attempt to promote myself as something I was not, but I think some had come to question if I truly was this black-hearted beast they had learned to hate. Now that Katherine was gone, there was no other Queen but me, and it seemed, at least to some, that I might in truth be not an agent of evil, but one of good.

And I was confident. Parliament had closed, and again my rights and titles had been enshrined in people's minds. If Henry had truly considered annulling our marriage, he would need Parliament to do so. Nothing had been said or done to lead me to that conclusion.

*

"I have news," said my brother as we walked in the gardens at Greenwich.

"Of Mother?" My voice emerged strained and hard.

"Of that, I have little," my brother said. "But Father has told me that Butts is doing her good, and she has recovered a little."

"God be praised!" My heart was in my mouth. For a moment I had thought George might be about to tell me she was dying. I wanted to go to her, but I could not. My power was hanging by a thread, and if I left, my enemies would cut it.

"But it is not that I have news of," he said.

"What, then?"

"I have a spy in Cromwell's house," said George. "Who tells me that Chapuys came to meet Cromwell, and they had a most interesting discussion."

"What did the pirate promise the hapless hare?"

"Much, and all of it without the King's authority."

George went on to explain that Chapuys had gone to Cromwell's house with authority invested in him by the Emperor to go ahead with negotiations of alliance. Chapuys had said that his master would intercede with the Pope on Henry's behalf, and in return Henry would aid the Emperor in a crusade against the Turks and the French. Mary would be restored to her *rightful place* in the succession, and Charles would accept my marriage to Henry. There was also to be reconciliation between Rome and England, and Henry would become part of a defensive league with the Emperor against any enemies.

"And Cromwell *promised* all this?" I asked.

Even I was shocked. To agree to these terms without the authorisation of the King was truly remarkable. Henry had given him no leave to do so. He was still wavering on who would make the best ally, but Cromwell was forging ahead without royal sanction.

"Indeed," said my brother. He grinned, wide and dangerous, like a wolf. "You should also know that the Emperor asked Chapuys to ferret out your opinion, knowing that it would go much smoother if you were on his side."

I smiled. It was good to know the Emperor understood my influence, even if his ambassador could not. "But he would want Mary made legitimate, and England's heir, in return for his acceptance of me as Queen," I said. "That has not changed."

"That has not changed," said my brother. "But much else has. Cromwell has gone too far. This will enrage the King."

"That it will."

"The time is ripe, Anne," George said. "If you wish to follow Father's advice and strike Cromwell again, this must be taken to the King."

"He will be furious," I gloated. "Cromwell has gone too far this time."

"We must move fast."

"We will go to Henry now."

We did just that. We told him all, and he was incensed.

"How *dare* he make promises to the ambassador and the Emperor?" Henry demanded, striding about his bedchamber. As he walked, he limped, his leg paining him.

"He thinks he can do as he wishes," I said. "And not only in this matter, as you have seen, my lord." I had given Henry all the information people had told me over the past months. He was now aware of the depths of Cromwell's ambitions, and subterfuge.

Henry's face snapped. There was suspicion blazing in his eyes, as well as deep, rich rage. "I will call him here... now," he roared. "And he will answer for this!"

"If so you wish, my love," I said. "But perhaps it might do Master Cromwell more good to be scolded before the court when he comes to Greenwich on the morrow with his ally Chapuys."

Henry stared at me for a moment and then laughed. It was a cruel sound. "Aye," he said. "Perhaps you are right, Anne. It is time to teach my servant his place, and have all men witness it."

Henry smiled, it grew, a thin wound running up his face; the swipe of a rapier. "You and your good brother will help me," he said. "And, what's more, my love, we shall achieve something that until now has been sadly neglected."

"What do you wish to do, my love?"

Henry's torn smile stretched. "We shall make Chapuys receive the Queen of England," he said. "And pay homage to her."

As we were about to leave, a messenger arrived from Cromwell. It informed the King that Cromwell had *"brought the best news in the world."*

Henry crumpled the parchment in his great hands. "We will see about that," he said, throwing it to the floor.

Chapter Sixty

Greenwich Palace
Easter Monday
April 18ᵗʰ 1536

Easter Monday dawned. A steady breeze blew, casting out sudden gusts that took many by surprise as they prepared to attend Mass.

They were not the only ones taken by surprise that blustery morning. Before he had risen from his bed, Henry received two visitors. Cromwell and Chapuys, eager to put to him all they had discussed without his knowledge, came to call, with no notion that George and I had already informed Henry of their plotting.

As we had discussed, Henry welcomed them and listened to their plans. He was receptive and polite, for he had no intention of offending the Emperor by rejecting overtures of friendship… but he also had no intention of allowing Cromwell to get away with usurpation of power.

Thinking their task well done, Cromwell departed and Chapuys prepared to do the same, but Henry stopped him, asking that in the interests of friendship, the ambassador should to come to Mass and kiss my hand, to demonstrate Spain and the Emperor accepted me as Queen.

Cromwell, who had paused at the door, was called upon by Chapuys to support him in expressing that such an encounter would be premature and inadvisable. Between them, they seemed to convince Henry that such an encounter might damage relations.

But we were ready for them.

Henry had known that Chapuys would try to wriggle out of his request, and had instructed George and my father to wait at the door of the chapel. Since George often sought Chapuys out, to engage in mischievous conversations about faith, the hare was not suspicious at first. They captured Chapuys with warm greetings, taking his arm as though they were the best of friends, and escorted him to a prearranged spot in the chapel. Chapuys suddenly realised he was trapped. Surrounded by courtiers, and with no polite way to flee, he was forced to stand as Henry and I descended from the royal pew and walked towards the altar to give offerings. As we passed Chapuys, we made as though we might walk on with little more than a polite nod… but just as the ambassador was set to expel a great sigh of relief, I turned, and so did Henry.

Chapuys, the man who had avoided me for seven years, was forced to bow and greet me as Queen.

The fraught look upon his face was almost more than I could bear! How I managed to keep from breaking into howling laughter I will never know. Chapuys was flustered, chagrined, but his back took over his wits, forcing him to bow.

I returned the honour, and dipped to a curtsey. "I am pleased to see you looking *so well*, my lord ambassador," I purred, struggling desperately to keep my face calm so it would not betray my smirking soul.

"Thank you, Your Majesty," said Chapuys. I could hear him grit his teeth to name me *Majesty*, and relished his discomfort.

"I hope I will see more of you at court," I said, "now that our gracious King and his cousin are to be friends again. I must tell you of the time I spent at the court of the magnificent Archduchess Margaret, for I am told you and I share a bond, in having known and loved her."

"That would please me greatly, Your Majesty."

Oh, little hare! I thought. *How well you lie!*

He handed me two altar candles to use in my offerings, and I accepted gracefully. Henry and I walked on, stopping here and there to talk to courtiers, and as we did, I could hear tongues wagging on how the Imperial ambassador had accepted me as Queen.

I could also feel the mortification of Chapuys, floating behind me on the incense-scented air, suffusing my spirit with joy.

*

That afternoon, Chapuys dined with my brother and Henry's councillors. I asked Henry why we did not build on our success, and have him dine with us, and his reply was strange. "It is not without good reason," was all he would say.

Elation seeped from me as I worried Henry had lost heart about the plan to teach Cromwell a lesson, or that I might have done something to offend him.

Why do you always blame yourself? I asked. *Just because that is what your husband does, that does not mean this is the path you should take. Have faith in yourself, Anne Boleyn!*

During that meal I took care to speak warmly of the Emperor and to say I had abandoned much hope for France. "It seems the King of France, tired on account of his *unfortunate* illness, wants to shorten his days by going to war," I said, causing Norris and others to titter. They knew I was speaking of the rumour François had contracted syphilis. But still, I was unnerved. I wondered why Henry would not push our advantage. Chapuys' acknowledgement had been a public endorsement of our marriage and me as Queen.

But later, as people began to assemble in Henry's Privy Chamber, my hope was restored. Edward Seymour escorted Chapuys in, to join Cromwell and Chancellor Audley, who were already in attendance. Chapuys put forth the four proposals that he and Cromwell had woken Henry with, and agreed in his absence. They thought that since he had accepted them so readily that morn, they would be publicly supported by the King.

Oh, how wrong they were…

Henry listened quietly, but as the ambassador finished by explaining that all the Emperor wanted was the peace and tranquillity of Christendom, he started to laugh. It was an uncanny sound, devoid of humour. He snapped his fingers at Cromwell. Drawing him to a window seat, he started to berate him, loud enough for all to hear. I looked on as Edward Seymour attempted to engage Chapuys in awkward conversation and Henry rebuked his chief minister.

He accused Cromwell of overstepping his authority, and forgetting who was King. "Your authority comes from *me*!" I heard Henry shout. "I told you to maintain cordial relations with Spain, not offer promises in my name! You forget yourself, Cromwell! You would be my master, is that it?"

I was delighted. Wolsey might have got away with such an audacious move. Cromwell could not. My once-friend was about to find out just what influence meant; favour, or death.

Cromwell attempted to respond, but Henry shut him down, time and time again. Eventually, Cromwell excused himself. He hastened to the other side of the room where he gulped down two cups of ale, his face feral and pale.

Henry looked as though he might go after him, but as he crossed the room he made for Chapuys. He sternly informed the ambassador that his issues with Rome were none of the Emperor's business, and since Mary was *his* daughter, and England was *his* country, he would do with both as he saw fit.

"And as for joining my royal brother in a war against his enemies," Henry went on, his angry contempt glaring like the noon sun. "It is necessary first for peace and amity to be restored between friends before favours are asked! I shall not put my people to ruinous expense and potential suffering for the restoration of friendship. The Emperor has worked much ill against me, lord ambassador. It is up to him to make peace with me!"

Henry went on to tell Chapuys he was not a child to be struck with a stick and then played with as a friend. He mocked Chapuys, acting out a little game with his fingers. It was strange, wild behaviour. Everyone stared. This was a side of their King they had not seen, or only witnessed in short spurts. He seemed deranged.

Henry demanded that the Emperor accept me and Elizabeth *in writing*, for the world to see. Chapuys attempted to calm him, but he got nowhere. Henry launched into a list of all the trials he had faced because of the Emperor. He abused his royal cousin, saying that Charles had failed him in the past when he betrayed him after his victory at Pavia, and had proved a poor friend and ally numerous times.

Even I was shocked. I was not sure what had got into Henry. He was like a man possessed. But as I watched, I saw him leaning slightly to one side. His leg was vexing him, and this, added to his rage at Cromwell, was making him so full of wrath that he knew not what to do with it.

Chapuys tried to say that the past was in the past, and could not be undone, but this only encouraged Henry to dig up more wrongs. He looked about, seeking support, but everyone was staring at him in dumb disbelief.

He looked insane. Henry truly looked as though he had lost his mind.

Eventually, he agreed to look over the proposals again, and the ambassador made a hasty escape, closely followed by Cromwell. Cromwell was hardly able to speak. Everyone could see he was terrified.

Outside the chamber, George heard the two men. Chapuys advised Cromwell to leave well alone. Their focus should switch, the ambassador said, to selecting a suitable husband for Mary. My brother did not catch Cromwell's response, but he could hear his mortified uncertainty, a strained, desperate note in his tone.

Cromwell left court. I did not sorrow. If he knew what was good for him he would cease to play me at this game. I thought I had won. I thought I had bested him.

I was wrong. I did not know that Cromwell would take that time to work against me.

Nor did I know I had only one month to live.

Chapter Sixty-One

Greenwich Palace
April 1536

Chapuys and Cromwell were not the only ones to come under fire from Henry's wrath. The French Ambassador received a generous helping of Henry's frustration later that same day, and Henry wrote to François, insisting he abandon his pursuit of Mary and accept Elizabeth.

As the humiliated ambassador departed, I found myself satisfied that finally my husband was standing up to his rivals, and at the same time, oddly disturbed.

Henry was acting in a most erratic manner. I could understand the sense in playing both sides, but the way in which he accosted the various ambassadors was striking in its ferocity. His leg pained him, and I understood that was why his temper was so changeable, but had he not been becoming harder for me to read over the past few years without injury playing a part?

In truth, Henry was taxing even those who had known him his whole life. No one knew what he might do.

But for the moment, I was pleased. Henry was fighting for Elizabeth's rights, and he had crushed Cromwell into submission. When Cranmer wrote to Cromwell, saying he was troubled about what the dissolution of the lesser houses would do for the poor, I was infused with new confidence. Cranmer had stood firm behind Cromwell for many years. To have him question the chief minister now, when he was vulnerable, would only enforce the fact that without my support Cromwell's position was precarious. The Church and her leaders were on my side, and although my allies were few and far between, those who stood with me were strong in Henry's love and favour. I was also assured that the people of England would soon know I was on their side; the side of cautious, careful reform.

I insisted that if any rapprochement were to be made with Spain, Charles would have to accept the supremacy, the succession, Elizabeth and me. Henry agreed wholeheartedly. No more would we talk about peace with Rome. No more would we accept people questioning Henry's right to his title. If foreign princes desired England's friendship they would have to accept us as we were; one kingdom, one state, one spirit, ruled by Henry.

Since Henry agreed with me, Cromwell swiftly understood his foreign policy was in peril. He was willing to compromise Henry's position and his sanctions on Mary in order to gain alliance. We were not.

Cromwell could not see England had the upper hand at that moment, and we had to use it. He feared to leave England alone in the vast oceans of the world. Perhaps he had a point, but since France and Spain were clamouring for our affection, Henry and I believed we should use this. Politics change overnight, and when a country finds itself in a position of authority, that should always be used to the best advantage.

When Cromwell returned to court, he was found in the company of arch-conservatives; the Courtenays, the Poles and Nicholas Carewe. He also seemed rather friendly with the Seymours. But I was not overly concerned. Henry and I were aligned in policy and passion, and as I supported him he turned to me like a flower opening her petals to the sun.

Henry needed me. I was never more assured of that fact than in those first days of April. He fed from my strength and courage, and although we did not see eye to eye on the closures of the monasteries, we were united in purpose.

Or so I thought.

I did not see what was coming. I did not note Henry's opposition to much I said about the monasteries or his wavering fear about foreign policy. I thought he was with me, that we were as solid in purpose as we were in heart.

I did not see. I was blind… Caught up in Henry's love and my own battle plans, I was oblivious.

My enemies were working in secret.

I had not yet learned to grow eyes in the back of my head.

*

"I am worried for my son," Henry said as we dined.

I glanced up. Henry's plate was full, yet he had touched nothing. For my husband to shy from food was a rare event. As some men seek out drink when they experience any emotion, happy or sad, Henry turned to food.

Fitzroy was ailing. Consumption, the curse that had carried away many male Tudors, had come for him. His lungs were weak. He hacked up phlegm, sometimes laced with blood, and was pale and thin. None dared say it, but the young Duke of Richmond was fading fast.

I took Henry's hand. "Doctor Butts is the best physician I have ever known," I said. "He is lately back at court after tending to my beloved mother. He made her well again. Send him to the Duke." I saw terror in his eyes, barely hidden in his sea-blue spheres. "And study your old books of physic, my lord," I said. "For you know more than many doctors. If there is a cure you will find it."

"Perhaps after the meeting of the Order of the Garter I should send him to the coast. They say sea air is beneficial for those who suffer complaints of the lungs."

"A good notion," I said. "And you could tell your son that you want him to inspect your ships and defences. That way he will not think he is being sent as an invalid."

Henry brightened. "Aye," he said. "The lad does not like anyone to note his troubles."

"He emulates his father," I said. "I remember when you were thrown from your horse many years ago, and, although you had a face full of splinters, you rode six more matches to assure your nervous people you were hale." I smiled at Henry and was greeted by one in return. "Your son is the same. He has all your courage, Henry, and your noble pride."

"I like the idea of sending him with a mission. But I would not want him to exhaust himself."

"Arrange his visit ahead of time," I suggested, warming to the subject. "Talk to your men on the docks. You know they will do anything for you. Ask them to stagger his visits, the paperwork, and his trips onto the ships. That way he will have plenty to keep him occupied, but not enough to exhaust him, and he will not suspect that this is done for the benefit of his health alone."

"You think of everything," he said. "At times, your mind is so devious, Anne, I wonder what other secrets you keep."

"With you alone, my lord, do I have no cause to hide," I replied. "With others, for sake of security and policy, I often have to mask my true intentions, but not with you."

This was not entirely true, especially of the past few years, but Henry and I seemed to be entering a time where honesty was indeed the better policy. I had held nothing back about the monasteries and I believed he respected me for it. The days when he had tried to mould me into his perfect ideal of a Queen seemed behind us. I believed he had accepted me for who I was, in return for me turning, at least some of the time, if he was careful, a blind eye to his affairs.

It was a strange compromise. An odd, unfair deal, for he gained all as I lost much. But I was willing to make it, for the sake of peace, and to retain part of the great love we had fought for.

I felt I was becoming my true self; the amalgamation of the Queen and Anne Boleyn. I understood my power now, and I drew on it. There was a new strength inside me, a new courage. At that time, I was more at peace with myself than I had ever been. I knew how to survive. I understood what was expected of me, and believed Henry respected me for the woman I had become. I was starting to reconcile myself to the twin aspects of my character, starting to understand the light and the darkness within. But I had forgotten someone. The broken one. So long had she been lost in the darkness that she had slipped my mind.

*

The annual meeting of the Order of the Garter took place on the 23rd of April. A vacancy had arisen, and I had put George forward as a candidate. To my chagrin, Henry had explained before the meeting that he could not support this.

"I promised François that the next vacancy would go to Nicholas Carewe," he told me. "Your brother will have the next slot, I swear it."

Many people took this as a sign that the Boleyns were out of favour, but since Henry was with me all the time, I knew not why they thought this. *Perhaps it is but wishful thinking*, I thought as I watched Henry leave for the meeting. *They see what they want to see.*

They, obviously, were not alone.

There was much I should have seen, and failed to.

As Henry and his knights met at Greenwich to discuss Carewe's appointment, I had a chance encounter of my own. There was a gathering of Henry's men, who, without their master requiring them that day, wanted to spend time with my ladies. My women were always ready to have handsome gallants in their company and the gathering was merry and bright.

As Brereton regaled me with another tale of his wild adventures on the Irish Sea, I noted Weston flirting with Mary Shelton. "Master Weston," I said, beckoning him over. "I desire that you would spend less time attempting to engage my cousin and her attention. Mary is betrothed to Norris now, and as such it is not fitting that she spend so much time with other men."

Weston smiled, for he saw I was partly teasing him. "I show attention to the lady, Majesty, for she is sadly neglected by her future husband."

I frowned. That much was true. Norris had asked for Mary's hand and her father had given permission, but he did not seem overly rushed to make her his wife. Others were keen, not only Weston but Tom, too. He had recently written a poem for Mary, included in the book of poetical warfare, wherein the first letter from each stanza spelt out *Sheltun*, when extracted. Once, he had written a similar poem for me, speaking of how I was constant, never-changeable and true. In this one for Mary, he wrote how he suffered without her love and wanted her to ease his pain. Mary had written a reply underneath, rejecting him, and signed it. So she had many admirers, but her future husband was not the most ardent amongst them.

"It is true there has been a delay," I said. "I wonder why Norris would tarry? Mary is a beautiful girl, and a clever one. They would make a handsome couple."

A little strike of pain flashed into my heart for the thought of Norris married. *Foolishness, Anne,* I told myself. *Would you keep him to yourself for your idle fancy for him, never allowing him to know happiness with others?*

A part of my heart said it wanted just that; for Norris to remain unwed, and therefore somehow mine.

"Norris comes more to your chamber for Your Grace than he does for Mary," said Weston with an impish grin.

I attempted to ignore that comment, yet I could not deny it brought a burst of sunshine to my heart. "Are you in love with Mary yourself, Weston?" I asked. "Do you not love your wife, Anne Pickering? She has lately granted you a son. Is that not all a man could ask?"

"I love one in your household better than both."

"And who is that?"

"It is yourself," said the cheeky young man, making me laugh.

"Hush now," I said. "Your love is like the love of all young men who would charm women into their power. You shall not catch me, Weston. I am old to all your tricks."

"You could never be anything but young and glorious to me, madam."

"Then your eyes fade in the pursuit of the glittering fiction you seek," I said. "Or your flattery tricks your mind into flights of fancy."

"It is not so," said he. "I am in possession of all my senses, and each and every one tells me you are the brightest star in the skies of court."

I rolled my eyes at Brereton. "What is a lady to do, my lord, when men let loose lies with such careless ease from their mouths?"

"Young Weston says nothing that is not true," said the old rogue. "I am daily dazzled by Your Majesty, sometimes so greatly that I stumble down dark stairs upon being removed from your brilliance."

"A conspiracy!" I laughed. "You all unite against me, then?" I emitted a dramatic sigh. "If I am to believe myself a normal woman again, I must seek Cromwell out, for he does not see me bathed in the glorious radiance you are all bemused by."

They laughed. This kind of battle went on every day, between many men and women.

"And here let this end," I said as Weston opened his mouth. "Speak no more, gentlemen. I will lose sight of all that is real if I dwell in your sweet fantasies."

The music played on. The dance resumed. We drank and we laughed. We moved between parties, trading quips and jests.

This was what we did. It was what everyone did. Men flattered women with more years, power and money, and gained a step up the ladder of court in doing so. We female patrons were marked out by such attentions, gaining fame and acclaim for the courtly love of our worshippers.

It was life. It was courtly love. It was how we whiled away dull hours, and how we structured the world in which we lived.

It was nothing. Nothing.

And yet to someone, it would become everything.

Chapter Sixty-Two

Greenwich Palace
April 1536

The next day, Chancellor Audley gave authorisation for Cromwell and Norfolk to form a commission to investigate cases of treason in Middlesex and Kent. The commission would examine commoners, and in truth, although it was put forth as a means to investigate those who would stand against the supremacy, it was really a means to *try* suspects swiftly. A grand jury would examine the offence, approving a bill of indictment if there was sufficient evidence, and the case would then be taken to the oyer and terminer commission to try the offender.

"Why is it needed, beloved?" I asked Henry. Commissions of oyer and terminer were not required by the Crown, nor were they commonplace. The King could authorize arrests and interrogations without one, as had been done in the case of Thomas More, who had been held for eight weeks before the oyer was issued, leading to his trial. Such commissions were only used for those of common blood. Nobles were tried by a high steward and a jury of their peers. Oyer and terminer commissions were also usually convened only after a person had been arrested, and no one had.

"Cromwell and Audley *insisted* on it," he replied. "I granted them leave to go ahead and sign the patents themselves. They tell me that with the commission already set up, trials of treason will move faster."

"Well, it will give Norfolk something useful to do," I said. "It is better my uncle is occupied. When he is free about court, he only gets himself into trouble."

Henry chuckled. "From all reports, he will be kept busy. We will weed out the traitors in our realm as we cleanse the Church. With the commission in place, we can have justice served in as little as four days." He paused, stroking his short beard. There were strands of silver amongst the golden-red fire now. "We will also call Parliament to sit again soon, to tie up the last strands of the rejection of the Pope's authority. From this point onwards, those who speak for the Bishop of Rome will find themselves facing charges of *praemunire*."

"Good," I said. "Let all men know and respect their true master."

I did not see. *I did not see*. The sands of time were moving against me. I was blinded by the dust rising in the skies.

I thought this commission could have little to do with me. Foolishly, I thought it was a means to protect me and Elizabeth. I did not know this commission would be used against my friends.

Canny Cromwell understood, where I did not, that swift speed would be required to take me down.

*

"Let Stokesley swallow that!" I crowed as I read a note from Henry. "And I hope he will choke on it!"

The Bishop of London would not be pleased with me. Since I suspected him of involvement in the arrest of Tyndale, who we were still trying to have released, I was pleased to have done the Bishop some harm.

Thomas Partmore, another former graduate of Gonville Hall, was a parson in Hadham, Hertfordshire. He had been accused of heresy by the Bishop of London almost six years ago, and held in the Lollards' Tower without trial. Butts had heard of his imprisonment even though the Bishop had tried to keep it secret, and had come to me, pleading for his release.

Henry had been most irritated to hear of *yet another* subject being held illegally, and had sent Cranmer, Hugh Latimer and Cromwell to investigate. Their findings were that there was not enough evidence to proceed to trial, and Henry had sent a note that morning to say Partmore was being released.

I was sure Stokesley had worked with More to get Tyndale arrested. More was dead, but if certain men were set on keeping alive the unjust ways he had used, this was a sign that times had changed.

*

After the oyer and terminer commission was set up, Henry wrote to Gardiner in France and Richard Pate in Rome. He called me *"our most dear and entirely beloved wife the Queen,"* and spoke of his hope that I would soon provide him with a son.

"Is there any sign of our boy, as yet?" he asked after showing me the letter.

"I nurture hope," was all I would say. In truth, our unions had been hampered by Henry's leg for the past few weeks, and his stamina was waning.

Our bed was tense. At times he could not coax his manhood into full strength, and would enter me in a manner that unpleasantly reminded me of someone trying to press a loose, raw sausage into a keyhole. We were awkward when this happened, which helped Henry not at all.

"Do you think we should speak to a doctor?" I had hesitantly asked, my blushing cheeks concealed by the gloom of the bedchamber.

"About what?" His tone should have warned me, but I tried again.

"Beloved," I cooed, putting a trembling hand to his shoulder. "Perhaps we should seek aid, in confidence."

He shook his shoulder and my hand dropped upon the covers. "There is nothing wrong with *me*," he had said pointedly. "I am not the one whose womb destroys our children."

"Perhaps we should speak to a cunning person," I said, trying again. "Such problems may be brought on by witchcraft, my lord. Mayhap Katherine has sought out someone to…"

"You will talk to no one about this." His tone was hard, twisted.

I was left in no doubt that to raise the subject again would be dangerous.

I had to pretend that everything was well, that I was satisfied. Until Henry was ready to accept there was a problem, there was nothing I could do.

"Come to me tonight," I said, touching his leg. "And we will set a prince in my belly."

Henry winced. I had not thought of his injury. His legs were monstrous. The bruises that his horse had inflicted were fading, but the risen veins had not fallen, and an ulcer had formed. It was a great, ugly hole in his leg, burrowing deep into the flesh. Weeping and bleeding, this ulcer was a fright to look upon and caused him pain, and discomfort. It itched fiercely, and the bandages had to be changed several times a day, for the substances that leeched from the open wound were putrid, rank and vile.

Henry did not like me to see his leg. He would not allow me to tend to it, change his dressings or apply ointment. Any infirmity was a horror to him, and, were I to look upon it, he thought I might love him less.

It was foolish to think that this would deter me from loving him. It was only when he betrayed me that I felt love slip from my hands. I would have nursed him and cared for him, had he let me. But he would not. Only trusted men would he allow to see his wound. Norris, Weston and Culpepper were three of them. He trusted few others.

Just as with his issues with his manhood, Henry thought if he could hide this frailty from me, from his people, then it did not exist. He thought he could keep the image of the hale young man who had come to the throne riding a wave of hope and glory firmly imbedded in his people's minds. He did not know that we all had eyes to see and ears to hear. That young man was no more, but there was no shame in that. Could a young buck, without experience of the world, have done all that Henry had for his country and his people?

But Henry could not glory in his present state. He looked to the past, when he had been upheld as a paragon of youth and loveliness. He did not care to think that he was no longer the prince he had once been.

I should have paid more attention. I respected Henry for the man he had become, and for all he had done. My love was not based on the way he looked. It was the inner light I worshipped. It was the soul and the heart of this man who had much potential for good within him.

But there were others who did see this. There were others who took note.

There were men who would push a woman at him who would flatter his self-image and speak of him as though he were still that strong, bold young prince.

There were others less honest than me who would tell him lies. And their falsehoods did not only stretch over his physical being... Their lies would stretch over everything, raining destruction and chaos upon innocent souls.

Chapter Sixty-Three

Greenwich Palace
April 1536

"I am much sorrowed by this news."

Henry's voice was hard and cold, it made me shiver just to hear it. Despite his hope that I was miraculously with child despite our problems, my laundresses had imparted news I had hoped they would not; my courses had arrived. I was not with child.

He sat upon his throne. My ladies and his men were but a whisker away, yet he did not trouble himself to drop his voice. The object of this lesson was to shame me for the inadequacies of my body; to humiliate me for not having caught his fragile seed, so sparely granted, to cultivate in my womb.

"Do you think I do not grieve?" I asked in a low tone. "Long have I yearned to hold another child in my arms." I looked up at him. "This is a *shared* sorrow, my lord. Allow me to bear it with you."

Henry grunted. His eyes, like gimlets, bored into the windowpanes. He would not look at me.

I left for my chambers, barely holding on to the grief welling inside me. Did he think I could be happy to see blood come, knowing another chance was lost?

But no. When Henry was mired in his own sorrows, he cared for those of no other. Not even mine.

"I will see my daughter," I said, suddenly veering from the path to my chambers and heading for Elizabeth's. My ladies did not even break step as they followed. They knew I would go to Elizabeth when I was distraught.

Sometimes I believed she was the only thing holding me to the world. She was my tether, my rock… the reason I woke with fire in my blood and courage in my soul. She was what I fought for, and what kept me sane.

In the company of my gentle child, my heart started to warm. In Henry's presence, with his cold cruelty pervading my heart, I had become chilled, but Elizabeth was warmer than any fire, lighter than any breaking dawn. She was the light of the world. The candle in my darkness.

That afternoon, I called Matthew Parker to Elizabeth's rooms. "I have a task for you," I said to this quiet man. "Should anything happen to me, I would entrust you with the spiritual welfare of my daughter. Watch over her, Matthew, and keep her safe… for me."

He started in surprise and glanced at my daughter, playing on the floor with her silver rattle. Light from the windows glittered as the toy danced in her long fingers. The light spilled, shining on my face and his as we watched her.

"Your Majesty," he said, stammering. "I… am honoured, but I know not why you would have me appointed to this task."

I smiled sadly. In truth, I was not entirely sure why I had asked it of him. But something in Henry's eyes had shaken my faith. Until Henry had called me to him, I had been sure and bold. But as Henry's sun departed my skies, I was left unsure.

If I was in danger, if Henry turned from me, Elizabeth had to be protected.

"You are gentle and kind, by nature, Matthew. The other men who serve me as chaplains… some are made of fire and some of ice, but you are soft, warm embers. If anyone should watch over my daughter, and ensure that her spiritual awakening comes with realisation of the truth of the Word of God, as well as the kindness to guide others, it should be you."

"What do you fear, madam?" he asked softly. "You think you will not be here to do this yourself?"

I watched my daughter play. The silver rattle passed through her long, straight fingers and her large black eyes never let it out of sight. She glanced up and beamed to see me watching. Elizabeth never smiled with anyone else as much as she did in my company.

"I know not," I murmured, and it was the truth. "But I think I must make sure she is safe."

"With you guarding her, madam, she will always be so."

"Yes," I said. "Perhaps I am being foolish. Thoughts of dying in childbirth come to me now and then, but if such a fate should befall me, Matthew, promise me you will care for my daughter."

"I promise, my lady," he said, watching little Elizabeth as she set down the rattle and deftly took up a bright ribbon. "I will protect your daughter and tend to her spiritual needs."

My daughter held out the ribbon and chuckled, as though it were the most amusing thing she had ever seen. "Pretty!" she exclaimed, holding it out to me. "Pretty ribbon."

"So it is," I said. I put the ribbon in my palm and surreptitiously slipped it inside my sleeve. Holding out my hands, I asked her where the ribbon was. She giggled and slapped her hands on mine. I opened them to show her the ribbon had vanished.

"How?" she asked, her pretty little mouth a perfect 'o'.

"Magic," I whispered.

Parker laughed and Elizabeth joined him. "Again!" my daughter commanded. "Again, Mama!"

If only I could work magic, I thought as I performed for my daughter. *If I could weave a spell to keep my husband constant, I would.*

Constancy is a much overlooked virtue. I do not know if I had ever known it whilst married to Henry. If I gave him a son, he would be true. But in this slipstream of waiting for an heir, he was as changeable as the temper of my infant child... as unpredictable as the winter seas, and perhaps, just as dangerous.

*

On the 27th of April, Parliament was recalled and Cranmer attended. On that same day, George came to Greenwich from Dover, with a grim look on his face.

"I heard something disturbing from one of my men," he said, throwing his cloak to Nan who caught it with a giggle. "That is why I came to court."

"What?" I led him to an alcove to one side of the chamber and we sat in it together.

"Anne," he said. "You must prepare yourself. This will not be easy to hear."

My heart stumbled. "What?" I whispered.

"One of my men overheard Montague talking to Stokesley," he said. "He said that the King had asked if there was any legal impediment to your union that might be preventing the birth of a son."

My heart seemed to have stopped beating. "But all sin of close acquaintance was removed by dispensation," I protested. "And the sin was Henry's, not mine!"

"Keep your voice low," he cautioned. "And smile, Anne. Pretend we talk of nothing serious."

I forced a smile onto my lips. It hurt to strain my mouth into such a position when all I felt was fear. If he set me aside, what would become of me, what would become of Elizabeth?

"I thought you and the King were on good terms?" my brother asked. "He has been so loving and sweet to you of late."

"He found out two days ago that my monthly courses have arrived," I said. "He was displeased. Although he has done little that might succeed in putting a child within me."

"Still he struggles in the bedchamber?" asked my brother. "Sometimes, with all you tell me I wonder how he managed to plant Elizabeth in you. Are you sure it was he?"

My brother's wife set a goblet of wine at his elbow and walked away again, joining Jane Seymour and Margery Horsman who were close by.

"And when he fails, he blames me," I said, my tone rising with anger as I ignored my brother's dangerous jest. "Strange is it not, that we are told all fertility and life comes from the male seed. That women hold nothing but the soil that will grow the child, but as soon as anything goes wrong, it *must* be the fault of the woman. If I am indeed nothing but a vessel, then how is it my fault there is no child within me? Henry blames me for he cannot face the truth... that he has not virility or strength to imbed a child in me, or give satisfaction to a woman."

George guffawed, despite himself, but his face swiftly fell. "With Cromwell in retreat," he said, "you must turn your attention to the King once more."

"Do you not think I know that?" I said. "But he does not send for me. Since he accosted me he has sent only for Jane Seymour. She makes him feel like a man. She plays to his sense of protectiveness, and pretends not to note that he is growing old and feeble."

"Then you must pretend too," he said. "Flirt with his men, throw entertainments in your chambers. Lure him back to your bed." My brother sighed. "Anne… if he continues to think this way, you know what will happen. Once he gets an idea in his head, nothing may uproot it. The same thing happened with Katherine when he got the notion into his mind that their union was ungodly."

"It was!" I exclaimed.

"That matters not," he said. "Do you not see that? This is not about what is fact and fiction, this is about what Henry *believes*. If he believes your marriage is cursed in the eyes of God, he may abandon it. The only hope is to prove this is not so, by bearing a child, and for that to happen, he must come to your bed."

"When the bleeding ceases, I will invite him to my chamber."

"And if he cannot perform?"

"I have learnt many tricks to entice him," I said. "But one thing works better than anything else. When I support him politically, he is granted strength and courage. When Parliament sits, I will support him in all ways, on whatever comes up. Then he will know that he cannot do without me. Then he will know he cannot leave me."

I glanced up to look at my ladies and gentlemen. They were singing and laughing, flirting and conversing, as though they had all the time in the world for pleasure. I envied them.

"All these years," I said. "All these years and I have never felt safe. Since the moment Henry first came to me with words of love on his lips, I have not known peace. Not even when I was made Queen, or when I carried my children."

I smiled mirthlessly. "I thought Henry would bring me safety, in the end. But it has never been so. Since first I fell in love, I have been falling, and never knew it. I have been tumbling down a cliff, in the dark of night. I have been exposed and slandered, defamed and abused, and all for love. I thought he would make me safe. I thought he would safeguard our future, but I was wrong."

I looked away from my brother. "He promised once to be my knight," I whispered. "But I come to think the days of chivalry are dead."

My brother left me to talk with Henry about the meeting with François. Much postponed had this meeting been, but now the final preparations were being put together, and I had been excited to think that I would soon be publicly accepted. But now… I was anxious.

I ordered more clothes, when my brother left me, thinking that if I had to draw Henry back to me, I would need enticements. Venice gold trim for gowns of silk, yards of cloth of gold and satin in shades of green and gold I ordered, along with a saddle with round buttons of gold for Lady Margaret Douglas.

"It is a fine gift, Majesty," said the girl when I showed her my drawings.

"You should have some consolation," I replied, glancing at her with sympathetic eyes. Her dalliance with my young uncle was continuing in secret, but Margaret had drawn back of late, fearing Henry's reaction if their love should become known.

Her eyes went to my Howard kinsman. The naked affection in them burned. "I know not what to do," she said.

"When the King is in a good mood, we will go to him together." I followed the track of her eyes. "There should be love, in this world. There should be constancy."

She looked baffled, but heartened. I sent her to my uncle to speak about preparations for the meeting in France, and she was pleased to have an excuse to talk to him.

I went back to my drawings, trying to lose myself in my plans... It did not work. *Perhaps he was not seeking annulment,* I thought as I sketched. *Perhaps he was simply worried, as you have been, as to why a son has not been granted by God.*

New clothes I ordered, planning to enchant Henry with my body and support him with my mind.

Those clothes would never be worn.

*

A day later, as I entered Henry's chamber to talk with him about the trip to France, I found he was not there. His men were embarrassed when I enquired where he was, and I knew then that he must be with Jane Seymour.

Turning about, and promising to return soon, I caught sight of Smeaton sitting by himself in an alcove in the Throne Room. He looked sad, so I went to him. "Why so grim, Master Smeaton?" I asked.

He glanced up, not bothering to rise from his seat to bow, as he should have done. "It makes no matter," he said, looking away with pensive eyes.

My frayed temper snapped. Smeaton was no equal of mine, and this behaviour was not acceptable. He should have risen and bowed, at the very least. "You may not expect to have me speak to you as I might a nobleman," I said. "You are a lesser person in this household."

My rebuke stung. A glimmer of anger crossed his eyes. Smeaton never liked to be reminded of his humble origins. "No, madam," he said, rising to bow. "From you, a look suffices me, and thus fare you well." He excused himself and left, leaving me staring after him with bemused eyes.

"He tells us all that he loves you, Majesty," said Norris, appearing behind me.

"Puppy love," I said, turning. "He sees the courtly love that others offer, and thinks it is real. He thinks himself in love with me for that is what is expected of gentlemen at court, and he yearns to be known as a noble."

"Do you not trust in any of the men about you?" Norris asked softly, drawing near.

"In whom should I trust?" I asked. "In my husband, who runs off to enjoy the company of whores? In men like Weston who seek advancement by pretending love they feel not?"

"What of me?"

"What of you, Norris?" I whispered. My ladies were on the other side of the chamber, not paying attention. For once, there was no one near us.

"Would you not believe in me?"

"Are you not to wed my fair cousin?"

Norris glanced at Mary, laughing with Brereton. "She is beautiful," he said, making my heart drop. Then he looked at me. "But she is not you."

"I know what you would say, and I beg you not to," I said quickly. "Life is full of lost liaisons, my friend. Had fate been different for either of us, there might be a chance for what you suggest, but it is not, and never will it be so."

He looked away. "I know," he said. "And I came to you not with hope, for I know your heart is dedicated to the King alone, and I, too, as his friend of twenty years would never betray him." Norris looked at me. "But know that I love you," he said. "And not for show, as Smeaton does, or for favours as Weston looks for... I admire and esteem you. I think you all that is good in this world."

"I think the same of you," I whispered. "And nothing will alter that."

"Then trust in the love of those who offer their hearts to you without motive or purpose. And although I will go to the altar and promise myself to your cousin, I will worship you in my heart for the rest of my days."

"Then know the same is true for me," I said sadly.

"I will stand by you, always... Anne."

Norris bowed and left to talk to Mary Shelton. I watched him walk across the chamber, knowing he carried a heavy heart, just as I did.

Nothing could come of it, but at such a time, as my husband questioned our union and as I struggled to bear a child, it was a comfort to know that amongst the lies and the shadows, amongst the illusions and deceit, there was an honest heart that beat for me, sounding its reckless call in the darkness, bringing light to my world. I hoped I brought Norris the same comfort.

As I went to join my ladies, I caught sight of Richard Rich, standing in a corner, talking to Carewe. I followed the path of their eyes. They were staring at Smeaton.

Something in their watchful eyes made me shudder... as though I had seen a cat with her eyes upon a mouse that stood in plain sight, oblivious to her stalking gait.

Chapter Sixty-Four

Greenwich Palace
April 29th 1536

The next day, everyone was gathered in my rooms. Smeaton was playing for my ladies to dance, and as I watched them, Norris drew near.

Mary and Margaret Shelton were dancing with George and Weston, their steps light and carefree. Mary was so vivacious and pretty that day, and I saw Norris' eyes linger on her. A spark of jealousy ignited in my heart.

"Why do you not go ahead with your marriage, Norris?" I asked him, sipping from a goblet of wine. I had already drunk more than was good for me, attempting to drown my fear. "It is clear you are attracted to my cousin, and her father has given his consent."

Norris did not look at me, but I saw his jaw twitch. Given that he had explained his reasons for delaying only the day before, and promised his heart to me, no doubt he thought my question arbitrary. I thought I caught a glimmer of resentment, too.

"I will tarry a time, Majesty," he said.

I sipped again and let out a short laugh that made people look our way. Unthinkingly, I made to tease him. "You look for dead men's shoes," I said, none too quietly. "For if aught were to come to the King but good, you would look to have me."

The moment I said it, my hand flashed to my mouth and my eyes dropped wide and wild. I looked about. Everyone standing nearby, and there were *many*, had heard me. It was treason to speak of the death of the King, and still more dangerous that I had suggested Norris might seek to take me, the Queen, as his wife.

Norris did not even turn his head. His face drained and his eyes bulged.

For a moment, there was silence.

Why had I said that? What was I thinking?

The truth is, I was not. I was caught up in fear and worry. Norris' admission of love on the previous day had brought me a fragment of joy. Jealous of Mary, I had sought to gain a compliment or another protestation of love from him, to heal my heart. But I had not thought. *I had not thought.* I had allowed such a scandalous statement to leave my lips unheeded. It was one thing for men to protest they loved me, but quite another for me to take the masculine role and go on the attack. And in saying Norris looked for a time when Henry was dead was dangerous to us both.

"If I thought any such thing," Norris said, turning, his grey eyes blazing with terror and rage. "I would that my head were taken from me."

"It was a jest, nothing more," I said desperately, grasping about for some way to salvage the situation.

"Then it was a foolish one." Norris glanced about, trying to ascertain who might have heard us.

"Do not think to speak to me as though you were my master!" I said loudly. "I am your Queen!"

"And as such I serve you, madam, but look for nothing more." Norris was looking wildly about. I stopped him, clutching his arm with a desperate claw.

"Hold still," I said. "Act as though something is wrong and more people will notice."

"Plenty heard you, Anne," he said through gritted teeth.

"Do as I say or I will undo you," I threatened.

"You may have done that already."

"We must remedy this," I said, swallowing hard. The intoxication of the wine left me swiftly. I had never felt more sober than I did in that moment. "The King must not hear of it."

"There are people here with connections to Cromwell," Norris whispered. "They will be only too pleased to take such a tale to him and he *will* use it."

"Then I must have a witness to speak for me. We will go to John Skip, and you will bear witness that I am a good woman, beyond reproach."

"What good will this do?"

"I know not. *I know not*," I said, wringing my hands. "But for my sake and yours, Norris, do this for me, I beg of you."

His eyes softened as he took in my distress. "I will," he said. "And it will be nothing but the truth in any case." He took my goblet of wine and passed it to my sister-in-law. "Drink no more," he said. "It brings you no peace." He gazed at me. I swear I could see his heart in his eyes. "All will be well, Anne," he said softly. "I will not let harm come to you."

And with that, Norris went to Skip to swear on his soul that I was a good woman.

My most trusted women, I knew, would say nothing of my hideous slip. But it was a fool's hope to think Henry would not find out.

I watched Norris leave and my mind called up an image; a drop of blood falling from the body of a deer into a pool of water.

Black falling to black. Blood on blood… A ripple in a pool, casting out from the first impression of liquid upon liquid, undulating out from the centre, washing in waves to touch all and everything.

Rumour would spread.

What had I done?

Later that day, Henry sent for me. As I walked to his chamber, my heart pounding like a drum, I knew my slip would cost me.

Just how much, I did not then know.

I knew it not, but I had granted Cromwell his chance. I had handed Henry his excuse. I had thought my enemies were what I should fear, but I should have looked within, to the unguarded tongue in my mouth. I was my own worst enemy, and this slip, no matter how foolish, no matter how silly, slim, slight and spare, would be used against me. I knew not that Cromwell had the bow ready in his hands.

I had just handed him an arrow.

*

"It was but a jest, Henry!" I cried, running to him and trying to take his sleeve. "A jest! It was a conversation on courtly love that got out of hand, but it meant nothing!"

He pulled his arm from me and glared. I had never seen him so angry. He lifted a hand, as though to strike my face, and I cringed from him.

"A *jest*?" he roared, gazing at me in disgust as I cowered. "You would jest about my death, would you, madam? You think it a subject of light importance? You think to make yourself a new husband from amongst my own men? My *closest friend*?"

"It was foolish," I said, my words tumbling over one another. "I was teasing Norris about not being yet wed to my cousin, and the words just came out."

"Perhaps this is what you hope for?" he demanded. "For me to die so you might take a new husband?"

"I love you!" I cried, tears bursting from my eyes. "And if I spoke wild, it was because you made me! You want a new wife, do you not? You have spoken to my enemies about setting me aside! In rage and sorrow did my heart lash out, and if I said something foolish, it was because you made me do it!"

"I? I made you say that you desired my demise?"

"I did not say such a thing," I protested. "I did not, Henry, and any who tells you otherwise is lying! I said to Norris that if aught were to come to you but good, he might think to have me. That is not a *wish* that you would die! It was a tease… I thought to push him into finally agreeing to wed my cousin."

Henry twisted away, his nostrils flaring, tipped with white, and his face a mangled mess of purple and red. I tried to take his arm again and he shook me off. "Get off me!" he shouted. "I cannot bear to even look at you, creeping after me, trying to placate me as all the while you plot my death with my men!"

"How can you think that?" I screamed, my wailing voice floating all through court. "For all these long years, I have remained true. For all these years you and Elizabeth have been my only thought. There is no sun in my sky without you, Henry. There is no light in this world. When you offered me your heart, I took it up, and I kept it safe. I offered you the same, but you trampled on my heart and derided my love for you. You mocked my affection by taking mistresses, and you have given leave to my enemies to work against me, and still, whilst I endured pain upon pain and agony on agony, I have never faltered. I am your wife, Henry of England! I swore myself to you and only you, and I have never broken that promise!"

I was sure any moment he would call his guards and have me arrested. I would be defamed and disgraced. Elizabeth would be taken from me.

I fell to my knees and gazed up at him. "For all the love once you bore me," I said. "For all that was pleasing when you saw my face, or heard my voice, *hear me now*. I love you, I would never harm you, and whilst I might at times speak recklessly out of fear and pain and hurt, I would never, *never* do anything to imperil your life."

I looked up at him. "You are my only protection and salvation, Henry," I whispered. "I love you."

"I cannot look at you," he muttered.

He swept out of the room, leaving me on my knees. I put my face into my hands and wept bitter, terrified tears. Was this the end? Would I find myself packed off to a nunnery, or under arrest? What would become of Elizabeth? I knew not.

I was petrified.

What would Henry do to me… this wife who had failed to grant him a son? This woman who had spoken of his death? This Queen who no longer pleased him and whose enemies were watching from the shadows, waiting to strike?

Chapter Sixty-Five

Greenwich Palace
April 29th 1536

There is still time to mend this. There is still time to mend this.

That was all that went through my head as I walked from Henry's chambers. I had to demonstrate that I loved him. I had to prove my words were but a jest. I had to show him I was, in heart, an honest women and a good wife. I had to remind him of all that once had been ours.

I went to the nursery and asked to take Elizabeth into the gardens. She loved to see the fish in the ponds. If her nursemaids noted the wildness of my eyes, they said nothing, but dressed my two-year-old daughter in warm layers, and brought her to me in the gardens at Greenwich.

We sat in a courtyard, beside a pond where little golden fish swam, their backs and sides flashing and glinting in the afternoon light as they turned to catch the warmth of the sun. Elizabeth was in my lap, her tiny, chubby hand reaching out as she tried to touch the fish. A small gurgle of mirth escaped her lips and she looked up, trying to share the moment with me. She waved her hands.

"Fishes!" she said with a simplicity of joy that caught at my heart. "Pretty fishes!"

I looked down at her.

A mirror of my black eyes came up to greet me, and inside her eyes, I saw my own. I saw the tired rings under my eyes, and the paleness of my skin. I saw the horrors I had faced and the terror I now lived with. And yet, as I saw all that, I saw too the purity and grace of my only child. My little girl. My sweet, sacred babe.

Her hand reached up to touch my face, as though she wanted to take hold of the black eyes that shone into hers with a love so strong I could barely contain it. I moved my face towards her hand, so her palm rested on my cheek, pressing my flesh against hers, feeling the warmth of her skin, smelling the scent of rose perfume, and the sweet smell all children possess, born of purity and innocence.

Elizabeth crowed with delight, her little laugh bounding about the gardens. The fine spring afternoon held a slight chill, as darkness loomed upon us, but the air remained warm. My eyes closed. For a moment, just a moment, I sought to draw peace from my daughter.

When I opened my eyes, they swam with tears.

Elizabeth's tiny face crumpled. Her head bobbed to one side as she tried to make sense of what she saw. My daughter was used to me laughing, for I was ever-joyous in her company, and yet now I was sad. It made no sense to her, I could see that. I wanted to stop my tears, to keep from scaring her, but I could not. Through a filmy haze I watched as she reached out both hands to touch my face. I smiled, trying to reassure her that all was well, but the smile petrified upon my face.

"Be not sad," she said in a commanding tone. "Mamma be not sad."

I was about to tell her that all was well when I caught a movement at the window. It was Henry. He was standing in his rooms, looking out onto us. His expression was dark, full of loathing.

His clothes and fingers sparkled with jewels and gold, flashing and twinkling as the sun caught them with her light fingers. But his face was grim as the sky before a summer storm.

Elizabeth saw him, and cooed with pleasure. Next to me, Henry was her favourite person in all the world. I pulled her to me, rose, and turned with her in my arms. I pushed our daughter out, holding her up so her father could see her. So he might be reminded of the love that had made this perfect, beautiful little girl.

She is my shield, I thought. *She will protect me.*

His dark face faltered. He looked down at the floor, then up again. He frowned. Then he turned away and walked away, disappearing into the darkness.

The window was empty. He had gone.

Like a statue, I held Elizabeth in the air, my palms slick with clammy fear. She grumbled, breaking the spell of terror upon me. I brought her down. When I turned her to face me, she started. As I looked into her eyes, I knew she had seen the naked horror in mine.

Reflected in Elizabeth's eyes, I was a hunted animal who knew not where to run.

Black falling to black… Blood on blood… the ripple was spreading.

My daughter leaned against me and I kissed her. "May God bless you, sweet one," I whispered. "And may He ever keep you safe. Remember that I love you, Elizabeth. Always remember that."

Quickly, before she could see more, I handed her to her maids. Elizabeth howled to be set aside, and cried out for me. But I could not go back. I could not allow her to be touched, tainted, by my fear. I walked away.

Had I known that was the last time I would hold her, I would never have let go.

I heard her maids tell her to be a good girl. They said that I was the Queen, and had many affairs to tend to. As they took her back to the palace, I walked on through the gardens. I did not know where I was going or what I would do. Everything was falling apart.

My gown of deep green whispered as I walked, its slashes of crimson velvet embroidered with golden thread catching the afternoon light, just as the fishes in the pond had. Little seed pearls glimmered in the waning light, and my French hood, lined with more pearls, was hot upon my head.

As I walked my hands clenched into fists, and then splayed out again.

I caught sight of the Scottish reformer, Alexander Aless. He lifted a hand to me and bowed, but I marched on. My ladies ran behind me, trying to keep up.

I knew not where I was going. I had no path, no purpose, and no plan. For the first time in my life, I was utterly lost. A vast desert was opening before me. I knew not my way home.

That was my *selva oscura*, the time I had lost my way.

Elizabeth went back to Eltham that night, on Henry's command.

I never saw her again.

Chapter Sixty-Six

Greenwich Palace
April 30th 1536

I barely slept that night.

Long hours of wakeful terror came one after the other. I stared at the rich hangings over my bed, those that Henry had presented me with years ago, flush with the arms of the Rochfords and motifs of honeysuckle and acorns. I stared at our entwined initials, and I thought on all I had done.

How could I have spoken so wild and untamed before witnesses? How could I have placed not only myself but Norris in danger? Guilt assailed me for what might become of him, but I told myself over and over that Henry loved Norris. He was his greatest friend, the man he trusted more than any other. He would not, surely, believe that I would plot his death, and Norris with me? He would not think that I had ceased to love him?

But his eyes…. But that expression of pure loathing when I had held up Elizabeth. That disgust was not directed at his daughter. His hatred burned for me.

When I rose, I was told I was not alone in sharing Henry's anger. That morning he had shouted at Cromwell for forgetting to send a letter, a most unusual slip for careful Cromwell, which, had I thought on it more, might have told me he had other things on his mind.

"The King boxed his ears," Jane informed me with some delight.

"He has become heavy handed with those who displease him," I agreed, hoping this would not be the case with me. In his pain and changeable temper, Henry had taken to abusing those who served him. It was not unusual for masters to slap, pinch or strike servants if they displeased them, but Henry had never before been so free with his hands.

I tried to see Henry, but I was curtly informed he was with his Council, and they would be some hours. When I said I would wait, I was told there was no point. "The King will be busy for the rest of the day," said one of his guards. "He told us to inform you, Majesty, if you came calling, that he would see you tomorrow."

If I came. If. He knew I would. Gone were the days when he would come running to me. Our roles had switched. He held all the power now.

I could not help but wonder, as I walked away, if Henry and his Council were meeting about what was to be done with me. Every imaginable terror was within me as I went back to my rooms.

That afternoon my chambers felt hollow and stark. The usual musicians and crowds were present, but the anxious fear and sorrow seeping from me infected everyone. Eventually my sister-in-law came to me. "Come, Majesty," she said in a kindly tone. "There is a dog fight due to begin soon in the gardens. Let us go and watch."

I did not want to go, but I did not want to stay. I was twitchy, restless... there was a rising wave of panic inside me, trying consume me. I allowed my ladies to dress me in a warm cloak lined with fur and we went to the fight.

The ring was dusty. No rain had fallen that day and the stands were packed with courtiers, roaring for their beasts. Coins jangled, changing hands, as men placed wagers and ladies crowed. The dogs were brought in. Two mastiffs, that growled and gnashed their teeth, competing with the cheering crowds for who could make the most noise.

The fight began. Whipped towards each other, starved for days, and regularly abused to be always ready to fight, the hounds fell upon each other.

Blood dripped. Scathing spittle flew. They tore chunks from one another with startling voracity, seeking to take hold of each other's throats and rend life into death.

As I watched the hounds rip at each other with claw and tooth, I did not know Cromwell was making his way to Henry. I did not know my absence would be taken advantage of, and my ladies were being questioned.

I wagered on the fight, but in truth it made me sick. As one dog slumped to the ground, blood beating from wounds too numerous to count, I turned my face away. A feral cry exploded. Men and women screamed for joy or sorrow as the dog breathed its last. Forgotten as soon as it died, its body was scraped from the earth, black with its blood, and thrown into a pit. Another dog was brought out. Another fight began.

I went back to my chambers, but the empty silence had not abated. Thinking I would run mad, I sent for musicians. But when I called for Smeaton, I was told he could not be found.

"Where is he?" I asked.

No one knew. Some said he was with the King, others said they thought he might be playing in a private house this night, as he had said something to make them think he had received a private commission.

That was the night Smeaton vanished.

*

"The trip to France has been cancelled," said my brother as he came to my rooms late that night.

It was twelve of the clock. I had been about to prepare for bed. Without Smeaton to play for us, the evening had passed in quiet strain. I had tried to read my Bible, but found my eyes travelling across the same sentence over and over again. Eventually I had set it aside, and passed the time simply staring at the tapestry. Conversation had dimmed, and soon everyone made excuses, leaving me alone with my ladies until my brother arrived.

"Why?" My voice was strange. It sounded like a lost child, a child who was afraid.

"The King gave no reason," he said. "But something is going on. The Council sat until eleven, and I was not permitted to enter. There is a great crowd gathered about the King's rooms. I saw Master Aless there, and he said they were battling with some issue about France, but all I was told was that the meeting has been postponed again."

"He will set me aside," I said, my tone hollow. "He will forsake me."

George was at my side in a flash, his hands curled about mine. "That is not so," he said. "You surrender to fear, but you should not."

"He knows what I said to Norris. He thinks I wish for his death."

"You must speak to him."

"Do you not think I have tried?" I wailed. "I go to him and am told he cannot see me. I chase him and he walks away." I paused, wiping clammy hands on my gown. "I am in trouble, George. I feel the hot breath of my enemies on my neck. They are circling. They will bring me down. I will be set aside, and Henry will take Jane Seymour as his wife. That is what they want. That is what he wants."

I burst into tears as my brother took me in his arms. "Will they take Elizabeth from me?" I sobbed into his coat. "Will they take her away?"

"All is not lost," he murmured into my hair.

As I was about to reply, there was a knock at the door. A messenger in Henry's livery appeared with a note.

"It is from Henry," I breathed, my shaking hands tearing the parchment as I opened it. I scanned the note, hoping for reassurance, but it was spare and short. "He wants to see me."

"*There*," said my brother, forcing a smile. "Perhaps he wishes to make it right between you."

I hastened to Henry's rooms, and found him still dressed, even though the hour was late. "Sit," he commanded, his face grim.

Feeling feeble, I scurried to a chair.

"I have cancelled the trip to France," he said. "I thought you should know, since we are due to depart in two days."

"Will you not look at me?" I asked softly.

He obliged, and suddenly I wished I had not asked him to. His eyes were deep, dark caves, a fire burning in the belly of their darkness.

"Have you done this because you mean to set me aside?" I asked.

"I have not."

I breathed in a welcome gulp of air. "I swear upon my soul… upon the soul of our daughter, whom you know I love more than anything, that I meant nothing when I spoke out of turn."

"I believe you."

My head darted up and I searched his eyes for any spark of love still left in his heart. "Then you know that I love you?"

He did not answer. His jaw clenched.

"I love you, Henry," I said, cursing my voice for sounding like a lost lamb bleating in the fields.

"Then all is well. I spoke with Norris. He too assures me there was nothing in your conversation. John Skip came too, to plead for you. You have many admirers."

There was something lurking in his tone I did not like. But he brushed off his coat and turned to stare into my eyes. "You should have more care of your tongue. What you said was not becoming of a wife or a queen."

"I know that," I said. "All I can do is tell you how sorry I am. I meant nothing by my words, but you are right. I am too unguarded, too brazen at times. I allowed my hurt and pain to master me. It will never happen again."

"You will preside over the May Day entertainments," he said. "I will expect to see you there, on the morrow."

"I will be there," I said, rising, for I heard dismissal in his voice. "And I will watch with a thankful heart, knowing that my husband is the greatest man in the world." I reached out to touch his sleeve, and this time he did not shrink away. His eyes rested on my hand and then flickered up and into my eyes.

"You are the best man I have ever known," I said. "And if I have not always shown you the humility and grace that I should have, I will from this day on."

He nodded, and there were tears in his eyes.

As I reached the door, I turned back. "I love you," I said.

He did not answer. With his back to me, I saw his shoulders hunch. I believe he was crying and did not want me to see.

"I love you," I said again. "And I will spend the rest of my life showing you my devotion."

I felt better as I went to my rooms. I thought we might put this behind us, that I would be given a second chance. Exhausted, I fell into slumber with ease. I walked in dreams of the tower and the desert.

Katherine came to me again. We stood in the shadow of the tower, looking out across the boundless desert. The tower was bathed in red light, reflected from the angry sun above and the bloody sand below. Dust rose, spiralling into tiny whirlwinds, streaking across the planes. There was a strange light, glowing and eerie. All was red and orange… the colours of flame and fire.

"The sands are running short," she said.

"The sands will never run short," I replied. "Layer upon layer… Dust upon dust. The winds make no impression. Never will they dissipate, never will they die."

"The sands are running short," she said again and turned to me.

In her eyes I saw two hourglasses, upturned. The glass vials at the top held sand, running into the bottom. It was almost spent.

"Time is running out," Katherine whispered.

Chapter Sixty-Seven

Greenwich Palace
May 1st 1536

May Day dawned fresh, warm, and with a touch of wildness. A celebration of love and renewal, its customs were entrenched in England's blood; a time for new beginnings. That was what I wanted.

Breathing a sigh of relief that Henry had sent for me, and that even if we were not entirely easy with one another, we were talking, I dressed with great care. I wanted to show him this could be our new beginning.

Early that morning, I sat on a chair with a blanket over my lap, sewing a shirt for Henry. I found myself marvelling upon the benevolence and purity of my husband's heart. *Truly, he is a man like no other. He has the best heart... the most forgiving nature.*

I told myself that day that I must be more like Henry. I should emulate his example, and become a better person. I dressed, thinking of this time of renewal and joy.

All over England people would celebrate. As dawn emerged, pink and gold on the skyline, maids would bathe their faces in morning dew, hoping to bring good fortune and beauty upon them. Villagers would march out into the forests to gather foliage; budding branches of blooms, flowers, twisted ivy and boughs of green leaves. The ringing sound of hunters' horns would blast in the woods. Doorsteps of scolds would be marked by alder boughs, and jades would find their steps decorated with a scattering of nuts. In the West Country, young lads would take a bucket of water and head into the streets, dunking any person they came across, especially if he be high ranking, into their brimming buckets. Only those with a piece of May, a flower or a tree sprig pinned to their coats, might escape their tricks.

Dairy women would dress their milk buckets with leaves and fresh flowers. Every door held a garland of buds and branches, and children would scatter blooms on neighbours' doorsteps to bring good fortune. Ritual battles would be enacted, with villagers jostling on hilltops to fight for the ancient right to control a glen. Wagons and carts were decked with flowers and trundled through the dirty streets, and maypoles would be erected, where people would take hands and dance about them in a circle. The base of the pole would be strewn with flowers and the pole itself bound in gay ribbon. Some reformers wanted to banish these customs, thinking them pagan, but I greeted such sights with joy. May Day was the coming of the new world. Why would God not want us to celebrate it?

And court was far from looking down upon the merry dance of May. Jousting and dancing were traditional on this day, and long ago, Henry and Katherine had gone a-Maying, enacting a masque where Henry and his men dressed up as Robin Hood and his merry band, as Katherine and her ladies sighed on flowery meads.

Perhaps one day, I thought, *Henry and I will do this.*

I processed from my chambers with a line of thirty ladies in my wake. Dressed in royal purple and cloth of gold, with a French hood trimmed with pearls upon my head, I looked magnificent, every inch a queen. I had taken care with my jewels, selecting those that Henry had given me with our initials entwined, so he might see that I was his alone. I set Norris out of mind. I had told him that nothing could come of our affections. I would cease to feel jealousy for something that could never be mine. I would hold my heart for my husband alone, setting foolish wishes and desires away. *You have not betrayed Henry,* I told myself. *When temptation came, you refused it. You did as you should, as was worthy of you.*

Guilt remained, however. No matter if Henry had forgotten his vows and betrayed me, I should not have nurtured affection, no matter how innocent, for another. Henry's forgiveness made me feel this shame. *Goodness lies in seeing our faults and rectifying them,* I thought. *You know your faults now, Anne Boleyn. Set them to mending.*

As we reached the jousting grounds, a crowd was already gathered, watching the knights with greedy eyes, to see whom they might wager upon to bring the greatest spoils.

The fresh wind blew, flouncing over the stands where pretty, plump cushions sat waiting. Despite the wind, the air was warm, and a balmy breeze fluttered through the streaming pennants of the nobles upon the field. I took my seat in the stands between the twin towers of the tiltyard, and looked out onto the gaily-coloured tents where knights were preparing for battle. Their horses were attended by young pages, brushing chestnut or white coats to shimmer like burnished copper or luminous pearl under the May sunshine.

Norris was leading the defenders as my brother led the answerers. Henry, still recovering from his injuries, was not to ride that day. He sat beside me as the lists were read, smiling at me with warmth in his eyes. At one point he took my hand. It was hesitant, but he laced his fingers through mine.

My heart pulsed with untamed gratitude and boundless, aching relief, thinking he was one of the best men in the world. *You will emerge from this ill event only stronger,* I thought. *There is nothing that can drive you apart.* Later, he went to speak to the knights, standing in the shadow of the green and white striped tents, whose sides flapped and billowed in the breeze.

I watched a squirrel as he ran over the dark earth, his red tail and coat buffeted by the breeze. Oblivious to the knights, he scampered happily over the earth, pausing to sniff the air, and, sensing no danger, ran on to clamber up a tree, his step light and fresh as the wind.

At one stage, Norris' horse became uncontrollable, and he could not ride him. Henry came forth with his own steed and handed the reins to Norris, a clear sign of favour, and one I celebrated. I had not placed Norris in danger.

The joust went on. The challengers were fierce and true. Their horses thundered across the earth, making the crowds scream with joy and terror. The answerers came back, breaking stout lances time and time again on the bodies of their foes. Splinters flew into the air, taken by the wind to cascade over the stands, falling upon the crowds as snowflakes raining from the skies. Ladies laughed and gallants screamed, each supporting their champion.

There was nothing to suggest anything was wrong.

But then, suddenly, Henry mounted his horse and turned from the field. A messenger had come, handed him a scrap of parchment, and then stepped back, his young face wary, as though he feared to be punished. Henry read the note and his face darkened. He glanced at me. I lifted a hand to wave, but he had already turned away.

Abruptly, he left the field, taking with him only six attendants and calling for Norris to follow. As they rode away I could see Henry questioning Norris closely, and from the distant glimpse I had of Norris' face, his questions brought my friend only horror.

That was the last time I saw my husband.

With the King gone, the joust tumbled to an ungainly close. Puzzled and worried, I rose and departed with my ladies, only to see Norfolk watching me with a strange smile on his face. He bowed as I passed, but as he rose that smirk lingered.

"Where is the King?" I asked when I arrived back at the palace.

"Gone to Westminster, Majesty," said Henry's servant.

"But... we are supposed to preside over the entertainments together."

The man stared blankly at me. What more could he say? Henry had chosen not to attend and that was that. No servant controls their master.

Neither Henry nor Norris resurfaced. I presided over the entertainments with a heart that beat like a drum in my breast. Anxiety rose again, consuming me. What was going on? Had this been any other time, I would have taken to a boat and gone to Henry, but something in me told me that I would not like what I found there.

I was told later that Henry had signed conditions for a treaty with France, and had gone to Westminster to tie up the last strands of this agreement.

"It requires François to end his alliance with Rome," my father told me.

I breathed in relief. Any agreement confirmed now would alter if Henry meant to set me aside. *You worry without cause,* I told myself. All was well. Henry believed in our innocence. There was nothing wrong.

But another voice was not so reassuring. It whispered, spilling much I did not want to hear. I sent for my brother.

"I want you to go to the King," I said. "And find out what is happening."

"He is working on the treaty," said George. "That is all."

"I fear it may not be." My eyes flashed to the dark panes in the windows. Night had fallen. Blackness covered the world like despair. "Please, George," I went on. "Go to Westminster."

"I will go on the morrow," he said. "I have to call at Whitehall first, to meet with Father."

"And then you will go to the King?"

He kissed my forehead. "I will," he said. "To calm you."

That was the last night of our liberty.

It took me hours to sleep. I tossed in my bed, wondering what was going on. Poor Mary Howard who shared my bed that night found no rest. But eventually I must have fallen into the realm of dreams, for I found myself on a horse, on a dusty road.

I looked up to see a palace. In one of the windows stood Katherine, watching me. I glanced at the road and there was Henry, waiting on his horse.

It was the day he had left her… The day he had committed himself to me.

I glanced up at Katherine again, and I saw the hourglasses in her eyes. As I watched, the last grain of sand fell.

Time is spent.

Katherine's mouth did not form the words, but they sounded in my head. I turned from her, urging my horse to follow Henry. But as I drew near, his horse raced ahead. He was calling for me, but I could not reach him. On and on I chased him, whipping my horse hard, as I never did in life. My hair billowed, thrashing my face and striking my hands. My breath was hard in my ears, as was the thundering of my heart.

I came to a stop on a long, dusty road. Henry had vanished, as had the palace holding Katherine.

There was no one and nothing there, but in the distance I could see the tower of blood. On the wind there were voices, crying out in terrible pain. But I could see no one.

I was alone.

Chapter Sixty-Eight

Greenwich Palace
May 2nd 1536

Early the next morning, I went to watch a tennis match. Henry was supposed to be playing, and I hoped to talk to him during a break in the matches, but when I arrived, I found his name had been taken from the lists.

"Is the King not competing today?" I asked Weston, who was.

"The King is at Whitehall, madam," he said. "Apparently there was an emergency Council meeting about France. The King means to sign a treaty with them."

"I wish I had known," I said, thinking that at least George would find Henry, as he had left for Whitehall with the dawn. "I could have counselled the King with my opinion."

"I believe it is not yet set in stone, my lady," the young man said, clearly itching to get to his match.

"Go, young Weston," I said, offering him a watery smile. "Play your best, for I will lay a wager on you to win."

"Then I will play for *you*, Your Majesty," he said. "And you will be my good luck charm."

Poor Weston. He did not know my luck had run out.

I caught his arm before he left. "Was Norris not meant to be partnering you?" I asked.

"He, too, is at Whitehall," said Weston.

It seemed strange that so many men who were supposed to be a part of these matches were absent, but I released Weston's arm. As he walked away I saw there was a hand print on his sleeve. I had not noted how wet my palms were.

I forgot to place my wager. When Weston won, I said to my ladies I was sad to have missed my chance. It was then that a messenger arrived. He handed me a note, telling me to present myself before the King's Privy Council immediately. They were waiting in the King's Council Chamber upstairs, it said, upon my pleasure.

Although I reasoned that this might have something to do with the treaty, I could not help but be frightened. It was rare for the Council to summon the Queen. Everything was strange. The air, the faces of the people… the atmosphere was palpable with suspense. I felt watched.

Something was going on.

I walked to the Council Chamber and as I entered I saw three men standing there, with faces grave as ghosts; Norfolk, Sir William FitzWilliam and Sir William Paulet.

"My lords," I said. "Is there news of the treaty?"

"That is not what we are here to speak of," said my uncle.

My head snapped up as he failed to address me as Majesty, and I liked not the smug look on his face. "Do you forget to whom you speak, Uncle?" I asked.

"Queen Anne," he said. I thought he was merely stating my title in answer to my reprimand, but he went on, "... you are accused of adultery with three men and treason against the King, your gracious husband. We are commanded to take you under arrest, and escort you to the Tower of London, where you will await trial and judgement for your incontinent living."

I stared at him, unable to speak. Unable to think. Unable to formulate a response.

"Do you have nothing to say?" asked my uncle.

"I deny all these charges… upon my very soul," I stammered. "Never have I betrayed the King, and never have I engaged in any act that might be construed as treason." My skin began to quiver. My heart was loud in my ears.

The men glanced at each other. I could see they did not believe me, or perhaps, they did not want to. I stepped forward and FitzWilliam pushed me back.

"Take your rude hands from the person of your Queen, sir!" I exclaimed. "I have done nothing to warrant such abuse of my name or person. Let me to the King. He must know that all of this is nonsense."

"It is on the King's order that we arrest you," said Norfolk.

My heart stalled. *Henry* had ordered this? Henry believed I was a traitor, an *adulterer*? On the basis of what? One unguarded jest? I stared at them in blind, dumb terror.

"You knew Norris and the musician, Smeaton, carnally, did you not?" FitzWilliam demanded, stepping forwards, satisfaction glimmering in his eyes. Once he had been Wolsey's creature. The Cardinal had named him his "treasure" and he had risen in favour because of him. Now he had a chance for revenge, he was not going to miss a moment of the pleasure it granted his restless heart.

"Norris?" I stuttered. "And Smeaton? *Smeaton*? You think I would lower myself so far as to not only betray my husband with *two* men, but to stoop so low beneath my station?"

"Was Norris a better lover then, my lady?" FitzWilliam taunted. "You will admit to him but not to the musician?"

"I admit to nothing, for nothing have I done!" I cried. My hands flailed, useless at my sides.

"Both men have confessed."

"Then they are liars. I have done nothing." *Confessed?* I thought. *To what?* What had they said? What had they accused me of?

"*Tut, tut, tut.*" Norfolk *tsked*, shaking his head. "Adding the sin of falsehood to those you already hold will not endear you to God, my lady."

His was the face of evil. He delighted in my pain, fear and confusion. He took pleasure in it. Norfolk's eyes were long and dark; tunnels which reached not only into his mind, but further, into all minds linked and bonded by the same iniquity ... to the darkness and chaos of Hell, where all evil becomes as one.

"I have done nothing!" I cried, my heart beating wild. "*Nothing*! Let me to the King. Let me see him! He cannot believe this of me!"

"He does not wish to see you, nor to associate with such a whore as you." FitzWilliam's voice was scathing and I blinked to hear him accuse me of being a jade.

It was then I realised. It was a hideous, dawning realisation... I was never going to get to Henry. They would not allow it. Had I not always said that when Henry put someone out of sight they went out of mind? He was leaving me, just as he had left Katherine. He was throwing me to the wolves of court.

"Am I to have no justice?" I asked, my voice shaking. "Am I to be condemned before I am tried?"

"You will have justice, Majesty," said Paulet, stepping forwards and scowling at the other two. I could see he did not approve of their harsh handling of this meeting, and he was the only one to use my royal title. "You will have a trial."

"I will be tried, for this? For lies?" I could have wept. I was shaking. From where had all this horror sprung? At what point had I deserved this? I was about to be ushered into Hell, on Henry's command.

"You will have a chance to defend yourself, before a jury," he said.

The commission... I thought, the court that was already set up, already prepared to try and condemn in matters of treason. And they had Norris and Smeaton under arrest... was this why it had been arranged? So they might move with swift speed to convict not only me, who would be tried by my peers, but Norris and Smeaton, men of common blood...

And it was then I realised whose snare I had run blindly into.

Cromwell.

He had set up the commission. He and Audley had insisted on it. Was it for this purpose? Had I been blithely thinking that I had bested him as he worked in the shadows against me?

They questioned me for more than an hour, repeating the same charges until they were branded into my brain. I denied everything. I said over and over that I had done nothing. It made no impression.

"You will be taken to your apartments, Majesty," Paulet said, seeing I was close to fainting. "And there you will await the tide to take you to the Tower."

"No," I said, my head swimming. I felt sick, dizzy, lost... I had wandered into a nightmare. "*Please*. Let me see my husband."

"I have not the authority to allow that," Paulet said. "I am sorry, madam."

I was marched to my apartments under guard. My ladies were taken away. I had not a moment to explain before they were bundled out, their faces white and drawn.

The door banged shut.

I heard guards take their places outside. Armour jangling against sword sheaths, footsteps taking position. I stared at the door with wide, wild eyes. I looked to the windows, and thought about breaking one, clambering out onto the turrets, and climbing down to run through the parks, to run away.

But I could not. I did not have strength or means to break the glass and climb out. I would never survive. I would die. For a moment it seemed this might be a better fate than waiting for what would come.

I walked about the chamber, my footsteps echoing in the oppressive silence. *My God, Norris!* I thought. *What have you told them?* Had he spoken of his feelings for me? Of mine for him? And what had Smeaton said? I could think of nothing I had ever said to the young lad that might be construed as treason, or evidence of adultery. Norris had told me that Smeaton thought himself in love with me… had this fantasy turned into reality in his mind?

They brought dinner to me. Only three ladies served and they shuffled about, silent as death, not meeting my eyes. Henry's messenger did not arrive to wish me his best, as was normal. I could eat nothing. I stared at the food until it was taken away.

That afternoon, I sank down on my throne. I could feel nothing but pure terror.

How could Henry believe this of me?

He believes because he wants to believe, said Katherine.

They came for me just after my dismal dinner, entering with a warrant for my arrest. Almost the whole Council had come. Until the moment I saw Henry's signature on the warrant, I had thought all this might just be a trick. It was then I knew it was not. I wanted to think it was a forgery… that someone else had commanded this, but I knew Henry's signature. Even if someone else had convinced him to sign, he had put his name to this paper.

I was not given leave to pack belongings, or take any money, but was told everything would be provided.

"If this is the King's pleasure," I said, thinking that if I cooperated, if I was submissive, Henry might see reason. "I am ready to obey."

I will never know how I stayed so calm. I think I was numb, numb with shock. My blood was frozen, my mind was deadened. There was no sensation in me. Common noises, my breathing, the sound of my heart, were so loud, so intense. I followed the guards like a little puppy; subservient and obedient… everything Henry had always wanted me to be, I became. Perhaps it was a shame that he was not present to witness his victory over me.

As I walked from the chamber, I caught Cromwell's eye. He was not standing at the back, but near the front, next to Audley. There was nothing in his eyes that suggested he was behind this, but I knew he was. I could feel a sense of excitement and apprehension wafting from him, perfume on his skin.

It was then I knew.

Henry did not mean to abandon me, leave me, desert me… I would not be sent to a castle like Katherine. I would not be offered a life in a convent. Henry did not mean to merely cast me aside.

He was going to kill me.

Chapter Sixty-Nine

The Tower of London
May 2nd 1536

The waters of the Thames lapped at the side of the little boat. They seemed to whisper, taunting me. *Trapped, trapped, trapped*, they murmured as they flowed past. *Trapped, trapped, trapped.*

A hare caught in a snare. A doe chased into a corner. A woman, accused of the vilest of sin, the rankest of living, being taken to a prison where once she had stayed before being made Queen.

Just as I had learned to stand, Henry had pushed me to my knees. Just as I had found my strength, he took it from me. And how would he ensure that I never rose to stand against him again? He would take my life.

Once, I had sworn I would never again be made a victim, as I had in France. In all the years that had passed, I had left victimised Anne behind. I had become a survivor, taking revenge in living my life, in restoring my soul. But my husband had made me a victim again. He had stolen my power. He had taken it from me, just as that monster had tried to in the arbour on that dark night. Once more I was rendered powerless, helpless. Once more my soul was in peril of being stolen from my body.

I stared at the water. The afternoon light was grainy and thin. The sun was high in the heavens, but its warmth did not reach me. Banks of clouds held it back, mist swathed it in a veil of white. There was no warmth left for me in this world.

It was usual for prisoners of rank to go to the Tower under cover of darkness. Not so for me. My enemies wanted the world to witness my disgrace, shame and fear. They sent me in broad daylight.

Not quite three years ago I had taken this same route, travelling by barge from Greenwich to the Tower before my coronation. Had my enemies sent me by water to remind me of those days of glory? To remind me how far I had fallen?

I knew what happened to people who went to the Tower under the shadow of treason. Once, it had been but a royal residence, but now, with the ghosts of Fisher and More, with the wailing wraiths of the monks in its dungeons, with phantoms of all those accused of heresy and treason trapped inside its stone confines, it was a place not of royal, sumptuous living, but of common, ugly death.

And now the Queen would join those ghosts.

Crowds had gathered at the river banks. News of my arrest had spread, and everyone who had ever hated me had turned out to jeer as my barge passed by. Norfolk stood at one end of the boat, with Oxford, Henry's Great Chamberlain, and Sandys, the Lord Chamberlain. Norfolk had attempted to lecture me as we set off, saying that my paramours had confessed, and I might as well do the same. I turned my face from him. I could not bear the glee in my uncle's eyes.

I had heard tales of mystical night creatures who fed on blood. I had never heard of one who supped on pain and fear.

I told myself not to stare at my hands, to keep my head up and my eyes fixed on the waters ahead. I did not look at the crowds. I did not look at my uncle to witness his barely concealed relish at my distress. *A sinner would look at their hands,* I told myself. I had done nothing wrong. Everyone must see there was no guilt in me.

We landed at the Water Gate, and I was greeted by Master Kingston, the Lieutenant of the Tower. Once, Henry had been here to meet me. He had taken me in his arms and kissed me, one hand upon the lump of our daughter on my front. But there was no husband waiting with love in his eyes. Now there was only Kingston. They called him the Angel of Death.

Trapped, trapped, trapped, said the little waves of the river as they broke against the boat. *Trapped, trapped, trapped.*

My mind was seething. Thoughts swarmed, blood rushed, and mindless, heedless, raw and naked panic washed over me.

Kingston helped me from the boat and I stumbled against him, weakened by terror. "Master Kingston," I said, my voice shaking. "Shall I be taken to a dungeon?"

"No, madam," he said, holding me up. "You shall go to the royal lodgings that you lay in at your coronation."

"It is too good for me," I cried, faint with relief that I would not see the inside of a grim cell. "*Jesu, have mercy on me!*"

I fell to my knees and started to pray. My words fell over each other, bursting from my mouth in panicked breaths. My hands were trembling, clasped together. Every drop of blood in my body quaked, an earthquake inside me. "God in Heaven protect me," I said. "Sweet Lord Jesus, help me. God in Heaven hear me. Cast Your light upon me."

Prayers became jumbled in my brain. I could not call any one psalm to mind. They had become as one. "Put not your trust in princes, nor in the son of man, in whom there is no help… But be not far from me, O Lord; O my strength, hasten Thee to help me. Deliver my soul from the sword… O my God, I trust in thee, let me not be ashamed, let not my enemies triumph over me… The Lord is my light and my salvation; whom shall I fear? The Lord is the strength of my life; of whom shall I be afraid?... Deliver me not over into the will of mine enemies; for false witnesses are risen up against… Forsake me not, O Lord. O my God be not far from me. Make haste to help me, O Lord, my salvation… They have sharpened their tongues like a serpent, adder's poison is under their lips. Keep me, O Lord, from the hands of the wicked; preserve me from the violent man…"

I looked up. No rain had fallen that day. Small clouds, like tousled wool, drifted in the skies. The Tower was bathed in the red light of the sun, breaking through the clouds. As I stared at it, I seemed to see the tower that had come to my dreams, oh, so many times.

The tower of blood stood in the sandy desert.

A cannon sounded, telling the world that a prisoner of high rank had been brought to the Tower. I wept and then I started to laugh. I could not stop.

Everyone stared at me. Everyone looked. The shell of Anne Boleyn cracked. The broken one crashed free.

Waves of strange, shattered laughter spilled from my mouth, drifting over the Tower, over the walls, shattering against stone, breaking into dust.

Dust of my dreams. Dust of my love. All was dust and ashes. All was burned and destroyed.

*

"Mistress Aucher," I breathed as the ladies who were to serve me were brought into the dim chamber I had been taken to. Her familiar face was a boon to my ruptured spirits. The women brought to me that day were all creatures of Cromwell, save her.

Mistress Stoner was the wife of Sir Walter, Henry's Sergeant-at-arms. Elizabeth Wood, Lady Boleyn, was my aunt, but her husband, James, my father's younger brother, was a staunch supporter of Lady Mary. Lady Shelton was the mother of Mary and Margaret, but she had turned against me long ago because of my endless demands about chastising Lady Mary, and perhaps, too, because I had made her daughter a whore. Mistress Margaret Coffin, a hideously appropriate name, was wife to William, my Master of Horse, but no friend to me, and Mary Scrope, Lady Kingston, was the wife of Sir William Kingston. She had once served Katherine.

They were all hostile. I could feel aggression emanating from them. The only exception was Mistress Aucher, and she, a mere chamberer, was not permitted to speak to me.

"You may speak only when my wife is present, madam," Kingston said as I was ushered in.

"Why?" My voice sounded so light, as though it were already an echo.

"So that all you might say can be recorded. For the sake of your honesty, and for what may come in your trial, madam."

"The King seeks to test me," I said, hysterically groping in the tangle of my mind for a reason I was sent here. "I think the King seeks to prove me. He tests my love and the courage of my love. I will show him I am true."

I did not know what I was saying. My mind was unravelling. Twisted, long, dark spirals and spindles of lurid misery were loose inside my head. Disjoined horror, unreal, *unreal* suffused me. There was nothing structured, nothing of sense. My mind succumbed to the labyrinth of perdition I had kept locked away. It was a twisted knot of dark tunnels, pits and traps, spiralling out from one central core where I, a quivering, huddled creature, lay curled about myself like an infant. Outside the labyrinth, keening winds howled, screaming at me. Thoughts, memories, events... they all raced past me on the wings of the wind. Bare trees heaved against infinite blackness, their branches thrashing the ground, snapping into the air. The skies above were grey and dark. There was no sun in my world.

A world of nightmares washed over me, claiming my wits. Everything was strange and unnatural, yet too uncontrolled, too uncompromising to be fiction. There is nothing so strange as life. Books must make sense. Tales must flow as the straightest, most clement of streams. There was nothing of that now. Life is not as pretty as tales told to children. Life is chaos; dawn, dusk, twilight and moon, bound and bonded together as one.

This must be real, I thought, *for it is too strange and wild to be a story.*

"Now abideth faith, hope and love," I muttered, quoting the Bible as though it could save me. "But the chief of these is love." I stared with glazed eyes at Lady Kingston, who glanced at her husband in fright. "Corinthians chapter one, verse thirteen," I said. "Chief of these is love."

I knew not what I was saying. The broken one was not a creature of reason, but of chaos. I thought Henry was trying to test me, trying to punish me. My mind was wild, lost and shattered. The light from the candles was too bright, so was that from the windows. I could not look at it. My eyes flickered from one woman to the next, searching for any scrap of compassion. I found none.

Mistress Aucher clasped my shaking hand, but Lady Kingston drove her away. As her hand dropped, I saw barren fright in my old nurse's eyes. They would not let her comfort me, but I felt the love within her heart. It was good to feel something other than hate, for that was all the others bore for me.

"My bishops and chaplains will speak for me," I said, gabbling on, even though I had just been informed my words would be recorded. "They will speak. They will tell the King I am an honest woman, who has done no wrong. They will speak for me."

They just stared.

"Will you bring the Sacrament to my chambers?" I asked Kingston, suddenly serene at the thought. I knew not that I was hysterical. "I would have the comfort of God within me. I will pray for mercy, for I am as clear from the company of any man as I am clear from you. I am the King's true, wedded wife."

"Such a request will have to go through the King," he told me.

"And as with Fisher, it will be denied." I stared at Kingston and then my eyes flickered to the ceiling. "My God, bear witness there is no truth in these charges, for I am as clear from the company of man as from sin. I am clear of sin. I am free of sin."

Reason abandoned me. I had only held a thread of it in my hands for a moment, and it was gone. I started to talk. I could not stop. "Why am I here?" I asked. "For what I said to Norris? It was nothing. The King cannot suspect me. I cannot be accused on slight words. I *cannot*."

I stared at the window. For a moment, there was silence.

"Master Kingston," I said turning to him. He stepped back as he saw my glittering, unhinged eyes. "Why am I here?"

The man thought I had lost my senses. I could feel the blankness on my face. I must have looked like a witless fool.

"Madam, I know not why," he said. "But it is my office to guard and tend to you."

"When saw you last the King?"

"At the Tiltyard at Greenwich," he said.

"I pray you, Master Kingston, tell me where my husband is?"

"At Whitehall, madam."

"Where is my lord father?"

"At court, my lady."

"And my brother? Where is my sweet brother?"

"Also at Whitehall, my lady."

"My brother will speak for me," I said, a burst of relief flooding through me. "He will tell the King I am a good woman, without sin of which I am accused. He will tell the King. He *will*. My good brother would never abandon me. He would always protect me. O, where is my sweet brother? I left him at Whitehall but I know not why he is not here."

I looked about wildly. My hands went to my gown and started to tear at the crimson silk and cloth of gold, ripping it from me as though in escaping it, I could flee my doom. Kingston tried to stop me, but I went on, my hands as claws, rending the fabric at my breast. "I hear I am accused of three men," I wailed. "*Three*! I can say no more but if I should open my body and reveal my heart."

Kingston tried to take hold of me and I fell across his arm. "Oh, Norris!" I cried. "Hast thou accused me? Thou art here in this Tower, and thou and I shall die together!"

"Mark, thou art here too," I murmured, thinking of that young, handsome man who had wanted nothing more than to be allowed into the ring of bright people at court. "My mother will die of sorrow!" I cried out. "She is not well, and this will end her! My friend, Elizabeth Browne, my Lady of Worcester… will her child not stir in her body to hear of my fate?" Sobbing, I lay across his arm.

"What should be the cause of that?" asked Lady Kingston.

"It was for the sorrow she took of me," I murmured. "When I lost my baby. Her child has not quickened, for sadness for me, and now it will not live within her."

The ladies exchanged loaded glances. There was great suspicion in their eyes. What I had said might have sounded like prophecy… as a witch would make.

"Will I know no justice?" I asked Kingston.

"Even the meanest subject in this kingdom receives the King's justice, madam."

I stared into his face for a moment, and again I started to laugh. Eerie and strange, mirth burst from me, and once unleashed, I could not hold it back. I slipped from his hands and landed with a dull thud on the floor. I sat there laughing, demented, lost and utterly alone.

They gathered me up from the floor, almost carrying me into my coronation chambers. I was still laughing.

Justice… was that what I would receive? I knew it was not so. I had no access to legal counsel. There would be no one to speak for me unless my brother could reach Henry. And Henry… he was a mass of paranoia at the best of times. What would he do in the throes of this anger and rage, of jealousy and lies? Never before had an English Queen been arrested in such a way for adultery and treason; never had one been imprisoned like this. And they would not stop there. I was too dangerous to be left alive. Henry would be kept from me, and my enemies would destroy me.

I saw Wolsey laughing in my mind. I saw Fisher, More and the monks. I saw Katherine and her daughter. Justice would not be served. It never had before.

Henry had sent me here to be rid of me. Cromwell had granted him the means. No more would England have to stand for a queen who could not bear a son. No more would Cromwell have to fear being removed. No more would my foes have to scrape and bow to me.

No more. No more.

I was undone.

My mind was warped and frayed… broken and bent… my enemies had taken a stick to the sand, merging stories that did not belong together into one of their own creation. The sands of my story were flowing into that of another.

Once my mouth opened, it would not close. Many times had I thought that my tongue was my greatest enemy, and now it proved itself. Trying to find light in the shadowlands of my mind, I babbled incoherently, saying that Henry meant to test me; that Henry wanted proof of my love. I spoke of Norris. I spoke of Smeaton and my encounter with him in Henry's chambers.

I talked and I talked, trying to find a reason for my imprisonment. In the corner of my eye I could see Mistress Aucher watching, silently commanding me to stop. Voices in my mind told me the same, told me to be quiet, for all that I said would be used against me.

But I could not.

I garbled on. It was all nothing. Nothing more than words exchanged at court. Of meaningless, chance encounters. But it would all be used against me.

As I cast my face from the women who stared at me, I thought I saw a movement. Draughts blew in the chambers, moving the tapestry from the wall. I saw eyes. Fisher and More. Wolsey and Katherine… they were all there, as real as the women sent to guard me.

I was not alone.

Ghosts and spies surrounded me.

Chapter Seventy

The Tower of London
May 3rd 1536

Kingston had lied. My brother was in the Tower.

The women who sat with me told me that my brother arrived on the same day as I, and was imprisoned in one of the towers. Norris and Smeaton, too, were here. George was the third man with whom I stood accused.

I was not only an adulterer in the eyes of these people. I was guilty of incest.

When they told me George was, too, under arrest, I thought I might fly apart. There was nothing that could have horrified me more, nothing that could have scared me as that did. The thought that George was in danger and I could not reach him, could not even *speak* to him, was sickening. I tried to tell them of all the goodness in him, but they just watched me with blank eyes. What were they to do? They were not my judges.

When I failed to convince them, I fell upon a stool.

How could anyone think this? I thought. *How could the thought have even reached anyone's mind?*

I knew not how anyone had come to these conclusions. I was surrounded by my women at court, guarded by them as much as I was tended to. How I could have lain with even one man, let alone three, was unknown to me, and to accuse me of having sex with my brother was obscene. There was nothing perverse in our relationship. He was my brother and I loved him as such. How could anyone think I would do something that went against everything of faith and honour within me?

Do you know me so little, Henry? I wondered. *That you would think this of me?*

But I wondered if he did believe it. He was a jealous man. Ample proof of that had I had over the years. Jealousy can lead to all kinds of false nightmares being produced by the mind. Or, as Katherine had whispered, did he simply *want* to believe? Was he so desperate to be rid of me that he would take any story, no matter how wild, and accept it?

My guards had ceased to try to stop me talking. It was not in their interests. Despite the warning, ringing sound of clamouring voices inside me telling me to hush my mouth, on and on I talked; a dam broaching its defences; a lamb bleating as the wolf bears down upon her.

They realised that Mistress Aucher was trying to send me eye signals to stop me talking. They had her removed.

Within twelve hours of coming to this grim, stark Tower, I had told them much. I spoke of Norris and Smeaton. I told them of my brother's love, no more to me than the love of a sibling; chaste and proper, without hint of scandal, but as I spoke of George they could see the naked fright in my heart. They took note of all I said, hoping to report it to their masters, to gain rich rewards by incriminating me only further in this fantasy.

And they told me much. I was accused of adultery, incest and treason, and my husband believed I was guilty. They told me that Henry had gone to his mistress, and become enfolded in her warm arms. Jane's family of vipers kept him close. They said I would be divorced on the basis of my pre-contract with Percy. They said on the night I was taken, Henry had called Fitzroy to him, and wept upon his shoulder, telling his son I had been about to poison him, and that I had had more than one hundred lovers.

"I fear Weston," I burbled. "I spoke to him because he loved my kinswoman, Mary Shelton, and not his wife."

On and on I rambled. I did not know my enemies had not formulated their plans; that my incoherent burbling would condemn more innocents.

"Weston said that he loved one amongst all I named better than the rest," I said, wringing my hands. "And that was me."

Soon, Weston would join our gathering in the Tower.

*

"What of my father?" I asked Kingston and his wife that night.

I sat at their table. A gross parody of honour was enacted as servants waited upon me. Prisoner I was, but still was I Queen. There had to be at least a feeble offering of respect.

I ate nothing. I could not even bear the smell. Everything made me sick.

"My father," I pressed. "He is not also here, is he?"

Kingston's eyes were troubled. It was his duty to tend to my needs, and to report to Cromwell and Henry, but my distress unnerved him. He did not want me to fall into chaos again. Perhaps that would have been to my advantage, for it was illegal to execute those whose minds had come unhinged.

"Your father is not here," said Kingston. "Nor has he or any of your Howard kin been accused of anything."

I understood. Father had bought his liberty. Would he dare trouble himself for me? For George, his heir? I doubted it.

I chuckled without humour. Kingston did not like my laugh. He feared it. It broke from my mouth like a greyhound coursing hares. The women who sat with me welcomed it not either. They thought it was the sound of the witch they had been told I was.

"The King sends me here to prove me," I said. Kingston nodded. He had heard my desperate quest for meaning too many times to be astonished.

"Perhaps that is so, my lady."

"He wants to know my love is true," I went on. "I will show him it is."

"I am sure, my lady."

Kingston and his wife went back to their dinners. I began to eat, and found I was suddenly ravenous. I drank deep of the wine that was offered, ate until my plate was empty, but nothing filled me, not the meat, not the bread, not the wine.

There was an emptiness within me. It had been there for a long time. I had kept it hidden, but it had claimed me. I was not Anne Boleyn, the construct I had created to protect myself… I was the shattered soul, the defeated heart.

My head spinning with wine, I was taken back to my chambers, and there I burst out laughing again. "The King will kill me," I announced to the grim faces of the watching women. "He will kill me, and yet I have done nothing to deserve this ill treatment."

"You have done much," one murmured.

"To whom?" I demanded. "To you? Tell me when I ever raised hand to you, and I will say I am sorry, good Mistress. Tell me whom I have offended and I will set it right." I wrapped my arms around my body and began to weep.

"I am undone," I murmured as they took my clothes from me. "I am undone and you would have me lose still more. You would take everything from me. My brother is here. What will they do to us?"

My belief that Henry was testing me was receding swift as the flesh on a dead man's hands.

They had no answer for me and again I laughed. "You cannot accuse me of anything," I said. "The Lord God knows my innocence, and He will tell the King. They are close in mind and spirit. The Almighty will speak for me."

They led me to the bed. "Someone will speak for me. Someone will. I am not alone, as you all think me."

I fell into the bed and turned my face from them, staring at the wall. For a moment, a flash of memory danced before my eyes. Another wall. Another time. Another moment when I had stared at a wall, seeing crumbling plaster hidden behind the cloth of tapestry. The day I had lost my child.

The eyes returned. Fisher and More stared, their ghostly faces pale, unmoved by my distress. I could flee my demons no more. They were all around me.

"I am not alone," I murmured.

Chapter Seventy-One

The Tower of London
May 4th 1536

"They say he wears his cuckold horns with merriness," murmured Lady Shelton to Mistress Coffin.

Coffin… had they picked her for her name? To remind me of the fate of traitors? My ears pricked up. I had been silent for a few hours, lapsed into a state of numb disbelief, but as they spoke, I knew they were talking of Henry.

I looked around. Why here? Why send me to the chambers prepared for my coronation? To torture me with memories of happiness and joy? My cruel captors knew how to whip me with their chains. I looked down at my hands. They trembled no more. The shaking which I had thought might tear me apart when I first entered these rooms had subsided. Now, it was an inward tremor, a constant itch I could not scratch. Every now and then it would erupt, making my teeth shake.

"My daughter came to deliver clothes to me this morning," Lady Shelton went on. "She said the King has announced he was seduced into marriage by witchcraft, and now is released." She drew her needle through the cloth she was working on, thinking I was in such a stupor of dread that I could not hear. "But he gambols at court, feasting with ladies until midnight and spending time with his men upon his barge…" she smiled. "Or, at least, those who are left with him."

"I have been told he will not marry again, unless his Council ask it of him," said Mistress Coffin.

"He has moved Mistress Seymour to another house," said Lady Shelton. "And he *will* marry her. The people know it. You have heard the ballads they sing… the ones from those pamphlets."

The pamphlets… I had all but forgotten I had asked them to be issued. It must have gone ahead whilst I was busy being arrested. I forced myself to swallow the laughter that wanted to rise from within. So now everyone would know that Henry had a mistress, and he was seeking to put her on my throne. That was why he had moved Jane, as once he had sent me to Hever; he wanted to distance her from scandal… to pretend he was not simply switching one wife for another.

"He sneaks out of Greenwich to visit Mistress Seymour," said Lady Shelton. "Mark my words, there will be a new Queen soon."

By God, the effort it was to contain my laughter! It was not happiness, but an expression of horror wanting escape. Henry was to wed again, and I was not yet gone. Would he take my life, or send me to the hallowed nunnery Katherine had never accepted?

How long had this been planned? How long had I sat with Henry, waited on him and shared his bed as he plotted against me? How had it come to this?

Mistress Aucher rose and went to the bag of silks which sat near me. Stooping, she rummaged in the bag, pretending to select a new thread. "Archbishop Cranmer has written to the King, protesting your innocence," she whispered, her voice scarcely more than a breath as I continued to stare at the wall. "The people… they do not believe the charges either, Majesty."

With that, she stood and went back to her seat.

Was it so? Did the people of England, who had never liked or supported me, know what was being done? Had they read the pamphlets and understood that Henry wanted rid of his wife, so he might take another? Did it matter? It had not before, with Katherine.

I stared at my hands. My long fingers. The rings upon them. The three I wore for my dead children shone. I thought of Elizabeth, and then tried not to. It was too much to bear to think that she might too be in danger.

I looked up as all the women moved to the window. Ghosting behind them, a frail shadow of myself, I followed. Looking down into the courtyard, I saw two new prisoners being brought in.

Weston… and Brereton.

More of my lovers? I had feared that my talk about Weston might have brought him here, but I had little expected he would come as a prisoner. I had thought he had spoken against me, and that was why I stood accused, but he, too, was a prisoner.

And Brereton? When had I even mentioned him as I rambled on?

"Weston and *Brereton*," said Mistress Stoner, her tone rising with surprise.

"He opposed Cromwell in Wales," I said numbly, making them start. They had not realised I was behind them.

"If he is here, it is because of *you*, madam, not Master Cromwell," said Mistress Stoner.

"He is here to get him out of the way," I said dully. "Another of my friends taken so that Cromwell might gather more power into his hands." They stared at me and I chuckled. "You are fools to think otherwise," I said. "Listen to the ditties sung in the streets, and you will find the true reason we are all brought here to die." I laughed harder. "What?" I asked. "You will not take notes on what I say now? For what reason? Because you fear your master? Because you fear the truth?"

"You are losing your sense again," she said.

"No, indeed," I said. "I think at last I am restored."

The smoke had cleared. The broken one fell back. I could see.

I could never have been brought down alone. Those who would speak for me, those who might reach Henry, they had to fall too. Norris, George, Weston, Brereton… They were all here because of me. Smeaton was the weakest link. He had vanished before the May Day celebrations, some said to play in a noble house. I would wager that house had been Cromwell's, and once Mark was there, he was made to say much. Weston was here because I had spoken of him in my fevered angst, and Norris for my conversation with him. George was imprisoned because my brother would never rest if harm was coming for me. And Brereton? He was my ally, it was true, but we had never been so close that this pirate could be considered an intimate. He was a boon for Cromwell. Remove Brereton, and all Cromwell's problems in Wales and Cheshire would fade away.

Smeaton had been the catalyst, but we would all be thrown into Cromwell's crucible. From the molten fire of our destruction would Cromwell forge a new world, one where he owned all the power.

I watched them taken to their separate towers and went back to my seat. My mind was whirring, and although the fug of terror was still upon me, rationality was breaking through.

I would not be condemned without trial. I held small hope that this would aid me, for in the courts it was for the accused to prove their innocence, rather than for the court to prove guilt. Most who were brought to trial knew that their end was a foregone conclusion, and pleaded guilty in order to receive mercy.

I would not give Henry that satisfaction.

I would not go quietly to my death. I would stand. I would fight, if not for my life, for my good name.

*

"Your brother's wife has sent a letter to the King," said Mistress Aucher as she helped me in the privy. This was the only place we could talk without the others hearing. We had not much time. They would come looking if we tarried too long, and would stop her doing even this slight duty.

"Jane will do all she can for my brother," I said, thinking at least we had one ally, no matter how insignificant, on the outside. "She loves him."

"She sent a letter," Mistress Aucher said, rustling my skirts so it sounded like we were busy. "And he wept over it. Your cousin, Bryan, delivered it."

A wash of coldness swept over me. "Bryan is no friend to us," I whispered. "Why would Jane have asked him to bring the message?"

"I know nothing more, my lady."

"Is she at court?"

"She is in the company of Cromwell, often, so I hear."

Another wave of chilly cold. Was it possible Jane, like my father, had turned on us in return for clemency? I could not believe it. Me, she might abandon, but not George. Surely not George. He was her light in the darkness, her North Star. What would she do without him?

But as I remembered those green glinting eyes full of pain and jealousy, I had cause to ponder again. George had talked of setting her aside... was she doing that to him? Would she take revenge?

"Come," I said. "We must not be too long."

"My lady…" Mistress Aucher's voice fractured. "I know you are innocent, even if no one else will believe me. I came here as ordered, and I told them I would report on you, but I will say nothing."

"Say *something*," I urged, "*anything*. If they think you feel for me, they will take you away. I cannot be without you. You are my only comfort."

She nodded, tears leaching from her crinkled eyes.

"Are you done in there, my lady?" called Mistress Coffin.

"Almost, good Mistress." I grasped Mistress Aucher's hand. "You must get word to my mother," I whispered. "I cannot send a letter, but at some stage, when you are not watched, when my fate is decided, you must tell her. Tell her George and I are innocent, as are all the others. Tell her I love her."

"I will."

We emerged and I was surrounded once more. They did not like leaving me with Mistress Aucher, but she was the only one I would allow into the privy with me. I had to be attended. No matter how unlikely, there was a chance I might squeeze myself down the foul-smelling tunnel that ran into the waters of the Thames, or sneak myself into the gardens where once I had strolled thinking of the good I might do England.

What good I might do, I thought bitterly. *I cannot even do good for myself.*

I returned to my seat and took up my Bible. "The Lord is my shepherd, I shall not want," I murmured. "He maketh me to lie down in green pastures; He leadeth me beside the still waters. He restoreth my soul; He leadeth me in the paths of righteousness for His name's sake. Yea, though I walk through the valley of the shadow of death, I shall fear no evil, for Thou art with me…"

I tried to lose myself in the Word of God, tried to draw comfort, but all I could think of was the men in this tower and wonder what Henry would do to them, and to me.

Chapter Seventy-Two

The Tower of London
May 5th – 6th 1536

As the fifth day of May dawned, new prisoners arrived.

Tom Wyatt and Richard Page.

Page had done many services for me in the past. He was Fitzroy's Vice-Chamberlain, and Captain of Henry's bodyguard. He had been absent from court since April, busy at his estates, but clearly now they thought he was another of my lovers. Tom, of course, all knew was my close friend, and once-admirer. *You spiteful little boy,* I said to my husband in my mind. Was Henry willing to remove a man he had once been jealous of from life in order to be rid of me? And Page? He was a servant, a sometime friend, but hardly a close acquaintance. Had he done something to annoy Cromwell, or would *any* man I had ever spoken to be committed to this stark tower?

I watched them arrive with a bleak expression. I gave nothing more to the women who watched. What more could I offer? Seven men were now in this tower. Seven souls brought to defame my name and pay the price of Cromwell's ambition in blood and ignominy.

"Inventories of their estates are already drawn up, so my daughters say," said Lady Shelton to Mistress Stoner.

"The King will take the price of their treason in blood and in coin," was her reply.

"Not yet tried," I said. "Not yet found guilty, but already ravens circle for rich pickings."

They stared at me in surprise. Did my words shock them? Surprise them by proclaiming that when men were condemned others would profit? Or was it just that I had spoken... that I, a woman accused of sexual impropriety, would *dare* lift my voice?

That night I was taken to dine with Kingston and his lady again. Their table was fine, set with rich pewter and holding birds of the forests and beasts of the bracken. Lady Kingston was trying to disguise her terror of me, and not succeeding. The women who watched had told her of my strange talk and feral laughter. She thought me a witch, as they did.

"The King wist what he did when he put two such about me as Lady Boleyn and Mistress Coffin," I said in a scathing tone. "They tell me nothing about my lord father, nor anything of comfort." I gazed at Kingston. "I asked them if my father was likely to be arrested, and Lady Boleyn said that my intrigues had brought me to this. They told me that Smeaton was chained, and I told them that is because he is no gentleman. I know nothing of him. He was a musician in the King's household. He played for me sometimes, but I did not know him well."

Kingston and his lady said nothing.

"Tell me," I said, taking wine from a server. "The men accused with me, will they have to shift for themselves… make their own beds?"

"Nay, I warrant you, my lady," Lady Kingston said, her eyes fixed on her pewter plate. "They have maids to serve."

"They might well make *ballets* now," I said, gravely insulting the name of all puns by rhyming *ballad* with *pallet*; the type of beds used in the Tower. Kingston and his lady offered polite smiles and I went on. "But there is none who could offer ballads but Rochford," I said, speaking of my brother.

"Could not Wyatt do the same?" asked Lady Kingston.

I stared. "Aye…" I said cautiously. "You speak right there, Lady Kingston. Wyatt could do a ballad of this time of injustice."

I went back to my plate. Were they trying to trick me? Get me to say something to incriminate Tom? Already I had condemned Weston. I would not allow another to fall.

"My lord my brother will die," I said, staring at my plate.

They said nothing, but I knew they thought I was correct. And they knew I would die, too.

*

The next day I asked for parchment and a quill.

"You are not permitted to write to anyone in this tower," said Lady Kingston.

"I will write to my husband," I said. "For I am his one, true wife still, am I not? Would you deny me this?"

Kingston approved the request, and although I doubted if it would reach Henry, I wrote. My flesh shook, despoiling my usually fine hand. The end result looked as though a spider had fallen in ink and crept across the page.

"Sire," I wrote. *"Your Grace's displeasure, and my imprisonment are things so strange unto me, as to what to write, or what to excuse, I am altogether ignorant. Whereas you sent unto me, willing me to confess a truth, and so obtain your favour, by such a one whom you know to be my ancient and professed enemy; I no sooner received the message by him than I rightly conceived your meaning, and if, as you say, confessing truth may procure my safety, I shall with willingness and duty perform your command.*

But let not Your Grace ever imagine that your poor wife will ever be brought to acknowledge a fault, where not so much as thought thereof proceeded. And to speak a truth, never Prince had wife more loyal in all duty, and in all true affection, than you have found in Anne Boleyn, with which name and place could willingly have contented myself, as if God, and Your Grace's pleasure had been so pleased. Neither did I, at any time, so far forge myself in my exaltation, or received Queenship, but that I always looked for such an alteration as now I find, for the ground of my preferment being on no surer foundation than Your Grace's fancy, the least alteration I knew, was fit and sufficient to draw that fancy to some other subject.

You have chosen me, from a low estate, to be your Queen and companion, far beyond my desert or desire. If then you found me worthy of such honour, good Your Grace, let not any light fancy, or bad counsel of mine enemies, withdraw your princely favour from me. Neither let that stain, that unworthy stain of a disloyal heart towards your good Grace, ever cast so foul a blot on your most dutiful wife, and the infant Princess, your daughter.

Try me, good King, but let me have a lawful trial, and let not my sworn enemies sit as my accusers and judges. Yes, let me receive an open trial, for my truth shall fear no open shame; then you shall see either mine innocence cleared, your suspicion and conscience satisfied, the ignominy and slander of the world stopped, or my guilt openly declared. So that whatsoever God or you may determine of me, Your Grace may be freed from an open censure, and mine offence being so lawfully proved, Your Grace is at liberty, both before God and man, not only to execute worthy punishment on me as an unlawful wife, but to follow your affection already settled on that party, for whose sake I am now as I am, whose name I could some good whilst since have pointed unto; Your Grace not being ignorant of my suspicion therein."

I was not about to let Henry get away with marrying Jane Seymour. Not without sending him knowledge that I knew this was why I was held here.

"But if you have already determined of me, and that not only my death, but an infamous slander must bring you the enjoying of your desired happiness, then I desire of God that He will pardon your great sin therein, and likewise mine enemies, the instruments thereof, that He will not call you to a strict account for your unprincely and cruel usage of me, at His general judgement-seat, where both you and myself must shortly appear, and in whose judgement, I doubt not, whatsoever the world may think of me, mine innocence shall be openly known, and sufficiently cleared.

My last and only request shall be, that myself may only bear the burthen of Your Grace's displeasure, and that it may not touch the innocent souls of those poor gentlemen, who, as I understand, are likewise in strait imprisonment for my sake.

If ever I found favour in your sight. If ever the name of Anne Boleyn hath been pleasing to your ears, then let me obtain this request. And I will so leave to trouble Your Grace no further, with mine honest prayers to the Trinity, to have God in His good keeping, and to direct all your actions.

Your most loyal and ever faithful wife,
Anne Bullen.

From my doleful prison, the Tower, this 6th of May."

Kingston assured me it would be delivered to Henry. Perhaps he thought this was the case, but I knew otherwise. You may question, with this in mind, why I troubled myself to write at all. I wondered that myself. Parchment may be destroyed in fire with such ease. My words might well go no further than Cromwell's bright hearth, but he would read it, if no one else did, and he would know.

He would know God was watching him.

Chapter Seventy-Three

The Tower of London
May 7th - 12th 1536

"I must be allowed the peace of the Sacrament," I said to Kingston. "Why will you not grant me this?"

I had been permitted this honour on the night of my arrival, but since then there had seemed to be some confusion about whether I was allowed the peace of God's blessing or not.

"Madam," he said. "It is to my utmost sorrow that I cannot offer you this consolation, but it is not permitted. You are accused of a sexual offence and have not confessed, so you may not take the Sacrament."

"Accused but not proven," I pointed out. "You would have me confess to something I did not do, and do penance for a falsehood too? I will confess no such thing, for nothing have I done. I am the King's one, true wife. I will confess no *lies* to satisfy my enemies. They withhold this to push me to confess, do they not? That is why it is denied. They think to make me desperate, and force me to confess false deeds in my terror. I will not."

"The Bishop of London says that it would be inappropriate for you to have the host in your chambers."

"*Stokesley*," I hissed in a sibilant whisper. "He withholds God from me, does he? And not for fear of displeasing the Almighty, Master Kingston. No... He wants me to suffer as his friends More and Fisher did. But it will not be so. God sees all, and He knows I am without guilt. If I must wait, then, so shall I. I will not come to God with a false heart, as others will."

"John Skip will also not be permitted to see you," he said, speaking of my other request.

"Nor Parker, Latimer or any of the others?" I asked. "Poor men. They stand without my protection, and those who would do them harm will do their utmost to inflict pain and suffering on those good men."

"I cannot answer for that which I know not," said Kingston. "I am only granted such information as I pass on to you."

"You do not have to answer for my enemies. They will answer to God." I looked away. "Vengeance is mine, sayeth the Lord," I murmured. "I shall repay."

*

From the whispers of Lady Shelton I had surmised that there was already much clamouring at court for the spoils of our disgrace. At court, if not everywhere in England, it must have seemed as though I and the men accused with me were already dead. Lady Shelton said Council meetings were being held and people were grappling to be appointed to posts that would fall vacant *when* my friends lost their lives… it was done. It was a treaty signed and sealed. We were doomed.

I heard that the sheriffs of London had been called to assemble. They would examine the evidence, decide whether there was enough to proceed to trial, and, in theory, they would choose the jury. But I knew Cromwell would have a hand in that. He was not about to allow friendly faces into the courtroom. The jury would eventually decide on the allegations against us. Spare little of these allegations had I heard, and my enemies did not intend me to. It was normal for prisoners to be examined before a trial, so they might hear the charges. This had not happened.

Cromwell and Henry wanted us unarmed.

I was sure it was both of them. This plot had all the marks of Cromwell upon it, but never would it have gone this far without Henry's approval. All I could think was that he was so eager to take Jane Seymour to bed that he was willing to murder not only me, but his closest friends in order to achieve that goal.

On the evening of the 11th, I was informed that the trial of Weston, Brereton, Norris and Smeaton would go ahead the next day. "They try commoners before peers?" I asked Kingston. "Why? Why will my brother and I not stand first?"

I knew the answer, of course. If those of common blood were tried before us and found guilty, we had no chance. We would be found guilty by association. The trials George and I would face afterwards would have already been decided.

"I know not why the change in practice has been made, madam," he said. "But be of good cheer. Your father is amongst those who will sit in judgement, and your uncle with him. Therefore there are friends in the jury, are there not?"

Friends… what an interesting euphemism to describe my father and uncle. Norfolk would have gladly murdered me years ago, and my father would save himself. The best way to do that was to do all Henry wanted.

They would not speak for me. They would not defend my friends.

"I much marvel," I said to Kingston, breaking into tears. "That the King's Council have not come to examine me."

"They have said they will put forth all the evidence at your trial, my lady," he said, although I could see he, too, thought this strange.

They already had what they wanted. Lies would convict us. Torture could not be used on my brother or me because of our noble status, and without that they knew they would not be able to bully us into confession. But they had Smeaton's confession, no doubt procured through torture, for he, a commoner, was fair game to be abused. Oh… they would have been cautious… careful to abuse only parts of his body that might be concealed, so none would know what they had done.

And they had more… they had all that had been ever said against me, all the shouts of *whore* that had rung in the long streets of London, all the people who had said I drew Henry to me with sexual wiles. All the infamy that I had withstood in order to become Henry's wife.

How little was loyalty rewarded in those dark and violent days…

They also had reputations. Weston, George, Brereton… all were known for keeping mistresses. If they had kept one, why would they hesitate to keep another, the

Queen? When a person is accused of sexual depravity any accusation will stick. This, too, applied fearfully to my child in some ways. Everyone knew the date of Elizabeth's birth; born seven months after our marriage was announced. This meant everyone also knew I had engaged in pre-marital sex. If I was willing to do that, even if it *was* with the man I had married, why could I not be guilty of more? Henry would not be condemned for also engaging in sex before marriage. The rules were different for men. Men walked in another world to that of women.

And there was my time in the French Court, which was known for loose morals. No matter that I had served Claude, and her court was not as François' was… No… The truth did not matter, only scandal did.

Most importantly, they had me; the manner in which I had risen to become Queen. I had done much that was unusual, extreme and never before heard of. Why, therefore could I not be guilty of treason against my husband, incest with my brother, and adultery with many, so many men? I had changed the world to my liking, so therefore it was possible that I would break any blockade, leap any bridge, ford any gully… If I could alter the world to make myself Queen, why would I hesitate to smash through any barrier of virtue?

Guilty of one thing was guilty of another.

*

That night, Cranmer, Norfolk and Audley came to my prison. No more would I call those rooms my chambers, for as opulent as they were, their furnishings and carpets, their gold plate and fine pewter were nothing but bars.

My gilded cage. My pretty prison. The falcon had been caught. Finally, I was the true servant of the King, just as he had always desired.

You have me in your power now, I said to Henry in my mind as I watched the men file in. *This is what you always wanted, isn't it? For me to bow to you? To know that I am your slave?*

He had never had this when I was with him. How greatly he must have desired it, to treat me so ill, to murder his best friends, in order to gain it.

Cling to this feeble power, Henry of England, I thought. *But know you have not broken me, and never will. I am not your possession, not your tool, nor your slave. You may take my life, but you will never claim my soul.*

"We have visited the others already, my lady," said Cranmer, his eyes boring into me. I wondered what lies he had been told to make him look on me with such distaste.

"I must say to you, madam," he went on. "There is no one in the realm, after my lord, the King, who is so distressed at your bad conduct as I am, for all these gentlemen well know I owe my dignity to your good will and…"

"My lord Bishop," I interjected, cutting him off. "I know well what is your errand. Waste no more time. I have never wronged the King, but I know well he is tired of me, as he was before of the good lady Katherine."

"Say no such thing, madam," he said, his brow furrowing, although I could see doubt forming in his eyes. "Your evil courses have been clearly seen and if you desire to read the confession which Mark has made, it will be shown to you."

"*Confession*," I spat. "Has any other man spoken against me, my lord Archbishop, or am I to be condemned on the lies of one man alone? One man who vanished from court and was taken to Cromwell? One man who was no doubt abused to extract what they wanted from him?"

I stared at my old friend and shook my head. "Go to!" I cried. "It has all been done as I say. The King has fallen in love with Jane Seymour and does not know how to get rid of me. Well, let him do as he likes. He will get nothing more from me and any confession that has been made is false, as God is my witness!"

Norfolk broke in. "Madam, if it be true that your brother has shared your guilt, a great punishment indeed should be yours and his as well."

"Duke, say no such thing," I retorted, rounding on him. "My brother is blameless, and if he has, at times, come to my chamber to speak with me, surely he might do so without suspicion, being my brother, and they cannot accuse him for that. I know that the King has had him arrested, so that there should be none left to take my part and speak for me. You need not trouble to speak with me, for you will find out no more. There is no more to tell. We are innocent, and if the court finds us guilty, it will be not for the sake of any evidence, but for the will and wants of the King, who wants to be rid of me, and for Cromwell, who would remove his rivals from court."

Cranmer was looking from Audley to Norfolk as though he had heard none of this. Had he expected me to announce my guilt? Did my old friend think so little of me?

"Did they not allow you to visit the others, Cranmer?" I asked. "Did you not hear this from the mouths of my brother, Norris, Weston and Brereton? Or did they only allow you to see Mark, snivelling in his cell?" I turned to my uncle. "What did you promise him, my lord, to make him confess? Clemency… a pardon… or will he be granted the death of a noble person?"

I laughed as I saw a flicker pass through Norfolk's eyes. "That is it, is it not?" I asked, my tone sardonic and jaunty. "You will grant Mark the position in death he ever envied in life. He will die as a noble where he lived as a commoner. A pretty pass, my lords. I congratulate you. You have done your task well and I have no doubt you will make sure you profit from it."

"You show courage, niece," drawled Norfolk, content in the knowledge it mattered no more what I said. "But it will do you no good. You will pay for all you have done."

"God will be my judge," I said. "If not here on earth then in Heaven. And He will be yours, Norfolk, and yours, Audley." I looked at Cranmer. "And He will judge you too, Eminence, you and the King. I have no fear of what the Almighty will find in my heart. Will you be able to say the same?"

As Cranmer left, I could see I had made an impression. I had no doubt he had been lied to, and Cromwell must have been convincing in order to turn my faithful friend from me in such short time, but I had laced doubt in his mind, and that pleased me. I cared nothing for Norfolk, for Audley or for Cromwell. Let them believe what they liked. But Cranmer I did care for. He was the last friend I had on the outside, and perhaps that was why they had tried to turn him.

There was nothing he could do, but I did not want to go to my grave with him thinking ill of me. A part of me, still untainted with the brush of hatred, could not bear that I would die and he would go on living, thinking me this monster they had created.

That night I dreamt of the tower again. Katherine stood at my side, her hourglass eyes fixed on me.

"My time is almost spent," I said.

"It is."

"You are my death as I am yours."

She smiled. "Finally, you understand."

I did. Whilst she had lived, Henry had been forced to stay with me. Set me aside, and they would send him back to her. When Katherine died, the last shadow of her protection had fallen. A protection she never intended to offer, and yet had. With her gone, Henry could take a new wife. He could get his sons.

"I saw this tower so many times in these dreams," I said. "I never understood that it was Fate."

"Fate… Time… Life…" she said, looking at the flowing blood, the dusty sand and the tower. "They are one."

She looked at me. "We are dust," she said. "Specks driven into the winds of Fate. We know it not, but our paths were decided long ago, before we were born, before those who sired us were… before time began and before Death came for men."

"And soon will come death," I said. "And the end."

She smiled wider. The hourglasses in her eyes gleamed under the light of the burning sun.

"This is not the end, my sister," she said. "Nor is it the beginning. There is no end and no beginning to the sands of time or the thread of destiny. There is only continuation. There is only eternity, infinity… perseverance… and you must surrender to it."

"Surrender…" I said. It was not a word I had ever welcomed.

Katherine smiled. "This is the one battle, sister, where you gain more from surrender than you will by waging war. Surrender to the infinite, and you will gain your true self."

"This is not the end," I said, watching blood as it flowed from the stones.

"This is not the end," Katherine said.

Chapter Seventy-Four

The Tower of London
May 12th 1536

Defying common practice, the trials of those of common blood were held first. This would allow our accusers to establish my guilt before I even came to trial, for how could these men, Norris, Weston, Smeaton and Brereton, have committed adultery with me if I was not involved? My brother and I would be condemned before we had a chance to defend ourselves. None of us were going to escape with our lives, or honour, intact.

But that did not mean we should not try.

My one consolation, and it was a slight one, was that Tom and Page were not called to trial. Perhaps there had not been time to fabricate evidence against them, or they had made a deal with Cromwell. I knew not which. If they had made a deal, I could not think ill of them. Smeaton, I despised, for having spoken against me and my friends, but now that had happened, there was little that could be done for us. If Tom and Page had found a way to save themselves, so be it. At least there would be two fewer deaths.

I watched the men taken from their towers and led to the river. They were to be tried at Westminster, in the great hall where not so many years ago I had sat before the court to feast on my first night as Queen.

I already knew what the judgement would be. Cromwell had assembled a hostile jury. Kingston had informed me who was to sit, and the names brought a cold shudder to my bones. The foreman was Edward Willoughby, a man much in debt to Brereton. William Askew was a friend of the Lady Mary. Walter Hungerford was a dependant of Cromwell's, widely rumoured to favour the company of men, which, in light of the new laws on sodomy, granted Cromwell ample leverage. Giles Alington was wed to Thomas More's stepdaughter, and therefore had reason to look for revenge. Sir John Hampden was related to William Paulet, Comptroller of the royal household, and was in Cromwell's pocket. William Musgrave was after Cromwell's favour for failing to deliver charges of treason against Lord Dacre. Thomas Palmer and William Drury were great friends of Henry's. Robert Dormer was known to oppose the break with Rome. Richard Tempest was Cromwell's friend, and Thomas Wharton was an ally of Henry Percy's, who, by now, was no doubt terrified that his offer of marriage, made to me so long ago, would see him too in the Tower.

Theoretically, defendants had the right to refuse any member of the jury they thought biased. But it was frowned upon in trials related to treason, incurring more ill-will from the panel of jurors. I was told that John Champnes, the ex-lord mayor, who was almost blind, had been replaced by William Sidney, but Sidney was close to Suffolk, and so this replacement had done us no good. There was only hope that Henry might show mercy, for it was clear no quarter would be granted from those who sat in judgement.

And there was a catch… in previous cases, such as with Wolsey, clemency had been offered if the defendant did not show resistance, and pleaded guilty. Wolsey had done so. He had thrown himself on the mercy of the King. I feared Norris and the others might do the same, might walk the same path as craven Mark, and plead guilty to sway Henry into mercy.

They were at a disadvantage from the start. In legal courts, there was no assumption of innocence, with guilt to be proved. Our courts were not so fair.

There was no counsel for the defence, as there were in some other countries. The accused had to defend themselves. Hearsay would be admitted as fact, and they had no prior knowledge of the evidence or accusations they would face… but the jury would. They would be well-prepared, and willing to give whatever sentence the King desired.

Of course, by now, my friends must have known some of the accusations. They had been pressured to confess and it is hard to confess to something without knowing what it is. But the evidence and full list of accusations had not been shown to me, and I suspected, not to any of us.

Those men walked into Westminster Hall without shield or sword, without understanding or preparation. Lambs to the slaughter…

But my fear that they would plead guilty, to save themselves, was misplaced. In terror, I misjudged my friends.

"They *all* pleaded not guilty, my lady," said Kingston that night. "All besides Mark Smeaton." His voice was incredulous. It was almost unique to find prisoners declaring they were innocent.

For a moment I could not breathe. I put my hand to my heart, thinking it would burst from within me. That these men, my friends, would stand with honour and plead innocence was beyond my reckoning. What nobility was theirs!

They had defied Henry, defied Cromwell. And even if this would not save our lives, the people would hear, and remark upon it. God would hear them.

They had shown their true hearts. They had stood for me and for their honour, even to the detriment of their lives.

All besides Mark. He had damned us all. With just one voice crying out that he had, indeed, had relations with me, the jury would convict, and convict they had. Kingston told me that Mark had said he deserved to die. I wondered if he thought so because he had betrayed us all.

"Many thought Brereton would be acquitted," Kingston said. "He said he deserved to die a thousand deaths for his sins, but that he was not guilty of what he was accused of. He asked the people to judge the best of him."

Judge the best, I thought. A pale, thin, yet sacred cry in this wicked world.

"Alas for Mark," I said. "I fear his soul will suffer punishment for his false confession."

"They were all found guilty," said Kingston. "And sentenced to death."

"It was already decided," I said. "Long before they went to trial. It matters not. The people will hear of this and so will God. I tell you, Master Kingston, it will not rain in

England until we are released. God will send a plague upon these lands that look no more to His justice or will, but to greed, want and lust."

He could not tell me more. I, too, would go unarmed to my trial. I would have two days to wait, as the court did not sit on a Saturday or Sunday. Two days to prepare myself. No doubt my foes would think that, being a *weak woman* and hearing of the sentence upon my friends, I would fall to pieces, and be a poor, easy opponent. They thought that leaving me here, to sit and wait for days, would unhinge me. I would come to them a weeping, distraught woman. Easy prey. Easy pickings.

They were wrong.

I would not go quietly to my own death. I would stand and proclaim my innocence as these brave men had done before me. They would not find a weak and feeble woman cowering before them, but a strong one. One who knew her worth and her virtue. One who understood she had nothing to fear, for even if they sent me to death, I would be upheld in the hands of God.

Finally, in the face of death, I had found true power. It was not something to be found at court, or in a bag of gold. It was in the strength and courage of my heart, and the endurance of my everlasting soul.

"They have been sentenced to be hung, drawn and quartered," said Kingston. "But many say the King will show mercy and commute the sentences to beheading."

"Mercy," I laughed. "Is that *mercy*, then, Master Kingston? To send an innocent soul to death by swift means rather than slow? The King may commute the sentence on these good, guiltless men, but God will not commute His sentence upon the King. For His Majesty is guilty still of *murder*, is he not? He takes lives not for justice and peace, but for the wishes and wants of his heart. He will murder to be rid of me and take a little wife who will play the sweet and humble Queen. God sees his heart, Master Kingston. There is no hiding from the Almighty."

Kingston looked worried, and I waved a hand. "Go to," I said. "Listen not, if you have not the stomach... But all I say is truth. Your lord and master has allowed himself to be deceived in order to have what he wants; a quiet life and a quiet wife. He will have obedience, he will have submission, for after this, who will dare to defy him? He will have me as he always wanted me; subject to his will. He will have the life he desires. And he will murder his friends and the woman he protested he loved in order to have it."

I laughed. "What small goals are these after all we did together! How tiny can ambitions become! He will have what he thinks he wants, but it will not satisfy him. He will become bored of dull, plain, Jane, and what then? If, in a few years' time, she does not bear a son, I think you will have a new guest here, Kingston. Another Queen to entertain in the days before her death. When she comes here, tell her what I said. Tell her I am glad she has come to the same fate. I understood only when I suffered as Katherine did what I had done to her. Little Jane, my pallid cousin, she will endure the same. But I will forgive her, for perhaps she, like me, thought she was doing all she did for love. Tell her that, Master Kingston, when she is sent here on trumped up charges so Henry might be rid of another wife who did not live up to his ridiculous fantasies."

"My lady, if any were to know what you say ..."

"What? The King would be *unmerciful*?" I laughed loudly.

"I will report nothing of this conversation," he said, glancing at me with both sympathy and fear. "But you must collect yourself."

He was right. That was what I had to do. If I was to face trial, with a jury led by my enemies, I had to be calm.

If, I thought, *for no other reason than to give them all a good scare.*

I started laughing again, and I could not stop. They fed me a potion of opium, which I did not want to take lest I said things that were untrue, or they claimed I had, but as I insisted Mistress Aucher was to sit with me, I was assured I would have some protection.

In truth, I should not have feared. What more did they need from me to cement their falsehoods in the minds of others? They had a web of lies and I was stuck fast in its centre. They had painted a portrait, with me as Guinevere and the men as Lancelot. Thrust into that frame, I was bound, held captive by the poor reputation I had earned and by Henry's abandonment. What more did they need? Nothing.

They had Henry. That was enough.

The next day I was told my household had been broken up. This could only be done on Henry's orders. I had not faced trial, but Henry was already assured I would be found guilty.

Will you call them back on the day I die? I asked Henry in my mind. *Will that be your wedding day, Lord of loss? Lord of spite? Lord of pain? Will you take to the altar on a carpet of blood as the one you loved breathes her last?*

I had not been found guilty, yet I had a home no more.

I had not been condemned, yet Death was already coming for me.

My women thought I did not hear them when they said a messenger had been sent on the 9th, summoning an expert swordsman from France. But I did hear. I had not yet faced trial, but my executioner was already on his way.

The sword… a graceful death. The axe was clumsy, and often chopped at the neck, the shoulders and the body before taking the head. The sword was quicker, cleaner… it was a noble death.

The sword was for me. Henry's last gift… a swift, quick death.

This act of mercy told me all I needed to know. Somewhere, perhaps buried deep inside him, Henry knew I was innocent. Had he thought me guilty, there was no pain, no agony, he would have denied me.

Norfolk was made Lord High Steward of England, in preparation for him to preside over our trial. I was told that my father would not sit in judgement upon George and me, as this was thought inappropriate.

What did that matter? My father had passed sentence on Weston, Smeaton, Norris and Brereton, *knowing* that to do so was to sign the death warrants of his children.

For my part, I would have had him sit, pass judgement and face us. At least that would have been honest. But no… our father crawled like the worm he was, currying favour by slaughtering his own children.

Our allies had deserted us. Our goods, property and offices were being handed to others. The sword was on its way. Judgement was already passed.

Henry was wasting no time.

*

"Your chaplain, William Latimer, was searched when he returned to England, my lady," Mistress Aucher whispered to me in the privy.

"For what reason?"

"They were looking for banned books, but found nothing."

Mistress Aucher had told me that Latimer had been detained for a day. Latimer was returning from a business trip to Flanders, and since all knew my reformist leanings, no doubt Cromwell had hoped to discover something incriminating on my chaplain. Clever Latimer had known to hide any books he might have brought back for me. They would have been shipped separately, for he understood the risks he took.

What was the purpose of this? Did they hope to add charges of heresy to my trial? Did they want to accuse me of being a witch? I knew not, but they had found nothing. What did it matter if they had? Were not charges of adultery, treason and incest damning enough?

"What have they done with him?" I asked.

"He was taken to London and placed under guard," said Mistress Aucher. "I know no more."

But I heard more. More from the watchers who thought I had gone deaf. Jane Seymour had been installed in Carewe's house at Beddington, and Henry visited her in secret. Jane had been dressed in great finery, when last the court had seen her, and, as Henry grew assured that I would be executed, she was moved closer to him, to Chelsea, where she was served by Henry's personal cook and other officers.

Henry was sending Jane love tokens, and notes, promising that the pamphlets and their printers would be destroyed and punished. Promising also, no doubt, that his love for her would sustain her, as once it had me.

"They say he will marry her, as soon as…" Mistress Coffin cast a look in my direction, but I was staring at my Bible, apparently unaware of them.

"Say what you will," said Lady Shelton, ruffling her stout shoulders. "I think it ill that he parades his love for this woman when his wife has not yet stood trial."

So, I thought. *Even those who guard me think badly of Henry. If that is so, I wonder what is said in the streets?*

They must know, I thought. *Just as they did with Katherine.* They must know that Henry was seeking to rid himself of one wife, in order to take another.

Chapter Seventy-Five

The Tower of London
May 15th 1536

I took another glance in the hand-held mirror before I left my rooms.

It was the morning of my trial. After me, George would stand. There was no hope of being found innocent, but I would not go quietly. A meek wife was all Henry wanted now, and I would not be so. Not for him. Not for a demon willing to sacrifice me, his friends, and our good names on the altar of his wants.

I was not to be tried in Westminster Hall. Henry and Cromwell did not want me to be seen by the people. They did not want further ditties to be sung, or the pale flesh of my face to engender sympathy. I would be tried in the King's Hall in the Tower. I would not leave this place, in life or in death.

The face in the mirror was hollow and pale, but her bright eyes shone from their sockets. There was something fearful about my beauty that day… something morbid, unearthly. As though Death had already taken up residence inside me, and my body shone with the last light of life and His immortal soul.

Doomed I may be, but falter, I would not. I would not fail to present myself as innocent. I did not deserve to die.

I waited at the doorway as they read the Crown's commission. Beside me was the Yeoman Gaoler of the Tower, his ceremonial axe turned away from me, to signify I was not yet condemned.

"Gentleman Gaoler of the Tower, bring forth your prisoner!" came Norfolk's voice.

I entered accompanied by Lady Boleyn, Kingston, Lady Kingston and Sir Edmund Walsingham. Mistress Aucher followed, taking a place in the packed stands. Upon entering, I had to steel my heart. I had not been informed how many people would be there to witness my trial. The stands were stocked full, piled with people like stacks of cloth waiting to be cut.

Later, I was told there were two thousand people present. At the time, all I could see was a sea of eyes, staring at me.

I swallowed hard, trying to diminish the frantic beating of my heart as I faced the stage on which my jury sat.

It was my privilege to be judged by a jury of my peers. Unlike Norris, Smeaton, Weston and Brereton, who had faced the commission of oyer and terminer, so *conveniently* established weeks before we were arrested, I would face lords and dukes. I looked upon them, twenty-six in all. I saw few I would name friends.

Norfolk, sitting as Lord Steward and representing Henry, was on a throne under a cloth of estate with his son at his feet. In Norfolk's hands was his white staff of office, and in Surrey's, the golden rod of the Earl Marshal. Norfolk looked pleased.

So finally you have a throne, Uncle, I thought with sneering contempt, *and will see me done to death too… what a good day for you!*

Norfolk had no doubt been chosen not only for his rank, but to provide a modicum of justice. As my kinsman, he might be viewed by any who knew nothing of our true relationship, as sympathetic. But he was not. It was his *delight* to sit in judgement over me. Had he not always wished to subdue me? This was Norfolk's grand day out.

You think to confirm your power, by crushing me this day, I thought. *But you do not understand, Uncle. Killing someone does not grant you power over them. My strength is greater than yours. My soul is vaster than you can possibly imagine. Even if you take my life, you will always be weak, as I will always be strong.*

Sir Thomas Audley and Suffolk were on either side of Norfolk. At their backs were more men. More enemies.

Henry Courtenay, Marquis of Exeter, and his cousin, Lord Montague, were firmly on the side of traditional religion, and Gertrude, Montague's wife, had long been my foe. Both had supported Katherine whilst she lived, and her daughter now she was dead. Both had plotted against me with Chapuys and Cromwell, as both had supported Jane Seymour.

John de Vere was the kinsman of Frances, one of my ladies, and he had borne the crown at my coronation, so might be thought of as a potential ally, but he was Henry's good friend, and shrewd enough to understand what was expected of him. Ralph Neville, too, was Henry's friend, as was Henry Somerset, Earl of Worchester, who was also husband to my good friend Elizabeth Browne. Robert Radcliff, Earl of Sussex, Thomas Manners, Earl of Rutland and George Hastings, Earl of Huntington were related to Henry and often in his company. Thomas Fiennes, Lord Dacre, had come up against Henry under charges of treason, which, uniquely, had been quashed for lack of evidence. Dacre needed to prove himself. This was his chance.

Henry Parker, Lord Morley, was George's father-in-law, but he had loved Thomas More and was a staunch supporter of Lady Mary, as were Lord Windsor and Lord Cobham. Edward Grey, Baron of Powys and Thomas Stanley, Lord Mounteagle, were Suffolk's sons-in-law. Edward Clinton was married to Bessie Blount. If I died, if Henry despaired of an heir, Clinton's stepson, Fitzroy, would be a step closer to the throne. Thomas Wentworth was a cousin of Jane Seymour, and therefore had good reason to think his prospects might improve with my destruction.

I almost faltered to see so many foes, but I thought of Katherine. I remembered Blackfriars. Unlike her, I would not walk out of here and be free, but like her I would stand. I would fight. I would be heard.

One face made me start. Sitting with a pale face and shaking hands was Henry Percy. His eyes would not meet mine, and I knew the reason. With all the arrests that had gone on of late, Percy must have thought he was but a whisker from the Tower himself. His appearance here, I had no doubt, had been commanded so he might prove his loyalty. Whatever his feelings had been for me in the past, or were now, he could not find me innocent. To do so might turn Henry's hungry eye upon him.

I doubted he would think on me with any affection. Percy had been trying to squeeze into the ranks of my enemies for some time… but there was something shameful in his expression. Something which made me think he was unwilling to be there.

Tom and Page had not been tried with the others. I wondered if they might be tried next, after George and me, but something in me told me they would not. It was to Cromwell's benefit to slaughter Brereton, Weston and Norris. Norris and Weston were part of my faction, and their removal would lead Cromwell closer to Henry than he had ever been. He had never liked Weston, in any case, and I was sure now he had been jealous of Norris. Brereton's death would grant Cromwell free rein in Wales and Cheshire. Mark was but a passing addition. He was of no importance in life, but in death he would grant Cromwell all he needed.

But as for the other two … Cromwell was friends with Tom, and had no grievance against Page. They would be reprieved, I was sure, and then they would owe Cromwell. He liked to have men in his debt.

And there was an added benefit. To allow *some* men to escape might secure the idea that those who were tried *were* guilty. Execute too many, and incredulity might overcome scandalous delight.

I stood before them, my head high as I curtseyed. I gazed on them with a stout face, unwilling to show fear. My gown was black velvet, with a scarlet kirtle and a cap decorated with a black feather and a white one. Black for mourning, and red for the colour of Catholic martyrs. I looked magnificent, as was intended.

We exchanged standard, cordial greetings and I took my seat on the chair provided. Only Norfolk had a throne this day, but I drew myself up. I would not cower and quake. I would show my innocence in all that I did.

Beside Suffolk was my crown on a cushion. It was the one made for my coronation; gold studded with sapphires, rubies and pearls. Crosses of gold and *fleurs-de-lis* surrounded the rim. They did not mean for me to wear it, but to surrender it, when I was condemned. There was no *if*.

"Queen Anne of England," Sir Christopher Hales said loudly. "You come here accused of high treason, adultery and carnal incest with five men, including your own brother. How do you plead?"

My chin rose as did my breast as I drew in air. I would ensure everyone heard me. I raised my right hand. "I plead not guilty, my lord," I announced.

A buzzing noise of muttering erupted in the stalls. The muffled mumbling sounded shocked. Had they been told I would plead guilty, or had they just supposed it?

I glanced to one side and saw Mistress Aucher in the stands, her face stark. I fixed my eyes on her, drawing strength and courage. At least one person there knew I was innocent.

"Despising her marriage and entertaining malice against the King," droned Norfolk, "and following daily her frail and carnal lust, the Queen did falsely and traitorously procure by base conversations and kisses, touching, gifts, and other infamous incitations, divers of the King's daily and familiar servants to be her adulterers and concubines, so that several of the King's servants yielded to her vile provocations."

I was not allowed to question witnesses if they were brought against me. Not permitted to call anyone to speak for me, and not allowed to offer evidence on my own behalf. All I could do was answer their questions.

I was to fight without a weapon.

They laid out the case against me. And how specific were the charges. *Too* specific to any who had a mind…

I was accused of lying with Norris at Westminster in October of 1533; Brereton at Greenwich that November and again at Hampton Court in December. Smeaton and I had apparently rutted at Westminster in April of 1534, followed by Weston in May and June at Westminster and Greenwich. That April of the same year, apparently unsatisfied by Weston, I had lain with Smeaton at Westminster. For some reason, I had taken a break from my whoring, and had resumed my affair with Smeaton only in the April of 1535. That November I had abandoned all virtue and sense, enticed my brother into incest by putting my tongue in his mouth, and had lain with George at Westminster and again in December at Eltham Palace.

They also mentioned, each time a date and charge was read, that I had fornicated with these men *at other times*, which were unspecified… which also meant it was impossible for me to offer any defence.

In return, I had promoted their careers, using them as my whores to be paid for services rendered.

Aside from these accusations, it was said that in October of 1535 I had conspired to kill Henry at Westminster, had given gifts to my lovers that November, and this January, and had plotted to murder Henry with my brother, Norris, Weston and Brereton whilst at Greenwich. I had also brought injury upon the King's body, harmed him through stress and strain.

Oh, Henry, I thought. *Poor you. Poor little boy… You have suffered, have you?*

They used ridiculous evidence against me: I had danced with these men, many times and often; George had been in my chambers; someone had seen me kiss my brother; I had been handed from man to man in the dance; I had written to George; I had given money and medals to these men; I had laughed with them, smiled at them… shown friendship.

Cromwell had no need to prove me guilty of treason, not really. All he needed to do was to thrust forth charges that would unseat the security of any man. Make me appear as a woman who had flouted the normal behaviour of women, as one who had mocked her husband, called his power and lineage into question, and emasculated him in doing so, and he could make me into their worst fear; a woman who threatened the apparently so-fragile power of men.

When I made no answer, one of the men said I could not deny that I had written to my brother to tell him I was pregnant. "Why should I not write with such wonderful news to my brother?" I asked. "Does your wife not write to kin to tell them when she is with child by her *lawful* husband?"

He had no answer for me.

One might have asked why Westminster was such a *particular* favourite place of mine to indulge my sinful appetite. Did its walls infect me with carnal lust so strong that I could not restrain it? Another pertinent question was how I could have committed adultery in October of 1533 whilst I was still confined in bed, recovering from Elizabeth's birth. I was sure a man had formed these accusations, for no woman would ever believe that a woman who had just given birth would entertain the notion of sex for a while…

But I could not question them on this basis. These charges were made to make me appear incontinent of virtue, for to lie with a man whilst recovering from childbed was detestable and against the laws of God. It would only have condemned me further, and possibly put my daughter in peril to attack them on this point.

Had I had the time or the *right* to examine their evidence, I could have made up a list of the palaces where I had stayed during this time from court records. I could have defended myself. A few, I was certain I had not been in at the times and dates proclaimed. In October of 1533, I was at Greenwich, not Westminster, as this had been where I had given birth and where I was churched. I was fairly sure I had been at Greenwich that December, and not at Hampton Court. During April, May and June of 1534, I had been with child, and indeed in June, just one month before I lost my first son, I had been very heavy with child. If I would not lie with my husband during those months, for fear of harming our baby, why would I risk the child who might save me from a horror such as this, by rutting with these men?

Apparently, according to these charges, I was so lost in lust that I could not stop enticing men into my bed, even when pregnant, or recovering from childbirth. There was also the implication that the children I had lost, my sweet, innocent babes, were not Henry's, but had been fathered by these men.

And as for plotting Henry's death in October of 1535, it was absurd. Katherine had still been alive then. Henry's death would have brought about rebellion, on behalf of Mary, and Katherine, daughter of the Most Catholic Kings, surely would have been enlisted to aid her child. The Emperor would have been called to defend his cousin's rights, England would have risen for Mary, and all I would have had in my arsenal was a babe only just in my belly, and my infant daughter.

It was also notable that I had apparently not committed adultery until after Elizabeth's birth. Only then had I begun my reign of scandal.

This is one thing I may thank you for, Henry, I thought. He did not want his daughter included in this nightmare. He was sure she was his, and would allow no man to take her from him. At least I could thank him for that. If he would not protect me, at least he was sheltering our child.

But why had this carnal passion suddenly burst from me after her birth? Had I always been a woman of frail temptation, yet had somehow kept it imprisoned until the birth of my daughter had set it free? And *how* had I done all this? They said nothing of the *mechanics*, of the plotting, the planning and the *work* that this career of vice would have required. As Queen, I was surrounded by women and men all day and night. My ladies slept in my bed. Guards followed my every step. Even in the privy I was never alone! There were servants about me every hour, every minute, every second of every day. How had I managed to slip in a lover, or *five*, not once, but many times, without their notice?

And there was my husband. Jealous, envious, covetous Henry. My husband whose eyes glittered with suspicion to see another man look at me, read verse for me, or dance with me. Would he not have known immediately if I was bedding all the men in his chambers? Would he not have strangled me with his bare hands?

But it is easier to believe in evil than in good. The world contains so much ill that we become used to it, we expect it. That which is good is harder to believe, yet it is just as possible. A thousand tiny deeds of goodness are done each and every day, yet go unnoticed. We should pay more attention to that which is good. Then, we might recognise what is true and what is fiction.

Strangely, the conversation I had with Norris, the one bit of evidence that I had, albeit unwisely, actually said, was not listed in the charges. I realised then it was not included for a good reason. I had handed Cromwell something to use against me. He must have been plotting this for some time, but had nothing solid to take to Henry. My reckless words had given him fodder to feed the beast of accusation, and he did not want it now to be known.

Presented here, it might sound damning to those who wanted me to be found guilty, but to others it would not. They would think it was perhaps but a foolish jest. They might think all this was made up, and they would be right.

"I have never offended against the King with my body," I said. "I have never been unfaithful. I have never plotted his demise, nor encouraged any soul to do so."

"Did you promise to marry Henry Norris when the King was dead?"

"I did not."

"Did you send tokens and messages to your lovers?"

"I have no lovers, other than the King, my husband, and I sent no such items to any other man than he."

"Did you hope for the King's death, that you might marry your lover, Norris?"

"I have no lover, and all I have ever wished for the King was peace and happiness."

"Did you give love tokens to Francis Weston, as well as money?"

"I gave money to Sir Francis," I said. "As I have to many men and women in my royal household who have served me well, such is my privilege as Queen."

"So you admit giving him money and love tokens?"

"I admit granting him money and a medal when he served me and my gracious husband well," I said. "Have you never rewarded a servant, Your Grace?"

"That is not the issue in contention."

"If you have not," I said. "I pity your servants. All men should serve generous masters, as it is the will of God for those more fortunate to support those less able."

They ignored me.

"Master Smeaton has confessed to his crimes," Suffolk said.

"Yet none of the other men have," I said. "And the false witness of one man is not enough to convict a person of high treason."

"In your case, madam, it is sufficient."

"Will you not call witnesses to affirm the charges against me?" I asked. "It is usual, is it not, when a person pleads not guilty?"

"It is not required in this case."

"How strange," I said. "It would seem the rules of our courts have been altered, just for me."

I made each answer with a calm voice. I held up my head. I answered well. The muffled hum in the stalls was growing, rumbling over the stands, reverberating about the hall, and, sensing they were losing the crowds, who might report my courage to England, they changed tactics.

"Did you poison Lady Katherine, Dowager of Wales?" asked Suffolk.

"I did not."

"Did you plot to murder her daughter, Lady Mary?"

"I did not."

On and on they went. The 'evidence' they had was spare at best, entrenched in innuendo and rumour. Much that was old and forgotten had been rooted out by these hogs. At one point they said that my old friend, Bridget Wingfield, had made a deathbed confession against me. They said her son had witnessed it, and Bridget had spoken about my sins.

"The Lady Wingfield is now dead," I said. "And unable to speak for herself. But she was a good friend to me, and I to her. I cannot believe she would have said anything against me, especially when she was about to meet God."

If Bridget had said anything, it was more likely to be in sorrow about the problems between us. Besides which, she had died after a terrible and bloody childbirth. Perhaps fever had stripped her of reason, and she had spoken ill of me, but something in me did not believe it.

A letter was produced. It was the missive I had written to her before my trip to Calais. There was nothing in it which could possibly be construed as evidence, but not having any knowledge of the reason it had been penned they tried to wield it against me.

"This is evidence of blackmail," said Suffolk after the letter had been read. "The Lady found out about your affairs and was attempting to blackmail you."

"It is not so," I said. "I was counselling the lady, who is now dead and cannot defend me, that there were rumours about her relationship with her third husband. Some said they had started courting before the death of her second, and it had been much talked of at court, damaging her reputation. I had heard the rumours and was saddened by them, but wrote that letter to say that I believed in her protests of purity, and would hear them no more. That is the trouble I mention."

You never liked me, did you, Tyrwitt? I thought. *How long did you dig through Bridget's old papers to find this ridiculous 'evidence'? And how happily did you skip on the way to hand this letter to Cromwell, betraying not only me, but your wife too, who loved me? I hope her ghost comes for you, wails at your gate each night and grants you no rest.*

I fixed a glittering eye on Suffolk. "Besides, my lord," I went on. "The false accusations you put to me say nothing of anything before October 1533. Lady Tyrwitt died in January of 1534 and was not at court for some time before that as she was with child. How could she have witnessed anything to give cause for blackmail? And that letter was written in 1532 before the King and I went to Calais, which is before any of the dates you have specified. This, then, has no bearing on the accusations I am judged upon, accusations which I say again are false."

Suffolk leant backwards to whisper something to the scribe. I was certain he told him to strike what I had said from the court records.

"Some of the ladies of your bedchamber, when questioned, said that you had lived a life of gross impropriety," said Suffolk.

"May I know who these women are, or what their allegations were, so I might answer them?"

"You may not. They are to be protected, by order of the King."

"Then all I can say against this *unfounded* and *unsupported* allegation is that I have never done anything to warrant such treatment as this," I said. "I am the King's one, true and devoted wife. Since the day he offered me marriage, I have been his alone, and before that I knew no man carnally. One man alone has come to my bed, my lords, and that is my husband. As God is my witness, I was a maid when I gave myself to him and true to His Majesty thereafter. Whatever has been said of me by these women, who were no doubt terrified into speaking against me, is false." I looked to the stands. "I am being condemned on rumour and hearsay, procured through threat and intimidation," I said. "On the word of people unnamed and not presented to this court, and on the basis of fiction, not fact."

Again, that whisper, that docking of the records. When Henry saw these papers, they would no doubt say that I had said nothing in my defence.

No witnesses were called to give evidence. Nothing firm was said. It was all rumour, all unfounded slander, and it was *all* accepted as fact. At one stage they accused me of *lèse-majesté*, by mocking Henry's clothes and poetry. I could not deny I had done this, but I wondered.

Is this your true reason for wanting me dead? I asked my husband in my mind. *Did I damage that fragile pride, Henry? Did I hurt your poor, insecure, little heart? Is your illusion of power damaged because I thought your poems poor and your clothes garish? How weak you are, dear husband. How small is your soul.*

Do you forget you hurt me too? I lashed you with ill words, but you betrayed me, betrayed me over and over, and told me to remain silent.

I had wounded Henry's male pride, not only in accosting him about his affairs, but by his belief in these false charges. If he believed Cromwell, then I had held him in the deepest of contempt, for I was able to disregard our sworn vows of love and had lain with other men. *How frail is your majesty and your authority, husband,* I thought. *That mere lies, fantastic in their fabrication, may unseat you from your throne of power.*

"Did you mock the King, your husband, with your brother about his clothes and his poetry?" asked Suffolk.

A light flush spread over my cheeks. I could think of only two people who might have overheard that conversation; the two Janes. I hoped for my sister-in-law's sake that she had not been the one to betray us.

"If I commented on the King's clothing, it would have been in passing and never meant with disrespect." I looked up at them. "I do not say I have always been the wife I should have been. But if I spoke with any disrespect, it was not intended."

Thankfully, there were no accusations of witchcraft. At least that stain was not upon my name. But there was plenty that was; plenty to paint me a black-hearted villain.

Over and over they repeated the dates of the alleged offences and asked me anew if I had allowed these men to violate me. I was painted as the *instigator*, the one who had run after these men, tempting them with my feminine wiles into lust so strong it could not be contained. I had played the *masculine* role, the *aggressor*, and so I was doubly guilty, not only of adultery, but of failing to behave as a woman should.

Would it be so hard for those who hated me to believe all this? Like a man, I had altered the world to my liking, rather than taking a woman's passive role, so why should it come as a surprise to hear that I had become as a man in other ways… Taking lovers as a man would, whilst retaining the womanly charm that had seduced men into the vilest of sins?

The phrase *"treasonably violated the Queen"* was said over and over and over again until it was secured in the minds of everyone there. As though lies might become truth, the more they are said. I wondered if the same had been done in the first trial. To have consensual intercourse with a married woman, even a queen, was not something punishable by courts of law, but by Church courts and the charge would have been moral impropriety, not treason. A death sentence was also highly unlikely.

These charges of adultery were there to make it seem possible that I would have committed treason by plotting Henry's death, for if I had committed adultery, why not treason? Treason carried a death sentence. If they could secure the notion of guilt for one charge, it would bring the other along with it.

And they were abusing the law… attempting to extend the notion of treason by saying these men had *"treasonably* violated the Queen." The legal term for rape, *felonice rapuit*, was avoided at all costs, for then I would be the innocent. Being violated was not a crime, but adding *treasonably* made it seem as though it was. They were trying to dupe the common people.

A piece of parchment was handed to me. On it was a question they dared not speak aloud. It asked if I had questioned Henry's strength and virility in bed.

"Without reference to the question," said Suffolk. "How do you answer the charge?"

They did not want me to read it aloud to save Henry's pride, and if I dared, I would be doubly condemned. It was common knowledge that impotence was caused by witchcraft. If I said anything about this, it would be believed I had cast a spell on Henry, so I might get a child by one of my other lovers, and pollute the royal line. I was tempted to read it out. What did I have to lose? But for all that he had done, I would not shame my husband as he had done to me.

I was better than that, even if he was not.

"Without being able to respond," I said. "How may I answer? At times I was made sorrowful as my husband sought the company of other women…" The buzzing muttering in the stands grew loud. Everyone knew of Jane Seymour by now. "… but as an honest and true wife, I was joyous when he returned to me in love and affection, forsaking those who would lead him from the just and good path of marriage."

Again the nod. Again the strike. Henry would hear what they wanted him to hear. I almost pitied him. They would have him send me to death thinking I was untrue, unfaithful and did not love him.

I almost pitied him… but not quite.

I despised him. There was no love left in me for this monster.

The morning wore thin and eventually Norfolk called for the verdict. Starting with the most junior peer, he went to each and asked them to pronounce their sentence.

Their voices rang out through the hushed chamber; *Guilty… Guilty… Guilty… Guilty…*

Only Percy's voice was strained. I let my eyes settle on him. I did not smile but he knew my eyes well. Once he had looked into them with love and seen that emotion returned.

I stood composed. I would not grant them the satisfaction of seeing me weep.

But if I wept not, another did. To my vast and unending surprise, Norfolk had tears in his eyes as he pronounced the verdict. For a moment I was stunned, but a bare second later I realised they were not tears of grief, but of relief. Norfolk had been unnerved by my calm manner and honourable answers. He had feared I might be found innocent, set loose to exact vengeance upon him.

"Because thou hast offended against our sovereign, the King's Grace, in committing treason against his person, and here attained of the same, the law of the realm is this; that thou hast deserved death, and the judgement is this; that thou shalt be burned here, within the Tower of London, on the Green, or else to have thy head smitten off, as the King's pleasure shall be further known of the same."

I struggled to keep a hold on myself. *Burned.* Would I be burned? Tied to a stake to cough and splutter, to melt and crisp my way to death? How often had my name been linked to the prophecy that a Queen of England would die in such a way? How often had Henry heard me say it? And now that might be my fate. To burn to death as all those worthier than me had done before for the faith.

As I stared at Norfolk, there was a cry from the stands. I looked up to see Mistress Aucher leaning forwards, her hands on the banister. Her eyes were wild and her mouth open as she stared in dumb disbelief. I offered her a light smile, knowing that after this they would not allow her back to me. She had shown horror at my death, and if they did not suspect before, they knew now she was my friend.

Then there was a noise from the jury. Percy collapsed. They tried to get him back on his chair, but he was shaking so violently that he could not. He was carried from the hall.

Poor man. Did he love me still, or was he simply horrified to have perjured himself?

I was commanded to relinquish my crown, the one upon the cushion, but also the symbolic nature of it. "I surrender it," I said. "But I do so as an innocent. I have never offended the King with my body." I cast my eyes up to Heaven. "O Father, O Creator, Thou who art the way, the life and the truth, knowest whether I have deserved this death."

Suffolk turned to me. "Henceforth, you, Anne Boleyn shall be stripped of your noble titles," he said. "The title of Queen remains yours, as it is not in the authority of this court to remove it, no matter how unjustly you deserve such a noble title. You will be taken from this place and returned to your quarters in the Tower until such a time as the King has decided your sentence. Do you have anything to say?"

I drew myself up and set my shoulders back.

"My lords," I said loudly. "I will not say your sentence is unjust, nor presume that my reason can prevail against your convictions. I am willing to believe that you have sufficient reasons for what you have done, but they must be other than those which have been pronounced in this court."

I looked about. "For I am clear of all the offences which you have lain to my charge. I have ever been a faithful wife to the King, though I do not say I have always shown him that humility which his goodness to me and the honour to which he raised me merited. I confess I have had jealous fancies and suspicions of him which I had not the discretion and wisdom to conceal at all times. But God knows, and is my witness, that I never sinned against him in any other way. Think not I say this in the hope to prolong my life. God hath taught me how to die and He will strengthen my faith. Think not that I am so bewildered in my mind as not to lay the honour of my chastity to heart now in mine extremity, when I have maintained it all my life long, much as ever a queen did. I know these, my last words, will avail me nothing, but for the justification of my chastity and honour."

"As for my brother and those who are unjustly condemned," I said, sticking my chin in the air. "I would willingly suffer many deaths to deliver them, but since I see it so pleases the King, I shall willingly accompany them in death, with this assurance; that I shall lead an endless life with them in peace, under the light of God."

I stared into the crowds. "The Judge of all the world, in Whom abounds justice and truth, knows all, and through His love I beseech that He will have compassion on those who have condemned me to this death."

I could see heads shaking, for many had been sure I would escape with my life. Nothing of this kind had ever been done before. I would be the first Queen of England to die for treason. This was a strange and different thing… But Henry had already done much that had never been done before.

I curtseyed to my judges, my heart hammering as though it meant to take flight from my body and flee to freedom. But I would not show my terror. I would not. They had taken my titles, my family, and they would take my life, but they would not take my dignity. They would not claim my soul.

I was escorted from the court by Kingston. As I left, the guards at the door turned the blades of their axes to face me, to show I had been sentenced to death. Behind me, the roar of voices became a deafening wave of sound. Londoners were already talking about the trial being held so quickly, and now such a swift sentence of death to follow… it was clear my husband wanted me gone, and quickly.

I was to die. To burn to death or be beheaded, at my husband's pleasure.

Chapter Seventy-Six

The Tower of London
May 15th 1536

George was taken in after me. I was escorted back to my rooms to sit and attempt to digest the notion that I was to die.

I could not. There was nothing within my mind that would latch on to that thought. Yet terror was within me. I kept hoping that Henry would arrive, to say it had all been but a jest or a test; something to scare me witless and make me meek and compliant.

But such grace did not come. There was no hero left for me. All my knights were here, sentenced as was I, to death.

Like my ancestor, Thomas Beckett, I would be killed by my King. One day, would people know I had died innocent, as he had?

Would Henry burn me? Would he? Would I die in flames as I had lived in them? I thought back to the day when I had told Jane Seymour that I was a phoenix. It was not so. This was no way for me to stand unburned in these flames. She had achieved that. She was the phoenix, not I.

Mistress Aucher was not brought back to the chambers. I would not see her again. They would not allow one who had shown public sorrow at my fate to return to me. There was little more she could do for me in any case. My fate was sealed.

I heard whispers of George's trial. He had acquitted himself well, calmly, and as a gentleman, and many had thought he might escape death. He, like me, had denied all the charges and spoken of his innocence. But George had gone further. They had handed him a note, as they had to me, but my bold brother had read it aloud, calling the question of Henry's potency into clear and public knowledge. I laughed when I heard that. George was not about to go to his death without insulting the friend who demanded it.

He was convicted on the evidence of one woman, apparently, although no one would tell me whom. It could have been one of the women who spoke against me, these anonymous creatures, more likely to be a figment of Cromwell's imagination than real people. George had objected, saying, much as I had about Smeaton, that he was being found guilty on the evidence of just one person.

I had to wonder who the person was. If they were real… and if they were, then who? I could not but help suspect Jane. I would never find out if it was the truth, but she had overheard our conversations. She was always listening at doors. And although we had been close at one point, her banishment had made her only more bitter. Had she, like Henry, found her heart had turned to hatred for the one she loved, and had taken revenge? Had she, like my father, capitulated to save herself when she realised we were doomed? Had she been forced to confess against us, like Smeaton? Or had she wanted to… Wanted to bring us down after lingering so long on the fringes of friendship and family?

Who was to know? For her sake, I hoped my suspicions were incorrect. For when George died, no matter what hatred she nurtured for him now, her life would be empty and bereft.

"Your brother was accused of saying the Princess Elizabeth was not the King's daughter," Kingston told me.

"My brother would never have said such a thing," I replied. The only time I could remember was when George had jested of it. That was no accusation, if it were every fool in England should be in this Tower.

"He was also most concerned about his debts, and read a list of them in court," Kingston went on. "He is troubled that if the King takes his property, as is likely, the people he owes money to will face ruin."

"Let us hope the King shows more mercy to George's debtors than he does to us."

"Your brother said that since he must die he would no more claim innocence," said Kingston. For a moment I wondered if George's hale spirit had deserted him, but the man went on. "He said all men were sinners and deserved death."

George was simply admitting he had sinned in life, like any man aware of his soul. Pride and adultery lay upon him. My brother, a staunch reformer and evangelical, was more than aware of the ills upon his conscience. In admitting them, he was confessing, cleansing his soul so it might be received by the Almighty.

But I was glad; glad he had insulted Henry with his last breath. Let the people know their King was not the man he pretended to be! Let them know that he betrayed me with others and found himself wanting! Let them know… Let them know… It was, too, a strike against Cromwell. He had ordered that this note be given to George, so he had provided the means for my brother to publicly insult Henry.

I'll wager you squirmed when you heard of this! My mind exulted. *Will you fear the wrath of your King, Master Cromwell? Fear that you allowed this to be said before his people?*

I hoped this was the case.

"He was found guilty," said Kingston. "Like the others, he will be taken to Tyburn to be hung, drawn and quartered, or beheaded on Tower Green, as the King decides."

"Of course," I said, amazing myself with my collected tone. "We were condemned before the moment of arrest, Master Kingston. His Majesty decided we were to die long ago. These trials were but a formality to procure a doom already decided… a way to defame us, so His Majesty might trick his people into thinking he is justified."

I flicked my chin up as I saw his face grow pale with fright. "Leave me," I said. "I wish to pray for the King. He needs my prayers."

*

That night, I sat at my window, thinking.

Why *these* charges? Would it not have been easier, simpler than slipping from a step, to accuse me of heresy? The penalty was the same, after all.

But I had taught my pupil well.

"In recognising necessity, my lady, and setting it above our most ardent wishes, a soul shows itself wise." That was what he had said to me.

Cromwell the pragmatist had done what was necessary to remove me before I came for him, but he had also done what he could to save the reform that had brought him and Henry such wealth. Accuse me of heresy and all his plans for England's monasteries might go awry, for all knew I had supported the investigations. Were I accused of heresy, Cromwell's investigations might become suspect by association. Accuse me of adultery and only I and those accused with me would die. I had told him this, had I not? When I said that to accuse a woman of being a whore allowed people to believe anything against her? My apprentice once told me he had learnt something from each of his masters. I had shown him how to allow Henry to leave people; I had taught Cromwell how to destroy me.

He had used my most powerful weapon against me; Henry's love. He had told him that I loved others. To accuse me of adultery would lace seeds of doubt and horror into Henry's paranoid mind. He would fly into a rage, deeper and darker than anything he had suffered before. It was enough… enough to drive him to murder. Enough to destroy me.

Cromwell knew he had to be rid of me now, and with speed… so quickly that none could have the chance to rise to stand and speak for me, least of all the King. If Henry forgave me, Cromwell would be ruined.

I had no doubt Cromwell had been convincing. His life depended on his tales. Henry would have been convinced of my unfaithfulness, of imagined betrayals… perhaps he would have seen his own sins in mine, and been revolted by them. Perhaps he would have thought of all the times I had disappointed him, argued against him, defied him, and had decided his life might be easier without Anne Boleyn.

Perhaps he had finally heard my enemies, who whispered I was a witch, who had seduced him from the side of light to that of dark. Perhaps he had listened to all those who called me whore, looked at the way the men of court worshipped me in games of courtly love, and wondered if it was not all a game, and I had indeed betrayed him. Our arrests and trials had been so quick. There had not been time for Henry's rage to dim, and questions to break through.

Cromwell must have known he had to move fast. He could not allow doubt to overcome the wrath in Henry's soul. Could not allow there to be a chance he might consider my innocence. The ruthless nature of the slanders, and the speed at which he had moved showed how greatly Cromwell feared me. But never would it have gone this far, without Henry.

My husband must have *wanted* rid of me, otherwise he would have immediately dismissed Cromwell's accusations. Henry was far from foolish. He must have known how absurd the charges were. But there were many times he had believed in the absurd over the rational. This was his excuse. Just as my pregnancy had given him a reason to betray me, so now these lies would allow him to kill me.

The monster in Henry was tired of me. He was older now, looking for an easier life than the one of fire and blood we had forged together. No more fire for Henry. He wanted cool, cold water. He thought I could not give him a child, and he would not make the same mistake he had with Katherine… No more wives left living to call his children's inheritance into question. No more women to cause upset, hurt and embarrassment.

The monster would sweep the sand clean.

Henry's *madam* would die. It was easier for Henry that way… to think of me as the shrew he had despised, rather than the woman he had loved.

Had he asked Cromwell to come up with a reason to cast me off? I knew not, but I suspected such was the case. Henry had asked his men if there was reason to think our marriage illegal. Perhaps he had asked Cromwell to investigate and Cromwell had told him that as he looked for a reason, he *had* found one, a terrible one. Cromwell could not leave me at liberty, nor send me to a nunnery. My influence over Henry was too compelling… too addictive. No. I had to die. That was the only way to ensure I never came creeping back to court and into Henry's life.

Henry wanted me gone.

That was the truth. I had shown him how a mere court lady might rise to become a queen. I had shown him how to leave those he loved behind. And he would make a new queen. Henry wanted peace, obedience, and meekness. I brought none of those things. The royal supremacy made him convinced of his righteousness, and all who questioned him were wrong. Therefore I must be wrong, for I challenged him.

He wanted submission. He would get that in Jane.

I harboured no doubt that part of him did not believe Cromwell's tales. Henry would convince himself that he *believed*. But there would always remain a part of him that would doubt. I knew it was there, in him. That was why I would die by the sword. Because he knew I was innocent.

Cromwell should watch that doubt, I thought. *This is the lesson he has not learned.*

Henry knew when Wolsey fell that some of the charges against him were false. When More and Fisher died, he knew they did not die for treason, but because they were in the way.

In time, he will come to doubt the tales against me, I thought. *That doubt will make him suspicious of Cromwell and the stories he spins.*

Cromwell would be judged one day, by God if not by Henry. And he would be punished, but he would also learn something important.

Setting Henry on this path was dangerous. Cromwell had granted leave to others to bring false charges against foes.

Watch your master close, Cromwell, my mind whispered. *Watch that doubt, that suspicion. One day they will come for you, and who will defend you then? All now know you will turn on anyone, even those who were your allies and friends, even those who helped you. Will any sorrow to see you fall? Will any protect you? I think not.*

Chapter Seventy-Seven

The Tower of London
May 16th 1536

The morning after George's trial, I overheard Lady Shelton talking to Mistress Coffin again. "They say the King demonstrated great joy to hear the sentences," she whispered. "My daughter heard him say that he was certain the Queen had betrayed him with hundreds of men, and he had composed a tragedy about it, which he was carrying in a little book in his pocket."

More poor, dull verse to show your ladies, Henry? I thought.

I remained in my royal chambers, the Queen's lodgings, and there Cranmer came to me. "I must beg your forgiveness, Majesty," he said, his tone humble and meek. I looked at him with surprise. The watchers had gone to the other end of the room and could not hear us, but I was shocked to hear him say such a thing. I thought he was sure of my guilt.

"Then… you do not believe?"

"I do not." His voice was calm but troubled. "I have been lied to, madam, as have many at court."

"I am glad you understand," I said, taking his hand. "I would not have wished to die with you thinking ill of me."

"I wrote to the King, when first you were taken into custody," he said. "I protested, although not as vehemently as I should, that I could not believe the charges against you." His voice dropped still lower. "I have not seen the King since all this began," he whispered. "I, and many others, have been kept away from him."

"And then Cromwell came," I said. "And told you tales."

Cranmer nodded. "He did," he said. "And to my disgrace, I believed him. It all seemed too much to be false. He gave me evidence upon evidence until I was so bemused that I accepted it."

"And therein lies the strength in the story," I said. "He thinks to compound me and those accused with me with a pestle so strong that we will become as paste with his falsehoods. But there, too, he made his mistake. He bombards people now with a stream of such horrors that they can do nothing but nod to hear them, but a lie, in order to be truly convincing, must be simple. This one is not. Whilst the fire of scandal hangs over us, many will be swept along in the hot wind's breath, and they will believe. But when the dust settles, when people have a moment to think, there will be questions. Their questions may never be asked openly, but they will be there, rotting and festering beneath the pretty skin of court. And I thank God for the questioning minds of England! One day will my innocence and that of my friends be as prominent in the minds of our people as Cromwell's lies are now. He has spread evil, but there is no darkness over which the light of God may not shine. The truth will come, Eminence, and Cromwell, that man of shadows, will fear its light."

"I should have seen through him," said my sad friend.

"He *had* to lie well," I said. "He has the world to convince that I and the innocent men to die with me were guilty." I smiled. "It is the way of the world, is it not, Eminence? Accuse a woman of being a whore, and you can convince the world she is guilty of anything… any lies, any disgrace, any misdemeanour… she is condemned for the thought that she is without morals, even when the charges are so false, so ridiculous."

"You are as free of sin as the Virgin," he said, "and as holy."

"I am not she, Eminence," I said. "Not virgin saint, but neither the whore-witch they call me at court. I am not wholly good nor wholly evil. I am neither, but something in between. A woman, just a woman, made of good and evil, of light and dark, but with as much right to stand upon this earth as any man."

"I should have protected you," he mourned. "I should go to the King and tell him all I know now."

"You will not," I said, tears breaking from my eyes. "You cannot fall too, old friend." His hand sought mine and was clammy to the touch. "You must survive, or all that has been done will be in vain. One of us must live, to guide the King in the right direction, for England, for my daughter, and for the faith." I looked up into his eyes. "Do what must be done to protect yourself, Cranmer. There is no hope for me, but I will not die knowing that I took more from England than I gave. I will not have you sacrifice yourself for me. Live for your faith. Protect the people, protect the King. However much I find it hard to hold anything but hatred for him in my heart, he must have counsellors who are good and just, or all is lost."

I smiled. "In some ways, old friend, I die a martyr, do I not? With my death, the true faith may still be upheld, as long as I bear no further association with it. And you must keep it alive. You must protect it. For my daughter, for the future, I will go to my death."

"You are, to the end, a better soul than this world deserves."

"What have you been sent to tell me?" I asked, looking from the window where a bloody sun was setting. "Will the King show mercy, or will he lash me to a pyre and burn me?"

"The King offers mercy," he said. "He offers that you might, instead of dying, be sent to a nunnery and live out your days in prayer."

"How can that be true?"

"That is what I have been sent to offer," said Cranmer.

"But it is not what you believe will happen."

He cast his hands out. "I know not, my lady, but I dare to hope."

"And what do they want in return?"

"You are to say you were never married to the King. That your relationship with Henry Percy was a formal pre-contract of marriage, making yours to the King invalid." He gazed at me. "If you admit this, the King will show mercy and save you from the flames. He may spare the men too. He will also protect your daughter, keeping her as his acknowledged child, and shielding her from harm."

I almost laughed. If I had never been married to Henry, how could I have committed adultery?

I knew my death was a foregone conclusion. The swordsman was already sent for and Cromwell could not allow me to live. But I agreed. If there was even the slightest hope that my disgrace would bring mercy to my friends, to my daughter, any lie was worth it. I signed the parchment. I declared I had been promised to Percy, and had never married the man I loved.

I submitted in the hope that Henry would treat Elizabeth well, and for the slighter, vainer hope that he might spare me and my friends. But even then I knew it was not so. This, much as it was with Katherine, was a way to wipe clean the past, to make it as though I had never been. This was Henry's way of forgetting me. He would cast me from his mind, never to return.

In truth, there could not have been a surer sign I would die.

But that night, as I dined with Kingston and his wife, I spoke brightly of the notion I might go to a nunnery and the men in the Tower would be pardoned. I knew it was false hope, but I spoke of it, hoping the servants would tell their friends of all they had heard, and everyone would know when I died how little the mercy and promises of the King meant.

When I returned to my rooms, I looked out over London. Dusk had given way to night and the little lights of the houses glowed in the darkness. In the distance I could make out a barge, its light dappled over the flowing, dark waters, the sound of music wafting from it as it sailed.

"The King," said Mistress Coffin, a strange look of mingled disgust and approval on her face. "He makes merry."

Henry had filled his barge with courtiers and ladies. He had set sail onto the waters, knowing I would see him. Henry was celebrating as his friends awaited death.

I left the window and went to my bed, exhausted. Did he truly care so little for any of us? Or had his heart turned as cold as the water on which he sailed?

*

As it transpired, it was not Percy they used against me, but Mary.

Cranmer told me that Henry Percy had written too many times to deny that he had ever promised me marriage, and the volume of letters was becoming embarrassing. Despite the fact that Henry and I had had a dispensation for marriage, which nullified his relationship with my sister, his dalliance with her was upheld. They made me twice a sinner, for this meant Henry was my brother, and I had married him. My daughter was the product of incest. Another shade of black to paint me in…

The dispensation that had allowed us to marry had been granted by Clement, on the understanding it would be used after the trial of Henry's marriage in Rome. In the year we married, Parliament had passed an Act, permitting our union, but had held that previous dispensations granted by the Pope would not be upheld if they went against God's law. They ignored this, and used the old canon law to be rid of me, to make me no more Henry's wife. They used me, and my last shred of hope that submission might buy life for the men accused with me, or clemency for my daughter.

But I hoped Elizabeth was safe, not only because of Henry's love for her, but by law. Even if our union had held impediments, we had married on the basis of the Pope's dispensation. I had some hope that she might be recognised as legitimate, for marriages made in good faith upheld the resulting children as lawful.

It would, however, aid Cromwell if Elizabeth was defamed. It would be easier to have Lady Mary restored to the succession, appeasing Spain, and making safe all the threatened trade. If both of Henry's daughters were bastards, why not restore Mary to the succession? My only hope was that Henry would save Elizabeth from harm. I knew he loved her, although clearly, love was not enough to ensure his protection, but I hoped my last submission would aid her.

"Your brother and the others die on the morrow," said Kingston. "We have been told to take you to another place, so you might watch." Kingston's granite face did not look happy about this task.

"There is no word of a reprieve?" I asked.

"The King has commanded the sentences be carried out, my lady."

Of course he had. I had known it was a fool's hope, but perhaps I had always been a fool. Fool to fall for Henry. Fool to believe in him, to think that he would lead England to a time of grace and godliness, when all he wanted was to steal from the poor, and murder those he loved.

Fool to think that I meant as much to him as he did once to me.

"You are to face the sword the next day," said Kingston. "The King has commuted your sentence to beheading."

Was I supposed to be grateful? That I was to die by a sword, sent for before my trial had taken place, rather than by burning? Perhaps I was grateful. At least I would not suffer much. That spare consolation could I take for the others too, that they would not be hung, drawn and quartered, but beheaded.

But we would die. For Henry's lust for quiet we would die. For the faith to continue unburdened, we would die.

Martyrs we were... for faith, for truth, and for love.

Chapter Seventy-Eight

The Tower of London
May 17th 1536

The wind whipped past the window, startling me from memories of the past. I jumped upon my stool, causing a single knock from its wooden leg to sound about the chamber. The maids on the floor did not wake.

Night had fallen on this terrible day. The day I lost my brother.

That morning, I had been led to a cold room in the Devilin Tower overlooking Tower Hill. I watched them lead out the prisoners. My brother stood in the sunlight, brought out from the Beauchamp Tower. The others walked out slowly, their eyes blinking owlishly in the harsh, bright sun, after days in the gloom of their prisons. Guards surrounded them; their presence laughable. As if these prisoners could flee.

I pressed my hand to the window as I saw my brother. He looked around, at the final sights his warm hazel eyes would see. His clothing was his best, he was freshly shaven; even in death my brother was the image of a gentleman.

My warm hand imprinted sweat onto the window as I cried out to him silently; my eyes awash with grief. As though he heard my silent cry, George looked up, and our eyes locked; our last goodbye in this world. He inclined his head to me and bowed. The guards did not try to hold him. The others, standing near him, bowed to me also; Weston, Norris, Brereton…. all but Smeaton, who stood snivelling, wiping his nose on his sleeve, his face turned from mine.

Smeaton had not been racked, as was rumoured. It was clear enough to see. Had he been, his limbs would have been distended, and he would have had trouble walking. Most people who were tortured had to be carried to their deaths. He stood tall and graceful, as ever. I had no doubt, however, that he had been made to talk somehow. Unless, my first thought of him had been true, and he had tripped a fantasy of love from his imagination.

But I could never have loved a man such as he. Not because he was low born. Because he was a coward.

The nobility Smeaton had hoped for had never come to him. Nobility, as he had never understood, is not something born of blood, titles, or wealth. It is defined by one's actions. Smeaton would get the death of a nobleman this day, but he would never be noble. The meanest peasant in the backstreets of London who offers a crust of bread to a starving dog had more nobility than him. Coward souls are not welcomed by God.

I watched them walk through the crowds, watched them put on a cart to be taken to Tower Hill. Thousands had gathered to watch them die; a national pastime, an entertainment… Such was our grief, such were our deaths… an hour's diversion for the low of this land, and the high.

How small and meaningless life becomes when others sport with it.

There were swarms of people on that hill. Thousands had come to watch the high brought low and rejoice in the spectacle of death. My hand still at the window, I felt panic rise in me as it must have in the men climbing the platform on Tower Hill, trying to keep their dignity as they walked towards Death.

I wanted to scream to them to run... run far away. But no sound came. There was nowhere to run. There was no one to help us.

I watched George as he climbed the steps to the platform amidst the roaring of the crowds. It had been built high, so none would miss a single moment. He stepped forward, and started to speak. I was too far away to hear him, but the crowds listened closely. There was a dull hush in the air. Tears rolled down my face and a noise, not quite a scream, not quite a whisper, escaped my throat as I watched his distant figure kneel before the executioner and bow his head in prayer. He lowered his head, and held out his hands.

Then there was the flash of the axe in the sun's light. Then there was blood.

George's body fell sideways. The roar of the crowd signalled that my brother's light had been extinguished.

My throat cried out again, the hollow, raw, dark noise of sorrow.

They pulled his body, heavy with death, rudely from the platform and another figure stood.

Norris... my sweet friend.

I thought of all the looks and glances between us. I thought of him telling me that he loved me. Did he regret those feelings as he went to his death? I hoped he did not, for I clung to them. I grasped them with the slippery ends of my fingers, and hugged them to my heart. This day, Henry would take the lives of those I had loved, and tomorrow he would take my head, but my heart was his no more.

It was in Norris' keeping, and he would hold it safe, even in death.

He knelt, his head in George's blood. He mumbled prayers, but none were needed. The Lord of Heaven knew what a fine man would come to Him that day. The axe flashed. The blood came.

Henry Norris, this man of goodness and grace, was lost to the world.

Weston came next. The platform was red, shining, sticky and slippery with blood. He was too young to die, if one can ever be too old... Is there ever a time when death is welcome? Even in old bones we strive to exist.

His head took some time to chop from his body. Perhaps the handle of the axe had grown slippery with blood, or the executioner was tired from killing George and Norris. Poor Weston... his was not a clean death.

Then there was Brereton, such an old rogue. His face was pale but he stood true and still as he faced the crowds. His head came off clean.

Then Smeaton stood. His blood would finally mix with those he had envied. In death, finally Smeaton was where he had always desired to be; in the company of great men.

His lips muttered as he died. I hoped he prayed for forgiveness.

I slid to the floor, weak and overwhelmed. Tears would not come. I sat upon the dusty floor and stared at my hands, listening to the roaring of the crowds.

Mistress Coffin, Cromwell's beast, came to me. For a moment I thought she sought to comfort me, as her arm reached around the back of my slim shoulders, but instead she leaned close. "Master Wyatt watched this also," she whispered.

I raised my head slowly. I saw a gleam of excitement in her pale eyes. Suddenly I felt more tired than I had ever been before. Here, at the point where so much grief met with such destruction, here, this woman sought to trap me. To trick me into expressing something that might harm Tom.

"Why do you say this to me?" I asked in a clear voice, anger flooding past the weary sorrow of my heart. "Do you seek rich pickings of flesh to take to your master, the wolf?"

I stood up and faced her, my lip curled in derision. "I have watched friends and kin die innocent this day; great men, greater than you or your master could ever hope to know or understand. Soon I shall be held in the mighty and gentle hand of God with them, for He knows the truth that you all seek to ignore. Take *those* words to your master, leech, and seek not to spill the blood of more innocents."

I walked to the door, turned and pointed at her. Her crafty face stalled as my eyes, always my greatest weapons, glinted. "God watches all you do," I said, "and He will reward or punish all you have done in this life." I lowered my hand. "I will pray for you," I said and turned to leave.

"Pray for yourself, my lady," she said.

I looked at her and smiled. "Although I am closer to death, you are more in need of prayer than I." I turned to be taken back to my apartments.

There I sat on a window seat and watched the bodies brought back and buried in the churchyard behind the Chapel of St Peter's on the Tower green. As I watched their lifeless bodies, wrapped in cloth stained with blood, being immured in the ground, I began to laugh. Not from any humour within my heart, but from desperation, fear, from the terror of what awaited me.

"Soon I shall be Queen Anne *sans-tete*.... the Lady Anne *lack-head*," I said. "I shall be the first Queen to rule without her head… perhaps that will serve me better, for trying to rule *with* a head did me no good."

I laughed wildly, my fine eyes afire with desperation and fear, cheeks flushed with unusual colour. My laughter bounced and echoed around the rooms. They stared, wondering if I had finally lost my senses, and I laughed louder still to see their fearful expressions, to watch them shrink from my glorious eyes, wicked and sparkling with hysteria and terror.

They are afraid I shall curse them, perhaps, I thought. As though I had access to those types of powers! As though I had access to any of even my earthly powers here. *Who is there that I can charm here? Who is there that I can dance for, or sing for… for my life?*

My laughter faltered, and I returned to stare from the window.

Rain splattered the window that afternoon. As I watched the grey skies, a leaf was flung by the winds against the window. Desiccated and broken, its fresh green was fading, but not gone. Against the window it moved in the wind, slipping on the diamond pane. Up and down it shifted, crooked like a bent finger beckoning me unto death.

New ghosts walked amongst the old in the Tower compound that night. I saw them, flitting in the darkness, pale light against the shadows. They were all there, waiting for me to join them. I stared out, at the platform on which I was to die, and I felt panic rising in me once more.

I stared from the window, but I did not see the green before me. I saw the past. I saw a girl leaving home for the glittering courts of Europe, and I saw her return. She knew not what would come, but I did.

Soon, that girl would have what all of us long for in this life; to have another's heart beat only for yours, to know the overwhelming power love can bring to a soul… to feel, even for the briefest of moments, that you are adored, wanted and held above all others.

That girl… would I tell her to go back? I knew not. Her story would lead her to death. But if she had taken another path, would her life have ever been as miraculous, as strange and wonderful, as mine had been?

These questions could not be answered. They would never be known. But I would not tell her to run… No. For then there would be no Elizabeth. For all that I had faced, for all I had endured, for all the pain, misery and suffering, I would not surrender my daughter. She was my one hope for this broken world.

I sat by the window and thought of my life. I watched them building the scaffold. They had told me I would die. I was glad of it.

Tomorrow I die, I thought. *Tomorrow I shall be free.*

Chapter Seventy-Nine

The Tower of London
May 18th 1536

I thought I was to die that day.

I was ready… eager, even… I was prepared for the end of life; ready to take the skeletal hand of Death and step into the light of Heaven. I had steeled myself to face the crowds who would come to watch me die. I welcomed the thought of seeing my brother once again. I thought I would be free of my mortal pain and fear, that I would find relief from this terror of death, this consuming, unyielding, fear.

At dawn, I took the Sacrament and made my last confession. I called Master Kingston to witness it as I swore, upon my eternal soul, before witnesses and before God that I had never offended the King with my body, that I had never betrayed him. Unlike Katherine, I was not afraid to confess this upon my soul.

And I told no lies. I could not, not with my soul about to be judged. I never offended with my body, but perhaps I did with my heart. A man I thought to love had died.

Never would I have allowed Norris to be to me what the court accused me of, and yet, did I not love him? Did I not care for his good opinion, for many more years than I cared to count? So I was specific, for I would not lie before God. Unlike Henry, when I felt something for another, I had not allowed them to share my bed. Unlike him, I had remained true to our vows.

But when my confession was done, they did not come for me… I sat upon my stool. I waited.

The women about me told me Henry had already become engaged. Their words struck deep into me, tearing into the last strands of love I had borne for him, shredding them from my heart. My mind whispered, reminding me he did such once before… with me… with Katherine.

I thought on my poor mother and sister… what were they thinking now? Hiding at Hever and in Calais, hoping this tempest would pass them by. On my father, I tried not to think. He would scrabble about in the dirt that stained my name for a chance at redemption. Redemption in life, he might achieve, but God would judge him. He would put the loss of his heir, George, from his mind. But I could not. The empty hole my brother left was a gaping wound in my heart; raw and bloody, it tore, it rent, it ripped when I thought of him.

His smile… his laugh… the way we used to talk… walks promised, now never to be taken. His soft friendship armed me against a hard world. I could not forget him. My brother… He was my courage… my best friend.

I had thought that morning I would feel his hand, soft and warm, curled about my own; that I would see them all again, all the innocents who had died for my sake as we stood before the Almighty in the soft light of Heaven. But it was not to be. My execution was delayed. The small hope I had left, to swiftly leave this life and enter the next, was ripped from my hands.

What did they hope to achieve with this delay? Would Henry relent? Were I to believe the worst, I would consider my enemies wished to offer me false hope, just so they could snatch it away, so I might understand their power over me. Hope… it can become a weapon, when it is used well.

When Master Kingston told me my execution was postponed, I gazed at him with glassy eyes brimming with disbelief. I rose unsteadily from my stool, my legs numb. My mind swam with the knowledge that I must wait another day, another night, for the blessed release of death. My courage faltered. My face fell. Outside the Tower, the wind blew strong and fast, whipping about the walls. Its scream of despair echoed in my frail heart.

I turned to Kingston, regarding him with my weary, red-rimmed eyes and tired mind. "Master Kingston," I murmured. "You say I shall not die afore noon and I am very sorry therefore, for I thought to be dead and past my pain."

"I am sorry," he said. "Your execution will come on the morrow, at nine o' clock, my lady," Kingston continued, glancing at me with troubled eyes.

His words sparked something of my old humour. I chuckled. Strange emotions were bubbling within my breast. "I have heard the executioner is very good." My lips quivered with eerie mirth. "And I have a little neck."

I put my hands about the slim contours of my throat and pressed them into the soft skin. Once, Katherine had called me a swan for the elegance of my bearing… Many times, Henry had kissed me there, his warm lips lingering on my flesh as he muttered words of love and devotion. It all seemed so far away… that person was another Anne, one who was loved so deeply by her King that she could never fall from grace. I started to laugh louder. The sheer ridiculousness of my fate overtook me.

Master Kingston stared at me as mirth spilled out over my lips, over my form, bouncing from the walls. It sounded unearthly… unnatural. I was nearing the edge of my capacity for calmness. I forced the laugh to end, shutting my lips over it, and turned my feral, dark eyes away. "I will return to my prayers, for the rest of the day, Master Kingston," I whispered, seeking to claim control over the broken one again. "If you would be so good as to leave me with my almoner."

The swordsman had not yet arrived. That was why the execution was delayed. I would die in the French fashion, as ever I had lived. All along, Henry had known I would die. His offers of mercy were a feint. He had known from the start that he was going to kill me.

I returned to my prayers. I prayed for myself, for Elizabeth, and for Henry. My sweet daughter did not need my prayers, but Henry did. He needed them more than anyone.

But if Death did not come, others did; Mary and Margaret Shelton, Nan Gainsford and Mary Lee. Cranmer brought them. His last gift.

I talked to my friends, I unleashed my heart. My part was done. I was ready for death.

Later that day I was told that my marriage had been announced as null and void. There was nothing left to me, but Elizabeth. All that Henry and I did, all we achieved together was gone, swept away by the breath of wolves and jackals, lain bare and crisp, for Henry to write his new tale upon.

"They say the King has already asked for a dispensation," Mary Shelton said to me that afternoon.

"Why does he need one to wed Jane?"

She shrugged. "I know not… but it is rumoured that the King once had an affair with someone related to her." She dropped her voice. "Or that Mistress Seymour once had a liaison with one of his family."

I chuckled. "So he will take another woman he is related to," I said, my mouth twisting into a smile as bitter as winter. "That will make it easier for him to be rid of his wife when he tires of her."

Chapter Eighty

The Tower of London
The Night of the 18th of May 1536

And so it has come. The night before the day I am to die.

I find myself strangely comforted by the notion of death; that at last I will be free of my mortal bonds, free of pain and suffering… free to forget that the man I trusted with my heart has betrayed me unto death.

What is death? What lies behind the veil before me? This whispering, silken sheet which obscures the last truth, the final end? Will I go to God as my true self, I wonder, with the same dreams and hopes and loves and fears that I held so dear in life? Will I leave all such cares behind me? Will I care not that I leave this world of such beauty and majesty and grace, of toil and heartbreak and hardship? Will I mourn to no more walk amidst the willowed wood, sorrow to never again feel the earth beneath my hand? Will I ever again witness the breaking of the bright dawn, pink and golden over the skies? Shall I feel the salt breath of the sea upon my skin, or know the comfort of a heart beating close to mine?

Will the world miss me? Will oak trees mourn not to hear my step below them? Will the streams weep and the clouds grieve, knowing that I will never pass by?

What is death? How shall I meet it? How can I go willingly into the darkness set before me, trusting that God's light will find me? How do I find the courage to do this?

And how shall I surrender the world… this beauteous, graceful, creation that I thought on so little when I was a part of it, and now I am to lose? No more to know the last light of day, or the first. No more to see birds swoop in the heavens, or catch sight of creatures of briar and bracken as they scuttle about their days. No more to watch the stars of the night sky as they dance about the moon. No more to stand in sunlight, witnessing the brilliance and glory of the day.

No more to live. No more to dance, or sing… to lift my voice in company, or trill in happiness when in solitude. Never again to put my soft palm under the velvet of a horse's mouth and feel its silky touch upon my skin. No more to know the caress of rain upon my face, or the warmth of the afternoon sunlight on my back. Never to see the soft hush of purple and grey upon moorland, or flowing water in a blue stream washing over pale grey rocks, smoothed by eons of time and tumbling water.

Never again… Never again.

No more to love. No more to hate. No more to live, and no more to die. Perhaps there is my answer, perhaps there I will find my courage. For in death there will be peace. No more will my restless heart know pain and suffering. God will take that from me. He will grant me peace.

"Death, where is thy sting?" says the Bible. I come to think now that I understand finally what these words mean. It is not in looking forward to a life everlasting alone that such words have meaning, but in the release of a soul from earthly torment.

All along, I thought Henry's love was my salvation. All along, I have been wrong. Henry is not my saviour. I am. His last act, intended to suppress me, to master me, to subdue me, will do nothing of the sort. No more do I hate Henry, for hatred indicates equality, and equals we are no more. Henry is beneath me, and I despise him.

Katherine told me to surrender, to accept, and to set myself free. That is what I will do, as well as I am able. Henry's last act of fragile fear will set me free.

I want to do her bidding. I want to follow Katherine without terror, and yet still I falter. I am become dusk, that unearthly state where all becomes unclear, unfocused, unformed. Wavering between states of being I am held. Half of me is ready, half trembles with fear.

But I can die. I will die. Everything will. Everything must. Death is the price we pay for life. It is the sacrifice we offer, to lose all that was once ours and surrender to the darkness of earth and the light of Heaven. We must accept that we are transitory, that we are mortal; that no matter our deeds and accomplishments, we are not eternal. In surrendering this, this fragile thread we cling to, this illusion that the person inside the vessel is immortal, we may accept death, we may leave life behind, with a blessing for those who follow on our lips.

My soul is prepared. My confession is made. Tyndale once wrote, when arguing with More, that the Church had misused the term penance. It was *repentance*, he argued, that mattered. To find release from sin a soul must confess their ills to God, not to a priest, and repent in the presence of the Almighty. There must be sorrow for sins committed, faith that God will hear and offer forgiveness and mercy, and the making of amends to those who have suffered at the sinner's hands.

Repentance, sorrow, faith and making amends… in these ways does a soul know peace.

I have told my story. I have asked forgiveness. I concealed nothing, I have told all my wrongdoings and I find Tyndale is right… for I have found release.

I wonder if Henry will ever be able to say the same? Will he tell his story to others before his death, seeking absolution, seeking to make amends? I know not, but I doubt it. Henry dwells in fiction and it in him. He believes what he wants to, and thinks people he wronged are to blame. He is not honest enough to look on his own sins and recount them.

Perhaps he knows that I am innocent and does not care. Perhaps the monster has won, and Henry the good knight is lost. For my daughter's sake, for England's sake, I hope this is not so. I hope there is something of the man I loved left in the shell of the demon.

Long have we all taught him to think of himself as not man but God. He has taken those lessons into his soul, and believes all he does is with the approval of the Almighty. But he is wrong. There are forces beyond his control which will judge him on the day he dies. And when we stand together, reunited, he will know.

I find myself wishing for Death to have speed. It will be done. An hour of courage, a moment of pure terror, a flash of agony… and it will be done. It will be over. No more will any man have the power to harm me.

Were it not for Elizabeth, I would go gladly, happily, to my death.

There is something seductive, beautiful, in the notion of knowing pain no more, but only everlasting peace. I have never had peace. Only in brief, passing moments have I felt its hush fall upon me, but it was never secure in my hands. I can hardly imagine it, yet I yearn for it. God the Father will take me in His arms and keep me safe, as my own father failed to. I will hold my brother again, see his smile, feel his hand in mine. I will see Brereton and Weston, and I will thank them for their nobility. I will laugh with Norris again. Beside a bright fire, in the kingdom of God, I will sit with Bridget, Queen Claude and the Archduchess, telling tales throughout the endless eons of existence. Katherine will be there, and I will beg her forgiveness.

I will see my three lost sons play in a place where shadows cannot reach us. We will walk in blessed light, leaving Henry's darkness far behind.

And Henry? He will have what he thinks he wants. Never again will he have to endure a wife challenging him, berating him, questioning him, answering him back. Never again will he be held accountable for his sins. No one will accost him now. Jane Seymour will not dare. She will feel my ghost at her back and fear to become like me. He will render her weak with dread, as he tried to do to me, so he may think himself strong, so he may think himself powerful.

And he will get what he deserves; a hollow shell to encase his fragile spirit in, a mask to hide behind. But a part of him dies with me.

All will know the truth, as will he. They will see the monster that has been bred in the blackness of his soul. They will see through the illusion of his power, and know that he is not strong. They will see his frailty, his terror… they will see that there is nothing in him, that he is empty, that he is lost.

For the rest of his life, Henry will have his people tell him what he wants to hear… and so much the worse for him. His world will become small, pale, and faded. There will be no horizon. No dawn and no dusk. There will be only the noon sun, eradicating all other shades, and lessening the glory of his world. For there must be light and dark, there must be shadow and sun. There must be variance, there must be variety; we must know the light and the dark within, and accept them, if we are to truly be whole.

Tomorrow, he will kill me, but he will become the ghost in truth; a pale imitation of the great man he could have been. A demon set upon a throne where a godly king might have ruled. He will become a wraith, without friends or love to warm his fickle, festering soul.

He will live without love. There is no worse fate.

I would never live under such a condition, even if it brought me all I could ever want. I am braver than Henry. For I know that a life lived without love is no life. It is living death, and I would rather die truly, than face all the years of my life utterly and completely alone.

Henry has surrounded himself with dim echoes of the people he once truly loved. About him, the phantoms he has created move and shift in the shadows. Henry rules a realm of ghosts, and all of them are of his making. He has told himself stories. But there is a problem, when we turn people into stories, when we turn people into *things*. Writers are not the masters of their tales, their characters are. If they are not permitted freedom, the world they inhabit is not real. Henry's fiction is incomplete, for he tries to hold dominion over his players. In lack of liberty, they will die, not on the block as my friends have, or by the sword as I will, but in the stagnant lack of imagination Henry dwells in.

Let Henry sit upon his throne of bones. Let Jane Seymour fill her pallid cheeks with the blood of my kin and friends. Let them lift a veil of shadow over them. The sun will no more reach them. The stars will no more shine. The wind and the rain and the storms will shy from them, shuddering to touch living death. They will abide in lies, in falsehoods, in their fractured, unreal reality, until the day they are called to answer for all they have done.

I am sure Henry thinks he hates me. I am sure he believes in his lies. Hatred feels simple. People think of it as red, like rage, but it is not. The purest hatred glows white; the brightest of flames. Burning, blazing, glorious beauty… the beauty of clarity, of pure and undiluted odium… A beauty that is too pure, too perfect, not to be dangerous. That is hatred. It feels pure, it seems simple and exquisite, but it is not.

And once revenge is won, white fire turns to ash. So will the same be true of Henry's heart, his life, and his soul. Dust will I become as I die, but dust will he be as he lives. He will see the glory of the world, and know no joy in it; he will witness beauty and feel none of its majesty. This is a worse fate than death, and it is Henry's.

The night draws close and cold. The stars are sharp in the chilled blackness. Their lights are darts in the clear, dark skies. I stare into the darkness and it stares right back. It is made of eyes, but I fear to be watched no more.

I should rest. I should eat and sleep, but I will do neither. Little sleep have I had since first I was brought by water to this place. Little slumber do I require. Soon I will rest for all the days of existence, held tight in the embrace of God.

The swordsman from France will be here soon; they have prepared a stage upon which my life will end with the sudden sweep of a sword. It stands on the ground north of the White Tower, fulfilling the Abbot of Garadon's prophecy that a queen would meet her doom "where one tower is white and another green". I will not die in flames, as he predicted, not in physical ones at least. But the flames of my heart are enough to make me think this prophecy has been brought to life.

To the people, I will become a myth; vilified and tainted. I will become a story used to make children behave, eat their dinner, or go to bed. I will become a demon; Evil Queen Anne, the betrayer, the traitor, the whore, the witch. They will not remember my charity, my loyalty, my zeal for reform. They will not recall my desire to protect the Church, from Rome, from Henry, from Cromwell. They will not remember my love for my family, for my daughter, or my love for my husband.

I will be painted in shades of shadow and gloom; in blackened night and the green-blue of black raven wing. I will become the portrait of a woman who risked much and lost all. People will shiver to look upon me. No light will illuminate my portrait. I will be lost in mists of lies and the fog of falsehood. My virtues will be forgotten, and my false vices will be lauded in the notes of history.

But there are those who will mourn me. They will mourn my death in secret, but there will be some in this world to sorrow at my passing.

My mother… will she walk through the chamber that Mary and I once shared as girls, hear the floorboards creak under her soft footfall, and remember us dancing there as children, welcoming in Midsummer as we pranced about a silken scarf of crimson, pretending we were at the village bonfires? Will Mary, safe in Calais with her husband, think on me as she hears I have died? Will her little girl, named for me, grow up in the knowledge of my true character, or the false one they have granted me?

And what of our child… my poor Elizabeth? Will Henry truly be kind? When I think of my child I fear I shall lose my mind. I cannot run to her, cannot protect her. I cannot hold her. She will be made a bastard, no more a princess… stigmatised as my daughter. But she is still the daughter of the King, and he cannot deny her that. No, he cannot deny that she was the true fruit of our love. She is the image of him…

But the eyes in that little face are mine, those dark, deep, black pools. When I am gone, my eyes will still look on the world from within her face.

In Elizabeth, at least, something good of me will continue to live in this world. I pray to God that she will lead a quieter, happier life than mine.

The dust from the scaffold's construction scatters gently in the night's wind. The fire burns and the winds whisper around the Tower. The skies are ominous, but there will be some sun to light the heavens tomorrow.

I will not die as my enemies wish me to. I will not let all that is Anne Boleyn slip away from me. I will not walk out as only the broken one, with my head hanging or scream and struggle in fear at the face of Death. I will die well and gracefully, just as I have lived. I go to death as myself, the three women in me joined as one, in the knowledge of my power, in acceptance of the light and dark within me… The power that Henry will never know.

Katherine is with me. Enemies and rivals we were in life, yet sisters of fate we are, united in death. She is ash as I am yet ember. Come the morrow, I shall be ash too. Floating into forgetfulness, in the realm where those lost to life linger.

The brittle grass upon the sandy plain will blow. Its leaves will mark out another circle. Particles of sand will tumble away, reaching new places, forming new circles, new stories, new tales… new beginnings and new ends.

All is one. As I scatter from the place my story began, so a new circle will form. And another, and another… going on through time, dancing in the light of destiny.

I wrote a poem, and left it on my desk.

Oh Death, rock me asleep,
Bring on my quiet rest,
Let pass my very guiltless ghost
Out of my careful breast.
Toll on thou passing bell,
Ring out my doleful knell,
Let thy sound my death tell,
Death doth draw nigh,
There is no remedy.

My pains who can express?
Alas, they are so strong.

My dolour will not suffer strength
My life for to prolong.
Toll on thou passing bell,
Ring out my doleful knell,
Let thy sound my death tell,
Death doth draw nigh,
There is no remedy.

Alone in prison strange,
I wail my destiny;
Well worth this cruel hap that I
Should taste this misery.
Toll on thou passing bell,
Ring out my doleful knell,
Let thy sound my death tell,
Death doth draw nigh,
There is no remedy.

Farewell my pleasures past,
Welcome, my present pain,
I feel my torments so increase
That life cannot remain.
Cease now, thou passing bell,
Rung is my death knell,
For its sound my death doth tell.
Death doth draw nigh;
Sound the knell dolefully, for now I die.

"George, you are in Heaven," I whisper. "And soon will I join you there."

I place a hand on the window. "So let us go," I whisper. "Let us go, you and I, to where the greenwood grows. To where the new buds burst and blossom sings. Let us take hands and walk, the warmth of the setting sun upon our backs. Let our feet trip over soft moss and fresh grass. Let us leave the world behind."

A vision of Heaven comes to me. It is a perfect field, strewn with flowers bobbing in a gentle wind. It will always be the hour before sunset there. The warmth of the day will not have left, and the chill of night not yet come. There will be poppies, their crimson blooms dusky in the falling light. Honeysuckle will bring light to the shade, daisies will sparkle in the grass like stars. Celandine will bring hope, and the scent of flowers and rough bark will fill the air. There will be a crystal stream, burbling at the edge of the field, flowing over rocks smoothed by the passage of time.

Beyond, there will be a forest, spun with spindles of soft, dappled light. There will be hillsides and groves, sweet blossom and hidden glens. We will hear my children in the distance, laughing as they play, as they tease, as they live. Purkoy will chase them, barking at their heels. Over the field and the stream and the forest the sound of their mirth will wander, breaking through the musical chatter of birds; a tender sound, as one with the warmth of the sun.

And there we will find our friends. Brereton will tell us stories of adventure, brash deeds and bold times. Weston will play for us to dance. I will take Norris' hand, and offer him my heart. George and I will read to each other, our backs against rocks heated by the warmth of the day, as we listen to the words of those wiser than us, and hear the sound of my three sons tearing through the still woods.

And if I see Smeaton there, I will try to forgive.

There will be our kingdom. There will we live as the world continues on without us. We will be united and reunited, brought together, never to lose each other again.

There will be peace, there will be love, there will be life, everlasting.

"Take my hand," I whisper to George. "Take my hand, brother mine, and together we will run as once we did as children. Let our laughter rock the gentle trees and race through the grass. There we will rejoice, as innocent as children, as pure as the fresh, new leaves, our souls as free as the soft wind, and our hearts at liberty."

I close my eyes. "Take my hand," I whisper to my brother. "Let us go, George, let us go. There we will go, and there we will stay, as this cruel, cold world ebbs, and flows away."

Chapter Eighty-One

The Tower of London
The Morning of the 19th of May 1536

I have not slept. There is no need. What rest does a soul about to depart for Heaven require?

I went to Mass. I heard the words of the Lord for the last time in this feeble life. This fragile, mortal world. They brought food for me to eat, but I could do no more than pick at it.

I am scared. My soul is prepared. I want death. I want release. But there is a part of me that is terrified of death. The broken one wants to run… to flee this place upon the wings of a falcon sent by God to save me. Yet I know there is no such creature. I will die and I must prepare myself to face death and show courage. The broken one will die with me. I will bring her to courage with my strength.

Will it hurt? This thought plagues me… that the pain that will come will terrify me into quaking before the crowds already gathering outside. I have been granted the honour of facing death inside the Tower confines. Not for me a death on Tower Hill, as my brother and friends endured. No screaming crowds of commoners, no… but I will see familiar faces, the faces of my enemies, as I walk into the arms of Death.

I will not cower before them. I will not falter. I will die as Anne Boleyn.

Eight o'clock rings in the Tower chapel, and Kingston comes to the door. I have been waiting for the sound of his footsteps, and now they are here, I do not want to hear them…. the deathly knell that announces my time has come.

I had dressed with care. My gown of dark, heavy grey silk strikes bold against the kirtle of crimson underneath. I wear red for it is the colour of Catholic martyrs. But there is another reason. I feared red for a long time; feared to remember my children and their deaths through it; feared to unleash the broken one, feared to lose myself to her. Today I need to fear it no more. My blood will rush from my neck, and it will join theirs in the soil. Today, I will see my dead children again.

My robe resembles the one I wore in Calais, on the first night Henry and I were together. He will not miss this when they tell him of it. Yet I wear it not for him, but for Elizabeth. I wear it to remember the moment when this glorious gift was granted to me. For the love, which then existed, which brought her to life.

Upon my head is not the French hood that I wore so often in life, but an English gable one. It was the first hood I wore, so perhaps it makes sense that it will be the last covering upon my raven hair. But it also proclaims my link to England, the country that gave birth to me, the place where I rose to glory and where I fell due to the machinations of wicked men.

My cloak is lined with ermine, the fur of royalty, for I am still the Queen. Under the Act of Succession, which has not been rescinded, I was made Queen by statutory right, not by virtue of my marriage to Henry. This has not been repealed, therefore I go to my death a queen. I meet Death as a woman accused of adultery, even though I never had a husband, as a queen who was never married to her King. Perhaps it is fitting. I was ever a creature of contradictions. And I will die as such.

But I am the Queen.

They cannot take that from me, just as they cannot take my power, my dignity, or my honour. Now, at the close, I finally understand. I have found the balance between the women within me. I have balanced the light and the dark.

They are twins of the same mother. For in the blackest, deepest night there shine the brightest stars. I defy you to look upon their blazing brilliance and tell me that darkness has more power than light. It seems that way at times, but it is not true. They own equal power and equal weakness. For every night ends with a dawn, and every day dies with dusk. They cannot live without each other, nor we without them. They are within us. We must see them, accept their influence, and use both to strive to do the best we can with all we are granted.

I am free although I am a prisoner. I am more alive at the moment of my death than I was in life. Henry will have my head, but my heart is his no more. My soul, my heart, myself, they are mine alone.

Finally, I am free of him.

I have prepared my speech. I will speak not of innocence, but I will admit no guilt. I will protect my daughter. To decry Henry in the last moments of my life would bring danger to Elizabeth. I will not allow that. But I will not admit guilt. Those who attend my execution, conditioned to prisoners proclaiming their guilt, whether they were or not, will understand.

Kingston comes for me. "Acquit yourself of your charge," I say. "I have been long prepared."

He hands me a purse with twenty pounds in it, so I might give alms before my death. It is usual for a condemned person to pay their own executioner, but I have already been informed his fee has been taken care of by Henry. How sweet of him.

As we make to leave, I turn to Lady Kingston. "Commend me to His Majesty," I say. "Tell him that he hath ever been constant in his career of advancing me. From a private gentlewoman, he made me a Marquess and from Marquess to a queen. And now he hath left no higher degree of honour, for he gives my innocency the crown of martyrdom as a saint in Heaven."

"I dare not carry such a message to the King," she breathes.

I merely smile. I knew that would be her answer, but we are surrounded by guards, my ladies and Kingston's men. By the fall of night, most of London will hear my last declaration.

Escorted by two hundred Yeomen, Kingston takes me from my lodgings and we walk past the Great Hall, through Cole Harbour Gate, to the western side of the White Tower. We wait in an alcove. There are crowds ahead, I can see them, hungry faces lit up in the morning light. The wind blows soft and the clouds part, illuminating the scaffold where the executioner stands. I cannot see his famous sword, and that worries me. I wish to know when death is coming.

I turn to Margaret Lee, handing her a book of hours. "This is for you," I murmur, trying to still my reckless heart.

She opens it at the page I have marked. *Remember me when you do pray, That hope doth lead from day to day.*

Her eyes fill with tears.

"Feel no pity for me," I say to Margaret as her face pales. She turns, her eyes wild and wide. "Pity me not," I say again, taking her hand. "I have lived and I have loved. I have done all that I could with my time. I opened my heart and I risked all. I do not fear the eyes of God upon me."

I smile. "Pity Henry. Pity all those at court. Pity creatures that live without love, for all they know is the aching darkness of agony. Some say a man can be measured by his friends. What will men say of one who has killed all his friends?" I stroke her pale hand, "of a man who murdered the woman he loved?"

"You should take care, my lady," says Kingston's gruff voice at my back.

"For what purpose, my lord?" I turn, a ghost of a smile on my face. "What more could be done against me now?"

He has no answer for me. He knows no more could be done to me. My name is spoken now in a whisper, my daughter is stolen from me, my friends are dead, my family disgraced and in a moment I will die. Nothing more can Henry take from me in life. But nothing that is me is left to him. I am free.

But he is not. Never will he be able to forget what we once were… all that we once had. The power and the glory that between us changed England… perhaps the world. He will try to forget me, try to lose memories of me in the arms of another woman. He will listen to all his sycophantic courtiers tell him, and he will think himself content.

But I know Henry.

So often does he cry out about his conscience that many think it is another of his fantasies, but it is not. In the dark of night, in the realm between dreaming and waking, he will remember me. When he gazes on our daughter, I will stare back at him from behind Elizabeth's black eyes. As he moves about his court, with that pale wisp of a woman at his side, he will remember me dancing, singing, laughing… The clothes I made will be upon his skin, my cushions and bed hangings about his chamber. He will pick up a goblet that once I used and I will come to him, as my sons did to me, a flash of memory striking through his carefully constructed fantasy.

No, this will not be easy for him. He will pretend it is, but I will haunt him. Katherine, Wolsey, Fisher, More, George, Brereton, Norris, Weston and perhaps even the craven Smeaton will come for him.

No man may murder his friends, and rest easy.

There are many wraiths in Henry's mind, and today I join them. By nightfall, Henry will have another presence at his back, another voice in his mind, another set of eyes watching him. Today he gains another ghost.

"It is almost the end," Margaret whispers, her face a blank mask of horror.

"You think this is the end?" I ask with a smile, touching Margaret's cheek.

Did Katherine place that thought in your mind, sweet friend? I wonder. *Does my sister of fate seek to bring me courage?*

"It is not the end," I say. "All endings are beginnings, old friend… all dusks but dawns of another day. The strands of stories are frayed. There is a circle which forms about the lives of men. It takes from one story a thread, and loops it upon another, so the story never truly ends, as it never begins."

I look from the window at the gathering crowds. I thought I would feel fear at this moment before death, but strangely, I am calm.

This is not the end. Not for me, not for my soul, and not for my blood. As my soul ascends into Heaven, so my body will become of the earth. My blood will seep into the soil, my flesh will melt into the water. My bones will rest atop the caverns of the world.

I will become England.

For as much as the earth is the source of all life, it is also where we go to die. She is a womb and a tomb; creation and destruction, light and dark… a circle with no end and no beginning. A snake swallowing its tail. The love of a mother to her daughter, returned and reflected back, as two mirrors held before one another.

From the earth springs all life and into her flows death. She is the maiden and the mother, the infant and the death crone.

Elizabeth will not lose me. I will always be with her.

I will be in the earth, the wind, the water… in the skies, the air and the ground beneath her feet.

I will be upon the wind she breathes; in the green, undulating fields bending to the bright skyline. My bones will stand amongst the last line of trees on the horizon. In the sigh of the oceans, slipping up the sandy beach, I will wait for her. Every pebble she plays with will hold a part of me. My energy will be in the grey skies and the blue; in crashing thunder and feral lightening. From within the clouds I will watch over her. I will dwell in the kind sun and the glaring, in lashing rain and creeping mist, in birdsong and the whispering woods.

My blood will be in the earth on which she walks. The flowers she plucks will be born of my body. The warm air of the day and the blessed coolness of night will be fed by my bones.

Heaven claims my soul, and there I will wait for my daughter, but England will take my blood, my flesh, my bone, marrow and sinew… and they will surround her. They will bind Elizabeth to England. They will hold her close, they will keep her safe.

I will be everything and nothing, a presence not at her side, but surrounding her, suffusing her, filling her… a part of her life, her future and her past.

All things are joined. Nothing is wasted.

So cry not, Elizabeth, I think. *The dead do not die. They become a part of the world around you, part of the majesty and beauty of life. Look for me in the wild places. Find me in the hush of midnight. When you reach out to feel the wind, you will take my hand. When you stand on a hilltop, I will stand beside you. When you take to your bed, I will lead you to gentle dreams. When you laugh, I will laugh with you.*

I will dwell in the peak of honest laughter, and the crisp, fresh scent of a new book. In the birdsong of dusk I will linger. In the life of the world will I live. There I shall wait for you. I will be your comfort.

Crown me not with henbane, as the ancients did to their dead. I have no wish to forget those I loved or the memories of my life. I will remember and I will linger. I will not forget you, nor you me.

Cry not, my blessed daughter. I will always be with you. I will always love you.

"This is not the end," I whisper. "I go back to the earth from which I was taken. Dust I am, and to dust I will return."

Epilogue

The Tower of London
The Bell Tower
May 19th 1536

Thomas Wyatt

I watched them kill the woman I loved today.

Watched her walk, brave as a lion, pale as a ghost. Through the streets of the Tower she came, past the crowds where she distributed alms, and onto the platform where her killer stood in the bright light of day.

Anne had never been more beautiful. She was afraid, even at this distance I could see that, but she was brave, she was powerful; as fragile as she was forceful, as light as she was dark.

Cromwell stood in the front row. No coward heart was he. He would face the woman he had brought down, as his master never would dare to. As Anne mounted the scaffold, she saw him. Their eyes met. She inclined her head. It was brief as the passing breeze, yet it was there; two foes acknowledging each other; acceptance of what had passed.

Did she know the King demanded her removal, and Cromwell found a way? I suspect so. Clever Anne… she missed little. Falsehoods have convinced others. Lost in this web, they think they see truth, but they are surrounded, wrapped tight, by lies. The greatest power is to make people see what you wish them to. But even that may be thwarted by one more potent.

By love.

Love allows me to see through this mist. The King wants her gone, and so will it be. He wants an empty vessel, to shape and fill as he wishes. Anne would never have been that to anyone. That is why she had to die.

This is his true reason. Those who have been fooled will say she died for her sins. Those who have not will say it was because she could not grant him a son. But these are not the true reasons.

He feared her. He always did. From the first moment he set eyes on her, from the first stirring of lust, it was there… a canker in his soul. He wanted to possess her so he might control her, and control his fear… but even when she became his, even when he won her heart, he did not own her. Her strength made him feel weak. Her courage made him a coward. He could not diminish Anne, so he took the craven path, and murdered what he could not master.

This is no victory. He is still the same, as is she. He has not triumphed, he has not won. The fear in his heart will not lessen as she dies. The craven soul within him will never grow strong.

She walked to the front of the platform and spoke gently, her sweet voice ringing against the stone walls of the Tower. She chilled the crowds with her majesty. And she was smiling; a gentle, contemplative expression. She was ready to die.

"Good Christian people," her voice rang out, that lilt of France which had never abandoned her, sung against the white walls of the Tower.

"I have not come here to preach a sermon. I have come here to die. For according to the law and by the law I am judged to die, and therefore I will speak nothing against it. I come here only to die, and thus to yield myself humbly to the will of the King, my lord. And if, in my life, I did ever offend the King's grace, surely with my death I do now atone. I am come hither to accuse no man, nor to speak of that whereof I am accused and condemned to die, as I know full well that aught I say in my defence doth not appertain to you. I pray and beseech you, good friends, to pray for the life of the King, my sovereign lord and yours. I pray to God to save the King, and send him long to reign over you, for a gentler nor a more merciful prince was there never, and to me he was ever a good, a gentle, and sovereign lord."

Her chin came up, displaying her long white neck. In how many dreams had I kissed that throat? In how many dreams had I longed to hold her... hold this wild, strange creature, this vision of beauty and grace?

"And if any person will meddle of my cause," she said loudly, "I require them to judge the best. And thus I take my leave of the world and of you all. I heartily desire you all to pray for me. Jesus Christ have mercy on me. To God I commend my soul."

The crowds were crying. They had all noted she had admitted no guilt, which was striking at such a time. As bold as she had lived, would Anne die.

She handed a prayer book to her maids, thanking them, and spoke to the executioner. She was asking him to wait until she had finished her prayers. The woman I love would command even Death to wait until she was ready.

Her mantle was removed, stripping away the last touch of royalty granted to her. Her gable hood was taken too, replaced with a linen coif. She covered her glorious hair, shining midnight against the sun's cruel light.

She knelt and prayed. I could almost hear her melodious voice, so charming, even when used in rage. Her face was bowed. I could not see her beautiful eyes, those deep, dark pools glittering like the sea under moonlight.

Many was the time I thought myself lost in those eyes. I could have drowned in them. There, I could have died a contented man.

I could not look away. I had to see her, no matter how much it hurt.

She was the breaking dawn, the light to which we were all drawn.

The crowds were moved to pity. They had witnessed many executions, yet this one touched them. Women wept and men grumbled. As she sank to her knees, they did too, even Cromwell. Only Suffolk and Fitzroy remained standing.

The swordsman waited, respecting her last request. He was no clumsy child brought to kill her, but an expert sent for from France. She was nervous as her lips sped over their prayers. Her eyes searched for the sword. If she wanted to die quick and clean, she had to keep still, but she could not. She glanced back time and time again, fearing he would steal upon her before she was ready.

"O Lord have mercy on me," she said, her eyes flashing forth and back. "To God I commend my soul. To Jesus Christ I commend my soul. Oh Lord God, receive my soul. Lord Jesu, receive my soul…" Her eyes were dazed. She swayed like a stalk of golden hay in the summer wind. I held my breath. If she faltered it would take more than one strike to kill her. She would suffer horrible, unimaginable agony.

"Madam," said the executioner. "Do not fear. I will wait until you tell me."

"You will have to take this off," she said, gesturing to her coif, but he shook his head. He knew he would be quicker than she imagined.

"O Lord, have mercy on me," she said, her prayers stumbling as they blindfolded her. "To God I commend my soul…"

He called to a boy to bring his sword; tricked, she turned her neck. She could see nothing through her blindfold, but still she looked. Swiftly, he pulled the great, blunt-tipped, sharp-sided sword from under a pile of hay. He came up, bare of shoes, upon her.

Anne was still looking blindly behind her, her neck twisted, elongated at just the right angle. "Into Thy hands…" she said as the sword swung.

The blade caught the sun as it flew up. Silver glinting against gold. She did not see Death as he stole upon her. He was quick, He was clean. The sword cleaved her neck. Her head fell into a stack of hay.

Her lips were still moving in prayer.

She was not born a Queen, but she died as one.

Her beautiful body remained upright for a moment, then fell, slumped on the dusty platform, pumping bright red blood onto the ground. Her head thumped to the floor, bouncing on the dusty surface. Her maids rushed to cover their fallen mistress with cloths and with their tears. There was a dull cheer from the crowd, but it held no enthusiasm.

There was no casket. No one had thought to provide one. An old elm chest, used for storing arrows, was heaved out, and she was put in it. Her ladies stumbled to do their work, hands shaking, faces numbed by grief.

The cannons on the walls of the Tower fired, telling London, telling England, and the waiting King that the Queen was dead.

She was gone.

I fell back from the window and sat on the stool in my bare cell. I put my face into my hands and wept. Hours passed. The crowds dispersed.

*

I am alone.

I know I am safe. Cromwell has told me so. He wants me to work for him, for the King.

To work for the men who slew this lady of fire and grace? Nothing could disgrace me more. Once I loved her. Did I ever cease to? Once she asked me if a heart may stop loving when love has been unleashed. I told her then that it could, but now I know not.

I remember much. The days we spent as children together, playing in the bright gardens at Hever, riding our horses, pretending to be kings and queens, lords and dukes… people of consequence who altered the world.

She had been one of those people.

I remember the night I opened the door to my hunting lodge and found the child I remembered had become a woman; sultry and seductive, beautiful and wise, canny, witty and enticing. She never understood her power. Never saw that those who loved her were bound to her, lashed to the rocks beneath her feet, looking up at this confident, curious creature. This woman so unlike every other we had ever known.

No… she wielded power but did not understand it. Anne was a glorious being. She was not perfect, but that which we love never is. It is the faults in a person that make them real. Flawed as she was fascinating, Anne Boleyn would never leave a heart when she had claimed it.

My friends are dead. The woman I loved is dead. A new world is dawning, and I cannot believe it will be a better one. Not without her, not without them.

Dark clouds are gathering. I know not what the future may bring.

All I know, is what we have lost.

I take up my pen, but I cannot write about her. I cannot bring myself to. To the world, she may become forgotten, but not to me. I will honour her in my heart for the rest of my days.

> *"These bloody days have broken my heart,*
> *My lust, my youth, did them depart,*
> *And blind desires of estate.*
> *Who hastens to climb seeks to rest,*
> *Of truth, circa Regna tonat."*

About the throne, thunder rolls. About the throne, there is now only death.

We must live with what has been done. Is this life… what is left to me? I know not. Sometimes life becomes but existence. Sometimes in death a person becomes only more alive.

The winter winds will blow, summer light will dim. The spring and autumn will be less bright. But she will not fade.

"And I watched as he opened the sixth seal," I murmur, "… and the skies became black as sackcloth, and the moon waxed as blood. The stars fell… and Heaven vanished away. Mountains and trees moved, and the kings of the earth, and the great men, and the rich men… every bond man and free man hid themselves in dens, in the rocks of the hills. They said to the hills and rocks 'fall on us and hide us… for the great day of His wrath cometh, and who can endure it'."

I walk to the window. A dull hush has fallen. It is night. The skies seem darker than ever before. The stars do not want to shine. The streets of the Tower are empty, smoke tumbles into the air from chimney pots.

Specks of ash float in the skies. Silver particles dancing against the stars.

Amongst them is one of amber, glowing in the night.

Author's Notes

I started writing this series almost ten years ago. Little ideas, inconsistent scribbles here and there turned into lines and chapters and books. When I first found I wanted to write the story of Anne Boleyn I was deterred; it had been done so many times before, I wondered if I had anything to contribute. But I realised that I did. I had read so many tales of Anne that painted her either as the ice-cold witch-queen who destroyed a marriage and strove only for burning ambition, and others that upheld her as a saint, and, in reading all these tales, I thought something was missing; a portrait of a woman who was not a saint nor a sinner, but was like all of us, something in between.

I also thought that single books on her life skipped over too much that I felt was important. From this thought, the series *Above all Others, The Lady Anne*, was born.

Anne Boleyn died on the 19th of May 1536. Her name was defamed. Everything that was important to her had been stripped away and her enemies ensured that her name would go down in history as that of a vilified, shamed and fallen Queen.

I believe she died innocent of what she was accused. Much ill had Anne done in her life, to Katherine, to Mary, Wolsey and to many others, but I do not believe she committed adultery or treason, still less do I believe that a woman of such zealous faith would ever have committed incest.

The charges against her were brought for reasons other than what was protested. Anne was standing in the way. She could not give Henry the son he wished for, at least not in the time frame he desired, and this was her most fatal 'flaw'. She was standing, too, in the way of peace with Spain and Cromwell's plans for the monasteries. Although Charles of Spain had agreed to acknowledge Anne as Queen, with her removal, peace would be easier to achieve, and her opposition to the wealth of the monasteries being tossed into the Crown coffers put her in direct conflict with Cromwell, but more importantly, with Henry. Anne did not oppose the investigations, or dissolution, but thought the money or property confiscated should go back into charitable works. Any houses shut down should be used for education, and some houses should be saved. This was what Anne thought, and is upheld by her actions.

But for all this, there was another reason. Henry had grown older, and did not want a wife who behaved like Anne. I believe he wanted peace, quiet, and a meek and submissive woman who would obey him. All this he found in Jane Seymour. Any time Jane attempted to become more, or tried to assert herself, she was put firmly in her place and reminded of the fate of the woman she had supplanted.

Anne has been criticised for never becoming a wife in the model the times expected. This criticism is unfair. I believe Anne loved Henry, and their marriage came about not for ambition, even though I will not deny she held that vice or virtue, but because he fell for her and she for him. Anne could not cope with Henry taking mistresses, and told him so. What she failed to see was that she had married a man who, despite his many extreme acts, was deeply conventional. Anne was anything but. Their courtship and relationship had been nothing short of radical, so why should their marriage be conventional? In his early letters to Anne, Henry wrote of a relationship which was not only exclusive, but unique. Anne believed him. I have no doubt Henry, too, believed this at the time of writing, but later, as his lust for a wife who would obey him, as all people should, overcame his passionate, romantic ideal of a marriage of equals, he wanted her to submit to him.

Anne commented on his infidelity in public, and reproached Henry for it. This led to her being seen as unnatural, but she was, in fact, only reacting with understandable hurt as the man she loved betrayed her trust and broke his promises.

I believe Anne thought their love would forge a different kind of marriage, one where a husband and wife were equal, would not betray each other as so many did, and would stand the test of time. Anne was wrong.

Today, some people say that Anne should have accepted her role as wife and Queen and should not have criticised Henry for his marital failings, but would we slander a wife today, who, finding her husband with another women, protested? We would not. Strangely, we allow Katherine of Aragon to have been hurt and wounded by Henry's infidelities, but deny this to Anne. Some people who support 'Team Katherine' over 'Team Anne' would say Anne got what she deserved, as she had done the same to Katherine. Perhaps this is true, but no one deserved the fate Anne was dealt. I think Anne fell in love with Henry, and believed all her subsequent actions to bring about their marriage and protect it were justified by that love. Love can bring out the best in us, but also the worst.

I, myself, am neither Team Anne nor Katherine. I like to think of myself as "Team of the Six Wives". Never will I stand on "Team Henry".

Anne's Innocence and Legacy

Anne was the most controversial of Henry's wives, both in her times and ours; people either love her or hate her.

But even her detractors admitted that Anne showed courage in life and death, and most serious historians now dismiss the accusations against her. Indeed, three quarters of the charges against Anne can be proved false by court records. Going back through them, we find that when she was accused of sleeping with men at Westminster, she was at Greenwich, and vice versa. She was also pregnant during a lot of the alleged offences. Some writers have protested that she might have taken a lover in order to conceive a son, and save herself, but if she was pregnant *at the time* of the alleged offence, why would she take the risk? The notion she took lovers whilst in her lying-in chamber, after the birth of Elizabeth, is also ridiculous. Not only was she segregated from the court, she was recovering from childbirth.

In the book, I had George visit her in her lying-in chamber. This was for narrative purposes, and was unlikely to have been permitted.

Even Chapuys did not believe the charges against her. One of his dispatches about Henry read; *"You never saw a prince or husband show or wear his [cuckold] horns more patiently and lightly than this one does. I leave you to guess the cause of it"*, and of the trial of George Boleyn, *"no proof of his guilt was produced except that of his having once passed many hours in her [Anne's] company, and other little follies."*

After Anne's death, he wrote, *"No one ever showed more courage or greater readiness to meet death than she did."*

In his last notes on Anne, there is a tone of respect. Although people are fond of saying that Chapuys only ever referred to her as 'the concubine' or other derogatory names, it is not really so. Certainly he used those terms, but he also called her by name more often. Chapuys had no reason to like Anne, but he was not quite as unfair to her as many suppose. Chapuys, her enemy, showed more emotion and reverence about Anne's death than her husband. He also understood the cause. *"The executioner's sword and her own death were virtually to separate and divorce man and wife. However, if such was their intention, it strikes me that it would have been a far more decent and honest excuse to allege that she had been married to another man still alive."*

This, of course, had been done. Anne's alleged pre-contract with Henry Percy was first used to attempt to annul her marriage to Henry, but it had not worked, so Cranmer was called upon to use Mary Boleyn instead. Since Anne had admitted in the Tower, that on this basis she and Henry were not married, we may ask why it was needful that she be executed at all. At the time of her trial, adultery, even for a queen, was not a capital crime, and if she had never been married to Henry she could not have committed adultery. The accusation of treason was still there, but it was clearly the weaker charge, with little to substantiate it, which is why her accusers tried to prove her guilty of adultery; if she was guilty of adultery, they could make the charges of treason stick. Guilty of one thing was guilty of another.

The truth is that Anne had to die because Henry did not want another Katherine of Aragon on his hands. Were Anne to be locked up in a nunnery, she might prove just as embarrassing as Katherine had, and might cause dispute about the legitimacy of any children Henry had with Jane, just as Katherine had with Anne. Anne's enemies, Cromwell in particular I imagine, would also not have been keen for this to happen, as even during the last months of her life, Anne exerted a power over Henry that was hard to match. Indeed, no one would ever have the same influence over him again, not even Cromwell. If she were allowed to live, she might find a way to reach him, and if that happened, her foes would be in serious trouble. The only safe solution was death.

According to Chapuys, Cromwell later admitted he had made up the accusations, the events and dates which led to her death. *"It was he [Cromwell] who, in consequence of the disappointment and anger he had felt on hearing the King's answer to me on the third day of Easter, had planned and brought about the whole affair."*

Even allowing for Chapuys to be transcribing Cromwell's words, this is a pretty revealing admission.

Another reason I believe in Anne's innocence is because of her last confession. It is all too easy, in these days, to think that Anne might have faked her last confession and protested she had not sinned against Henry in order to bring about a pardon, or to clear her name. But to think such is to ignore that Anne was a woman of faith. God, Heaven and the afterlife were not theories to her and many of her contemporaries, they were *truths*. To die with a sin on one's conscience, such as a lie, was to risk not being allowed into Heaven. Her immortal soul was at risk. Anne would not have gambled.

Another reason is the strikingly accurate nature of her last confession; that she had not offended against Henry *with her body*. Alison Weir postulates this may mean that she had grown to love another, but had not acted, physically, upon it… a theory I decided to follow in this book, threading together this idea along with Anne's ramblings in the Tower about Norris. I do not know if she truly had feelings for him, but if she had fallen for another man I hardly blame her. Henry had been repeatedly unfaithful, had wounded her trust and love, and had shamed and threatened her. His threats we would now term as emotional or psychological abuse. It is not unsurprising to think that she may have taken comfort in a platonic, or romantic, love, but I think it went no further, and her last confession should be accepted as genuine.

There is a possibility that Henry's crimes were worse than often believed. In Alison Weir's book *King and Court*, the historian theorises that Anne might have been pregnant when she went to her death, having conceived again when the couple were reconciled after Anne's miscarriage in January 1536. I chose not to follow this line of theory, as the evidence is by no means certain, but there are some facts that may cause one to wonder.

1. After her arrest, Anne was not subject to an inspection of her body, standard for the time, to ascertain if she was pregnant. This is unusual and worth note. It might seem impossible that if Anne was carrying his child, Henry would have moved against her. But if he believed she was unfaithful, and the child was not his, it remains possible that this insecure, jealous, and often shallow man might have seen her execution, and that of her child, as justice.

2. Various documents about Anne's trial are missing, presumed destroyed. It is dangerous to suppose that mention of her pregnancy could be amongst them, and evidence was destroyed to protect Henry and Cromwell, but it remains a possibility. It is also possible these records were simply lost, or were destroyed in Queen Elizabeth's reign.

3. A letter Henry wrote, speaking in high praise of his wife in February 1536, seems to suggest a child may come soon.
4. The favour Anne had in early 1536 seems odd when you look at the fact she had miscarried again.

I chose not to include this theory in my book because other historians disagree, and there is therefore a weight of doubt. Another reason is Anne herself. I cannot bring myself to believe that if she were pregnant she would have said nothing. There were 2,000 people at her trial, so had she said something there, *pleaded her belly*, as it was known, her execution would have been postponed until she bore the child. It is possible she might have said something in private, and it was ignored because Henry wanted her dead, but even if she was consumed by an intense desire to die, as she was at the end, having lost everything, Anne was a woman of abiding, genuine faith. She would not have taken an innocent to death with her. One could argue that three miscarriages/ premature births (some say only two, and some one, but I chose to follow the theory of three) may have brought her to a place where she could not bear the thought of trying again, but I do not think this would have been the case. Since she was so careful to confess her sins, and absolve herself of the accusations against her, I don't think she would have allowed a child to die with her.

Another point in favour of her innocence is that on the scaffold, Anne made no protestation of innocence, which has sometimes been held against her, but she also made *no admission of guilt*, which was standard practise for the Tudor era. This omission is striking. In saying nothing, Anne proclaimed she was not guilty.

Anne's choice of wardrobe, ever a high concern of this elegant woman's, on the day of her death was also salient. Her ermine robe proclaimed her as royalty, and her kirtle, the Tudor under-skirt, was crimson. Red was the colour of Catholic martyrs. Anne was proclaiming to the world that she went to her death an innocent.

She was also demonstrating her faith. People claim Anne Boleyn for the Protestant faith, but she was an evangelical Catholic who believed in the rites of the traditional Church. Some points of faith she may have disagreed with, but Anne Boleyn lived and died a Catholic.

Another fact for Anne is that when she was arrested, none of her ladies were. Not one of them stood accused of aiding their mistress in adultery, and none were sent to the Tower. To understand how difficult it would have been for a queen of this era to commit adultery, one has to understand that this was not the sultry world portrayed in *The Tudors*, or racy films. This was reality. Queens were closely guarded. The women who served them were not there for show, nor were they there to merely provide handkerchiefs and serve drinks. They were usually chosen by the King, and were there to guard the reputation of the Queen. When Queen Catherine Howard was arrested on charges of adultery, her ladies, including the unfortunate Lady Jane Rochford, were arrested, and Jane Rochford died for aiding her mistress. With Anne, none of her ladies were. There is, naturally, the possibility that any ladies detained turned King's evidence in return for their statements, but nowhere in the documents of the time does it seem this happened, and if it had, why would her accusers not troop out these women to speak against Anne in court? The truth is, because there were none who were detained, and none who were accused, because everything Anne, and the five men who died with her, were accused of, was nonsense.

The fact is, Henry sent his wife to her death, and he knew she was innocent. This is borne out when, much later, Jane Seymour, then his wife, begged for him to spare the ring-leaders of the *Pilgrimage of Grace*, a rebellion of peasants and lords which rose against Henry in 1537 in response to the dissolution of the monasteries. When Jane begged for these men, Henry allegedly told her not to meddle in politics, as her predecessor had done the same, and this had led to her death.

Henry knew what had been done to Anne, and to his friends, and he allowed it to happen.

About Europe, there was general rejoicing amongst Catholic monarchs about Anne's death. She had been, in the eyes of many, the sole reason Henry had broken from Rome, and was a heretic husband-stealer. Not long after, however, in the wake of her execution, there was dissent in opinion. Chapuys, I have already mentioned, but there were others. A man named John Hill was brought to court a month after Anne's fall for saying that Henry had put her and the men to death *"only of pleasure"*, and reformists thought her death was part of a plot dreamed up in Rome. Mary of Hungary, sister to the Emperor Charles said, *"As none but her organist [Smeaton] confessed, nor herself either, people think [Henry] invented this device to be rid of her."* When Christine of Denmark was approached as a potential wife for Henry in 1538, she responded by saying that if she had two heads, *one* would be at the disposal of the King of England, and in 1544, the Abbot of Lvry frankly claimed that Henry had murdered his wife.

George Constantine, no supporter of Anne's, said he had *"never heard of queens that they should be thus handled,"* and *"there was much muttering of Queen Anne's death"*. Alexander Aless, speaking of her execution, said that Anne *"exhibited such constancy, patience and faith towards God that all the spectators, even her enemies and those persons who had previously rejoiced at her misfortune, testified and proclaimed her innocence and chastity."* Aless went on to report that there were a lot of suspicions about the evidence, as it was no new thing for men to dance in the Queen's chambers, and that George Boleyn had taken Anne's hand in the dance was not proof of incest. Aless thought it was Henry's desire for an heir which had led to Anne's downfall, combined with the failure of the embassy to the Schmalkalden League, as he would tell her daughter, Queen Elizabeth I, some years later.

In the summer after Anne's death, Parliament was concerned with showing Anne as guilty and re-working the succession. Elizabeth was declared a bastard, like her half-sister Mary, and excluded from the succession. Henry would later restore them, but he never made them legitimate. Mary, upon her succession, attempted to turn back time by proclaiming her mother's union to her father legal, rendering Mary legitimate. Elizabeth, never one to live in the past, did not do this for Anne, probably realising that to dig up the past would do her fragile reputation more harm than good.

The great irony of Henry's quest for a male heir is that it was his daughter by Anne who would go on to be remembered as the greatest monarch of the Tudor dynasty, rather than his son, or even himself.

One of the reasons Anne remains so fascinating is because of the mystery surrounding her fall. I based my story on my own theories and those of historians, but no one truly knows whether Cromwell was the only author of Anne's death, or if Henry asked him to get rid of her. I should also note that no one knows for sure if Anne was innocent, although from the evidence I have collected I believe she was.

Anne was the first Queen of England to be tried, condemned and executed. She remains but one of two, her cousin Catherine being the second. Anne was a political player, and in the last game she lost. I have no doubt that Henry wanted her gone, and this was why her fall was brought about so easily, but the swiftness of her fall was down to Cromwell. My theory is that he was asked to find a reason for Henry and Anne to separate by Henry himself, but, realising that a mere annulment would be dangerous, Cromwell took the game to its final conclusion, told Henry that Anne had been unfaithful, and had plotted his death.

Anne's conversation with Henry Norris provided the last scrap of evidence Cromwell required. Henry Tudor was a paranoid man. To hear that Anne had jested about "dead men's shoes" was enough to make him think, even for a short while, that she had plotted against him. And the idea that she might love another, or others, was unbearable. No matter who he betrayed or how often, Henry expected absolute love and devotion from his people, his wife most of all. And I think he loved her, and at least a trace of that love, which had endured so long and stood so many trials, was still within him. Reports, even from Chapuys, suggest that Anne and Henry were united in the last months of her life, and Henry was even seeking further recognition of her status and titles, a fact which is borne out by his insistence that Chapuys recognise her as Queen only a month before her arrest. Henry's continued insistence that Elizabeth be recognised as Princess also show that until Cromwell provided the 'evidence' that Anne had been unfaithful, Henry was dedicated to Anne as his wife and Elizabeth as his daughter. Provisions had been put in place to ensure Elizabeth's future, such as the request that a son of France be sent to England to be raised according to Henry's ideals. The idea quite clearly was that Elizabeth and her future husband would rule England in place of a legitimate son.

Henry's reaction to Cromwell's accusations stemmed, I think, from jealousy and hurt. Cromwell told him she had been unfaithful, and Henry, in rage and anger, accepted it, turning with murderous fire upon her and the men accused with her.

It may be that Henry quickly realised he was being played, and went along with it because he knew that killing Anne would get him all he wanted. Until Cromwell granted Henry the means to be rid of his wife, he was thinking of keeping her. When granted an excuse, he took it.

This is my belief. You may hold a different one. That is your right.

*

There are a lot of ghost stories about Anne Boleyn, and Anne, as a phantom, is apparently *very* busy. She has been seen at Hever Castle, The Tower of London, Blickling Hall, Windsor Castle, Bollin Hall, on a barge on the River Thames, at Marwell Hall, Hampton Court, and Durham House. She is said to have even visited what is now a shoe shop in Wisbech. Perhaps, seeing as she was a true and dedicated follower of fashion in life, she decided to continue this in death.

Anne is often described as wearing grey. She sometimes talks to those who see her, and sometimes simply walks on by, or is seen reading.

Her father, too, has stories about his ghost, and supposedly drives a coach along the country roads to Blickling Hall up to the gates, where it vanishes. There is a legend he is doomed to repeat this each year, in payment for abandoning his children. Another story has him appearing with his head under his arm. Unfortunately for these legends, carriages only came into use in Elizabeth's reign, and Thomas Boleyn died in his bed rather than by beheading, but then, ghosts do not have to follow the same rules as mortals.

In Elizabeth's reign, Anne's tomb was investigated, and the remains of the Duke of Northumberland, Catherine Howard, Anne Boleyn, Lady Jane Grey, Jane Rochford,

Lord Sudeley, and George Boleyn were found. Queen Victoria agreed to another investigation on the condition that any remains were treated with respect. One lot of bones (those resting beneath the chapel floor had been disturbed as others were buried there) was thought to be those of Anne Boleyn, based on the fact they were slender and the skull had *"an intellectual forehead"* with hands that had tapering fingers. There is some doubt about the identification, as Anne's remains may have become confused with those of Catherine Howard.

Each year, on the anniversary of her death, roses arrive at the Tower of London, to be placed upon her grave. Roses were a part of Anne Boleyn's arms of the crowned falcon sitting on a stump surrounded by roses, and it is likely the sender knew this. They are sent on the request of an anonymous benefactor, who left instructions for this honour to a board of trustees. They come with a card which says: *Queen Anne Boleyn, 1536.* The Yeomen place the flowers on her tomb, and take them away only when they have withered.

No one knows who set this order up. Whoever it was, was I suspect, a person like me who read of Anne and decided she deserved more honour in death than she was granted in life.

These books are my roses. My way of honouring Queen Anne Boleyn.

The Aftermath

The day after Anne died, Henry had Jane Seymour brought to him at Hampton Court. There, they were formally betrothed. Ten days after the execution of his second wife, they were married.

Although she died in 1536, Anne's memory lived on, despite the very best efforts of her husband. Upon Anne's death, Henry purged his palaces of every picture, portrait, item of jewellery, dress and all her embroidery work. Stained glass bearing the saint whose name she shared was taken down. Anne's badge of the leopard was adapted to become Jane's of the panther. Henry obliterated Anne's initials entwined with his, leaving only a very few, at Hampton Court and other palaces, which he missed, and they survive to this day. Although the portraits we have of Anne are not contemporary, there is a medal of her which is.

A few other traces remained. Henry kept a bed which featured his arms and Anne's, along with a set of bed hangings; the 'Greenwich bed', as it is known. I can't imagine Jane Seymour felt very secure getting into bed surrounded by the arms and monograms of the woman she had helped displace.

Henry remained an active man, despite his failing health. He became bald, and his eyes became lost in his face as his weight overtook him. The strains of the past years had taken their toll on his body, but also on his character. He became secretive, suspicious, and dangerously changeable. This is understandable. We don't know if Henry was truly convinced that Anne and the men accused with her had actually betrayed him, but there is the possibility he *allowed* himself to be persuaded. If he thought they had betrayed him that meant there were few he could trust. If he knew they were innocent that meant he could not trust the people advising him. Either way, it is not surprising he became so suspicious.

Whether he believed in their guilt or not, by 1536 he had executed many of his close friends, and a woman he loved. It is common practise to put the changes in his behaviour down to the jousting accident he had in 1536, or other head injuries (more in jousting, and one when he tried to vault a stream and ended up with his head stuck in the mud) he suffered, but the strain of sending basically every friend he had to death must also have had some psychological effects.

Whether or not Henry was impotent is debatable. During his time with Katherine, she became pregnant many times, and Anne conceived three or four times during their union. But it is probable, given Anne's fatal words that he lacked virility and strength, that he had some form of sexual dysfunction. This is hardly surprising. The stress that he was under for much of the time, coupled with his growing weight problems, could have led to partial impotence, perhaps caused by emotional as well as physical problems. Clearly, if it existed, it was also intermittent.

Henry's reputation, which he took so much care to uphold, was ruined by 1537. He was known as a lecher, and tales that he took some women by force were also common knowledge. No more would Henry be the good, chaste and virtuous knight. He became a tyrant, ruling England with an iron will.

Henry went into a steady decline in health. His legs were terrible to behold. The ulcer or abbess that formed in January 1536 never healed. It would seal over, causing terrible pain and discomfort, then burst, leeching out foul smelling pus and blood. The wound caused him constant agony. It is no wonder he became changeable, for constant pain and suffering would have not helped that famous Tudor temper at all. The rumour that Henry had syphilis is false. He was never treated with mercury, the 'cure or kill' method used on syphilis, and neither his children nor wives showed any signs of the disease.

When Jane died, Henry declared himself distraught, but despite this, marriage negotiations began almost immediately. Henry was turned down by Christine of Milan, but there were others, such as unsubstantiated rumours he once intended to marry Mary Shelton. Henry also became interested in five French princesses, and, unable to choose between them, asked that they be shipped to Calais so he might inspect them. François was insulted by this, and told Henry quite bluntly that it was not French custom to send royal woman to be inspected as though they were horses at a market.

Henry, by this time, seems to have only wanted to marry a partner he had seen, something his daughter, Elizabeth, would also insist upon during her many dalliances with the wedded state. Although this is odd, seeing as most kings and queens only met their future partner when they were already married by proxy and could not escape the match, for Henry it is less so. No matter how delusional his heart, Henry was a romantic. He wanted to marry for love.

This aim would be frustrated time and time again: Anne of Cleves either did not measure up to his desires, or saw through his web of fabrication; Catherine Howard turned out to be a woman with a past he could not accept, and Katherine Parr, although he might have convinced himself that she loved him, loved Thomas Seymour. Henry's quest for a woman who combined the best elements of Katherine of Aragon, Anne Boleyn, and Jane Seymour, would prove fruitless.

The truth was no woman could live up to the ideal he desired.

Those who had truly loved him were dead. Those who were left feared him. For a man who had always been desperate to be loved, as I think Henry was, this was the worst fate. A part of me believes this was no less than he deserved.

Henry VIII died in 1547, eleven years after Anne. He left behind his son, Edward, as well as his two daughters, Mary and Elizabeth, who were restored to the succession. Henry had done much that was remarkable, and is remembered to this day not only for his marital career, but for his break with Rome, and suppression of the monasteries.

The Wives of Henry VIII

Henry took many remarkable women and made them his wives. Katherine of Aragon was a courageous, upstanding woman who did not deserve to be locked away in a castle for the rest of her life, or separated from her only daughter. Anne Boleyn was an extraordinary, almost modern woman, living in Tudor times, who displayed a myriad of virtues and vices, ending her life as one of the most infamous women in history, but she too did not deserve her fate, nor subsequent reputation.

Jane Seymour is hard to pin-point in character, but she must have had some determination to step into Anne's place. Jane splits opinion, with some seeing her as an innocent, perhaps naïve, woman thrown at Henry by powerful relations, who had little choice in the matter, and others who theorise she may well have been a great deal more cunning, ruthless and spirited than is thought, but managed, as Anne never could, to hide her intelligence under a mask of subservience and obedience. These are two very different personalities, and it is hard to know which option is the truth, since little is known of Jane's early life, and she did not survive long as Queen. It may be the truth is somewhere in between.

There is something in me that pities Jane Seymour, especially after her wedding. Jane had no easy time with Henry. Only a week after his marriage to Jane, Henry was heard to say that he had noted two or three beautiful ladies at court. He sighed and said he was *"sorry he had not seen them before he was married."* Jane was insecure on her throne, and was not crowned, as Anne and Katherine were before her. Hearing comments like this could hardly have made her feel happy, and indeed, would have been chilling. Henry saw his partners as disposable now, and Jane was well aware of that.

Jane tried to be all that Henry wanted. She was meek, mild, ductile and malleable. Her motto, fittingly, was *"Bound to Obey and Serve"* and she tried to live up to it. But from the very start, she was in a perilous position. Her family were even lower on the slippery Tudor social scale than Anne's, so she would not have been hard to get rid of, and her efforts in the political arena were dismissed by Henry. The only success she had was in the domestic sphere, the only place Henry would allow her a little power. Jane managed to engineer Lady Mary's return to court, and showed great honour to her. Jane all but ignored Elizabeth, who was kept at Hatfield, but this should not be surprising. Jane was unlikely to be able to look at Anne's tiny daughter without guilt.

The only time Jane was secure was when she found she was with child, but even this ended in tragedy when she died. Rumours that Prince Edward was born by caesarean section are false. Although this procedure was not unknown, it was only done in extremis, when the mother was already dead, or was certain to die. It also caused almost immediate death for the mother, and Jane lived for ten days after Edward was born. It is most likely that she succumbed to puerperal fever, known at the time as *childbed fever*, brought on by poor hygiene. Jane's moment of glory was therefore also her downfall.

She died on the 24th of October 1537 and was buried at St George's Chapel at Windsor Castle. She was the only one of Henry's wives to receive a queen's funeral. An inscription above her tomb reads,

Here lieth a Phoenix, by whose death

Another Phoenix life gave breath
It is to be lamented much
The world ne'er knew two such.

Her son became the short-lived Edward VI of England. When Henry died in 1547, he was buried with Jane at his request. He claimed she was the love of his life, and his one, true Queen. Since he wasn't always very nice to her whilst she lived, I think this declaration has more to do with Henry's world of abiding and ridiculous fantasy, in which he dwelled for the rest of his life.

Anne of Cleves, who I often feel is the most underestimated of Henry's wives, showed great political survival skills and pragmatism, ending up as his most fortunate wife in many ways. She secured a generous annulment settlement, outlived him and died in Mary's reign. In accepting the separation Henry offered, Anne became his 'sister' and a rich woman. She is often overlooked, discredited because of the short period of her marriage, and the fact she was apparently not good looking, but there are other virtues than beauty.

Henry may in fact have been more upset that, at their first meeting, when he presented himself to her in disguise, she failed to recognise him as the King. What Henry did not realise was by this point he was no oil portrait himself. So, in coming to her in disguise, thinking she would immediately know he was the King, he deluded himself. He was fat, bald, aged, his leg ulcer was rotten and pungent and he apparently had bad breath, so he was not an attractive proposition. Immediately after that first meeting, he began to complain he didn't like her. It is far more likely he didn't like the truth he saw in her eyes; that he was no more the romantic young knight he had once been.

Anne was a clever woman. She submitted to Henry's wishes and profited from her sheer guile and pragmatism. She did the best of all his queens and was the only one buried in Westminster Abbey.

Anne was succeeded by the unfortunate **Catherine Howard**, another of Norfolk's nieces, who was executed in 1542 for adultery. Catherine was accused of adultery with Thomas Culpeper, and of engaging in pre-marital sexual intercourse with Francis Dereham, as well as promising to marry him before her marriage. Whether or not Catherine committed adultery is unknown, but it appears she was sexually active before her marriage, something Henry, who called this young girl his *Rose without a Thorn*, could not cope with. Whether or not her sexual activity was consensual or not, is another question.

During her confessions after her arrest, Catherine told her accusers she had been repeatedly molested by her music teacher, Henry Mannox, when she was a child of thirteen, then living in her grandmother's house at Horsham. Both she and Mannox (who gave evidence against her) said that actual sex, or more accurately, rape, had not taken place.

When Catherine was fifteen, she was sent to another of her grandmother's houses in Lambeth, and there met Francis Dereham. Catherine claimed that Dereham raped her, and denied there was a pre-contract of marriage between them. Dereham claimed they had agreed to marry, and on the basis of that had become lovers. It is not impossible, even if she was raped by Dereham that Catherine might have agreed to marry him. It was standard for the Tudor age, and for some cultures now, that if a woman is raped, the method used to remove the stain of that assault is to marry her to her rapist. The fact that this condemns a woman to a life with her attacker is apparently less important than making the accusation of rape disappear, rendered dissolved, apparently, by making a predator and his victim into man and wife. If Catherine agreed to marry Dereham, she may well have simply been playing into this myth, seeking to remove the stain on her character, since survivors of abuse were (and sadly still are) often held responsible for the actions of their attackers. If Dereham and Catherine exchanged vows and consummated their promises with sexual intercourse, consentual or not, this would have constituted a pre-contract, rendering Henry and Catherine's marriage invalid.

But adultery and pre-marital sex still did not offer Henry a reason to kill her.

This was swiftly solved. Henry and his Parliament passed an Act called *The Royal Assent by Commission Act*, in 1542, which authorised Catherine's execution on the grounds of adultery. This Act made it treason for a queen consort to fail to disclose her sexual history to the King, and also to incite someone to commit adultery with her. This Act was only repealed by the British Government in 1967, and in the Republic of Ireland in 2007.

If her confessions were true, Catherine was a child who had been sexually abused by her music teacher, and then raped by Francis Dereham. If she did commit adultery with Culpeper, it is possible this was a reaction to her experience of abuse. Some people who endure abuse come to fear and hate the act of sex, and shy from it. Others develop a different response, sometimes becoming sexually aggressive or promiscuous in future relationships; if they can control the act of sex, they can control the fear they feel of it.

We should also remember that even if these encounters were consensual, which I think they were not, were Catherine to be judged by *male* extra-marital or pre-marital relationships, which often were numerous, she would come up as an example of restraint. The simple fact is that women then, and even now, are judged differently to men in terms of sexuality. It stems from deep-rooted, antiquated religious and societal beliefs and misogyny. In Tudor times, women were censured, punished, and often branded for promiscuity and men were usually celebrated for engaging in it. And although change is coming, it continues to this day, sadly.

People see Catherine as the flighty, wanton temptress of Henry's wives, and perhaps she was a flirt, but perhaps this should be seen as another response to abuse. Perhaps she, like so many who suffer abuse early in life, learned how to exert a measure of control over men by playing into the behaviour expected of women. Maybe Catherine learnt to appease men, in an effort to protect herself.

There is also doubt as to whether she actually committed adultery with Thomas Culpeper, or if the affair was merely romantic. Since most historians take the accusations against Anne with a pinch of salt, it seems strange we do not offer the same courtesy to Catherine Howard. Is it so hard to believe that Henry, hearing of her past relationships, might have wanted to rid himself of her? He had used an accusation of adultery against Anne, and got away with it, so why not with Catherine Howard? Perhaps his ego could not cope with his fantastical illusion of the perfect woman becoming soiled by the knowledge she did not come to his bed a virgin, and took revenge. When he heard of her pre-marital affairs, he swore he would take a sword to her himself.

Something else that should be considered is that if Catherine was in a relationship, sexual or not, with Thomas Culpeper, this is perhaps something to be pitied rather than condemned. Culpeper had been accused of rape, but had been pardoned by the King due to Henry's affection for him. If this is so, then Catherine, a potential survivor of childhood sexual abuse, was attracted to another abuser in adulthood. This is not uncommon. Abuse can become a cyclical monster; victims of abuse occasionally (the majority of childhood sexual abuse survivors do not become adult abusers) victimise others, or sometimes end up in abusive relationships which mirror the suffering they endured. Often this is entirely subconscious. If Catherine was attracted to Culpeper, this, as much as his looks, may have been the reason. We would not now judge a person who had suffered as she may have done, for ending up in a cycle of abuse. We would pity them, and attempt to help them. I feel Catherine Howard is one of the original 'slut-shamed' women of the past, and also think it is time to end this. Depending on what date is taken for her birth, Catherine was between sixteen and twenty years of age when she was executed. She was a child. This, I think is the way we should see her, rather than putting her down as the Tudor wild-child, and dismissing her.

On the night before her death, Catherine asked that the block be brought to her rooms, so she could practice walking to it and putting her head on it, so she might die with the same courage her cousin had shown. Unlike Anne, Catherine never got a trial. She was condemned by Act of Attainder, and executed by the clumsy axe. Her family utterly abandoned her. Catherine's death is one of the most tragic of the Tudor age, in my opinion, and remembering this young girl as nothing but a silly flirt is reductive and damaging. We should remember her death as one of Henry's most awful crimes.

Katherine Parr, Henry's last wife, was too a remarkable woman. Sadly, and unfairly, called the 'blue-stocking' or the 'nurse', Katherine was a lively, witty, pretty woman with a great deal of intelligence. One of the first female authors in England, she produced books of devotion and prayer.

Her religious beliefs were reformist and radical, and she held salon meetings where she and her women discussed Scripture and religious beliefs. Stephen Gardiner worked on a plot to destroy her, as he did not like her influence over the King.

It came horrifyingly close to succeeding. Henry had grown tired of Katherine's habit of debating Scripture with him, and agreed to order an investigation into her beliefs. That Katherine escaped with her life was only due to two things; luck and her own wits. The warrant for her arrest was found, dropped by Gardiner, so Katherine had forewarning of what was coming. She saved her life by taking to her bed. Her illness may have been feigned, or not. She might have played ill in order to rouse Henry's pity, but by this time two queens had gone to their deaths. It is therefore not unfeasible that she might have truly suffered hysteria or sickness. When Henry came to her, she told him she only sought to discuss faith with him in order to distract him from his bodily pains, and learn more for herself, since he was such a wise man.

I doubt Katherine thought this in actual fact. She submitted to her husband because she knew it was what he wanted, and it saved her. Henry bought it, and when Gardiner arrived to take her under arrest the next day, Henry hit him with his walking stick and sent him packing.

Katherine was careful for the rest of his reign, and managed to outlive him, but she was not to end her life happily. Her marriage to Thomas Seymour, and his subsequent 'wooing' as it is called in many books of Princess Elizabeth, led to Katherine falling into deep depression. Today, were a forty year-old man to hunt a thirteen year old girl, his own stepdaughter, by giving presents, touching her, jumping into her bed, and, quite literally, ripping a dress from her body, we would call it grooming and abuse. Katherine's death in childbirth was only more tragic as she felt she had lost the love she had yearned for so long, and never become a mother; something she had always wanted.

Henry was attracted to outstanding women; women of courage, spirit and intelligence. Once married, however, he wanted them to abandon those traits and become submissive, obedient and awed by him. Those who obeyed, like Jane Seymour, Anne of Cleves and Katherine Parr, did as well as could be expected. Those who did not, Anne Boleyn, Katherine of Aragon, and Catherine Howard, were defamed, punished and sent to their deaths; two by execution, and one by insidious neglect.

Although Henry is famous for having six wives, to his mind, he had only had two; Jane Seymour and Katherine Parr. The reasoning behind this is that all his other unions were annulled, making them non-existent in law, if never in our minds. I have no doubt it eased his conscience to believe this, but if he thought that belief would stick in the minds of his people, he was a fool.

But Henry believed what he wanted to believe, and never was this more true than when it came to killing his wives.

The Other Players in the Story

Richard Page and **Thomas Wyatt** were set free. Cromwell secured the release of both men. Page stayed away from court for some time, but was later granted positions and became a regularly attending courtier again. Wyatt returned to court quite swiftly, but was left haunted by the executions of his friends, as may be attested from his poetry. He went back to his father's estates, wrote heartbreaking sonnets about his experiences and fallen friends, but returned to court later, and was knighted by Henry. He spent the latter years of his life as an ambassador and spy in the court of Spain, and died in 1542. His poetry is still studied in schools and universities to this day.

Thomas Cranmer, Archbishop of Canterbury, continued to serve Henry, and furthered the fight for reform. Henry protected him during his reign, as there were many who considered Cranmer a heretic. During Henry's reign Cranmer published the first vernacular service, *The Exhortation and Litany*.

Cranmer was successful in the reign of King Edward, too, promoting major reforms and writing the first two editions of the *Book of Common Prayer*. But when Queen Mary came to the throne and instigated her counter-reformation, Cranmer was arrested on charges of treason and heresy. He recanted his beliefs, but on the day of his execution withdrew them, choosing to die as a Protestant. He was burned at the stake in 1556. As the flames crept higher, he put his right hand, the one which had signed the recantation of his beliefs, into the flames, saying his unworthy hand should go first to death for its crimes. His last words were, "Lord Jesus, receive my spirit. I see the heavens open and Jesus standing at the right hand of God."

Thomas Howard, Duke of Norfolk, was banished from court for a while after Anne's fall, but continued in service later. His influence was nominal until his niece, Catherine Howard, became Queen. Her fall was disastrous for him, and he abandoned her to save himself. His son, Surrey, managed to get into trouble often at court. He was proud, and had a rather inflated notion of the importance of his family. Surrey commissioned more portraits from Holbein than anyone else, and displayed the royal arms of England along with his own. Henry was remarkably tolerant of this for many years, but it was not to last.

In 1546, Norfolk and his son, Surrey, were arrested on charges of treason. Norfolk's mistress, Bess Holland, as well as his daughter, Mary Howard, gave evidence against them. Surrey was executed; the last victim of Henry VIII, but Norfolk escaped, as Henry held back from signing his death warrant, and had not put quill to parchment by the time he himself died in 1547.

Norfolk survived into Mary's reign, when he was released from the Tower and restored to favour. That he was the uncle of the woman who had displaced her mother mattered less to Mary than his rigid Catholicism. He died in 1554.

Thomas Cromwell was knighted, became Lord Cromwell of Wimbledon, and later the Earl of Essex. He also held the posts of Lord Privy Seal (taken from Thomas Boleyn), Vicar-General and Vice-Regent of the King in spirituals. His son married one of Jane Seymour's sisters.

Quickly, Cromwell became in charge of all the major administrative departments of England, enabling him to bring about sweeping reform. In 1536, Convocation laid out the King's wishes for religion. A middle path was forged between the teachings of the Catholic Church and the radical one of reformers. The dissolution of the monasteries began in force after Anne's death. Over the span of four years, every religious house in England, five hundred and sixty-three in all, were closed down and their monks, nuns and abbots were either pensioned off or simply sent out into the streets. Dissolution brought Henry great wealth, and the people of England great suffering. Clergymen and women became beggars, and the educational, medical and pastoral care they had offered, in differing scales, was lost.

Some houses were re-founded, but many of them were dissolved later. All the money, lands, estates and goods from the monasteries went into Henry's pocket, as Cromwell had intended, making him one of the richest kings in the world. One of the gemstones confiscated was a ruby donated by Louis VII for the tomb of Anne's ancestor, Thomas Becket, at Canterbury. Henry had it set into a thumb ring.

Many abbeys were pulled down or became fashionable estates for noblemen. Nobles had to pay for the estates, so the King did not miss out on any money.

The *Pilgrimage of Grace*, a rebellion led by commoners, erupted in October 1536 in response to the closures of the monasteries and the religious changes in England. It was a huge, and extremely dangerous, uprising. Terms of peace were made in December, where Henry agreed to all the rebels' demands, and Robert Aske, the ringleader, was invited to court. Afterwards, Aske went back north, telling everyone that Henry was on their side, but in January 1537 another rebellion broke out, and martial law was imposed on England. Two hundred rebels were executed, Aske amongst them. To celebrate, Henry dubbed forty-eight new knights. Henry emerged from this horror more powerful than ever, but if his people loved him as they had when he was a young prince, is doubtful. They had learned to fear their King.

Cromwell became a powerful man, but he never exerted the same influence over Henry as Wolsey and Anne had. There are unsubstantiated tales that Henry hit Cromwell at times and told him that his common birth meant he was unfit to meddle with the affairs of Kings.

In 1540, just four years after Anne's execution, Cromwell was brought down by his enemies. On the 10th of June, whilst sat at the Council table, Cromwell was arrested by the Captain of the Guard. Norfolk and the Earl of Southampton tore Cromwell's badge of the Order of the Garter from his chest, saying, *"A traitor must not wear it."*

In reply, Cromwell said, *"This, then is my reward for faithful service."*

There was a boat already waiting by the river, and he was taken to the Tower.

Attained for treason and heresy, Cromwell was sentenced to death. His fall, much like his career, echoed Wolsey's. The failure of the Cleves marriage was his true undoing, granting his enemies the opportunity to unseat him. They told Henry he supported Anabaptists, Lutherans, and had even plotted to marry the Lady Mary. His last letter to Henry survives, *"Most gracious Prince, I cry for mercy, mercy, mercy!"* it reads.

But there was none to be had.

Cromwell did not get a trial. He was condemned by Act of Attainder and died on the 28th of June 1540. Not for Cromwell was a private death granted. He died on Tower Hill, before thousands, and was given an inexperienced executioner. It took two blows to sever his head, and he would have suffered greatly. His head was set upon a spike on London Bridge.

Henry regretted beheading his most able minister not long later, but obviously it was far too late.

Ironically, one of Cromwell's descendants would return the favour of beheading to another King. Oliver Cromwell, the great general and leader of the Parliamentarian cause in the English Civil War, was the great-grandson of Richard Cromwell, Cromwell's nephew. King Charles I was beheaded after losing the war against his own Parliament, and Oliver Cromwell became Lord Protector of England. He was offered the crown, and the title of King, but turned it down.

Stephen Gardiner continued as ambassador to France for some time, and was also sent to Germany. Returning to England, he took part in the *Six Articles*, which led to Anne's bishops, Latimer and Shaxton, resigning from their posts. After Cromwell was executed, Gardiner became Chancellor of Cambridge University, and spent a great deal of time trying to make charges of heresy stick to Cranmer. He became the face of the Catholic faction at court, tried to bring down Queen Katherine Parr, but failed, and when Henry died Gardiner found himself excluded from the Council. He opposed the reforms of Edward Seymour as Lord Protector, and eventually ended up in the Tower, where he was deprived of his bishopric.

Gardiner was released when Mary came to the throne. His bishopric was restored and he became Lord Chancellor. He sat in judgement on several bishops accused of heresy as Mary's counter-reformation got underway, and there is some suggestion he was behind the arrest of Princess Elizabeth, and may have petitioned Mary to have her executed.

Gardiner died at Westminster in 1555.

Charles Brandon, Duke of Suffolk, had two sons with Katherine Willoughby, who, very sadly, both died on the same day in 1551 of the sweating sickness. Charles had no other male heirs, so the title of Duke of Suffolk was granted to his eldest daughter's husband, Henry Grey. From Frances Brandon and Henry Grey came Lady Jane Grey, as well as her sisters, Katherine and Mary, who became famous, or infamous, in the reign of Elizabeth I due to their unsanctioned marriages.

Charles remained in favour, and died in 1545.

Richard Rich became Chancellor of the Court of Augmentations in 1536, and was a part of the dissolution of the monasteries. He was also a participant in the torture of Anne Askew, who was arrested in conjunction with investigations into heresy. Askew was tortured, at least in part, to provide evidence to bring down Queen Katherine Parr. Askew did not provide the evidence, and burned to death. She was the only woman to be tortured at the Tower of London.

Rich became a Baron in 1547 and then Chancellor of England. He was a supporter of Protector Somerset (Edward Seymour) and helped to prosecute Thomas Seymour. He joined forces with the Duke of Northumberland in 1549, but Northumberland's later *coup* to place Lady Jane Grey on the throne failed.

Under Mary, Rich took an active role in the restoration of the Catholic faith, showing his ease at switching sides, and was a member of the Privy Council, but did not attend regularly. He also served Elizabeth in a minor role, and died in 1567.

Chiefly remembered for his part in the death of Sir Thomas More, Rich has not done well in the pages of history. The historian Hugh Trevor-Roper called Rich a man *"of whom nobody has ever spoken a good word."*

Thomas Boleyn retained his place at court, attended the christening of Prince Edward, and helped to suppress the *Pilgrimage of Grace*. He died in 1539 and Henry ordered Masses to be sung for his soul. His wife, Elizabeth, died before him in 1538. There is no record of her coming to court after the executions of her children.

Thomas is, quite rightly, not remembered with affection. He thrust one, if not two, daughters at the King, and completely abandoned Anne and George when they were arrested. He never reconciled with Mary, either. Justly, Thomas Boleyn is remembered as a self-serving social climber, happy to sacrifice his offspring for his own gain. His wife and children deserved better.

Mary Boleyn lived in Calais for some years, returning to England later, and died at Rochford Hall in 1543. Although there are tales that Mary was reconciled with her father after her clandestine marriage, there is no evidence to support this. In fact, upon his death, Thomas Boleyn left all his property to his granddaughter, Elizabeth, leaving Mary and her children with nothing.

Mary's daughter, Anne, whose existence is contested, must have died young if she existed, as there is no further mention of her, but Catherine Carey and **Henry Carey** would go on to serve their cousin, and possibly half-sister, Queen Elizabeth, and were high-fliers in her reign. Henry Carey became the first Baron Hudson and patron of the Lord Chamberlain's Men. He married Anne Morgan, and had six children. He served as a Member of Parliament for Buckingham, and was knighted in November 1558. He was also Master of the Queen's Hawks, and Captain of the Gentlemen Pensioners.

Elizabeth was very fond of Henry, and called him *"my Harry"*. He was instrumental in crushing rebellions in her reign, and was appointed Warden of the Eastern Marches, becoming a Privy Councillor in 1581.

He died in Somerset House, on the 23rd of July, 1596, and was buried at Westminster Abbey. On his deathbed, he refused Elizabeth's offer to make him Earl of Wilshire, saying that if he had not been deemed worthy in life, he would not consider himself worthy in death.

Catherine Carey became a maid of honour to both Anne of Cleves and Catherine Howard. In 1540, she married Sir Francis Knollys, who was knighted in 1547 and later became a Knight of the Garter. Francis also became treasurer to the royal household for Queen Elizabeth I.

During the reign of Queen Mary I, Catherine and Francis, along with some of their children, fled abroad. As Protestants they knew they were in danger. When Elizabeth came to the throne they returned, and Catherine became one of the highest ranking of Elizabeth's women. She was a great favourite of Elizabeth's and despite problems that later occurred with her children, they remained close throughout life.

Catherine had about fourteen children, the most famous of which was Lettice, her eldest surviving daughter, who secretly married Robert Dudley, Elizabeth's favourite, and Lettice found herself perpetually banished from court for daring to marry the man the Queen loved. Lettice's son, Robert Devereaux, the Earl of Essex, was also a great favourite of Elizabeth's, but was a rather bold, reckless and foolish young man. He was executed in 1601, becoming the second man carrying the title of Earl of Essex to die for treason.

Catherine Carey died on the 15th of January, 1569, at Hampton Court. She was buried the following April in Westminster Abbey with full honours. Elizabeth talked of her almost constantly after her death, betraying a deep and abiding love for the woman who may have been her sister.

Jane Boleyn, or Lady Rochford as she is better known, carried on at court, and remained a lady in waiting perhaps to Jane Seymour, but certainly to Anne of Cleves and Catherine Howard. The extent to which she was involved in Anne and George's fall cannot be known, but despite recent attempts to clear her name, the fact that she remained in favour is highly suspicious. Cromwell saw to it that Jane was well provided for when she encountered crippling debt after George's death. I cannot think there was good reason for this kindness unless she had helped him to bring Anne and George down. If Jane did give evidence against her husband and sister-in-law, we must judge her as we do Thomas Boleyn for abandoning his children to save himself. It may be that they both understood they could not save George and Anne, and simply worked to save themselves, but if we judge Thomas Boleyn harshly for this, Jane must be included if she did the same.

Jane died as Anne and George did, on the block. Embroiled in Catherine Howard's love affair, she was arrested with her mistress, gave evidence against Catherine, and died for her part in the liaison. Jane may have suffered a mental breakdown in the Tower before her execution, which, under normal circumstances, would have led to at least a postponement in her execution, as it was illegal to execute those who were insane. It is possible she was faking, in full knowledge of this, and equally as possible she was not. It made no matter. Henry had his Parliament pass an Act of Attainder, which condemned her to death. On the 13th of February 1542, Jane died.

On the scaffold, she is supposed to have said, *"Good Christians, God has permitted me to suffer this shameful death as punishment for having contributed to my husband's death. I falsely accused him of loving, in an incestuous manner, his sister, Queen Anne Boleyn. For this I deserve to die. But I am guilty of no other crime."*

If this speech is accurate, then at least, at the end, Jane vindicated Anne and George.

Mary Tudor, later Queen Mary I, found to her utmost shock and disgust, that the fall of Anne Boleyn did not alter Henry's attitude towards her or to religion. Mary may well have expected to be immediately reconciled with her father, and to find him heading back to Rome with open arms. Neither happened. In fact, Henry continued the same method of abuse with his daughter he had started many years before. He was tired of women defying him, and he would have obedience.

His treatment of Mary after Anne's death also goes to show that it was not only Anne who urged harsh treatment for the Princess. Many historians claim that it was Anne alone who made Mary suffer. It was not. Henry played an equal, if not greater part in her suffering.

Mary was only reconciled to her father when she submitted to him and signed a declaration that her parents' marriage was unlawful and she was a bastard. She also had to repudiate papal authority. Eventually, Mary submitted, but it was to haunt her for the rest of her life. She came back to court and was granted a household. She had many supporters, and one of the conditions of the *Pilgrimage of Grace* was that she be recognised as legitimate.

Mary became Prince Edward's godmother, which was ironic considering the troubles they encountered in his reign about their differing faiths. There were numerous suggestions of husbands for her, but they were all turned down by Henry. Upon the death of her father, Mary became Edward's heir and a rich woman, but due to her dedication to the Catholic faith, she and King Edward, a zealous and committed Protestant, came to blows. She retired from court and more than once considered fleeing England as her brother was determined to make her cede to the Protestant faith.

In 1553, Edward died at the age of just fifteen. He did not want Mary on his throne, fearing she would undo all his work for reform. He left a will in contradiction of the Act of Succession, which made Lady Jane Grey, his cousin and the granddaughter of Mary Tudor, Duchess of Suffolk, his heir.

In a *coup* led by John Dudley, the Duke of Northumberland, Jane Grey was placed on the throne, and Mary was to be captured. But Mary knew what was going on. Rather than head to London, as invited, she went to her estates in East Anglia, and raised an army. Northumberland's support collapsed, his followers fled, and Mary, accompanied by her sister, Elizabeth, entered London carried on a wave of popular support.

Initially clement in matters of religion, Mary was, at first, a popular Queen. It is, perhaps, pleasingly ironic that the fate Henry attempted to escape in his unending search for a male heir was utterly thwarted by his daughter. Mary became England's first Queen regnant, in defiance of her father's quest.

But Mary's reign was tragic in many ways. She was forced to execute Lady Jane Grey. Initially it seemed Mary would spare her, but when Jane's father, Henry Grey, embarked on repeated rebellion in the name of his daughter, Mary knew Jane was too high-risk to leave alive.

Mary brought about a counter-reformation, trying to turn back time, and married Phillip of Spain. She loved her husband, but he did not return her affection. She suffered two false pregnancies, which brought many to censure her for the supposed failings of her body. The first may have been a phantom pregnancy brought about by her intense desire to be a mother and the second was almost certainly the illness that killed her, either a form of cancer or an infection. She was also repeatedly separated from her husband.

Mary burned somewhere around 300 men and woman for their faith and went down in history for religious genocide. Her reign also saw England joining with Spain to make war on France, which lost England a great deal of money, men, and the territory of Calais. She almost executed her half-sister, the wily Elizabeth, several times, and kept her under house arrest for a long time, fearing her Protestant half-sister would undo all her work to restore England to Rome. But she did leave her throne to her sister, and refused to execute her, despite the many troubles Elizabeth presented.

Mary died in 1558. She was vastly unpopular at the time of her death, and her husband was not with her. She lies in Westminster Abbey and shares a tomb with her half-sister, Elizabeth.

Henry Fitzroy died in the same year as Anne, most likely of consumption (tuberculosis), on the 22nd of July 1536. His death was kept secret, and his corpse was taken to Thetford Priory in Norfolk for burial. The secrecy was due to the fact that with the succession in doubt, many people had thought Henry would legitimise him. With both his daughters disinherited, and Prince Edward not yet born, there was no clear heir to the throne, and Fitzroy was a grown man, capable of taking on the weight of the crown. Had he lived, England might have had a different future. Cromwell claimed that Henry certainly intended to make him his heir.

After the funeral, Henry exploded at Norfolk and accused him of not burying his son with the honour he deserved, even though the commands about secrecy had come from Henry. Surrey mourned his friend, and wrote many beautiful verses about him, sorrowing for his death.

William Tyndale died in 1536 in the Duchy of Brabant, convicted of heresy. He was strangled to death and his corpse was burnt at the stake. He used his last words to pray that the eyes of the King of England would be opened.

Two years after Tyndale's death, one of his greatest wishes came true when Henry authorised an English Bible. The work was largely Tyndale's with other segments provided by Miles Coverdale. It became known as the *Tyndale Bible*, and was a driving force in spreading reformist ideas. The 1611 *King James Bible* was also based on Tyndale's text, and the *New American Standard Bible*, and the *English Standard Bible* draw on his work too. He introduced words to the English language such as *passover, scapegoat,* and phrases such as *a moment in time, let there be light, judge not that ye be judged, the powers that be, a sign of the times*, and many others.

There is no denying that Tyndale was a vital part of the Reformation, and his genius in translating is almost unmatched. He has been recognised as one of the most influential people of Britain, and there are monuments to him in Vivloorde where he died (along with a museum), at the London Victoria Embankment Gardens, on a hill in North Nibly, the alleged place of his birth, and in Millennium Square, Bristol.

Although a humble man, his legacy may not have displeased him.

Despite rising high at court, the Seymour brothers were to die ignominiously. **Thomas Seymour** came under suspicion first for marrying the widowed Queen Katherine Parr after the death of Henry. Luckily for Thomas, King Edward was fond of him, and excused this illicit union. He was less forgiving, however, when he heard his uncle had been in hot pursuit of both Mary and Elizabeth, and Edward Seymour became equally mistrustful of his brother. When Katherine Parr died, and their child with her, (although there is some evidence to suggest the baby might have survived for a few years), all sense abandoned Thomas. He was executed for treason on 20th of March 1549 after attempting to gain physical control of King Edward by kidnapping him.

Edward Seymour followed his younger brother to the block on the 22nd of January 1552, accused of "ambition, vainglory," as well as negligence, stealing King Edward's wealth and following his own opinion. The Lord Protector had risen to become one of the most powerful men in England, ruling for his nephew, King Edward, during his minority, but he made powerful enemies, and was not popular in England. His fall saw the Duke of Northumberland rise and gain control of the young King.

Margaret and Mary Shelton often become confused in the pages of history. There is contention about which sister was Henry's mistress, but from recent research it seems it was Mary rather than Margaret. The reason for the confusion is that Henry's mistress was known as *Marg*, which would seem to point to Margaret, but it was common practise to write *y's* as similar to *g's* in the sixteenth century, which makes Mary the more likely candidate.

There is no evidence to firmly suggest that Anne asked Mary to become Henry's mistress in an effort to unseat her rivals, but it is possible, and I chose to follow this in this book. Anne might not have liked it, but she would have understood by that point Henry was going to take mistresses, and it was better to have one in place who was her friend, than allow an enemy to warm his bed.

There is also no firm identification of the four ladies who attended Anne in her last days in the Tower. They are not named in sources, and only described as 'young'. I chose to make them Mary and Margaret Shelton, Nan Gainsford and Margaret Wyatt/Lee, as these women had been shown as Anne's closest friends, aside from her brother, during the course of the books.

After Anne's death, Mary retired from court and entered a convent. She was engaged to a poet, named Thomas Clere, but he died before they could marry. She instead married Anthony Heveningham and had seven children, one of which, Abigail, went on to attend upon Queen Elizabeth I. Mary may have served as a chamberer (a royal cleaning lady) to Queen Elizabeth too. She died in 1571 and is buried in Suffolk.

Margaret is much harder to trace. It is thought she died before 1555.

Nan Gainsford, Lady Zouche went on to serve Jane Seymour. There were rumours she was one of the women who gave evidence that led to Anne's arrest, although if she did, and how much choice she had in the matter is unknown. She and her husband, George, had eight children and there are claims (probably untrue) that she raised Bess of Hardwick in her household. George died in 1557, and Nan followed in or around 1590.

Mary Aucher vanishes from records after Anne's trial. It is likely she went back to Hever and cared for Elizabeth Boleyn.

Mary Howard had a most unfortunate time after Anne's death. When her husband, Fitzroy, died, their match has still not been consummated, and was therefore not binding by law. Mary was not allowed to keep the lands and properties that should have been granted to her. She stayed at court and was one of the women chosen to meet Anne of Cleves upon her arrival in England in 1539.

Upon the disgrace of Catherine Howard, Mary along with most of her family ended up in the Tower. She was released, and her father petitioned for her to marry Thomas Seymour, but Edward Seymour and his wife objected, and the marriage never took place. At a later date, her brother, Surrey, told Mary to seduce the King, and use him to wield power. Mary replied that she would rather cut her own throat. Later, she testified against her brother, leading to his execution.

Mary did not re-marry. She remained at court, but retired at some later stage, and died in the reign of Queen Mary, in 1557. She raised Surrey's son, who went on to become the Duke of Norfolk in the reign of Queen Elizabeth.

Margaret Douglas found herself in a great deal of trouble not long after Anne's death. Her love affair with Thomas Howard, Anne's uncle, was uncovered, and when Henry learned of it, he was enraged. Both of them were sent to the Tower. Thomas wrote poetry to her from within his prison.

This event caused Henry to add a clause to the Act of Succession, which stated that it was treason to espouse, marry or deflower any woman of the royal family without knowledge and consent of the King. Thomas was attained by Parliament and sentenced to death. There was word that Margaret would face the same fate, but since actual sex had not taken place, she was reprieved.

In the autumn of 1537, Thomas and Margaret caught a fever in the Tower. Margaret was released into the care of the nuns of Syon, but Thomas died in the Tower. Eventually, Margaret was allowed to return to court.

Another clandestine love affair saw Margaret return to the Tower. In 1540, she fell in love with Charles, the brother of Catherine Howard, and Henry was incensed when he found out.

She went on to marry Matthew Stewart, the Count of Lennox; a match which, finally, had the permission of her royal uncle. During the reign of Queen Mary, Margaret was recognised by the Queen as the best suited to be her heir. Mary did not want Elizabeth on the throne. Margaret was Catholic, and, in Mary's eyes, carried more royal blood than her Protestant half-sister. Margaret was never named as heir, however, and when Elizabeth became Queen, Margaret, perhaps in resentment, became a constant problem, involved in intrigues and plots, mostly on behalf of her sons.

Margaret became mother to Henry Darnley, the obnoxious and ill-fated second husband of Mary, Queen of Scots. The marriage was not supported by Elizabeth, as it united the twin claims of the Douglas and Stewart families, posing a danger to her throne. Darnley was murdered in 1567 in an explosion, (although he was probably suffocated or strangled after the blast), and Margaret denounced Mary of Scots as the murderer. Margaret later became reconciled to her daughter-in-law, and her husband became Regent of Scotland, but he was assassinated in 1571.

In 1574, Margaret's second son, Charles, married Elizabeth Cavendish, daughter of Bess of Hardwick, without the permission of Queen Elizabeth. Margaret went *again* to the Tower of London, but was pardoned when her son died a few years later. Margaret's granddaughter by Charles, Arbella Stewart, was a potential claimant to the throne during Elizabeth's reign, but her cousin, King James of Scotland, was seen as the more desirable successor.

Margaret died in 1578 and was granted a royal funeral in Westminster Abbey. She lies in the same grave as her son, Charles. Margaret's grandson, King James, went on to become King of England and Scotland.

Agnes Howard, *nee* Tilney, Dowager Duchess of Norfolk got in a lot of trouble when her ward, Catherine Howard, fell from grace. When Catherine's pre-marital activities became known, lax guardianship was blamed, and Agnes came under fire. She protested that if there had been no offence since the marriage then Catherine had not committed adultery, but no one listened. Her step-son, Norfolk, was sent to her house to investigate, and found that Agnes had burned papers belonging to Dereham and his friends, although what these contained, we do not know. She was sent to the Tower and questioned. Later she admitted to have promoted Catherine to the King as a bride in full knowledge that she had been sexually active before marriage, and had persuaded Catherine to offer Dereham a place in her royal household. The position Dereham was offered at court is generally seen as a means to buy his silence.

Many of her family were also taken to the Tower, and lost property and money in the wake of Catherine's fall. Agnes was not brought to trial, but she was sentenced to imprisonment and forfeiture of her lands, estates and goods.

Although the King was of a mind to convict her for treason, Agnes was released. She died in 1545 and is buried at Thetford Priory.

Nicholas Carewe fell out of favour in 1538 after responding with anger to something Henry VIII said, but the real reason was his support for Princess Mary. Cromwell had decided to move against his former allies, and presented letters to Henry, supposedly written by Carewe, showing that he had been involved in a plot to depose Henry and put Cardinal Reginald Pole (who had Plantagenet blood) on his throne instead. This became known as the Exeter Conspiracy.

Carewe was arrested and found guilty of high treason. He was beheaded on Tower Hill in 1539

Gertrude Courtenay was imprisoned in the Tower along with her husband and their son in 1538, suspected of involvement in the Exeter Conspiracy. Her husband was executed and Gertrude and her son remained in prison. She was released in 1540 and died somewhere around 1558.

Reginald Pole was made a Cardinal by Rome in late 1536, and published his tract defaming Henry as a heretic and adulterer. Pole was appointed by the Pope to lead a European offensive against Henry, and since Henry was at that time rather busy with the *Pilgrimage of Grace*, and other uprisings, he did not take well to this. Henry chose to take revenge on Pole's family, since he could not reach the Cardinal himself.

Reginald Pole returned to England when Queen Mary took the throne, and became Archbishop of Canterbury. His involvement in the infamous Marian burnings is disputed, as he was known to be lenient towards heretics, but he does not appear to have done anything to stop them. He died, possibly of influenza, on the 17th of November 1558, a bare twelve hours after Queen Mary.

Margaret Pole, **Countess of Salisbury**, once Katherine's great friend and the governess of Princess Mary, was executed on trumped up charges of treason, ostensibly to do with a plot her son Reginald was involved in, but also, and more likely, because she was one of the last surviving Plantagenets. She was an old woman at the time of her death, and was confused and panicked at her execution. Her headsman was inexperienced, and hacked her to death, delivering blows to her arms, shoulders and neck, which led to agony and suffering. **Henry Courtenay**, Marquess of Exeter, and **Henry Pole**, Baron Montague, were also arrested, tried, and executed for treason at the same time.

Henry Percy, Earl of Northumberland, was constantly ill with ague, and his marriage was unhappy. He made the King his heir, for want of children, and in 1536 was created Lord President of the Council of the North and vice-regent of the Order of the Garter, perhaps for appearing at Anne's trial as a jury member. His brothers and mother were deeply involved on the rebel side in the *Pilgrimage of Grace*, but Percy remained loyal to his King. The rebel leader, Robert Aske came to him and asked that he resign his command of the north, but Percy refused.

By early 1537, he was very ill. Percy died on the 29th of June, 1537 and was buried in Hackney church.

Anne's daughter, of course, went on to become Queen of England. **Elizabeth Tudor** reigned for forty-five years, longer than any of her forebears, and is widely recognised as the greatest of the Tudor monarchs.

Elizabeth was born into a perilous world. Just a child of two and a half at the time of her mother's death, she grew up in an uncertain time. Her brother, Edward, was born when she was four, and he took the place she was denied in the succession. Her childhood, whilst her father lived, was fairly happy, I believe. Henry accepted her as his daughter, and although she was labelled a bastard, she enjoyed his love and favour. Elizabeth was a remarkably precocious girl, who possessed a fierce intelligence and will to survive. She came to the throne as a young woman, and ruled well, if not always fairly. But she was a great deal more balanced and just than her father or siblings.

Elizabeth rewarded her Boleyn and Howard relatives when she came to the throne, as well as children of the men who fell with her mother, and this, combined with several other facts, such as Elizabeth wearing a necklace of Anne's in the *Whitehall Portrait*, and the discovery of a ring upon her finger when she died, which bore twin portraits of Anne and Elizabeth, point me towards thinking that Elizabeth remembered her mother with a private, enduring love, and perhaps did not believe the accusations against her.

Elizabeth was not without fault; her reign saw England become involved not only with piracy on a breathtaking scale against Spain, but also in the slave trade. Despite slavery being illegal in England, Elizabeth sent men to plunder slaves from Spanish and Portuguese plantations, supposedly taking them to better owners, but in reality profiting from human misery. The slaves were not to be brought to England, but could be traded outside English waters without upsetting the law. English involvement with the slave trade was minimal at this stage, and after a disastrous mission led by John Hawkins, was largely abandoned in favour of piracy, only to emerge again in force about one hundred years later.

I may argue that slavery was already established, and even the Pope kept slaves, that Elizabeth's part in the trade was lesser than that of Spain or Portugal, but England was still involved, and this should not be brushed over. Horrors were done in Ireland, too, which are much overlooked in English history. Queen Mary is remembered for all the ills she did, with any good being ignored, and Elizabeth for all the good she did, whilst the ills are brushed under a convenient carpet. But if we judge Mary harshly, we must judge Elizabeth in the same manner. Elizabeth did a great deal that was good, and should be remembered, but we should not forget the wrongs that were done.

What can be said of Elizabeth is that she took an England which, by the time she came to the throne, was impoverished and fragile, and made it strong. The idea of

Empire was brought up in her time, and however much damage that ideal did to other countries, it made England a world power to be reckoned with.

As a person Elizabeth is hard to see, and she kept it that way. A precocious child became a hardened survivor and she learned early on that it was better to be obscure than frank, and hid many of her actions under a cloak of lies, courtly subterfuge and deft political manoeuvring. Elizabeth was a superb spin doctor, and always made the best of what she was handed. She was resourceful, witty, clever, and knew how to rule. She chose highly skilled men to serve her, and promoted the arts and education. It is a testament to her reign, that by the time she died, nearly 60% of the population was literate, compared to 15% at the start of her grandfather's. Many of her methods were sneaky and underhand, but she was playing a dangerous game. Many wanted her deposed and replaced with a Catholic, and she was under almost constant threat of her life. Her religious settlement, forged after years of switching from Catholic to Protestant and back again under her siblings and father, was brought about to try to bring peace between the faiths. And she was remarkably tolerant in comparison to her siblings and father. She executed traitors, but did not burn them for their faith, and often pardoned those who had plotted against her. In the early years of her reign, Catholics were left alone in England, and it was only when the Pope excommunicated her, effectively making all Catholics in England potential assassins, that she took any action against them as a whole.

During her reign, the infant beginnings of the British Secret Service were also born. Walsingham, her spymaster, and Cecil, her greatest and longest-lasting advisor, saw to this.

She famously never married. Elizabeth admitted that she hated the state, and said it was better to remain a virgin, and single, than become a wife. Elizabeth had witnessed first-hand what it was for a woman to be in the complete control of a husband, and she did not want to enter into any state that would imperil her life, her freedom or her power. Unlike many others, I think Elizabeth was a virgin, as she claimed. Her experiences of her father's many unions, the fear of losing her power, the terrible example of the humiliation her sister Mary suffered when she failed to bear a child, and the early abuse she suffered at the hands of Thomas Seymour, I think convinced Elizabeth that it was safer to remain single.

Elizabeth died an old woman in March 1603. She was the last of the Tudors.

But not the last of the Boleyns… Although Anne's direct line died out, Mary Boleyn's did not. The house of Spencer, that of Princess Diana, is directly related to Mary Boleyn, as were notables of history such as William Churchill, Lord Nelson, Charles Darwin, P.G. Woodhouse, and Sarah Ferguson, the Duchess of York.

The Windsor Princes Harry and William carry Boleyn blood through their mother, but also their father. Queen Elizabeth II is related to Mary Boleyn though her mother, who was a direct descendant of Catherine Carey. The Boleyns, somewhat ironically therefore, still sit upon the throne of England, and will continue to do so, and if Catherine Carey was the daughter of Henry VIII, then so do the Tudors.

The past, at times, is not as far away as we think.

Changes Made in the Books to Historical Fact

I must note here that this book is historical fiction, and therefore not to be taken as a blueprint of that time. I try to stick to facts, but conversations, and various plots and subplots in this book, are based on theories I have developed after ten years of study.

One of the striking variations from fact is Anne's visit to the Abbey of Syon. Anne did go there, and appeared to make an impression on the nuns, leading to a partial (although this is contested) submission to Henry as Supreme Head of the Church. I have no evidence that she made a deal with the nuns of Syon, but I think it is reasonable that since she had more success than the many, *many* delegations sent to Syon, she negotiated with them, and her propensity to uphold the Church, even against Henry, makes this a reasonable, in my eyes, supposition.

Anne suffers, in the book, from what we would now call PTSD in response to the deaths of her three children. There is no firm evidence of this, but PTSD can affect women in the aftermath of miscarriages, and Anne's often erratic behaviour, such as high anxiety, irritability, and emotional outbursts, could be symptoms of PTSD. Often, the emotional and psychological effects of suffering three miscarriages are set aside as we concentrate on her terror of being abandoned by Henry. I think three losses, in such a short space of time, were likely to have adversely affected her.

With regards to her first lost son, and the failure to baptise him at birth, this was something I chose to include which cannot be proven, and is fairly unlikely. I chose to include this as it granted a way to introduce Anne questioning aspects of traditional faith, and it is a possibility, but midwives were trained to bless or baptise any part of the child which emerged from the mother, sometimes a hand or foot, if it was likely the child would die. The silence about her children I think was genuine. There is doubt about how many pregnancies she had, and therefore how many miscarriages/ premature births, but since they are barely recorded in court records, and were not publicly announced, I think it likely that Henry ordered them to not be spoken of, something that did not allow Anne time or opportunity to grieve or heal.

The identification of Mary Perrot as the *Imperial Lady* is based on supposition. In the book *The Other Tudors*, by Philippa Jones, Mary Perrot is identified as the mother of John Perrot, who was widely believed to be Henry's son. The *Imperial Lady* was said to have been a woman Henry had had a previous affair with, and had resumed it later. No one actually knows who she was, as she is not named in sources, but I stitched together these scraps, and made Mary his mistress. The name of *the parrot* is just an invention of mine, much like the *hapless hare* for Chapuys, and in earlier books, the *fat bat*, for Wolsey. Joanna Dingley was thought to have been Henry's mistress, and her daughter was possibly his child.

The part where Anne sits for Holbein, and he sketches her with fair hair, is based on a drawing which some think may be Anne, and some do not. The fair hair would seem to indicate it is not her. I put in a reason for why it might still be her, but admit this part was more to do with accentuating her sorrow about her child than it is based on real fact.

There is only slight evidence that Anne and her sister Mary reconciled after their argument about Mary's marriage. I chose to include the idea so that Mary would not simply disappear from the books, as I was very fond of her, but also because Mary called her daughter Anne, and because there is disputed evidence that Anne sent Mary money and a golden cup. Anne Carey, Mary's daughter, may not have lived, and may not have been called Anne, but there is some evidence to suggest she was. One could argue that Mary might have named her daughter after her sister to gain back favour, or it may have been out of genuine affection. I think the latter.

Jane Boleyn, Lady Rochford, was likely to have been involved in the demonstration in favour of Princess Mary, but was perhaps not held in the Tower. This situation has been disputed by so many historians that I chose to include a compromise; Jane was involved, was arrested, but her arrest was wiped from the Tower records. This last idea is my invention.

The pamphlets that were distributed about Henry and Jane Seymour after Anne's arrest came from an unknown source. I chose to make Anne the author. She had links to a Southwark printing house, so I thought it not impossible. She also had the best motive. I think it was either her, or one of her faction, who set the order up.

The meeting between Chapuys, Cromwell and Henry at Easter in 1536 was not attended by Anne. I chose to place her there so that the encounter where Cromwell was berated by Henry, leading to him deciding to work against Anne for fear of his life, was done in the first person. She was not present.

Anne's last letter to Henry in the Tower may be a fake. There are disputes about the handwriting, and the fact she called herself *Anne Bullen*, rather than other spellings of her name, or indeed instead of using her title of Queen, but recent studies have put forward suggestions that it was her work. The recklessness of the letter certainly suggests Anne's hand to me. She was not always talented at hiding her emotions, even when she knew she was in danger.

In the Tower, I granted Anne a great deal of insight into her predicament and who was behind her arrest. Anne was a clever woman, and it is likely she understood Cromwell was behind her fall, but how far she understood Henry's culpability was another matter.

In her trial, I added the accusation about Bridget Wingfield's letter, that it was evidence of blackmail. This is actually a modern theory, and one I wanted to demonstrate was erroneous. That letter holds nothing firm in it that could be evidence that Bridget found out Anne was having affairs and blackmailed her. The reports that Bridget made a death-bed confession against her friend were brought up in court, although they are likely to be false.

As for the other books, I will not go into detail here, but I have a few points to make.

In *La Petite Boulain,* Anne's early life and her time in Mechelen and France are described. I placed Anne at Henry's coronation and the funeral of Prince Henry, as it is a possibility she was present, and also so I could describe these events in detail. I tried to stick to what was known about her time in Mechelen and France, but most of the events in those sections are based on theories rather than facts.

Her relationship with Marguerite de Navarre is likely to have happened, but the depths of that relationship are unknown. Considering that Anne owned several of Marguerite's books, spoke warmly of her in later life, and helped in the plan to free Bourbon, however, are points to indicate that they were indeed friends.

The attack on Anne in the gardens in France is fiction. There is no evidence it happened, but due to the French King slandering her later in life, despite her stout defence of her virginity whilst Henry pursued her, made me think that perhaps there was a reason beyond the political for his accusations.

Despite numerous suggestions and slanders that Anne was loose of morals, and had been the mistress of many a man before Henry, I think she was, as she protested, careful of her honour. Her upbringing was different to that of her sister and brother, and in Mechelen she was brought up with a set of ideals that valued courtly love, but resisted sex. I think that when Henry set his sights on her, her protestations that she could not become a man's mistress were entirely genuine.

In *The Lady Anne,* Anne's relationship with Tom Wyatt is shown as innocent. It may not have been, but I think it was. I think she did perhaps promise to marry Percy, but unlike some other historical novelists, I do not think they consummated their oaths.

During her time of banishment, after she and Percy were found out, there is little record of what Anne did or where she was. Some postulate she may have gone back to France, but I think it more likely, given the political issues at the time, that she was simply at Hever. Her visit to the house of Edmund Howard, her uncle, is fiction. It may have happened, since it was not unusual that female kin visited others in times of need, such as during births, but really I wanted a way to introduce Catherine Howard, and used this premise to do so.

All of her encounters with Henry are from my imagination. No one knows at what exact point he saw Anne, nor exactly when he decided to move from trying to make her his mistress to offering her the title of Queen.

In *Above all Others,* Anne is intimately involved in the fall of Wolsey. Some dispute how far she was embroiled in this, preferring to see the hand of the men in her life rather than Anne's, but I think she became more and more involved as time went on and she realized Wolsey was a true impediment to her marriage.

Her dramatic flight from court at one stage in the book is fiction. She was known to stay at Hever for a lot of the time in this book, and threatened to leave Henry, so I thought including this would emphasise that fact.

The name she grants Wolsey (and the later one she gives Chapuys) came from my imagination. Elizabeth was known for granting pet names to favourites, and I thought Anne granting them to enemies would offer another link between them.

In *The Scandal of Christendom,* I tried to show that it was not only Anne who was responsible for the suffering of Mary and Katherine, but that she was involved. Anne was certainly responsible for some of their suffering and since the premise of the books was that she was essentially confessing by telling her story before death, I thought it important to note both her good and bad acts.

All conversations are also a product of my imagination. Where possible, I have inserted things people actually said, and were recorded, at others, I allowed myself free rein.

If you have a question, or think I have omitted a change I made in the books here, then please contact me if you wish to discuss it further. There is an email address at the end section, and I try to reply promptly. Besides, I love a good discussion on Tudor history!

Select Bibliography for the Series

Ackroyd, Peter, *The Life of Thomas More*
Baldwin-Smith, Lacey, *Anne Boleyn: Queen of Controversy*
Bernard, G.W, *Anne Boleyn: Fatal Attractions*
Bordo, Susan, *The Creation of Anne Boleyn*
Borman, Tracy, *Thomas Cromwell, Elizabeth's Women, The Private Lives of the Tudors*
Brigden, Susan, *Thomas Wyatt: The Heart's Forest*
Brears, Peter, *Cooking and Dining in Medieval England, All the King's Cooks*
Breverton, Terry, *The Tudor Kitchen*
Castiglione, Baldesar, *The Book of the Courtier*
Chapman, Lissa, *Anne Boleyn in London*
Childs, Jessie, *Terror and Faith in Elizabethan England*
Cummings, John, *The Hound and the Hawk: The Art of Medieval Hunting*
Denny, Joanna, *Anne Boleyn: A New Life of England's Most Tragic Queen*
Duffy, Eamon, *The Stripping of the Altars*
Evans, Jennifer and Read, Sarah, *Maladies and Medicines*
Fletcher, Catherine, *The Divorce of Henry VIII: The Untold Story*
Fletcher, Stella, *Cardinal Wolsey: a Life in Renaissance Europe*
Fox, Julia, *Jane Boleyn: The Infamous Lady Rochford, Sister Queens: Katherine of Aragon and Juana, Queen of Castile*
Friedmann, P, *Anne Boleyn*
Fraser, Antonia, *The Six Wives of Henry VIII*
Gelis, Jacques, *History of Childbirth*
Goodman, Ruth, *How to be a Tudor*
Gunn, Steven, *Charles Brandon,*
Green, Monica (editor and translator), *The Trotula: An English Translation of the Medieval Compendium of Women's Medicine*
Grueninger, Natalie, *Discovering Tudor London*
Gwyn, Peter, *The King's Cardinal: The Rise and Fall of Thomas Wolsey*
Hammond, Peter, *Food and Feast in Medieval England*
Hart, Kelly, *The Mistresses of Henry VIII*
Haynes, Alan, *Sex in Elizabethan England*
Hayward, Maria, *Rich Apparel: Clothing and the Law in Henry VIII's England*
Hieatt, Constance and Butler, Sharon, (editors), *Curye on Inglysch*
Hutchinson, Robert, *Thomas Cromwell*
Ives, Eric, *The Life and Death of Anne Boleyn*
Jones, Philippa, *The Other Tudors*
Knecht, R.J, *Renaissance Prince and Warrior: The Reign of Francis I*
Licence, Amy, *Catherine of Aragon, Anne Boleyn: Adultery, Heresy, Desire, The Tudors, The Six Wives and Many Mistresses of Henry VIII: The Women's Stories*
Lipscomb, Suzannah, *A Visitor's Companion to Tudor England*
Loades, David, *Jane Seymour: Henry VIII's Favourite Wife, The Seymours of Wolf Hall, The Six Wives of Henry VIII, The Boleyns*
Lofts, Norah, *Anne Boleyn*
Machiavelli, Niccolo, *The Prince*
Mackay, Lauren, *Inside the Tudor Court*
MacCulloch, Diarmaid, *Reformation: Europe's House Divided, 1490-1700, Thomas Cranmer*
Markham, Gervase, *The English Housewife*
Matusiak, John, *Wolsey: The Life of Henry VIII's Cardinal*
Moorhouse, Geoffrey, *Great Harry's Navy*
Morris, Sarah and Grueninger, Natalie, *In the Footsteps of Anne Boleyn*

Moynahan, Brian, *Book of Fire*
Murphy, Beverley, *Bastard Prince: Henry VIII's Lost Son*
Navarre, Marguerite of, *The Heptameron, The Glass of the Sinful Soul*
Norton, Elizabeth, *Jane Seymour, The Lives of Tudor Women, Anne Boleyn: Henry VIII's Obsession, Anne Boleyn: In her own words and those of who knew her, The Boleyn Women*
Norris, Herbert, *Tudor Costume and Fashions*
Perry, Maria, *Sisters to the King*
Plat, Hugh, *Delightes for Ladies*
Plowden, Alison, *The House of Tudor, Tudor Women: Queens and Commoners*
Porter, Linda, *Mary Tudor*
Power, Eileen (translator), *The Goodman of Paris*
Ridgeway, Claire, *George Boleyn, The Anne Boleyn Collection, The Anne Boleyn Papers, The Fall of Anne Boleyn*
Ridley, Jasper, *The Tudor Age*
Roud, Steve, *The English Year*
Roth, Erik, *With a Bended Bow*
Sharp, Jane, *The Midwives Book*
Shulman, Nicola, *Graven with Diamonds*
Sim, Alison, *The Tudor Housewife, Food and Feast in Tudor England, Pleasures and Pastimes in Tudor England,*
Siraisi, Nancy, *Medieval and Early Renaissance Medicine*
Seward, Desmond, *Prince of the Renaissance*
Skidmore, Chris, *Edward VI: The Lost King of England*
Starkey, David, *Six Wives: The Queens of Henry VIII, The Reign of Henry VIII: Personalities and Politics, Henry: Virtuous Prince*
Thomas, Keith, *Religion and the Decline of Magic*
Tremlett, Giles, *Catherine of Aragon: Henry's Spanish Queen*
Tudor, Henry, *The Love Letters of Henry VIII, Asserto Septem Sacramentorium*
Tyndale, William, *The Obedience of a Christian Man, the Tyndale New Testament*
Watkins, Sarah-Beth, *The Tudor Brandons*
Weir, Alison, *Henry VIII, King and Court, The Lady in the Tower: The Fall of Anne Boleyn, Mary Boleyn, The Great and Infamous Whore, The Children of Henry VIII,*
Wilkinson, Josephine, *Anne Boleyn: The Young Queen To Be, The Early Loves of Anne Boleyn,*
Williams, Patrick, *Katherine of Aragon*
Wilson, Derek, *Henry VIII: Reformer and Tyrant, Hans Holbein: Portrait of an Unknown Man*
Wyngaerde, Anthonis, *The Panorama of London circa 1544*

About the Author

I find people talking about themselves in the third person to be entirely unsettling, so, since this section is written by me, I will use my own voice rather than try to make you believe that another person is writing about me to make me sound terribly important.

I am an independent author, publishing my books by myself, with the help of my lovely proof reader. I write every day, and became a full time author in 2016. I briefly tried entering into the realm of 'traditional' publishing but, to be honest, found the process so time consuming and convoluted that I quickly decided to go it alone and self-publish.

My passion for history, in particular perhaps the era of the Tudors, began early in life. As a child I lived in Croydon, near London, and my schools were lucky enough to be close to such glorious places as Hampton Court and the Tower of London to mean that field trips often took us to those castles. I think it is hard not to find the Tudors infectious when you hear their stories, especially when surrounded by the bricks and mortar they built their reigns within. There is heroism and scandal, betrayal and belief, politics and passion and a seemingly never-ending cast list of truly fascinating people. So when I sat down to start writing, I could think of no better place to start than somewhere and sometime I loved and was slightly obsessed with.

Expect *many* books from me, but do not necessarily expect them all to be of the Tudor era. I write as many of you read, I suspect; in many genres. My own bookshelves are weighted down with historical volumes and biographies, but they also contain dystopias, sci-fi, horror, humour, children's books, fairy tales, romance and adventure. I can't promise I'll manage to write in *all* the areas I've mentioned there, but I'd love to give it a go. If anything I've published isn't your thing, that's fine, I just hope you like the ones I write which *are* your thing!

The majority of my books *are* historical fiction however, so I hope that if you liked this volume you will give the others in this series (and perhaps not in this series), a look. I want to divert you as readers, to please you with my writing and to have you join me on these adventures.

A book is nothing without a reader.

As to the rest of me; I am in my thirties and live in Cornwall with a rescued dog and a rescued cat. I studied Literature at University after I fell in love with books as a small child. When I was little I could often be found nestled half-way up the stairs with a pile of books and my head lost in another world between the pages. There is nothing more satisfying to me than finding a new book I adore, to place next to the multitudes I own and love… and nothing more disappointing to me to find a book I am willing to never open again. I do hope that this book was not a disappointment to you; I loved writing it and I hope that showed through the pages.

This is only one in a large selection of titles coming to you on Amazon. I hope you will try the others.

If you would like to contact me, please do so.

On twitter, I am @TudorTweep and am more than happy to follow back and reply to any and all messages. I may avoid you if you decide to say anything worrying or abusive, but I figure that's acceptable.

Via email, I am tudortweep@gmail.com a dedicated email account for my readers to reach me on. I'll try and reply within a few days.

I publish some first drafts and short stories on Wattpad where I can be found at www.wattpad.com/user/GemmaLawrence31 . Wattpad was the first place I ever showed my stories, *to anyone*, and in many ways its readers and their response to my works were the influence which pushed me into self-publishing. If you have never been on the site I recommend you try it out. Its free, its fun and its chock-full of real emerging talent. I love Wattpad because its members and their encouragement gave me the boost I needed as a fearful waif to get some confidence in myself and make a go of a life as a real, published writer.

Thank you for taking a risk with an unknown author and reading my book. I do hope now that you've read one you'll want to read more. If you'd like to leave me a review, that would be very much appreciated also!

Gemma Lawrence
Cornwall
2018

Thank You

...to so many people for helping me make this book possible... to my proof reader, Julia Gibbs, who gave me her time, her wonderful guidance and also her encouragement. To my family for their ongoing love and support; this includes not only my own blood in my mother and father, sister and brother, but also their families, their partners and all my nieces who I am sure are set to take the world by storm as they grow. To my friend Petra who took a tour of Tudor palaces and places with me back in 2010 which helped me to prepare for this book and others; her enthusiasm for that strange but amazing holiday brought an early ally to the idea I could actually write a book. To all my wonderful readers, who took a chance on an unknown author, and have followed my career and books since. To those who have left reviews or contacted me by email or Twitter, I give great thanks, as you have shown support for my career as an author, and enabled me to continue writing. Thank you for allowing me to live my dream.

And lastly, to the people who wrote all the books I read in order to write this book... all the historical biographers and masters of their craft who brought Anne, and her times, to life in my head.

Thank you to all of you; you'll never know how much you've helped me, but I know what I owe to you.

Gemma
Cornwall
2018

Printed in Great Britain
by Amazon